THE JOHN HARVARD LIBRARY

BERNARD BAILYN
Editor-in-Chief

OLDTOWN FOLKS

Harriet Beecher Stowe

EDITED BY HENRY F. MAY

The John Harvard Library

THE BELKNAP PRESS OF
HARVARD UNIVERSITY PRESS

CAMBRIDGE, MASSACHUSETTS

1966

CONTENTS

EDITOR'S NOTE

I assume that the purpose of editing a novel is to make it more and not less readable, and that the way to read a novel is straight through, stopping as little as possible. I have therefore avoided footnotes in the text, though Mrs. Stowe allowed herself a few. The materials the author uses, some of them reproduced literally with or without quotations, are identified in the Introduction whenever it has proved possible to locate them. I have further assumed that this Introduction is to be read either immediately before or after reading the novel, and have not peppered it with page numbers each time I have referred to a particular passage.

In the large mass of writing about Mrs. Stowe, there are four indispensable books. Charles Edward Stowe's life of his mother, published in 1889, incorporates a great deal of family knowledge. Annie Fields' *Life and Letters* (1898) is written by Mrs. Stowe's close friend, the wife of her publisher, and makes use (sometimes inaccurately) of letters and personal memories. Forrest Wilson's 1941 biography, *Crusader in Crinoline,* was the first good academic account and rests on voluminous research. Finally, Charles H. Foster's *The Rungless Ladder* (1954) is a brilliant interpretation of Mrs. Stowe's religious development through her works. My introduction depends on all these, and especially the last, though I think my emphasis and purpose somewhat different from Mr. Foster's. Three other biographical works deserve some mention. Florence Thayer McCray's rhapsodic description of *The Life-Work of the Author of Uncle Tom's Cabin,* published in 1889, was detested by its subject but contains some information not available elsewhere. The 1911 biography by Charles E. and Lyman Beecher Stowe is largely a rehash of Charles Stowe's earlier work, but contains some additional details. John R. Adams, for his University of Southern California dissertation of 1940 on "The Literary Achievements of Harriet Beecher Stowe" has performed the heroic task of going through Mrs. Stowe's magazine writing. For main facts on which the biographers agree I have cited no sources. All facts or insights which come from one particular author are identified in footnotes.

The text followed is that of the first edition, published in 1869 by Fields, Osgood and Co. The plates for this edition were used by Houghton Mifflin for most of their many reprintings of the book. The 1896 Fireside Edition in two volumes used new plates and departs from the original in a number of unimportant ways.

Mrs. Stowe was a careless author, and even her trusted proof-reader nodded. I have made changes only in obvious cases of careless errors in the 1869 edition. These include, for instance, proper names spelled different ways in successive uses, and in one case a necessary word omitted. I have not however tried to correct usages I believe Mrs. Stowe intended, even when these are obsolete or dubious. In the use of dialect she was a pioneer and had no rules or customs to follow. It has seemed right, therefore, to leave her odd but fairly consistent contractions as her readers found them in 1869.

Thanks are due to the staff of the Huntington Library for permitting me to make use of the library's collection of Stowe papers, which includes Mrs. Stowe's correspondence with her publisher during the writing of *Oldtown Folks*, and to my research assistant, David Lundberg, for some thorough and successful detective work.

H.F.M.

INTRODUCTION
BY
HENRY F. MAY

INTRODUCTION

In 1865 Harriet Beecher Stowe wrote her friend and publisher, James T. Fields, that she could not accept an invitation from his wife, her dear Annie, to pay a visit. Her reason was that she felt it was finally time to get seriously to work, in quiet and concentration, on the New England novel she had been brooding over for many years.[1] From then on until the book was finished early in 1869 Mrs. Stowe gave herself, her publisher, and her family a very hard time. Her letters to both the Fields are full of apologies, complaints about distractions, hesitations about the title, and exultation about the quality of what was being painfully achieved. In December 1867 she thought that the book was almost done, but in 1868 she was still struggling: "*My own book*, instead of cooling, boils and bubbles daily and nightly, and I am pushing and spurring like fury to get to it. I work like a dray-horse, and I'll *never* get in such a scrape again." [2] On Christmas Eve 1868 she again saw the end in sight, this time correctly, and again insisted she had never put so much work upon anything before. In February 1869 she finally finished the job, still complaining: "I have struggled with every kind of difficulty in writing it, and it has seemed some times as if it were going to take my life to do it, and I wish to live to write two or three more, and intend to, P.P. [Providence permitting?]" [3]

In many authors, all this display of agony and temperament would be part of a standard drama of parturition. Mrs. Stowe, however, had come a long way since she had scribbled *Uncle*

[1] H.B.S. to Fields, 1865. Stowe letters, Huntington Library. The letters in this collection are ordinarily dated only very roughly if at all, except when they are written by Mrs. Stowe's secretary. All letters referred to below and not otherwise identified are in this collection. Quotations are by permission of the Huntington Library.

[2] H.B.S. to Fields, 1868.

[3] H.B.S. to Fields, "per sect.," February 18, 1869.

Tom's Cabin on her kitchen table in Brunswick under — she later insisted — immediate Divine dictation. She was a well-to-do, prolific, experienced authoress who could command comfort and solitude either in her new big house in Hartford or her orange grove in far-off, undiscovered Florida. Moreover she was never a meticulous writer; she left it to lesser folk to fuss and fret over style. Why then had she suffered so acutely over *Oldtown Folks?* Partly because she intended, as she repeatedly told the Fields and others, that it should be her masterpiece. Partly, also because of its subject matter. The center of *Oldtown Folks* is the center of Mrs. Stowe's whole life, her long and agonizing struggle with the religion of her fathers, and more particularly with the religion of her father.

She herself did not doubt that the book was worth the struggle; others have made varying judgments. Two important contemporary reviewers were tired of New England. E. L. Godkin's *The Nation*, the new organ of the intellectual and political elite, found the book one more indication of the region's decay. Surely, said the anonymous reviewer in a tone of weary tolerance, we have had enough of the Puritan parson and the deacon "and the Puritan tithing man; and the Puritan Thanksgiving, and 'Lection cake, and May Training; and the Puritan 'revivals,' and 'doctrines,' and 'donation parties'" and the rest of the overworked provincial paraphernalia. Moreover, Mrs. Stowe's characters (especially, the reviewer added, the male characters) were as tired as her plot devices — the mysterious child of vaguely aristocratic antecedents, the brilliant and wicked fascinator, duly punished in the end.[4] Bret Harte, who could not take his dislike of New England as lightly as a New York reviewer, looked forward in an anonymous review in *The Overland Monthly* to the day when "we shall probably hear less of Jonathan Edwards and Governor Winthrop, and even begin to understand that they have as little to do with the present civilization as the aborigines." [5]

Mrs. Stowe was wounded by the *Nation's* review, but the book was praised by her friend Lowell and her correspondent George Eliot, and there was never any doubt about its popular success. Soon the town of Natick, original of Oldtown, was making money

[4] *Nation*, June 3, 1869, pp. 437–438.
[5] *The Overland Monthly*, 3 (1869): 3.

out of visits to places celebrated in the novel, and Mrs. Stowe was at work satisfying the demand for more New England stories, this time narrated by Sam Lawson, the celebrated town loafer of *Oldtown*.[6] Moreover, the book was being imitated; despite the *Nation's* weariness with New England, literary historians place the book near the beginning of the local color movement rather than at its end. For several generations the book's reputation rose and fell — and mostly it was a slow decline — with the literary fortunes of New England local color in general. Artistically inferior to the work of Sarah Orne Jewett, it was remembered if at all as an early specimen of the genre, and the best of the *other* books by the author of *Uncle Tom's Cabin*.

In the 1920's and 1930's a major re-examination of the American past took place. Its main focus was on literature, and one of its main themes was a bitterly hostile indictment of Puritanism. For the few who read it, *Oldtown Folks* became an important anti-Puritan novel. Constance Rourke's amusing, sometimes penetrating, and sketchy portrait of the Beechers probably did more than any other book to set this pattern.[7] It was powerfully revived in 1962 by Edmund Wilson, who rediscovered Mrs. Stowe along with the American Civil War, and correctly said that Puritanism had a lot to do with both.[8]

Well before this, however, Puritanism was itself being reassessed. Instead of a mere mask for sexual repression or hatred of the arts it began to be seen as a profound effort to come to grips with permanent metaphysical and moral problems, and as the source of much of America's greatest literature. Perry Miller, who played a heroic role in this reassessment, gave it as his opinion that "Harriet Beecher Stowe, brought up in the Edwardsian tradition, understood many of its implications better than the theologians who endeavored to follow him [Edwards], and could evaluate his achievements in terms that are fundamental for understanding

[6] The *Nation* review (and the editor's subsequent apology) and also the Natick celebration are discussed in Mrs. Stowe's letter to Annie Fields of May 9, 1869. *Sam Lawson's Oldtime Fireside Stories* was published in 1872.

[7] Rourke, *Trumpets of Jubilee* (New York, 1927).

[8] Wilson, *Patriotic Gore* (New York, 1963). Midway between these two rediscoveries of Mrs. Stowe, Ruth Suckow, herself a regional novelist and the daughter of a Congregational minister, argued for the importance of the book as a religious novel from a somewhat less anti-Puritan point of view. Suckow, "An Almost Lost American Classic," *College English*, 14 (1952–1953): 315–325.

American culture." [9] Following his lead, Charles H. Foster in 1954 published a brilliant and thorough survey of the whole body of Mrs. Stowe's writing, concentrating on her deeply ambivalent relation to her ancestral faith and calling *Oldtown Folks* a "central New England and American book." [10] This has become a widespread judgment; yet the book has not been reprinted, and its rediscovery has been largely limited, like that of many American classics, to professional students of the American past.

This continuing neglect does not seem to me surprising. Though I agree with much of the recent praise, especially that of such deeply informed scholars as Miller and Foster, I cannot altogether disagree with the 1869 judgment of the *Nation. Oldtown Folks* .is not a good novel. It is, however, an important and highly interesting book, in some ways all the more interesting because of its author's limited capacity for invention. Mrs. Stowe lacked creative talent but had in large measure other literary gifts. In the first place she was, as James Russell Lowell told her, one of "the few persons lucky enough to be born with eyes in your head." [11] She was a keen observer and often a penetrating historian. Even more important, she was a Beecher, and therefore first and foremost a preacher. Her treatment of New England Calvinism in *Oldtown Folks* is far more than expert local color; it is more even than intellectual history. It is a record of the intense and painful experience of a gifted woman to find her way through the difficult issues of her day. This effort was carried on in terms of her inherited Calvinist tradition, and illuminates that tradition in a way that no later scholar, looking at Puritanism from outside, could entirely emulate.

Mrs. Stowe, in dealing with declining Calvinism of the early nineteenth century, is not studying a bygone social and religious pattern primarily for literary or scholarly purposes. She is discussing the way a people — and she herself above all — had tried to deal with the perennial problems of the meaning of life and death. By the time she wrote *Oldtown Folks* she had fought her way out — or almost out — of the thorny tangle of post-Edwardsian

[9] Jonathan Edwards, *Images or Shadows of Divine Things* (Perry Miller, ed., New Haven, 1948), p. 44.

[10] Charles H. Foster, *The Rungless Ladder* (Durham, N.C., 1954), p. 202.

[11] Lowell to H.B.S. February 4, 1859, quoted in Charles Edward Stowe, *The Life of Harriet Beecher Stowe* (Boston, 1889).

theology. She treats New England religion with respect and affection, but always wryly. She is not sorry that the formulations
taught her in her youth are dead, or almost dead, but she cannot
dismiss the outlook of which these formulations were a passing
symbol. Ambivalence — usually the most fruitful perspective for
a historian — had grown in this instance out of Harriet Beecher's
upbringing and Mrs. Stowe's whole experience of life. *Oldtown
Folks* could have been written only when New England Calvinism
was still warm in its grave and its ghost still walked through the
memories and emotions of a generation. To understand the book,
to discuss its relation to historical reality, and to assess its author's
achievement we must look first at the religion in which Mrs. Stowe
was brought up, and then at her own struggle with its stern teachings.

For Harriet Beecher, as for most of her generation, the founders
of New England were holy men, enshrined by patriotism as well as
piety. The *Nation's* skepticism or Bret Harte's Western rebellious-
ness were still fairly new, and later kinds of anti-Puritanism un-
imaginable. New England was "the seedbed of this great American
republic," and as such the pattern for progressive society everywhere. To a Beecher, the especially important pattern was that set
by rural New England, paradoxical as always, at once democratic
and traditional. Here, despite the rough equality, ministers and
other leading citizens were respected. Within the surviving Congregational order, lively religious and political dispute was taken
for granted. To Emerson, brought up in Boston where most of the
old arguments seemed to be swallowed up in the new liberalism,
the beginning of the nineteenth century was a dead period without a book or a thought. To Harriet Beecher Stowe, the villages
of her youth were "burning like live coals under this obscurity
with all the fervid activity of an intense, newly kindled, peculiar,
and individual life." These were the coals that burst into blaze in
the period of Emerson's own maturity.

Her idea of the founders was based on mythology, living oral
tradition, and limited but intense reading, especially of Cotton
Mather's *Magnalia Christi Americana*, to which she repeatedly
refers. Her version of New England religious history blurs some
episodes and skips others, but contains some vivid and correct

insights. Knowing something of the earthy side of a preacher's problems, she knew that a society entirely made up of intensely introspective saints would fall apart, and its churches would perish with it. Thus she strongly approved the Halfway Covenant, under which the church was kept in existence by admitting to a halfway status not only the children but also the grandchildren of church members without requiring the definite experience of Divine Grace demanded by Puritan theology. This compromise, the work of the practical second generation of American Puritans, she pushes back to the founding of New England. She also associates it, in Chapter 28, with Cotton Mather himself, who was born in the year the Halfway Covenant was adopted. (It was, however, defended by him and both his father and grandfather had played a part in its adoption.) Lavishing on Mather her highest praise — in Chapter 28 he is "good, motherly Cotton Mather" and in Chapter 19 he has already been called a "delightful New England grand-mother" — she laments that Edwards undid his maternal work, throwing out of the church the children of the saints and demand-ing, as the condition of readmission, an experience of regeneration which one could do nothing to earn.

When Mrs. Stowe dealt with Edwards, she was dealing with a subject she understood more deeply than she did the earlier his-tory of New England religion. She was no intellectual, and did not concern herself with Edwards' awesome metaphysical system. His theology, however, was the background of her father's and her husband's careers, and furnished the terms for the most severe inner conflicts of her life. Because she approached Edwards not as an academic student but as a person who had tried to live by his teachings, she understood one thing that has only recently become clear to historians of American religion. Not just because he helped destroy the Halfway Covenant, but for many reasons, Edwards was at least as much an aberration as a culmination in the history of American religion. This is, after all, usually true of religious genius when it appears within an established church.

Modern admirers of Edwards are often affected by Protestant neo-orthodoxy. It is important in understanding Mrs. Stowe's treatment to remember that this approach was not available to her. She and her generation had to confront not neo-orthodoxy, but orthodoxy. Hell was not a metaphysical necessity or an absence from God, but a real place full of real fire, described accurately and not just poetically by preachers of great dramatic talent. In this place oneself and most of the people one loved were probably destined to spend an eternity of torture. To accept this concrete fact as a necessary consequence of the nature of things, and yet to love that nature of things with all one's heart, took a man of Edwards' own spiritual and intellectual gifts. The surprising thing, as Mrs. Stowe fully understood, was not that he had failed to convert all his countrymen to his own austere views — nothing could be more contrary to his own estimate of depraved humanity — but rather that his work had dominated and inspired the religious leaders of a hardheaded community for so long. Some of Mrs. Stowe's generation, looking back in revulsion to their early religious training, were able to dismiss Edwards as a primitive malevolent monster with no relevance to their lives or to reality. However successful this dismissal was for some — and it was seldom entirely successful — Mrs. Stowe could not echo it. The power and beauty of Edwards' system was too much a part of her education, her understanding of parts of his achievement was too acute, and her view of life too close to his own.

Mrs. Stowe knew that Edwards broke up, once and for all, "the crust of formalism and mechanical piety" which had been one inevitable consequence of the compromise arrangement she so much admired in itself. With still greater penetration, she knew that his fearless and uncompromising search for ultimate truth had "sawed the great dam and let out the whole waters of discussion all over New England," and thus given rise even to the pantheistic heresies of Emerson and Parker.[12] She also knew — it was the problem central to her father's career — that the conquest of many of the churches by the New Divinity had driven away large numbers of members. Nobody knew better or from harsher experience the toll taken among the most sensitive by the effort to live up to the impossible. All these consequences of the work of New England's major prophet had to be weighed against each other, and they are so weighed in the superb *obiter dicta* which constitute the chief enduring interest of *Oldtown Folks.*

[12] This daring insight is repeated in Perry Miller's essay, "From Edwards to Emerson," reprinted in his *Errand into the Wilderness* (Cambridge, Mass., 1956), pp. 184–203. It is tempting to speculate whether the first suggestion of it may have come from Miller's highly sympathetic reading of Mrs. Stowe.

Both this novel and *The Minister's Wooing,* Mrs. Stowe's other main effort to deal in literature with Edwardsian theology, are still more directly concerned with Edwards' disciples than with their master. As Mrs. Stowe's husband, in a penetrating sketch of her father, points out, President Edwards' writings almost took the place of St. Paul's for a generation of New England divines, and gave rise to arguments of almost proportionate intensity.[13]

The chief problem of the Edwardsian school of theologians was to bring divine sovereignty and foreknowledge into some sort of relation to human responsibility, and to reconcile both of these with God's benevolence. Like their predecessors for two millennia, they labored to understand the necessity of evil and sin. Why, they asked — never doubting that there was an answer — must most of God's creatures be made in such a way that it was impossible for them to fulfill the duties God had prescribed for them. Facing boldly up to the most sacred mysteries, they asked why the sacrifice of Christ and the whole work of redemption was necessary. Instead of saving a small remnant at this vast price, could not God have saved all by a different sort of creation? The most dangerous way to answer this question, as well as the most profound, is to deny that God's right and wrong are those with which men are familiar. To Edwards, whose ultimate standards according to his modern biographer were aesthetic rather than moralistic, it was enough to say that the scheme was the means of exhibiting God's greatest glory.

Practical preachers, concerned more with preserving the moral order of the community and less with contemplation of ultimate truth, had to search for some less exalted way to demonstrate that the terrible fate awaiting most of mankind made some sort of sense. Joseph Bellamy, whose *True Religion Delineated* ("my grandmother's blue book") is quoted at length and accurately in *Oldtown Folks,* was a didactic simplifier of the Edwardsian system. Nobody is harsher in insisting on man's total depravity and the limitation of Christ's Atonement to the elect. Almost scolding the presumptuous advocates of universal salvation who were already rampant in New England, Bellamy insists that "the door is not

---

[13] C. W. Stowe, "Sketches and Recollections of Dr. Lyman Beecher," *Congregational Quarterly,* 23 (1864): 226–229. Mrs. Stowe echoes, in *Oldtown Folks,* her husband's complaint that New England neglects Biblical study for exegesis of Edwards.

opened wider than Christ desired it should be." [14] Yet he demonstrates, in somewhat Panglossian fashion, that sin and its inevitable consequences are a means of the greatest possible good of the universe; that it is actually better, in terms understandable to us, that the world be as dreadful as it is.

Samuel Hopkins, Edwards' favorite and perhaps his most gifted disciple, is the principal character in Mrs. Stowe's *The Minister's Wooing*. A major systematic theologian, Hopkins is best known — or rather *was* best known when he was known at all — for carrying to a terrifying conclusion Edwards' most compelling doctrine, that all virtue consists in an austere, mystical, completely disinterested love of being in general, and thus ultimately in love of God. [15] To attain this kind of virtue, Hopkins and Edwards agree, human beings need direct and continuous Divine help. Without it all such trivialities as self-love, natural affections, or even good done for the purpose of achieving reward, earthly or heavenly, are evil in God's sight. Hopkins pushes this one step farther. We must, he argues, so love holiness that if our own eternal damnation be a necessary part of God's scheme, we must willingly acquiesce in it. If we cannot meet this test, all is hopeless for us.

This doctrine, and its inevitable corollary that we must also acquiesce willingly in the damnation of others, is represented in *Oldtown Folks* by another major New England theologian, who plays a recurrent and important part in the novel, this time in disguise, as "Dr. Stern." Dr. Stern is Nathaniel Emmons, a follower of Hopkins and a dry and dull theologian, but the most extraordinary specimen of the Calvinist personality ever developed in the historic seedbed. [16]

[14] Quoted in Frank Hugh Foster, *A Genetic History of New England Theology* (Chicago, 1907), p. 117.

[15] Mrs. Stowe's novel makes it clear that this austere notion of virtue was far from a deterrent to action for the improvement of this world. Oliver Wendell Elsbree has pointed out that the Hopkinsian school, acting under this direct injunction to strive after disinterested benevolence, made a distinctive and disproportionately large contribution to several kinds of New England reform, including antislavery. Elsbree, "Samuel Hopkins and His Doctrine of Benevolence," *New England Quarterly*, 8 (1935): 534–550.

[16] There are two editions of Emmons' works. The first, edited by his son-in-law Jacob Ide (6 vols., Boston, 1842), contains in volume 1 Emmons' autobiography. The second, expanded edition (5 vols., Boston, 1863) was re-edited by Edwards Amasa Park, a Calvinist theologian, Andover professor, and friend of Mrs. Stowe. The entire first volume of this edition is a biography of Emmons by Park. This biography, which had been published separately in 1861, is an excellent account

Emmons' theological system, indefatigably worked out over a long life, was a variant of Hopkins' and need not concern us much. With almost none of Edwards' metaphysical interest, Emmons insisted on crystal-clear logic and specialized in pushing the Edwardsian paradoxes to an almost perverse extreme. He took an extreme view of Divine agency in regeneration, and held firmly to complete individual moral responsibility. A moral activist, he taught that regeneration was shown through a series of moral exercises, not general inclination or taste. Though God was completely sovereign, He was yet limited by the categories of right and wrong, whose nature we were able correctly to perceive through intuition. (Here Emmons, like most of his contemporaries, was influenced by the Scottish common-sense philosophers.) Underlying these paradoxes was the fundamental contradiction common to the post-Edwards school: God was an utterly unlimited ruler; yet his opinions and conduct were laid down for Him in detail by His humble creature, Nathaniel Emmons.

Nowhere does Emmons discuss God's purposes in more excruciating detail than in his many funeral sermons. Always addressing the bereaved directly, as Parson Lothrop does at the funeral in *Oldtown Folks*, Emmons was wont to outline the many ways in which God might have intended the bereavement for their good. If, as was often the case, the deceased had made no profession of religion and might well be damned, God's purpose in so decreeing was laid down all the more scrupulously. The sermon of Dr. Stern's quoted in *Oldtown Folks* is a real one, and its severity is if anything understated by the quotations Mrs. Stowe has chosen.[17] If the saved are not willing properly to enjoy the sufferings of the damned, this proves that they do not really want to go to heaven, or have an incorrect conception of it. "How must Moses feel in seeing Pharaoh! How must Paul feel in seeing Pilate! How must parents feel in seeing children, and children in seeing parents, and friends in seeing friends, separated from them, and doomed to unutterable and unending misery! What gratitude must the happy ones feel, and how sincerely will they praise God for his sovereign and distinguishing mercy?"[18]

---

of Emmons' life, personality, and doctrine and a neglected source for New England social and religious history.

[17] Emmons, *Works* (1842 ed.), VI, 177–189.

[18] *Ibid.*, p. 183.

This reference to children was particularly telling, since as Emmons once pointed out in a child's funeral sermon, few families failed to experience the loss of a child.[19] Having described, with feeling, the sufferings occasioned by such losses, Emmons went on in his usual systematic fashion to list eight ways in which God might intend such deaths to work to the edification of the bereaved parents and the eternal advantage of mankind.

It is tempting to us, and it must have been still more tempting to Mrs. Stowe, to make Emmons simply an unfeeling monster. She knew, however, that this would be completely false. Personally kind and compassionate, Emmons was revered, even perhaps loved, by his long succession of theological students. He was also particularly in demand as a funeral preacher and, in his strange uncompromising way, comforter of the bereaved. His congregation knew that his view of death and the proper attitude toward it by no means rested on his logic-chopping theology alone. Mrs. Stowe mentions Dr. Stern's "most affecting autobiography," and Emmons' own memoir indeed deserves quotation at length. In his "domestic concerns" Emmons "experienced uncommon favors and uncommon frowns of providence." Marrying early a young woman to whom he was deeply devoted, he became the father of two sons. His wife however fell into a decline after the birth of the second and shortly died. Emmons undertook the care of the two children, whom he "loved to excess." He was forced helplessly to watch one after the other die of dysentery, in convulsions and "extreme agonies."

It is impossible to describe what I felt. I stood a few moments, and viewed the remains of my two darlings, who had gone to their mother and to their long home, never to return. But I soon found the scene too distressing and retired to my chamber, to meditate in silence upon my forlorn condition. I thought there was no sorrow like unto my sorrow. I thought my burden was greater than I could bear. I felt as though I could not submit to such a complicated affliction. My heart rose in all its strength against the government of God, and then suddenly sunk under its distress, which greatly alarmed me. I sprang up, and said to myself, I am going into immediate distraction; I must submit, or I am undone for ever. In a very few minutes my burden was removed, and I

[19] "A celebrated European physician," he said, had calculated that more than half those born in the world die before the age of 8, and even in New England the majority die before reaching 20. Occasionally a whole family survives; as often a whole family is cut down. *Works* (1863 ed.), V, 777–792.

felt entirely calm and resigned to the will of God. I soon went down, attended to my family concerns, and gave directions respecting the interment of my children. I never enjoyed greater happiness in the course of my life, than I did all that day and the next. My mind was wholly detached from the world, and altogether employed in pleasing contemplation of God and divine things. I felt as though I could follow my wife and children into eternity, with peculiar satisfaction.[20]

Like many another widowed New England minister, Emmons married twice more. In due time he became the father of six more children. He had been taught a lesson, however, and "never indulged such high hopes concerning my present family, as I presumptuously indulged with respect to the family I have laid in the dust. I have likewise learned, by past painful experience, to mourn with those who mourn, and to weep with those who weep."[21] He had learned particularly, he said, to follow the mourners from the funeral to their dwellings, where they sat alone, and to try to bring them some of the consolation which he had himself experienced in his worst trial. In his old age he preached funeral sermons over two of his own children by his second marriage, expressing his own grief but steadfastly setting forth the will of God in these events for the edification of his hearers.

Emmons lived to be 95, conceding nothing to changing times, maintaining a spiritual monopoly of the village of Franklin (in *Oldtown Folks,* "Adams") against Unitarians, Arminians, and all challengers; and even wearing to the end the ancient clerical costume of cocked hat and buckled shoes. In his ninety-first year, on his first visit to New York City, he made the dramatic contribution to the antislavery cause which is briefly described in the novel.

This was the supreme example of the Calvinist pattern of improving the lessons taught by God in death, and this was the pattern which was to be set before the Beecher family in a very special way.

The Calvinist theologian who most influenced Harriet Beecher's upbringing was, of course, Lyman Beecher ("Mr. Avery" in the novel).[22] Beecher was no Emmons. Indeed, if he had been, his

[20] *Works* (1842 ed.), I, xxxi–xxxii.
[21] *Ibid.,* I, xxxii.
[22] The best source for Beecher, and for his children's upbringing, is his *Autobiography,* which is actually a composite work by several of his children, including Harriet, incorporating their father's oral reminiscences recorded by them. The

daughter's life might have been easier; she would either have been compelled into submission or driven into outright revolt. Beecher was one of the principal adapters of the Calvinist heritage to the nineteenth century, and his career marks a sort of halfway house between the austere religion of Edwards and the sentimental, anti-intellectual liberalism of his son Henry Ward Beecher.

As a theologian, Lyman Beecher was not especially interesting or profound. He followed the more liberal branch of the Edwards school, through the influence of his teacher, President Timothy Dwight of Yale, and his close friend Nathaniel Taylor. Taylor, like Beecher, knew that in the democratic and pluralistic age in which he lived Calvinism could survive only if its moral soundness could be demonstrated in terms acceptable to many. Thus sin, to Taylor, was not as it was to Bellamy and Hopkins and Emmons, a means deliberately chosen by God, in preference to other possibilities, as the best way of carrying out His plan. It was instead unpreventable in the nature of things: even God could not choose human freedom without including freedom to do evil. Taylor's favorite formula for explaining what was left of predestination was that man's propensity to do evil amounted to "certainty with power to the contrary." His motto was "Follow Truth if it carries you over Niagara."

Beecher followed Taylor in these theoretical matters. His own great role was not that of theologian but that of a preacher, revivalist, and above all fighter. His successive fights, however, amounted in the long run to a compromise, since his enemies were successively infidels (meaning eighteenth-century Deists), Episcopalians, Unitarians, ultrarevivalists, and finally, and most bitterly, ultraorthodox Calvinists. He also campaigned fervently against Sabbath-breaking, duelling, and (after giving up the genial practices described in the Cloudland consociation meeting in the novel) drink. Thus Beecher played a major part in opening the doors of New England religion to emotionalism, moralism, and reform. Yet in his own mind he remained loyal to Edwards, Dwight, and Bellamy.

John Harvard Library edition is edited by Barbara Cross (2 vols., Cambridge, Mass., 1961). This can be supplemented by various recollections by contemporaries. For Beecher's theology and that of his closest friend, see Sidney Earl Mead, *Nathaniel William Taylor, 1786–1858* (Chicago, 1942). Beecher's attitude toward Emmons is set forth in the *Autobiography*, I, 374–375.

Above all, as Beecher's fascinating autobiography reveals, he was a man of superlative vigor and gusto, who kept a gun beside him to shoot birds if any flew over while he was writing a sermon, delighted in fishing or roughhousing with his boys, wept over Scott and (with regret for the poet's failings) over Byron, and even, in private, played the fiddle and danced out of sheer exuberance. As a father, he was unbearably demanding. The colorful and lively center of the household, a pattern for affectionate emulation by his children, he of course insisted like his contemporaries on instant obedience, drastically enforced once and for all and then taken for granted. In dealing with his children's souls, his views made outright coercion impossible. Leaving them free to accept or reject Divine Grace, all-important and freely offered, he watched indefatigably with them for signs of a changing heart, and once he found such signs played his children like the skilled professional fisher of souls he was, alternating pulling them in and slackening the line, but never letting them off the hook.

The results were impressive. Of Beecher's children four were preachers, and at least two of these achieved wide public notice. One child became a college president, one an important female educator, and one of the most influential author of her day and the uncrowned queen of Anglo-American evangelical antislavery reform. Rather surprisingly, only one was a suicide. But all the ministerial sons and all but one of the daughters eventually rejected even the loose kind of orthodoxy represented by their father. Some of them wandered far indeed. (One daughter, Isabella, eventually became convinced that she herself was destined to be the new Messiah, an equal partner with Jesus Christ.) Of them all, the closest to Harriet was Henry, whose gushy religion of unlimited hope and undiscriminating love becomes more understandable when one sees it against the background of Edwards, Emmons, and Lyman Beecher.[23]

Harriet Beecher was brought up in Litchfield, Connecticut, and in Edwardsian Calvinism as taught and modified by her father. According to a contemporary biographer she had committed to memory twenty-seven hymns and two long chapters of the Bible

[23] Lyman Beecher Stowe, *Saints, Sinners and Beechers* (Indianapolis, 1934) is a breezy but sometimes informative family history.

by the time she was four.[24] An early alternative to her father's Presbyterianism was furnished by the Episcopalianism of her mother's family, and visits to "Nutplains," the house of her mother's cultivated and comparatively easy-going family, were among her most pleasant childhood recollections.

The most important part of her religious education was, however, that provided by death, which visited the Beecher family as often as it did most large families of the day. The first important disaster of her childhood was the death of her mother, Lyman Beecher's first wife, Roxana. From every record a simple, saintly, and beautiful woman, Roxana, mourned tempestuously but with real and deep grief by Lyman, became a sort of ethereal cult figure to the Beecher children. Henry Ward, who was two when she died, said that his feeling for her was comparable to that of a devout Catholic for the Virgin Mary.[25] To Harriet she formed the pattern for an angelic mother dying in her offspring's early childhood, a figure that recurs in her novels, among them *Oldtown Folks*. There were of course other family tragedies, but the one which circumstances made most crucial was that of a young man Harriet herself probably barely knew, Alexander Metcalf Fisher. Death, Emmons had said in sermon after sermon, should be sanctified to the living. In a statement which unconsciously echoed this doctrine, Mrs. Stowe's son and grandson said a long time later that Fisher's death provided "an epoch in the history of the Beecher family, and in the history of the New England theology." After this episode, they said, even Lyman Beecher's serenity may never have recovered, but without it, at least one novel of Mrs. Stowe's and at least one important heretical work of Edward Beecher's would never have been written.[26]

Fisher, a youthful prodigy, was named adjunct professor of

[24] Florence Thayer McCray, *The Life-Work of the Author of Uncle Tom's Cabin* (New York, 1889), p. 27.

[25] Quoted in Stowe, *Saints, Sinners and Beechers,* p. 241.

[26] Charles E. and Lyman B. Stowe, *Harriet Beecher Stowe* (Boston, 1911), p. 49. This judgment repeats an earlier one by Charles Stowe. It should be noted that his estimate of the episode's importance meets only qualified agreement in Charles H. Foster's well-informed article, "The Genesis of Harriet Beecher Stowe's 'The Minister's Wooing,'" *New England Quarterly,* 21 (1948): 493–517. The Fisher episode is discussed in the standard Stowe biographies, Lyman Beecher's *Autobiography,* and also at some length in Stowe, *Saints, Sinners and Beechers* and in Elizabeth Harveson, *Catharine Esther Beecher, Pioneer Educator* (Philadelphia, 1932).

mathematics and natural philosophy at Yale at twenty-three. He
fell in love with Catharine Beecher, the most vivacious and one
of the most gifted of the Beecher children. Since he was a young
man of great promise, impeccable morals, and sound religion
(though his efforts to receive assurance of saving Grace were as
yet unrewarded) he was more than acceptable to Catharine's
father. In 1822 Fisher said good-bye to his fiancée for a brief
professional trip to England. It became Lyman Beecher's duty to
tell his daughter that the ship *Albion,* with Fisher aboard, had
sunk off the Irish coast.

Lyman Beecher, like any Calvinist ministerial father, did his
very best to see that this loss was sanctified to his daughter. He
could not, however, depart from his life's teachings and his idea
of plain honesty enough to tell her that the young man was in
Heaven. In a long series of tender, considerate letters he tried to
persuade her of the justice of God's ways and her duty, whatever
Fisher's eternal destiny, to turn this grief to her own spiritual
advantage. In her long, agonized, and spirited answers to her
father's letters Catharine declared herself unable willingly to accept the possible damnation of her impeccably virtuous fiancé.[27]

On a visit to Fisher's family, Catharine found in his papers
evidence of his unsuccessful struggle for assurance of salvation,
which seemed to rivet his fate. And since the village the Fisher
family lived in was Franklin, Fisher's funeral sermon was preached
by no lesser figure than Nathaniel Emmons. It was as mild as any
Emmons sermon.[28] The preacher pictured graphically the anguish
of the ship's company, but devoted most of his time to an abstract
demonstration of "Divine Sovereignty in the Death of Men." He
ended with a great deal of praise of Fisher, and even, stretching a
point farther than Beecher had, suggested that "Though he never
professed, yet there is some ground to hope that he had experienced a saving change." Either way, of course, it was necessary
for his father and friends to learn the lesson taught by the death
of this excellent young man, and Emmons particularly hoped that
"It may have a happy effect upon a very sensible and highly
accomplished young lady, who may imagine she has the largest
share of affliction in this instance of mortality."

[27] Beecher, *Autobiography,* I, 355–384.
[28] Emmons, *Works* (1842 ed.), III, 246–259.

In a sense Emmons' hope that Fisher's death might be improved to Catharine's advantage was fulfilled, but the ways of Providence are more inscrutable than he realized, and things hardly turned out as he could have wished. Catharine, as her letters make clear, listened patiently and at length to Emmons' preaching and her father's pleas, and by both was gradually persuaded not to accept but to reject the whole Calvinist scheme. In a long series of able arguments she denied that God requires of us anything He does not give the ability to perform. (One essay was considered by some competent theologians the ablest refutation of Edwards on the Will.)[29] She later contrasted the entire Augustinian system with what she considered the system of common sense, and was even capable, in a letter, of a prim New England blasphemy: "I must have *proof* that all this horrible misery and wrong resulting from the wrong construction or nature of mind is not attributable to the Creator of All Things. His mere word is nothing from the Author of a system which is all ruined and worse than good for nothing. He must clear his character before he can offer me a Revelation!"[30]

The main result of her departure from her ancestral religion was still more in a New England vein. She became convinced that mankind can be made perfect if, and only if, a sufficiently intense effort is made on behalf of education. Catharine Beecher therefore became a school principal, and later a tireless, belligerent promoter of education in general, particularly for women and for the West. In the first stage of this career, desiring a wider sphere of usefulness as part of her recovery from Fisher's death, she established a school at Hartford, where her sister Harriet joined her, as an apprentice teacher, in 1824.

It was in Hartford, in close consultation with Catharine and, by letter, with her far more heretical brother Edward, that Harriet Beecher underwent her own two successive experiences of conversion. The first was conventional in everything except its ease. Hearing her father preach, on a "dewey, fresh summer morning" during her first vacation, she became ecstatically convinced that she had the friend she needed, and told her father that she had

[29] Stowe, *Saints, Sinners and Beechers*, p. 97. See also Harveson, *Catharine Esther Beecher*.
[30] Catharine to Edward Beecher, 1857, quoted in Harveson, p. 99.

given herself to Jesus, and he had taken her. " 'Is it so?" he said, holding me silently to his heart, as I felt the hot tears fall on my head. 'Then has a new flower blossomed in the kingdom this day.' " [31]

But Lyman Beecher's religion was not yet Henry Ward Beecher's, and hot tears and blossoms were only a small part of it. Instances of delusions of conversion were many and familiar, and he felt obliged to question her further about her willingness to be alone in the universe with God, and her acceptance of her own possible sin and misery. She went back to Hartford full of doubts, and argued them out painfully with Catharine and, by letter, with Edward. She was afraid that her own actions rose too much from a wish to be loved, but, like Catharine, found it more and more difficult to understand how God could have required heights of virtue which he had purposely made people unable to obtain. By 1830, however, she again thought she had reached a certainty of happiness and rest in the love of Christ.[32] This certainty, as far as we can tell, she never quite lost and never securely held.

In her mature life Harriet Beecher was to see clearly, as she repeatedly indicates in the novel before us, that Edwardsian Calvinism of the Emmons variety drove the majority into religious indifference, the most courageous minority into active hostility, and the most sensitive minority into hell on earth. Yet she was far too close to her father and his religion, and too deeply convinced about the faithfulness of Calvinist pessimism to actual life, to abandon the inherited doctrine soon, easily, or ever completely. Essentially brave and intelligent, introspective, given to emotional storms in the Victorian manner but not without a good deal of hardness and egotism, she was forced increasingly to give up the search for complete understanding of God's ways. According to her own repeated statements, she was able to conclude, in the worst crisis of her life, that the mystery of God's dealing with men was swallowed up in the greater mystery of the love of Christ.[33] To the extent that she really achieved this conviction, she was surely a better Christian, and perhaps even a better Christian theologian, than Nathaniel Emmons. The genuineness

---

[31] C. E. Stowe, *Life*, p. 34.

[32] The narrative from which most later accounts of these two conversions are drawn is *ibid.*, pp. 33–52.

[33] H.B.S. to Catharine Stowe, undated, quoted *ibid.*, p. 322.

of her somewhat insistent serenity is beyond our search and essentially irrelevant to our purpose. What is certain is that her inner experience was sufficiently rich and intense to give rise to the best of her writing.

As much as any Beecher, Harriet Beecher Stowe during the time of her own struggles felt called to minister to the spiritual needs of others. Though she wrote hymns and called some of her essays sermons, convention barred her from the pulpit and opened the way, not without some shaking of heads, to ladylike literary work. Furthermore, as the wife of a distinguished but impractical theologian and soon enough the mother of a struggling family, she felt the need to supplement the family income. From about 1840 Mrs. Stowe's life centered, at least on a worldly level, in a literary career. Yet this career itself could never be separated entirely from her spiritual Pilgrim's Progress and the many severe personal trials still in store. We must now consider at once her inner and her outer life, in the period when both were leading toward *Oldtown Folks*.[34]

Mrs. Stowe's early sketches, written while her father was president of Lane Seminary in Cincinnati, exploit her nostalgic feeling for the New England scene and do not venture into religion or theology beyond a few platitudes. *Uncle Tom's Cabin*, however, was written like most of her best books at a time of personal crisis and therefore plunged deeper. Once more God's mysterious ways had been exhibited in death, this time in her loss by cholera of a small son. *Uncle Tom*, written in the midst of poverty and the distractions of housekeeping, much of it nonetheless in a state of religious exaltation, is haunted by the deaths of children. Sometimes, as in the case of Little Eva, these deaths are models of holy and happy death reminiscent of thousands of contemporary tracts. Sometimes, however, they are grim and terrible. The slave Prue, who laconically reports the death of her own child as a result of her mistress's cruelty and neglect, is absolutely unsentimentalized. Prue knows that she is ugly, and wicked, and supposes she

[34] In this section even more than elsewhere I am influenced by the religious interpretation of Mrs. Stowe's entire literary development in Foster's *Rungless Ladder*. I discuss below only those works which seem to me to be directly relevant to *Oldtown Folks*.

is going to torment; but she is so miserable here and now that she does not care.

Much of the overt religious content of *Uncle Tom's Cabin* is in the tearful revivalistic vain which had, with the partial support of Lyman Beecher, become increasingly dominant in American Christianity. But the mark of Calvinism is there in the harsh realism about human nature that gives the book its lasting bite. Only Eva and Uncle Tom are capable of any dependable goodness. For less favored characters, the book again and again makes clear, "temptations to hardheartedness . . . always overcome frail human nature when the prospect of sudden and rapid gain is weighed in the balance, with no heavier counterpoise than the interests of the helpless and unprotected." [35]

After Uncle Tom, Mrs. Stowe's name became, in Annie Fields's phrase, "A sacred talisman, especially in Old and New England," [36] and the great authoress set off on a triumphal tour of Old England and Europe. Like most American authors, Mrs. Stowe found Europe somewhat overwhelming. She was fussed over by duchesses, and never quite got over making inept references to aristocratic glamour. (There are a few in *Oldtown Folks,* more in some of her other novels.) Dutifully doing the galleries, she set down her impressions in her travel journal, which is a mixture of conventional rhapsody, extreme provincial naïveté, and shrewd observation. At her shrewdest, she compared art critics to practitioners of the science she knew best and drew a characteristic conclusion. "Divided into little cliques, each with his shibboleth, artists excommunicate each other as heartily as theologians, and a neophyte who should attempt to make up a judgment by their help would be obliged to shift opinions with every circle. I therefore look with my own eyes, for if not the best that might be, they are the best that God has given me." [37]

For a Beecher recording her impressions of Europe, however, other issues were involved than those of aesthetics, issues which could not be so easily dismissed. Defending her ancestral loyalties against Europe's powerful blandishments, Mrs. Stowe harked back dutifully to the oppressions of feudalism and the horrors of the

[35] *Uncle Tom's Cabin* (Boston, 1852), p. 23.
[36] Fields, *Harriet Beecher Stowe* (London, 1898), p. 376.
[37] Stowe, *Sunny Memories of Foreign Lands* (Boston, 1854), II, 353.

Inquisition. Unless many American tourists, however, she remembered that slavery was a blemish on New World institutions which might well qualify any contempt for other countries.[38] Despite herself, she was attracted by the majestic ceremonial and uncontroversial preaching she encountered in the Church of England, and, still more, by the color and drama of continental Catholicism. Putting the question "if we *could,* would we efface from the world such cathedrals as Strasbourg and Cologne," she answered it easily enough in the negative.[39] Like many Protestant voyagers, she wondered whether Puritanism's hostility to art and enjoyment was necessary to religious truth, and she even found something innocent and attractive in the French Sunday. In Scotland, however, she was recalled to her usual sentiments by encountering again Sabbatarianism and doctrinal preaching. She reminded herself that only Protestant countries had achieved republican government and that unfortunately, "as a country is free and self-governed it has fewer public amusements. America and Scotland have the fewest of any, and Italy the most." [40] (Both these last two judgments are repeated in passing in *Oldtown Folks.*)

Finally, musing in Switzerland about the strength and weaknesses of the Genevan system and of Calvinism in general, giving due weight to the burning of Servetus and the Salem witchcraft trials, she reiterated her firm, if ambivalent loyalty:

Calvinism, in its essential features, will never cease from the earth, because the great fundamental facts of nature are Calvinistic, and men with strong minds and wills always discover it. The predestination of a sovereign will is written over all things. The old Greek tragedians read it, and expressed it. So did Mahomet, Napoleon, Cromwell. Why? They found it so by their own experience; they tried the forces of nature enough to find their strength . . . To him who strives in vain with the giant forces of evil, what calm in the thought of an overpowering will, so that will be crowned by goodness! However grim, to the distrusting, looks this fortress of sovereignty in times of flowery ease, yet in times when 'the waters roar and are troubled, and the mountains shake with the swelling thereof,' it has always been the refuge of God's people. All this I say, while I fully sympathize with the causes which incline many fine and beautiful minds against the system.[41]

[38] *Ibid.,* II, 417.
[39] *Ibid.,* II, 329.
[40] *Ibid.,* II, 359.
[41] *Ibid.,* II, 277. This passage is quoted in part in Foster, *Rungless Ladder,* p. 68.

This conclusion was shortly to be tested again by a further shaking of Harriet's foundations. After completing, in 1856, her second antislavery novel, *Dred,* which contained a strong attack on ministers lukewarm to the cause, as her father had been, she was turned sharply back to the problem that had always haunted her most deeply. In 1857 her favorite son Henry was drowned at Dartmouth in a swimming accident. Not only was she almost overwhelmed with grief; all the old questions were again raised, and they were still theological questions. Not without difficulty, with the help of Catharine among others of her family, she managed to settle in her mind the question of Henry's eternal state. In one desperate letter she hinted that God could not be so unfair as to punish one who was not only innocent but "the child of one who had trusted and confided in him for years." [42] She really knew, however, that this was pushing the idea of a hereditary covenant too far, and it was in the same letter that she was able to make the statement, quoted earlier, that Christ's love must swallow up the mystery of God's ways with us.[43] Nevertheless, neither then nor later was this an easy conclusion for Mrs. Stowe to reach and hold, and it was in part her renewed pondering of the problem that sent her back to ancestral ground for her novels. From this point on, her main overt subject was what her main implied subject had always been, God's ways and New England's perception of them.

In 1858, asked for a contribution to the first issue of the *Atlantic Monthly,* that organ of Boston Unitarianism and uplift, Mrs. Stowe sent in, incongruously enough, a parable of death as teacher in the traditional orthodox mold, only slightly softened. A father, sending a package of presents from town to his cheerful family, includes a black mourning veil. Most of the children think it ugly, but a minister who turns up says that until one has seen the world through such a veil, he has not truly lived. Sure enough, family catastrophe provides an opportunity for its use, and the sketch ends with the mother, who has lost a child, putting away the veil with her sad mementoes "in solemn thankfulness." Sentimental as

[42] H.B.S. to Catharine Beecher, no date, quoted in C. E. Stowe, *Life,* p. 322.
[43] *Ibid.* It should be pointed out that she attributes this insight partly to a sermon of her husband's.

it may seem, this story is much more succinct and effective than the great bulk of Mrs. Stowe's potboiling occasional pieces.[44]

Her next contribution to the *Atlantic* was a review article about the first two volumes of that delightful mine of American clerical lore, W. B. Sprague's *Annals of the American Pulpit*. Not only does she demonstrate by affectionate retelling of Sprague's anecdotes the provincial eccentricity of New England ministers over two centuries, she also emphasizes their unrelenting and courageous search for complete, logical answers to the most difficult questions. Increasingly free herself from the need to struggle with the particular formulations of New England theology, she insists (doubtless with some *Atlantic* authors in mind) that "It is a mark of a shallow mind to scorn these theological wrestlings and surgings; they have had in them something even sublime." [45] Mrs. Stowe was a thrifty author, and she was to incorporate a large section of this excellent essay verbatim into chapter 19 of *Oldtown Folks*.

In 1859 Mrs. Stowe published *The Minister's Wooing*, which prefigures *Oldtown Folks* more completely than any of her other works. The book's main character is Samuel Hopkins, and Mrs. Stowe had done some historical research. Her main, though not her only, source of information was Edwards Amasa Park, the last major developer and defender of Edwardsian theology. Park had written a useful biography of Hopkins and was working on one of Emmons which was to be still better. Since he taught at Andover Seminary, whose faculty Calvin Stowe had recently joined, Mrs. Stowe was able to read him parts of her manuscript. As a novelist may, she took her historical research lightly, and altered to fit her plot the incidents of Hopkins' life. For this she was criticized by orthodox reviewers. Yet her liberties with Hopkins' doctrines were few, and her attitude toward them far from completely hostile.

One subplot of the book is concerned with Hopkins' brave and early (and actual) denunciation of slavery. The major plot is a recapitulation of the loss of Fisher, seen through Mrs. Stowe's own mourning veil. The fiancé of a devoted Puritan maiden is drowned at sea, or seems to be (the fact that he turns up later is an unim-

[44] "The Mourning Veil," *Atlantic Monthly*, 1 (1858): 63–70.
[45] *Atlantic Monthly*, 1 (1858): 485–492.

portant concession to public taste). The girl, a saintly character modeled not on Catharine but on Mrs. Stowe's mother, Roxana Beecher,[46] accepts the loss in the proper spirit, but the boy's mother is unable to do so. Like Catharine, and perhaps a little like Mrs. Stowe herself, the bereaved mother goes most convincingly through torments of despair and near-blasphemy, only to be saved in the end, rather unconvincingly, by the simple heart-religion of a Negro slave.

The Minister's Wooing has its share of gush and melodrama and conventional piety, and is further marred by the introduction of a stock French countess, doubtless to show the author's ability to handle a high European style. Yet in at least two chapters the author anticipates and equals the best of *Oldtown Folks*. Chapter 4, "Theological Tea," develops successfully the new genre of dialect folk theology. And the first part of Chapter 24, "Views of Divine Government," is Mrs. Stowe's most direct and most powerful piece of theological criticism so far. Grand and impressive as the New England systems are, she is now sure that they differ from the New Testament "as the living embrace of a friend does from his lifeless body, mapped out under the knife of the anatomical demonstrator." "All systems," moreover, "that deal with the infinite are, besides, exposed to danger from small, unsuspected admixtures of human error, which become deadly when carried to such vast results."[47] Deadly, that is, to the most sensitive spirits, who take them most to heart in the concerns of life and death.

Attacked by the orthodox, Mrs. Stowe was reassured by Lowell, who not only praised her for going back to ground she knew but, as somebody who himself had to confess "a strong sympathy with many parts of Calvinist orthodoxy," gave her his own rather odd theological imprimatur: "If, with your heart and brain, you are not orthodox, in Heaven's name, who is? If you mean 'Calvinistic,' no woman could ever be such, for Calvinism is logic, and no woman worth the name could ever live by syllogisms."[48]

[46] As Foster shows, Mrs. Stowe characteristically ascribes to her heroine the entire text of a letter from Roxana to Lyman Beecher. The letter expresses Roxana's simple and confident faith in Christ in response to Beecher's Calvinist inquiries. Foster, *Rungless Ladder*, pp. 114–116.

[47] *The Minister's Wooing* (Riverside ed.), p. 274.

[48] Lowell to H.B.S., February 4, 1859, quoted in full in C. E. Stowe, *Life*, pp. 333–336.

In 1862 Mrs. Stowe published another New England novel, *The Pearl of Orr's Island.* This was again a half-success, and was less directly concerned with theology than *The Minister's Wooing.* Her other work of the same year, *Agnes of Sorrento,* transferred the familiar theological issues with no great success to Renaissance Italy. It was time for her to bring her favorite theme and her favorite locale back together, and she was now ready to do so.

Through the sixties, through the strains of the Civil War (in which Mrs. Stowe called for the destruction of the ungodly as fiercely as any Old Testament prophet), through the drudgery of prolific professional authorship, through the difficulties of emerging into a grander style of living, Mrs. Stowe was brooding over her major New England novel, and in her own phrase "skimming and saving the cream" for it.[49] By 1865 she was ready to start the actual writing of it. With her religious and literary development in mind, it is possible for us to see clearly some of the many sources on which she drew.

Once more, a major work coincided with a major grief, this time the destruction by alcoholism of her son Fred.[50] She was by now, however, accustomed to grief, and there is no evidence that this disaster hit her as hard as Henry's death had. *Oldtown Folks* does not, like *The Minister's Wooing,* show the effects of obsession with a particular loss, though the general problem of accepting whatever is Divinely ordained is constantly present to its Calvinist characters, and several of Mrs. Stowe's past griefs are occasionally reflected. For some years she had been tending more and more toward something like her mother's religion of accepting, unanalytic love. Increasingly, she was finding the Protestant Episcopal Church the proper vessel for this kind of piety. To Mrs. Stowe, and to many other New Englanders of her generation, Anglicanism seemed to offer far more than ritual and decorum. There was, as Ellery Davenport points out in *Oldtown Folks,* plenty of Calvinism in the Thirty-Nine Articles. There was also, however, confession and absolution in the service, and the assurance, which former Edwardsians badly needed, that God hates nothing he has made. Yet Mrs. Stowe still retained a certain detachment, and was able

---

[49] H.B.S. to Mrs. Fields, undated, apparently 1864.
[50] C. E. and L. B. Stowe, *Harriet Beecher Stowe,* p. 278.

in *Oldtown Folks* to make fun of the more extreme claims of the Church of England in Revolutionary America.[51]

More than ever before, she was attracted at the end of the fifties by her father's archenemy, Bostonian liberalism, especially in the person of its reigning favorite, Dr. Oliver Wendell Holmes. Understandably, Holmes had been a little worried when in 1859 he had been deputed to escort the Stowes to a meeting of the Saturday Club. The teetotal and straitlaced Stowes were indeed gently baited by the discreetly jocular assembly, and Holmes hoped that Mrs. Stowe would not disapprove of him *very* much.[52]

Holmes was worried about more fundamental matters than the wine and wit of the Saturday Club. Like Mrs. Stowe, he was the son of a moderate Calvinist minister, but he had reacted against his upbringing far more strongly. In his *Autocrat,* and still more in its sequel *The Professor at the Breakfast Table,* he was unable to resist baiting the orthodox, urbanely but none the less sharply. His article on Jonathan Edwards was an eloquent version of the usual liberal caricature. And his lectures are full of his own bland synthesis of uplift, relativism, mechanism, and the ethics of the New Testament — a system at least as full of paradox as that of Nathaniel Emmons.[53]

Mrs. Stowe, however, answered Holmes' letter with great cor-

[51] In her last New England novel, *Poganuc People,* she was to treat Anglicanism more gently and more at length. Here the scene is Litchfield, and the main character a much idealized version of her father, whose battle with the Episcopalians is softened almost beyond recognition. In a fairly acute passage about the various reasons people joined the Episcopal Church, she suggests her own increasingly sentimental attitude toward it: "Then, too, there came to them gentle spirits, cut and bleeding by the sharp crystals of doctrinal statement, and courting the balm of devotional liturgy and the cool shadowy indefiniteness of more aesthetic forms of worship." *Poganuc People* (Boston, 1878), p. 27.

[52] Eleanor M. Tilton, *Amiable Autocrat: A Biography of Dr. Oliver Wendell Holmes* (New York, 1947), pp. 250f.

[53] The essay on Edwards can be found in Holmes's *Pages from an Old Volume of Life* (Boston, 1892), pp. 361–401. The best single statement of his religious-philosophical position is probably "Mechanism in Thought and Morals," his Harvard Phi Beta Kappa address of 1870, to be found in the same volume, pp. 260–314. Though not yet delivered when *Oldtown Folks* was being written, this address summarizes long-held views. His biographer believes that a reference in *The Professor at the Breakfast Table* to a "beautiful and affecting letter" from one whose name "is known to all, in some of its representations" refers to Mrs. Stowe. The letter apparently protests unduly harsh treatment of ministers. Holmes gently stated his respect for the cloth, and then grew on to the usual effective attack. Tilton, *Amiable Autocrat,* p. 250. The number of the *Professor* referred to was originally published in the *Atlantic Monthly,* 3 (1859): 609–620, immediately before a chapter of *The Minister's Wooing.*

diality and some sprightliness, and he became her closest literary friend. Both the Stowes defended Holmes against the attacks of the orthodox when in 1861 he published his novel *Elsie Venner,* an odd parable of determinism and moral irresponsibility in which the heroine's character is shaped by a prenatal rattlesnake bite.[54] As both Holmes and Mrs. Stowe realized, both were struggling with the same upbringing, and neither was completely victorious in the struggle. "I have been," said Holmes

in the doctrinal boiler at Andover, and the rational ice-chest at Cambridge. I have been hung with my head downwards, from the hook of a theological dogma, and set on my feet again by the hand of uninspired common-sense. I have found myself like a nursery-tree, growing up with labels of this and that article of faith wired to my limbs. The labels have dropped off, but the wires are only buried in my flesh, which has grown over them . . . I do not say that you have been through all this . . . Yet, I say we have had some experiences in common, and however imperfectly I express myself by word or by letter, now or at any time, there are mental and emotional states which you can understand as none can do who have not been through the chronometer of experience.[55]

I do not believe you or I can ever get the iron of Calvinism out of our souls.[56]

More than Holmes was quite able to realize, this was true of Mrs. Stowe, and there is one indication that, despite her cordiality, she was stung by his constant belaboring of the orthodox. Identifying herself fully, for the first time in a long while, with her father's people rather than with his Bostonian enemies, she wrote Fields refusing to have *Oldtown Folks* published in the *Atlantic:*

There are several objections to the plan you propose. In the first place, as to the success of the book *as* a book. It is more to me than a story; it is my resume of the whole spirit and body of New England — a country that now is exerting such an influence on the civilized world that to know it truly becomes an object.

But the Atlantic has on the part of *my* people (i.e., the orthodox) prejudices to encounter that would *predispose* them to look suspiciously on it, more than ever by the fact of its being by a Beecher.

Dr. Holmes has stung and irritated them by his sharp, scathing irony and keen ridicule; and, after all, they are not ridiculous, and the estimate

[54] Foster, *Rungless Ladder,* pp. 131–132.
[55] Holmes to H.B.S., May 29, 1867, quoted in John T. Morse, Jr., *Life and Letters of Oliver Wendell Holmes* (2 vols., Boston, 1896), p. 226.
[56] Holmes to H.B.S., no date, *ibid.,* p. 246.

of New England life and principles and orthodoxy, as dramatically set forth, must be graver and wider than he has revealed it.

Under all the drollery that is to be found in it, this book will be found to have in it the depths of the most solemn tragedy of life, and I shall make it my means of saying many things which I hope will be accepted pacifically on all sides. It will answer my purpose better to be read at once in a book. To spend two years in getting my story before the world, before half of my friends will read or judge, would not suit my views.[57]

By the sixties, Mrs. Stowe was indeed ready to write about all the varieties of New England religious experience: agnosticism, Episcopalianism, Arminianism, and various shades of orthodoxy, with remarkable detachment. It is worth noticing however that the variety that comes off worst, despite the personal worth of its representative, is Parson Lothrop's Arminianism. This kind of liberal optimism, the ancestor of Holmes' Brahminism, proves inadequate to deal with death, and that is still for Mrs. Stowe the main test. Even Ellery Davenport, the scoffer, is allowed to speak more convincingly than the liberal Christian optimist.

One major remaining source both for Mrs. Stowe's opinions and her facts, and one whose importance is often minimized, was the author's husband. Professor Calvin Stowe, by no means the henpecked mediocrity he is sometimes turned into (even by his wife), accepted with a good deal of grace the difficult role of attendant to a literary lioness. A man of considerable Biblical learning (he was so fond of Hebrew studies that Mrs. Stowe referred to him as "My old Rab," for Rabbi), he remained more definitely than his wife a follower of Edwards. Yet, like her and like many of the most intelligent members of his generation, he hung onto his loyalties with difficulty. In letters to his father-in-law, he expressed his tormenting doubts about God and Christ, and his concern over his own sensual tendencies.[58] Outwardly serene enough, he had a reputation as a narrator in New England dialect of odd incidents from his boyhood in Natick, Massachusetts. These formed the main basis of incident and minor character in *Oldtown Folks,* and Calvin Stowe was permitted to criticize the manuscript as it was written.

The most surprising fact about Calvin Stowe is that he saw

[57] H.B.S. to James B. Fields, August 16, 1868, Stowe papers. Quoted in full with minor inaccuracies by Forrest Wilson, *Crusader in Crinoline* (New York, 1941), pp. 530–531.
[58] See Edmund Wilson's essay on Calvin Stowe in *Patriotic Gore,* pp. 59–70.

visions, strange appearances he had learned to take for granted, sometimes a man and woman, sometimes a boy, sometimes vague cloudy shapes. He was also occasionally visited by clairvoyant intuitions about death and the dead. From time to time Mrs. Stowe, partly because of her husband's gift but more out of her own griefs, gave serious consideration to spiritualism. In the long run, however, she largely rejected it. Edwards, after all, had had no use for visions, and Dr. Park of Andover was sure Calvin Stowe's visions came from a disease of the optic nerve.[59] Nonetheless, the visions were included in *Oldtown Folks* with the rest of Calvin Stowe's memories, and were the part of the book which occasioned the most contemporary discussion. To later readers, it seems probable that the author was not much more interested in them than we are.

With her husband's reminiscences, Mrs. Stowe mixed episodes from her own childhood and her father's, incidents already used in her earlier works, and items drawn from research. This eclecticism, besides providing harmless work for the literary detective, seems to raise some doubt not only about the authenticity but about the dating of Mrs. Stowe's principal account of New England society. Pointers scattered through the text of *Oldtown Folks* — mentions of the Constitutional Convention, then of Washington as President, then of the French Revolution and the Terror — date the story precisely; it takes place in the years from 1787 to 1793. For the book's most important purposes, it does not matter a great deal that some of its incidents occurred in the Beecher family twenty and thirty years later. Its main subject is the twilight of New England's Calvinist order. That order declined over a long period, and at a different pace in different places. Mrs. Stowe knew this decline both at first hand and through her father's reminiscences. Her own life extended from 1811 almost until the end of the century. More important, by the time she wrote *Oldtown Folks,* her immediate and acute experience ran from Nathaniel Emmons to Oliver Wendell Holmes.

For whatever it is worth, many of the book's particular incidents and characters have long been assigned real antecedents, and we can assign a few more. Local tradition, alive in the time of Mrs. Stowe's early biographers, identified many of the minor *Oldtown*

[59] McCray, *Life-Work,* p. 379.

characters.[60] Parson Lothrop, whose real name was Stephen Badger, was an Arminian, avoided doctrinal preaching, and modeled his style on that of Addison.[61] Parson Badger did have a wife whose Tory sympathies were tolerated as the eccentricity of a great lady. Uncle Fly is modeled on a Natick tavernkeeper, and Sam Lawson on a real village character named Sam Lawton. The narrator's jovial Harvard uncle is William Bigelow, a real "Uncle Bill" of Calvin Stowe's and a Natick wit and occasional poet. Mrs. Stowe herself refers her readers to a source for the town's haunted house and the legend of Sir Harry Frankland that explains the haunting.[62] The book's Indians have actual counterparts even to their names. Natick was founded in 1651 as a refuge for John Eliot's "praying Indians," and only Indians were at first permitted to own land there. As the American story so often goes, by 1750 most of the land was in white hands, and the Indians hung on as a sort of ragged fringe on village society. The details of daily life in Oldtown — food, clothes, speech, and so forth — are no doubt part of both Stowes' common memories of their separate upbringings. A few such details are apparently drawn from Lyman Beecher's reminiscences of a still earlier time.[63]

Of the three child characters on whom the plot is loosely hung, Horace Holyoke, the useful but colorless narrator, is of course poor Calvin Stowe himself. Tina is Mrs. Stowe's liveliest child, her daughter Georgiana. As for Harry, with his ringlets and his ineffable smile, if he is anybody he is little Eva, with perhaps some echoes, when he is patiently enduring affliction and defending only his religion, of Uncle Tom. This religion, which combines a remarkable certainty of God's love with a strong taste for Epis-

---

[60] For this purpose the most useful of the biographies is C. E. and L. B. Stowe, *Harriet Beecher Stowe,* esp. pp. 258–260. Local tradition and two early town histories are drawn upon to identify *Oldtown* characters in "The Story of Natick," a pamphlet published by the Natick Federal Savings and Loan Association (Natick, 1948). One of the early histories, Oliver N. Bacon, *A History of Natick* (Boston, 1856), contains "A Brief Account of the Customs and Manners of Living in the Days of Our Forefathers" which, with other material in this book, may have been used by Mrs. Stowe to supplement her husband's reminiscences.

[61] Bacon, *Natick,* p. 66. An earlier history makes him both an Arminian and a Unitarian, adding that he thought it politic to conceal the latter belief. William Biglow, *History of the Town of Natick* (Boston, 1830), p. 61.

[62] Elias Nason, *Sir Charles Frankland, Baronet, or Boston in the Colonial Times* (Albany, 1865).

[63] For instance the preparation of pies for Thanksgiving, and freezing them for use all winter. *Autobiography,* I, 15.

copalian formulations, is that of Roxana Beecher and her earlier literary incarnations. It is the kind of religion for which Mrs. Stowe herself had struggled all her life with only partial success.

Miss Rossiter manages, as Mrs. Stowe was trying to do, to move from Calvinism through doubt to a religion of love. But her younger sister Emily is, like Catharine Beecher, unable to recover from exposure to Dr. Stern's (Emmons') "appalling doctrines," made still more devastating by the loss of a favorite brother (not a fiancé). Instead of becoming a heretic like Catharine, Emily takes the road to moral ruin. The story is told in the exchange of letters between the Rossiter brother and sister, with the brother concluding that the family had done wrong to allow Emily to be "baited and tortured with ultra-Calvinism."

The supreme example of this kind of ultra-Calvinism is Dr. Stern, who haunts the book as Nathaniel Emmons himself haunted the Beecher family. Immediately before Stern, who is actually Emmons, is introduced, there is a reference to "the deepest tragedy" in "our own family," which cannot be understood without reference to a peculiar society conditioned by a peculiar theology. Apparently this refers to the disastrous flight of Miss Rossiter's sister Emily, which results in her moral downfall. This flight was associated with Emily's reaction to Stern's sermons. Since, however, the episode does not actually occur in the narrator's family, it seems possible that Mrs. Stowe may here be referring — perhaps by a slip — to the greatest disaster in her own family, the loss of Fisher and Catharine's reaction to it. This also, it will be remembered, was made especially poignant by Emmons' preaching.

Throughout the book, Mrs. Stowe's references to Stern are undoubtedly sharpened by her own recollections of Emmons and her family's association with him. Her major account of his life, in Chapter 29, is, however, drawn from Professor Park's biography of Emmons, first published in 1861. It is a measure of the balance achieved by Mrs. Stowe that she is able to treat Stern with such detached and sympathetic irony. Robust people like "Grandmother Badger" are able to live with arch-Calvinist doctrines and retain their humanity, but for the sensitive, preaching like Stern's has a devastating effect. Nonetheless, and despite her own and her sister's sufferings at his hands, Mrs. Stowe pays tribute to Stern's courage and consistency: "In all this if there is something terrible and painful, there is something also which is grand, and in which we can take pride, as the fruit of our human nature. Peace to his ashes: he has learned better things ere now." To reach this point, Mrs. Stowe had traveled a long and painful journey.

The Boston Episcopalian establishment the children visit is partly modeled on "Nutplains," Harriet Beecher's mother's house. At "Nutplains," where some of Harriet Beecher's happiest childhood memories were centered, there was both a kind grandmother who was a defender of King George, and a strong-minded aunt who insisted that visiting children learn *both* catechisms, their father's and hers, and conceded that dissenting clergymen could be saved by God's "uncovenanted mercies" outside the Church. "Nutplains" undergoes a magic upgrading in the novel into a more than Bostonian mansion; in her own reminiscences Mrs. Stowe refers to it affectionately as "a lonely little farmhouse under the hill." [64]

Cloudland, where the children go to school, is Litchfield, with its beautiful hill country, its unusually cultivated society (mainly brought there by the famous law school), and its Academy.[65] The school in the book is a somewhat rose-colored version of the real one, but many of its actual graduates fervently praised Litchfield Female Academy. It had been founded in 1750 by Miss Sarah Pierce, with the purpose of teaching young ladies not only embroidery and music but such branches as Latin, sacred and profane history, and geography, which were usually considered essential only for young gentlemen. The school was not, as Mrs. Stowe implies, representative of New England academies, nor was it on principle coeducational, though some boys (including some male Beechers) were admitted. Most of its educational innovation was the work of Miss Pierce's nephew, John Pierce Brace, who is the original of Jonathan Rossiter. Under his regime the Litchfield Female Academy did indeed display some of the social liberalism

[64] Mrs. Stowe's reminiscences of "Nutplains" are in Lyman Beecher's *Autobiography,* I, 228–234.
[65] The best sources on Litchfield Female Academy, in addition to the standard Stowe material, are Alain C. White, *The History of the Town of Litchfield, Connecticut, 1720–1920* (Litchfield, 1920), and Elizabeth C. Barney Buel, ed., *The Chronicles of a Pioneer School* (Cambridge, Mass., 1903), which puts together a mass of primary material. Both are supplemented by Harveson, *Catharine Esther Beecher,* and by descriptions of the school by both Catharine and Harriet Beecher in their father's *Autobiography,* I, 164–166, 397–399.

and some of the academic seriousness attributed to it in the novel. There were, for instance, dancing parties which were open to the young gentlemen from the law school, and plays with Biblical subjects, including the one about Jephthah's daughter described in the novel. On the other hand pupils had to memorize a long and strict set of rules, accurately quoted in the novel, and Miss Pierce sometimes threatened the unruly with the penalties of the next world as well as this. As in the novel, ambitious themes were assigned for discussion and writing. Harriet Beecher herself, at twelve, wrote a logical, highly conventional essay answering in the negative the question debated in the novel by Harry and Esther: "Can the Immortality of the Soul Be Proved by the Light of Nature?" [66]

Religious instruction in the Academy was attended by Lyman Beecher, as it is in the novel by his prototype Dr. Avery. The Beecher theological position, stretching Calvinism to provide hope for nearly everybody, is described accurately enough in the novel, as are Beecher's methods of argument. The "Minister's wood-spell" comes from the *Autobiography*, as does the consocation meeting, with liquor and argument flowing freely (in the *Autobiography*, Beecher remembers this as a background for the prohibitionist movement that swept the clergy soon after).[67] Esther, Dr. Avery's intellectual daughter, is somehow unable to yield to the religious pressures even of such an admirable father, and refuses to be converted until she falls in love. Obviously she is an idealized combination of Catharine (whose middle name was Esther) and Harriet herself.

A number of characters and incidents are warmed over from previous use. The repetition of long passages from Mrs. Stowe's 1858 essay on "New England Ministers" has already been mentioned. *Uncle Tom's Cabin* provides the quite irrelevant "Raid on Oldtown" in Chapter 28, and is echoed less precisely by the children's flight from Old Crab Smith. In *The Pearl of Orr's Island*, Mrs. Stowe had already made use of a mysterious but unmistakably aristocratic child, who like Harry and Tina is adopted by a New England town when the mother dies. *The Minister's Wooing* provided still more material for *Oldtown Folks*, including one of its

[66] The essay is printed in full in C. E. Stowe, *Life*, pp. 15–21.
[67] *Autobiography*, I, 179, 238–239.

major characters, the satanic, brilliant grandson of Jonathan Edwards who in the later book is called Ellery Davenport but in *The Minister's Wooing* is identified as Edwards' actual grandson, Aaron Burr.

It is clear that Mrs. Stowe intended this book, for which she ransacked so ruthlessly her own and her husband's memories and her own earlier works, to be a masterpiece. It is less than that, and in some ways it is more interesting than if it were written with the control that masterpieces demand. It is most obviously interesting to students of American mores and religion. As Lowell told her, Mrs. Stowe could use her eyes, and she could, much of the time, use her imagination. Frequently she shows a talent for the evocative detail. One does not forget the dog's paws ticking up and down the meetinghouse aisle; or the turkey, languid from the cold, his wattles turned blue, lying over Caesar's shoulder while he is taken to the house so that grandmother can force down his throat Indian-meal mixed with peppercorns. A rather richer mixture of imagination with memory produces all Mrs. Stowe's best characters — all unfortunately minor characters and most, as the *Nation* observed, women. Lavishly, she gives her readers not one New England old maid but five: Miss Asphyxia, Aunt Lois, Miss Rossiter, the maid Polly, and the Anglican Miss Deborah. Each is different from the rest, and each is far more than a caricature out of stock. Sam Lawson, so much admired by nineteenth-century readers, is also more than a stock rendition of a cracker-barrel philosopher, though he is given too much of the story to carry, and at times breaks down under the burden.

Mrs. Stowe's imaginative perception extends from individuals to society. Her systematic review of the village social structure, illustrated in the church's seating arrangements, beginning neatly with the minister and leading families and trailing off into the Indian fringe, is a tour de force. Her explanation of the kind of pre-eminence which old families like the Rossiters enjoy, despite Oldtown's quite real social democracy, is more acute than a good deal of New England social research.

Above all, Mrs. Stowe uses her imagination effectively in dealing with history. In seeing Edwardsian Calvinism as an aberration from the New England tradition of bargaining with God, an aberration both triumphant and disastrous, Mrs. Stowe long anticipates the findings of historians. To do so took an enviable combination of firsthand knowledge and long-range vision. The opening image of New England's live coals, burning in isolation and obscurity beneath the surface, is the kind of image that is more than useful; it is illuminating.

Mrs. Stowe, moreover, has a point to make about intellectual history in general that is well worth the attention of historians. Ideas, she points out, though they do indeed dominate communities and nobody is immune from their influence, affect different people in different ways; as she puts it, "temperament gradually, but with irresistible power," modifies creed. As for the origins of "temperament," Mrs. Stowe knows well that individuality is partly a product of social forces, but of forces too complex to weigh and measure with confidence: "The humblest human being is the sum total of a column of figures which go back through centuries before he was born. Old Crab Smith and Miss Asphyxia, if their biographies were rightly written, would be found to be the result and out-come of certain moral and social forces, justly to discriminate which might puzzle a philosopher." This balance between determinism and freedom, one which many recent historians might well envy, is of course derived from Mrs. Stowe's theological inheritance. She does far more than simply to proclaim the necessity and fruitfulness of such a balanced vision; she triumphantly illustrates it again and again.

There is no question that *Oldtown Folks* is a valuable, and at times a masterly, piece of social and intellectual history. The question remains whether it is a good novel, or even a novel at all. Certainly Mrs. Stowe lacked some of the kinds of talent a novelist needs. She was never, for one thing, much interested in plot; except in *Uncle Tom's Cabin* (and there the success is partial) her plots are a failure; her dramatic structure is not only uninteresting, but even gets in the way of what she wants to say. In *Oldtown Folks* the plot has little to do with her announced purpose of recapturing ante-railroad New England and even, finally, takes her clear out of her chosen locale. The book is best where it is static, as in the first seven chapters, largely descriptive of Oldtown. In the next section, chapters 8 through 15, the children find a new home and the major characters are in motion. This part is saved from dullness only by minor characters like Miss Asphyxia. In the next and longest section, in which everybody settles down again in Oldtown, the superb observation of village life generally makes the adventures of the children tolerable, and is interrupted only by the unconvincing excursion into Boston high life. In chapters 32 to 39 the book's pace again slows down while Cloudland, its school and its minister, are described almost as successfully as Oldtown. Then, in the last chapters, the pace of events quickens and the book runs rapidly downhill. By this time, all Mrs. Stowe wanted was to mail the last chapters. Since she has no more to say, she relies on coincidence and melodrama, heavily coated with sentimentality and liberally spiced with high life. Harry turns out to be a missing heir and even Tina preaches — and she preaches moreover the simplest of moralities with no undergirding of theology. Inevitably, when the Oldtown people come to Boston for the wedding and are forced again to go through their paces, now in the presence of the quality, they become quaint.

Mrs. Stowe's style cannot very profitably be discussed in terms of conventional literary influences. Like everybody who writes, she was influenced by what she had read. Like everybody who read at all and was brought up when she was, she was influenced by Scott — in her case not the Scott of *Ivanhoe,* whose influence in America Mark Twain and others deplore, but the Scott of *The Heart of Mid-Lothian,* the Scott who turned to native subjects and the lives of the humble, the Scott for whom Lyman Beecher raised his ban on fiction. She read Maria Edgeworth early, as a young woman learned to like Madame de Staël's *Corinne,* and never got over the Byron craze that swept New England in her youth.

Mrs. Stowe, as some of her biographers point out, was not much interested in literature. She was a prolific professional author, but much of her production, in tracts and magazine pieces, can be called subliterary. Despite her friendship with Holmes and her warm relations with the Fields, she took almost no part in New England literary life. In the heyday of the Genteel Tradition, when veneration for the past and conscious imitation of approved models were all too common, it was not really a disadvantage to live outside literary circles.

Most of the time Mrs. Stowe frankly refused to bother about style at all, except for a few specific purposes. She insisted that her

best work came from God. In his own way, even so skeptical a
critic as Edmund Wilson accepts this statement: her best writing
came from her subconscious.

In *Oldtown Folks,* she uses at least three styles. One, the one in
which she labors her way through the plot, is the standard polite
diction of her day. She is more informal than most of her contemporaries. Setpieces of elaborate description are rare, and mock-
heroic diction, that favorite device of Victorian authors dealing
with the humble, is employed only rarely, when she is tired of her
material.

The style Mrs. Stowe worked at hardest, and one in which she
was a pioneer, is dialect. Sam Lawson at his best, Miss Nervy
teaching Latin, and Grandmother needling Aunt Lois speak with
originality and point. Their utterance is not at all in the already
conventional vein of the comic Yankee, because Mrs. Stowe's purpose is not patronizing or trivial. It is significant that some of her
sharpest theological criticism is delivered through characters who
speak dialect. Miss Asphyxia, accused by Grandmother of having
a hard heart, tellingly asks what else she *could* have, not being
elected, but makes it clear that she considers herself quite as good
for all worldly purposes as any church member. Sam Lawson puts
the perennial question graphically: "Ef a man's cut off his hands,
it ain't right to require him to chop wood. Wal, Polly, she says he'd
no business to cut his hands off; and so he ought to be required
to chop the wood all the same. Wal, I told her it was Adam
chopped our hands off."

In dealing with rural New England speech, Mrs. Stowe made
an exception to her usual carelessness about detail. Writing Fields,
just as she was finishing *Oldtown Folks* and while batches of proof
were coming in, she complained about the proofreader she usually
trusted:

There is one thing I wish to have you expound to my accurate friend
and family connection Mr. Bigelow, when he sends my proof of yankee
talk. The genuine yankee always calls things this ere and that are.

This ere woman and that 'are man.

Now I always spell them according to the sound this *ere* and that *are*
— but my accurate friend Mr. Bigelow always alters it & wont let me
print 'that *are*' simply because being a contraction of *there* it is more

accurate to spell it 'that 'ere'. Now please ask him to have it printed *my* way in future." [68]

The third style Mrs. Stowe uses, and the one that comes most clearly from her subconscious, is the prophetic. If we cannot accept her own view of her inspiration, we can perhaps admit that she was a prophetess at third hand. As she says, the taste of all New Englanders was formed on the King James Bible, and in her case the Bible was mediated through a tradition of lively evangelical preaching. In *Oldtown Folks* Mrs. Stowe puts on the prophetic mantle only briefly and rarely, and when she does it fits; she is talking about her Israel and its decline.

In terms of American literary history, Mrs. Stowe's New England novels are a part of the beginning of the local color movement.[69] She could draw, it is true, on a considerable number of minor genre pieces, a large repertory of Yankee dialect humor, and an oral tradition of folklore. She did make use of all these. Mrs. Lydia Sigourney, for one — an author known to Mrs. Stowe — made some attempt to treat religious history in dialect. A comic farmer, in her *Sketch of Connecticut,* criticizes the ways of Episcopalians and Methodists.[70] But Mrs. Sigourney's treatment, both of Connecticut and its religion, is from outside. She plays the role of an aristocratic visitor, who finds rustic ways morally admirable but stylistically amusing.

Mrs. Stowe usually avoids this tone, and is among the first writers to render the scene and speech of an American region with respect as well as fidelity. *Oldtown Folks* barely antedates the principal works of Bret Harte, who does not attain this standard, and of Edward Eggleston, who does. All the New England local writers who followed Mrs. Stowe were, like her, motivated by

[68] H.B.S. to Fields, March 2, 1869. Stowe papers. Her injunction was followed in her next book, *Sam Lawson's Oldtown Fireside Stories.*

[69] For estimates of Mrs. Stowe's position in the local color movement, see Walter Blair, *Native American Humor* (New York, 1937); Perry D. Westbrook, *Acres of Flint* (Washington, 1961); and Richard M. Dorson, *Jonathan Draws the Long Bow* (Cambridge, Mass., 1946).

[70] Lydia H. Sigourney, *Sketch of Connecticut Forty Years Since* (Hartford, 1824), p. 116. Mrs. Sigourney was a Hartford authoress, and probably known personally by Harriet Beecher during her first Hartford stay. Catharine Beecher wrote her asking help in promoting her treatise on Domestic Economy: see Harveson, *Catharine Esther Beecher,* p. 77. Mrs. Stowe certainly read Mrs. Sigourney, and borrowed as was her custom. A pair of twins in the *Sketch* are called Roxy and Ruey, the names used for the two old maids in *The Pearl of Orr's Island.*

nostalgia for what was passing, but most were much more sentimental than their predecessor. Until *Poganuc People*, Mrs. Stowe
does not use the sturdy New England virtues, as many others did,
to attack the faults of newcomers.

Judged solely as a specimen of regional literature, *Sam Lawson's
Oldtown Fireside Stories*, in which Mrs. Stowe used up her surplus
Oldtown material, may contain her best work.[71] The dialect is
meticulous, the folklore and legend rich, the touch fairly light.
Fireside Stories gives us an idea of what *Oldtown Folks* might
have amounted to, if Mrs. Stowe had been trying to portray the
surface of a time and a place, and trying nothing more.

If we see *Oldtown Folks* in relation to the regional movement,
it achieves an honorable place. To compare it to the greatest works
of American fiction is equally illuminating, but the result is less
flattering. Hawthorne, Melville, and Mark Twain have all been
occasionally invoked in the course of the recent revival of interest
in Mrs. Stowe. It is true that both *Moby Dick* and the *Scarlet
Letter* deal with the same problem as *Oldtown Folks*, the evil in
the universe and man's perception of it through the medium of
Christian theology. But there the resemblance stops. Melville and
Hawthorne were able to organize a novel to make their philosophical and theological points; Mrs. Stowe had to make her points
either through minor characters or in her own person; her narrative has little to do with them.

Neither Melville nor Hawthorne, though both nodded, could
ever have written the most conventional and sentimental parts
of *Oldtown Folks*. Mark Twain, the most uneven of major writers,
could, and the comparison of Mrs. Stowe with her Hartford neighbor has something to tell us. *Huckleberry Finn*, like most of *Oldtown Folks*, was written in the prosperous section of Hartford
known as Nook Farm, a place of mansions, ample grounds, liberal
Beecherized religion, and other evidences of Victorian culture.[72]
Like Mrs. Stowe, Clemens looked back from this Hartford to the
time and place of his childhood, and sometimes he looked with

---

[71] Foster considers this book her most artistic performance, *Rungless Ladder*,
p. 218.

[72] For a highly interesting discussion of this phase of Mrs. Stowe's career, in
which the relation between her work and Mark Twain's is discussed at length,
see Kenneth R. Andrews, *Nook Farm, Mark Twain's Hartford Circle* (Cambridge,
Mass., 1950).

regret for what had gone. Like her, he alternated between a lofty and a colloquial style.[73] At her best she used regional speech almost as effectively as he did, and she did it first.

There is, however, one big difference between the two Hartford neighbors in addition to the obvious one in creative capacity. This is in their attitude toward the American past. Mark Twain, harking back to the time and place of his youth, praised it even less whole-heartedly than Mrs. Stowe. Like her, he subscribed fully to the official American goals of liberty and democracy. Again like Mrs. Stowe, Clemens loved and sometimes exaggerated the uncomplicated kind of freedom and equality which seemed in retrospect characteristic of a preindustrial society. But Clemens, like most major American writers, was in some moods far more skeptical than Mrs. Stowe about the degree to which prewar America — or perhaps any society — had ever achieved real freedom or equality.

No doubt Clemens' greater alienation is explainable partly in regional terms, and partly in the far more complicated terms of individual development. There is, however, at least one clear source for this difference. Clemens probably felt somewhat ambivalent about the secular half of American tradition. About the religious half he felt no ambivalence at all: Protestant orthodoxy he obsessively hated. Mrs. Stowe, despite her sufferings and her doubts, found New England Calvinism more than half admirable, and its view of the world more than half true.

Clemens' more alienated stance was not always to his advantage as a writer. He could not deal as convincingly as Mrs. Stowe with some kinds of people. Aunt Polly is a conventional figure and not much more; she is not nearly as interesting as Mrs. Stowe's old maids. But Huck, who has seceded from society, sees it more clearly than does Sam Lawson, who does not secede but hangs around on the fringes. Huck cannot be tolerated by solid citizens, and cannot be patronized; Sam is tolerated and patronized, occasionally even by his author. Thus Huck's outside vision can serve as the main instrument for Mark Twain's comments on society and its official beliefs. Mrs. Stowe has much to say about these matters, and much of it is shrewd and original, but she cannot say it

---

[73] For an authoritative discussion of Mark Twain's formal and colloquial styles and their significance, see Henry Nash Smith, *Mark Twain, the Development of a Writer* (Cambridge, Mass., 1962).

through any of her characters. The main figures of her story are trivial constructs, and the minor characters, who are often believable and interesting, are part of her social picture and cannot look straight at it. Thus she has to interrupt herself, forget her story, and comment on New England in her own person — as historian or prophetess but not as novelist.

Oldtown Folks is not a great novel or a great work of art; it may not be a novel at all. Whatever it be called — a series of sketches, a historical essay with interpolated plot — it is an uneven performance. With all its faults it is an interesting and important book. In it a woman of keen intelligence and sharp perception has drawn on a lifetime of outward observation and inner experience. As a New England writer should, and as few writers of any kind manage to do successfully, Mrs. Stowe gives us a look beneath the surface of a society: at the live coals glowing.

OLDTOWN FOLKS

BY

Harriet Beecher Stowe

PREFACE

Gentle reader, — It is customary to omit prefaces. I beg you to make an exception in my particular case; I have something I really want to say. I have an object in this book, more than the mere telling of a story, and you can always judge of a book better if you compare it with the author's object. My object is to interpret to the world the New England life and character in that particular time of its history which may be called the seminal period. I would endeavor to show you New England in its *seed-bed*, before the hot suns of modern progress had developed its sprouting germs into the great trees of to-day.

New England has been to these United States what the Dorian hive was to Greece. It has always been a capital country to emigrate from, and North, South, East, and West have been populated largely from New England, so that the seed-bed of New England was the seed-bed of this great American Republic, and of all that is likely to come of it.

New England people cannot be thus interpreted without calling into view many grave considerations and necessitating some serious thinking.

In doing this work, I have tried to make my mind as still and passive as a looking-glass, or a mountain lake, and then to give you merely the images reflected there. I desire that you should see the characteristic persons of those times, and hear them talk; and sometimes I have taken an author's liberty of explaining their characters to you, and telling you why they talked and lived as they did.

My studies for this object have been Pre-Raphaelite, — taken from real characters, real scenes, and real incidents. And some of those things in the story which may appear most romantic and like fiction are simple renderings and applications of facts.

Any one who may be curious enough to consult Rev. Elias Nason's book, called "Sir Charles Henry Frankland, or Boston in the Colonial Times," will there see a full description of the old manor-house which in this story is called the Dench House. It was by that name I always heard it spoken of in my boyhood.

In portraying the various characters which I have introduced, I have tried to maintain the part simply of a sympathetic spectator. I propose neither to teach nor preach through them, any farther than any spectator of life is preached to by what he sees of the workings of human nature around him.

Though Calvinist, Arminian, High-Church Episcopalian, sceptic, and simple believer all speak in their turn, I merely listen, and endeavor to understand and faithfully represent the inner life of each. I myself am but the observer and reporter, seeing much, doubting much, questioning much, and believing with all my heart in only a very few things.

And so I take my leave of you.

HORACE HOLYOKE.

CHAPTER I

—◆—

OLDTOWN AND THE MINISTER

It has always been a favorite idea of mine, that there is so much of the human in every man, that the life of any one individual, however obscure, if really and vividly perceived in all its aspirations, struggles, failures, and successes, would command the interest of all others. This is my only apology for offering my life as an open page to the reading of the public.

Besides this, however, every individual is part and parcel of a great picture of the society in which he lives and acts, and his life cannot be painted without reproducing the picture of the world he lived in; and it has appeared to me that my life might recall the image and body of a period in New England most peculiar and most interesting, the impress of which is now rapidly fading away. I mean the ante-railroad times, — the period when our own hard, rocky, sterile New England was a sort of half Hebrew theocracy, half ultra-democratic republic of little villages, separated by a pathless ocean from all the civilization and refinement of the Old World, forgotten and unnoticed, and yet burning like live coals under this obscurity with all the fervid activity of an intense, newly kindled, peculiar, and individual life.

My early life lies in one of these quiet little villages, — that of Oldtown, in Massachusetts. It was as pretty a village as ever laid itself down to rest on the banks of a tranquil river. The stream was one of those limpid children of the mountains, whose brown, clear waters ripple with a soft yellow light over many-colored pebbles, now brawling and babbling on rocky bottoms, dashing hither and thither in tiny cascades, throwing white spray over green mossed rocks, and then again sweeping silently, with many a winding curve, through soft green meadows, nursing on its bosom troops of water-lilies, and bordering its banks with blue and white violets, snow-flaked meadow-sweet, and wild iris. Hither and thither, in the fertile tracts of meadow or upland through which this little stream wound, were some two dozen farm-houses, hid in green hollows, or perched on breezy hill-tops; while close alongside of the river, at its widest and deepest part, ran one rustic street, thickly carpeted with short velvet green grass, where stood the presiding buildings of the village.

First among these was the motherly meeting-house, with its tall white spire, its ample court of sheds and stalls for the shelter of the horses and the various farm-wagons which came in to Sunday services. There was also the school-house, the Academy, and Israel Scran's store, where everything was sold, from hoe-handles up to cambric needles, where the post-office was kept, and where was a general exchange of news, as the different farm-wagons stood hitched around the door, and their owners spent a leisure moment in discussing politics or theology from the top of codfish or mackerel barrels, while their wives and daughters were shopping among the dress goods and ribbons, on the other side of the store. Next to the store was the tavern, — with a tall signpost which used to creak and flap in the summer winds, with a leisurely, rich, easy sort of note of invitation, — a broad veranda in front, with benches, — an open tap-room, where great barrels of beer were kept on draft, and a bar where the various articles proscribed by the temperance society were in those days allowed an open and respectable standing. This tavern veranda and tap-room was another general exchange, not in those days held in the ill repute of such resorts now. The minister himself, in all the magnificence of his cocked hat and ample clerical wig, with his gold-headed cane in his hand, would sometimes step into the tap-room of a cold winter morning, and order a mug of flip from obsequious Amaziah the host, and, while he sipped it, would lecture with a severe gravity a few idle, ragged fellows who were spending too much time in those seductive precincts. The clergy in those days felt that they never preached temperance with so warm a fervor as between the comfortable sips of a beverage of whose temperate use they intended to be shining examples. The most vivid image of respectability and majesty which a little boy born in a Massachusetts village in those early days could form was the minister. In the little theocracy which the Pilgrims established in the wilderness, the ministry was the only order of nobility. They were the only privileged class, and their voice it was that decided *ex cathedra* on all questions both in Church and State, from the choice of a Governor to that of the district-school teacher.

Our minister, as I remember him, was one of the cleanest, most gentlemanly, most well bred of men, — never appearing without all the decorums of silk stockings, shining knee and shoe buckles, well-brushed shoes, immaculately powdered wig, out of which shone his clear, calm, serious face, like the moon out of a fleecy cloud.

Oldtown was originally an Indian town, and one of the most numerous and powerful of the Indian tribes had possessed the beautiful tracts of meadow and upland farms that bordered the Sepaug River. Here the great apostle of the Indians had established the first missionary enterprise among them, under the patronage of a society in England for the propagation of the Gospel in foreign parts; here he had labored and taught and prayed with a fervor which bowed all hearts to his sway, and gathered from the sons of the forest a church of devoted Christians. The harsh guttural Indian language, in the fervent alembic of his loving study, was melted into a written dialect; a Bible and hymn-book and spelling-book seemed to open a path to an Indian literature. He taught them agriculture, and many of the arts and trades of civilized life. But he could not avert the doom which seems to foreordain that those races shall dry up and pass away with their native forests, as the brook dries up when the pines and hemlocks which shaded its source are torn away.

In my boyhood, three generations had passed since the apostle died. The elms which two grateful Indian catechumens had set out as little saplings on either side of his gateway were now two beautiful pillars, supporting each its firmament of leafy boughs, and giving a grand air of scholarly retirement to the plain, old-fashioned parsonage; but the powerful Indian tribe had dwindled to a few scattered families, living an uncertain and wandering life on the outskirts of the thrift and civilization of the whites.

Our minister was one of those cold, clear-cut, polished crystals that are formed in the cooling-down of society, after it has been melted and purified by a great enthusiasm. Nobody can read Dr. Cotton Mather's biography of the first ministers of Massachusetts, without feeling that they were men whose whole souls were in a state of fusion, by their conceptions of an endless life; that the ruling forces which impelled them were the sublimities of a world to come; and that, if there be such a thing possible as perfect faith in the eternal and invisible, and perfect loyalty to God and to conscience, these men were pervaded by it.

More than this, many of them were men of a softened and tender spirit, bowed by past afflictions, who had passed through the refining fires of martyrdom, and come to this country, counting not home or kindred dear to them, that they might found a commonwealth for the beloved name and honor of One who died for them. *Christo et Ecclesiæ*, was the seal with which they consecrated all their life-work, from the founding of Harvard College down to the district school in every village. These men lived in the full spirit of him who said, "I am crucified with Christ, nevertheless I live: yet not I, but Christ liveth in me"; and the power of this invisible and mighty love shed a softening charm over the austere grandeur of their lives. They formed a commonwealth where vice was wellnigh impossible; where such landmarks and boundaries and buttresses and breastworks hedged in and defended the morality of a community, that to go very far out of the way would require some considerable ingenuity and enterprise.

The young men grew up grave and decorous through the nursing of church, catechism, and college, all acting in one line; and in due time many studious and quiet youths stepped, in regular succession, from the college to the theological course, and thence to the ministry, as their natural and appointed work. They received the articles of faith as taught in their catechism without dispute, and took their places calmly and without opposition to assist in carrying on a society where everything had been arranged to go under their direction, and they were the recognized and appointed leaders and governors.

The Rev. Mr. Lothrop had come of good ministerial blood for generations back. His destination had always been for the pulpit. He was possessed of one of those calm, quiet, sedate natures, to whom the temptations of turbulent nerves or vehement passions are things utterly incomprehensible.

Now, however stringent and pronounced may be the forms in which one's traditional faith may have been expressed, it is certain that temperament gradually, and with irresistible power, modifies one's creed. Those features of a man's professed belief which are unsympathetic with his nature become to his mind involved in a perpetual haze and cloud of disuse; while certain others, which are congenial, become vivid and pronounced; and thus, practically, the whole faith of the man changes without his ever being aware of the fact himself.

Parson Lothrop belonged to a numerous class in the third generation of Massachusetts clergy, commonly called Arminian, — men in whom this insensible change had been wrought from the sharply defined and pronounced Calvinism of the early fathers. They were mostly scholarly, quiet men, of calm and philosophic temperament, who, having from infancy walked in all the traditions of a virtuous and pious education, and passed from grade to grade of their progress with irreproachable quiet and decorum, came to regard the spiritual struggles and conflicts, the wrestlings and tears, the fastings and temptations of their ancestors with a secret scepticism, — to dwell on moralities, virtues, and decorums, rather than on those soul-stirring spiritual mysteries which still stood forth unquestioned and uncontradicted in their confessions of faith.

Parson Lothrop fulfilled with immaculate precision all the proprieties exacted in his station. Oldtown having been originally an Indian missionary station, an annual stipend was paid the pastor of this town from a fund originally invested in England for the conversion of the Indians; and so Parson Lothrop had the sounding-board of Eliot's pulpit put up over the great arm-chair in his study, and used to call thither weekly the wandering remnants of Indian tribes to be catechised. He did not, like his great predecessor, lecture them on the original depravity of the heart, the need of a radical and thorough regeneration by the Holy Spirit of God, or the power of Jesus as a Saviour from sin, but he talked to them of the evil of drunkenness and lying and idleness, and exhorted them to be temperate and industrious; and when they, notwithstanding his exhortations, continued to lead an unthrifty, wandering life, he calmly expressed his conviction that they were children of the forest, a race destined to extinction with the progress of civilization, but continued his labors for them with automatic precision.

His Sunday sermons were well-written specimens of the purest and most elegant Addisonian English, and no mortal could find fault with a word that was in them, as they were sensible, rational, and religious, as far as they went. Indeed, Mr. Lothrop was quite an elegant scholar and student in literature, and more than once surprise had been expressed to him that he should be willing to employ his abilities in so obscure a town and for so inconsiderable a salary. His reply was characteristic. "My salary is indeed small, but it is as certain as the Bank of England, and retirement and quiet give me leisure for study."

He, however, mended his worldly prospects by a matrimonial union with a widow lady of large property, from one of the most aristocratic families of Boston. Mrs. Dorothea Lucretia Dixwell was the widow of a Tory merchant, who, by rare skill in trimming his boat to suit the times, had come through the Revolutionary war with a handsome property unimpaired, which, dying shortly after, he left to his widow. Mrs. Dixwell was in heart and soul an Englishwoman, an adorer of church and king, a worshipper of aristocracy and all the powers that be. She owned a pew in King's Chapel, and clung more punctiliously than ever to her prayer-book, when all other memorials of our connection with the mother country had departed.

Could it be thought that the elegant and rich widow would smile on the suit of an obscure country Congregational clergyman? Yet she did; and for it there were many good reasons. Parson Lothrop was a stately, handsome, well-proportioned man, and had the formal and ceremonious politeness of a gentleman of the old school, and by family descent Mrs. Dorothea's remembrance could trace back his blood to that of some very solid families among the English gentry, and as there were no more noblemen to be had in America, marrying a minister in those days was the next best thing to it; and so Mrs. Dixwell became Mrs. Parson Lothrop, and made a processional entrance into Oldtown in her own coach, and came therein to church the first Sunday after her marriage, in all the pomp of a white brocade, with silver flowers on it of life-size, and white-satin slippers with heels two inches high. This was a great grace to show to a Congregational church, but Mrs. Lothrop knew the duty of a wife, and conformed to it heroically. Nor was Parson Lothrop unmindful of the courtesies of a husband in this matrimonial treaty, for it was stipulated and agreed that Madam Lothrop should have full liberty to observe in her own proper person all the festivals and fasts of the Church of England, should be excused from all company and allowed to keep the seclusion of her own apartment on Good Friday, and should proceed immediately thereafter in her own coach to Boston, to be present at the Easter services in King's Chapel. The same procession to Boston in her own coach took place also on Whitsunday and Christmas. Moreover she decked her house with green boughs and made mince-pies at Christmas time, and in short conducted her housekeeping in all respects as a zealous member of the Church of England ought.

In those days of New England, the minister and his wife were considered the temporal and spiritual superiors of everybody in the parish. The idea which has since gained ground, of regarding the minister and his family as a sort of stipendiary attachment and hired officials of the parish, to be overlooked, schooled, advised, rebuked, and chastened by every deacon and deacon's wife or rich and influential parishioner, had not then arisen. Parson Lothrop was so calmly awful in his sense of his own position and authority, that it would have been a sight worth seeing to witness any of his parish coming to him, as deacons and influential parishioners now-a-days feel at liberty to come to their minister, with suggestions and admonitions. His manner was ever gracious and affable, as of a man who habitually surveys every one from above, and is disposed to listen with indulgent courtesy, and has advice in reserve for all seekers; but there was not the slightest shadow of anything which encouraged the most presuming to offer counsel in return. And so the marriage with the rich Episcopal widow, her processional entry into Oldtown, the coach and outriders, the brocade and satin slippers, were all submitted to on the part of the Oldtown people without a murmur.

The fact is, that the parson himself felt within his veins the traditional promptings of a far-off church and king ancestry, and relished with a calm delight a solemn trot to the meeting-house behind a pair of fat, decorous old family horses, with a black coachman in livery on the box. It struck him as sensible and becoming. So also he liked a sideboard loaded with massive family plate, warmed up with the ruby hues of old wines of fifty years' ripening, gleaming through crystal decanters, and well-trained man-servants and maid-servants, through whom his wig, his shoes, and all his mortal belongings, received daily and suitable care. He was to Mrs. Dorothea the most deferential of husbands, always rising with stately courtesy to offer her a chair when she entered an apartment, and hastening to open the door for her if she wished to pass out, and passing every morning and evening the formal gallantries and inquiries in regard to her health and well-being which he felt that her state and condition required.

Fancy if you can the magnificent distance at which this sublime couple stood above a little ten-year-old boy, who wore a blue checked apron, and every day pattered barefoot after the cows, and who, at the time this story of myself begins, had just, by reaching up on his little bare tiptoes, struck the great black knocker on their front door.

The door was opened by a stately black servant, who had about him an indistinct and yet perceptible atmosphere of ministerial gravity and dignity, looking like a black doctor of divinity.

"Is Mr. Lothrop at home," I said, blushing to the roots of my hair.

"Yes, sonny," said the black condescendingly.

"Won't you please tell him father's dying, and mother wants him to come quick?" and with that, what with awe, and what with grief, I burst into tears.

The kind-hearted black relaxed from his majesty at once, and said: "Lord bress yer soul! why, don't cry now, honey, and I'll jes' call missis"; — and in fact, before I knew it, he had opened the parlor door, and ushered me into the august presence of Lady Lothrop, as she used to be familiarly called in our village.

She was a tall, thin, sallow woman, looking very much like those portraits by Copley that still adorn some old houses in Boston; but she had a gentle voice, and a compassionate, womanly way with her. She comforted me with a cake, which she drew from the closet in the sideboard; decanted some very choice old wine into a bottle, which she said I was to carry to my mother, and be sure and tell her to take a little of it herself. She also desired me to give her a small book which she had found of use in times of affliction, called "The Mourner's Companion," consisting mainly of choice selections from the English Book of Common Prayer.

When the minister came into the room I saw that she gave a conjugal touch to the snowy plaited frill of his ruffled shirt, and a thoughtful inspection to the wide linen cambric frills which set off his well-formed hand, and which were a little discomposed by rubbing over his writing-table, — nay, even upon one of them a small stain of ink was visible, as the minister, unknown to himself, had drawn his ruffles over an undried portion of his next Sunday's sermon.

"Dinah must attend to this," she said; "here's a spot requiring salts of lemon; and, my dear," she said, in an insinuating tone, holding out a richly bound velvet prayer-book, "would you not like to read our service for the Visitation of the Sick, — it is so excellent."

"I am well aware of that, my love," said the minister, repelling her prayer-book with a gentle stateliness, "but I assure you, Dorothea, it would not do, — no, it would not do."

I thought the good lady sighed as her husband left the house, and looked longingly after him through the window as he walked down the yard. She probably consoled herself with the reflection that one could not have everything, and that her spouse, if not in the Established Church of England, was every way fitted to adorn it had he only been there.

CHAPTER II

MY FATHER

My good reader, it must sometimes have fallen under your observation that there is a class of men who go through life under a cloud, for no other reason than that, being born with the nature of gentlemen, they are nevertheless poor. Such men generally live under a sense of the dissatisfaction and rebuke of our good mother world; and yet it is easy to see all the while that even a moderate competence would at any moment turn their faults into virtues, and make them in everybody's opinion model characters.

Now you know there are plants to whom poor soil or rich soil seems to make no manner of difference. Your mullein and your burdock do admirably on a gravelly hillside, and admirably in rich garden soil. Nothing comes amiss with them. But take a saffrano rose or a hyacinth and turn it out to shift for itself by the roadside, and it soon dwindles and pines, and loses its color and shape, till everybody thinks such a wretched, ragged specimen of vegetation had better be out of the world than in it.

From all I remember of my poor father, he had the organization and tastes of a scholar and a gentleman; but he was born the son of a poor widow, who hardly knew from week to week where the few hard-earned dollars were to come from which kept her and her boy in the very plainest food and clothing. So she thought herself happy when she apprenticed him to a paper-maker. Thence he had fought his way up with his little boy hands towards what to him was light and life, — an education. Harvard College, to his eyes, was like the distant vision of the New Jerusalem to the Christian. Thither he aspired, thither he meant to go. Through many a self-denial, many an hour of toil, — studying his Latin grammar by night in the paper-mill, saving his odd pennies, and buying book after book, and treasuring each one as a mine of wealth, — he went on, till finally he gained enough of a standing to teach, first the common school, and then the Academy.

While he was teacher of the Academy he made his first false step, which was a false step only because he was poor, — he fell in love with my mother. If he had been well to do in the world, everybody would have said that it was the most natural and praiseworthy thing possible. It was some extenuation of his fault that my poor mother was very pretty and attractive, — she was, in fact, one of my father's prettiest scholars. He saw her daily, and so the folly grew upon him, till he was ready to sacrifice his life's object, and consent to be all his days a poor academy teacher in Oldtown, that he might marry her.

One must be very much of a woman for whom a man can sacrifice the deepest purpose of his life without awaking to regret it. I do not say that my father did so; and yet I could see, from the earliest of my recollection, that ours was a household clouded by suppressed regrets, as well as embarrassed by real wants.

My mother was one of those bright, fair, delicate New England girls who remind us of the shell-pink of the wood-anemone, or the fragile wind-flower; and every one must remember how jauntily they toss their gay little heads as they grow in their own mossy dells, at the root of old oaks or beeches, but how quickly they become withered and bedraggled when we gather them.

My mother's gayety of animal spirits, her sparkle and vivacity all went with the first year of marriage. The cares of housekeeping, the sicknesses of maternity and nursing, drained her dry of all that was bright and attractive; and my only recollections of her are of a little quiet, faded, mournful woman, who looked on my birth and that of my brother Bill as the greatest of possible misfortunes, and took care of us with a discouraged patience, more as if she pitied us for being born than as if she loved us.

My father seemed to regard her with a half-remorseful tenderness, as he strove by extra reading and study to make up for the loss of that education the prospect of which he had sacrificed in his marriage. In common with a great many scholars of that day and of this, he ignored his body altogether, and tasked and strained his brain with night studies till his health sank under it; and Consumption, which in New England stands ever waiting for victims, took his cold hand in hers, and led him quietly but irresistibly downward.

Such, to this moment, was my father's history; and you will see

the truth of what I have been saying, — that a modest little property would have changed all his faults and mistakes into proprieties
and virtues.

He had been sick so long, so very long, it seemed to my child-
mind! and now there was approaching him that dark shadow so
terrible to flesh and heart, in whose dimness every one feels an
instinctive longing for aid. That something must be done for the
dying to prepare them for their last lonesome journey is a strong
instinct of every soul; and I had heard my mother pathetically
urging my father that morning to send for the minister.

"What good will it do, Susy?" had been his answer, given with
a sort of weary despondence; but still he had assented, and I had
gone eagerly to bring him.

I was, for my part, strong in faith. I wanted to do something
for my father, and I felt certain that the minister would know
what was the right thing; and when I set forth with him, in his
full panoply, — wig and ruffles and gold-headed cane, — I felt
somehow as if the ark of the covenant was moving down the street
to our house.

My mother met the minister at the door, with tears yet undried
in her eyes, and responded in the fullest manner to the somewhat
stately, but yet gracious, inquiries which he made as to my father's
health and condition, and thanked him for the kindly messages
and gifts of Lady Lothrop, which I had brought.

Then he was shown into the sick-room. My father was lying
propped up by pillows, and with the bright flush of his afternoon
fever on his cheeks. He was always a handsome man, fastidious
about his person and belongings; and as he lay with his long thin
hands folded together over the bed-clothes, his hair clinging in
damp curls round his high white forehead, and his large, clear
hazel eyes kindled with an unnatural brightness, he formed on my
childish memory a picture that will never fade. There was in his
eyes at this moment that peculiar look of deep suffering which I
have sometimes seen in the eyes of wounded birds or dying animals, — something that spoke of a quiet, unutterable anguish.

My father had been not only a scholar, but a thinker, — one of
those silent, peculiar natures whose thoughts and reasonings too
often wander up and down the track of commonly received opinion, as Noah's dove of old, without finding rest for the sole of their

foot. When a mind like this is approaching the confines of the eternal unknown, there is often a conflict of thought and emotion, the utterance of which to a receptive and sympathizing soul might bring relief. Something there was of intense yearning and inquiry in the first glance he threw on the minister, and then it changed to one of weary languor. With the quick spiritual instincts of that last dying hour, he had seen into the soul of the man, — that there was nothing there for him. Even the gold-headed cane was not the rod and staff for him in the dark valley.

There was, in fact, something in the tranquil, calm, unpathetic nature of that good man, which rendered him peculiarly inapt to enter into the secret chamber of souls that struggle and suffer and doubt. He had a nature so evenly balanced, his course in life had been so quiet and unruffled, his speculations and doubts had been of so philosophical and tranquil a kind, that he was not in the least fitted to become father confessor to a sick and wounded spirit.

His nature was one that inclined to certain stately formalities and proprieties; and although he had, in accordance with his station in the Congregational church, put from him the forms of the Church of England, and was supposed to rely on the extemporaneous movements of the hour, his devotional exercises, nevertheless, had as much a stereotype form as if they had been printed in a book. We boys always knew when the time for certain familiar phrases and expressions would occur in his Sunday morning prayer, and exactly the welcome words which heralded the close of the afternoon exercise.

I remember now, as he knelt by my father's bedside, how far off and distant the usual opening formula of his prayer made the Great Helper to appear. "Supremely great, infinitely glorious, and ever-blessed God," it said, "grant that we may suitably realize the infinite distance between us, worms of the dust, and thy divine majesty."

I was gazing earnestly at my father, as he lay with his bright, yearning, troubled eyes looking out into the misty shadows of the eternal world, and I saw him close them wearily, and open them again, with an expression of quiet endurance. The infinite distance was a thing that he realized only too well; but who should tell him of an infinite *nearness* by which those who are far off are made nigh?

After the prayer, the minister expressed the hope that my father would be resigned to the decrees of infinite wisdom, and my father languidly assented; and then, with a ministerial benediction, the whole stately apparition of ghostly aid and comfort departed from our house.

One thing, at all events, had been gained, — my father had had the minister and been prayed with, and nobody in Oldtown could say that everything had not been properly done, according to the code of spiritual etiquette generally established. For our town, like other little places, always kept a wide-awake eye on the goings and doings of her children. Oldtown had had its own opinion of my father for a great while, and expressed it freely in tea-drinkings, quiltings, at the store, and at the tavern. If Oldtown's advice had been asked, there were a hundred things that he did which would have been left undone, and a hundred things done which he did not do. Oldtown knew just whom he ought to have married instead of marrying my mother, and was certain he could have had her too. Oldtown knew just how and when he might have made himself a rich man, and didn't. Oldtown knew exactly when, how, and why he caught the cold that set him into a consumption, and what he ought to have taken to cure it, and didn't. And now he was, so to speak, dying under a cloud, just as Oldtown always knew he would. But one thing was certain, and Oldtown was glad to hear of it, — he wasn't an infidel, as had been at different times insinuated, for he had had the minister and been prayed with; and so, though he never had joined the church, Oldtown indulged some hope for his hereafter.

When the minister was gone, my father said, with a weary smile: "There, Susy dear, I hope you are satisfied now. My poor child," he added, gently drawing her to sit down by him, and looking at her with the strange, solemn dispassionateness of dying people, who already begin to feel that they are of another sphere, — "my poor dear little girl! You were so pretty and so gay! I did you a great wrong in marrying you."

"O, don't say that Horace," said my mother.

"It's true, though," said my father. "With a richer and more prosperous man, you might have been blooming and happy yet. And this poor little man," said my father, stroking my head, — "perhaps fate may have something better in store for him. If I had

had but the ghost of a chance, such as some men have, — some who do not value it, who only throw it away, — I might have been something. I had it in me; but no one will ever know it now. My life is a miserable, disgusting failure. Burn all my papers, Susy. Promise me that."

"I will do just what you say, Horace."

"And, Susy, when I am gone, don't let all the old gossips of Oldtown come to croak and croon over me, and make their stupid remarks on my helpless body. I hate country funerals. Don't make a vulgar show of me for their staring curiosity. Death is dreary enough at best, but I never could see any sense in aggravating its horrors by stupid funeral customs. Instead of dressing me in those ghostly, unnatural grave-clothes that people seem to delight in, just let me be buried in my clothes and let the last look my poor children have of me be as natural and familiar as possible. The last look of the dead ought to be sacred to one's friends alone. Promise, now, Susy," he said earnestly, "promise to do as I say."

"O Horace, I do promise, — I promise to do all you say. You know I always have."

"Yes, poor dear child, you have; you have been only too good for me."

"O Horace, how can you say so!" and my poor mother fell on my father's neck in a paroxysm of weeping.

But his great, bright eyes gathered no tears; they were fixed in an awful stillness. "My darling, you must not," he said tenderly, but with no answering emotion. "Calm yourself. And now, dear, as I am sure that to-morrow I shall not be with you, you must send for your mother to be with you to-night. You know she will come."

"Father," said I earnestly, "where are you going?"

"Where?" said he, looking at me with his clear, mournful eyes. "God knows, my son. I do not. It ought to be enough for me that God does know."

CHAPTER III

───◆◇◆───

MY GRANDMOTHER

"Now, Horace," said my mother, "you must run right up to your grandfather's, and tell your grandmother to come down and stay with us to-night; and you and Bill must stay there."

Bill, my brother, was a year or two older than I was; far more healthy, and consequently, perhaps, far more noisy. At any rate, my mother was generally only too glad to give her consent to his going anywhere of a leisure afternoon which would keep him out of the house, while I was always retained as her own special waiter and messenger.

My father had a partiality for me, because I was early an apt reader, and was fond of the quiet of his study and his books. He used to take pride and pleasure in hearing me read, which I did with more fluency and understanding than many children of twice my age; and thus it happened that, while Bill was off roaming in the woods this sunny autumn afternoon, I was the attendant and waiter in the sick-room. My little soul was oppressed and sorrowful, and so the message that sent me to my grandmother was a very welcome one, for my grandmother was, in my view, a tower of strength and deliverance. My mother was, as I have said, a frail, mournful, little, discouraged woman; but my grandmother belonged to that tribe of strong-backed, energetic, martial mothers in Israel, who brought to our life in America the vigorous bone and muscle and hearty blood of the yeomanry of Old England. She was a valiant old soul, who fearlessly took any bull in life by the horns, and was ready to shake him into decorum.

My grandfather, a well-to-do farmer, was one of the chief magnates of the village, and carried on a large farm and certain mills at the other end of it. The great old-fashioned farm-house where they lived was at some distance from my father's cottage, right on the banks of that brown, sparkling, clear stream I have spoken of.

My grandfather was a serene, moderate, quiet man, upward of sixty, with an affable word and a smile for everybody, — a man of easy habits, never discomposed, and never in a hurry, — who had a comfortable faith that somehow or other the affairs of this world in general, and his own in particular, would turn out all right, without much seeing to on his part.

My grandmother, on the contrary, was one of those wide-awake, earnest, active natures, whose days were hardly ever long enough for all that she felt needed to be done and attended to. She had very positive opinions on every subject, and was not at all backward in the forcible and vigorous expression of them; and evidently considering the apostolic gift of exhortation as having come straight down to her, she failed not to use it for the benefit of all whom it might concern.

Oldtown had in many respects a peculiar sort of society. The Indian tribe that once had been settled in its vicinity had left upon the place the tradition of a sort of wandering, gypsy, tramping life, so that there was in the town an unusual number of that roving, uncertain class of people, who are always falling into want, and needing to be helped, hanging like a tattered fringe on the thrifty and well-kept petticoat of New England society.

The traditions of tenderness, pity, and indulgence which the apostle Eliot had inwrought into the people of his day in regard to the Indians, had descended through all the families, and given to that roving people certain established rights in every household, which in those days no one ever thought of disowning. The wandering Indian was never denied a good meal, a seat by the kitchen fire, a mug of cider, and a bed in the barn. My grandfather, out of his ample apple-orchard, always made one hogshead of cider which was called the Indian hogshead, and which was known to be always on tap for them; and my grandmother not only gave them food, but more than once would provide them with blankets, and allow them to lie down and sleep by her great kitchen fire. In those days New England was such a well-watched, and schooled and catechised community, and so innocent in the general tone of its society, that in the rural villages no one ever locked the house doors of a night. I have lain awake many a night hearing the notes of the whippoorwills and the frogs, and listening to the sighing of the breeze, as it came through the great wide-open front-door of the house, and swept up the staircase. Nobody ever thought of being afraid that the tramper whom he left asleep on the kitchen floor would rouse up in the night and rob the house. In fact, the poor vagrants were themselves tolerably innocent, not being guilty of very many sins darker than occasional drunkenness and habitual unthrift. They were a simple, silly, jolly set of rovers, partly Indian and partly whites who had fallen into Indian habits, who told stories, made baskets, drank cider, and raised puppies, of which they generally carried a supply in their wanderings, and from which came forth in due time an ample supply of those yellow dogs of old, one of whom was a standing member of every well-regulated New England family. Your yellow dog had an important part to act in life, as much as any of his masters. He lay in the kitchen door and barked properly at everything that went by. He went out with the children when they went roving in the woods Saturday afternoon, and was always on hand with a sober face to patter on his four solemn paws behind the farm-wagon as it went to meeting of a Sunday morning. And in meeting, who can say what an infinite fund of consolation their yellow, honest faces and great, soft eyes were to the children tired of the sermon, but greatly consoled by getting a sly opportunity to stroke Bose's yellow back? How many little eyes twinkled sympathetically through the slats of the high-backed pews, as the tick of their paws up and down the broad aisle announced that they were treating themselves to that meditative locomotion allowed to good dogs in sermon-time!

Surrounded by just such a community as I have described, my grandmother's gifts never became rusty for want of exercise. Somebody always needed straightening up and attending to. Somebody was to be exhorted, rebuked, or admonished, with all long-suffering and doctrine; and it was cheering to behold, after years of labors that had appeared to produce no very brilliant results on her disciples, how hale and vigorous her faith yet remained in the power of talking to people. She seemed to consider that evil-doers fell into sins and evils of all sorts merely for want of somebody to talk to them, and would fly at some poor, idle, loafing, shiftless object who staggered past her house from the tavern, with the same earnestness and zeal for the fortieth time as if she had not exhorted him vainly for the thirty-nine before.

In fact, on this very Saturday afternoon, as I was coming down the hill, whence I could see the mill and farm-house, I caught sight of her standing in the door, with cap-border erect, and vigorous gesticulation, upbraiding a poor miserable dog commonly called Uncle Eph, who stood swaying on the bridge, holding himself up by the rails with drunken gravity, only answering her expostulations by shaking his trembling fist at her, irreverently replying in every pause of her expostulation, "You — darned — old sheep you!"

"I do wonder now, mother, that you can't let Uncle Eph alone," said my Aunt Lois, who was washing up the kitchen floor behind her. "What earthly good does it do to be talking to him? He always has drank, and always will."

"I can't help it," quoth my grandmother; "it's a shame to him, and his wife lying there down with rheumatism. I don't see how folks can do so."

"And I don't see as it's any of our business," said Aunt Lois. "What is it to us? We are not our brother's keeper."

"Well, it was Cain that said that to begin with," said my grandmother; "and I think it's the spirit of Cain not to care what becomes of our neighbors!"

"I can't help it if it is. I don't see the use of fussing and caring about what you can't help. But there comes Horace Holyoke, to be sure. I suppose, mother, you're sent for; I've been expecting it all along. — Stand still there!" she called to me as I approached the door, "and don't come in to track my floor."

I stood without the door, therefore, and delivered my message; and my grandmother promptly turned into her own bedroom, adjoining the kitchen, to make herself ready to go. I stood without the door, humbly waiting Aunt Lois's permission to enter the house.

"Well," said Aunt Lois, "I suppose we've got to have both boys down here to-night. They've got to come here, I suppose, and we may as well have 'em first as last. It's just what I told Susy, when she would marry Horace Holyoke. I saw it just as plain as I see it now, that we should have to take care of 'em. It's aggravating, because Susy neglected her opportunities. She might have been Mrs. Captain Shawmut, and had her carriage and horses, if she'd only been a mind to."

"But," said my Aunt Keziah, who sat by the chimney, knitting, — "but if she couldn't love Captain Shawmut, and *did* love Horace Holyoke — "

"Fiddlestick about that. Susy would 'a' loved him well enough if she'd 'a' married him. She'd 'a' loved anybody that she married well enough, — she's one of the kind; and he's turned out a very rich man, just as I told her. Susy was the only handsome one in our family, and she might have done something with herself if she'd had sense."

"For my part," said Aunt Keziah, "I can't blame people for following their hearts. I never saw the money yet that would 'a' tempted *me* to marry the man I didn't love."

Poor Aunt Keziah had the reputation of being, on the whole, about the homeliest woman in Oldtown. She was fat and ill-shapen and clumsy, with a pale, greenish tinge to her complexion, watery, whitish-blue eyes, very rough thin hair, and ragged, scrubby eyebrows. Nature had been peculiarly unkind to her; but far within her ill-favored body she had the most exalted and romantic conceptions. She was fond of reading Young's Night Thoughts, Mrs. Rowe's Meditations, and Sir Charles Grandison, and always came out strong on the immaterial and sentimental side of every question. She had the most exalted ideas of a lofty, disinterested devotion, which she, poor soul! kept always simmering on a secret altar, ready to bestow on some ideal hero, if ever he should call for it. But, alas! her want of external graces prevented any such application. The princess was enchanted behind a hedge of ragged and unsightly thorns.

She had been my mother's aid and confidante in her love affair, and was therefore regarded with a suppressed displeasure by Aunt Lois, who rejoined, smartly: "I don't think, Kezzy, that you are likely to be tempted with offers of any sort; but Susy did have 'em, — plenty of 'em, — and took Horace Holyoke when she might 'a' done better. Consequence is, we've got to take her and her children home and take care of 'em. It's just our luck. Your poor folks are the ones that are sure to have children, — the less they have to give 'em, the more they have. I think, for my part, that people that can't provide for children ought not to have 'em. Susy's no more fit to bring up those boys than a white kitten. There never was a great deal to Susy," added Aunt Lois, reflectively, as, having finished the ablution of the floor, she took the dish of white sand to sand it.

"Well, for my part," said Aunt Kezzy, "I don't blame Susy a mite. Horace Holyoke was a handsome man, and the Holyokes are a good family. Why, his grandfather was a minister, and Horace certainly was a man of talents. Parson Lothrop said, if he'd 'a' had early advantages, there were few men would have surpassed him. If he'd only been able to go to college."

"And why wasn't he able to go to college? Because he must needs get married. Now, when people set out to do a thing, I like to see 'em do it. If he'd a let Susy alone and gone to college, I dare say he might have been distinguished, and all that. I wouldn't have had the least objection. But no, nothing would do but he must get married, and have two boys, and then study himself into his grave, and leave 'em to us to take care of."

"Well now, Lois," said my grandmother, coming out with her bonnet on, and her gold-headed cane in her hand, "if I were you, I wouldn't talk so. What do you always want to fight Providence for?"

"Providence!" said my Aunt Lois, with a sniff. "I don't call it Providence. I guess, if folks would behave themselves, Providence would let them alone."

"Why, everything is ordered and foreordained," said Aunt Keziah.

"Besides that," said my grandmother, setting down her stick hard on the floor, "there's no use in such talk, Lois. What's done's done; and if the Lord let it be done, we may. We can't always make people do as we would. There's no use in being dragged through the world like a dog under a cart, hanging back and yelping. What we must do, we may as well do willingly, — as well walk as be dragged. Now we've got Susy and her children to take care of, and let's do it. They've got to come here, and they shall come, — should come if there were forty-eleven more of 'em than there be, — so now you just shut up."

"Who said they shouldn't come?" said Aunt Lois. "I want to know now if I haven't moved out of the front room and gone into the little back chamber, and scoured up every inch of that front-room chamber on my hands and knees, and brought down

the old trundle-bed out of the garret and cleaned it up, on purpose to be all ready for Susy and those children. If I haven't
worked hard for them, I'd like to have any one tell me; and I
don't see, for my part, why I should be scolded."

"She wasn't scolding you, Lois," said Aunt Keziah, pacifically.

"She was, too; and I never open my mouth," said Lois, in an
aggrieved tone, "that you all don't come down on me. I'm sure
I don't see the harm of wishing Susy had married a man that
could 'a' provided for her; but some folks feel so rich, nothing
comes amiss with 'em. I suppose we are able to send both boys
to college, and keep 'em like gentlemen, aren't we?"

My grandmother had not had the benefit of this last volley, as
she prudently left the house the moment she had delivered herself of her reproof to Aunt Lois.

I was listening at the door with a troubled spirit. Gathering
from the conversation that my father and mother, somehow, had
been improperly conducted people, and that I and my brother
Bill had no business to have been born, and that our presence on
the earth was, somehow or other, of the nature of an imperti-
nence, making everybody a vast deal of trouble. I could not bear
to go in; and as I saw my grandmother's stately steppings in the
distance, I ran after her as fast as my little bare feet could patter,
and seized fast hold of her gown with the same feeling that makes
a chicken run under a hen.

"Why, Horace," said my grandmother, "why didn't you stay
down at the house?"

"I didn't want to, grandma; please let me go with you."

"You mustn't mind Aunt Lois's talk, — she means well."

I snuffled and persisted, and so had my own way, for my grandmother was as soft-hearted to children as any of the meekest of
the tribe who bear that revered name; and so she didn't mind
it that I slid back into the shadows of my father's room, under
cover of her ample skirts, and sat down disconsolate in a dark
corner.

My grandmother brought to the sick-room a heavier responsibility than any mere earthly interest could have laid on her.
With all her soul, which was a very large one, she was an earnest Puritan Calvinist. She had been nourished in the sayings
and traditions of the Mathers and the Eliots, and all the first

generation of the saints who had possessed Massachusetts. To these she had added the earnest study of the writings of Edwards and Bellamy, and others of those brave old thinkers who had broken up the crust of formalism and mechanical piety that was rapidly forming over the New England mind.

My remembrances of her are always as a reader. In her private chamber was always a table covered with books; and though performing personally the greater share of the labors of a large family, she never failed to have her quiet hour every afternoon for reading. History and biography she delighted in, but she followed with a keen relish the mazes of theology.

During the days of my father's health and vigor, he had one of those erratic, combative minds that delight in running logical tilts against received opinions, and was skilled in finding the weak point in all assertions. My grandmother, who believed with heart and soul and life-blood everything that she believed at all, had more than once been worsted by him in arguments where her inconsiderate heat outran her logic. These remembrances had pressed heavily on her soul during the time of his sickness, and she had more than once earnestly sought to bring him to her ways of thinking, — ways which to her view were the only possible or safe ones; but during his illness he had put such conversation from him with the quick, irritable impatience of a sore and wounded spirit.

On some natures theology operates as a subtle poison; and the New England theology in particular, with its intense clearness, its sharp-cut crystalline edges and needles of thought, has had in a peculiar degree the power of lacerating the nerves of the soul, and producing strange states of morbid horror and repulsion. The great unanswerable questions which must perplex every thinking soul that awakes to consciousness in this life are there posed with the severest and most appalling distinctness. These awful questions underlie all religions, — they belong as much to Deism as to the strictest orthodoxy, — in fact, they are a part of human perception and consciousness, since it cannot be denied that Nature in her teaching is a more tremendous and inexorable Calvinist than the Cambridge Platform or any other platform that ever was invented.

But in New England society, where all poetic forms, all the

draperies and accessories of religious ritual, have been rigidly and unsparingly retrenched, there was nothing between the soul and these austere and terrible problems; it was constantly and severely brought face to face with their infinite mystery. When my grandmother came into the room, it was with an evident and deep emotion working in her strong but plain features. She came up to the bed and grasped my father's hand earnestly.

"Well, mother," he said, "my time is come, and I have sent for you to put Susy and the children into your hands."

"I'll take 'em and welcome, — you know that," said my grandmother heartily.

"God bless you, mother, — I do know it," he said; "but do have a special eye on poor little Horace. He has just my passion for books and study; and if he could be helped to get an education, he might do what I have failed to do. I leave him my books, — you will try and help him, mother?"

"Yes, my son, I will; but O my son, my son!" she added with trembling eagerness, "how is it with you now? Are you prepared for this great change?"

"Mother," he said in a solemn voice, yet speaking with a great effort, "no sane man ever comes to my age, and to this place where I lie, without thinking a great deal on all these things. I have thought, — God knows how earnestly, — but I cannot talk of it. We see through a glass darkly here. There perhaps we shall see clearly. You must be content to leave me where I leave myself, — in the hands of my Creator. He can do no wrong."

CHAPTER IV

———◄◆►———

THE VILLAGE DO-NOTHING

"Wal naow, Horace, don't ye cry so. Why, I'm railly concerned for ye. Why, don't you s'pose your daddy's better off? Why, sartin *I* do. Don't cry, there's a good boy, now. I'll give ye my jack-knife now."

This was addressed to me the day after my father's death, while the preparations for the funeral hung like a pall over the house, and the terror of the last cold mystery, the tears of my mother, and a sort of bustling dreariness on the part of my aunts and grandmother, all conspired to bear down on my childish nerves with fearful power. It was a doctrine of those good old times, no less than of many in our present days, that a house invaded by death should be made as forlorn as hands could make it. It should be rendered as cold and stiff, as unnatural, as dead and corpse-like as possible, by closed shutters, looking-glasses pinned up in white sheets, and the locking up and hiding out of sight of any pleasant little familiar object which would be thought out of place in a sepulchre. This work had been driven through with unsparing vigor by Aunt Lois, who looked like one of the Fates as she remorselessly cleared away every little familiar object belonging to my father, and reduced every room to the shrouded stillness of a well-kept tomb.

Of course no one thought of looking after me. It was not the fashion of those days to think of children, if only they would take themselves off out of the way of the movements of the grown people; and so I had run out into the orchard back of the house, and, throwing myself down on my face under an apple-tree in the tall clover, I gave myself up to despair, and was sobbing aloud in a nervous paroxysm of agony, when these words were addressed to me. The speaker was a tall, shambling, loose-jointed man, with a long, thin visage, prominent watery blue eyes, very fluttering and seedy habiliments, who occupied the responsible position of

first do-nothing-in-ordinary in our village of Oldtown, and as such
I must introduce him to my readers' notice.

Every New England village, if you only think of it, must have
its do-nothing as regularly as it has its school-house or meeting-
house. Nature is always wide awake in the matter of compensation. Work, thrift, and industry are such an incessant steam-
power in Yankee life, that society would burn itself out with
intense friction were there not interposed here and there the
lubricating power of a decided do-nothing, — a man who won't
be hurried, and won't work, and will take his ease in his own
way, in spite of the whole protest of his neighborhood to the contrary. And there is on the face of the whole earth no do-nothing
whose softness, idleness, general inaptitude to labor, and everlasting, universal shiftlessness can compare with that of this worthy,
as found in a brisk Yankee village.

Sam Lawson filled this post with ample honor in Oldtown. He
was a fellow dear to the souls of all "us boys" in the village,
because, from the special nature of his position, he never had
anything more pressing to do than croon and gossip with us. He
was ready to spend hours in tinkering a boy's jack-knife, or mending his skate, or start at the smallest notice to watch at a wood-
chuck's hole, or give incessant service in tending a dog's sprained
paw. He was always on hand to go fishing with us on Saturday
afternoons; and I have known him to sit hour after hour on the
bank, surrounded by a troop of boys, baiting our hooks and taking
off our fish. He was a soft-hearted old body, and the wrigglings
and contortions of our prey used to disturb his repose so that it was
a regular part of his work to kill the fish by breaking their necks
when he took them from the hook.

"Why, lordy massy, boys," he would say, "I can't bear to see
no kind o' critter in torment. These 'ere pouts ain't to blame for
bein' fish, and ye ought to put 'em out of their misery. Fish hes
their rights as well as any on us."

Nobody but Sam would have thought of poking through the
high grass and clover on our back lot to look me up, as I lay sobbing under the old apple-tree, the most insignificant little atom
of misery that ever bewailed the inevitable.

Sam was of respectable family, and not destitute of education.

He was an expert in at least five or six different kinds of handicraft, in all of which he had been pronounced by the knowing ones to be a capable workman, "if only he would stick to it." He had a blacksmith's shop, where, when the fit was on him, he would shoe a horse better than any man in the county. No one could supply a missing screw, or apply a timely brace, with more adroitness. He could mend cracked china so as to be almost as good as new; he could use carpenter's tools as well as a born carpenter, and would doctor a rheumatic door or a shaky window better than half the professional artisans in wood. No man could put a refractory clock to rights with more ingenuity than Sam, — that is, if you would give him his time to be about it.

I shall never forget the wrath and dismay which he roused in my Aunt Lois's mind by the leisurely way in which, after having taken our own venerable kitchen clock to pieces, and strewn the fragments all over the kitchen, he would roost over it in endless incubation, telling stories, entering into long-winded theological discussions, smoking pipes, and giving histories of all the other clocks in Oldtown, with occasional memoirs of those in Needmore, the North Parish, and Podunk, as placidly indifferent to all her volleys of sarcasm and contempt, her stinging expostulations and philippics, as the sailing old moon is to the frisky, animated barking of some puppy dog of earth.

"Why, ye see, Miss Lois," he would say, "clocks can't be druv; that's jest what they can't. Some things can be druv, and then agin some things can't, and clocks is that kind. They's jest got to be humored. Now this 'ere's a 'mazin' good clock; give me my time on it, and I'll have it so't will keep straight on to the Millennium."

"Millennium!" says Aunt Lois, with a snort of infinite contempt.

"Yes, the Millennium," says Sam, letting fall his work in a contemplative manner. "That 'ere's an interestin' topic now. Parson Lothrop, he don't think the Millennium will last a thousand years. What's your 'pinion on that pint, Miss Lois?"

"My opinion is," said Aunt Lois, in her most nipping tones, "that if folks don't mind their own business, and do with their might what their hand finds to do, the Millennium won't come at all."

"Wal, you see, Miss Lois, it's just here, — one day is with the Lord as a thousand years, and a thousand years as one day."

"I should think you thought a day was a thousand years, the way you work," said Aunt Lois.

"Wal," says Sam, sitting down with his back to his desperate litter of wheels, weights, and pendulums, and meditatively caressing his knee as he watched the sailing clouds in abstract meditation, "ye see, ef a thing's ordained, why it's got to be, ef you don't lift a finger. That 'ere's *so* now, ain't it?"

"Sam Lawson, you are about the most aggravating creature I ever had to do with. Here you've got our clock all to pieces, and have been keeping up a perfect hurrah's nest in our kitchen for three days, and there you sit maundering and talking with your back to your work, fussin' about the Millennium, which is none of your business, or mine, as I know of! Do either put that clock together or let it alone!"

"Don't you be a grain uneasy, Miss Lois. Why, I'll have your clock all right in the end, but I can't be druv. Wal, I guess I'll take another spell on 't to-morrow or Friday."

Poor Aunt Lois, horror-stricken, but seeing herself actually in the hands of the imperturbable enemy, now essayed the tack of conciliation. "Now do, Lawson, just finish up this job, and I'll pay you down, right on the spot; and you need the money."

"I'd like to 'blige ye, Miss Lois; but ye see money ain't everything in this world. Ef I work tew long on one thing, my mind kind o' gives out, ye see; and besides, I've got some 'sponsibilities to 'tend to. There's Mrs. Captain Brown, she made me promise to come to-day and look at the nose o' that 'ere silver teapot o' hern; it's kind o' sprung a leak. And then I 'greed to split a little oven-wood for the Widdah Pedee, that lives up on the Shelburn road. Must visit the widdahs in their affliction, Scriptur' says. And then there's Hepsy: she's allers a castin' it up at me that I don't do nothing for her and the chil'en; but then, lordy massy, Hepsy hain't no sort o' patience. Why jest this mornin' I was a tellin' her to count up her marcies, and I 'clare for 't if I did n't think she'd a throwed the tongs at me. That 'ere woman's temper railly makes me consarned. Wal, good day, Miss Lois. I'll be along again to-morrow or Friday, or the first o' next week." And away he went with long, loose strides down the village street, while the leisurely wail of an old fuguing tune floated back after him, —

> "Thy years are an
> Etarnal day,
> Thy years are an
> Etarnal day."

"An eternal torment," said Aunt Lois, with a snap. "I'm sure, if there's a mortal creature on this earth that I pity, it's Hepsy Lawson. Folks talk about her scolding, — that Sam Lawson is enough to make the saints in Heaven fall from grace. And you can't *do* anything with him: it's like charging bayonet into a wool-sack."

Now, the Hepsy thus spoken of was the luckless woman whom Sam's easy temper, and a certain youthful reputation for being a capable fellow, had led years before into the snares of matrimony with him, in consequence of which she was encumbered with the bringing up of six children on very short rations. She was a gnarly, compact, efficient little pepper-box of a woman, with snapping black eyes, pale cheeks, and a mouth always at half-cock, ready to go off with some sharp crack of reproof at the shoreless, bottom-less, and tideless inefficiency of her husband. It seemed to be one of those facts of existence that she could not get used to, nor find anywhere in her brisk, fiery little body a grain of cool resignation for. Day after day she fought it with as bitter and intense a vigor, and with as much freshness of objurgation, as if it had come upon her for the first time, — just as a sharp, wiry little terrier will bark and bark from day to day, with never-ceasing pertinacity, into an empty squirrel-hole. She seemed to have no power within her to receive and assimilate the great truth that her husband was essen-tially, and was to be and always would be, only a do-nothing.

Poor Hepsy was herself quite as essentially a do-something, — an early-rising, bustling, driving, neat, efficient, capable little body, — who contrived, by going out to day's works, — washing, scrub-bing, cleaning, — by making vests for the tailor, or closing and binding shoes for the shoemaker, by hoeing corn and potatoes in the garden at most unseasonable hours, actually to find bread to put into the mouths of the six young ravens aforesaid, and to clothe them decently. This might all do very well; but when Sam

— who believed with all his heart in the modern doctrines of woman's rights so far as to have no sort of objection to Hepsy's sawing wood or hoeing potatoes if she chose — would make the small degree of decency and prosperity the family had attained by these means a text on which to preach resignation, cheerfulness, and submission, then Hepsy's last cobweb of patience gave out, and she often became, for the moment, really dangerous, so that Sam would be obliged to plunge hastily out of doors to avoid a strictly personal encounter.

It was not to be denied that poor Hepsy really was a scold, in the strong old Saxon acceptation of the word. She had fought life single-handed, tooth and nail, with all the ferocity of outraged sensibilities, and had come out of the fight scratched and dishevelled, with few womanly graces. The good wives of the village, versed in the outs and ins of their neighbors' affairs, while they admitted that Sam was not all he should be, would sometimes roll up the whites of their eyes mysteriously, and say, "But then, poor man, what could you expect when he hasn't a happy home? Hepsy's temper is, you know," etc., etc.

The fact is, that Sam's softly easy temper and habits of miscellaneous handiness caused him to have a warm corner in most of the households. No mothers ever are very hard on a man who always pleases the children; and every one knows the welcome of a universal gossip, who carries round a district a wallet of choice bits of neighborhood information.

Now Sam knew everything about everybody. He could tell Mrs. Major Broad just what Lady Lothrop gave for her best parlor carpet, that was brought over from England, and just on what occasions she used the big silver tankard, and on what they were content with the little one, and how many pairs of long silk stockings the minister had, and how many rows of stitching there were on the shoulders of his Sunday shirts. He knew just all that was in Deacon Badger's best room, and how many silver table-spoons and teaspoons graced the beaufet in the corner; and when each of his daughters was born, and just how Miss Susy came to marry as she did, and who wanted to marry her and couldn't. He knew just the cost of Major Broad's scarlet cloak and shoe-buckles, and how Mrs. Major had a real *Ingy* shawl up in her "camphire" trunk, that cost nigh as much as Lady Lothrop's. Nobody had made love, or married, or had children born, or been buried, since Sam was able to perambulate the country, without his informing himself minutely of every available particular; and his unfathomable knowledge on these subjects was an unfailing source of popularity.

Besides this, Sam was endowed with no end of idle accomplishments. His indolence was precisely of a turn that enjoyed the excitement of an occasional odd bit of work with which he had clearly no concern, and which had no sort of tendency toward his own support or that of his family. Something so far out of the line of practical utility as to be in a manner an artistic labor would awaken all the energies of his soul. His shop was a perfect infirmary for decayed articles of *virtu* from all the houses for miles around. Cracked china, lame tea-pots, broken shoe-buckles, rickety tongs, and decrepit fire-irons, all stood in melancholy proximity, awaiting Sam's happy hours of inspiration; and he was always happy to sit down and have a long, strictly confidential conversation concerning any of these with the owner, especially if Hepsy were gone out washing, or on any other work which kept her at a safe distance.

Sam could shave and cut hair as neatly as any barber, and was always in demand up and down the country to render these offices to the sick. He was ready to go for miles to watch with invalids, and a very acceptable watcher he made, beguiling the night hours with endless stories and legends. He was also an expert in psalmody, having in his youth been the pride of the village singing-school. In those days he could perform reputably on the bass-viol in the choir of a Sunday with a dolefulness and solemnity of demeanor in the highest degree edifying, — though he was equally ready of a week-evening in scraping on a brisk little fiddle, if any of the thoughtless ones wanted a performer at a husking or a quilting frolic. Sam's obligingness was many-sided, and he was equally prepared at any moment to raise a funeral psalm or whistle the time of a double-shuffle.

But the more particular delight of Sam's heart was in funerals. He would walk miles on hearing the news of a dangerous illness, and sit roosting on the fence of the premises, delighted to gossip over the particulars, but ready to come down at any moment to do any of the odd turns which sickness in a family makes necessary; and when the last earthly scene was over, Sam was more

than ready to render those final offices from which the more nervous and fastidious shrink, but in which he took almost a professional pride.

The business of an undertaker is a refinement of modern civilization. In simple old days neighbors fell into one another's hands
for all the last wants of our poor mortality; and there were men
and women of note who took a particular and solemn pride in
these mournful offices. Sam had in fact been up all night in our
house, and having set me up in the clover, and comforted me with
a jack-knife, he proceeded to inform me of the particulars.

"Why, ye see, Horace, I ben up with 'em pretty much all night;
and I laid yer father out myself, and I never see a better-lookin'
corpse. It's a 'mazin' pity your daddy hed such feelin's 'bout havin'
people come to look at him, 'cause he does look beautiful, and
it's been a long time since we've hed a funeral, anyway, and
everybody was expectin' to come to his'n, and they'll all be dis-
sipinted if the corpse ain't show'd; but then, lordy massy, folks
oughtn't to think hard on 't ef folks hes their own way 'bout their
own funeral. That 'ere's what I've been a tellin' on 'em all, over
to the tavern and round to the store. Why, you never see such a
talk as there was about it. There was Aunt Sally Morse, and Betsey
and Patsy Sawin, and Mis' Zeruiah Bacon, come over early to look
at the corpse, and when they wasn't let in, you never heerd sich a
jawin'. Betsey and Patsy Sawin said that they allers suspected your
father was an infidel, or some sich, and now they was clear; and
Aunt Sally, she asked who made his shroud, and when she heerd
there wasn't to be none, he was laid out in his clothes, she said
she never heerd such unchristian doin's, — that she always had
heerd he had strange opinions, but she never thought it would
come to that."

"My father isn't an infidel, and I wish I could kill 'em for talking
so," said I, clenching my jack-knife in my small fist, and feeling
myself shake with passion.

"Wal, wal, I kind o' spoke up to 'em about it. I wasn't a-goin'
to hear no sich jaw; and says I, 'I think ef there is anybody that
knows what's what about funerals I'm the man, fur I don't s'pose
there's a man in the county that's laid out more folks, and set up
with more corpses, and ben sent for fur and near, than I have,
and my opinion is that mourners must always follow the last direc-

tions gi'n to 'em by the person. Ef a man hasn't a right to have the say about his own body, what hes he a right to?' Wal, they said that it was putty well of me to talk so, when I had the privilege of sittin' up with him, and seein' all that was to be seen. 'Lordy massy,' says I, 'I don't see why ye need envi me; 't ain't my fault that folks thinks it's agreeable to have me round. As to bein' buried in his clothes, why, lordy massy, 't ain't nothin' so extraordinary. In the old country great folks is very often laid out in their clothes. 'Member, when I was a boy, old Mr. Sanger, the minister in Deerbrook, was laid out in his gown and bands, with a Bible in his hands, and he looked as nateral as a pictur. I was at Parson Rider's funeral, down to Wrentham. He was laid out in white flannel. But then there was old Captain Bigelow, down to the Pint there, he was laid out regular in his rigimentals, jest as he wore 'em in the war, epaulets and all.' Wal now, Horace, your daddy looks jest as peaceful as a psalm-tune. Now, you don't know, — jest as nateral as if he'd only jest gone to sleep. So ye may set your heart at rest 'bout him."

It was one of those beautiful serene days of October, when the earth lies as bright and still as anything one can dream of in the New Jerusalem, and Sam's homely expressions of sympathy had quieted me somewhat. Sam, tired of his discourse, lay back in the clover, with his hands under his head, and went on with his moralizing.

"Lordy massy, Horace, to think on 't, — it's so kind o' solemnizin'! It's one's turn to-day, and another's to-morrow. We never know when our turn'll come." And Sam raised a favorite stave,—

> "And must these active limbs of mine
> Lie moulderin' in the clay?"

"Active limbs! I guess so!" said a sharp voice, which came through the clover-heads like the crack of a rifle. "Well, I've found you at last. Here you be, Sam Lawson, lyin' flat on your back at eleven o'clock in the morning, and not a potato dug, and not a stick of wood cut to get dinner with; and I won't cut no more if we never have dinner. It's no use a humorin' you, — doin' your work for you. The more I do, the more I may do; so come home, won't you?"

"Lordy massy, Hepsy," said Sam, slowly erecting himself out

of the grass, and staring at her with white eyes, "you don't ought
to talk so. I ain't to blame. I hed to sit up with Mr. Holyoke all
night, and help 'em lay him out at four o'clock this mornin'."

"You're always everywhere but where you've business to be,"
said Hepsy; "and helpin' and doin' for everybody but your own.
For my part, I think charity ought to begin at home. You're everywhere, up and down and round, — over to Shelbun, down to
Podunk, up to North Parish; and here Abram and Kiah Stebbins
have been waitin' all the morning with a horse they brought all
the way from Boston to get you to shoe."

"Wal now, that 'ere shows they know what's what. I told Kiah
that ef they'd bring that 'ere hoss to me I'd 'tend to his huffs."

"And be off lying in the mowing, like a patridge, when they
come after ye. That's one way to do business," said Hepsy.

"Hepsy, I was just a miditatin'. Ef we don't miditate sometimes
on all these 'ere things, it'll be wus for us by and by."

"Meditate! I'll help your meditations in a way you won't like,
if you don't look out. So now you come home, and stop your
meditatin', and go to doin' somethin'. I told 'em to come back
this afternoon, and I'd have you on the spot if 't was a possible
thing," said the very practical Hepsy, laying firm hold of Sam's
unresisting arm, and leading him away captive.

I stole into the darkened, silent room where my father had lain
so long. Its desolate neatness struck a chill to my heart. Not even
a bottle remained of the many familiar ones that used to cover the
stand and the mantel-piece; but he, lying in his threadbare Sunday coat, looked to me as I had often seen him in later days, when
he had come from school exhausted, and fallen asleep on the bed.
I crept to his side and nestled down on the floor as quietly as a
dog lies down by the side of his master.

CHAPTER V

———◆———

THE OLD MEETING-HOUSE

The next day was the funeral, and I have little remembrance in it of anything but what was dreary. Our Puritan ancestors, in the decision of their reaction from a dead formalism, had swept away from the solemn crises of life every symbolic expression; and this severe bareness and rigid restriction were nowhere more striking than in funeral services, as conducted in these early times in Massachusetts.

There was at the house of mourning simply a prayer, nothing more; and then the procession of relatives, friends, and towns-people walked silently to the grave, where, without text, prayer, or hymn, the dust was forever given to its fellow-dust. The heavy thud of the clods on the coffin, the rattling of spades, and the fall of the earth, were the only voices that spoke in that final scene. Yet that austere stillness was not without its majesty, since it might be interpreted, not as the silence of indifference, but as the stillness of those whose thoughts are too mighty for words. It was the silence of the unutterable. From the grave my mother and her two boys were conducted to my grandfather's house, — the asylum ever ready for the widowed daughter.

The next day after was Sunday, and a Sunday full of importance in the view of Aunt Lois, Aunt Keziah, and, in fact, of every one in the family. It was the custom, on the first Sabbath after a bereavement, for the whole family circle to be present together in church, to request, in a formal note, the prayers of the congregation that the recent death might be sanctified to them. It was a point of honor for all family connections to be present at this service, even though they should not attend the funeral; and my Uncle Bill, a young Sophomore in Cambridge College, had come down duly to be with us on the occasion. He was a joyous, spirited, jolly, rollicking young fellow, not in the slightest degree given to

funereal reflections, and his presence in the house always brought
a certain busy cheerfulness which I felt to lighten my darkness.

One thing certainly had a tendency in that direction, which
was that Aunt Lois was always perceptibly ameliorated by Uncle
Bill's presence. Her sharp, spare features wore a relaxed and smiling aspect, her eyes had a softer light, and she belied her own
frequent disclaimer, that she never had any beauty, by looking
almost handsome.

Poor Aunt Lois! I am afraid my reader will not do justice to
her worth by the specimens of her ways and words which I have
given. Any one that has ever pricked his fingers in trying to force
open a chestnut-burr may perhaps have moralized at the satin
lining, so smooth and soft, that lies inside of that sharpness. It is
an emblem of a kind of nature very frequent in New England,
where the best and kindest and most desirable of traits are enveloped in an outside wrapping of sharp austerity.

No person rendered more deeds of kindness in the family and
neighborhood than Aunt Lois. She indeed bore the cares of the
whole family on her heart; she watched and prayed and fretted
and scolded for all. Had she cared less, she might perhaps have
appeared more amiable. She *invested* herself, so to speak, in others;
and it was vital to her happiness, not only that they should be
happy, but that they should be happy precisely on her pattern and
in her way. She had drawn out the whole family chart, and if she
had only had power to make each one walk tractably in the path
she foreordained, her sharp, thin face might have had a few less
wrinkles. It seemed to her so perfectly evident that the ways she
fixed upon for each one were ways of pleasantness and paths of
peace, that she scarcely could have patience with Providence for
allowing things to fall out in a way so entirely different from her
designs.

Aunt Lois was a good Christian, but she made that particular
mistake in repeating the Lord's Prayer which so many of us quite
unconsciously do, — she always said, *My* will be done, instead of
Thy will. Not in so many words, of course, — it was the secret
inner voice of her essential nature that spoke and said one thing,
while her tongue said another. But then who can be sure enough
of himself in this matter, to cast the first stone at Aunt Lois?

It was the fashion of the Calvinistic preaching of that time to

put the doctrine of absolute and unconditional submission to God
in the most appalling forms, and to exercise the conscience with
most severe supposititious tests. After many struggles and real
agonies, Aunt Lois had brought herself to believe that she would
be willing to resign her eternal salvation to the Divine glory; that
she could consent to the eternal perdition of those on whom her
heart was most particularly set, were it God's will; and thus her
self-will, as she supposed, had been entirely annihilated, whereas
it was only doubled back on itself, and ready to come out with
tenfold intensity in the unsuspected little things of this life, where
she looked less at Divine agency than human instrumentality. No
law, as she supposed, required her to submit to people's acting
foolishly in their worldly matters, particularly when she was able
and willing to show them precisely how they ought to act.

Failing of a prosperous marriage for my mother, Aunt Lois's
heart was next set upon a college education for my Uncle Bill,
the youngest and brightest of the family. For this she toiled and
economized in family labor, and eked it out by vest-making at
the tailor's, and by shoe-binding at the shoemaker's, — all that she
might have something to give to Bill for spending-money, to keep
up his standing respectably in college. Her antagonistic attitude
toward my brother and myself proceeded less from hardness of
heart than from an anxious, worrying fear that we should trench
on the funds that at present were so heavily taxed to bring Uncle
Bill through college. Especially did she fear that my father had
left me the legacy of his own ungratified desire for an education,
and that my grandmother's indulgence and bountifulness might
lead her to encourage me in some such expectations, and then
where was the money to come from? Aunt Lois foresaw contingen-
cies afar off. Not content with the cares of the present day and
hour, she dived far into the future, and carried all sorts of imaginary
loads that would come in supposititious cases. As the Christian
by the eye of faith sees all sorts of possible good along the path
of future duty, so she by the eye of cautiousness saw every possible
future evil that could arise in every supposable contingency. Aunt
Lois's friends often had particular reason to wish that she cared
less for them, for then, perhaps, she might give them some peace.
But nothing is so hopeless as your worthy domestic house-dog,
every hair of whose fur bristles with watchfulness, and who barks

at you incessantly from behind a most terrible intrenchment of faithful labors and loving-kindnesses heaped up on your behalf.

These dear good souls who wear their life out for you, have they not a right to scold you, and dictate to you, and tie up your liberty, and make your life a burden to you? If they have not, who has? If you complain, you break their worthy old hearts. They insist on the privilege of seeking your happiness by thwarting you in everything you want to do, and putting their will instead of yours in every step of your life.

Between Aunt Lois and my father there had been that constant antagonism which is often perceptible between two human beings, each good enough in himself, but of a quality to act destructively upon the other. A satin vest and a nutmeg-grater are both perfectly harmless, and even worthy existences, but their close proximity on a jolting journey is not to be recommended.

My father never could bear my Aunt Lois in his house; and her presence had such an instant effect in developing all the combative element in him, that really the poor woman never saw him long enough under an agreeable aspect to enable her even to understand why my mother should regard him with affection; and it is not to be wondered at, therefore, that she was not a deep mourner at his death. She regarded her sister's love for my father as an unfortunate infatuation, and was more satisfied with the ways of Providence than she usually was, when its object was withdrawn.

It was according to all the laws of moral gravitation that, as soon as my father died, my mother became an obedient satellite in Aunt Lois's orbit. She was one of those dear, helpless little women, who, like flowers by the wayside, seem to be at the disposal of the first strong hand that wants to gather them. She was made to be ruled over; and so we all felt this first Sunday morning that we had come home to be under the dominion of Aunt Lois. She put on my mother's mourning-bonnet and tied it under her meek, unresisting chin, turning her round and round to get views of her from different points, and arranging her ribbons and veil and pins as if she had been a lay figure going to exhibition; and then she tied our collars, and gave a final twitch to our jackets, and warned us not to pull out the pins from the crape bands on our new hats, nor to talk and look round in meeting, strengthening the caution with, "Just so sure as you do, there's Mr. Israel Scran, the tithing-man, will come and take you and set you on the pulpit stairs."

Now Mr. Israel Scran on week-days was a rather jolly, secular-looking individual, who sat on the top of a barrel in his store, and told good stories; but Israel Scran on Sundays was a tithing-man, whose eyes were supposed to be as a flame of fire to search out little boys that played in meeting, and bring them to awful retribution. And I must say that I shook in my shoes at the very idea of his entering into judgment with me for any misdemeanor.

Going to church on the present occasion was rather a severe and awful ceremony to my childish mind, second only to the dreary horror of the time when we stood so dreadfully still around the grave, and heard those heavy clods thud upon the coffin. I ventured a timid inquiry of my mother as to what was going to be done there.

Aunt Lois took the word out of her mouth. "Now, Horace, hush your talk, and don't worry your mother. She's going to put up a note to be prayed for to-day, and we are all going to join; so you be a good boy, and don't talk."

Being good was so frequently in those days represented to me as synonymous with keeping silence, that I screwed my little mouth up firmly as I walked along to the meeting-house, behind my mother, holding my brother Bill's hand, and spoke not a word, though he made several overtures towards conversation by informing me that he saw a chipmunk, and that if it was only Monday he'd hit him smack; and also telling me that Sam Lawson had promised to go pout-fishing with us on Tuesday, with other boy temporalities of a nature equally worldly.

The meeting-house to which our steps were tending was one of those huge, shapeless, barn-like structures, which our fathers erected apparently as a part of that well-arranged system by which they avoided all resemblance to those fair, poetic ecclesiastical forms of the Old World, which seemed in their view as "garments spotted by the flesh."

The interior of it was revealed by the light of two staring rows of windows, which let in the glare of the summer sun, and which were so loosely framed, that, in wintry and windy weather, they rattled and shook, and poured in a perfect whirlwind of cold air, which disported itself over the shivering audience.

It was a part of the theory of the times never to warm these buildings by a fire; and the legend runs that once in our meeting-house the communion was administered under a temperature which actually froze the sacred elements while they were being distributed. Many a remembrance of winter sessions in that old meeting-house rose to my mind, in which I sat with my poor dangling feet perfectly numb and paralyzed with cold, and blew my finger-ends to keep a little warmth in them, and yet I never thought of complaining; for everybody was there, — mother, aunts, grandmother, and all the town. We all sat and took our hardships in common, as a plain, necessary fact of existence.

Going to meeting, in that state of society into which I was born, was as necessary and inevitable a consequence of waking up on Sunday morning as eating one's breakfast. Nobody thought of staying away, — and, for that matter, nobody wanted to stay away. Our weekly life was simple, monotonous, and laborious; and the chance of seeing the whole neighborhood together in their best clothes on Sunday was a thing which, in the dearth of all other sources of amusement, appealed to the idlest and most unspiritual of loafers. They who did not care for the sermon or the prayers wanted to see Major Broad's scarlet coat and laced ruffles, and his wife's brocade dress, and the new bonnet which Lady Lothrop had just had sent up from Boston. Whoever had not seen these would be out of society for a week to come, and not be able to converse understandingly on the topics of the day.

The meeting on Sunday united in those days, as nearly as possible, the whole population of a town, — men, women, and children. There was then in a village but one fold and one shepherd, and long habit had made the tendency to this one central point so much a necessity to every one, that to stay away from "meetin'" for any reason whatever was always a secret source of uneasiness. I remember in my early days, sometimes when I had been left at home by reason of some of the transient ailments of childhood, how ghostly and supernatural the stillness of the whole house and village outside the meeting-house used to appear to me, how loudly the clock ticked and the flies buzzed down the window-pane, and how I listened in the breathless stillness to the distant psalm-singing, the solemn tones of the long prayer, and then to the monotone of the sermon, and then again to the closing echoes of the last hymn, and thought sadly, what if some day I should be left out, when all my relations and friends had gone to meeting in the New Jerusalem, and hear afar the music from the crystal walls.

As our Sunday gathering at meeting was a complete picture of the population of our village, I shall, as near as possible, daguerreo-type our Sunday audience, as the best means of placing my readers in sympathy with the scene and actors of this history.

The arrangement of our house of worship in Oldtown was some-what peculiar, owing to the fact of its having originally been built as a mission church for the Indians. The central portion of the house, usually appropriated to the best pews, was in ours devoted to them; and here were arranged benches of the simplest and most primitive form, on which were collected every Sunday the thin and wasted remnants of what once was a numerous and powerful tribe. There were four or five respectable Indian families, who owned comfortable farms in the neighborhood, and came to meeting in their farm-wagons, like any of their white neighbors.

Conspicuous among these, on the front bench, facing the pulpit, sat the Indian head-magistrate, Justice Waban, — tall and erect as an old pine-tree, and of a grave and reverend aspect. Next to him was seated the ecclesiastical superior of that portion of the congregation, Deacon Ephraim. Mild, intelligent, and devout, he was the perfect model of the praying Indian formed in the apos-tolic traditions of the good Eliot. By his side sat his wife, Keturah, who, though she had received Christian baptism, still retained in most respects the wild instincts and untamed passions of the savage. Though she attended church and allowed her children to be baptized, yet, in spite of minister, elder, and tithing-man, she obstinately held on to the practice of many of her old heathen superstitions.

Old Keturah was one of the wonders of my childhood. She was spoken of among the gossips with a degree of awe, as one who possessed more knowledge than was good for her; and in thunder-storms and other convulsions of nature she would sit in her chimney-corner and chant her old Indian incantations, to my mingled terror and delight. I remember distinctly three syllables that occurred very often, — "ah-mah-ga, ah-mah-ga," — sometimes pronounced in wild, plaintive tones, and sometimes in tones of menace and denunciation. In fact, a century before, Keturah must have had a hard time of it with her Christian neighbors; but our minister was a gentleman and a scholar, and only smiled benignly when certain elderly ladies brought him terrible stories of Keturah's proceedings.

Next to Keturah was seated Deborah Kummacher, an Indian woman, who had wisely forsaken the unprofitable gods of the wild forest, and taken to the Christian occupation of fruit-growing, and kept in nice order a fruit farm near my grandfather's, where we children delighted to resort in the season, receiving from her presents of cherries, pears, peaches, or sweet apples, which she informed us she was always ready to give to good children who said their prayers and made their manners when they came into her house. Next behind her came Betty Poganut, Patty Pegan, and old Sarah Wonsamug, — hard-visaged, high-cheek-boned females, with snaky-black eyes, principally remarkable, in my mind, for the quantity of cider they could drink. I had special reason to remember this, as my grandmother's house was their favorite resort, and drawing cider was always the work of the youngest boy.

Then there was Lem Sudock, a great, coarse, heavy-moulded Indian, with gigantic limbs and a savage face, but much in request for laying stone walls, digging wells, and other tasks for which mere physical strength was the chief requisite. Beside him was Dick Obscue, a dull, leering, lazy, drinking old fellow, always as dry as an empty sponge, but with an endless capacity for imbibing. Dick was of a class which our modern civilization would never see inside of a church, though he was in his seat in our meeting-house as regularly as any of the deacons; but on week-days his principal employment seemed to be to perambulate the country, making stations of all the kitchen firesides, where he would tell stories, drink cider, and moralize, till the patience or cider-pitchers of his hosts ran dry, when he would rise up slowly, adjust his old straw hat, hitch up his dangling nether garments a little tighter, and, with a patronizing nod, say, "Wal, naow, 'f you can spare me I'll go."

Besides our Indian population, we had also a few negroes, and a side gallery was appropriated to them. Prominent there was the stately form of old Boston Foodah, an African prince, who had been stolen from the coast of Guinea in early youth, and sold in Boston at some period of antiquity whereto the memory of man runneth not. All the Oldtown people, and their fathers and grandfathers, remembered old Boston just as he then existed, neither older nor younger. He was of a majestic stature, slender and proudly erect, and perfectly graceful in every movement, his woolly hair as white as the driven snow. He was servant to General Hull in the Revolutionary war, and at its close was presented by his master with a full suit of his military equipments, including three-cornered hat, with plume, epaulets, and sword. Three times a year, — at the spring training, the fall muster, and on Thanksgiving day, — Boston arrayed himself in full panoply, and walked forth a really striking and magnificent object. In the eyes of us boys, on these days, he was a hero, and he patronized us with a condescension which went to our hearts. His wife, Jinny, was a fat, roly-poly little body, delighting in red and yellow bonnets, who duly mustered into meeting a troop of black-eyed, fat, woolly-headed little negroes, whom she cuffed and disciplined during sermon-time with a matronly ferocity designed to show white folks that she was in earnest in their religious training.

Near by was old Primus King, a gigantic, retired whaleman, black as a coal, with enormous hands and feet, universally in demand in all the region about as assistant in butchering operations.

Besides these, let me not forget dear, jolly old Cæsar, my grandfather's own negro, the most joyous creature on two feet. What could not Cæsar do? He could gobble like a turkey so perfectly as to deceive the most experienced old gobbler on the farm; he could crow so like a cock that all the cocks in the neighborhood would reply to him; he could mew like a cat, and bark like a dog; he could sing and fiddle, and dance the double-shuffle, and was *au fait* in all manner of jigs and hornpipes; and one need not wonder, therefore, that old Cæsar was hugged and caressed and lauded by me in my childhood as the most wonderful of men.

There were several other colored families, of less repute, who also found seats in the negro gallery. One of them was that of Aunt Nancy Prime, famous for making election-cake and ginger-pop, and who was sent for at all the great houses on occasions of high festivity, as learned in all mysteries relating to the confection of cakes and pies. A tight, trig, bustling body she, black and polished as ebony, smooth-spoken and respectful, and quite a favorite with everybody. Nancy had treated herself to an expensive luxury in the shape of a husband, — an idle, worthless mulatto man, who was owned as a slave in Boston. Nancy bought him by intense labors in spinning flax, but found him an undesirable acquisition, and was often heard to declare, in the bitterness of her soul, when he returned from his drinking bouts, that she should never buy another nigger, she knew.

The only thing she gained by this matrimonial speculation was an abundant crop of noisy children, who, as she often declared, nearly wore the life out of her. I remember once, when I was on a visit to her cottage, while I sat regaling myself with a slice of cake, Nancy lifted the trap-door which went down into the cellar below. Forthwith the whole skirmishing tribe of little darkies, who had been rolling about the floor, seemed suddenly to unite in one coil, and, with a final flop, disappeared in the hole. Nancy gave a kick to the door, and down it went; when she exclaimed, with a sigh of exhausted patience, "Well, now then, I hope you'll be still a minute, anyway!"

The houses of the colored people formed a little settlement by themselves in the north part of the village, where they lived on most amicable terms with all the inhabitants.

In the front gallery of the meeting-house, opposite the pulpit, was seated the choir of the church. The leader of our music was old Mump Morse, a giant of a man, in form not unlike a cider-hogshead, with a great round yellow head, and a voice like the rush of mighty winds, who was wont to boast that he could chord with thunder and lightning better than any man in the parish. Next to him came our friend Sam Lawson, whose distinguishing peculiarity it was, that he could strike into any part where his voice seemed most needed; and he often showed the miscellaneous nature of his accomplishments by appearing as tenor, treble, or counter, successively, during the rendering of one psalm. If we consider that he also pitched the tunes with his pitch-pipe, and played on his bass-viol, we shall see increasing evidence of that versatility of genius for which he was distinguished.

Another principal bass-singer was old Joe Stedman, who asserted his democratic right to do just as he had a mind to by always appearing every Sunday in a clean leather apron of precisely the form he wore about his weekly work. Of course all the well-conducted upper classes were scandalized, and Joe was privately admonished of the impropriety, which greatly increased his satisfaction, and caused him to regard himself as a person of vast importance. It was reported that the minister had told him that there was more pride in his leather apron than in Captain Brown's scarlet cloak; but Joe settled the matter by declaring that the apron was a matter of conscience with him, and of course after that there was no more to be said.

These leading characters, with a train of young men and maidens who practised in the weekly singing-school, used to conduct the musical devout exercises much to their own satisfaction, if not always to that of our higher circle.

And now, having taken my readers through the lower classes in our meeting-house, I must, in order of climax, represent to them our higher orders.

Social position was a thing in those days marked by lines whose precision and distinctness had not been blurred by the rough handling of democracy. Massachusetts was, in regard to the aroma and atmosphere of her early days, an aristocratic community. The seeds of democratic social equality lay as yet ungerminated in her soil. The State was a garden laid out with the old formal parallelograms and clipped hedges of princely courts and titled ranks, but sown with seeds of a new and rampant quality, which were destined to overgrow them all.

Even our little town had its court circle, its House of Lords and House of Commons, with all the etiquette and solemn observances thereto appertaining. At the head stood the minister and his wife, whose rank was expressed by the pew next the pulpit. Then came Captain Browne, a retired English merchant and ship-owner, who was reported to have ballasted himself with a substantial weight of worldly substance. Captain Browne was a tall, upright, florid man, a little on the shady side of life, but carrying his age with a cheerful greenness. His long, powdered locks hung in a well-tended queue down his back, and he wore a scarlet coat, with a white vest and stock, and small-clothes, while long silk stockings with knee and shoe buckles of the best paste, sparkling like real diamonds, completed his attire. His wife rustled by his side in brocade which might almost stand alone for stiffness, propped upon heels that gave a majestic altitude to her tall, thin figure.

Next came the pew of Miss Mehitable Rossiter, who, in right of being the only surviving member of the family of the former minister, was looked upon with reverence in Oldtown, and took rank decidedly in the Upper House, although a very restricted and limited income was expressed in the quality of her attire. Her Sunday suit in every article spoke of ages past, rather than of the present hour. Her laces were darned, though still they were laces; her satin gown had been turned and made over, till every possible capability of it was exhausted; and her one Sunday bonnet exhibited a power of coming out in fresh forms, with each revolving season, that was quite remarkable, particularly as each change was somewhat odder than the last. But still, as everybody knew that it was Miss Mehitable Rossiter, and no meaner person, her queer bonnets and dyed gowns were accepted as a part of those inexplicable dispensations of the Providence that watches over the higher classes, which are to be received by faith alone.

In the same pew with Miss Mehitable sat Squire Jones, once, in days of colonial rule, rejoicing in the dignity of Sheriff of the County. During the years of the Revolutionary war, he had mysteriously vanished from view, as many good Tories did; but now that the new social status was well established, he suddenly reappeared in the neighborhood, and took his place as an orderly citizen, unchallenged and unquestioned. It was enough that the Upper House received him. The minister gave him his hand, and Lady Lothrop courtesied to him, and called on his wife, and that, of course, settled the manner in which the parish were to behave; and, like an obedient flock, they all jumped the fence after their shepherd. Squire Jones, besides, was a well-formed, well-dressed man, who lived in a handsome style, and came to meeting in his own carriage; and these are social virtues not to be disregarded in any well-regulated community.

There were certain well-established ranks and orders in social position in Oldtown, which it is important that I should distinctly define. People who wore ruffles round their hands, and rode in their own coaches, and never performed any manual labor, might be said to constitute in Oldtown our House of Lords, — and they might all have been counted on two or three of my fingers. It was, in fact, confined to the personages already enumerated. There were the minister, Captain Browne, and Sheriff Jones.

But below these, yet associating with them on terms of strict equality, were a more numerous body of Commons, — men of substance and influence, but who tilled the earth with their own hands, or pursued some other active industrial calling.

Distinguished among these, sitting in the next pew to the Sheriff, was Major Broad, a practical farmer, who owned a large and thriving farm of the best New England type, and presented that true blending of the laboring man and the gentleman which is nowhere else found. He had received his military rank for meritorious services in the late Revolutionary war, and he came back to his native village with that indefinable improvement in air and manner which is given by the habits of military life. With us he owed great prestige to a certain personal resemblance to General Washington which he was asserted to have by one of our townsfolk, who had often seen him and the General on the same field, and who sent the word abroad in the town that whoever wanted to know how General Washington looked had only to look upon Major Broad. The Major was too much of a real man to betray the slightest consciousness of this advantage, but it invested him with an air of indefinable dignity in the eyes of all his neighbors, especially those of the lower ranks.

Next came my grandfather's family pew; and in our Oldtown House of Commons I should say that none stood higher than he. In his Sunday suit my grandfather was quite a well-made, handsome man. His face was marked by grave, shrewd reflection, and a certain gentle cast of humor, which rarely revealed itself even in a positive smile, and yet often made me feel as if he were quietly and interiorly smiling at his own thoughts. His well-brushed Sunday coat and small-clothes, his bright knee and shoe buckles, his long silk stockings, were all arranged with a trim neatness refreshing to behold. His hair, instead of being concealed by a wig, or powdered and tied in a queue, after the manner of the aristocracy, fell in long curls on his shoulders, and was a not unbecoming silvery frame to the placid picture of his face. He was a man by nature silent and retiring, indisposed to anything like hurry or tumult, rather easy and generously free in his business habits, and quietly sanguine in his expectations. In point of material possessions he was reputed well to do, as he owned a large farm and two mills, and conducted the business thereof with a quiet easiness which was often exceedingly provoking to my grandmother and Aunt Lois. No man was more popular in the neighborhood, and the confidence of his fellow-townsmen was yearly expressed in town-meeting by his reappointment to every office of trust which he could be induced to accept. He was justice of the peace, deacon of the church, selectman, — in short, enjoyed every spiritual and temporal office by the bestowal of which his fellow-men could express confidence in him. This present year, indeed, he bore the office of tithing-man, in association with Mr. Israel Scran. It had been thought that it would be a good thing, in order to check the increasing thoughtlessness of the rising generation in regard to Sunday-keeping, to enlist in this office an authority so much respected as Deacon Badger; but the manner in which he performed its duties was not edifying to the minds of strictly disposed people. The Deacon in his official capacity was expected to stalk forth at once as a terror to evil-doers, whereas he seemed to have no capacity for terrifying anybody. When a busy individual informed him that this or that young person was to be seen walking out in the fields, or picking flowers in their gardens of a Sabbath afternoon, the Deacon always placidly answered that he hadn't seen them; from which the ill-disposed would infer that he looked another way, of set purpose, and the quiet internal smile that always illuminated the Deacon's face gave but too much color to this idea.

In those days the great war of theology which has always divided New England was rife, and every man was marked and ruled as to his opinions, and the theologic lines passed even through the conjugal relation, which often, like everything else, had its Calvinistic and its Arminian side.

My grandfather was an Arminian, while my grandmother was, as I have said, an earnest, ardent Calvinist. Many were the controversies I have overheard between them, in which the texts of Scripture flew thick and fast, until my grandfather at last would shut himself up in that final fortress of calm and smiling silence which is so provoking to feminine ardor. There intrenched, he would look out upon his assailants with a quiet, imperturbable good-humor which quite drove them to despair.

It was a mystery to my grandmother how a good man, as she knew my grandfather to be, *could* remain years unmoved in the very hearing of such unanswerable arguments as she had a thousand times brought up, and still, in the very evening of his days, go on laying his serene old head on an Arminian pillow! My grandfather was a specimen of that class of men who can walk amid the opinions of their day, encircled by a halo of serene and smiling individuality which quarrels with nobody, and, without shocking any one's prejudices, preserves intact the liberty of individual dissent. He silently went on thinking and doing exactly as he pleased, and yet was always spoken of as the *good* Deacon. His calm, serene, benignant figure was a sort of benediction as he sat in his pew of a Sunday; and if he did not see the little boys that played, or, seeing them, only smilingly brought them to a sense of duty by passing them a head of fennel through the slats of the pews, still Deacon Badger was reckoned about the best man in the world.

By the side of my grandfather sat his eldest born, Uncle Jacob, a hale, thrifty young farmer, who, with his equally hale and thrifty wife, was settled on a well-kept farm at some distance from ours. Uncle Jacob was a genuine son of the soil, whose cheeks were ruddy as clover, and teeth as white as new milk. He had grown up on a farm, as quietly as a tree grows, and had never been ten miles from his birthplace. He was silent, contented, and industrious. He was in his place to be prayed for as one of a bereaved family, of course, this morning; but there was scarcely more capability of mourning in his plump, healthy body than there is in that of a well-fed, tranquil steer. But he took his weekly portion of religion kindly. It was the thing to do on Sunday, as much as making hay or digging potatoes on Monday. His wife by his side displayed no less the aspect of calm, respectable, well-to-do content. Her Sunday bonnet was without spot, her Sunday gown without wrinkle; and she had a great bunch of fennel in her pocket-handkerchief, which, from time to time, she imparted to us youngsters with a benevolent smile.

Far otherwise was the outward aspect of my grandmother's brother, Eliakim Sheril. He was a nervous, wiry, thin, dry little old man, every part of whose body appeared to be hung together by springs that were in constant vibration. He had small, keen black eyes, a thin, sharp hooked nose, which he was constantly buffeting, and blowing, and otherwise maltreating, in the fussy uneasiness which was the habit of the man.

Uncle 'Liakim was a man known as Uncle to all the village, — the kindest-souled, most untiringly benevolent, single-hearted old body that could be imagined; but his nervous activity was such as to have procured among the boys a slight change in the rendering of his name, which was always popularly given as Uncle Fliakim, and, still more abbreviated, Uncle Fly.

"Can you tell me where Mr. Sheril is," says an inquirer at the door of my grandfather's mill.

"If you want to find 'Liakim," says my grandfather, with his usual smile, "never go after him, — you'll never catch him; but stand long enough on any one spot on earth, and he's sure to go by."

Uncle 'Liakim had his own particular business, — the overseeing of a soap and candle factory; but, besides that, he had on his mind the business of everybody else in town, — the sorrows of every widow, the lonely fears of every spinster, the conversion of every reprobate, the orthodoxy of every minister, the manners and morals of all the parish, — all of which caused him to be up early and down late, and flying about confusedly at all hours, full of zeal, full of kindness, abounding in suggestions, asking questions the answers to which he could not stop to hear, making promises which he did not remember, and which got him into no end of trouble with people who did, telling secrets, and letting innumerable cats out of countless bags, to the dismay and affright of all reserved and well-conducted people. Uncle Fliakim, in fact, might be regarded in our village of Oldtown as a little brown pudding-stick that kept us in a perpetual stir. To be sure, it was a general stir of loving-kindness and good intentions, yet it did not always give unlimited satisfaction.

For instance, some of the more strictly disposed members of the congregation were scandalized that Uncle Fliakim, every stormy Sunday, nearly destroyed the solemnity of the long prayer by the officious zeal which he bestowed in getting sundry forlorn old maids, widows, and other desolate women to church. He had a horse of that immortal species well known in country villages, — made of whalebone and india-rubber, with a long neck, a hammer-head, and one blind eye, — and a wagon which rattled and tilted and clattered in every part, as if infected with a double portion of its owner's spirits; and, mounting in this, he would drive miles in the rain or the snow, all for the pleasure of importing into the congregation those dry, forlorn, tremulous specimens of female mortality which abound in every village congregation.

Uncle Fliakim had been talked to on this subject, and duly admonished. The benevolence of his motives was allowed; but why, it was asked, must he always drive his wagon with a bang against the doorstep just as the congregation rose to the first prayer? It was a fact that the stillness which followed the words, "Let us pray," was too often broken by the thump of the wagon and the sound, "Whoa, whoa! take care, there!" from without, as Uncle Fly's blind steed rushed headlong against the meeting-house door, as if he were going straight in, wagon and all; and then there would be a further most unedifying giggle and titter of light-minded young men and damsels when Aunt Bathsheba Sawin and Aunt Jerusha Pettibone, in their rusty black-crape bonnets, with their big black fans in their hands, slowly rustled and creaked into their seats, while the wagon and Uncle 'Liakim were heard giggiting away. Then the boys, if the tithing-man was not looking at them, would bet marbles whether the next load would be old Mother Chris and Phœbe Drury, or Hetty Walker and old Mother Hopestill Loker.

It was a great offence to all the stricter classes that Uncle Fly should demean his wagon by such an unedifying character as Mother Hopestill Loker; for, though her name intimated that she ought to have charity, still she was held no better than a publican and sinner; and good people in those days saw the same impropriety in such people having too much to do with reputable Christians that they used to years ago in a country called Palestine.

For all these reasons Uncle Fliakim was often dealt with as one of good intentions, but wanting the wisdom which is profitable to direct. One year his neighbors thought to employ his superfluous activity by appointing him tithing-man; and great indeed in this department were his zeal and activity; but it was soon found that the dear man's innocent sincerity of heart made him the prey of every village good-for-naught who chose to take him in. All the naughty boys in town were agog with expectancy when Joe Valentine declared, with a wink, that he'd drive a team Sunday right by Uncle Fly's house, over to Hopkinton, with his full consent. Accordingly, the next Sunday he drove leisurely by, with a solemn face and a broad weed on his hat. Uncle Fly ran panting, half dressed, and threw himself distractedly on the neck of the horse. "My young friend, I cannot permit it. You must turn right back."

"My dear sir," said Joe, "haven't you heard that my mother is lying dead in Hopkinton at this very moment?"

"Is it possible?" said my uncle, with tears in his eyes. "I beg your pardon. I hadn't heard it. Proceed, by all means. I'm sorry I interrupted you."

The next morning wicked Joe careered by again. "Good morning, Mr. Sheril. I s'pose you know my mother's been lying dead these five years; but I'm equally obliged for your politeness."

Vain was Uncle Fly's indignation. Greater men than he have had to give up before the sovereign power of a laugh, and erelong he resigned the office of tithing-man as one requiring a sterner metal than he possessed. In fact, an unsavory character, who haunted the tavern and was called by the boys Old Mopshear, gave a résumé of his opinions of tithing-men as seen from the camp of the enemy.

"Old Deacon Badger," he said, "was always lookin' 't other way, and never saw nothin' 't' was goin' on. But there was Uncle Fliakim, — wal, to be sure the gals couldn't tie up their shoes without he was a lookin'; but then, come to railly doin' anythin', it was only a snap, and he was off agin. He wa'n't much more'n a middlin'-sized grasshopper, arter all. Tell you what," said Mopshear, "it takes a fellow like Israel Scran, that knows what he's about, and 's got some *body* to do with. When old Jerusalem Ben swore he'd drive the stage through the town a Sunday, I tell you it was fun to see Israel Scran. He jest stood out by the road and met the hosses smack, and turned 'em so quick that the stage flopped over like a wink, and Ben was off rolling over and over in the sand. Ben got the wust on 't that time. I tell you, it takes Israel Scran to be tithing-man!"

Good Uncle Fliakim had made himself extremely busy in my

father's last sickness, dodging out of one door and in at another, at all hours; giving all manner of prescriptions for his temporal and spiritual state, but always in too much of a hurry to stop a minute, — a consideration which, I heard my father say, was the only one which made him tolerable. But, after all, I liked him, though he invariably tumbled over me, either in coming into or going out of the house, and then picked me up and gave me a cent, and went on rejoicing. The number of cents I acquired in this way became at last quite a little fortune.

But time would fail me to go on and describe all the quiddities and oddities of our Sunday congregation. Suffice it to say, that we all grew in those days like the apple-trees in our back lot. Every man had his own quirks and twists, and threw himself out freely in the line of his own individuality; and so a rather jerky, curious, original set of us there was. But such as we were, high and low, good and bad, refined and illiterate, barbarian and civilized, negro and white, the old meeting-house united us all on one day of the week, and its solemn services formed an insensible but strong bond of neighborhood charity.

We may rail at Blue Laws and Puritan strictness as much as we please, but certainly those communities where our fathers carried out their ideas fully had their strong points; and, rude and primitive as our meeting-houses were, this weekly union of all classes in them was a most powerful and efficient means of civilization. The man or woman cannot utterly sink who on every seventh day is obliged to appear in decent apparel, and to join with all the standing respectability of the community in a united act of worship.

Nor were our Sunday services, though simple, devoid of their solemn forms. The mixed and motley congregation came in with due decorum during the ringing of the first bell, and waited in their seats the advent of the minister. The tolling of the bell was the signal for him that his audience were ready to receive him, and he started from his house. The clerical dress of the day, the black silk gown, the spotless bands, the wig and three-cornered hat and black gloves, were items of professional fitness which, in our minister's case, never failed of a due attention. When, with his wife leaning on his arm, he entered at the door of the meeting-house, the whole congregation rose and remained reverently standing until he had taken his seat in the pulpit. The same reverential decorum was maintained after service was over, when all remained standing and uncovered while the minister and his family passed down the broad aisle and left the house. Our fathers were no man-worshippers, but they regarded the minister as an ambassador from the great Sovereign of the universe, and paid reverence to Him whose word he bore in their treatment of him.

On the Sunday following the funeral of any one in the parish, it was customary to preach a sermon having immediate reference to the event which had occurred, in the course of which the near-est friends and relatives were directly addressed, and stood up in their seats to receive the pastoral admonition and consolation. I remember how wan and faded, like a shimmering flower, my poor mother rose in her place, while I was forcibly held down by Aunt Lois's grasp on my jacket till the "orphan children" were men-tioned, when I was sent up on my feet with an impetus like a Jack in a box; and afterward the whole family circle arose and stood, as the stream of admonition and condolence became more general. We were reminded that the God of the widow and orphan never dies, — that this life is the shadow, and the life to come the substance, — that there is but one thing needful, — that as our departed friend is to-day, so we may all be to-morrow; and then the choir sung, to the tune of old Darwen,

> "Shall man, O God of life and light,
>   Forever moulder in the grave?
> Hast thou forgot thy glorious work,
>   Thy promise and thy power to save?"

I cannot say much for our country psalmody. Its execution was certainly open to severe criticism; and Uncle Fliakim, on every occasion of especial solemnity, aggravated its peculiarities by tuning up in a high, cracked voice a weird part, in those days called "counter," but which would in our days insure his being taken out of the house as a possessed person. But, in spite of all this, those old minor-keyed funeral hymns in which our fathers delighted always had a quality in them that affected me power-fully. The music of all barbarous nations is said to be in the minor key, and there is in its dark combinations something that gives piercing utterance to that undertone of doubt, mystery, and sorrow by which a sensitive spirit always is encompassed in this life.

I was of a peculiarly sensitive organization; my nerves shivered
to every touch, like harp-strings. What might have come over me
had I heard the solemn chants of cathedrals, and the deep pulsa-
tions of the old organ-hearts that beat there, I cannot say, but
certain it is that the rude and primitive singing in our old meeting-
house always excited me powerfully. It brought over me, like a
presence, the sense of the infinite and eternal, the yearning and
the fear and the desire of the poor finite being, so ignorant and
so helpless. I left the church lifted up as if walking on air, with
the final words of the psalm floating like an illuminated cloud
around me, —

> "Faith sees the bright eternal doors
> Unfold to make His children way;
> They shall be crowned with endless life,
> And shine in everlasting day."

CHAPTER VI

FIRE-LIGHT TALKS
IN MY GRANDMOTHER'S KITCHEN

My grandmother's kitchen was a great, wide, roomy apartment, whose white-sanded floor was always as clean as hands could make it. It was resplendent with the sheen of a set of scoured pewter plates and platters, which stood arranged on a dresser on one side. The great fireplace swept quite across another side. There we burned cord-wood, and the fire was built up on architectural principles known to those days. First came an enormous back-log, rolled in with the strength of two men, on the top of which was piled a smaller log; and then a fore-stick, of a size which would entitle it to rank as a log in our times, went to make the front foundation of the fire. The rearing of the ample pile thereupon was a matter of no small architectural skill, and all the ruling members of our family circle had their own opinions about its erection, which they maintained with the zeal and pertinacity which become earnest people. My grandfather, with his grave smile, insisted that he was the only reasonable fire-builder of the establishment; but when he had arranged his sticks in the most methodical order, my grandmother would be sure to rush out with a thump here and a twitch there, and divers incoherent exclamations tending to imply that men never knew how to build a fire. Frequently her intense zeal for immediate effect would end in a general rout and roll of the sticks in all directions, with puffs of smoke down the chimney, requiring the setting open of the outside door; and then Aunt Lois would come to the rescue, and, with a face severe with determination, tear down the whole structure and rebuild from the foundation with exactest precision, but with an air that cast volumes of contempt on all that had gone before. The fact is, that there is no little nook of domestic life which gives snug harbor to so much self-will and self-righteousness as the family hearth; and this is particularly the case with wood fires, because, from the miscellaneous nature of the material, and the sprightly activity of the combustion, there is a constant occasion for tending and alteration, and so a vast field for individual opinion.

We had come home from our second Sunday service. Our evening meal of smoking brown bread and baked beans had been discussed, and the supper-things washed and put out of sight. There was an uneasy, chill moaning and groaning out of doors, showing the coming up of an autumn storm, — just enough chill and wind to make the brightness of a social hearth desirable, — and my grandfather had built one of his most methodical and splendid fires.

The wide, ample depth of the chimney was aglow in all its cavernous length with the warm leaping light that burst out in lively jets and spirts from every rift and chasm. The great black crane that swung over it, with its multiplicity of pot-hooks and trammels, seemed to have a sort of dusky illumination, like that of old Cæsar's black, shining face, as he sat on his block of wood in the deep recess of the farther corner, with his hands on the knees of his Sunday pantaloons, gazing lovingly into the blaze with all the devotion of a fire-worshipper. On week-day evenings old Cæsar used to have his jack-knife in active play in this corner, and whistles and pop-guns and squirrel-traps for us youngsters grew under his plastic hand; but on Sunday evening he was too good a Christian even to think of a jack-knife, and if his hand casually encountered it in his pocket, he resisted it as a temptation of the Devil, and sat peacefully winking and blinking, and occasionally breaking out into a ripple of private giggles which appeared to spring purely from the overflow of bodily contentment. My Uncle Bill was in that condition which is peculiarly apt to manifest itself in the youth of well-conducted families on Sunday evenings, — a kind of friskiness of spirits which appears to be a reactionary state from the spiritual tension of the day, inclining him to skirmish round on all the borders and outskirts of permitted pleasantry, and threatening every minute to burst out into most unbecoming uproariousness. This state among the youngsters of a family on Sunday evening is a familiar trial of all elders who have had the task of keeping them steady during the sacred hours.

My Uncle Bill, in his week-day frame, was the wit and buffoon of the family, — an adept in every art that could shake the sides, and bring a laugh out on the gravest face. His features were flexible, his powers of grimace and story-telling at times irresistible. On the present occasion it was only my poor mother's pale, sorrowful face that kept him in any decent bounds. He did not wish to hurt his sister's feelings, but he was boiling over with wild and elfish impulses, which he vented now by a sly tweak at the cat's tail, then by a surreptitious dig at black Cæsar's sides, which made the poor black a helpless, quivering mass of giggle, and then he would slyly make eyes and mouths at Bill and me behind Aunt Lois's chair, which almost slew us with laughter, though all the while he appeared with painful effort to keep on a face of portentous gravity.

On the part of Aunt Lois, however, there began to be manifested unequivocal symptoms that it was her will and pleasure to have us all leave our warm fireside and establish ourselves in the best room, — for we had a best room, else wherefore were we on tea-drinking terms with the high aristocracy of Oldtown? We had our best room, and kept it as cold, as uninviting and stately, as devoid of human light or warmth, as the most fashionable shut-up parlor of modern days. It had the tallest and brightest pair of brass and-irons conceivable, and a shovel and tongs to match, that were so heavy that the mere lifting them was work enough, without doing anything with them. It had also a bright-varnished mahogany tea-table, over which was a looking-glass in a gilt frame, with a row of little architectural balls on it; which looking-glass was always kept shrouded in white muslin at all seasons of the year, on account of a tradition that flies might be expected to attack it for one or two weeks in summer. But truth compels me to state, that I never saw or heard of a fly whose heart could endure Aunt Lois's parlor. It was so dark, so cold, so still, that all that frisky, buzzing race, who delight in air and sunshine, universally deserted and seceded from it; yet the looking-glass, and occasionally the fire-irons, were rigorously shrouded, as if desperate attacks might any moment be expected.

Now the kitchen was my grandmother's own room. In one corner of it stood a round table with her favorite books, her great work-basket, and by it a rickety rocking-chair, the bottom of which was of ingenious domestic manufacture, being in fact made by interwoven strips of former coats and pantaloons of the home circle;

but a most comfortable and easy seat it made. My grandfather had also a large splint-bottomed arm-chair, with rockers to it, in which he swung luxuriously in the corner of the great fireplace. By the side of its ample blaze we sat down to our family meals, and afterwards, while grandmother and Aunt Lois washed up the tea-things, we all sat and chatted by the firelight. Now it was a fact that nobody liked to sit in the best room. In the kitchen each member of the family had established unto him or her self some little pet private snuggery, some chair or stool, some individual nook, — forbidden to gentility, but dear to the ungenteel natural heart, — that we looked back to regretfully when we were banished to the colder regions of the best room.

There the sitting provisions were exactly one dozen stuffed-seated cherry chairs, with upright backs and griffin feet, each foot terminating in a bony claw, which resolutely grasped a ball. These chairs were high and slippery, and preached decorum in the very attitudes which they necessitated, as no mortal could ever occupy them except in the exercise of a constant and collected habit of mind.

Things being thus, when my Uncle Bill saw Aunt Lois take up some coals on a shovel, and look towards the best-room door, he came and laid his hand on hers directly, with, "Now, Lois, what are you going to do?"

"Going to make up a fire in the best room."

"Now, Lois, I protest. You're not going to do any such thing. Hang grandeur and all that.

> "'Mid pleasures and palaces though we may roam,
>   Be it ever so humble, there's no place like home,'

you know; and home means right here by mother's kitchen-fire, where she and father sit, and want to sit. You know nobody ever wants to go into that terrible best room of yours."

"Now, Bill, how you talk!" said Aunt Lois, smiling, and putting down her shovel.

"But then, you see," she said, the anxious cloud again settling down on her brow, — "you see, we're exposed to calls, and who knows who may come in? I shouldn't wonder if Major Broad, or Miss Mehitable, might drop in, as they saw you down from College."

"Let 'em come; never fear. They all know we've got a best room, and that's enough. Or, if you'd rather, I'll pin a card to that effect upon the door; and then we'll take our ease. Or, better than that, I'll take 'em all in and show 'em our best chairs, andirons, and mahogany table, and then we can come out and be comfortable."

"Bill, you're a saucy boy," said Aunt Lois, looking at him indulgently as she subsided into her chair.

"Yes, that he always was," said my grandfather, with a smile of the kind that fathers give to frisky sophomores in college.

"Well, come sit down, anyway," said my grandmother, "and let's have a little Sunday-night talk."

"Sunday-night talk, with all my heart," said Bill, as he seated himself comfortably right in front of the cheerful blaze. "Well, it must be about 'the meetin',' of course. Our old meeting-house looks as elegant as ever. Of all the buildings I ever saw to worship any kind of a being in, that meeting-house certainly is the most extraordinary. It really grows on me every time I come home!"

"Come, now, Bill," said Aunt Lois.

"Come, now! Ain't I coming? Haven't said anything but what you all know. Said our meeting-house was extraordinary, and you all know it is; and there's extraordinary folks in it. I don't believe so queer a tribe could be mustered in all the land of Israel as we congregate. I hope some of our oddities will be in this evening after cider. I need to study a little, so that I can give representations of nature in our club at Cambridge. Nothing like going back to nature, you know. Old Obscue, seems to me, was got up in fine fancy this morning; and Sam Lawson had an extra touch of the hearse about him. Hepsy must have been disciplining him this morning, before church. I always know when Sam is fresh from a matrimonial visitation: he's peculiarly pathetic about the gills at those times. Why don't Sam come in here?"

"I'm sure I hope he won't," said Aunt Lois. "One reason why I wanted to sit in the best room to-night was that every old tramper and queer object sees the light of our kitchen fire, and comes in for a lounge and a drink; and then, when one has genteel persons calling, it makes it unpleasant."

"O, we all know you're aristocratic, Lois; but, you see, you can't be indulged. You must have your purple and fine linen and your Lazarus at the gate come together some time, just as they do in the meeting-house and the graveyard. Good for you all, if not agreeable."

Just at this moment the conversation was interrupted by a commotion in the back sink-room, which sounded much like a rush of a flight of scared fowl. It ended with a tumble of a row of milk-pans toward chaos, and the door flew open and Uncle Fly appeared.

"What on earth!" said my grandmother, starting up. "That you, 'Liakim? Why on earth *must* you come in the back way and knock down all my milk-pans?"

"Why, I came 'cross lots from Aunt Bathsheba Sawin's," said Uncle Fly, dancing in, "and I got caught in those pesky blackberry-bushes in the graveyard, and I do believe I've torn my breeches all to pieces," he added, pirouetting and frisking with very airy gyrations, and trying vainly to get a view of himself behind, in which operation he went round and round as a cat does after her tail.

"Laws a-massy, 'Liakim!" said my grandmother, whose ears were startled by a peculiar hissing sound in the sink-room, which caused her to spring actively in that direction. "Well, now, you have been and done it! You've gone and fidgeted the tap out of my beer-barrel, and here's the beer all over the floor. I hope you're satisfied now."

"Sorry for it. Didn't mean to. I'll wipe it right up. Where's a towel, or floor-cloth, or something?" cried Uncle Fly, whirling in more active circles round and round, till he seemed to me to have a dozen pairs of legs.

"Do sit down, 'Liakim," said my grandmother. "Of course you didn't mean to; but next time don't come bustling and whirligigging through my back sink-room after dark. I do believe you never will be quiet till you're in your grave."

"Sit down, uncle," said Bill. "Never mind mother, — she'll come all right by and by. And never mind your breeches, — all things earthly are transitory, as Parson Lothrop told us to-day. Now let's come back to our Sunday talk. Did ever anybody see such an astonishing providence as Miss Mehitable Rossiter's bonnet to-day? Does it belong to the old or the new dispensation, do you think?"

"Bill, I'm astonished at you!" said Aunt Lois.

"Miss Mehitable is of a most respectable family," said Aunt

Keziah, reprovingly. "Her father and grandfather and great-grand-father were all ministers; and two of her mother's brothers, Jeduthun and Amariah."

"Now, take care, youngster," said Uncle Fly. "You see you young colts mustn't be too airy. When a fellow begins to speak evil of bonnets, nobody knows where he may end."

"Bless me, one and all of you," said Bill, "I have the greatest respect for Miss Mehitable. Furthermore, I like her. She's a real spicy old concern. I'd rather talk with her than any dozen of modern girls. But I do wish she'd give me that bonnet to put in our Cambridge cabinet. I'd tell 'em it was the wing of a Madagascar bat. Blessed old soul, how innocent she sat under it! — never knowing to what wandering thoughts it was giving rise. Such bonnets interfere with my spiritual progress."

At this moment, by the luck that always brings in the person people are talking of, Miss Mehitable came in, with the identical old wonder on her head. Now, outside of our own blood-relations, no one that came within our doors ever received a warmer welcome than Miss Mehitable. Even the children loved her, with that instinctive sense by which children and dogs learn the discerning of spirits. To be sure she was as gaunt and brown as the Ancient Mariner, but hers was a style of ugliness that was neither repulsive nor vulgar. Personal uncomeliness has its differing characters, and there are some very homely women who have a style that amounts to something like beauty. I know that this is not the common view of the matter; but I am firm in the faith that some very homely women have a certain attraction about them which is increased by their homeliness. It is like the quaintness of Japanese china, — not beautiful, but having a strong, pronounced character, as far remote as possible from the ordinary and vulgar, and which, in union with vigorous and agreeable traits of mind, is more stimulating than any mere insipid beauty.

In short, Miss Mehitable was a specimen of what I should call the good-goblin style of beauty. And people liked her so much that they came to like the singularities which individualized her from all other people. Her features were prominent and harsh; her eyebrows were shaggy, and finished abruptly half across her brow, leaving but half an eyebrow on each side. She had, however, clear, trustworthy, steady eyes, of a greenish gray, which impressed one with much of that idea of steadfast faithfulness that one sees in the eyes of some good, homely dogs. "Faithful and true," was written in her face as legibly as eyes could write it.

For the rest, Miss Mehitable had a strong mind, was an omnivorous reader, apt, ready in conversation, and with a droll, original way of viewing things, which made her society ever stimulating. To me her house was always full of delightful images, — a great, calm, cool, shady, old-fashioned house, full of books and of quaint old furniture, with a garden on one side where were no end of lilies, hollyhocks, pinks, and peonies, to say nothing of currants, raspberries, apples, and pears, and other carnal delights, all of which good Miss Mehitable was free to dispense to her child-visitors. It was my image of heaven to be allowed to go to spend an afternoon with Miss Mehitable, and establish myself, in a shady corner of the old study which contained her father's library, over an edition of Æsop's Fables illustrated with plates, which, opened, was an endless field of enchantment to me.

Miss Mehitable lived under the watch and charge of an ancient female domestic named Polly Shubel. Polly was a representative specimen of the now extinct species of Yankee serving-maids. She had been bred up from a child in the Rossiter family of some generations back. She was of that peculiar kind of constitution, known in New England, which merely becomes drier and tougher with the advance of time, without giving any other indications of old age. The exact number of her years was a point unsettled even among the most skilful genealogists of Oldtown. Polly was a driving, thrifty, doctrinal and practical female, with strong bones and muscles, and strong opinions, believing most potently in early rising, soap and sand, and the Assembly's Catechism, and knowing *certainly* all that she did know. Polly considered Miss Mehitable as a sort of child under her wardship, and conducted the whole business of life for her with a sovereign and unanswerable authority. As Miss Mehitable's tastes were in the world of books and ideas, rather than of physical matters, she resigned herself to Polly's sway with as good a grace as possible, though sometimes she felt that it rather abridged her freedom of action.

Luckily for my own individual self, Polly patronized me, and gave me many a piece of good advice, sweetened with gingerbread, when I went to visit Miss Rossiter. I counted Miss Mehitable among my personal friends; so to-night, when she came in, I came quickly and laid hold of the skirt of her gown, and looked admiringly upon her dusky face, under the portentous shadow of a great bonnet shaded by nodding bows of that preternatural color which people used to call olive-green. She had a word for us all, a cordial grasp of the hand for my mother, who sat silent and thoughtful in her corner, and a warm hand-shake all round.

"You see," she said, drawing out an old-fashioned snuff-box, and tapping upon it, "my house grew so stupid that I must come and share my pinch of snuff with you. It's windy out to-night, and I should think a storm was brewing; and the rattling of one's own window-blinds, as one sits alone, isn't half so amusing as some other things."

"You know, Miss Rossiter, we're always delighted to have you come in," said my grandmother, and my Aunt Lois, and my Aunt Keziah, all at once. This, by the way, was a little domestic trick that the females of our family had; and, as their voices were upon very different keys, the effect was somewhat peculiar. My Aunt Lois's voice was high and sharp, my grandmother's a hearty chest-tone, while Aunt Keziah's had an uncertain buzz between the two, like the vibrations of a loose string; but as they all had corresponding looks and smiles of welcome, Miss Mehitable was pleased.

"I always indulge myself in thinking I am welcome," she said. "And now pray how is our young scholar, Master William Badger? What news do you bring us from old Harvard?"

"Almost anything you want to hear, Miss Mehitable. You know that I am your most devoted slave."

"Not so sure of that, sir," she said, with a whimsical twinkle of her eye. "Don't you know that your sex are always treacherous? How do I know that you don't serve up old Miss Rossiter when you give representations of the Oldtown curiosities there at Cambridge? We are a set here that might make a boy's fortune in that line, — now aren't we?"

"How do you know that I do serve up Oldtown curiosities?" said Bill, somewhat confused, and blushing to the roots of his hair.

"How do I know? Can the Ethiopian change his skin, or the leopard his spots? and can you help being a mimic, as you were born, always were and always will be?"

"O, but I'm sure, Miss Mehitable, Bill never would, — he has too much respect," said Aunt Keziah and Aunt Lois, simultaneously again.

"Perhaps not; but if he wants to, he's welcome. What are queer old women for, if young folks may not have a good laugh out of them now and then? If it's only a friendly laugh, it's just as good as crying, and better too. I'd like to be made to laugh at myself. I think generally we take ourselves altogether too seriously. What now, bright eyes?" she added, as I nestled nearer to her. "Do you want to come up into an old woman's lap? Well, here you come. Bless me, what a tangle of curls we have here! Don't your thoughts get caught in these curls sometimes?"

I looked bashful and wistful at this address, and Miss Mehitable went on twining my curls around her fingers, and trotting me on her knee, lulling me into a delicious dreaminess, in which she seemed to me to be one of those nice, odd-looking old fairy women that figure to such effect in stories.

The circle all rose again as Major Broad came in. Aunt Lois thought, with evident anguish, of the best room. Here was the Major, sure enough, and we all sitting round the kitchen fire! But my grandfather and grandmother welcomed him cheerfully to their corner, and enthroned him in my grandfather's splint-bottomed rocking-chair, where he sat far more comfortably than if he had been perched on a genteel, slippery-bottomed stuffed chair with claw feet.

The Major performed the neighborly kindnesses of the occasion in an easy way. He spoke a few words to my mother of the esteem and kindness he had felt for my father, in a manner that called up the blood into her thin cheeks, and made her eyes dewy with tears. Then he turned to the young collegian, recognizing him as one of the rising lights of Oldtown.

"Our only nobility now," he said to my grandfather. "We've cut off everything else: no distinction now, sir, but educated and un-educated."

"It is a hard struggle for our human nature to give up titles and ranks, though," said Miss Mehitable. "For my part, I have a ridiculous kindness for them yet. I know it's all nonsense; but I can't help looking back to the court we used to have at the Government

House in Boston. You know it was something to hear of the goings
and doings of my Lord this and my Lady that, and of Sir Thomas
and Sir Peter and Sir Charles, and all the rest of 'em."

"Yes," said Bill; "the Oldtown folks call their minister's wife
Lady yet."

"Well, that's a little comfort," said Miss Mehitable; "one don't
want life an entire dead level. Do let us have one titled lady
among us."

"And a fine lady she is," said the Major. "Our parson did a good
thing in that alliance."

While the conversation was thus taking a turn of the most approved genteel style, Aunt Keziah's ears heard alarming premon-
itory sounds outside the door. "Who's that at the scraper?" said
she.

"O, it's Sam Lawson," said Aunt Lois, with a sort of groan.
"You may be sure of that."

"Come in, Sam, my boy," said Uncle Bill, opening the door.
"Glad to see you."

"Wal now, Mr. Badger," said Sam, with white eyes of veneration, "I'm real glad to see ye. I told Hepsy you'd want to see me.
You're the fust one of my Saturday afternoon fishin' boys that's
got into college, and I'm 'mazing proud on 't. I tell you I walk tall,
— ask 'em if I don't, round to the store."

"You always were gifted in that line," said Bill. "But come, sit
down in the corner and tell us what you've been about."

"Wal, you see, I thought I'd jest go over to North Parish this
arternoon, jest for a change, like, and I wanted to hear one of
them *Hopkintinsians* they tell so much about; and Parson Simpson,
he's one on 'em."

"You ought not to be roving off on Sunday, leaving your own
meeting," said my grandfather.

"Wal, you see, Deacon Badger, I'm interested in these 'ere new
doctrines. I met your Polly a goin' over, too," he said to Miss
Mehitable.

"O yes," said Miss Mehitable, "Polly is a great Hopkinsian. She
can hardly have patience to sit under our Parson Lothrop's preaching. It's rather hard on me, because Polly makes it a point of
conscience to fight every one of his discourses over to me in my
parlor. Somebody gave Polly an Arminian tract last Sunday, en-

titled, 'The Apostle Paul an Arminian.' It would have done you good to hear Polly's comments. ' 'Postle Paul an Arminian! He's the biggest 'lectioner of 'em all.' "

"That he is," said my grandmother, warmly. "Polly's read her Bible to some purpose."

"Well, Sam, what did you think of the sermon?" said Uncle Bill.

"Wal," said Sam, leaning over the fire, with his long, bony hands alternately raised to catch the warmth, and then dropped with an utter laxness, when the warmth became too pronounced, "Parson Simpson's a smart man; but, I tell ye, it's kind o' discouragin'. Why, he said our state and condition by natur was just like this. We was clear down in a well fifty feet deep, and the sides all round nothin' but glare ice; but we was under immediate obligations to get out, 'cause we was free, voluntary agents. But nobody ever had got out, and nobody would, unless the Lord reached down and took 'em. And whether he would or not nobody could tell; it was all sovereignty. He said there wa'n't one in a hundred, — not one in a thousand, — not one in ten thousand, — that would be saved. Lordy massy, says I to myself, ef that's so they're any of 'em welcome to my chance. And so I kind o' ris up and come out, 'cause I'd got a pretty long walk home, and I wanted to go round by South Pond, and inquire about Aunt Sally Morse's toothache."

"I heard the whole sermon over from Polly," said Miss Mehitable, "and as it was not a particularly cheerful subject to think of, I came over here." These words were said with a sort of chilly, dreary sigh, that made me turn and look up in Miss Mehitable's face. It looked haggard and weary, as of one tired of struggling with painful thoughts.

"Wal," said Sam Lawson, "I stopped a minute round to your back door, Miss Rossiter, to talk with Polly about the sermon. I was a tellin' Polly that that 'ere was puttin' inability a leetle too strong."

"Not a bit, not a bit," said Uncle Fly, "so long as it's moral inability. There's the point, ye see, — moral, — that's the word. That makes it all right."

"Wal," said Sam, "I was a puttin' it to Polly this way. Ef a man's cut off his hands, it ain't right to require him to chop wood. Wal, Polly, she says he'd no business to cut his hands off; and so he ought to be required to chop the wood all the same. Wal, I telled her it was Adam chopped our hands off. But she said, no; it was we did it *in* Adam, and she brought up the catechise plain enough, — '*We sinned in him,* and fell with him.' "

"She had you there, Sam," said Uncle Fly, with great content. "You won't catch Polly tripping on the catechism."

"Well, for my part," said Major Broad, "I don't like these doctrinal subtilties, Deacon Badger. Now I've got a volume of Mr. Addison's religious writings that seem to me about the right thing. They're very pleasing reading. Mr. Addison is my favorite author of a Sunday."

"I'm afraid Mr. Addison had nothing but just mere morality and natural religion," said my grandmother, who could not be withheld from bearing her testimony. "You don't find any of the discriminating doctrines in Mr. Addison. Major Broad, did you ever read Mr. Bellamy's 'True Religion Delineated and Distinguished from all Counterfeits'?"

"No, madam, I never did," said Major Broad.

"Well, I earnestly hope you will read *that* book," said my grandmother.

"My wife is always at me about one good book or another," said my grandfather; "but I manage to do with my old Bible. I haven't used that up yet."

"I should know about Dr. Bellamy's book by this time," said Miss Mehitable, "for Polly intrenches herself in that, and preaches out of it daily. Polly certainly missed her vocation when she was trained for a servant. She is a born professor of theology. She is so circumstantial about all that took place at the time the angels fell, and when the covenant was made with Adam in the Garden of Eden, that I sometimes question whether she really might not have been there personally. Polly is particularly strong on Divine sovereignty. She thinks it applies to everything under the sun except my affairs. Those she chooses to look after herself."

"Well," said Major Broad, "I am not much of a theologian. I want to be taught my duty. Parson Lothrop's discourses are generally very clear and practical, and they suit me."

"They are good as far as they go," said my grandmother; "but I like good, strong, old-fashioned doctrine. I like such writers as Mr. Edwards and Dr. Bellamy and Dr. Hopkins. It's all very well, your essays on cheerfulness and resignation, and all that; but I want something that takes strong hold of you, so that you feel something has got you that *can* hold."

"The Cambridge Platform, for instance," said Uncle Bill.

"Yes, my son, the Cambridge Platform. I ain't ashamed of it. It was made by men whose shoe-latchet we aren't worthy to unloose. I believe it, — every word on 't. I believe it, and I'm going to believe it."

"And would if there was twice as much of it," said Uncle Bill. "That's right, mother, stand up for your colors. I admire your spirit. But, Sam, what does Hepsy think of all this? I suppose you enlighten her when you return from your investigations."

"Wal, I try to. But lordy massy, Mr. Badger, Hepsy don't take no kind o' interest in the doctrines, no more'n nothin' at all. She's so kind o' worldly, Hepsy is. It's allers meat and drink, meat and drink, with her. That's all she's thinkin' of."

"And if *you* would think more of such things, she wouldn't have to think so much," said Aunt Lois, sharply. "Don't you know the Bible says, that the man that provideth not for his own household hath denied the faith, and is worse than an infidel?"

"I don't see," said Sam, slowly flopping his great hands up and down over the blaze, — "I railly don't see why folks are allers a throwin' up that 'ere text at me. I'm sure I work as hard as a man ken. Why, I was a workin' last night till nigh twelve o'clock, doin' up odd jobs o' blacksmithin'. They kind o' 'cumulate, ye know."

"Mr. Lawson," said my grandmother, with a look of long-suffering patience, "how often and often must I tell you, that if you'd be steadier round your home, and work in regular hours, Hepsy would be more comfortable, and things would go on better?"

"Lordy massy, Mis' Badger, bless your soul and body, ye don't know nothin' about it; — ye don't know nothin' what I undergo. Hepsy, she's at me from morning till night. First it's one thing, and then another. One day it rains, and her clothes-line breaks. She's at me 'bout that. Now I tell her, 'Hepsy, I ain't to blame, — I don't make the rain.' And then another day she's at me agin 'cause the wind's east, and fetches the smoke down chimbley. I tell her, 'Hepsy, now look here, — *do* I make the wind blow?' But it's no use talkin' to Hepsy."

"Well, Sam, I take your part," said Bill. "I always knew you was a regular martyr. Come, boys, go down cellar and draw a pitcher of cider. We'll stay him with flagons, and comfort him with apples. Won't we, Sam?"

As Sam was prime favorite with all boys, my brother Bill and I started willingly enough on this errand, one carrying the candle and the other a great stone pitcher of bountiful proportions, which always did hospitable duty on similar occasions.

Just as we returned, bearing our pitcher, there came another rap at the outside door of the kitchen, and Old Betty Poganut and Sally Wonsamug stood at the door.

"Well, now, Mis' Badger," said Betty, "Sally and me, we thought we must jest run in, we got so scar't. We was coming through that Bill Morse's woods, and there come such a flash o' lightnin' it most blinded us, and the wind blew enough to blow a body over; and we thought there was a storm right down on us, and we run jest as fast as we could. We didn't know what to do, we was so scar't. I'm mortal 'fraid of lightning."

"Why, Betty, you forgot the sermon to-day. You should have said your prayers, as Parson Lothrop tells you," said my grandfather.

"Well, I did kind o' put up a sort o' silent 'jaculation, as a body may say. That is, I jest said, 'O Lord,' and kind o' gin him a wink, you know."

"O, you did?" said my grandfather.

"Yes, I kind o' thought He'd know what I meant."

My grandfather turned with a smile to Miss Mehitable. "These Indians have their own wild ways of looking at things, after all."

"Well, now, I s'pose you haven't had a bit of supper, either of you," said my grandmother, getting up. "It's commonly the way of it."

"Well, to tell the truth, I was sayin' to Sarah that if we come down to Mis' Deacon Badger's I shouldn't wonder if we got something good," said Betty, her broad, coarse face and baggy checks beginning to be illuminated with a smile.

"Here, Horace, you come and hold the candle while I go into the buttery and get 'em some cold pork and beans," said my grandmother, cheerily. "The poor creturs don't get a good meal of victuals very often; and I baked a good lot on purpose."

If John Bunyan had known my grandmother, he certainly would have introduced her in some of his histories as "the housekeeper whose name was Bountiful"; and under her care an ample meal of brown bread and pork and beans was soon set forth on the table in the corner of the kitchen, to which the two hungry Indian women sat down with the appetite of wolves. A large mug was placed between them, which Uncle Bill filled to the brim with cider.

"I s'pose you'd like twice a mug better than once a mug, Sally," he said, punning on her name.

"O, if the mug's only big enough," said Sally, her snaky eyes gleaming with appetite; "and it's always a good big mug one gets here."

Sam Lawson's great white eyes began irresistibly to wander in the direction of the plentiful cheer which was being so liberally dispensed at the other side of the room.

"Want some, Sam, my boy?" said Uncle Bill, with a patronizing freedom.

"Why, bless your soul, Master Bill, I wouldn't care a bit if I took a plate o' them beans and some o' that 'ere pork. Hepsy didn't save no beans for me; and, walkin' all the way from North Parish, I felt kind o' empty and windy, as a body may say. You know Scriptur' tells about bein' filled with the east wind; but I never found it noways satisfyin', — it sets sort o' cold on the stomach."

"Draw up, Sam, and help yourself," said Uncle Bill, putting plate and knife and fork before him; and Sam soon showed that he had a vast internal capacity for the stowing away of beans and brown bread.

Meanwhile Major Broad and my grandfather drew their chairs together, and began a warm discussion of the Constitution of the United States, which had been recently presented for acceptance in a Convention of the State of Massachusetts.

"I haven't seen you, Major Broad," said my grandfather, "since you came back from the Convention. I'm very anxious to have our State of Massachusetts accept that Constitution. We're in an unsettled condition now; we don't know fairly where we are. If we accept this Constitution, we shall be a nation, — we shall have something to go to work on."

"Well, Deacon Badger, to say the truth, I could not vote for this Constitution in Convention. They have adopted it by a small majority; but I shall be bound to record my dissent from it."

"Pray, Major, what are your objections?" said Miss Mehitable.

"I have two. One is, it gives too much power to the President. There's an appointing power and a power of patronage that will play the mischief some day in the hands of an ambitious man. That's one objection. The other is the recognizing and encouraging of slavery in the Constitution. That is such a dreadful wrong, — such a shameful inconsistency, — when we have just come through a battle for the doctrine that all men are free and equal, to turn round and found our national government on a recognition of African slavery. It cannot and will not come to good."

"O, well," said my grandfather, "slavery will gradually die out. You see how it is going in the New England States."

"I cannot think so," said the Major. "I have a sort of feeling about this that I cannot resist. If we join those States that still mean to import and use slaves, our nation will meet some dreadful punishment. I am certain of it." *

"Well, really," said my grandfather, "I'm concerned to hear you speak so. I have felt such anxiety to have something settled. You see, without a union we are all afloat, — we are separate logs, but no raft."

"Yes," said Miss Mehitable, "but nothing can be settled that isn't founded on right. We ought to dig deep, and lay our foundations on a rock, when we build for posterity."

"Were there many of your way of thinking in the Convention, Major?" said my grandfather.

"Well, we had a pretty warm discussion, and we came very near to carrying it. Now, in Middlesex County, for instance, where we are, there were only seventeen in favor of the Constitution, and twenty-five against; and in Worcester County there were only seven in favor and forty-three against. Well, they carried it at last by a majority of nineteen; but the minority recorded their protest. Judge Widgery of Portland, General Thompson of Topsham, and Dr. Taylor of Worcester, rather headed the opposition. Then the town of Andover instructed its representative, Mr. Symmes, to vote against it, but he didn't, he voted on the other side, and I under-

---

* The dissent of Major Broad of Natick, and several others, on the grounds above stated, may still be read in the report of the proceedings of the Convention that ratified the Constitution.

stand they are dreadfully indignant about it. I saw a man from Andover last week who said that he actually thought Symmes would be obliged to leave the town, he was so dreadfully unpopular."

"Well, Major Broad, I agree with you," said my grandmother, heartily, "and I honor you for the stand you took. Slavery is a sin and a shame; and I say, with Jacob, 'O my soul, come not thou into their secret, — unto their assembly, mine honor, be not thou united.' I wish we may keep clear on 't. I don't want anything that we can't ask God's blessing on heartily, and we certainly can't on this. Why, anybody that sees that great scar on Cæsar's forehead sees what slavery comes to."

My grandmother always pointed her anti-slavery arguments with an appeal to this mark of ill-usage which old Cæsar had received at the hands of a brutal master years before, and the appeal never failed to convince the domestic circle.

"Well," said my grandfather, after some moments of silence, in which he sat gazing fixedly at the great red coals of a hickory log, "you see, Major, it's done, and can't be helped."

"It's done," said the Major, "but in my opinion mischief will come of it as sure as there is a God in heaven."

"Let's hope not," said my grandfather, placidly.

Outside the weather was windy and foul, the wind rattling doors, shaking and rumbling down the chimney, and causing the great glowing circle lighted by the fire to seem warmer and brighter. The Indian women and Sam Lawson, having finished their meal and thoroughly cleaned out the dishes, grouped themselves about the end of the ingle already occupied by black Cæsar, and began a little private gossip among themselves.

"I say," says Sam, raising his voice to call my grandfather's attention, "do you know, Deacon Badger, whether anybody is living in the Dench house now?"

"There wasn't, the last I knew about it," said my grandfather.

"Wal, you won't make some folks believe but what that 'ere house is haunted."

"Haunted!" said Miss Mehitable; "nothing more likely. What old house isn't? — if one only knew it; and that certainly ought to be if ever a house was."

"But this 'ere's a regular *haunt*," said Sam. "I was a talkin' the other night with Bill Payne and Jake Marshall, and they both on 'em said that they'd seen strange things in them grounds, — they'd seen a figger of a man — "

"With his head under his arm," suggested Uncle Bill.

"No, a man in a long red cloak," said Sam Lawson, "such as Sir Harry Frankland used to wear."

"Poor Sir Harry!" said Miss Mehitable, "has he come to that?"

"Did you know Sir Harry?" said Aunt Lois.

"I have met him once or twice at the Governor's house," said Miss Mehitable. "Lady Lothrop knew Lady Frankland very well."

"Well, Sam," said Uncle Bill, "do let's hear the end of this haunting."

"Nothin', only the other night I was a goin' over to watch with Lem Moss, and I passed pretty nigh the Dench place, and I thought I'd jest look round it a spell. And as sure as you're alive I see smoke a comin' out of the chimbley."

"I didn't know as ghosts ever used the fireplaces," said Uncle Bill. "Well, Sam, did you go in?"

"No, I was pretty much in a hurry; but I telled Jake and Bill, and then they each on 'em had something to match that they'd seen. As nigh as I can make it out, there's that 'ere boy that they say was murdered and thrown down that 'ere old well walks sometimes. And then there's a woman appears to some, and this 'ere man in a red cloak; and they think it's Sir Harry in his red cloak."

"For my part," said Aunt Lois, "I never had much opinion of Sir Harry Frankland, or Lady Frankland either. I don't think such goings on ever ought to be countenanced in society."

"They both repented bitterly, — repented in sackcloth and ashes," said Miss Mehitable. "And if God forgives such sins, why shouldn't we?"

"What was the story?" said Major Broad.

"Why," said Aunt Lois, "haven't you heard of Agnes Surridge, of Marblehead? She was housemaid in a tavern there, and Sir Harry fell in love with her, and took her and educated her. That was well enough; but when she'd done going to school he took her home to his house in Boston, and called her his daughter; although people became pretty sure that the connection was not what it should be, and they refused to have anything to do with her. So he bought this splendid place out in the woods, and built a great palace of a house, and took Miss Agnes out there. People that wanted to be splendidly entertained, and that were not particular as to morals, used to go out to visit them."

"I used to hear great stories of their wealth and pomp and luxury," said my grandmother, "but I mourned over it, that it should come to this in New England, that people could openly set such an example and be tolerated. It wouldn't have been borne a generation before, I can tell you. No, indeed, — the magistrates would have put a stop to it. But these noblemen, when they came over to America, seemed to think themselves lords of God's heritage, and free to do just as they pleased."

"But," said Miss Mehitable, "they repented, as I said. He took her to England, and there his friends refused to receive her; and then he was appointed Ambassador to Lisbon, and he took her there. On the day of the great earthquake Sir Harry was riding with a lady of the court when the shock came, and in a moment, without warning, they found themselves buried under the ruins of a building they were passing. He wore a scarlet cloak, as was the fashion; and they say that in her dying agonies the poor creature bit through this cloak and sleeve into the flesh of his arm, and made a mark that he carried to his dying day. Sir Harry was saved by Agnes Surridge. She came over the ruins, calling and looking for him, and he heard her voice and answered, and she got men to come and dig him out. When he was in that dreadful situation, he made a vow to God, if he would save his life, that he would be a different man. And he was a changed man from that day. He was married to Agnes Surridge as soon as they could get a priest to perform the ceremony; and when he took her back to England all his relations received her, and she was presented in court and moved in society with perfect acceptance."

"I don't think it ever ought to have been," said Aunt Lois. "Such women never ought to be received."

"What! is there no place of repentance for a woman?" said Miss Mehitable. "Christ said, 'Neither do I condemn thee; go and sin no more.'"

I noticed again that sort of shiver of feeling in Miss Mehitable;

and there was a peculiar thrill in her voice, as she said these words, that made me sensible that she was speaking from some inward depth of feeling.

"Don't you be so hard and sharp, Lois," said my grandmother; "sinners must have patience with sinners."

"Especially with sinners of quality, Lois," said Uncle Bill. "By all accounts Sir Harry and Lady Frankland swept all before them when they came back to Boston."

"Of course," said Miss Mehitable; "what was done in court would be done in Boston, and whom Queen Charlotte received would be received in our upper circles. Lady Lothrop never called on her till she was Lady Frankland, but after that I believe she has visited out at their place."

"Wal, I've heerd 'em say," said Sam Lawson, "that it would take a woman two days jest to get through cleaning the silver that there was in that 'ere house, to say nothing about the carpets and the curtains and the tapestry. But then, when the war broke out, Lady Frankland, she took most of it back to England, I guess, and the house has been back and forward to one and another. I never could rightly know jest who did live in it. I heard about some French folks that lived there one time. I thought some day, when I hadn't nothin' else to do, I'd jest walk over to old Granny Walker's, that lives over the other side of Hopkinton. She used to be a housekeeper to Lady Frankland, and I could get particulars out o' her."

"Well," said Miss Mehitable, "I know one woman that must go back to a haunted house, and that is this present one." So saying, she rose and put me off her knee.

"Send this little man over to see me to-morrow," she said to my mother. "Polly has a cake for him, and I shall find something to amuse him."

Major Broad, with old-fashioned gallantry, insisted on waiting on Miss Mehitable home; and Sam Lawson reluctantly tore himself from the warm corner to encounter the asperities of his own fireside.

"Here, Sam," said good-natured Bill, — "here's a great red apple for Hepsy."

"Ef I dares to go nigh enough to give it to her," said Sam, with a grimace. "She's allers a castin' it up at me that I don't want to set with her at home. But lordy massy, she don't consider that a fellow don't want to set and be hectored and lectured when he can do better elsewhere."

"True enough, Sam; but give my regards to her."

As to the two Indian women, they gave it as their intention to pass the night by the kitchen fire; and my grandmother, to whom such proceedings were not at all strange, assented, — producing for each a blanket, which had often seen similar service. My grandfather closed the evening by bringing out his great Bible and reading a chapter. Then we all knelt down in prayer.

So passed an evening in my grandmother's kitchen, — where religion, theology, politics, the gossip of the day, and the legends of the supernatural all conspired to weave a fabric of thought quaint and various. Intense earnestness, a solemn undertone of deep mournful awe, was overlaid with quaint traceries of humor, strange and weird in their effect. I was one of those children who are all ear, — dreamy listeners, who brood over all that they hear, without daring to speak of it; and in this evening's conversation I had heard enough to keep my eyes broad open long after my mother had laid me in bed. The haunted house and its vague wonders filled my mind, and I determined to question Sam Lawson yet more about it.

But now that I have fairly introduced myself, the scene of my story, and many of the actors in it, I must take my reader off for a while, and relate a history that must at last blend with mine in one story.

CHAPTER VII

OLD CRAB SMITH

On the brow of yonder hill you see that old, red farm-house, with its slanting back roof relieved against the golden sky of the autumn afternoon. The house lifts itself up dark and clear under the shadow of two great elm-trees that droop over it, and is the first of a straggling, irregular cluster of farm-houses that form the village of Needmore. A group of travellers, sitting on a bit of rock in the road below the hill on which the farm-house stands, are looking up to it, in earnest conversation.

"Mother, if you can only get up there, we'll ask them to let you go in and rest," said a little boy of nine years to a weary, pale, sick-looking woman who sat as in utter exhaustion and discouragement on the rock. A little girl two years younger than the boy sat picking at the moss at her feet, and earnestly listening to her older brother with the air of one who is attending to the words of a leader.

"I don't feel as if I could get a step farther," said the woman; and the increasing deadly paleness of her face confirmed her words.

"O mother, don't give up," said the boy; "just rest here a little and then lean on me, and we'll get you up the hill; and then I'm sure they'll take you in. Come, now; I'll run and get you some water in our tin cup, and you'll feel better soon." And the boy ran to a neighboring brook and filled a small tin cup, and brought the cool water to his mother.

She drank it, and then, fixing a pair of dark, pathetic eyes on the face of her boy, she said: "My dear child, you have always been such a blessing to me! What should I do without you?"

"Well, mother, now, if you feel able, just rest on my shoulder, and Tina will take the bundle. You take it, Tina, and we'll find a place to rest."

And so, slowly and with difficulty, the three wound their way up to the grassy top of the hill where stood the red house. This

house belonged to a man named Caleb Smith, whose character
had caused the name he bore to degenerate into another which
was held to be descriptive of his nature, namely, "Crab"; and the
boys of the vicinity commonly expressed the popular idea of the
man by calling him "Old Crab Smith." His was one of those sour,
cross, gnarly natures that now and then are to be met with in
New England, which, like knotty cider-apples, present a compound of hardness, sourness, and bitterness. It was affirmed that a
continual free indulgence in very hard cider as a daily beverage
was one great cause of this churlishness of temper; but be that as
it may, there was not a boy in the village that did not know and
take account of it in all his estimates and calculations, as much as
of northeast storms and rainy weather. No child ever willingly
carried a message to him; no neighbor but dreaded to ask a favor
of him; nobody hoped to borrow or beg of him; nobody willingly
hired themselves out to him, or did him cheerful service. In short,
he was a petrified man, walled out from all neighborhood sympathies, and standing alone in his crabbedness. And it was to this
man's house that the wandering orphan boy was leading his poor
sick mother.

The three travellers approached a neat back porch on the shady
side of the house, where an old woman sat knitting. This was Old
Crab Smith's wife, or, more properly speaking, his life-long bond-
slave, — the only human being whom he could so secure to himself that she should be always at hand for him to vent that residue
of ill-humor upon which the rest of the world declined to receive.
Why half the women in the world marry the men they do, is a
problem that might puzzle any philosopher; how any woman
could marry Crab Smith, was the standing wonder of all the neighborhood. And yet Crab's wife was a modest, industrious, kindly
creature, who uncomplainingly toiled from morning till night to
serve and please him, and received her daily allowance of grum-
bling and fault-finding with quiet submission. She tried all she
could to mediate between him and the many whom his ill-temper
was constantly provoking. She did surreptitious acts of kindness
here and there, to do away the effects of his hardness, and shrunk
and quivered for fear of being detected in goodness, as much as
many another might for fear of being discovered in sin. She had
been many times a mother, — had passed through all the trials

and weaknesses of maternity without one tender act of consideration, one encouraging word. Her children had grown up and gone from her, always eager to leave the bleak, ungenial home, and go out to shift for themselves in the world, and now, in old age, she was still working. Worn to a shadow, — little, old, wrinkled, bowed, — she was still about the daily round of toil, and still the patient recipient of the murmurs and chidings of her tyrant.

"My mother is so sick she can't get any farther," said a little voice from under the veranda; "won't you let her come in and lie down awhile?"

"Massy, child," said the little old woman, coming forward with a trembling, uncertain step. "Well, she does look beat out, to be sure. Come up and rest ye a bit."

"If you'll only let me lie down awhile and rest me," said a faint, sweet voice.

"Come up here," said the old woman, standing quivering like a gray shadow on the top doorstep; and, shading her wrinkled forehead with her hand, she looked with a glance of habitual apprehension along the road where the familiar cart and oxen of her tyrant might be expected soon to appear on their homeward way, and rejoiced in her little old heart that he was safe out of sight. "Yes, come in," she said, opening the door of a small ground-floor bedroom that adjoined the apartment known in New England houses as the sink-room, and showing them a plain bed.

The worn and wasted stranger sunk down on it, and, as she sunk, her whole remaining strength seemed to collapse, and something white and deathly fell, as if it had been a shadow, over her face.

"Massy to us! she's fainted clean away," said the poor old woman, quiveringly. "I must jest run for the camphire."

The little boy seemed to have that unchildlike judgment and presence of mind that are the precocious development of want and sorrow. He ran to a water-pail, and, dipping his small tin cup, he dashed the water in his mother's face, and fanned her with his little torn straw hat. When the old woman returned, the invalid was breathing again, and able to take a few swallows of camphor and water which had been mixed for her.

"Sonny," said the old woman, "you are a nice little nurse, — a good boy. You jest take care now; and here's a turkey-feather fan to fan her with; and I'll get on the kettle to make her a cup

of tea. We'll bring her round with a little nursing. Been walking
a long way, I calculate?"

"Yes," said the boy, "she was trying to get to Boston."

"What, going afoot?"

"We didn't mind walking, the weather is so pleasant," said the
boy; "and Tina and I like walking; but mother got sick a day or
two ago, and ever since she has been so tired!"

"Jes' so," said the old woman, looking compassionately on the
bed. "Well, I'll make up the fire and get her some tea."

The fire was soon smoking in the great, old-fashioned kitchen
chimney, for the neat, labor-saving cook-stove had as yet no being;
and the thin, blue smoke, curling up in the rosy sunset air, received prismatic coloring which a painter would have seized with
enthusiasm.

Far otherwise, however, was its effect on the eye of Old Crab
Smith, as, coming up the hill, his eye detected the luminous vapor
going up from his own particular chimney.

"So, burning out wood, — always burning out wood. I told her
that I wouldn't have tea got at night. These old women are crazy
and bewitched after tea, and they don't care if they burn up your
tables and chairs to help their messes. Why a plague can't she
eat cold pork and potatoes as well as I, and drink her mug of cider?
but must go to getting up her fire and biling her kettle. I'll see to
that. Halloa there," he said, as he stamped up on to the porch,
"what the devil you up to now? I s'pose you think I hain't got
nothing else to do but split up wood for you to burn out."

"Father, it's nothing but a little brush and a few chips, jest to
bile the kettle."

"Bile the kettle, bile the kettle! Jest like yer lazy, shif'less ways.
What must you be a bilin' the kettle for?"

"Father, I jest want to make a little tea for a sick woman."

"A sick woman! What sick woman?"

"There was a poor sick woman came along this afternoon with
two little children."

"Wal, I s'pose you took 'em in. I s'pose you think we keep the
poor-house, and that all the trampers belong to us. We shall have
to go to the poor-house ourselves before long, I tell ye. But you
never believe anything I say. Why couldn't you 'a' sent her to the
selectmen? I don't know why I must keep beggars' tavern."

"Father, father, don't speak so loud. The poor critter wa'n't able to stir another step, and fainted dead away, and we had to get her on to a bed."

"And we shall have her and her two brats through a fit of sickness. That's just like you. Wal, we shall all go to the poor-house together before long, and then you'll believe what I say, won't ye? But I won't have it so. She may stay to-night, but to-morrow morning I'll cart her over to Joe Scran's, bright and early, brats and all."

There was within hearing of this conversation a listener whose heart was dying within her, — sinking deeper and deeper at every syllable, — a few words will explain why.

A younger son of a family belonging to the English gentry had come over to America as a commissioned officer near the close of the Revolutionary war. He had persuaded to a private marriage the daughter of a poor country curate, a beautiful young girl, whom he induced to elope with him, and share the fortunes of an officer's life in America. Her parents died soon after; her husband proved a worthless, drunken, dissipated fellow; and this poor woman had been through all the nameless humiliations and agonies which beset helpless womanhood in the sole power of such a man. Submissive, gentle, trusting, praying, entreating, hoping against hope, she had borne with him many vicissitudes and reverses, — always believing that at last the love of his children, if not of her, would awaken a better nature within him. But the man steadily went downward instead of upward, and the better part of him by slow degrees died away, till he came to regard his wife and children only as so many clogs on his life, and to meditate night and day on a scheme to abandon them, and return, without their encumbrance, to his own country. It was with a distant outlook to some such result that he had from the first kept their marriage an entire secret from his own friends. When the English army, at the close of the war, re-embarked for England, he carried his cowardly scheme into execution. He had boarded his wife and children for a season in a country farm-house in the vicinity of Boston, with the excuse of cheapness of lodgings. Then one day his wife received a letter enclosing a sum of money, and saying, in such terms as bad men can find to veil devilish deeds, that all was over between them, and that ere she got this he should be on the ocean. The sorest hurt of all was that the letter denied the validity of their marriage; and the poor child found, to her consternation, that the marriage certificate, which she had always kept among her papers, was gone with her husband.

The first result of this letter had been a fit of sickness, wherein her little stock of money had melted almost away, and then she had risen from her bed determined to find her way to Boston, and learn, if possible, from certain persons with whom he had lodged before his departure, his address in England, that she might make one more appeal to him. But before she had walked far the sickness returned upon her, till, dizzy and faint, she had lain down, as we have described, on the bed of charity.

She had thought, ever since she received that letter, that she had reached the bottom of desolation, — that nothing could be added to her misery; but the withering, harsh sounds which reached her ear revealed a lower deep in the lowest depths. Hitherto on her short travels she had met only that kindly country hospitality which New England, from one end to the other, always has shown to the stranger. No one had refused a good meal of brown bread and rich milk to her and her children, and more often the friendly housewife, moved by her delicate appearance, had unlocked the sanctum where was deposited her precious tea-caddy, and brewed an amber cup of tea to sustain the sickly-looking wanderer. She and her children had been carried here and there, as occasion offered, a friendly mile or two, when Noah or Job or Sol "hitched up the critter" to go to mill or country store. The voice of harsh, pitiless rejection smote on her ear for the first time, and it seemed to her the drop too much in her cup. She turned her face to the wall and said, "O my God, I cannot bear this! I cannot, I cannot!" She would have said, "Let me die," but that she was tied to life by the two helpless, innocent ones who shared her misery. The poorest and most desolate mother feels that her little children are poorer and more desolate than she; and, however much her broken spirit may long for the rest of Paradise, she is held back by the thought that to abide in the flesh is needful to them. Even in her uttermost destitution the approaching shadow of the dark valley was a terror to the poor soul, — not for her own sake, but for theirs. The idea of a harsh, unpitiful world arose before her for the first time, and the thought of leaving her little ones in it unprotected was an anguish which rent her heart.

The little girl, over-weary, had eaten her supper and fallen asleep beside her, with the trusting, ignorant rest of early childhood; but her boy sat by her bedside with that look of precocious responsibility, that air of anxious thought, which seems unnatural in early childhood, and contrasted painfully with the slight childish figure, the little hands, and little voice. He was, as we have said, but nine years of age, well grown for his years, but with that style of growth which indicates delicacy of fibre rather than strength of organization. His finely formed head, with its clustering curls of yellow hair, his large, clear blue eyes, his exquisitely delicate skin, and the sensitiveness betrayed by his quivering lips, spoke of a lineage of gentle blood, and an organization fitted rather to æsthetic and intellectual development than to sturdy material toil. The little girl, as she lay sleeping, was a beautiful picture. Her head was a wilderness of curls of a golden auburn, and the defined pencilling of the eyebrows, and the long silken veil of the lashes that fell over the sleeping eyes, the delicate polished skin, and the finely moulded limbs, all indicated that she was one who ought to have been among the jewels, rather than among the potsherds of this mortal life. And these were the children that she was going to leave alone, without a single friend and protector in this world. For there are intuitions that come to the sick and dying which tell them when the end is near; and as this wanderer sunk down upon her bed this night, there had fallen upon her mind a perfect certainty that she should never be carried thence till carried to the grave; and it was this which had given her soul so deadly a wrench, and caused her to cry out in such utter agony.

What happens to desolate souls, who, thus forsaken by all the world, cry out to God, is a mystery, good brother and sister, which you can never fathom until you have been exactly where they are. But certain it is that there is a very near way to God's heart, and so to the great heart of all comfort, that sometimes opens like a shaft of light between heaven and the soul, in hours when everything earthly falls away from us. A quaint old writer has said, "God keeps his choicest cordials for the time of our deepest faintings." And so it came to pass that, as this poor woman closed her eyes and prayed earnestly, there fell a strange clearness into her soul, which calmed every fear, and hushed the voice of every passion, and she lay for a season as if entranced. Words of holy writ, heard years ago in church-readings, in the hours of unconscious girlhood, now seemed to come back, borne in with a living power on her soul. It seemed almost as if a voice within was saying to her: "The Lord hath called thee as a woman forsaken and grieved in spirit, and a wife of youth, when thou wast refused, saith thy God. For a small moment have I forsaken thee, but with great mercies will I gather thee. In a little wrath I hid my face from thee for a moment, but with everlasting kindness will I have mercy on thee, saith the Lord thy Redeemer. O thou afflicted, tossed with tempest, and not comforted, behold, I will lay thy stones with fair colors, and thy foundations with sapphires. And all thy children shall be taught of the Lord, and great shall be the peace of thy children."

It is fashionable now to speak of words like these as fragments of ancient Hebrew literature, interesting and curious indeed, but relating to scenes, events, and states of society long gone by. But it is a most remarkable property of this old Hebrew literature, that it seems to be enchanted with a divine and living power, which strikes the nerve of individual consciousness in every desolate and suffering soul. It may have been Judah or Jerusalem ages ago to whom these words first came, but as they have travelled down for thousands of years, they have seemed to tens of thousands of sinking and desolate souls as the voice of God to them individually. They have raised the burden from thousands of crushed spirits; they have been as the day-spring to thousands of perplexed wanderers. Ah! let us treasure these old words, for as of old Jehovah chose to dwell in a tabernacle in the wilderness, and between the cherubim in the temple, so now he dwells in them; and to the simple soul that seeks for him here he will look forth as of old from the pillar of cloud and of fire.

The poor, ill-used, forsaken, forgotten creature who lay there trembling on the verge of life felt the presence of that mighty and generous, that godlike spirit that inspired these words. And surely if Jehovah ever did speak to man, no words were ever more worthy of Him. She lay as in a blessed trance, as passage after passage from the Scriptures rolled over her mind, like bright waves from the ocean of eternal peace.

"Fear thou not, for I am with thee; be not dismayed, for I am thy God. When thou passest through the waters I will be with thee, and through the rivers, they shall not overflow thee. When thou walkest through the fire, thou shalt not be burned, neither shall the flame kindle upon thee; for I am the Lord thy God, the Holy One of Israel, thy Saviour."

The little boy, who had heard his mother's first distressful cry, sat by her anxiously watching the changes of her face as she lay there. He saw her brow gradually grow clear and calm, and every line of trouble fade from her face, as shadows and clouds roll up from the landscape at day-dawn, till at last there was a rapt, peaceful expression, an evenness of breathing, as if she slept, and were dreaming some heavenly dream. It lasted for more than an hour, and the child sat watching her with the old, grave, tender look which had come to be the fashion of his little face when he looked upon his mother.

This boy had come to this mother as a second harvest of heart, hope, and joy, after the first great love and hope of womanhood had vanished. She felt herself broken-hearted, lonely, and unloved, when her first-born son was put into her arms, and she received him as did the first mother, saying, "I have gotten a man from the Lord." To him her desolate heart had unfolded its burden of confidence from the first dawning hours of intelligence. His tiny faculties had been widened to make room for her sorrows, and his childish strength increased by her leaning. There had been hours when this boy had stood between the maniac rage of a drunken father and the cowering form of his mother, with an unchildlike courage and steadiness that seemed almost like an inspiration. In days of desertion and poverty he had gone out with their slender stock of money and made bargains such as it is pitiful to think that a little child should know how to make; and often, in moments when his mother's heart was overwhelmed, he would come to her side with the little prayers and hymns which she had taught him, and revive her faith and courage when it seemed entirely gone.

Now, as he thought her sleeping, he began with anxious care

to draw the coverlet over her, and to move his little sister back upon the bed. She opened her eyes, — large, clear blue eyes, the very mirror of his own, — and, smiling with a strange sweetness, stretched out her hand and drew him towards her. "Harry, my dear good boy, my dear, dear child, nobody knows what a comfort you have been to me."

Then holding him from her, and looking intently in his eyes, she seemed to hesitate for words to tell him something that lay on her mind. At last she said, "Harry, say your prayers and psalms."

The child knelt by the bed, with his hands clasped in his mother's, and said the Lord's Prayer, and then, standing up, repeated the beautiful psalm beginning, "The Lord is my shepherd." Then followed a hymn, which the Methodists had made familiar in those times: —

> "One there is above all others
>   Well deserves the name of Friend;
> His is love beyond a brother's,
>   Costly, free, and knows no end.
>
> "Which of all our friends, to save us,
>   Could or would have shed his blood?
> But this Saviour died to have us
>   Reconciled in him to God.
>
> "When he lived on earth abased,
>   Friend of Sinners was his name;
> Now, above all glory raised,
>   He rejoiceth in the same.
>
> "O for grace our hearts to soften!
>   Teach us, Lord, at length to love;
> We, alas! forget too often
>   What a friend we have above."

"Harry," said his mother, looking at him with an intense earnestness, "I want to tell you something. God, our Father, has called me to come home to him; and I am going. In a little while — perhaps to-morrow — I shall be gone, and you cannot find me. My soul will go to God, and they will put my body in the ground; and then you will have no friend but Jesus, and no father but the Father in heaven."

The child looked at her with solemn, dilated gaze, not really comprehending the full mystery of that which she was trying to explain; yet the tears starting in his eyes, and the twitching of the muscles of his mouth, showed that he partly understood.

"Mother," he said, "will papa never come back?"

"No, Harry, never. He has left us and gone away. He does not love us, — nobody loves us but our Father in heaven; but He does. You must always believe this. Now, Harry, I am going to leave your little sister to your care. You must always keep with her and take care of her, for she is a very little girl."

"Yes, mother."

"This is a great charge for a little boy like you; but you will live and grow up to be a man, and I want you never, as long as you live, to forget what I say to you now. Promise me, Harry, all your life to say these prayers and hymns that you have just been saying, every morning and every night. They are all I have to leave you; but if you only believe them, you will never be without comfort, no matter what happens to you. Promise me, dear."

"Yes, mother, I will."

"And, Harry, no matter *what* happens, never doubt that God loves you, — never forget that you have a Friend in heaven. Whenever you have a trouble, just pray to Him, and He will help you. Promise this."

"Yes, mother."

"Now lie down by me; I am very, very tired."

The little boy lay down by his mother; she threw her arms around him, and both sunk to sleep.

CHAPTER VIII

———— ◆◎◆ ————

MISS ASPHYXIA

"There won't be no great profit in this 'ere these ten year."

The object denominated "this 'ere" was the golden-haired child whom we have spoken of before, — the little girl whose mother lay dying. That mother is dead now; and the thing to be settled is, What is to be done with the children? The morning after the scene we have described looked in at the window and saw the woman, with a pale, placid face, sleeping as one who has found eternal rest, and the two weeping children striving in vain to make her hear.

Old Crab had been up early in his design of "carting the 'hull lot over to the poor-house," but made a solemn pause when his wife drew him into the little chamber. Death has a strange dignity, and whatsoever child of Adam he lays his hand on is for the time ennobled, — removed from the region of the earthly and commonplace to that of the spiritual and mysterious. And when Crab found, by searching the little bundle of the deceased, that there was actually money enough in it to buy a coffin and pay 'Zekiel Stebbins for digging the grave, he began to look on the woman as having made a respectable and edifying end, and the whole affair as coming to a better issue than he had feared.

And so the event was considered in the neighborhood, in a melancholy way, rather an interesting and auspicious one. It gave something to talk about in a region where exciting topics were remarkably scarce. The Reverend Jabez Periwinkle found in it a moving Providence which started him favorably on a sermon, and the funeral had been quite a windfall to all the gossips about; and now remained the question, What was to be done with the children?

"Now that we are diggin' the 'taters," said Old Crab, "that 'ere chap might be good for suthin', pickin' on 'em out o' the hills.

Poor folks like us can't afford to keep nobody jest to look at, and so he'll have to step spry and work smart to airn his keep." And so at early dawn, the day after the funeral, the little boy was roused up and carried into the fields with the men.

But "this 'ere" — that is to say, a beautiful little girl of seven years — had greatly puzzled the heads of the worthy gossips of the neighborhood. Miss Asphyxia Smith, the elder sister of old Crab, was at this moment turning the child round, and examining her through a pair of large horn spectacles, with a view to "taking her to raise," as she phrased it.

Now all Miss Asphyxia's ideas of the purpose and aim of human existence were comprised in one word, — work. She was herself a working machine, always wound up and going, — up at early cock-crowing, and busy till bedtime, with a rampant and fatiguing industry that never paused for a moment. She conducted a large farm by the aid of a hired man, and drove a flourishing dairy, and was universally respected in the neighborhood as a smart woman.

Latterly, as her young cousin, who had shared the toils of the house with her, had married and left her, Miss Asphyxia had talked of "takin' a child from the poor-house, and so raisin' her own help"; and it was with the view of this "raisin' her help," that she was thus turning over and inspecting the little article which we have spoken of.

Apparently she was somewhat puzzled, and rather scandalized, that Nature should evidently have expended so much in a merely ornamental way on an article which ought to have been made simply for service. She brushed up a handful of the clustering curls in her large, bony hand, and said, with a sniff, "These'll have to come right off to begin with; gracious me, what a tangle!"

"Mother always brushed them out every day," said the child.

"And who do you suppose is going to spend an hour every day brushing your hair, Miss Pert?" said Miss Asphyxia. "That ain't what I take ye for, I tell you. You've got to learn to work for your living; and you ought to be thankful if I'm willing to show you how."

The little girl did not appear particularly thankful. She bent her soft, pencilled eyebrows in a dark frown, and her great hazel eyes had gathering in them a cloud of sullen gloom. Miss Asphyxia did not mind her frowning, — perhaps did not notice it. She had it settled in her mind, as a first principle, that children never liked anything that was good for them, and that, of course, if she took a child, it would have to be made to come to her by forcible proceedings promptly instituted. So she set her little subject before her by seizing her by her two shoulders and squaring her round and looking in her face, and opened direct conversation with her in the following succinct manner.

"What's your name?"

Then followed a resolved and gloomy silence, as the large bright eyes surveyed, with a sort of defiant glance, the inquisitor.

"Don't you hear?" said Miss Asphyxia, giving her a shake.

"Don't be so ha'sh with her," said the little old woman. "Say, my little dear, tell Miss Asphyxia your name," she added, taking the child's hand.

"Eglantine Percival," said the little girl, turning towards the old woman, as if she disdained to answer the other party in the conversation.

"Wh — a — t?" said Miss Asphyxia. "If there ain't the beatin'est name ever I heard. Well, I tell you *I* ain't got time to fix *my* mouth to say all that 'ere every time I want ye, now I tell ye."

"Mother and Harry called me Tina," said the child.

"Teny! Well, I should think so," said Miss Asphyxia. "That showed she'd got a grain o' sense left, anyhow. She's tol'able strong and well-limbed for her age," added that lady, feeling of the child's arms and limbs; "her flesh is solid. I think she'll make a strong woman, only put her to work early and keep her at it. I could rub out clothes at the wash-tub afore I was at her age."

"O, she can do considerable many little chores," said Old Crab's wife.

"Yes," said Miss Asphyxia; "there can a good deal be got out of a child if you keep at 'em, hold 'em in tight, and never let 'em have their head a minute; push right hard on behind 'em, and you get considerable. That's the way I was raised."

"But I want to play," said the little girl, bursting out in a sobbing storm of mingled fear and grief.

"Want to play, do you? Well, you must get over that. Don't you know that that's as bad as stealing? You haven't got any money, and if you eat folks's bread and butter, you've got to work to pay for it; and if folks buy your clothes, you've got to work to pay for them."

"But I've got some clothes of my own," persisted the child, determined not to give up her case entirely.

"Well, so you have; but there ain't no sort of wear in 'em," said Miss Asphyxia, turning to Mrs. Smith. "Them two dresses o' hern might answer for Sundays and sich, but I'll have to make her up a regular linsey working dress this fall, and check aprons; and she must set right about knitting every minute she isn't doing anything else. Did you ever learn how to knit?"

"No," said the child.

"Or to sew?" said Miss Asphyxia.

"Yes; mother taught me to sew," said the child.

"No! Yes! Hain't you learned manners? Do you say yes and no to people?"

The child stood a moment, swelling with suppressed feeling, and at last she opened her great eyes full on Miss Asphyxia, and said, "I don't like you. You ain't pretty, and I won't go with you."

"O now," said Mrs. Smith, "little girls mustn't talk so; that's naughty."

"Don't like me? — ain't I pretty?" said Miss Asphyxia, with a short, grim laugh. "May be I ain't; but I know what I'm about, and you'd as goods know it first as last. I'm going to take ye right out with me in the waggin, and you'd best not have none of your cuttin's up. I keep a stick at home for naughty girls. Why, where do you suppose you're going to get your livin' if I don't take you?"

"I want to live with Harry," said the child, sobbing. "Where is Harry?"

"Harry's to work, — and there's where he's got to be," said Miss Asphyxia. "He's got to work with the men in the fields, and you've got to come home and work with me."

"I want to stay with Harry, — Harry takes care of me," said the child, in a piteous tone.

Old Mother Smith now toddled to her milk-room, and, with a melting heart, brought out a doughnut. "There now, eat that," she said; "and mebbe, if you're good, Miss Asphyxia will bring you down here some time."

"O laws, Polly, you allers was a fool!" said Miss Asphyxia. "It's all for the child's good, and what's the use of fussin' on her up? She'll come to it when she knows she's got to. 'T ain't no more than I was put to at her age, only the child's been fooled with and babied."

The little one refused the doughnut, and seemed to gather herself up in silent gloom.

"Come, now, don't stand sulking; let me put your bonnet on," said Miss Asphyxia, in a brisk, metallic voice. "I can't be losin' the best part of my day with this nonsense!" And forthwith she clawed up the child in her bony grasp, as easily as an eagle might truss a chick-sparrow.

"Be a good little girl, now," said the little gray woman, who felt a strange swelling and throbbing in her poor old breast. To be sure, she knew she was a fool; her husband had told her so at least three times every day for years; and Miss Asphyxia only confirmed what she accepted familiarly as the truth. But yet she could not help these unprofitable longings to coddle and comfort something, — to do some of those little motherly tendernesses for children which go to no particular result, only to make them happy; so she ran out after the wagon with a tempting seed-cake, and forced it into the child's hand.

"Take it, do take it," she said; "eat it, and be a good girl, and do just as she tells you to."

"I'll see to that," said Miss Asphyxia, as she gathered up the reins and gave a cut to her horse, which started that quadruped from a dream of green grass into a most animated pace. Every creature in her service — horse, cow, and pig — knew at once the touch of Miss Asphyxia, and the necessity of being up and doing when she was behind them; and the horse, who under other hands would have been the slowest and most reflective of beasts, now made the little wagon spin and bounce over the rough, stony road, so that the child's short legs flew up in the air every few moments.

"You must hold on tight," was Miss Asphyxia's only comment on this circumstance. "If you fall out, you'll break your neck!"

It was a glorious day of early autumn, the sun shining as only an autumn sun knows how to shine. The blue fields of heaven were full of fleecy flocks of clouds, drifting hither and thither at their lazy will. The golden-rod and the aster hung their plumage over the rough, rocky road; and now and then it wound through a sombre piece of woods, where scarlet sumachs and maples flashed out among the gloomy green hemlocks with a solemn and gorgeous light. So very fair was the day, and so full of life and beauty was the landscape, that the child, who came of a beauty-loving lineage, felt her little heart drawn out from under its burden of troubles, and springing and bounding with that elastic habit of happiness which seems hard to kill in children.

Once she laughed out as a squirrel, with his little chops swelled with a nut on each side, sat upon the fence and looked after them, and then whisked away behind the stone wall; and once she called out, "O, how pretty!" at a splendid clump of blue fringed gentian, which stood holding up its hundred azure vases by the wayside. "O, I do wish I could get some of that!" she cried out, impulsively.

"Some of what?" said Miss Asphyxia.

"O, those *beautiful* flowers!" said the child, leaning far out to look back.

"O, that's nothing but gentian," said Miss Asphyxia; "can't stop for that. Them blows is good to dry for weakness," she added. "By and by, if you're good, mebbe I'll let you get some on 'em."

Miss Asphyxia had one word for all flowers. She called them all "blows," and they were divided in her mind, in a manner far more simple than any botanical system, into two classes; namely, blows that were good to dry, and blows that were not. Elder-blow, catnip, hoarhound, hardhack, gentian, ginseng, and various other vegetable tribes, she knew well and had a great respect for; but all the other little weeds that put on obtrusive colors and flaunted in the summer breeze, without any pretensions to further useful-ness, Miss Asphyxia completely ignored. It would not be describ-ing her state to say she had a contempt for them: she simply never saw or thought of them at all. The idea of beauty as connected with any of them never entered her mind, — it did not exist there.

The young cousin who shared her housework had, to be sure, planted a few flowers in a corner of the garden; there were some peonies and pinks and a rose-bush, which often occupied a spare hour of the girl's morning or evening; but Miss Asphyxia watched these operations with a sublime contempt, and only calculated the loss of potatoes and carrots caused by this unproductive beauty. Since the marriage of this girl, Miss Asphyxia had often spoken to her man about "clearing out them things"; but somehow he always managed to forget it, and the thriftless beauties still remained.

It wanted but about an hour of noon when Miss Asphyxia set down the little girl on the clean-scrubbed floor of a great kitchen, where everything was even desolately orderly and neat. She swung her at once into a chair. "Sit there," she said, "till I'm ready to see to ye." And then, marching up to her own room, she laid aside her bonnet, and, coming down, plunged into active preparations for the dinner.

An irrepressible feeling of desolation came over the child. The elation produced by the ride died away; and, as she sat dangling her heels from the chair, and watching the dry, grim form of Miss Asphyxia, a sort of terror of her began slowly to usurp the place of that courage which had at first inspired the child to rise up against the assertion of so uncongenial a power.

All the strange, dreadful events of the last few days mingled themselves, in her childish mind, in a weird mass of uncomprehended gloom and mystery. Her mother, so changed, — cold, stiff, lifeless, neither smiling nor speaking nor looking at her; the people coming to the house, and talking and singing and praying, and then putting her in a box in the ground, and saying that she was dead; and then, right upon that, to be torn from her brother, to whom she had always looked for protection and counsel, — all this seemed a weird, inexplicable cloud coming over her heart and darkening all her little life. Where was Harry? Why did he let them take her? Or perhaps equally dreadful people had taken him, and would never bring him back again.

There was a tall black clock in a corner of the kitchen, that kept its invariable monotone of tick-tack, tick-tack, with a persistence that made her head swim; and she watched the quick, decisive movements of Miss Asphyxia with somewhat of the same respectful awe with which one watches the course of a locomotive engine.

It was late for Miss Asphyxia's dinner preparations, but she instituted prompt measures to make up for lost time. She flew about the kitchen with such long-armed activity and fearful celerity, that the child began instinctively to duck and bob her little head when she went by, lest she should hit her and knock her off her chair.

Miss Asphyxia raked open the fire in the great kitchen chimney, and built it up with a liberal supply of wood; then she rattled into the back room, and a sound was heard of a bucket descending into a well with such frantic haste as only an oaken bucket under Miss Asphyxia's hands could be frightened into. Back she came with a stout black iron tea-kettle, which she hung over the fire; and then, flopping down a ham on the table, she cut off slices with a martial and determined air, as if she would like to see the ham try to help itself; and, before the child could fairly see what she was doing, the slices of ham were in the frying-pan over the coals, the ham hung up in its place, the knife wiped and put out of sight, and the table drawn out into the middle of the floor, and invested with a cloth for dinner.

During these operations the child followed every movement with awe-struck eyes, and studied with trembling attention every feature of this wonderful woman.

Miss Asphyxia was tall and spare. Nature had made her, as she often remarked of herself, entirely for use. She had allowed for her muscles no cushioned repose of fat, no redundant smoothness of outline. There was nothing to her but good, strong, solid bone, and tough, wiry, well-strung muscle. She was past fifty, and her hair was already well streaked with gray, and so thin that, when tightly combed and tied, it still showed bald cracks, not very sightly to the eye. The only thought that Miss Asphyxia ever had had in relation to the *coiffure* of her hair was that it was to be got out of her way. Hair she considered principally as something that might get into people's eyes, if not properly attended to; and accordingly, at a very early hour every morning, she tied all hers in a very tight knot, and then secured it by a horn comb on the top of her head. To tie this knot so tightly that, once done, it should last all day, was Miss Asphyxia's only art of the toilet, and she tried her work every morning by giving her head a shake, before she left her looking-glass, not unlike that of an unruly cow. If this process did not start the horn comb from its moorings, Miss Asphyxia was well pleased. For the rest, her face was dusky and wilted, — guarded by gaunt, high cheek-bones, and watched over by a pair of small gray eyes of unsleeping vigilance. The shaggy eyebrows that overhung them were grizzled, like her hair.

It would not be proper to say that Miss Asphyxia looked ill-tempered; but her features could never, by any stretch of imagination, be supposed to wear an expression of tenderness. They were set in an austere, grim gravity, whose lines had become more deeply channelled by every year of her life. As related to her fellow-creatures, she was neither passionate nor cruel. We have before described her as a working machine, forever wound up to high-pressure working-point; and this being her nature, she trod down and crushed whatever stood in the way of her work, with as little compunction as if she had been a steam-engine or a power-loom.

Miss Asphyxia had a full conviction of what a recent pleasant writer has denominated the total depravity of matter. She was not given to many words, but it might often be gathered from her brief discourses that she had always felt herself, so to speak, sword in hand against a universe where everything was running to disorder, — everything was tending to slackness, shiftlessness, unthrift, and she alone was left on the earth to keep things in their places. Her hired men were always too late up in the morning, — always shirking, — always taking too long a nap at noon; everybody was watching to cheat her in every bargain; her horse, cow, pigs, — all her possessions, — were ready at the slightest winking of her eye, or relaxing of her watch, to fall into all sorts of untoward ways and gyrations; and therefore she slept, as it were, in her armor, and spent her life as a sentinel on duty.

In taking a child, she had had her eyes open only to one patent fact, — that a child was an animal who would always be wanting to play, and that she must make all her plans and calculations to keep her from playing. To this end she had beforehand given out word to her brother, that, if she took the girl, the boy must be kept away. "Got enough on my hands now, without havin' a boy trainin' round my house, and upsettin' all creation," said the grim virgin.

"Wal, wal," said Old Crab, " 't ain't best; they'll be a consultin' together, and cuttin' up didos. I'll keep the boy tight enough, I tell you."

Little enough was the dinner that the child ate that day. There were two hulking, square-shouldered men at the table, who stared at her with great round eyes like oxen; and so, though Miss Asphyxia dumped down Indian pudding, ham, and fried potatoes before her, the child's eating was scarcely that of a blackbird.

Marvellous to the little girl was the celerity with which Miss Asphyxia washed and cleared up the dinner-dishes. How the dishes rattled, the knives and forks clinked, as she scraped and piled and washed and wiped and put everything in a trice back into such perfect place, that it looked as if nothing had ever been done on the premises!

After this Miss Asphyxia produced thimble, thread, needle, and scissors, and, drawing out of a closet a bale of coarse blue home-made cloth, proceeded to measure the little girl for a petticoat and short gown of the same. This being done to her mind, she dumped her into a chair beside her, and, putting a brown towel into her hands to be hemmed, she briefly said, "There, keep to work"; while she, with great despatch and resolution, set to work on the little garments aforesaid.

The child once or twice laid down her work to watch the chickens who came up round the door, or to note a bird which flew by with a little ripple of song. The first time, Miss Asphyxia only frowned, and said, "Tut, tut." The second time, there came three thumps of Miss Asphyxia's thimble down on the little head, with the admonition, "Mind your work." The child now began to cry, but Miss Asphyxia soon put an end to that by displaying a long birch rod, with a threatening movement, and saying succinctly, "Stop that, this minute, or I'll whip you." And the child was so certain of this that she swallowed her grief and stitched away as fast as her little fingers could go.

As soon as supper was over that night, Miss Asphyxia seized upon the child, and, taking her to a tub in the sink-room, proceeded to divest her of her garments and subject her to a most thorough ablution.

"I'm goin' to give you one good scrubbin' to start with," said Miss Asphyxia; and, truth to say, no word could more thoroughly express the character of the ablution than the term "scrubbing." The poor child was deluged with soap and water, in mouth, nose, ears, and eyes, while the great bony hands rubbed and splashed, twisted her arms, turned her ears wrong side out, and dashed on the water with unsparing vigor. Nobody can tell the torture which can be inflicted on a child in one of these vigorous old New England washings, which used to make Saturday night a terror in good families. But whatever they were, the little martyr was by this time so thoroughly impressed with the awful reality of Miss Asphyxia's power over her, that she endured all with only a few long-drawn and convulsed sighs, and an inaudible "O dear!"

When well scrubbed and wiped, Miss Asphyxia put on a coarse homespun nightgown, and, pinning a cloth round the child's neck, began with her scissors the work of cutting off her hair. Snip, snip, went the fatal shears, and down into the towel fell bright curls, once the pride of a mother's heart, till finally the small head was despoiled completely. Then Miss Asphyxia, shaking up a bottle of camphor, proceeded to rub some vigorously upon the child's head. "There," she said, "that's to keep ye from catchin' cold."

She then proceeded to the kitchen, raked open the fire, and shook the golden curls into the bed of embers, and stood grimly over them while they seethed and twisted and writhed, as if they had been living things suffering a fiery torture, meanwhile picking diligently at the cloth that had contained them, that no stray hair might escape.

"I wonder now," she said to herself, "if any of this will rise and get into the next pudding?" She spoke with a spice of bitterness, poor woman, as if it would be just the way things usually went on, if it did.

She buried the fire carefully, and then, opening the door of a small bedroom adjoining, which displayed a single bed, she said, "Now get into bed."

The child immediately obeyed, thankful to hide herself under the protecting folds of a blue checked coverlet, and feeling that at last the dreadful Miss Asphyxia would leave her to herself.

Miss Asphyxia clapped to the door, and the child drew a long breath. In a moment, however, the door flew open. Miss Asphyxia had forgotten something. "Can you say your prayers?" she demanded.

"Yes, ma'am," said the child.

"Say 'em, then," said Miss Asphyxia; and bang went the door again.

"There, now, if I hain't done up my duty to that child, then I don't know," said Miss Asphyxia.

CHAPTER IX

HARRY'S FIRST DAY'S WORK

It was the fashion of olden times to consider children only as children pure and simple; not as having any special and individual nature which required special and individual adaptation, but as being simply so many little creatures to be washed, dressed, schooled, fed, and whipped, according to certain general and well-understood rules.

The philosophy of modern society is showing to parents and educators how delicate and how varied is their task; but in the days we speak of nobody had thought of these shadings and variations. It is perhaps true, that in that very primitive and simple state of society there were fewer of those individual peculiarities which are the result of the stimulated brains and nervous systems of modern society.

Be that as it may, the little parish of Needmore saw nothing in the fact that two orphan children had fallen into the hands of Crab Smith and his sister, Miss Asphyxia, which appeared to its moral sense as at all unsuitable. To be sure, there was a suppressed shrug of the shoulders at the idea of the little fair-haired, pleasant-mannered boy being given up to Old Crab. People said to each other, with a knowing grin: "That 'ere boy'd have to toe the mark pretty handsome; but then, he might do wus. He'd have enough to eat and drink anyhow, and old Ma'am Smith, she'd mother him. As to Miss Asphyxia and the girl, why, 't was jest the thing. She was jest the hand to raise a smart girl."

In fact, we are not certain that Miss Asphyxia, with a few modifications and fashionable shadings suitable for our modern society, is not, after all, the ideal personage who would get all votes as just the proper person to take charge of an orphan asylum, — would be recommended to widowers with large families as just the woman to bring up their children.

Efficiency has always been, in our New England, the golden

calf before which we have fallen down and worshipped. The great
granite formation of physical needs and wants that underlie life
in a country with a hard soil and a severe climate gives an intensity
to our valuation of what pertains to the working of the direct and
positive force that controls the physical; and that which can keep
in constant order the eating, drinking, and wearing of this mortal
body is always asserting itself in every department of life as the
true wisdom.

But what, in fact, were the two little children who had been
thus seized on and appropriated?

The boy was, as we have described, of a delicate and highly
nervous organization, — sensitive, æsthetic, — evidently fitted by
nature more for the poet or scholar than for the rough grind of
physical toil. There had been superinduced on this temperament
a precocious development from the circumstance of his having
been made, during the earliest years of his consciousness, the
companion of his mother. Nothing unfolds a child faster than
being thus taken into the companionship of older minds in the first
years of life. He was naturally one of those manly, good-natured,
even-tempered children that are the delight of nurses and the staff
and stay of mothers. Early responsibility and sorrow, and the
religious teachings of his mother, had awakened the spiritual part
of his nature to a higher consciousness than usually exists in childhood. There was about him a steady, uncorrupted goodness and
faithfulness of nature, a simple, direct truthfulness, and a loyal
habit of prompt obedience to elders, which made him one of those
children likely, in every position of child-life, to be favorites, and
to run a smooth course.

The girl, on the contrary, had in her all the elements of a little
bundle of womanhood, born to rule and command in a pure
womanly way. She was affectionate, gay, pleasure-loving, self-
willed, imperious, intensely fond of approbation, with great stores
of fancy, imagination, and an under-heat of undeveloped passion
that would, in future life, give warmth and color to all her
thoughts, as a volcanic soil is said to brighten the hues of flowers
and warm the flavor of grapes. She had, too, that capacity of
secretiveness which enabled her to carry out the dictates of a
strong will, and an intuitive sense of where to throw a tendril or
strike a little fibre of persuasion or coaxing, which comes early to

those fair parasites who are to live by climbing upon others, and to draw their hues and sweetness from the warmth of other hearts. The moral and religious faculties were as undeveloped in her as in a squirrel or a robin. She had lived, in fact, between her sorrowing mother and her thoughtful little brother, as a beautiful pet, whose little gladsome ways and gay pranks were the only solace of their poverty. Even the father, in good-natured hours, had caressed her, played with her, told her stories, and allowed all her little audacities and liberties with an indulgence that her brother could not dare to hope for. No service or self-denial had ever been required of her. She had been served, with a delicate and exact care, by both mother and brother.

Such were the two little specimens of mortality which the town of Needmore thought well provided for when they were consigned to Crab Smith and Miss Asphyxia.

The first day after the funeral of his mother, the boy had been called up before light in the morning, and been off at sunrise to the fields with the men; but he had gone with a heart of manly enterprise, feeling as if he were beginning life on his own account, and meaning, with straightforward simplicity, to do his best.

He assented to Old Crab's harsh orders with such obedient submission, and set about the work given him with such a steady, manly patience and good-will, as to win for himself, at the outset, golden opinions from the hired men, and to excite in Old Crab that discontented satisfaction which he felt in an employee in whom he could find nothing to scold. The work of merely picking up the potatoes from the hills which the men opened was so very simple as to give no chance for mistake or failure, and the boy was so cheerful and unintermitting in his work that no fault could be found under that head. He was tired enough, it is true, at night; but, as he rode home in the cart, he solaced himself with the idea that he was beginning to be a man, and that he should work and support his sister, — and he had many things to tell her of the result of his first day's labor. He wondered that she did not come to meet him as the cart drove up to the house, and his first inquiry, when he saw the friendly old woman, was, "Where is Tina?"

"She's gone to live with *his* sister," said Mrs. Smith, in an undertone, pointing to her husband in the back yard. "Asphyxia's took her to raise."

"To what?" said the boy, timidly.

"Why, to fetch her up, — teach her to work," said the little old woman. "But come, sonny, go wash your hands to the sink. Dear me! why, you've fairly took the skin off your fingers."

"I'm not much used to work," said the boy, "but I don't mind it." And he washed carefully the little hands, which, sure enough, had the skin somewhat abraded on the finger-ends.

"Do ye good," said Old Crab. "Mustn't mind that. Can't have no lily-fingered boys workin' for me."

The child had not thought of complaining; but as soon as he was alone with Mrs. Smith, he came to her confidentially and said, "How far is it to where Tina lives?"

"Well, it's the best part of two miles, I calculate."

"Can't I go over there to-night and see her?"

"Dear heart! no, you can't. Why, your little back must ache now, and he'll have you routed up by four o'clock in the morning."

"I'm not so very tired," said the boy; "but I want to see Tina. If you'll show me the way, I'll go."

"O, well, you see, they won't let you," said the old woman, confidentially. "They are a ha'sh pair of 'em, him and Sphyxy are; and they've settled it that you ain't to see each other no more, for fear you'd get to playin' and idlin'."

The blood flushed into the boy's face, and he breathed short. Something stirred within him, such as makes slavery bitter, as he said, "But that isn't right. She's my only sister, and my mother told me to take care of her; and I *ought* to see her sometimes."

"Lordy massy!" said Goody Smith; "when you're with some folks, it don't make no difference what's right and what ain't. You've jest got to do as ye ken. It won't do to rile *him*, I tell you. He's awful, once git his back up." And Goody Smith shook her little old head mysteriously, and hushed the boy, as she heard her husband's heavy tread coming in from the barn.

The supper of cold beef and pork, potatoes, turnips, and hard cider, which was now dispensed at the farm-house, was ample for all purposes of satisfying hunger; and the little Harry, tired as he was, ate with a vigorous relish. But his mind was still dwelling on his sister.

After supper was over he followed Goody Smith into her milk-room. "Please do ask *him* to let me go and see Tina," he said, persuasively.

"Laws a massy, ye poor dear! ye don't know the critter. If *I* ask him to do a thing, he's all the more set agin it. I found out that 'ere years ago. He never does nothin' *I* ask him to. But never mind; some of these days, we'll try and contrive it. When he's gone to mill, I'll speak to the men, and tell 'em to let ye slip off. But then the pester on 't is, there's Sphyxy; she's allers wide awake, and wouldn't let a boy come near her house no more than ef he was a bulldog."

"Why, what harm do boys do?" said the child, to whom this view presented an entirely new idea.

"O, well, she's an old maid, and kind o' set in her ways; and it ain't easy gettin' round Sphyxy; but I'll try and contrive it. Sometimes I can get round 'em, and get something done, when they don't know nothin' about it; but it's drefful hard gettin' things done."

The view thus presented to the child's mind of the cowering, deceptive policy in which the poor old woman's whole married life had been spent gave him much to think of after he had gone to his bedroom.

He sat down on his little, lonely bed, and began trying to comprehend in his own mind the events of the last few days. He recalled his mother's last conversation with him. All had happened just as she had said. She was gone, just as she had told him, and left him and little Tina alone in the world. Then he remembered his promise, and, kneeling down by his bedside, repeated the simple litany — psalm, prayer, and hymn — which his mother had left him as her only parting gift. The words soothed his little lonesome heart; and he thought what his mother said, — he recalled the look of her dying eyes as she said it, — "Never doubt that God loves you, whatever happens; and, if you have any trouble, pray to him." Upon this thought, he added to his prayer these words: "O dear Father! they have taken away Tina; and she's a very little girl, and cannot work, as I can. Please do take care of Tina, and make them let me go and see her."

CHAPTER X

MISS ASPHYXIA'S SYSTEM

When Miss Asphyxia shut the door finally on little Tina, the child began slowly to gather up her faculties from the stunning, benumbing influence of the change which had come over her life.

In former days her father had told her stories of little girls that were carried off to giants' houses, and there maltreated and dominated over in very dreadful ways; and Miss Asphyxia presented herself to her as one of these giants. She was so terribly strong, the child felt instinctively, in every limb, that there was no getting away from her. Her eyes were so keen and searching, her voice so sharp, all her movements so full of a vigor that might be felt, that any chance of getting the better of her by indirect ways seemed hopelessly small. If she should try to run away to find Harry, she was quite sure that Miss Asphyxia could make a long arm that would reach her before she had gone far; and then what she would do to her was a matter that she dared not think of. Even when she was not meaning to be cross to her, but merely seized and swung her into a chair, she had such a grip that it almost gave pain; and what would it be if she seized her in wrath? No; there was evidently no escape; and, as the thought came over the child, she began to cry, — first sobbing, and then, as her agitation increased, screaming audibly.

Miss Asphyxia opened the door. "Stop that!" she said. "What under the canopy ails ye?"

"I — want — Harry!" said the child.

"Well, you can't have Harry; and I won't have ye bawling. Now shut up and go to sleep, or I'll whip you!" And, with that, Miss Asphyxia turned down the bedclothes with a resolute hand.

"I will be good, — I will stop," said the child, in mortal terror, compressing the sobs that seemed to tear her little frame.

Miss Asphyxia waited a moment, and then, going out, shut the door, and went on making up the child's stuff gown outside.

"That 'ere's goin' to be a regular limb," she said; "but I must begin as I'm goin' to go on with her, and mebbe she'll amount to suthin' by and by. A child's pretty much dead loss the first three or four years; but after that they more 'n pay, if they're fetched up right."

"Mebbe that 'ere child's lonesome," said Sol Peters, Miss Asphyxia's hired man, who sat in the kitchen corner, putting in a new hoe-handle.

"Lonesome!" said Miss Asphyxia, with a sniff of contempt.

"All sorts of young critters is," said Sol, undismayed by this sniff. "Puppies is. 'Member how our Spot yelped when I fust got him? Kept me 'wake the biggest part of one night. And kittens mews when ye take 'em from the cats. Ye see they's used to other critters; and it's sort o' cold like, bein' alone is."

"Well, she'll have to get used to it, anyhow," said Miss Asphyxia. "I guess 't won't kill her. Ef a child has enough to eat and drink, and plenty of clothes, and somebody to take care of 'em, they ain't very bad off, if they be lonesome."

Sol, though a big-fisted, hard-handed fellow, had still rather a soft spot under his jacket in favor of all young, defenceless animals, and the sound of the little girl's cry had gone right to this spot. So he still revolved the subject, as he leisurely turned and scraped with a bit of broken glass the hoe-handle that he was elaborating. After a considerable pause, he shut up one eye, looked along his hoe-handle at Miss Asphyxia, as if he were taking aim, and remarked, "That 'ere boy's a nice, stiddy little chap; and mebbe, if he could come down here once and a while after work-hours, 't would kind o' reconcile her."

"I tell you what, Solomon Peters," said Miss Asphyxia, "I'd jest as soon have the great red dragon in the Revelations a comin' down on my house as a boy! Ef I don't work hard enough now, I'd like to know, without havin' a boy raound raisin' gineral Cain. Don't tell me! I'll find work enough to keep that 'ere child from bein' lonesome. Lonesome! — there didn't nobody think of no such things when I was little. I was jest put right along, and no remarks made; and was made to mind when I was spoken to, and to take things as they come. O, I'll find her work enough to keep her mind occupied, I promise ye."

Sol did not in the least doubt that, for Miss Asphyxia's reputation in the region was perfectly established. She was spoken of with applause under such titles as "a staver," "a pealer," "a roarer to work"; and Sol himself had an awful sense of responsibility to her in this regard. He had arrived at something of a late era in single life, and had sometimes been sportively jogged by his associates, at the village store, as to his opportunity of becoming master of Miss Asphyxia's person and property by matrimonial overtures; to all which he summarily responded by declaring that "a hoss might as soon go a courtin' to the hoss-whip as he court Miss Sphyxy." As to Miss Asphyxia, when rallied on the same subject, she expressed her views of the matrimonial estate in a sentence more terse and vigorous than elegant, — that "she knew t' much to put her nose into hot swill." Queen Elizabeth might have expressed her mind in a more courtly way, but certainly with no more decision.

The little head and heart in the next room were full of the rudiments of thoughts, desires, feelings, imaginations, and passions which either had never lived in Miss Asphyxia's nature, or had died so long ago that not a trace or memory of them was left. If she had had even the dawnings of certain traits and properties, she might have doubted of her ability to bring up a child; but she had not.

Yet Miss Asphyxia's faults in this respect were not so widely different from the practice of the hard, rustic inhabitants of Needmore as to have prevented her getting employment as a district-school teacher for several terms, when she was about twenty years of age. She was held to be a "smart," economical teacher, inasmuch as she was able to hold the winter term, and thrash the very biggest boys, and, while she did the duty of a man, received only the wages of a woman, — a recommendation in female qualification which has not ceased to be available in our modern days. Gradually, by incredible industries, by a faculty of pinching, saving, and accumulating hard to conceive of, Miss Asphyxia had laid up money till she had actually come to be the possessor of a small but neat house, and a farm and dairy in excellent condition; and she regarded herself, therefore, and was regarded by others, as a model for imitation. Did she have the least doubt that she was eminently fitted to bring up a girl? I trow not.

Miss Asphyxia, in her early childhood, had been taken to raise in the same manner that she had taken this child. She had been trained to early rising, and constant, hard, unintermitted work, without thought of respite or amusement. During certain seasons of the year she had been sent to the district school, where, always energetic in whatever she took in hand, she always stood at the head of the school in the few arts of scholarship in those days taught. She could write a good, round hand; she could cipher with quickness and adroitness; she had learned by heart all the rules of Murray's Grammar, notwithstanding the fact that, from the habits of early childhood, she habitually set at naught every one of them in her daily conversation, — always strengthening all her denials with those good, hearty double negatives which help out French and Italian sentences, and are unjustly denied to the purists in genteel English. How much of the droll quaintness of Yankee dialect comes from the stumbling of human nature into these racy mistakes will never be known.

Perhaps my readers may have turned over a great, flat stone some time in their rural rambles, and found under it little clovers and tufts of grass pressed to earth, flat, white, and bloodless, but still growing, stretching, creeping towards the edges, where their plant instinct tells them there is light and deliverance. The kind of life that the little Tina led, under the care of Miss Asphyxia, resembled that of these poor clovers. It was all shut down and repressed, but growing still. She was roused at the first glimmer of early dawn, dressing herself in the dark, and, coming out, set the table for breakfast. From that time through the day, one task followed another in immediate succession, with the sense of the ever-driving Miss Asphyxia behind her.

Once, in the course of her labors, she let fall a saucer, while Miss Asphyxia, by good fortune, was out of the room. To tell of her mischance, and expose herself to the awful consequences of her anger, was more than her childish courage was equal to; and, with a quick adroitness, she slipped the broken fragments in a crevice between the kitchen doorstep and the house, and endeavored to look as if nothing had occurred. Alas! she had not counted on Miss Asphyxia's unsleeping vigilance of hearing. She was down stairs in a trice.

"What have you been breaking?"

"Nothing, ma'am," was the trembling response.

"Don't tell me! I heard something fall."

"I think it must have been the tongs," said the little girl, — not over-wise or ingenious in her subterfuge.

"Tongs! likely story," said Miss Asphyxia, keenly running her eye over the cups and saucers.

"One, two, — here's one of the saucers gone. What have you done with it?"

The child, now desperate with fear, saw no refuge but in persistent denial, till Miss Asphyxia, seizing her, threatened immediate whipping if she did not at once confess.

"I dropped a saucer," at last said the frightened child.

"You did, you little slut?" said Miss Asphyxia, administering a box on her ear. "Where is it? what have you done with the pieces?"

"I dropped them down by the doorstep," said the sobbing culprit.

Miss Asphyxia soon fished them up, and held them up in awful judgment. "You've been telling me a lie, — a naughty, wicked lie," she said. "I'll soon cure you of lying. I'll scour your mouth out for you." And forthwith, taking a rag with some soap and sand, she grasped the child's head under her arm, and rubbed the harsh mixture through her mouth with a vengeful energy. "There, now, see if you'll tell me another lie," said she, pushing her from her. "Don't you know where liars go to, you naughty, wicked girl? 'All liars shall have their part in the lake that burns with fire and brimstone,' — that's what the Bible says; and you may thank me for keeping you from going there. Now go and get up the potatoes and wash 'em, and don't let me get another lie out of your mouth as long as you live."

There was a burning sense of shame — a smothered fury of resentment — in the child's breast, and, as she took the basket, she felt as if she would have liked to do some mischief to Miss Asphyxia. "I hate you, I hate you, I hate you," she said to herself when she got into the cellar, and fairly out of hearing. "I hate you, and when I get to be a woman, I'll pay you for all this."

Miss Asphyxia, however, went on her way, in the testimony of a good conscience. She felt that she had been equal to the emergency, and had met a crisis in the most thorough and effectual manner.

The teachers of district schools in those days often displayed a singular ingenuity in the invention of punishments by which the different vices of childhood should be repressed; and Miss Asphyxia's housewifely confidence in soap and sand as a means of purification had suggested to her this expedient in her school-teaching days. "You can break any child o' lying, right off short," she was wont to say. "Jest scour their mouths out with soap and sand. They never want to try it more'n once or twice, I tell you."

The intervals which the child had for play were, in Miss Asphyxia's calendar, few and far between. Sometimes, when she had some domestic responsibility on her mind which made the watching of the child a burden to her, she would say to her, "You may go and play till I call you," or, "You may play for half an hour; but you mustn't go out of the yard."

Then the child, alone, companionless, without playthings, sought to appropriate to herself some little treasures and possessions for the instituting of that fairy world of imagination which belongs to childhood. She sighed for a doll that had once belonged to her in the days when she had a mother, but which Miss Asphyxia had contemptuously tossed aside in making up her bundle.

Left thus to her own resources, the child yet showed the unquenchable love of beauty, and the power of creating and gilding an imaginary little world, which is the birthright of childhood. She had her small store of what she had been wont to call pretty things, — a broken teapot handle, a fragment of colored glass, part of a goblet that had once belonged to Miss Asphyxia's treasures, one or two smooth pebbles, and some red berries from a wild rose-bush. These were the darlings, the dear delights of her heart, — hoarded in secret places, gazed on by stealth, taken out and arranged and re-arranged, during the brief half-hours, or hours, when Miss Asphyxia allowed her to play. To these treasures the kindly Sol added another; for one day, when Miss Asphyxia was not looking, he drew from his vest-pocket a couple of milkweed pods, and said, "Them's putty, — mebbe ye'd like 'em; hide 'em up, though, or she'll sweep 'em into the fire."

No gloss of satin and glimmer of pearls ever made bright eyes open wider than did the exploring the contents of these pods. It was silk and silver, fairy-spun glass, — something so bright and soft that it really seemed dear to her; and she took the shining silk fringes out and caressed them against her cheek, and wrapped them in a little bit of paper, and put them in her bosom. They felt so soft and downy, — they were so shining and bright, — and they were her own, — Sol had given them to her. She meditated upon them as possessions of mysterious beauty and unknown value. Unfortunately, one day Miss Asphyxia discovered her gazing upon this treasure by stealth during her working hours.

"What have you got there?" she said. "Bring it to me."

The child reluctantly placed her treasure in the great bony claw.

"Why, that's milkweed silk," said Miss Asphyxia. " 'T ain't good for nothin'. What you doing with that?"

"I like it because it's pretty."

"Fiddlestick!" said Miss Asphyxia, giving it a contemptuous toss. "I can't have you making litter with such stuff round the house. Throw it in the fire."

To do Miss Asphyxia justice, she would never have issued this order if she had had the remotest conception how dear this apparent trash was to the hopeless little heart.

The child hesitated, and held her treasure firmly. Her breast heaved, and there was a desperate glare in her soft hazel eyes.

"Throw it in the fire," said Miss Asphyxia, stamping her foot, as she thought she saw risings of insubordination.

The child threw it in, and saw her dear, beautiful treasure slowly consumed, with a swelling and indignant heart. She was now sure that Miss Asphyxia hated her, and only sought occasion to torment her.

Miss Asphyxia did not hate the child, nor did she love her. She regarded her exactly as she did her broom and her rolling-pin and her spinning-wheel, — as an implement or instrument which she was to fashion to her uses. She had a general idea, too, of certain duties to her as a human being, which she expressed by the phrase, "doing right by her," — that is, to feed and clothe and teach her. In fact, Miss Asphyxia believed fully in the golden rule of doing as she would be done by; but if a lioness should do to a young lamb exactly as she would be done by, it might be all the worse for the lamb.

The little mind and heart were awakened to a perfect burning conflict of fear, shame, anger, and a desire for revenge, which now overflowed with strange, bitter waters that hitherto ignorantly happy valley of child-life. She had never had any sense of moral or religious obligation, any more than a butterfly or a canary-bird. She had, it is true, said her little prayers every night; but, as she said to herself, she had always said them to mother or Harry, and now there was nobody to say them to. Every night she thought of this when she lay down in her joyless, lonesome bed; but the kindly fatigue which hard work brings soon weighed down her eyes, and she slept soundly all night, and found herself hungry at breakfast-time the next morning.

On Sunday Miss Asphyxia rested from her labors, — a strange rest for a soul that had nothing to do in the spiritual world. Miss Asphyxia was past middle life, and, as she said, had never experienced religion, — a point which she regarded with some bitterness, since, as she was wont to say, she had always been as honest in her dealings and kept Sunday as strict as most church-members. Still, she would do her best at giving religious instruction to the child; and accordingly the first Sunday she was dressed in her best frock, and set up in a chair to be kept still while the wagon was getting ready to "go to meetin'," and Miss Asphyxia tried to put into her head the catechism made by that dear, friendly old lover of children, Dr. Watts.

But somehow the first question, benignly as it is worded, had a grim and threatening sound as it came from the jaws of Miss Asphyxia, somewhat thus: "Stop playing with your frock, and look right at me, now. 'Can you tell me, dear child, who made you?'"

Now the little one had often heard this point explained, but she felt small disposition to give up her knowledge at this demand; so she only looked at Miss Asphyxia in sulky silence.

"Say, now, after me," said Miss Asphyxia, "'The great God that made heaven and earth.'"

The child repeated the words, in that mumbling, sulky manner which children use when they are saying what does not please them.

"Tina Percival," said Miss Asphyxia, in warlike tones, "do you speak out plain, or I'll box yer ears."

Thus warned, the child uttered her confession of faith audibly enough.

Miss Asphyxia was peculiarly harsh and emphatic on the answer which described the omnipresence of the Supreme Being, and her harsh voice, croaking, "If I tell a lie, He sees me, — if I speak an idle or wicked word, He hears me," seemed to the child to have a ghastly triumph in it to confirm the idea that Miss Asphyxia's

awful tyranny was thoroughly backed up by that of a Being far
more mighty, and from whom there was no possible escape. Miss
Asphyxia enforced this truth with a coarse and homely eloquence,
that there was no getting away from God, — that He could see in
the night just as plain as in the daytime, — see her in the yard,
see her in the barn, see her under the bed, see her down cellar;
and that whenever she did anything wrong He would write it
down in a dreadful book, and on the Day of Judgment she would
have it all brought out upon her, — all which the child heard with
a stony, sullen despair. Miss Asphyxia illustrated what became of
naughty children by such legends as the story of the two she-bears
which came out of a wood and tare forty-and-two children who
mocked at old Elisha, till the rebellious auditor quaked in her little
shoes, and wondered if the bears would get Harry, and if Harry,
after all, would not find some way to get round the bears and
come to her help.

At meeting she at last saw Harry, seated, however, in a distant
part of the house; but her heart was ready to jump out of her
breast to go to him; and when the services were over she contrived
to elude Miss Asphyxia, and, passing through the throng, seized
his hand just as he was going out, and whispered, "O Harry, Harry,
I do want to see you so much! Why don't you come to see me?"

"They wouldn't let me, Tina," said Harry, drawing his sister into
a little recess made between the church and the horse-block, —
an old-fashioned structure that used to exist for the accommodation
of those who came to church on horseback. "They won't let me
come. I wanted to come, — I wanted to see you so much!"

"O Harry, I don't like her, — she is cross to me. Do take me
away, — do, Harry! Let's run away together."

"Where could we go, Tina?"

"O, somewhere, — no matter where. I hate her. I won't stay
with her. Say, Harry, I sleep in a little room by the kitchen; come
to my window some night and take me away."

"Well, perhaps I will."

"Here you are, you little minx," said Miss Asphyxia. "What you
up to now? Come, the waggin's waiting," — and, with a look of
severe suspicion directed to Harry, she seized the child and conveyed her to the wagon, and was soon driving off with all speed
homeward.

That evening the boy pondered long and soberly. He had worked well and steadily during the week, and felt no disposition to complain of his lot on that account, being, as we have said, of a faithful and patient nature, and accepting what the friendly hired men told him, — that work was good for little boys, that it would make him grow strong, and that by and by he would be grown up and able to choose his own work and master. But this separation from his little sister, and her evident unhappiness, distressed him; he felt that she belonged to him, and that he must care for her, and so, when he came home, he again followed Goody Smith to the retirement of her milk-room.

The poor woman had found a perfect summer of delight in her old age in having around her the gentle-mannered, sweet-spoken, good boy, who had thus marvellously fallen to her lot; and boundless was the loving-kindness with which she treated him. Sweet-cakes were slipped into his hands at all odd intervals, choice morsels set away for his consumption in secret places of the buttery, and many an adroit lie told to Old Crab to secure for him extra indulgences, or prevent the imposition of extra tasks; and many a little lie did she recommend to him, at which the boy's honest nature and Christian education inclined him greatly to wonder.

That a grown-up, good old woman should tell lies, and advise little boys to tell them, was one of those facts of human experience which he turned over in his mind with wonder, — thinking it over with that quiet questioning which children practise who have nobody of whom they dare make many inquiries. But to-day he was determined to have something done about Tina, and so he began, "Please, won't you ask him to let me go and see Tina to-night? It's Sunday, and there isn't any work to do."

"Lordy massy, child, he's crabbeder Sundays than any other day, he has so much time to graowl round. He drinks more cider; and Sunday night it's always as much as a body's life's worth to go near him. I don't want you to get him sot agin ye. He got sot agin Obed; and no critter knows why, except mebbe 'cause he was some comfort to me. And ye oughter seen how he used that 'ere boy. Why, I've stood here in the milk-room and heerd that 'ere boy's screeches clear from the stun pastur'. Finally the men, they said they couldn't stan' it, nor they wouldn't."

"Who was Obed?" said Harry, fearfully.

"Lordy massy! wal, I forgot ye didn't know Obed. He was the baby, ye see. He was born the eighteenth of April, just about nine o'clock in the evening, and Aunt Jerusha Periwinkle and Granny Watkins, they said they hadn't seen no sich child in all their nussing. Held up his head jest as lively, and sucked his thumb, he did, — jest the patientest, best baby ye ever did see, — and growed beautiful. And he was gettin' to be a real beautiful young man when he went off."

"Went off?" said Harry.

"Yes, he went off to sea, jest for nothin' but 'cause his father aggravated him so."

"What *was* the matter? what *did* he do it for?"

"Wal, Obed, he was allers round helpin' me, — he'd turn the cheeses for me, and draw the water, and was always on hand when I wanted a turn. And he took up agin him, and said we was both lazy, and that I kept him round waitin' on me; and he was allers a throwin' it up at me that I thought more of Obed than I did of him; and one day flesh and blood couldn't stan' it no longer. I got clear beat out, and says I, 'Well, father, why shouldn't I? Obed's allers a tryin' to help me and make my work easy to me, and thinkin' what he can do for me; and he's the greatest comfort of my life, and it ain't no sin if I do think more on him than I do of other folks.' Wal, that very day he went and picked a quarrel with him, and told him he was going to give him a stand-up thrashing. And Obed, says he, 'No, father, that you sha'n't. I'm sixteen year old, and I've made up my mind you sha'n't thrash me no more.' And with that he says to him, 'Get along out of my house, you lazy dog,' says he; 'you've been eatin' of my bread too long,' says he. 'Well, father, I will,' says Obed. And he walks up to me and kisses me, and says he, 'Never mind, mother, I'm going to come home one of these days and bring money enough to take care of you in your old age; and you shall have a house of your own, and sha'n't have to work; and you shall sit in your satin gown and drink your tea with white sugar every day, and you sha' n't be no man's slave. You see if I don't.' With that he turned and was off, and I hain't never seen him since."

"How long's he been gone?"

"Wal, it's four years come next April. I've hed one or two letters from him, and he's ris' to be mate. And he sent me his wages, —

biggest part on 'em, — but he hed to git 'em to me round by sendin'
on 'em to Ebal Parker; else *he*'d a took 'em, ye see. I couldn't have
nothin' decent to wear to meetin', nor my little caddy o' green tea,
if it hadn't been for Obed. He won't read Obed's letters, nor hear
a word about him, and keeps a castin' it up at me that I think so
much of Obed that I don't love him none."

"I shouldn't think you would," said the boy, innocently.

"Wal, folks seems to think that you must love 'em through thick
and thin, and I try ter. I've allers kep' his clothes mended, and his
stockings darned up, and two or three good pair ahead, and done
for him jest the best I know how; but as to lovin' folks when they's
so kind o' as he is, I don't reely know how ter. Except, ef he was
to be killed, I should feel putty bad, too, — kind o' used to havin'
on him round."

This conversation was interrupted by the voice of Crab, in the
following pleasing style of remark: "What the devil be you a doin'
with that boy, — keepin' him from his work there? It's time to be
to the barn seein' to the critters. Here, you young scamp, go out
and cut some feed for the old mare. Suppose I keep you round
jest to eat up the victuals and be round under folks' feet?"

CHAPTER XI

THE CRISIS

Matters between Miss Asphyxia and her little subject began to show evident signs of approaching some crisis, for which that valiant virgin was preparing herself with mind resolved. It was one of her educational tactics that children, at greater or less intervals, would require what she was wont to speak of as *good* whippings, as a sort of constitutional stimulus to start them in the ways of well-doing. As a school-teacher, she was often fond of rehearsing her experiences, — how she had her eye on Jim or Bob through weeks of growing carelessness or obstinacy or rebellion, suffering the measure of iniquity gradually to become full, until, in an awful hour, she pounced down on the culprit in the very blossom of his sin, and gave him such a lesson as he would remember, as she would assure him, the longest day he had to live.

The burning of rebellious thoughts in the little breast, of internal hatred and opposition, could not long go on without slight whiffs of external smoke, such as mark the course of subterranean fire. As the child grew more accustomed to Miss Asphyxia, while her hatred of her increased, somewhat of that native hardihood which had characterized her happier days returned; and she began to use all the subtlety and secretiveness which belonged to her feminine nature in contriving how *not* to do the will of her tyrant, and yet not to seem designedly to oppose. It really gave the child a new impulse in living to devise little plans for annoying Miss Asphyxia without being herself detected. In all her daily toils she made nice calculations how slow she could possibly be, how blundering and awkward, without really bringing on herself a punishment; and when an acute and capable child turns all its faculties in such a direction, the results may be very considerable.

Miss Asphyxia found many things going wrong in her establishment in most unaccountable ways. One morning her sensibilities were almost paralyzed, on opening her milk-room door, to find there, with creamy whiskers, the venerable Tom, her own model cat, — a beast who had grown up in the very sanctities of household decorum, and whom she was sure she had herself shut out of the house, with her usual punctuality, at nine o'clock the evening before. She could not dream that he had been enticed through Tina's window, caressed on her bed, and finally sped stealthily on his mission of revenge, while the child returned to her pillow to gloat over her success.

Miss Asphyxia also, in more than one instance, in her rapid gyrations, knocked down and destroyed a valuable bit of pottery or earthen-ware, that somehow had contrived to be stationed exactly in the wind of her elbow or her hand. It was the more vexatious because she broke them herself. And the child assumed stupid innocence: "How could she know Miss Sphyxy was coming that way?" or, "She didn't see her." True, she caught many a hasty cuff and sharp rebuke; but, with true Indian spirit, she did not mind singeing her own fingers if she only tortured her enemy.

It would be an endless task to describe the many vexations that can be made to arise in the course of household experience when there is a shrewd little elf watching with sharpened faculties for every opportunity to inflict an annoyance or do a mischief. In childhood the passions move with a simplicity of action unknown to any other period of life, and a child's hatred and a child's revenge have an intensity of bitterness entirely unalloyed by moral considerations; and when a child is without an object of affection, and feels itself unloved, its whole vigor of being goes into the channels of hate.

Religious instruction, as imparted by Miss Asphyxia, had small influence in restraining the immediate force of passion. That "the law worketh wrath" is a maxim as old as the times of the Apostles. The image of a dreadful Judge — a great God, with ever-watchful eyes, that Miss Asphyxia told her about — roused that combative element in the child's heart which says in the heart of the fool, "There is no God." "After all," thought the little sceptic, "how does she know? She never saw him." Perhaps, after all, then, it might be only a fabrication of her tyrant to frighten her into submission. There was a dear Father that mamma used to tell her about; and perhaps he was the one, after all. As for the bear story she had a private conversation with Sol, and was relieved by his confident assurance that there "hadn't been no bears seen round in them parts these ten year"; so that she was safe in that regard, even if she should call Miss Asphyxia a bald-head, which she perfectly longed to do, just to see what would come of it.

In like manner, though the story of Ananias and Sapphira, struck down dead for lying, had been told her in forcible and threatening tones, yet still the little sinner thought within herself that such things must have ceased in our times, as she had told more than one clever lie which neither Miss Asphyxia nor any one else had found out.

In fact, the child considered herself and Miss Asphyxia as in a state of warfare which suspends all moral rules. In the stories of little girls who were taken captives by goblins or giants or witches, she remembered many accounts of sagacious deceptions which they had practised on their captors. Her very blood tingled when she thought of the success of some of them, — how Hensel and Grettel had heated an oven red-hot, and persuaded the old witch to get into it by some cock-and-bull story of what she would find there; and how, the minute she got in, they shut up the oven door, and burnt her all up! Miss Asphyxia thought the child a vexatious, careless, troublesome little baggage, it is true; but if she could have looked into her heart and seen her imaginings, she would probably have thought her a little fiend.

At last, one day, the smothered fire broke out. The child had had a half-hour of holiday, and had made herself happy in it by furbishing up her little bedroom. She had picked a peony, a yellow lily, and one or two blue irises, from the spot of flowers in the garden, and put them in a tin dipper on the table in her room, and ranged around them her broken bits of china, her red berries and fragments of glass, in various zigzags. The spirit of adornment thus roused within her, she remembered having seen her brother make pretty garlands of oak-leaves; and, running out to an oak hard by, she stripped off an apronful of the leaves, and, sitting down in the kitchen door, began her attempts to plait them into garlands. She grew good-natured and happy as she wrought, and was beginning to find herself in charity even with Miss Asphyxia, when down came that individual, broom in hand, looking vengeful as those old Greek Furies who used to haunt houses, testifying their wrath by violent sweeping.

"What under the canopy you up to now, making such a litter on my kitchen floor?" she said. "Can't I leave you a minute 'thout your gettin' into some mischief, I want to know? Pick 'em up, every leaf of 'em, and carry 'em and throw 'em over the fence; and don't you never let me find you bringing no such rubbish into my kitchen agin!"

In this unlucky moment she turned, and, looking into the little bedroom, whose door stood open, saw the arrangements there. "What!" she said; "you been getting down the tin cup to put your messes into? Take 'em all out!" she said, seizing the flowers with a grasp that crumpled them, and throwing them into the child's apron. "Take 'em away, every one of 'em! You'd get everything out of place, from one end of the house to the other, if I didn't watch you!" And forthwith she swept off the child's treasures into her dust-pan.

In a moment all the smothered wrath of weeks blazed up in the little soul. She looked as if a fire had been kindled in her which reddened her cheeks and burned in her eyes; and, rushing blindly at Miss Asphyxia, she cried, "You are a wicked woman, a hateful old witch, and I hate you!"

"Hity-tity! I thought I should have to give you a lesson before long, and so I shall," said Miss Asphyxia, seizing her with stern determination. "You've needed a good sound whipping for a long time, miss, and you are going to get it now. I'll whip you so that you'll remember it, I'll promise you."

And Miss Asphyxia kept her word, though the child, in the fury of despair, fought her with tooth and nail, and proved herself quite a dangerous little animal; but at length strength got the better in the fray, and, sobbing, though unsubdued, the little culprit was put to bed without her supper.

In those days the literal use of the rod in the education of children was considered as a direct Bible teaching. The wisest, the most loving parent felt bound to it in many cases, even though every stroke cut into his own heart. The laws of New England allowed masters to correct their apprentices, and teachers their pupils, — and even the public whipping-post was an institution of New England towns. It is not to be supposed, therefore, that Miss Asphyxia regarded herself otherwise than as thoroughly performing a most necessary duty. She was as ignorant of the blind agony of mingled shame, wrath, sense of degradation, and burning for revenge, which had been excited by her measures, as the icy east wind of Boston flats is of the stinging and shivering it causes in its course. Is it the wind's fault if your nose is frozen? There is not much danger in these days that such measures will be the fashionable ones in the bringing up of children. But there is a class of coldly-conscientious, severe persons, who still, as a matter of duty and conscience, justify measures like these in education. *They*, at all events, are the ones who ought to be forbidden to use them, and whose use of them with children too often proves a soul-murder, — a dispensation of wrath and death. Such a person is commonly both obtuse in sensibility and unimaginative in temperament; but if his imagination could once be thoroughly enlightened to see the fiend-like passions, the terrific convulsions, which are roused in a child's soul by the irritation and degradation of such correction, he would shrink back appalled. With sensitive children left in the hands of stolid and unsympathizing force, such convulsions and mental agonies often are the beginning of a sort of slow moral insanity which gradually destroys all that is good in the soul. Such was the danger now hanging over the hapless little one whom a dying mother had left to God. Is there no stirring among the angel wings on her behalf?

As the child lay sobbing in a little convulsed heap in her bed, a hard, horny hand put back the curtain of the window, and the child felt something thrown on the bed. It was Sol, who, on coming in to his supper, had heard from Miss Asphyxia the whole story, and who, as a matter of course, sympathized entirely with the child. He had contrived to slip a doughnut into his pocket, when his hostess was looking the other way. When the child rose up in the bed and showed her swelled and tear-stained face, Sol whispered: "There's a doughnut I saved for ye. Darn her pictur'! Don't dare say a word, ye know. She'll hear me."

"O Sol, can't you get Harry to come here and see me?" said the child, in an earnest whisper.

"Yes, I'll get him, if I have to go to thunder for 't," said Sol. "You jest lie down now, there's a good girl, and I'll work it, — ye see if I don't. To-morrow I'll make her go off to the store, and I'll get him down here, you see if I don't. It's a tarnal shame; that 'ere critter ain't got no more bowels than a file."

The child, however, was comforted, and actually went to sleep hugging the doughnut. She felt as if she loved Sol, and said so to the doughnut many times, — although he had great horny fists, and eyes like oxen. With these, he had a heart in his bosom, and the child loved him.

CHAPTER XII

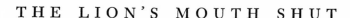

THE LION'S MOUTH SHUT

"Now, where a plague is that boy?" said Old Crab, suddenly bearing down, as evil-disposed people are always apt to do, in a most unforeseen moment.

The fact was that there had been a silent conspiracy among Sol and Goody Smith and the hired men of Old Crab, to bring about a meeting between the children. Miss Asphyxia had been got to the country store and kept busy with various bargains which Sol had suggested, and Old Crab had been induced to go to mill, and then the boy had been sent by Goody Smith on an errand to Miss Asphyxia's house. Of course he was not to find her at home, and was to stay and see his sister, and be sure and be back again by four o'clock.

"Where a plague is that lazy shote of a boy?" he repeated.

"What, Harry?"

"Yes, Harry. Who do you suppose I mean? Harry, — where is he?"

"O, I sent him up to Sphyxy's."

"*You* sent him?" said Old Crab, with that kind of tone which sounds so much like a blow that one dodges one's head involuntarily. "*You* sent him? What business *you* got interfering in the work?"

"Lord massy, father, I jest wanted Sphyxy's cards and some o' that 'ere fillin' she promised to give me. He won't be gone long."

Old Crab stood at this disadvantage in his fits of ill-temper with his wife, that there was no form of evil language or abuse that he had not tried so many times on her that it was quite a matter of course for her to hear it. He had used up the English language, — made it, in fact, absolutely of no effect, — while his fund of ill-temper was, after all, but half expressed.

"You've begun with that 'ere boy just as you allers did with all your own, gettin' 'em to be a waitin' round on you, — jest 'cause you're a lazy good-for-nothin'. We're so rich, I wonder you don't hire a waiter for nothin' but to stan' behind your chair. I'll teach him who his master is when he comes back."

"Now, father, 't ain't no fault o' his'n. *I* sent him."

"And *I* sot him to work in the fields, and I'd like to know if he's goin' to leave what I set him to do, and go round after your errands. Here 'tis gettin' to be 'most five o'clock, and the critters want fodderin', and that 'ere boy a dancing 'tendance on you. But he ain't a doin' that. He's jest off a berryin' or suthin' with that trollopin' sister o' his'n, — jes' what you bring on us, takin' in trampers. That 'ere gal, she pesters Sphyxy half to death."

"Sphyxy's pretty capable of takin' care of herself," said Goody Smith, still keeping busy with her knitting, but looking uneasily up the road, where the form of the boy might be expected to appear.

The outbreak that she had long feared of her husband's evil nature was at hand. She knew it by as many signs as one foretells the approach of hurricanes or rain-storms. She knew it by the evil gleam in his small, gray eyes, — by the impatient pacing backward and forward in the veranda, like a caged wild animal. It made little matter to him what the occasion was: he had such a superfluity of evil temper to vent, that one thing for his purpose was about as good as another.

It grew later and later, and Old Crab went to the barn to attend to his cattle, and the poor little old woman knitted uneasily.

"What could 'a' kep' him?" she thought. "He can't 'a' run off." There was a sudden gleam of mingled pleasure and pain in the old woman's heart as this idea darted through her mind. "I shouldn't wonder if he would, but I kind o' hate to part with him."

At last she sees him coming along the road, and runs to meet him. "How could you be so late? He's drefful mad with ye."

"I didn't know how late it was. Besides, all I could do, Tina would follow me, and I had to turn back and carry her home. Tina has bad times there. That woman isn't kind to her."

"No, dear, she ain't noways kind," said the old woman; "it ain't Sphyxy's way to be kind; but she'll do middlin' well by her, — anyway, she won't let nobody hurt her but herself. It's a hard world to live in; we have to take it as 't comes."

"Well, anyway," said the boy, "they *must* let us go to see each other. It isn't right to keep us apart."

"No, 't ain't, dear; but lordy massy, what can ye do?"

There was a great steady tear in the boy's large, blue eyes as he stopped at the porch, and he gave a sort of dreary shiver.

"Halleoah you there! you lazy little cuss," said Old Crab, coming from the barn, "where you been idling all the afternoon?"

"I've been seeing my sister," said the boy, steadily.

"Thought so. Where's them cards and the fillin' you was sent for?"

"There wasn't anybody at home to get them."

"And why didn't you come right back, you little varmint?"

"Because I wanted to see Tina. She's my sister; and my mother told me to take care of her; and it's wicked to keep us apart so."

"Don't you give me none of yer saace," said Old Crab, seizing the boy by one ear, to which he gave a vicious wrench.

"Let me alone," said the boy, flushing up with the sudden irritation of pain and the bitter sense of injustice.

"Let you alone? I guess I won't; talking saace to me that 'ere way. Guess I'll show you who's master. It's time you was walked off down to the barn, sir, and find out who's your master," he said, as he seized the boy by the collar and drew him off.

"O Lord!" said the woman, running out and stretching her hands instinctively after them. "Father, do let the boy alone."

She could not help this cry any more than a bird can help a shriek when she sees the hawk pouncing down on her nest, though she knew perfectly well that she might as well have shouted a petition in the angry face of the northeast wind.

"Take off your jacket," said Old Crab, as soon as he had helped himself to a long cart-whip which stood there.

The boy belonged to that class of amiable, good-natured children who are not easily irritated or often provoked, but who, when moved by a great injustice or cruelty, are thrown into convulsions of passion. The smallest and most insignificant animal, in moments of utter despair, when every fibre of its being is made vital with the energy of desperate resistance, often has a force which will make the strongest and boldest stand at bay. The boy retreated a pace or two, braced his back against the manger, while his whole form trembled and appeared to dilate, and it seemed as if blue streams of light glared from his eyes like sparks struck from burning steel.

"Strike me if you dare, you wicked, dreadful man," he shouted. "Don't you know that God sees you? God is my Father, and my mother is gone to God; and if you hurt me He'll punish you. You know I haven't done anything wrong, and God knows it. Now strike me if you dare."

The sight of any human being in a singular and abnormal state has something appalling about it; and at this moment the child really appeared to Old Crab like something supernatural. He stood a moment looking at him, and then his eyes suddenly seemed fixed on something above and beyond him, for he gazed with a strange, frightened expression; and at last, pushing with his hands, called out, "Go along; get away, get away! I hain't touched him," and, turning, fled out of the barn.

He did not go to the house again, but to the village tavern, and, entering the bar-room with a sort of distraught air, called for a dram, and passed the evening in a cowering state of quiet in the corner, which was remarked on by many as singular.

The boy came back into the house.

"Massy to us, child," said the old woman, "I thought he'd half killed ye."

"No, he hasn't touched me. God wouldn't let him," said the boy.

"Well, I declare for 't! he must have sent the angels that shut the lion's mouth when Daniel was in the den," said the woman. "I wouldn't 'a' had him struck ye, not for ten dollars."

The moon was now rising, large, white, and silvery, yet with a sort of tremulous, rosy flush, as it came up in the girdle of a burning autumn horizon. The boy stood a moment looking at it. His eyes were still dilated with that unnatural light, and his little breast heaving with waves of passion not yet tranquillized.

"Which way did he go?" said the woman.

"Up the road," said the boy.

"To the tavern," said the woman. "He's been there before this afternoon. At any rate, then, he'll let us alone awhile. There comes the men home to supper. Come in; I've got a turnover I made a purpose for ye."

"No, I must bid you good by, now," said the boy. "I can't stay here any longer."

"Why, where be ye going?"

"Going to look for a better place, where I can take care of Tina," said the boy.

"Ye ain't a going to leave me?" said the old woman. "Yet I can't want ye to stay. *I* can't have nothin' nor nobody."

"I'll come back one of these days," said the boy cheerfully, — "come and see you."

"Stay and get your supper, anyhow," pleaded the old woman. "I hate ter have ye go, drefful bad."

"I don't want any supper," said the child; "but if you'll give me a little basket of things, — I want 'em for Tina."

The old soul ran to her buttery, and crammed a small splint basket with turnovers, doughnuts, and ample slices of rye bread and butter, and the boy took it and trudged off, just as the hired men were coming home.

"Hulloah, bub!" shouted they, "where ye goin'?"

"Going to seek my fortune," said the boy cheerfully.

"Jest the way they all go," said the old woman.

"Where do you suppose the young un'll fetch up?" said one of the men to the other.

"No business of mine, — can't fetch up wus than he has ben a doin'."

"Old Crab a cuttin' up one of his shines, I s'pose?" said the other, interrogatively.

"Shouldn't wonder; 'bout time, — ben to the tavern this arternoon, I reckon."

The boy walked along the rough stony road towards Miss Asphyxia's farm. It was a warm, mellow evening in October. The air had only a pleasant coolness. Everything was tender and bright. A clump of hickory-trees on a rocky eminence before him stood like pillars of glowing gold in the twilight; one by one little stars looked out, winking and twinkling at the lonely child, as it seemed to him, with a friendly, encouraging ray, like his mother's eyes.

That afternoon he had spent trying to comfort his little sister, and put into her soul some of the childlike yet sedate patience with which he embraced his own lot, and the good hopes which he felt of being able some time to provide for her when he grew bigger. But he found nothing but feverish impatience, which all his eloquence could scarcely keep within bounds. He had, however,

arranged with her that he should come evenings after she had gone
to bed, and talk to her at the window of her bedroom, that she
should not be so lonesome nights. The perfectly demoniac violence
which Old Crab had shown this night had determined him not
to stay with him any longer. He would take his sister, and they
would wander off, a long, long way, till they came to better people,
and then he would try again to get work, and ask some good woman
to be kind to Tina. Such, in substance, was the plan that occurred
to the child; and accordingly that night, after little Tina had laid
her head on her lonely pillow, she heard a whispered call at her
window. The large, bright eyes opened very wide as she sat up in
bed and looked towards the window, where Harry's face appeared.

"It's me, Tina, — I've come back, — be very still. I'm going to
stay in the barn till everybody's asleep, and then I'll come and
wake you, and you get out of the window and come with me."

"To be sure I will, Harry. Let me come now, and sleep with you
in the barn."

"No, Tina, that wouldn't do; lie still. They'd see us. Wait till
everybody's asleep. You just lie down and go to sleep. I'll get in
at your window and waken you when it's time."

At this moment the door of the child's room was opened; the
boy's face was gone in an instant from the window. The child's
heart was beating like a trip-hammer; there was a tingling in her
ears; but she kept her little eyes tightly shut.

"O, here's that brown towel I gin her to hem," said Miss Asphyxia, peacefully. "She's done her stent this afternoon. That 'ere
whipping did some good."

"You'll never whip me again," thought the defiant little heart
under the bedclothes.

＊   ＊   ＊   ＊   ＊

Old Crab came home that night thoroughly drunk, — a thing
that did not very often occur in his experience. He commonly
took only just enough to keep himself in a hyena's state of temper, but not enough to dull the edge of his cautious, grasping,
money-saving faculties. But to-night he had had an experience
that had frightened him, and driven him to deeper excess as a
refuge from thought.

When the boy, upon whom he was meaning to wreak his diabolic passions, so suddenly turned upon him in the electric fury of enkindled passion, there was a sort of jar or vibration of the nervous element in the man's nature, that brought about a result not uncommon to men of his habits. As he was looking in a sort of stunned, stupid wonder at the boy, where he stood braced against the manger, he afterwards declared that he saw suddenly in the dark space above it, hovering in the air, the exact figure and form of the dead woman whom they had buried in the grave-yard only a few weeks before. "Her eyes was looking right at me, like live coals," he said; "and she had up her hand as if she'd 'a' struck me; and I grew all over cold as a stone."

"What do you suppose 't was?" said his auditor.

"How should I know," said Old Crab. "But there I was; and that very night the young'un ran off. I wouldn't have tried to get him back, not for my right hand, I tell you. Tell you what," he added, rolling a quid of tobacco reflectively in his mouth, "I don't like dead folks. Ef dead folks'll let me alone, I'll let them alone. That 'ere's fair, ain't it?"

CHAPTER XIII

THE EMPTY BIRD'S-NEST

The next morning showed as brilliant a getting up of gold and purple as ever belonged to the toilet of a morning. There was to be seen from Miss Asphyxia's bedroom window a brave sight, if there had been any eyes to enjoy it, — a range of rocky cliffs with little pin-feathers of black pine upon them, and behind them the sky all aflame with bars of massy light, — orange and crimson and burning gold, — and long, bright rays, darting hither and thither, touched now the window of a farm-house, which seemed to kindle and flash back a morning salutation; now they hit a tall scarlet maple, and now they pierced between clumps of pine, making their black edges flame with gold; and over all, in the brightening sky, stood the morning star, like a great, tremulous tear of light, just ready to fall on a darkened world.

Not a bit of all this saw Miss Asphyxia, though she had looked straight out at it. Her eyes and the eyes of the cow, who, with her horned front, was serenely gazing out of the barn window on the same prospect, were equally unreceptive.

She looked at all this solemn pomp of gold and purple, and the mysterious star, and only said: "Good day for killin' the hog, and I must be up gettin' on the brass kettle. I should like to know why Sol ain't been a stirrin' an hour ago. I'd really like to know how long folks *would* sleep ef I'd let 'em."

Here an indistinct vision came into Miss Asphyxia's mind of what the world would be without her to keep it in order. She called aloud to her prime minister, who slept in the loft above, "Sol! Sol! You awake?"

"Guess I be," said Sol; and a thundering sound of cowhide boots on the stairs announced that Sol's matutinal toilet was complete.

"We're late this morning," said Miss Asphyxia, in a tone of virtuous indignation.

"Never knowed the time when we wa'n't late," said Sol, composedly.

"You thump on that 'ere child's door, and tell her to be lively," said Miss Asphyxia.

"Yaas'm, I will," said Sol, while secretly he was indulging in a long and low chuckle, for Sol had been party to the fact that the nest of that young bird had been for many hours forsaken. He had instructed the boy what road to take, and bade him "walk spry and he would be out of the parish of Needmore afore daybreak. Walk on, then, and follow the road along the river," said Sol, "and it'll bring you to Oldtown, where our folks be. You can't miss your victuals and drink any day in Oldtown, call at what house you may; and ef you's to get into Deacon Badger's, why, your fortin's made. The Deacon he's a soft-spoken man to everybody, — white folks, niggers, and Indians, — and Ma'am Badger keeps regular poor-man's tavern, and won't turn even a dog away that behaves himself. Ye couldn't light on wus than ye have lit on, — for Old Crab's possessed of a devil, everybody knows; and as for Miss Asphyxia, she's one of the kind of sperits that goes walkin' through dry places seekin' rest and findin' none. Lordy massy, an old gal like her ain't nobody to bring up a child. It takes a woman that's got juice in her to do that. Why, that 'ere crittur's drier 'n a two-year-old mullen-stalk. There ain't no sap ris in her these 'ere thirty years. She means well; but, lordy, you might jest as well give young turkey chicks to the old gobbler, and let him stram off in the mowin' grass with 'em, as give a delicate little gal like your sister to her to raise; so you jest go long and keep up your courage, like a brave boy as ye be, and you'll come to somethin' by daylight"; — and Sol added to these remarks a minced pie, with a rye crust of a peculiarly solid texture, adapted to resist any of the incidents of time and travel, which pie had been set out as part of his own last night's supper.

When, therefore, he was exhorted to rap on the little girl's door, he gave sundry noisy, gleeful thumps, — pounding with both fists, and alternating with a rhythmical kick of the cowhide boots, calling out in stentorian tones: "Come, little un, — time you's up. Miss Sphyxy's comin' down on ye. Better be lively! Bless me, how the gal sleeps!"

"Don't take the door off the hinges," said Miss Asphyxia, sweeping down stairs. "Let me come; I'll wake her, I guess!" and with a dipper of cold water in her hand, Miss Asphyxia burst into the little room. "What! — what! — where!" she said, looking under the bed, and over and around, with a dazed expression. "What's this mean? Do tell if the child's re'lly for once got up of herself afore I called her. Sol, see if she's out pickin' up chips!"

Sol opened the door and gazed out with well-affected stolidity at the wood-pile, which, garnished with a goodly show of large chips, was now being touched up and brightened by the first rays of the morning sun.

"Ain't here," he said.

"Ain't here? Why, where can she be then? There ain't nobody swallowed her, I s'pose; and if anybody's run off with her in the night, I guess they'd bring her back by daylight."

"She must 'a' run off," said Sol.

"Run! Where could she 'a' run to?"

"Mebbe she's gone to her brother's."

"I bet you," said Miss Asphyxia, "it's that 'ere boy that's the bottom of it all. You may always know that there's a boy at the bottom, when there's any deviltry up. He was here yesterday, — now wa'n't he?"

"Wal, I reckon he was," said Sol. "But, massy, Miss Sphyxy, ef the pigs is to be killed to-day, we can't stan' a talkin' about what you nor me can't help. Ef the child's gone, why she's somewhere in the Lord's world, and it's likely she'll keep, — she won't melt away like the manna in the wilderness; and when the pigs is killed, and the pork salted down and got out o' the way, it'll be time enough to think o' lookin' on her up. She wa'n't no gret actual use, — and with kettles o' hot water round, it's jest as well not to have a child under yer feet. Ef she got scalded, why, there's your time a taking care on her, and mebbe a doctor to pay; so it's jest as well that things be as they be. *I* call it kind o' providential," said Sol, giving a hoist to his breeches by means of a tug at his suspenders, which gesture was his usual indication that he was girding up the loins of his mind for an immediate piece of work; and, turning forthwith, he brought in a mighty armful of wood, with massive back-log and fore-stick, well grizzled and bearded with the moss that showed that they were but yesterday living children of the forest.

The fire soon leaped and crackled and roared, being well fed with choice split hickory sticks of last year, of which Sol kept ample store; and very soon the big brass kettle was swung over, upon the old iron crane, and the sacrificial water was beginning to simmer briskly, while Miss Asphyxia prepared breakfast, not only for herself and Sol, but for Primus King, a vigorous old negro, famed as a sort of high-priest in all manner of butchering operations for miles around. Primus lived in the debatable land between Oldtown and Needmore, and so was at the call of all who needed an extra hand in both parishes.

The appearance of Primus at the gate in his butcher's frock, knife in hand, in fact put an end, in Miss Asphyxia's mind, to all thoughts apart from the present eventful crisis; and she hastened to place upon the table the steaming sausages which, with her usual despatch, had been put down for their morning meal. A mighty pitcher of cider flanked this savory dish, to which Primus rolled delighted eyes at the moment of sitting down. The time had not yet dawned, in those simple, old New England days, when the black skin of the African was held to disqualify him from a seat at the social board with the men whom he joined in daily labor. The strength of the arm, and the skill of the hand, and the willingness of the mind of the workman, in those days, were his passport to equal social rights; and old Primus took rank, in the butchering season, as in fact a sort of leader and commander. His word was law upon all steps and stages of those operations which should transform the plethoric, obese inhabitants of the sty into barrels of pink-hued salt-pork, or savory hams and tenderloins and spareribs, or immense messes of sausage-meat.

Concerning all these matters, Primus was an oracle. His fervid Ethiopian nature glowed with a broad and visible delight, his black face waxed luminous with the oil of gladness, while he dwelt on the savory subject, whereon, sitting at breakfast, he dilated with an unctuous satisfaction that soothed the raven down of darkness in Miss Asphyxia's perturbed mind, till something bearing a distant analogy to a smile played over her rugged features.

CHAPTER XIV

THE DAY IN FAIRY-LAND

Our little travellers, meanwhile, had had a prosperous journey along the rocky road between Needmore and Oldtown, in which Sol had planted their feet. There was a great, round-orbed, sober-eyed October moon in the sky, that made everything as light as day; and the children were alive in every nerve with the keen interest of their escape.

"We are going just as Hensel and Grettel did," said the little girl. "You are Hensel, and I am Grettel, and Miss Asphyxia is the old witch. I wish only we could have burnt her up in her old oven before we came away!"

"Now, Tina, you mustn't wish such things *really*," said the boy, somewhat shocked at such very extreme measures. "You see, what happens in stories wouldn't do *really* to happen."

"O, but Harry, you don't know how I *hate* — how I h—*ate* — Miss Sphyxy! I hate her — most as much as I love you!"

"But, Tina, mother always told us it was wicked to hate anybody. We must love our enemies."

"You don't love Old Crab Smith, do you?"

"No, I don't; but I try not to hate him," said the boy. "I won't think anything about him."

"I can't help thinking," said Tina; "and when I think, I am *so* angry! I feel such a burning in here!" she said, striking her little breast; "it's just like fire!"

"Then don't think about her at all," said the boy; "it isn't pleasant to feel that way. Think about the whippoorwills singing in the woods over there, — how plain they say it, don't they? — and the frogs, all singing, with their little, round, yellow eyes looking up out of the water; and the moon looking down on us so pleasantly! she seems just like mother!"

"O Harry, I'm so glad," said the girl, suddenly throwing herself on his neck and hugging him, — "I'm so glad we're together again! Wasn't it wicked to keep us apart, — we poor children?"

"Yes, Tina, I *am* glad," said the boy, with a steady, quiet, inward sort of light in his eyes; "but, baby, we can't stop to say so much, because we must walk fast and get way, way, way off before daylight; and you know Miss Sphyxy always gets up early, — don't she?"

"O dear, yes! She always poked me out of bed before it was light, — hateful old thing! Let's run as fast as we can, and get away!"

And with that she sprang forward, with a brisk and onward race, over the pebbly road, down a long hill, laughing as she went, and catching now at a branch of sweetbrier that overhung the road, and now at the tags of sweet-fern, both laden and hoary with heavy autumnal dews, till finally, her little foot tripping over a stone, she fell and grazed her arm sadly. Her brother lifted her up, and wiped the tears from her great, soft eyes with her blue check apron, and talked to her in that grandfatherly way that older children take such delight in when they feel the care of younger ones.

"Now, Tina, darling, you shouldn't run so wild. We'd better go pretty fast steadily, than run and fall down. But I'll kiss the place, as mother used to."

"I don't mind it, Hensel, — I don't mind it," she said, controlling the quivering of her little resolute mouth. "That scratch came for *liberty;* but this," she said, showing a long welt on her other arm, — "this was *slavery.* She struck me there with her great ugly stick. O, I never *can* forgive her!"

"Don't let's talk any more, baby; let's hurry on. She *never* shall get you again; I'll fight for you till I die, first!"

"You'd kill 'em all, wouldn't you? You would have knocked her down, wouldn't you?" said Tina, kindling up with that inconsiderate exultation in the powers of an elder brother which belongs to childhood. "I knew you would get me away from here, Harry, — I knew you would."

"But now," said Harry, "you just keep hold of my hand, and let's run together, and I'll hold you up. We must run fast, after all, because maybe they will harness up the wagon when daylight comes, and come out to look for us."

"Well, if it's only Sol comes," said the little girl, "I sha'n't care; for he would only carry us on farther."

"Ay, but you may be sure Miss Asphyxia would come herself."

The suggestion seemed too probable, and the two little pairs of heels seemed winged by it as they flew along, their long shadows dancing before them on the moonlit road, like spiritual conductors. They made such good headway that the hour which we have already recorded, when Miss Asphyxia's slumbers were broken, found the pair of tiny pilgrims five miles away on the road to Oldtown.

"Now, Tina," said the boy, as he stopped to watch the long bars of crimson and gold that seemed to be drawing back and opening in the eastern sky, where the sun was flaring upward an expectant blaze of glory, "only look there! Isn't it so wonderful? It's worth being out here only to see it. There! there! there! the sun is coming! Look! Only see that bright-red maple, — it seems all on fire! — now that yellow chestnut, and that old pine-tree! O, see, see those red leaves! They are like the story papa used to tell of the trees that bore rubies and emeralds. Aren't they beautiful?"

"Set me on the fence, so as I can see," said Tina. "O Harry, it's beautiful! And to think that we can see it together!"

Just at this moment they caught the distant sound of wheels.

"Hurry, Tina! Let me lift you over the fence," said the boy; "they are coming!"

How the little hearts beat, as both children jumped down into a thicket of sweet-fern, heavy and wet with morning dew! The lot was one of those confused jungles which one often sees hedging the course of rivers in New England. Groups of pine and hemlock grew here and there, intermixed with low patches of swampy land, which were waving with late wild-flowers and nodding swamp-grasses. The children tore their way through goldenrods, asters, and cat-tails to a little elevated spot where a great, flat rock was surrounded by a hedge of white-pine. This was precisely the shelter they wanted; for the pines grew so thickly around it as completely to screen it from sight from the road, while it was open to the warm beams of the morning sun.

"Cuddle down here, Tina," said Harry, in a whispering voice, as if he feared the driver in the rattling farm-wagon might hear them.

"O, what a nice little house the trees make here!" said Tina. "We are as snug here and as warm as can be; and only see what a nice white-and-green carpet there is all over the rock!"

The rock, to be sure, was all frothed over with a delicate white foam of moss, which, later in the day, would have crackled and broken in brittle powder under their footsteps, but which now, saturated by the heavy night-dews, only bent under them, a soft, elastic carpet.

Their fears were soon allayed when, peeping like scared partridges from their cover, they saw a farm-wagon go rattling by from the opposite direction to that in which Miss Asphyxia lived.

"O, it's nobody for us; it comes the other way," said the boy. It was, in fact, Primus King, going on his early way to preside over the solemnities of pig-killing.

"Then, Hensel, we are free," said the little girl; "nobody will catch us now. They could no more find us in this lot than they could find a little, little tiny pin in the hay-mow."

"No, indeed, Tina; we are safe now," said the boy.

"Why don't you call me Grettel? We will play be Hensel and Grettel; and who knows what luck will come to us?"

"Well, Grettel then," said the boy, obediently. "You sit now, and spread out your frock in the sun to dry, while I get out some breakfast for you. Old Aunty Smith has filled my basket with all sorts of good things."

"And nice old Sol, — he gave us his pie," said Tina. "I love Sol, though he is a funny-looking man. You ought to see Sol's hand, it's so big! And his feet, — why, one of his shoes would make a good boat for me! But he's a queer old dear, though, and I love him."

"What shall we eat first?" said the boy, — "the bread and butter, or the cookies, or the doughnuts, or the pie?"

"Let's try a little of all of them," said young madam.

"You know, Tina," said the boy, in a slow, considerate way, "that we must take care of this, because we don't know when we'll get any more. There's got to be a dinner and a supper got out of this at any rate."

"O, well, Hensel, you do just as you please with it, then; only let's begin with Sol's pie and some of that nice cheese, for I am so hungry! And then, when we have had our breakfast, I mean to lie down in the sun, and have a nap on this pretty white moss. O Harry, how pretty this moss is! There are bright little red things in it, as bright as mother's scarlet cloak. But, O Harry, look, quick! don't say a word! There's a squirrel! How bright his little eyes are! Let's give him some of our breakfast."

Harry broke off a crumb of cake and threw it to the little striped-backed stranger.

"Why, he's gone like a wink," said the girl. "Come back, little fellow; we sha'n't hurt you."

"O, hush, Tina, he's coming! I see his bright eyes. He's watching that bit of cake."

"There, he's got it and is off!" said Tina, with a shriek of delight. "See him race up that tree with it!"

"He's going to take it home to his wife."

"His wife!" said Tina, laughing so hard at Harry's wit that she was obliged to lay down her pie. "Has he got a wife?"

"Why, of course he has," said Harry, with superior wisdom.

"I'm *your* wife, ain't I?" said Tina, contentedly.

"No. You're my little sister, and I take care of you," said the boy. "But people can't have their sisters for wives; the Bible says so."

"Well, I can be just *like* your wife; and I'll mend your clothes and knit your stockings when I get bigger."

To which practical view of matrimonial duties Harry gave a grave assent.

Not a striped-backed squirrel, or a bobolink, or a cat-bird, in the whole pasture-lot, had better spirits than our two little travellers. They were free; they were together; the sun was shining and birds were singing; and as for the future, it was with them as with the birds. The boy, to be sure, had a share of forethought and care, and deemed himself a grown man acting with most serious responsibility for his light-headed little sister; but even in him this was only a half-awakening from the dream-land of child-hood.

When they had finished their breakfast, he bethought him of his morning prayers, and made Tina kneel down beside him while he repeated psalm and hymn and prayer, in which she joined with a very proper degree of attention. When he had finished, she said, "Do you know, Hensel, I haven't said my prayers a single once since I've been at Miss Asphyxia's?"

"Why, Tina!"

"Well, you see, there wasn't anybody to say them to, now mother is gone; and you were not there."

"But you say them to God, Tina."

"O, he's so far off, and I'm so little, I can't say them to him. I must say them to somebody I can see. Harry, where is mother gone?"

"She is gone to heaven, Tina."

"Where is heaven?"

"It's up in the sky, Tina," said the boy, looking up into the deep, cloudless blue of an October sky, which, to say the truth, is about as celestial a thing as a mortal child can look into; and as he looked, his great blue eyes grew large and serious with thoughts of his mother's last wonderful words.

"If it's up in the sky, why did they dig down into the ground, and put her in that hole?" said the little sceptic.

"It is her soul that went up. Her body is planted like a beautiful flower. She will come up by and by; and we shall see her again, if we are good children."

Tina lay back on the white moss, with only a fringy bough of white-pine between her and the deep, eternal blue, where the thinnest films of white clouds were slowly sailing to and fro. Her spiritual musings grew, to say the truth, rather confused. She was now very tired with her night tramp; and the long fringes fell over her great, dark eyes, as a flower shuts itself, and she was soon asleep.

The boy sat watching her awhile, feeling soothed by the calm, soft sunshine, and listening to the thousand sweet lullaby-notes which Nature is humming to herself, while about her great world-housework, in a calm October morning. The locusts and katydids grated a drowsy, continuous note to each other from every tree and bush; and from a neighboring thicket a lively-minded cat-bird was giving original variations and imitations of all sorts of bird voices and warblings; while from behind the tangled thicket which fringed its banks came the prattle of a hidden river, whose bright brown waters were gossiping, in a pleasant, constant chatter, with the many-colored stones on the bottom; and when the light breezes wandered hither and thither, as your idle breezes always will be doing, they made little tides and swishes of sound among the pine-trees, like the rising and falling of sunny waters on the sea-shore.

Altogether, it was not long before Harry's upright watch over his sister subsided into a droop upon one elbow, and finally the little curly head went suddenly down on to his sister's shoulder; and then they were fast asleep, — as nice a little pair of babes in the wood as ever the robins could cover up. They did not awake till it was almost noon. The sun was shining warm and cloudless, and every bit of dew had long been dried; and Tina, in refreshed spirits, proposed that they should explore the wonders of the pasture-lot, — especially that they should find out where the river was whose waters they heard gurgling behind the leafy wall of wild vines.

"We can leave our basket here in our little house, Hensel. See, I set it in here, way, way in among the pine-trees; and that's my little green closet."

So the children began picking their way through the thicket, guided by the sound of the water.

"O Tina!" said the boy; "look there, over your head!"

The object pointed out was a bough of a wild grape-vine, heavily laden with ripe purple grapes.

"O, wild grapes!" said Tina. "Harry, do get them!"

Harry soon pulled the bough down within reach, and the children began helping themselves.

"I'm going to take an apronful up to the tree, and put into our closet," said Tina; "and we shall have a nice store there."

"But, Tina, we can't live there on the rock," said the boy; "we must walk on and get to Oldtown some time."

"O, well, we have the whole long, long day for it," said the girl, "and we may as well have a good time now; so, when I've put up these grapes, we'll see where the river is."

A little scrambling and tearing through vines soon brought the children down to the banks of a broad, rather shallow river, whose waters were of that lustrous yellow-brown which makes every stone gleam up from the bottom in mellow colors, like the tints through the varnish of an old picture. The banks were a rampart

of shrubbery and trees hung with drapery of wild vines, now in
the brilliancy of autumnal coloring. It is not wonderful that exclamations of delight and wonder burst from both children. An
old hemlock that hung slantwise over the water opposite was
garlanded and interwoven, through all its dusky foliage, with
wreaths and pendants of the Virginia creeper, now burning in
the brilliant carmine and scarlet hues of autumn. Great, soft,
powdery clumps of golden-rod projected their heads from the
closely interwoven thicket, and leaned lovingly over the stream,
while the royal purple of tall asters was displayed in bending
plumage at their side. Here and there, a swamp-maple seemed
all one crimson flame; while greener shrubbery and trees, yet un-
touched by frosts, rose up around it, as if purposely to give background and relief to so much color. The rippling surface of the
waters, as they dashed here and there over the stones, gave back
colored flashes from the red, yellow, crimson, purple, and green
of the banks; while ever and anon little bright leaves came sailing
down the stream, all moist and brilliant, like so many floating gems.
The children clapped their hands, and began, with sticks, fishing
them towards the shore. "These are our little boats," they said. So
they were, — fairy boats, coming from the land of nowhere, and
going on to oblivion, shining and fanciful, like the little ones that
played with them.

"I declare," said Tina, "I mean to take off my shoes and stockings, and wade out to that little island where those pretty white
stones are. You go with me."

"Well, Tina, wait till I can hold you."

And soon both the little pairs of white feet were slipping and
spattering among the pebbles at the bottom. On the way, Tina
made many efforts to entrap the bright rings of sunlight on the
bottom, regardless of the logic with which Harry undertook to
prove to her that it was nothing but the light, and that she could
not catch it; and when they came to the little white gravelly bank,
they sat down and looked around them with great content.

"We're on a desolate island, aren't we, Hensel?" said Tina. "I
like desolate islands," she added, looking around her, with the
air of one who had had a wide experience of the article. "The
banks here are so high, and the bushes so thick, that Miss As-

phyxia could not find us if she were to try. We'll make our home here."

"Well, I think, Tina, darling, that it won't do for us to stay here very long," said Harry. "We must try to get to some place where I can find something to do, and some good, kind woman to take care of you."

"O Harry, what's the use of thinking of that, — it's so bright and pleasant, and it's so long since I've had you to play with! Do let's have one good, pleasant day alone among the flowers! See how beautiful everything is!" she added, "and it's so warm and quiet and still, and all the birds and squirrels and butterflies are having such a good time. I don't want anything better than to play about out in the woods with you."

"But where shall we sleep nights, Tina?"

"O, it was so pleasant last night, and the moon shone so bright, I would not be afraid to cuddle down under a bush with you, Harry."

"Ah, Tina! you don't know what may come. The moon don't shine all night, and there may be cold and wind and rain, and then where would we be? Come, darling, let's go on; we can walk in the fields by the river, and so get down to the place Sol told us about."

So at last the little fanciful body was persuaded to wade back from her desolate island, and to set out once more on her pilgrimage. But even an older head than hers might have been turned by the delights of that glorious October day, and gone off into a vague trance of bliss, in which the only good of life seemed to be in luxurious lounging and dreamy enjoyment of the passing hour. Nature in New England is, for the most part, a sharp, determined matron, of the Miss Asphyxia school. She is shrewd, keen, relentless, energetic. She runs through the seasons a merciless express-train, on which you may jump if you can, at her hours, but which knocks you down remorselessly if you come in her way, and leaves you hopelessly behind if you are late. Only for a few brief weeks in the autumn does this grim, belligerent female condescend to be charming; but when she does set about it, the veriest Circe of enchanted isles could not do it better. Airs more dreamy, more hazy, more full of purple light and lustre, never lay over Cyprus or

Capri than those which each October overshadow the granite rocks and prickly chestnuts of New England. The trees seem to run no longer sap, but some strange liquid glow; the colors of the flowers flame up, from the cold, pallid delicacy of spring, into royal tints wrought of the very fire of the sun and the hues of evening clouds. The humblest weed, which we trod under our foot unnoticed in summer, changes with the first frost into some colored marvel, and lifts itself up into a study for a painter, — just as the touch of death or adversity often strikes out in a rough nature traits of nobleness and delicacy before wholly undreamed of.

The children travelled onward along the winding course of the river, through a prairie-land of wild-flowers. The whole tribe of asters — white, lilac, pale blue, and royal purple — were rolling in perfect billows of blossoms around them, and the sprays of golden-rod often rose above their heads, as they crackled their way through the many-colored thickets. The children were both endowed with an organization exquisitely susceptible to beauty, and the flowers seemed to intoxicate them with their variety and brilliancy. They kept gathering from right to left without any other object than the possession of a newer and fairer spray, till their little arms were full; and then they would lay them down to select from the mass the choicest, which awhile after would be again thrown by for newer and fairer treasures. Their motion through the bushes often disturbed clouds of yellow butterflies, which had been hanging on the fringes of the tall purple asters, and which rose toying with each other, and fluttering in ethereal dances against the blue sky, looking like whirls and eddies of air-flowers. One of the most brilliant incidents in the many-colored pictures of October days is given by these fluttering caprices of the butterflies. Never in any other part of the season are these airy tribes so many and so brilliant. There are, in particular, whole armies of small, bright yellow ones, which seem born for no other purpose than to make effective and brilliant contrasts with those royal-purple tints of asters, and they hang upon them as if drawn to them by some law of affinity in their contrasting colors.

Tina was peculiarly enchanted with the fanciful fellowship of these butterflies. They realized exactly her ideal of existence, and she pointed them out to Harry as proof positive that her own notion of living on sunshine and flowers was not a bad one. She was quite sure that they could sleep out all night if the butterflies could, and seemed not to doubt that they would fancy her as a bedfellow.

Towards sundown, when the children were somewhat weary of wandering, and had consumed most of the provisions in their basket, they came suddenly on a little tent pitched in the field, at the door of which sat an old Indian woman weaving baskets. Two or three red-skinned children, of about the same age as our wanderers, were tumbling and kicking about on the ground, in high frolic, with about as many young puppies, who were scratching, rolling, and biting, with their human companions, in admirable spirits. There was a fire before the door, over which a pot was swung from a frame of crossed sticks, the odor of which steamed up, suggestive of good cheer.

The old Indian woman received the children with a broad, hearty grin, while Harry inquired of her how far it was to Oldtown. The old squaw gave it as her opinion, in very Indian English, that it was "muchee walkee" for little white boy, and that he had best stay with her that night and go on to-morrow.

"There, Harry," said Tina, "now you see just how it is. This is a nice little house for us to sleep in, and oh! I see such pretty baskets in it."

The old woman drew out a stock of her wares, from which she selected a small, gayly-painted one, which she gave to the children; in short, it was very soon arranged that they were to stop to supper and spend the night with her. The little Indians gathered around them and surveyed them with grins of delight; and the puppies, being in that state of ceaseless effervescence of animal spirits which marks the indiscreet era of puppyhood, soon had the whole little circle in a state of uproarious laughter.

By and by, the old woman poured the contents of the pot into a wooden trough, and disclosed a smoking mess of the Indian dish denominated succotash, — to wit, a soup of corn and beans, with a generous allowance of salt pork. Offering a large, clean clam-shell to each of the children, she invited them to help themselves.

Whether it was the exhilarating effect of a whole day spent on foot in the open air, or whether it was owing to the absolute perfection of the cookery, we cannot pretend to say, but certain it is that the children thought they had never tasted anything better; and Tina's spirits became so very airy and effervescent, that she laughed perpetually, — a state which set the young barbarians to laughing for sympathy; and this caused all the puppies to bark at once, which made more fun; so that, on the whole, a jollier supper company could nowhere be found.

After sundown, when the whole party had sufficiently fatigued themselves with play and laughing, the old woman spread a skin inside the tent, where Tina lay down contentedly between Harry and one of the puppies, which she insisted upon having as her own particular bedfellow. Harry kneeled down to his prayers outside the tent, which being observed by the Indian woman, she clasped her hands, and seemed to listen with great devotion; and when he had finished, she said, "Me praying Indian; me much love Jesus."

The words were said with a tender gleam over the rough, hard, swarthy features; and the child felt comforted by them as he nestled down to his repose.

"Harry," said Tina, decisively, "let's we live here. I like to play with the puppies, and the old woman is good to us."

"We'll see, Tina," said wise little Harry.

CHAPTER XV

———————◆———————

THE OLD MANOR-HOUSE

Alas! the next morning dawned wet and rainy. The wind flapped the tent-cover, and the rain put out the fire; and, what was worse, a cross, surly Indian man came home, who beat the poor old woman, and scattered the children and puppies, like partridges, into the bushes.

The poor old squaw took it all patiently, and seemed only intent on protecting the children from injuries and inconveniences on which she calculated as part of her daily lot. She beckoned them to her, and pointed across a field. "Go dat way. White folks dere be good to you." And she insisted on giving them the painted basket and some coarse corn bread.

They set off through the fields; but the wind was chilly and piercing, and the bushes and grass were wet, and Tina was in a doleful state. "O Harry, I wish we had a house to live in! Where do you suppose all the butterflies are staying that we saw yesterday? I'd like to go where they stay."

"Never mind, Tina; by and by we'll come to a house."

They passed a spot where evidently some Indians had been camping, for there were the remains of a fire; and Harry picked up some dry brush and refuse sticks around, and kindled it up bright for Tina to warm and dry herself. They sat there awhile and fed the fire, till they began to feel quite warm. In one of Harry's excursions for sticks, he came back and reported a house in sight.

Sure enough, concealed from view behind a pine thicket was a large, stately mansion, the approach to which was through an avenue of majestic trees. The path to this was all grown over with high grass, and a wilderness of ornamental shrubbery seemed to have twined and matted itself together in a wild labyrinth of utter desertion and neglect. The children made their way up the avenue through dripping grass, and bushes that reached almost to their shoulders, and that drizzled water upon their partially dried garments in a way that made Tina shiver. "I'm so cold!" she said, pitifully. "The folks must let us come in to dry us."

They at last stood before the front door, in a sort of porch which overshadowed it, and which rested on Corinthian pillars of some architectural pretension. The knocker was a black serpent with its tail in its mouth. Tina shuddered with some vague, inward dread, as Harry, rising on tiptoe, struck several loud blows upon it, and then waited to see who would appear.

The wind now rose, and tossed and swung the branches of the great trees in the avenue with a creaking, groaning sound. The shrubbery had grown around the house in a dense and tangled mass, that produced, in the dismal stormy weather, a sense of oppression and darkness. Huge lilacs had climbed above the chamber windows, and clumps of syringas billowed outward from the house in dense cascades; while roses and various kinds of more tender shrubbery, which had been deprived of light and air by their more hardy neighbors, filled up the space below with bare, dead branches, through which the wind sighed dolefully.

"Harry, do knock again," said Tina, when they had waited some time.

"It's no use," said the boy; "I don't think anybody lives here."

"Perhaps, if we go round to the back of the house, we shall find somebody," said Tina; "it's storming worse and worse." And the little girl plunged resolutely into the thicket of dead shrubbery, and began tearing her way through.

There was a door on the side of the house, much like that in front; and there were spacious back buildings, which, joining the house, stretched far away in the shrubbery. Harry tried this side door. It was firmly locked. The children then began regularly trying every door that presented itself to their view. At last one, after considerable effort, gave way before their united exertions, and opened to them a shelter from the storm, which was now driving harder and harder. It was a place that had evidently been used for the storing of wood, for there was then quite a pile of fuel systematically arranged against the wall. An ancient axe, perfectly red with rust, was also hanging there.

"Well, we're in at last," said Tina, "but wet through. What a storm it is!"

"Perhaps we can get to some better place in the house," said Harry; "here is wood, and we might make a fire and dry our clothes, and wait here till the storm is over."

He accordingly pushed against a door at the farther end of the wood-shed, and it opened before him into a large old kitchen. There was the ample fireplace of olden times, extending quite across one side, garnished with a crane having various hooks and other paraphernalia for the convenience of culinary operations.

"There, now," said Harry, "is a fireplace, and here is wood. Now we can dry ourselves. Just you wait here, and I'll go back and bring a brand from our fire, if the rain hasn't put it all out." And Harry turned, and hastily made the best of his way out of the house, to secure his treasure before it should be too late.

Tina now resolved to explore some of the other rooms. She opened a door which seemed to lead into a large dining-hall. A heavy dining-table of dark wood stood in the middle of this room, and a large, old-fashioned carved sideboard filled up an arched recess. Heavy mahogany chairs with stuffed leathern bottoms stood against the wall, but the brass nails with which they had been finished were green with rust. The windows of this room were so matted over with cobwebs, and so darkened by the dense shrub-bery outside, as to give the apartment a most weird and forlorn appearance. One of the panes of the window had been broken, perhaps by the striking of the shrubbery against it; and the rain and snow beating in there had ruined the chair that stood below, for the seat of it was all discolored with mould.

Tina shivered as she looked at this dreary room, and the tap-ping of her own little heels seemed to her like something ghostly; so she hastened to open another door. This led to a small apart-ment, which had evidently been a lady's boudoir. The walls were hung with tapestry of a dark-green ground, on which flowers and fruits and birds were represented in colors that yet remained brilliant, notwithstanding the dilapidated air of some portions of it. There was a fireplace in this room, and the mantel was choicely carved, of white Italian marble, and upon it were sundry flasks and vases of Venetian glass, of quaint and strange shapes, which the child eyed with awe-struck curiosity. By the side of the fire-place was a broad lounge or sofa, with a pile of cushions, covered with a rich but faded brocade, of a pattern evidently made to carry out the same design with the tapestry on the wall.

A harpsichord occupied another side of the room, and upon it were piled music-books and manuscript music yellow with age. There was a sort of Oriental guitar or lute suspended from the wall, of which one of the strings, being broken, vibrated with the air of the door when the child made her way into the room, and continued quivering in a way that seemed to her nervous and ghostly. Still she was a resolute and enterprising little body; and though her heart was beating at a terrible rate, she felt a sort of mixture of gratified curiosity and exultation in her discovery.

"I wish Harry would come back," she said to herself. "We might make a fire in this pretty little room, and it would be quite snug, and we could wait here till the folks come home." How glad she was when the sound of his voice and footsteps broke the terrible loneliness! She ran out to him, exclaiming, "O Harry, we won't make a fire in this great, doleful old kitchen. I've found such a nice little room full of pretty things! Let me bring in some wood"; — and, running to the wood-pile, she filled her arms.

"It was all I could do to find a brand with a bit of fire on it," said Harry. "There was only the least spark left, but I put it under my jacket and blew and blew, and now we have quite a bright spot in it," he said, showing with exultation a black brand with a round, fiery eye in it, which had much the appearance of a knowing old goblin winking at the children.

The desolate boudoir was soon a scene of much animation, as the marble hearth was strewn with chips and splinters.

"Let me blow, Harry," said Tina, "while you go and look for some more of this brushwood. I saw a heap in that wood-house. I'll tend the fire while you are gone. See," she said triumphantly to him, when he returned, dragging in a heavy pile of brushwood, "we'll soon have such a fire!" — and she stooped down over the hearth, laying the burnt ends of sticks together, and blowing till her cheeks were so aflame with zeal and exertion that she looked like a little live coal herself. "Now for it!" she said, as she broke bit after bit of the brushwood. "See now, it's beginning to burn, — hear it crackle! Now put on more and more."

Very soon, in fact, the brushwood crackled and roared in a wide sheet of flame up the old chimney; and being now reinforced with stout sticks of wood, the fire took a solid and settled and companionable form, — the brightest, most hopeful companion a mortal could ask for in a chill, stormy day in autumn.

"Now, Harry," said Tina, "let's dry our clothes, and then we will see what we can do in our house."

"But is it really ours?" said thoughtful Harry. "Who knows who it may belong to?"

"Do you think," said Tina, apprehensively, "that any giant lives here that has gone out and will come home again? Father used to tell us a story like that."

"There aren't really giants now-a-days, Tina," said Harry; "those are only stories. I don't think that it looks as if anybody had lived here for a great while. Things don't look as if anybody lived here, or was expecting to come back."

"Then we may as well live here as anybody," said Tina, "and I will keep house for you. I will roast some apples for our dinner, — I saw ever so many out here on the tree. Roast apples with our corn bread will be so good! And then we can sleep to-night on this great, wide sofa, — can't we? Here, let me sweep up the chips we have made, and make our little house look nice."

"It must be a long time since any one has lived here," said Harry, looking up at the cobwebbed window, against which the shrubbery was dashing and beating in the fury of the storm, "and there can't be the least harm in our staying here till the storm is over."

"Such a strange, pretty room this is!" said Tina, "and so many strange, pretty things in it! Do you know, Harry, I was almost afraid to be here while you were gone; but this bright, warm fire makes such a difference. Fire is company, isn't it?"

When the little one had dried her clothes, she began, with a restless, butterfly sort of motion, to investigate more closely the various objects of the apartment. She opened the harpsichord, and struck a few notes, which sounded rather discordantly, as an instrument which chill and solitude had smitten with a lasting hoarseness.

"O, horrid! This isn't pretty," she said. "I wonder who ever played on it? But, O Harry! come and look here! I thought this was another room in here, with a fire in it," she said, as she lifted a curtain which hung over a recess. "Look! it's only looking-glass in a door. Where does it go to? Let's see." And with eager curiosity she turned the knob, and the door opened, disclosing only a sort of inner closet, which had been evidently employed for a writing-cabinet, as a writing-table stood there, and book-cases filled with books.

What most attracted the attention of the children was a picture, which was hung exactly opposite the door, so that it met the children face to face. It was the image of a young girl, dressed in white, with long, black, curling hair falling down over her neck and shoulders. The dark eyes had an expression both searching and melancholy; and it was painted in that peculiar manner, which produces such weird effects on the beholder, in which the eyes seem to be fixed upon the spectator, and to follow him on whichever side he stands.

"What a pretty lady! But she looks at us so!" said Tina, covering her eyes. "I almost thought it was a real woman."

"Whichever way me move, she looks after us," said Harry.

"She looks as if she would speak to us," said Tina; "she surely wants to say something."

"It is something very sad, then," said the boy, studying the picture attentively. "She was not sad as mother was," said he, with a delicate, spiritual instinct reading the impression of the face. "Mother used to look very, very sad, but in a different way, — a better way, I think."

"Of course it isn't in the least like mother," said Tina. "Mother had soft, bright hair, — not black, like this; and her eyes were blue, like yours, Harry."

"I don't mean her hair or her eyes," said Harry; "but when mother was sad, she always used to pray. I don't think this one looks as if she would pray," said the boy, rather under his breath.

There was, in fact, a lurking sparkle of haughty determination in the depths of the mournful eyes, and a firm curve to the lines of the mouth, an arching of the neck, and a proud carriage of the head, that confirmed the boy's strictures, and indicated that, whatever sorrows might have crushed the poor heart that beat beneath that fair form, they were borne in her own strength, with no up-looking for aid.

Tina longed to open the drawers of the cabinet beneath the picture, but Harry held her hand. "Tina, dear, what would mother say?" he said, reprovingly. "This isn't our house. Whoever owns it wouldn't think it was wrong for us to stay here in such a storm, but we certainly ought not to touch their things."

"But we may go through the house, and see all the rooms," said Tina, who had a genuine feminine passion for rummaging, and whose curiosity was piqued to the extreme point by the discoveries already made. "I shall be afraid to sleep here to-night, unless I know all that is in the house."

So the children went, hand in hand, through the various apartments. The house was one of those stately manors which, before the Revolutionary war, the titled aristocracy of England delighted to reproduce on the virgin soil of America. Even to this modern time, some of the old provincial towns in New England preserve one or two of these monuments of the pride and pomp of old colonial days, when America was one of the antechambers of the English throne and aristocracy.

The histories of these old houses, if searched into, present many romantic incidents, in which truth may seem wilder than fiction. In the breaking of the ties between the mother country and America, many of these stately establishments were suddenly broken up, and the property, being subject to governmental claims yet undecided, lay a long time unoccupied; the real claimants being in England, and their possessions going through all the processes of deterioration and decay incident to property in the hands of agents at a distance from the real owners. The moss of legend and tradition grew upon these deserted houses. Life in New England, in those days, had not the thousand stimulants to the love of excitement which are to be found in the throng and rush of modern society, and there was a great deal more of story-telling and romancing in real life than exists now; and the simple villagers by their firesides delighted to plunge into the fathomless abyss of incident that came from the histories of grand, unknown people across the water, who had established this incidental connection with their neighborhood. They exaggerated the records of the pomp and wealth that had environed them. They had thrilling legends of romantic and often tragic incidents, of which such houses had been the theatres. More than one of them had its well-attested ghosts, which, at all proper hours, had been veritably seen to go through all those aimless ghostly perambulations and performances which, according to village legends, diversify the leisure of the spiritual state.

The house into which the children's wandering fortunes had led them was one whose legends and history formed the topic of many an excited hour of my childhood, as crooned over to me by different story-telling gossips; and it had, in its structure and arrangements, the evident impress of days nevermore to be reproduced in New England. Large and lofty apartments, some of them still hung with tapestry, and some adorned with arches and columns, were closed in from air and light by strong shutters, although a dusky glimmer came through the heart-shaped holes cut in them. Some of these apartments were quite dismantled and bare. In others the furniture was piled together in confusion, as if for the purpose of removal. One or two chambers were still thoroughly furnished, and bore the marks of having been, at some recent period, occupied; for there were mattresses and pillows and piles of bedclothing on the great, stately bedsteads.

"We might sleep in one of these rooms," said Harry.

"O, no, no!" said the child, clinging to him; "I should be afraid. That great, dreadful-looking, dark bed! And who knows what might be behind the curtains! Let me sleep in the bright little room, where we can see all around us. I should be afraid that lady in the closet would walk about these rooms in the night."

"Perhaps she did once," said Harry. "But come, let us go down. The wind blows and howls so about these lonesome rooms, it makes me afraid."

"How it rumbles down the chimneys!" said Tina; "and now it squeals just as if somebody was hurting it. It's a terrible storm, isn't it?"

"Yes, it's well we are in a house at any rate," said Harry; "but let's go down and bring in wood, and I'll get some apples and pears off the trees out by the back door."

And so the two poor little swallows chittered as they built their small, innocent nest in the deserted house, as ignorant of the great Before and After, as if they had had wings and feathers, and round, bright bird-eyes, instead of curly, golden heads. Harry brought in a quantity of fruit in Tina's little checked apron, and, like two squirrels, they stored it under the old brocade sofa.

"Now ever so much wood in the hall here," said Tina, with the providence of a little housewife; "because when the dark night comes we shall be afraid to go into the wood-house."

Harry felt very large and very provident, and quite like a householder, as he brought armful after armful and laid it outside the door, while Tina arranged some apples to roast on the marble hearth. "If we only could get something to eat every day, we might live here always," she said.

And so that evening, when the night shadows came down darkly on the house, though the storm without thundered and beat and groaned amid the branches of the old trees, and rumbled and shook the chimneys of the solitary manor-house, there was one nook that presented as bright and warm a picture as two fair child-faces, with a background of strange antique furniture and surroundings, could furnish. The fire had burned down into great splendid glowing coals, in which the children, seated before it on the tapestried hearth-rug, saw all sorts of strange faces. Tina had insisted on keeping open the door of the cabinet where the beautiful lady was, because, she said, she must be lonesome in that dark closet by herself.

"I wish she would only smile," she said, as the sharp spires of flame from a new stick of wood which she had just laid on, dancing up, made the face seem to become living and tremulous as if with emotion. "See, Hensel, she looks as if she were going to speak to us."

And hours later the fire still burned in the little boudoir; but the two pretty child-faces lay cheek to cheek in the wide, motherly arms of the sofa, and the shadowy lady seemed to watch over them silently from her lonely recess.

CHAPTER XVI

SAM LAWSON'S DISCOVERIES

The evening was closing in sharp and frosty, with a lowering of wind and cloud that rendered fire-light doubly dear and welcome, as we all drew our chairs round the great, glowing fire in my grandmother's kitchen. I had my little block of wood, which served as a footstool, far in the cavernous depths of one end of the fireplace, close by Black Cæsar, who was busy making me a popgun, while my grandmother sat at the other end in her rocking-chair, rattling her knitting-needles. Uncle Fly had just frisked in, and was perched, as was his wont, on the very tip of his chair, where he sat fussily warming and rubbing his hands, much as a meditative blue-bottle performs the same operation with his fore feet.

"So," said my grandmother to my grandfather, in reproachful tones, "you've gone and shut the calf up from its mother."

"To be sure," said my grandfather; "that was foreordained and freely predetermined."

"Well, I say it's a shame," sputtered my grandmother, — "poor creturs!"

It was a part of the farming ordinance, when the calf was fated to be killed, to separate it for a day from its mother, a proceeding which never failed to excite the indignation of my grandmother, which she expressed always with as much life and freshness as if she had never heard of such a matter before in her life. She was not, to be sure, precisely aware what was to be done about it; but in a general way she considered calf-killing as an abominable cruelty, and the parting of calf and cow for a day beforehand as an aggravation. My grandfather was fond of meeting her with a sly use of some of the Calvinistic theological terms which abounded in her favorite writers. The most considerate of husbands often enjoy any quiet method of giving a sly tweak to some cherished peculiarity of their yokefellows; and there was the least suggestion of a smile hovering over my grandfather's face, — which smile, in your quiet man, means two things, — first, that he is going to have his own way in spite of all you can say, and, secondly, that he is quietly amused by your opposition.

"I say it's a shame," quoth my grandmother, "and I always shall. Hear that poor cow low! She feels as bad as I should."

"Mother," said Aunt Lois, in an impatient tone, "I wonder that you can't learn to let things go on as they must. What would you have? We must have fresh meat sometimes, and you eat as much as any of us."

"I don't care, it's too bad," said my grandmother, "and I always shall think so. If I had things *my* way, folks shouldn't eat creatures at all."

"You'd be a Brahmin," said my grandfather.

"No, I shouldn't be a Brahmin, either; but I know an old cow's feelings, and I wouldn't torment her just to save myself a little trouble."

The conversation was here interrupted by the entrance of Sam Lawson, who came in with a long, lugubrious face, and an air of solemn, mysterious importance, which usually was the herald of some communication.

"Well, Sam," said my grandfather, "how are you?"

"Middlin', Deacon," said Sam, mournfully, — "only middlin'."

"Sit down, sit down," said my grandfather, "and tell us the news."

"Wal, I guess I will. How kind o' revivin' and cheerful it does look here," said Sam, seating himself in his usual attitude, with his hands over the fire. "Lordy massy, it's so different to our house! Hepsy hain't spoke a railly decent word to me since the gineral trainin'. You know, Deacon, Monday, a week ago, was gineral trainin' day over to Hopkinton, and Hepsy, she was set in the idee that I should take her and the young uns to muster. 'All right, Hepsy,' says I, 'ef I can borrow a hoss.' Wal, I walked and walked clean up to Captain Brown's to borrow a hoss, and I couldn't get none, and I walked clean down to Bill Peters's, and I couldn't get none. Finally, Ned Parker, he lent me his'n. Wal, to be sure, his hoss has got the spring-halt, that kind o' twitches up the waggin, and don't look so genteel as some; but, lordy massy, 't was all I could get. But Hepsy, she blamed me all the same. And then she was at me 'cause she hadn't got no gloves. Wal, I hadn't no gret o' change in my pocket, and I wanted to keep it for gingerbread and sich for the young uns, so I thought I'd jest borrow a pair for her, and say nothin'; and I went over and asked Mis' Captain Brown, and over to Mis' Dana's, and round to two or three places; and finally Lady Lothrop, she said she'd *give* me a old pair o' hern. And I brought 'em to Hepsy; and do you believe, she throwed 'em right smack in my face. 'S'pose I'm goin' to wear such an old dirty pair as that?' says she. Wal, arter all, we sot out, and Hepsy, she got clear beat out; and when Hepsy does get beat out she has *spells*, and she goes on awful, and they last day arter day. Hepsy's spells is jest like these 'ere northeast storms, — they never do railly clear off, but kind o' wear out, as 't were, — and this 'ere seems to be about one of her longest. She was at me this mornin' fust thing 'fore I was out o' bed, cryin' and goin' on, and castin' on it up at me the men she might 'a' hed if she hadn't 'a' hed me, and the things they'd 'a' done for her, jest as if 't was my fault. 'Lordy massy, Hepsy,' says I, 'I ain't t' blame. I wish with all my heart you hed 'a' hed any on 'em you'd ruther.' You see I wa'n't meanin' no 'fence, you know, but just a bein' kind o' sympathizin' like, and she flew at me 't oncet. Massy to us! why, you'd 'a' thought all them old Sodom and Gomorrah sinners biled down wa'n't nothin' to me. She did talk ridiculous. I tried to reason with her. Says I, 'Hepsy, see here now. Here you be in a good bed, in your own house, and your kindlin's all split to make your fire, — and I split every one on 'em after twelve o'clock last night, — and you a goin' on at this 'ere rate. Hepsy,' says I, 'it's awful.' But, lordy massy, how that 'ere woman can talk! She begun agin, and I couldn't get in a word edgeways nor crossways nor noways; and so I jest got up and went round to the tavern, and there I met Bill Moss and Jake Marshall, and we had some crackers and cheese and a little suthin' hot with it, and it kind o' 'curred to me, as Hepsy was in one o' her spells, it would be a good time to go kind o' Indianing round the country a spell till she kind o' come to, ye know. And so I thought I'd jest go t' other side o' Hopkinton and see Granny Walkers, — her that was housekeeper to Lady Frankland, ye know, — and see if I couldn't rake out the pertickelars of that 'ere Dench house. That 'ere house has been a lyin' on my mind considerable, along back."

My ears began to prick up with great liveliness and animation at this sound; and, deserting Cæsar, I went over and stood by Sam, and surveyed him with fixed attention, wondering in the mean time how a house could lie on his mind.

"Well," said my grandfather, "what did you hear?"

"Wal, I didn't get over to her house; but when I'd walked a pretty good piece I came across Widdah Peters's son, Sol Peters, — you know him, Mis' Badger, he lives over in Needmore with a great, spankin' old gal they call Miss Asphyxy Smith. You've heard of Miss Sphyxy Smith, hain't you, Mis' Badger?"

"Certainly I have," said my grandmother.

"Miss Asphyxia Smith is a smart, industrious woman," said Aunt Lois; "it isn't worth while to talk so about her. The world would be better off," she continued, eying Sam with an air of didactic severity, "if there were more people in it that keep to their own business, like Miss Sphyxy."

"Wal, spuz so," said Sam Lawson, with an innocent and virtuous droop, not in the slightest degree recognizing the hint; "but now, you see, I'm coming to a pint. Sol, he asked me if anybody over to Oldtown had seen or heard anything of a couple of children that had run away from Needmore. There was a boy and a gal about nine or ten or under, that had been put out by the parish. The boy was livin' with Old Crab Smith, and the gal with Miss Sphyxy."

"Well, I pity the child that Miss Sphyxy Smith has taken to bring up, I must say," said my grandmother. "What business have old maids a taking children to bring up, I want to know? Why, it isn't every hen that's fit to bring up chickens. How came the children there, anyway?"

"Wal, you see, there come a woman along to Crab Smith's with these 'ere children. Sol says they're real putty children, — putty-behaved as ever he see. The woman, she was took down and died there. And so Old Crab, he took the boy; and Miss Sphyxy, she took the gal."

"Too bad," said my grandmother; "poor motherless babes, and nobody but Crab and Sphyxy Smith to do for 'em! Somebody ought to see about it."

"Wal, ye see, Sol, he said that Miss Sphyxy was as hard as a grindstone on this gal, and they kep' the boy and gal apart, and wouldn't let 'em see nor speak to each other; and Sol says he never did pity any poor, lonesome little critter as he did that 'ere little gal. She used to lie abed nights, and sob and cry fit to break her little heart."

"I should like to go and talk to that woman!" said my grandmother, vengefully. "I wonder folks can be so mean! I wonder what such folks think of themselves, and where they expect to go to!"

"Wal, you see," continued Sam, "the young un was spicy; and when Miss Sphyxy was down on her too hard, the child, she fit her, — you know a rat'll bite, a hen will peck, and a worm will turn, — and finally it come to a fight between 'em; and Miss Sphyxy, she gin her an awful whippin'. 'Lordy massy, Sol,' says I, when Sol was a tellin' me, 'you needn't say nothin' about it. That 'ere gal's got arms like a windmill; she's a regular brown thrasher, she is, only she ain't got no music in her; and ef she undertook to thrash me, she'd make out.'"

"Well, what became of the children?" said my grandmother.

"Wal, you see, they run off together; fact is, Sol says he helped 'em off, and told 'em to come over to Oldtown. He says he told 'em to inquire for Deacon Badger's."

"I believe so," said Aunt Lois, severely. "Every man, woman, and child that wants taking care of is sent straight to our house."

"And good reason they should, Lois," said my grandmother, who was wide awake. "I declare, people ought to be out looking for them. 'Liakim, you are always flying about; why don't you look 'em up?"

Uncle Fly jumped up with alacrity. "To be sure, they ought to be looked after," he said, running to the window. "They ought to be looked after right off; they must be attended to." And Uncle Fly seemed to have an indefinite intention of pitching straight through the window in pursuit.

Sam Lawson eyed him with a serene gravity. He felt the importance of being possessed of all the information the subject in question admitted of, which he was determined to develop in an easy and leisurely manner, without any undue hurry or heat. "Mr. Sheril," he said, "the fust thing you'll hev to find out is *where they be*. It's no use tearin' round gen'lly. Where be they? — that's the question."

"To be sure, to be sure," said Uncle Fly. "Well, what you got to say about that?"

"Wal, you jest set down now, and be kind o' composed. I'm a comin' to that 'ere pint in time," said Sam. "That 'ere's jest what I says to Sol. 'Sol,' says I, 'where be they?' And Sol, he says to me, 'I dunno. They might 'a' gone with the Indians,' says Sol, 'or they might 'a' got lost in the Oldtown woods'; — and jest as we was a talkin', we see old Obscue a comin' along. He was out on a tramp over to Hopkinton, Obscue was, and we asked him about 'em. Wal, Obscue, he says that a gal and boy like what we talked of had slep' in his wife's hut not long sence. You know Obscue's wife; she makes baskets, and goes round sellin' on 'em. I couldn't fairly get out o' Obscue what day 't was, nor which way they went arter; but it was clear that them was the ones."

"Then," said Uncle Fly, "they must be somewhere. They may have lost their way in the Oldtown woods, and wandered up and down. There ought to be a party started out to look for 'em to-morrow morning."

"Now look here, Mr. Sheril," said Sam, "I think we'd better kind o' concentrate our idees on some one pint afore we start out, and I'll tell you what I'm a thinkin' of. You know I was a tellin' you that I'd seen smoke coming out o' the chimbly of the Dench house. Now I jest thought them poor little robins might have jest got in there. You know it stormed like vengeance last week, and the little critters might have took shelter in that 'ere lonesome old house."

"Poor babes!" said my grandmother. "'Liakim, you go up there and see."

"Well, I tell you," said Uncle Eliakim, "I'll be up bright and early with my old horse and wagon, and go over to the Dench house and see about it."

"Wal, now," said Sam, "if you wouldn't mind, I'll just ride over with you. I wanted to kind o' go over that 'ere house. I've had it on my mind a good while."

"Is that the haunted house?" said I, in a whisper.

"Wal, it's the one they call haunted, but 't ain't best to be 'fraid of nothin'," said Sam, surveying me paternally, and winking very obviously with one eye at Uncle Eliakim; quite forgetting the long roll of terrible suggestions he had made on the same subject a few evenings before.

"But you told about the man in a long red cloak, and the boy they threw in a well, and a woman in white."

"Lordy massy, what ears young ones has!" said Sam, throwing up his hands pathetically. "I never thought as you was round, Horace; but you mustn't never mind nothin' about it. There ain't really no such thing as ghosts."

"I want to go over and see the house," said I.

"Well, well, you shall," said Uncle Fly; "but you must wake up bright and early. I shall be off by six o'clock."

"Well, now, mother," said Aunt Lois, "I just want to know if you are going to make our house an asylum for all the trampers and all the stray children in the neighboring parishes? Have we got to keep these children, or are we going to send 'em back where they belong?"

"Send 'em back to Old Crab Smith and Miss Sphyxy?" said my grandmother. "I'd like to see myself doing that."

"Well, then, are *we* going to maintain 'em?" said Aunt Lois; "because I want to know definitely what this is coming to."

"We'll see," said my grandmother. "It's our business to do good as we have opportunity. *We* mustn't reap the corners of our fields, nor beat off all our olive-berries, but leave 'em for the poor, the fatherless, and the widow, Scripture says."

"Well, I guess our olive-berries are pretty well beaten off now, and our fields reaped, corners and all," said Lois; "and I don't see why we needs must intermeddle with children that the selectmen in Needmore have put out."

Now Aunt Lois was a first-rate belligerent power in our family circle, and in many cases carried all before her; but my grandmother always bore her down on questions like these, and it was agreed, *nem. con.*, that the expedition to look up the wanderers should take place the next morning.

The matter being thus arranged, Sam settled back with a jocular freedom of manner, surveying the fire, and flopping his hands over it, smiling to himself in a manner that made it evident that he had a further reserve of something on his mind to communicate. "This 'ere Miss Sphyxy Smith's a rich old gal, and 'mazin' smart to work," he began. "Tell you, she holds all she gets. Old Sol, he told me a story 'bout her that was a pretty good un."

"What was it?" said my grandmother.

"Wal, ye see, you 'member old Parson Jeduthun Kendall, that lives up in Stonytown: he lost his wife a year ago last Thanksgiving, and he thought 't was about time he hed another; so he comes down and consults our Parson Lothrop. Says he, 'I want a good, smart, neat, economical woman, with a good property. I don't care nothin' about her bein' handsome. In fact, I ain't particular about anything else,' says he. Wal, Parson Lothrop, says he, 'I think, if that's the case, I know jest the woman to suit ye. She owns a clear, handsome property, and she's neat and economical; but she's no beauty.' 'O, beauty is nothin' to me,' says Parson Kendall; and so he took the direction. Wal, one day he hitched up his old one-hoss shay, and kind o' brushed up, and started off a courtin'. Wal, the parson he come to the house, and he was tickled to pieces with the looks o' things outside, 'cause the house is all well shingled and painted, and there ain't a picket loose nor a nail wantin' nowhere. 'This 'ere's the woman for me,' says Parson Kendall. So he goes up and raps hard on the front door with his whip-handle. Wal, you see, Miss Sphyxy, she was jest goin' out to help get in her hay. She had on a pair o' clompin' cowhide boots, and a pitchfork in her hand, just goin' out when she heard the rap. So she come jest as she was to the front door. Now you know Parson Kendall's a little midget of a man; but he stood there on the step kind o' smilin' and genteel, lickin' his lips and lookin' *so* agreeable! Wal, the front door kind o' stuck, — front doors gen'ally do, ye know, 'cause they ain't opened very often, — and Miss Sphyxy, she had to pull and haul and put to all her strength, and finally it come open with a bang, and she 'peared to the parson, pitchfork and all, sort o' frownin' like.

" 'What do you want?' says she; for you see Miss Sphyxy ain't no ways tender to the men.

" 'I want to see Miss Asphyxia Smith,' says he, very civil, thinking she was the hired gal.

" 'I'm Miss Asphyxia Smith,' says she. 'What do you want o' me?'

"Parson Kendall, he jest took one good look on her, from top to toe. '*Nothin*',' says he, and turned right round and went down the steps like lightnin'.

"The way she banged that 'ere door, Sol said, was lively. He jumped into his shay, and I tell you his old hoss was waked up for once. The way that 'ere old shay spun and bounced was a sight. And when he come to Oldtown, Parson Lothrop was walkin' out in his wig and cocked hat and ruffles, as serene as a pictur, and he took off his hat to him as handsome as a gentleman could; but Parson Kendall, he driv right by and never bowed. He was awful riled, Parson Kendall was; but he couldn't say nothin', 'cause he'd got all he asked for. But the story got out, and Sol and the men heard it, and you'd a thought they'd never be done laughin' about it. Sol says, if he was to be hung for it the next minute, he never can help laughin' when he thinks how kind o' scared little Parson Kendall looked when Miss Asphyxia 'peared to him on the doorstep."

"Well, well, well," said Uncle Eliakim, "if we are going to the Dench house to-morrow morning, you must all be up early, for I mean to be off by daylight; and we'd better all go to bed." With which remark he fluttered out of the kitchen.

"'Liakim'll be along here by ten o'clock to-morrow," said my grandfather, quietly. "I don't suppose he's promised more than forty people to do something for them to-morrow morning."

"Yes," said Aunt Lois, "and the linch-pins of the wagon are probably lost, and the tire of the wheels sprung; but he'll be up before daylight, and maybe get along some time in the forenoon."

CHAPTER XVII

THE VISIT
TO THE HAUNTED HOUSE

My story now approaches a point in which I am soon to meet and begin to feel the force of a train of circumstances which ruled and shaped my whole life. That I had been hitherto a somewhat exceptional child may perhaps have been made apparent in the incidents I have narrated. I was not, in fact, in the least like what an average healthy boy ought to be. My brother Bill was exactly that, and nothing more. He was a good, growing, well-limbed, comfortably disposed animal, reasonably docile, and capable, under fair government, of being made to go exactly in any paths his elders chose to mark out for him.

It had been settled, the night after my father's funeral, that my Uncle Jacob was to have him for a farm-boy, to work in the summer on the farm, and to pick up his education as he might at the district school in the winter season; and thus my mother was relieved of the burden of his support, and Aunt Lois of his superfluous activity in our home department. To me the loss was a small one; for except a very slight sympathy of souls in the matter of fish-hooks and popguns, there was scarcely a single feeling that we had in common. I had a perfect passion for books, and he had a solid and well-pronounced horror of them, which seems to belong to the nature of a growing boy. I could read, as by a kind of preternatural instinct, as soon as I could walk; and reading was with me at ten years a devouring passion. No matter what the book was that was left in my vicinity, I read it as by an irresistible fascination. To be sure, I preferred stories, history, and lively narrative, where such material was to be had; but the passion for reading was like hunger, — it must be fed, and, in the absence of palatable food, preyed upon what it could find. So it came to pass that theological tracts, treatises on agriculture, old sermons, — anything, in short, that could be raked out of the barrels and boxes in my grandfather's garret, — would hold me absorbed in some shady nook of the house when I ought to have been out playing as a proper boy should. I did not, of course, understand the half of what I read, and miscalled the words to myself in a way that would have been laughable had anybody heard me; but the strange, unknown sounds stimulated vague and dreamy images in my mind, which were continually seething, changing, and interweaving, like fog-wreaths by moonlight, and formed a phantasmagoria in which I took a quaint and solemn delight.

But there was one peculiarity of my childhood which I have hesitated with an odd sort of reluctance to speak of, and yet which so powerfully influenced and determined my life, and that of all with whom I was connected, that it must find some place here. I was, as I said, dreamy and imaginative, with a mind full of vague yearnings. But beside that, through an extreme delicacy of nervous organization, my childish steps were surrounded by a species of vision or apparition so clear and distinct that I often found great difficulty in discriminating between the forms of real life and these shifting shapes, that had every appearance of reality, except that they dissolved at the touch. All my favorite haunts had their particular shapes and forms, which it afforded me infinite amusement to watch in their varying movements.

Particularly at night, after I had gone to bed and the candle was removed from my room, the whole atmosphere around my bed seemed like that which Raphael has shadowed forth around his Madonna San Sisto, — a palpitating crowd of faces and forms changing in dim and gliding quietude. I have often wondered whether any personal experience similar to mine suggested to the artist this living background to his picture. For the most part, these phantasms were agreeable to me, and filled me with a dreamy delight. Sometimes distinct scenes or visions would rise before my mind, in which I seemed to look far beyond the walls of the house, and to see things passing wherein were several actors. I remember one of these, which I saw very often, representing a venerable old white-headed man playing on a violin. He was always accompanied by a tall, majestic woman, dressed in a strange, outlandish costume, in which I particularly remarked a high fur cap of a peculiar form. As he played, the woman appeared to dance in time to the music.

Another scene which frequently presented itself to my eyes was that of a green meadow by the side of a lake of very calm water. From a grove on one side of the lake would issue a miniature form of a woman clothed in white, with a wide golden girdle around her waist, and long, black hair hanging down to her middle, which she constantly smoothed down with both her hands, with a gentle, rhythmical movement, as she approached me. At a certain point of approach, she always turned her back, and began a rapid retreat into the grove; and invariably as she turned there appeared behind her the image of a little misshapen dwarf, who pattered after her with ridiculous movements which always made me laugh. Night after night, during a certain year of my life, this pantomime never failed to follow the extinguishment of the candle, and it was to me a never-failing source of delight. One thing was peculiar about these forms, — they appeared to cause a vibration of the great central nerves of the body, as when a harp-string is struck. So I could feel in myself the jar of the dwarf's pattering feet, the soft, rhythmic movement of the little woman stroking down her long hair, the vibrations of the violin, and the steps of the dancing old woman. Nobody knew of this still and hidden world of pleasure which was thus nightly open to me. My mother used often to wonder, when, hours after she put me to bed, she would find me lying perfectly quiet, with my eyes widely and calmly open. Once or twice I undertook to tell her what I saw, but was hushed up with, "Nonsense, child! there hasn't been anybody in the room; you shouldn't talk so."

The one thing that was held above all things sacred and inviolable in a child's education in those old Puritan days was to form habits of truth. Every statement received an immediate and unceremonious sifting, and anything that looked in the least like a departure from actual verity was met with prompt and stringent discouragement. When my mother repeated before Aunt Lois some of my strange sayings, she was met with the downright declaration: "That child will be an awful liar, Susy, if you don't keep a strict lookout on him. Don't you let him tell you any stories like that."

So I early learned silence; but my own confidence in the reality of my secondary world was not a whit diminished. Like Galileo, who said, "It does move, nevertheless," so I, when I once had the candle out at night, snapped my fingers mentally at Aunt Lois, and enjoyed my vision.

One peculiarity of these appearances was that certain of them seemed like a sort of *genii loci*, — shapes belonging to certain places. The apparition of the fairy woman with the golden girdle only appeared in a certain room where I slept one year, and which had across one of its corners a sort of closet called a buffet. From this buffet the vision took its rise, and when my parents moved to another house it never appeared again.

A similar event in my shadow-world had marked our coming to my grandmother's to live. The old violin-player and his wife had for a long time been my nightly entertainers; but the first night after we were established in the apartment given up to our use by Aunt Lois, I saw them enter as they usually did, seeming to come right through the wall of the room. They, however, surveyed the apartment with a sort of confused, discontented movement, and seemed to talk to each other with their backs to me; finally I heard the old woman say, "We can't stay here," and immediately I saw them passing through the wall of the house. I saw after them as clearly as if the wall had dissolved and given my eyes the vision of all out of doors. They went to my grandfather's wood-pile and looked irresolutely round; finally they mounted on the pile, and seemed to sink gradually through it and disappear, and I never saw them afterwards.

But another of the companions of my solitude was more constant to me. This was the form of a young boy of about my own age, who for a year past had frequently come to me at night, and seemed to look lovingly upon me, and with whom I used to have a sort of social communion, without words, in a manner which seemed to me far more perfect than human language. I *thought* to him, and in return I received silent demonstrations of sympathy and fellowship from him. I called him Harvey, and used, as I lay looking in his face, mentally to tell him many things about the books I read, the games I played, and the childish joys and griefs I had; and in return he seemed to express affection and sympathy by a strange communication, as lovers sometimes talk to each other by distant glances.

Attendant on all these exceptional experiences, perhaps resulting from them, was a peculiar manner of viewing the human beings by whom I was surrounded. It is common now-a-days to speak of the sphere or emanation that surrounds a person. To my childish mind there was a vivid perception of something of this nature with regard to every one whom I approached. There were people for whom I had a violent and instinctive aversion, whose presence in the room gave me a pain so positive that it seemed almost physical, and others, again, to whom I was strongly attracted, and whose presence near me filled me with agreeable sensations, of which I could give no very definite account. For this reason, I suppose, the judgments which different people formed concerning me varied extremely. Miss Mehitable, for example, by whom I was strongly attracted, thought me one of the most amiable of boys; while my poor Aunt Lois was certain I was one of the most trying children that ever were born.

My poor mother! I surely loved her, and yet her deficient vital force, her continual sadness and discouragement, acted on my nerves as a constant weight and distress, against which I blindly and instinctively struggled; while Aunt Lois's very footstep on the stair seemed to rouse every nerve of combativeness in my little body into a state of bristling tension. I remember that when I was about six or seven years old I had the scarlet-fever, and Aunt Lois, who was a most rampant and energetic sick-nurse, undertook to watch with me; but my cries and resistance were so terrible that I was thought to be going deranged. Finally the matter was adjusted by Sam Lawson's offering to take the place, upon which I became perfectly tranquil, and resigned myself into his hands with the greatest composure and decorum. Sam was to me, during my childhood, a guide, philosopher, and friend. The lazy, easy, indefinite atmosphere of being that surrounded him was to me like the haze of Indian summer over a landscape, and I delighted to bask in it. Nothing about him was any more fixed than the wavering shadows of clouds; he was a boundless world of narrative and dreamy suggestion, tending to no point and having no end, and in it I delighted. Sam, besides, had a partiality for all those haunts in which I took pleasure. Near our house was the old town burying-ground, where reposed the bones of generations of Indian sachems, elders, pastors, and teachers, converted from the wild forests, who, Christianized and churched, died in the faith, and were gathered into Christian burial. On its green hillocks I loved to sit and watch and dream long after sundown or moonrise, and fancy I saw bands of wavering shapes, and hope that some one out of the crowd might have a smile of recognition or a spiritual word for me.

My mother and grandmother and Aunt Lois were horror-stricken by such propensities, indicating neither more nor less than indefinite coughs and colds, with early death in the rear; and however much in the way a little boy always seemed in those times in the active paths of his elders, yet it was still esteemed a primary duty to keep him in the world. "Horace, what do you go and sit in the graveyard for?" would my grandmother say. "I should think you'd be 'fraid something would 'pear to you."

"I want something to appear, grandmother."

"Pshaw, pshaw! no, you don't. What do you want to be so odd for? Don't you ever say such things."

Sam, however, was willing to aid and abet me in strolling and lounging anywhere and at any hour, and lent a willing ear to my tales of what I saw, and had in his capacious wallet a pendent story or a spiritual precedent for anything that I could mention.

On this night, after he had left me, I went to bed with my mind full of the haunted house, and all that was to be hoped or feared from its exploration. Whether this was the cause or not, the result was that Harvey appeared nearer and more friendly than ever; and he held by his hand another boy, whose figure appeared to me like a faintly discerned form in a mist. Sometimes the mist seemed to waver and part, and I caught indistinct glimpses of bright yellow curls and clear blue eyes, and then Harvey smiled and shook his head. When he began to disappear, he said to me, "Good by"; and I felt an inward assurance that he was about to leave me. I said my "Good by" aloud, and stretched out my hands.

"Why, Horace, Horace!" said my mother, waking suddenly at the sound of my voice, — "Horace, wake up; you've been dreaming."

I had not even been asleep, but I did not tell her so, and turning over, as I usually did when the curtain fell over my dreamland, I was soon asleep. I was wide awake with the earliest peep of dawn the next morning, and had finished dressing myself before my mother awoke.

Ours was an early household, and the brisk tap of Aunt Lois's footsteps, and the rattling of chairs and dishes in the kitchen, showed that breakfast was in active preparation.

My grandfather's prediction wih regard to my Uncle Eliakim proved only too correct. The fact was, that the poor man lived always in the whirl of a perfect Maelstrom of promises and engagements, which were constantly converging towards every hour of his unoccupied time. His old wagon and horse both felt the effects of such incessant activity, and such deficient care and attention as were consequent upon it, and were at all times in a state of dilapidation. Therefore it was that the next morning nine, ten, and eleven o'clock appeared, and no Uncle Eliakim.

Sam Lawson had for more than two hours been seated in an expectant attitude on our doorstep; but as the sun shone warm, and he had a large mug of cider between his hands, he appeared to enjoy his mind with great equanimity.

Aunt Lois moved about the house with an air and manner of sharp contempt, which exhibited itself even in the way she did her household tasks. She put down plates as if she despised them, and laid sticks of wood on the fire with defiant thumps, as much as to say that she knew some things that had got to be in time and place if others were not; but she spake no word.

Aunt Lois, as I have often said before, was a good Christian, and held it her duty to govern her tongue. True, she said many sharp and bitter things; but nobody but herself and her God knew how many more she would have said had she not reined herself up in conscientious silence. But never was there a woman whose silence could express more contempt and displeasure than hers. You could feel it in the air about you, though she never said a word. You could feel it in the rustle of her dress, in the tap of her heels over the floor, in the occasional flash of her sharp, black eye. She was like a thunder-cloud whose quiet is portentous, and from which you every moment expect a flash or an explosion. This whole morning's excursion was contrary to her mind and judgment, — an ill-advised, ill-judged, shiftless proceeding, and being entered on in a way as shiftless.

"What time do you suppose it is, mother?" she at last said to my grandmother, who was busy in her buttery.

"Massy, Lois! I daren't look," called out my grandmother who was apt to fall behindhand of her desires in the amount of work she could bring to pass of a morning. "I don't want to know."

"Well, it's eleven o'clock," said Lois, relentlessly, "and no signs of Uncle 'Liakim yet; and there's Sam Lawson, I s'pose he's going to spend the day on our doorstep."

Sam Lawson looked after my Aunt Lois as she went out of the kitchen. "Lordy massy, Horace, I wouldn't be so kind o' un-reconciled as she is all the time for nothin'. Now *I* might get into a fluster 'cause *I'm* kep' a waitin', but I don't. I think it's our duty to be willin' to wait quiet till things come round; this 'ere's a world where things can't be driv', and folks mustn't set their heart on havin' everything come out jes' so, 'cause ef they do they'll allers be in a stew, like Hepsy and Miss Lois there. Let 'em jest wait quiet, and things allers do come round in the end as well or better 'n ef you worried."

And as if to illustrate and justify this train of thought, Uncle Eliakim's wagon at this moment came round the corner of the street, driving at a distracted pace. The good man came with such headlong speed and vivacity that his straw hat was taken off by the breeze, and flew far behind him, and he shot up to our door, as he usually did to that of the meeting-house, as if he were going to drive straight in.

"Lordy massy, Mr. Sheril," said Sam, "don't get out; I'll get your hat. Horace, you jest run and pick it up; that's a good boy."

I ran accordingly, but my uncle had sprung out as lively as an autumn grasshopper. "I've been through a sea of troubles this morning," he said. "I lent my waggin to Jake Marshall yesterday afternoon, to take his wife a ride. I thought if Jake was a mind to pay the poor woman any attention, I'd help; but when he brought it back last night, one of the bolts was broken, and the harness gave out in two places."

"Want to know?" said Sam, leisurely examining the establish-ment. "I think the neighbors ought to subscribe to keep up your team, Mr. Sheril, for it's free to the hull on 'em."

"And what thanks does he get?" said Aunt Lois, sharply. "Well, Uncle 'Liakim, it's almost dinner-time."

"I know it, I know it, I know it, Lois. But there's been a lot o' things to do this morning. Just as I got the waggin mended come Aunt Bathsheba Sawin's boy and put me in mind that I promised to carry her corn to grind; and I had to stop and take that round to mill; and then I remembered the pills that was to go to Hannah Dexter — ”

"I dare say, and forty more things like it," said Aunt Lois.

"Well, jump in now," said Uncle Fly; "we'll be over and back in no time."

"You may as well put it off till after dinner now," said Aunt Lois.

"Couldn't stop for that," said Uncle 'Liakim; "my afternoon is all full now. I've got to be in twenty places before night." And away we rattled, while Aunt Lois stood looking after us in silent, unutterable contempt.

"Stop! stop! stop! Whoa! whoa!" said Uncle 'Liakim, drawing suddenly up. "There's that plaster for Widdah Peters, after all. I wonder if Lois wouldn't just run up with it." By this time he had turned the horse, who ran, with his usual straightforward, blind directness, in a right line, against the doorstep again.

"Well, what now?" said Aunt Lois, appearing at the door.

"Why, Lois, I've just come back to tell you I forgot I promised to carry Widdah Peters that plaster for lumbago; couldn't you just find time to run up there with it?"

"Well, give it to me," said Aunt Lois, with sharp precision, and an air of desperate patience.

"Yes, yes, I will," said Uncle Fly, standing up and beginning a rapid search into that series of pockets which form a distinguishing mark of masculine habiliments, — searching with such hurried zeal that he really seemed intent on tearing himself to pieces. "Here 't is! — no, pshaw, pshaw! that's my handkerchief! O, here! — pshaw, pshaw! Why, where is it? Didn't I put it in? — or did I — O, here it is in my vest-pocket; no, though. Where a plague!" and Uncle Fly sprang from the wagon and began his usual active round-and-round chase after himself, slapping his pockets, now before and now behind, and whirling like a dancing dervis, while Aunt Lois stood regarding him with stony composure.

"If you *could* ever think where anything was, before you began to talk about it, it would be an improvement," she said.

"Well, fact is," said Uncle Eliakim, "now I think of it, Mis' Sheril made me change my coat just as I came out, and that's the whole on 't. You just run up, Lois, and tell Mis' Sheril to send one of the boys down to Widdah Peters's with the plaster she'll find in the pocket, — right-hand side. Come now, get up."

These last words were addressed, not to Aunt Lois, but to the horse, who, kept in rather a hungry and craving state by his master's hurrying manner of life, had formed the habit of sedulously improving every spare interval in catching at a mouthful of anything to eat, and had been accordingly busy in cropping away a fringe of very green grass that was growing up by the kitchen doorstep, from which occupation he was remorselessly twitched up and started on an impetuous canter.

"Wal, now I hope we're fairly started," said Sam Lawson; "and, Mr. Sheril, you may as well, while you are about it, take the right road as the wrong one, 'cause that 'ere saves time. It's pleasant enough anywhere, to be sure, to-day; but when a body's goin' to a place, a body likes to get there, as it were."

"Well, well, well," said Uncle Fly, "we're on the right road, ain't we?"

"Wal, so fur you be; but when you come out on the plains, you must take the fust left-hand road that drives through the woods, and you may jest as well know as much aforehand."

"Much obliged to you," said my uncle. "I reely hadn't thought particularly about the way."

"S'pose not," said Sam, composedly; "so it's jest as well you took me along. Lordy massy, there ain't a road nor a cart-path round Oldtown that I hain't been over, time and time agin. I believe I could get through any on 'em the darkest night that ever was hatched. Jake Marshall and me has been Indianing round these 'ere woods more times 'n you could count. It's kind o' pleasant, a nice bright day like this 'ere, to be a joggin' along in the woods. Everything so sort o' still, ye know; and ye hear the chestnuts a droppin', and the wa'nuts. Jake and me, last fall, went up by Widdah Peters's one day, and shuck them trees, and got nigh about a good bushel o' wa'nuts. I used to kind o' like to crack 'em for the young uns, nights, last winter, when Hepsy'd let em sit up. Though she's allers for drivin' on 'em all off to bed, and makin' it kind o' solitary, Hepsy is." And Sam concluded the conjugal allusion with a deep sigh.

"Have you ever been into the grounds of the Dench house?" said Uncle Fly.

"Wal, no, not reely; but Jake, he has; and ben into the house too. There was a fellow named 'Biah Smith that used to be a kind o' servant to the next family that come in after Lady Frankland went out, and he took Jake all over it once when there wa'n't nobody there. 'Biah, he said that when Sir Harry lived there, there was one room that was always kept shet up, and wa'n't never gone into, and in that 'ere room there was the long red cloak, and the hat and sword, and all the clothes he hed on when he was buried under the ruins in that 'ere earthquake. They said that every year, when the day of the earthquake come round, Sir Harry used to spend it a fastin' and prayin' in that 'ere room, all alone. 'Biah says that he had talked with a fellow that was one of Sir Harry's body-servants, and he told him that Sir Harry used to come out o' that 'ere room lookin' more like a ghost than a live man, when he'd fasted and prayed for twenty-four hours there. Nobody knows what might have 'peared to him there."

I wondered much in my own quiet way at this story, and marvelled whether, in Sir Harry's long, penitential watchings, he had seen the air of the room all tremulous with forms and faces such as glided around me in my solitary hours.

"Naow, you see," said Sam Lawson, "when the earthquake come, Sir Harry, he was a driving with a court lady; and she, poor soul, went into 'tarnity in a minit, — 'thout a minit to prepare. And I 'spect there ain't no reason to s'pose but what she was a poor, mis'able Roman Catholic. So her prospects couldn't have been no-ways encouragin'. And it must have borne on Sir Harry's mind to think she should be took and he spared, when he was a cuttin' up just in the way he was. I shouldn't wonder but she should 'pear to him. You know they say there is a woman in white walks them grounds, and 'Biah, he says, as near as he can find out, it's that 'ere particular chamber as she allers goes to. 'Biah said he'd seen her at the windows a wringin' her hands and a cryin' fit to break her heart, poor soul. Kind o' makes a body feel bad, 'cause, arter all, 't wa'n't her fault she was born a Roman Catholic, — now was it?"

The peculiarity of my own mental history had this effect on me from a child, that it wholly took away from me all dread of the supernatural. A world of shadowy forms had always been as much a part of my short earthly experience as the more solid and tangible one of real people. I had just as quiet and natural a feeling about one as the other. I had not the slightest doubt, on hearing Sam's story, that the form of the white lady did tenant those deserted apartments; and so far from feeling any chill or dread in the idea, I felt only a sort of curiosity to make her acquaintance.

Our way to the place wound through miles of dense forest. Sir Harry had chosen it, as a retreat from the prying eyes and slanderous tongues of the world, in a region of woodland solitude. And as we trotted leisurely under the bright scarlet and yellow boughs of the forest, Uncle Eliakim and Sam discoursed of the traditions of the place we were going to.

"Who was it bought the place after Lady Frankland went to England?" said Uncle Eliakim.

"Wal, I believe 't was let a spell. There was some French folks hed it 'long through the war. I heerd tell that they was pretty high people. I never could quite make out when they went off; there was a good many stories round about it. I didn't clearly make out how 't was, till Dench got it. Dench, you know, got his money in a pretty peculiar way, ef all they says 's true."

"How's that?" said my uncle.

"Wal, they do say he got the great carbuncle that was at the bottom of Sepaug River. You've heard about the great carbuncle, I s'pose?"

"O, no! do pray tell me about it," said I, interrupting with fervor.

"Why, didn't you never hear 'bout that? want to know. Wal, I'll tell ye, then. I know all 'bout it. Jake Marshall, he told me that Dench fust told him, and he got it from old Mother Ketury, ye know, — a regelar old heathen Injun Ketury is, — and folks do go so fur as to say that in the old times Ketury'd 'a' ben took up for a witch, though I never see no harm in her ways. Ef there be sperits, and we all know there is, what's the harm o' Ketury's seein' on 'em?"

"Maybe she can't help seeing them," suggested I.

"Jes' so, jes' so; that 'ere's what I telled Jake when we's a talkin' it over, and he said he didn't like Dench's havin' so much to do with old Ketury. But la, old Ketury could say the Lord's Prayer in Injun, cause I've heard her; though she wouldn't say it when she didn't want to and she would say it when she did, — jest as the fit took her. But lordy massy, them wild Injuns, they ain't but

jest half folks, they're so kind o' wild, and birchy and bushy as a
body may say. Ef they take religion at all, it's got to be in their
own way. Ef you get the wild beast all out o' one on 'em, there
don't somehow seem to be enough left to make an ordinary smart
man of, so much on 'em's wild. Anyhow, Dench, he was thick
with Ketury, and she told him all about the gret carbuncle, and
gin him directions how to get it."

"But I don't know what a great carbuncle is," I interrupted.

"Lordy massy, boy, didn't you never read in your Bible about
the New Jerusalem, and the precious stones in the foundation, that
shone like the sun? Wal, the carbuncle was one on 'em."

"Did it fall down out of heaven into the river?" said I.

"Mebbe," said Sam. "At any rate Ketury, she told 'em what they
had to do to get it. They had to go out arter it jest exactly at
twelve o'clock at night, when the moon was full. You was to fast
all the day before, and go fastin', and say the Lord's Prayer in
Injun afore you went; and when you come to where 't was, you
was to dive after it. But there wa'n't to be a word spoke; if there
was, it went right off."

"What did they have to say the prayer in Indian for?" said I.

"Lordy massy, boy, I s'pose 't was 'cause 't was Indian sperits
kep' a watch over it. Any rate 't was considerable of a pull on 'em,
'cause Ketury, she had to teach 'em; and she wa'n't allers in the
sperit on 't. Sometimes she's crosser 'n torment, Ketury is. Dench,
he gin her fust and last as much as ten dollars, — so Jake says.
However, they got all through with it, and then come a moonlight
night, and they went out. Jake says it was the splendidest moonlight ye ever did see, — all jest as still, — only the frogs and the
turtles kind o' peepin'; and they didn't say a word, and rowed
out past the pint there, where the water's ten feet deep, and he
looked down and see it a shinin' on the bottom like a great star,
making the waters all light like a lantern. Dench, he dived for it,
Jake said; and he saw him put his hand right on it; and he was
so tickled, you know, to see he'd got it, that he couldn't help
hollerin' right out, "There, you got it!" and it was gone. Dench
was mad enough to 'a' killed him; 'cause, when it goes that 'ere
way, you can't see it agin for a year and a day. But two or three
years arter, all of a sudden, Dench, he seemed to kind o' spruce
up and have a deal o' money to spend. He said an uncle had died

and left it to him in England; but Jake Marshall says you'll never take him in that 'ere way. He says he thinks it's no better 'n witch-craft, getting money that 'ere way. Ye see Jake was to have had half if they'd 'a' got it, and not gettin' nothin' kind o' sot him to thinkin' on it in a moral pint o' view, ye know. — But, lordy massy, where be we, Mr. Sheril? This 'ere's the second or third time we've come round to this 'ere old dead chestnut. We ain't makin' no progress."

In fact there were many and crossing cart-paths through this forest, which had been worn by different farmers of the vicinity in going after their yearly supply of wood; and, notwithstanding Sam's assertion of superior knowledge in these matters, we had, in the negligent inattention of his narrative, become involved in this labyrinth, and driven up and down, and back and forward, in the wood, without seeming at all to advance upon our errand.

"Wal, I declare for 't, I never did see nothing beat it," said Sam. "We've been goin' jest round and round for this hour or more, and come out again at exactly the same place. I've heerd of places that's kep' hid, and folks allers gets sort o' struck blind and con-fused that undertakes to look 'em up. Wal, I don't say I believe in sich stories, but this 'ere is curious. Why, I'd 'a' thought I could 'a' gone straight to it blindfolded, any day. Ef Jake Marshall was here, he'd go straight to it."

"Well, Sam," said Uncle Eliakim, "it's maybe because you and me got so interested in telling stories that we've missed the way."

"That 'ere's it, 'thout a doubt," said Sam. "Now I'll just hush up, and kind o' concentrate my 'tention. I'll just git out and walk a spell, and take an observation."

The result of this improved attention to the material facts of the case was, that we soon fell into a road that seemed to wind slowly up a tract of rising ground, and to disclose to our view, through an interlacing of distant boughs, the western horizon, toward which the sun was now sinking with long, level beams. We had been such a time in our wanderings, that there seemed a prospect of night setting in before we should be through with our errand and ready to return.

"The house stan's on the top of a sort o' swell o' ground," said Sam; "and as nigh as I can make it out, it must be somewhere about there."

"There is a woman a little way before us," said I; "why don't you ask her?"

I saw very plainly in a turn of the road a woman whose face was hidden by a bonnet, who stood as if waiting for us. It was not the white woman of ghostly memory, but apparently a veritable person in the every-day habiliments of common life, who stood as if waiting for us.

"I don't see no woman," said Sam; "where is she?"

I pointed with my finger, but as I did so the form melted away. I remember distinctly the leaves of the trees back of it appearing through it as through a gauze veil, and then it disappeared entirely.

"There isn't any woman that I can see," said Uncle Eliakim, briskly. "The afternoon sun must have got into your eyes, boy."

I had been so often severely checked and reproved for stating what I saw, that I now determined to keep silence, whatever might appear to me. At a little distance before us the road forked, one path being steep and craggy, and the other easier of ascent, and apparently going in much the same general direction. A little in advance, in the more rugged path, stood the same female form. Her face was hidden by a branch of a tree, but she beckoned to us. "Take *that* path, Uncle 'Liakim," said I; "it's the right one."

"Lordy massy," said Sam Lawson, "how in the world should you know that? That 'ere is the shortest road to the Dench house, and the other leads away from it."

I kept silence as to my source of information, and still watched the figure. As we passed it, I saw a beautiful face with a serene and tender expression, and her hands were raised as if in blessing. I looked back earnestly and she was gone.

A few moments after, we were in the grounds of the place, and struck into what had formerly been the carriage way, though now overgrown with weeds, and here and there with a jungle of what was once well-kept ornamental shrubbery. A tree had been uprooted by the late tempest, and blown down across the road, and we had to make quite a little detour to avoid it.

"Now how are we to get into this house?" said Uncle Eliakim. "No doubt it's left fastened up."

"Do you see *that?*" said Sam Lawson, who had been gazing steadily upward at the chimneys of the house, with his eyes shaded by one of his great hands. "Look at that smoke from the middle chimbly."

"There's somebody in the house, to be sure," said Uncle Eliakim; "suppose we knock at the front door here?" — and with great briskness, suiting the action to the word, he lifted the black serpent knocker, and gave such a rat tat tat as must have roused all the echoes of the old house, while Sam Lawson and I stood by him, expectant, on the front steps.

Sam then seated himself composedly on a sort of bench which was placed under the shadow of the porch, and awaited the result with the contentment of a man of infinite leisure. Uncle Eliakim, however, felt pressed for time, and therefore gave another long and vehement rap. Very soon a chirping of childish voices was heard behind the door, and a pattering of feet; there appeared to be a sort of consultation.

"There they be now," said Sam Lawson, "jest as I told you."

"Please go round to the back door," said a childish voice; "this is locked, and I can't open it."

We all immediately followed Sam Lawson, who took enormous strides over the shrubbery, and soon I saw the vision of a curly-headed, blue-eyed boy holding open the side door of the house.

I ran up to him. "Are you Harvey?" I said.

"No," he answered; "my name isn't Harvey, it's Harry; and this is my sister Tina," — and immediately a pair of dark eyes looked out over his shoulder.

"Well, we've come to take you to my grandmother's house," said I.

I don't know how it was, but I always spoke of our domestic establishment under the style and title of the female ruler. It was grandmother's house.

"I am glad of it," said the boy, "for we have tried two or three times to find our way to Oldtown, and got lost in the woods and had to come back here again."

Here the female partner in the concern stepped a little forward, eager for her share in the conversation. "Do you know old Sol?" she said.

"Lordy massy, I do," said Sam Lawson, quite delighted at this verification of the identity of the children. "Yes, I see him only day afore yesterday, and he was 'quirin' arter you, and we thought we'd find you over in this 'ere house, 'cause I'd seen smoke a comin' out o' the chimblies. Had a putty good time in the old house, I reckon. Ben all over it pretty much, hain't ye?"

"O yes," said Tina; "and it's such a strange old place, — a great big house with ever so many rooms in it!"

"Wal, we'll jest go over it, being as we're here," said Sam; and into it we all went.

Now there was nothing in the world that little Miss Tina took more native delight in than in playing the hostess. To entertain was her dearest instinct, and she hastened with all speed to open before us all in the old mansion that her own rummaging and investigating talents had brought to light, chattering meanwhile with the spirit of a bobolink.

"You don't know," she said to Sam Lawson, "what a curious little closet there is in here, with book-cases and drawers, and a looking-glass in the door, with a curtain over it."

"Want to know?" said Sam. "Wal, that 'ere does beat all. It's some of them old English folks's grander, I s'pose."

"And here's a picture of such a beautiful lady, that always looks at you, whichever way you go, — just see."

"Lordy massy, so 't does. Wal, now, them drawers, mebbe, have got curous things in 'em," suggested Sam.

"O yes, but Harry never would let me look in them. I tried, though, once, when Harry was gone; but, if you'll believe me, they're all locked."

"Want to know?" said Sam. "That 'ere's a kind o' pity, now."

"Would *you* open them? You wouldn't, would you?" said the little one, turning suddenly round and opening her great wide eyes full on him. "Harry said the place wasn't ours, and it wouldn't be proper."

"Wal, he's a nice boy; quite right in him. Little folks mustn't touch things that ain't theirn," said Sam, who was strong on the moralities; though, after all, when all the rest had left the apartment, I looked back and saw him giving a sly tweak to the drawers of the cabinet on his own individual account.

"I was just a makin' sure, you know, that 't was all safe," he said, as he caught my eye, and saw that he was discovered.

Sam revelled and expatiated, however, in the information that lay before him in the exploration of the house. No tourist with

Murray's guide-book in hand, and with travels to prepare for publication, ever went more patiently through the doing of a place. Not a door was left closed that could be opened; not a passage unexplored. Sam's head came out dusty and cobwebby between the beams of the ghostly old garret, where mouldy relics of antique furniture were reposing, and disappeared into the gloom of the spacious cellars, where the light was as darkness. He found none of the marks of the tradional haunted room; but he prolonged the search till there seemed a prospect that poor Uncle Eliakim would have to get him away by physical force, if we meant to get home in time for supper.

"Mr. Lawson, you don't seem to remember we haven't any of us had a morsel of dinner, and the sun is actually going down. The folks'll be concerned about us. Come, let's take the children and be off."

And so we mounted briskly into the wagon, and the old horse, vividly impressed with the idea of barn and hay at the end of his toils, seconded the vigorous exertions of Uncle Fly, and we rattled and spun on our homeward career, and arrived at the farmhouse a little after moonrise.

CHAPTER XVIII

TINA'S ADOPTION

During the time of our journey to the enchanted ground, my Aunt Lois, being a woman of business, who always knew precisely what she was about, had contrived not only to finish meritoriously her household tasks, and to supplement Uncle Eliakim's forgetful benevolence, but also to make a call on Miss Mehitable Rossiter, for the sake of unburdening to her her oppressed heart. For Miss Mehitable bore in our family circle the repute of being a woman of counsel and sound wisdom. The savor of ministerial stock being yet strong about her, she was much resorted to for advice in difficult cases.

"I don't object, of course, to doing for the poor and orphaned, and all that," said Aunt Lois, quite sensibly; "but I like to see folks seem to know what they are doing, and where they are going, and not pitch and tumble into things without asking what's to come of them. Now, we'd just got Susy and the two boys on our hands, and here will come along a couple more children to-night; and I must say I don't see what's to be done with them."

"It's a pity you don't take snuff," said Miss Mehitable, with a whimsical grimace. "Now, when I come to any of the cross-places of life, where the road isn't very clear, I just take a pinch of snuff and wait; but as you don't, just stay and get a cup of tea with me, in a quiet, Christian way, and after it we will walk round to your mother's and look at these children."

Aunt Lois was soothed in her perturbed spirit by this proposition; and it was owing to this that, when we arrived at home, long after dark, we found Miss Mehitable in the circle around the blazing kitchen fire. The table was still standing, with ample preparations for an evening meal, — a hot smoking loaf of rye-and-Indian bread, and a great platter of cold boiled beef and pork, garnished with cold potatoes and turnips, the sight of which, to a party who had had no dinner all day, was most appetizing.

My grandmother's reception of the children was as motherly as if they had been of her own blood. In fact, their beauty and evident gentle breeding won for them immediate favor in all eyes.

The whole party sat down to the table, and, after a long and somewhat scattering grace, pronounced by Uncle Eliakim, fell to with a most amazing appearance of enjoyment. Sam's face waxed luminous as he buttered great blocks of smoking brown bread with the fruits of my grandmother's morning churning, and refreshed himself by long and hearty pulls at the cider-mug.

"I tell *you*," he said, "when folks hes been a ridin' on an empty stomach ever since breakfast, victuals is victuals; we learn how to be thankful for 'em; so I'll take another slice o' that 'ere beef, and one or two more cold potatoes, and the vinegar, Mr. Sheril. Wal, chillen, this ere's better than bein' alone in that 'ere old house, ain't it?"

"Yes, indeed," piped Tina; "I had begun to be quite discouraged. We tried and tried to find our way to Oldtown, and always got lost in the woods." Seeing that this remark elicited sympathy in the listeners, she added, "I was afraid we should die there, and the robins would have to cover us up, like some children papa used to tell about."

"Poor babes! just hear 'em," said my grandmother, who seemed scarcely able to restrain herself from falling on the necks of the children, in the ardor of her motherly kindness, while she doubled up an imaginary fist at Miss Asphyxia Smith, and longed to give her a piece of her mind touching her treatment of them.

Harry remained modestly silent; but he and I sat together, and our eyes met every now and then with that quiet amity to which I had been accustomed in my spiritual friend. I felt a cleaving of spirit to him that I had never felt towards any human being before, — a certainty that something had come to me in him that I had always been wanting, — and I was too glad for speech.

He was one of those children who retreat into themselves and make a shield of quietness and silence in the presence of many people, while Tina, on the other hand, was electrically excited, waxed brilliant in color, and rattled and chattered with as fearless confidence as a cat-bird.

"Come hither to me, little maiden," said Miss Mehitable, with a whimsical air of authority, when the child had done her supper. Tina came to her knee, and looked up into the dusky, homely face, in that still, earnest fashion in which children seem to study older people.

"Well, how do you like me?" said Miss Mehitable, when this silent survey had lasted an appreciable time.

The child still considered attentively, looking long into the great, honest, open eyes, and then her face suddenly rippled and dimpled all over like a brook when a sunbeam strikes it. "I do like you. I think you are good," she said, putting out her hands impulsively.

"Then up you come," said Miss Mehitable, lifting her into her lap. "It's well you like me, because, for aught you know, I may be an old fairy; and if I didn't like you, I might turn you into a mouse or a cricket. Now how would you like that?"

"You couldn't do it," said Tina, laughing.

"How do you know I couldn't?"

"Well, if you did turn me into a mouse, I'd gnaw your knitting-work," said Tina, laying hold of Miss Mehitable's knitting. "You'd be glad to turn me back again."

"Heyday! I must take care how I make a mouse of you, I see. Perhaps I'll make you into a kitten."

"Well, I'd like to be a kitten, if you'll keep a ball for me to play with, and give me plenty of milk," said Tina, to whom no proposition seemed to be without possible advantages.

"Will you go home and live with me, and be my kitten?"

Tina had often heard her brother speak of finding a good woman who should take care of her; and her face immediately became grave at this proposal. She seemed to study Miss Mehitable in a new way. "Where do you live?" she said.

"O, my house is only a little way from here."

"And may Harry come to see me?"

"Certainly he may."

"Do you want me to work for you all the time?" said Tina; "because," she added, in a low voice, "I like to play sometimes, and Miss Asphyxia said that was wicked."

"Didn't I tell you I wanted you for my little white kitten," said Miss Mehitable, with an odd twinkle. "What work do you suppose kittens do?"

"Must I grow up and catch rats?" said the child.

"Certainly you will be likely to," said Miss Mehitable, solemnly. "I shall pity the poor rats when you are grown up."

Tina looked in the humorous, twinkling old face with a gleam of mischievous comprehension, and, throwing her arms around Miss Mehitable, said, "Yes, I like you, and I will be your kitten."

There was a sudden, almost convulsive pressure of the little one to the kind old breast, and Miss Mehitable's face wore a strange expression, that looked like the smothered pang of some great anguish blended with a peculiar tenderness. One versed in the reading of spiritual histories might have seen that, at that moment, some inner door of that old heart opened, not without a grating of pain, to give a refuge to the little orphan; but opened it was, and a silent inner act of adoption had gone forth. Miss Mehitable beckoned my grandmother and Aunt Lois into a corner of the fireplace by themselves, while Sam Lawson was entertaining the rest of the circle by reciting the narrative of our day's explorations.

"Now I suppose I'm about as fit to undertake to bring up a child as the old Dragon of Wantley," said Miss Mehitable; "but as you seem to have a surplus on your hands, I'm willing to take the girl and do what I can for her."

"Dear Miss Mehitable, what a mercy it'll be to her!" said my grandmother and Aunt Lois, simultaneously; — "if you feel that you can afford it," added Aunt Lois, considerately.

"Well, the fowls of the air and the lilies of the field are taken care of somehow, as we are informed," said Miss Mehitable. "My basket and store are not much to ask a blessing on, but I have a sort of impression that an orphan child will make it none the less likely to hold out."

"There'll always be a handful of meal in the barrel and a little oil in the cruse for you, I'm sure," said my grandmother; "the word of the Lord stands sure for that."

A sad shadow fell over Miss Mehitable's face at these words, and then the usual expression of quaint humor stole over it. "It's to be hoped that Polly will take the same view of the subject that you appear to," said she. "My authority over Polly is, you know, of an extremely nominal kind."

"Still," said my grandmother, "you must be mistress in your own house. Polly, I am sure, knows her duty to you."

"Polly's idea of allegiance is very much like that of the old Spanish nobles to their king; it used to run somewhat thus: 'We, who are every way as good as you are, promise obedience to your government if you maintain our rights and liberties, but if not, not.' Now Polly's ideas of 'rights and liberties' are of a very set and particular nature, and I have found her generally disposed to make a good fight for them. Still, after all," she added, "the poor old thing loves me, and I think will be willing to indulge me in having a doll, if I really am set upon it. The only way I can carry my point with Polly is, to come down on her with a perfect avalanche of certainty, and so I have passed my word to you that I will be responsible for this child. Polly may scold and fret for a fortnight; but she is too good a Puritan to question whether people shall keep their promises. Polly abhors covenant-breaking with all her soul, and so in the end she will have to help me through."

"It's a pretty child," said my grandmother, "and an engaging one, and Polly may come to liking her."

"There's no saying," said Miss Mehitable. "You never know what you may find in the odd corners of an old maid's heart, when you fairly look into them. There are often unused hoards of maternal affection enough to set up an orphan-asylum; but it's like iron filings and a magnet, — you must try them with a live child, and if there is anything in 'em you find it out. That little object," she said, looking over her shoulder at Tina, "made an instant commotion in the dust and rubbish of my forlorn old garret, and brought to light a deal that I thought had gone to the moles and the bats long ago. She will do me good, I can feel, with her little pertnesses and her airs and fancies. If you could know how chilly and lonesome an old house gets sometimes, particularly in autumn, when the equinoctial storm is brewing! A lively child is a godsend, even if she turns the whole house topsy-turvy."

"Well, a child can't always be a plaything," said Aunt Lois; "it's a solemn and awful responsibility."

"And if I don't take it, who will?" said Miss Mehitable, gravely. "If a better one would, I wouldn't. I've no great confidence in myself. I profess no skill in human cobbling. I can only give house-room and shelter and love, and let come what will come. 'A man cannot escape what is written on his forehead,' the Turkish proverb says, and this poor child's history is all forewritten."

"The Lord will bless you for your goodness to the orphan," said my grandmother.

"I don't know about its being goodness. I take a fancy to her. I hunger for the child. There's no merit in wanting your bit of cake, and maybe taking it when it isn't good for you; but let's hope all's well that ends well. Since I have fairly claimed her for mine, I begin to feel a fierce right of property in her, and you'd see me fighting like an old hen with anybody that should try to get her away from me. You'll see me made an old fool of by her smart little ways and speeches; and I already am proud of her beauty. Did you ever see a brighter little minx?"

We looked across to the other end of the fireplace, where Miss Tina sat perched, with great contentment, on Sam Lawson's knee, listening with wide-open eyes to the accounts he was giving of the haunted house. The beautiful hair that Miss Asphyxia had cut so close had grown with each day, till now it stood up in half rings of reddish gold, through which the fire shone with a dancing light; and her great eyes seemed to radiate brightness from as many points as a diamond.

"Depend upon it, those children are of good blood," said Miss Mehitable, decisively. "You'll never make me believe that they will not be found to belong in some way to some reputable stock."

"Well, we know nothing about their parents," said my grandmother, "except what we heard second-hand through Sam Lawson. It was a wandering woman, sick and a stranger, who was taken down and died in Old Crab Smith's house, over in Needmore."

"One can tell, by the child's manner of speaking, that she has been brought up among educated people," said Miss Mehitable. "She is no little rustic. The boy, too, looks of the fine clay of the earth. But it's time for me to take little Miss Rattlebrain home with me, and get her into bed. Sleep is a gracious state for children, and the first step in my new duties is a plain one." So saying, Miss Mehitable rose, and, stepping over to the other side of the fireplace, tapped Tina lightly on the shoulder. "Come, Pussy," she said, "get your bonnet, and we will go home."

Harry, who had watched all the movements between Miss Mehitable and his sister with intense interest, now stepped for-

ward, blushing very much, but still with a quaint little old-fashioned air of manliness. "Is my sister going to live with you?"

"So we have agreed, my little man," said Miss Mehitable. "I
hope you have no objection?"

"Will you let me come and see her sometimes?"

"Certainly; you will always be quite welcome."

"I want to see her sometimes, because my mother left her under
my care. I sha'n't have a great deal of time to come in the daytime, because I must work for my living," he said, "but a little
while sometimes at night, if you would let me."

"And what do you work at?" said Miss Mehitable, surveying
the delicate boy with an air of some amusement.

"I used to pick up potatoes, and fodder the cattle, and do a great
many things; and I am growing stronger every day, and by and
by can do a great deal more."

"Well said, sonny," said my grandfather, laying his hand on
Harry's head. "You speak like a smart boy. We can have you down
to help tend sawmill."

"I wonder how many more boys will be wanted to help tend
sawmill," said Aunt Lois.

"Well, good night, all," said Miss Mehitable, starting to go
home.

Tina, however, stopped and left her side, and threw her arms
round Harry's neck and kissed him. "Good night now. You'll come
and see me to-morrow," she said.

"May I come too?" I said, almost before I thought.

"O, certainly, do come," said Tina, with that warm, earnest
light in her eyes which seemed the very soul of hospitality. "*She'll*
like to have you, I know."

"The child is taking possession of the situation at once," said
Miss Mehitable. "Well, Brighteyes, you may come too," she added,
to me. "A precious row there will be among the old books when
you all get together there"; — and Miss Mehitable, with the gay,
tripping figure by her side, left the room.

"Is this great, big, dark house yours?" said the child, as they
came under the shadow of a dense thicket of syringas and lilacs
that overhung the front of the house.

"Yes, this is Doubting Castle," said Miss Mehitable.

"And does Giant Despair live here?" said Tina. "Mamma showed me a picture of him once in a book."

"Well, he has tried many times to take possession," said Miss Mehitable, "but I do what I can to keep him out, and you must help me."

Saying this she opened the door of a large, old-fashioned room, that appeared to have served both the purposes of a study and parlor. It was revealed to view by the dusky, uncertain glimmer of a wood fire that had burned almost down on a pair of tall brass andirons. The sides of the room were filled to the ceiling with book-cases full of books. Some dark portraits of men and women were duskily revealed by the flickering light, as well as a wide, ample-bosomed chintz sofa and a great chintz-covered easy-chair. A table draped with a green cloth stood in a corner by the fire, strewn over with books and writing-materials, and sustaining a large work-basket.

"How dark it is!" said the child.

Miss Mehitable took a burning splinter of the wood, and lighted a candle in a tall, plated candlestick, that stood on the high, narrow mantel-piece over the fireplace. At this moment a side door opened, and a large-boned woman, dressed in a homespun stuff petticoat, with a short, loose sack of the same material, appeared at the door. Her face was freckled; her hair, of a carroty-yellow, was plastered closely to her head and secured by a horn comb; her eyes were so sharp and searching, that, as she fixed them on Tina, she blinked involuntarily. Around her neck she wore a large string of gold beads, the brilliant gleam of which, catching the firelight, revealed itself at once to Tina's eye, and caused her to regard the woman with curiosity.

She appeared to have opened the door with an intention of asking a question; but stopped and surveyed the child with a sharp expression of not very well-pleased astonishment. "I thought you spoke to me," she said, at last, to Miss Mehitable.

"You may warm my bed now, Polly," said Miss Mehitable; "I shall be ready to go up in a few moments."

Polly stood a moment more, as if awaiting some communication about the child; but as Miss Mehitable turned away, and appeared to be busying herself about the fire, Polly gave a sudden windy dart from the room, and closed the door with a bang that made the window-casings rattle.

"Why, what did she do that for?" said Tina.

"O, it's Polly's way; she does everything with all her might," said Miss Mehitable.

"Don't she like *me?*" said the child.

"Probably not. She knows nothing about you, and she does not like new things."

"But won't she *ever* like me?" persisted Tina.

"*That,* my dear, will depend in a great degree on yourself. If she sees that you are good and behave well, she will probably end by liking you; but old people like her are afraid that children will meddle with their things, and get them out of place."

"I mean to be good," said Tina, resolutely. "When I lived with Miss Asphyxia, I wanted to be bad, I tried to be bad; but now I am changed. I mean to be good, because you are good to me," and the child laid her head confidingly in Miss Mehitable's lap.

The dearest of all flattery to the old and uncomely is this caressing, confiding love of childhood, and Miss Mehitable felt a glow of pleasure about her dusky old heart at which she really wondered. "Can anything so fair really love *me?*" she asked herself. Alas! how much of this cheap-bought happiness goes to waste daily! While unclaimed children grow up loveless, men and women wither in lonely, craving solitude.

Polly again appeared at the door. "Your bed's all warm, and you'd better go right up, else what's the use of warming it?"

"Yes, I'll come immediately," said Miss Mehitable, endeavoring steadfastly to look as if she did not see Polly's looks, and to act as if there had of course always been a little girl to sleep with her.

"Come, my little one." *My* little one! Miss Mehitable's heart gave a great throb at this possessive pronoun. It all seemed as strange to her as a dream. A few hours ago, and she sat in the old windy, lonesome house, alone with the memories of dead friends, and feeling herself walking to the grave in a dismal solitude. Suddenly she awoke as from a dark dream, and found herself sole possessor of beauty, youth, and love, in a glowing little form, all her own, with no mortal; to dispute it. She had a mother's right in a child. She might have a daughter's love. The whole house seemed changed. The dreary, lonesome great hall, with its tall, solemn-ticking clock, the wide, echoing staircase, up which Miss Mehitable had crept, shivering and alone, so many sad nights, now gave back the chirpings of Tina's rattling gayety and the silvery echoes of her laugh, as, happy in her new lot, she danced up the stairway, stopping to ask eager questions on this and that, as anything struck her fancy. For Miss Tina had one of those buoyant, believing natures, born to ride always on the very top crest of every wave, — one fully disposed to accept of good fortune in all its length and breadth, and to make the most of it at once.

"This is *our* home," she said, "isn't it?"

"Yes, darling," said Miss Mehitable, catching her in her arms fondly; "it is *our* home; we will have good times here together."

Tina threw her arms around Miss Mehitable's neck and kissed her. "I'm so glad! Harry said that God would find us a home as soon as it was best, and now here it comes."

Miss Mehitable set the child down by the side of a great dark wooden bedstead, with tall, carved posts, draped with curious curtains of India linen, where strange Oriental plants and birds, and quaint pagodas and figures in turbans, were all mingled together, like the phantasms in a dream. Then going to a tall chest of drawers, resplendent with many brass handles, which reached almost to the ceiling, she took a bunch of keys from her pocket and unlocked a drawer. A spasm as of pain passed over her face as she opened it, and her hands trembled with some suppressed emotion as she took up and laid down various articles, searching for something. At last she found what she wanted, and shook it out. It was a child's nightgown, of just the size needed by Tina. It was yellow with age, but made with dainty care. She sat down by the child and began a movement towards undressing her.

"Shall I say my prayers to you," said Tina, "before I go to bed?"

"Certainly," said Miss Mehitable; "by all means."

"They are rather long," said the child, apologetically, — "that is, if I say all that Harry does. Harry said mamma wanted us to say them all every night. It takes some time."

"O, by all means say all," said Miss Mehitable.

Tina kneeled down by her and put her hands in hers, and said the Lord's Prayer, and the psalm, "The Lord is my shepherd." She had a natural turn for elocution, this little one, and spoke her words with a grace and an apparent understanding not ordinary in childhood.

"There's a hymn, besides," she said. "It belongs to the prayer."

"Well, let us have that," said Miss Mehitable.

Tina repeated, —

> "One there is above all others
>> Well deserves the name of Friend;
> His is love beyond a brother's,
>> Costly, free, and knows no end."

She had an earnest, half-heroic way of repeating, and as she gazed into her listener's eyes she perceived, by a subtle instinct, that what she was saying affected her deeply. She stopped, wondering.

"Go on, my love," said Miss Mehitable.

Tina continued, with enthusiasm, feeling that she was making an impression on her auditor: —

> "Which of all our friends, to save us,
>> Could or would have shed his blood?
> But the Saviour died to have us
>> Reconciled in him to God.
>
> "When he lived on earth abaséd,
>> Friend of sinners was his name;
> Now, above all glory raiséd,
>> He rejoiceth in the same."

"O my child, where did you learn that hymn?" said Miss Mehitable, to whom the words were new. Simple and homely as they were, they had struck on some inner nerve, which was vibrating with intense feeling. Tears were standing in her eyes.

"It was mamma's hymn," said Tina. "She always used to say it. There is one more verse," she added.

> "O for grace our hearts to soften!
>> Teach us, Lord, at length to love;
> We, alas! forget too often
>> What a Friend we have above."

"Is that the secret of all earthly sorrow, then?" said Miss Mehitable aloud, in involuntary soliloquy. The sound of her own voice seemed to startle her. She sighed deeply, and kissed the child. "Thank you, my darling. It does me good to hear you," she said.

The child had entered so earnestly, so passionately even, into the spirit of the words she had been repeating, that she seemed to Miss Mehitable to be transfigured into an angel messenger, sent to inspire faith in God's love in a darkened, despairing soul. She put her into bed; but Tina immediately asserted her claim to an earthly nature by stretching herself exultingly in the warm bed, with an exclamation of vivid pleasure.

"How different this seems from my cold old bed at Miss Asphyxia's!" she said. "O, that horrid woman! how I *hate* her!" she added, with a scowl and a frown, which made the angelhood of the child more than questionable.

Miss Mehitable's vision melted. It was not a child of heaven, but a little mortal sinner, that she was tucking up for the night; and she felt constrained to essay her first effort at moral training.

"My dear," she said, "did you not say, to-night, 'Forgive us our trespasses, *as* we forgive those who trespass against us'? Do you know what that means?"

"O yes," said Tina, readily.

"Well, if your Heavenly Father should forgive your sins just *as* you forgive Miss Asphyxia, how would you like that?"

There was a silence. The large bright eyes grew round and reflective, as they peered out from between the sheets and the pillow. At last she said, in a modified voice: "Well, I won't hate her any more. But," she added, with increased vivacity, "I may think she's hateful, mayn't I?"

Is there ever a hard question in morals that children do not drive straight at, in their wide-eyed questioning?

Miss Mehitable felt inclined to laugh, but said, gravely: "I wouldn't advise you to think evil about her. Perhaps she is a poor woman that never had any one to love her, or anything to love, and it has made her hard."

Tina looked at Miss Mehitable earnestly, as if she were pondering the remark. "She told me that she was put to work younger than I was," she said, "and kept at it all the time."

"And perhaps, if you had been kept at work all your life in that hard way, you would have grown up to be just like her."

"Well, then, I'm sorry for her," said Tina. "There's nobody loves her, that's a fact. Nobody can love her, unless it's God. He loves every one, Harry says."

"Well, good night, my darling," said Miss Mehitable, kissing her. "I shall come to bed pretty soon. I will leave you a candle," she added; "because this is a strange place."

"How good you are!" said Tina. "I used to be so afraid in the dark, at Miss Asphyxia's; and I was so wicked all day, that I was afraid of God too, at night. I used sometimes to think I heard something chewing under my bed; and I thought it was a wolf, and would eat me up."

"Poor little darling!" said Miss Mehitable. "Would you rather I sat by you till you went to sleep?"

"No, thank you; I don't like to trouble you," said the child. "If you leave a candle I sha'n't be afraid. And, besides, I've said my prayers now. I didn't use to say them one bit at Miss Asphyxia's. She would tell me to say my prayers, and then bang the door so hard, and I would feel cross, and think I wouldn't. But I am better now, because you love me."

Miss Mehitable returned to the parlor, and sat down to ponder over her fire; and the result of her ponderings shall be given in a letter which she immediately began writing at the green-covered table.

CHAPTER XIX

MISS MEHITABLE'S LETTER, AND THE REPLY, GIVING FURTHER HINTS OF THE STORY

My dear Brother: — Since I wrote you last, so strange a change has taken place in my life that even now I walk about as in a dream, and hardly know myself. The events of a few hours have made everything in the world seem to me as different from what it ever seemed before as death is from life.

Not to keep you waiting, after so solemn a preface, I will announce to you first, briefly, what it is, and then, secondly, how it happened.

Well, then, *I have adopted a child,* in my dry and wilted old age. She is a beautiful and engaging little creature, full of life and spirits, — full of warm affections, — thrown an absolute waif and stray on the sands of life. Her mother was an unknown Englishwoman, — probably some relict of the retired English army. She died in great destitution, in the neighboring town of Needmore, leaving on the world two singularly interesting children, a boy and a girl. They were, of course, taken in charge by the parish, and fell to the lot of old Crab Smith and his sister, Miss Asphyxia, — just think of it! I think I need say no more than this about their lot.

In a short time they ran away from cruel treatment; lived in a desolate little housekeeping way in the old Dench house; till finally Sam Lawson, lounging about in his general and universal way, picked them up. He brought them, of course, where every wandering, distressed thing comes, — to Deacon Badger's.

Now I suppose the Deacon is comfortably off in the world, as our New England farmers go, but his ability to maintain general charges of housekeeping for all mankind may seriously be doubted. Lois Badger, who does the work of Martha in that establishment, came over to me, yesterday afternoon, quite distressed in her mind about it. Lois is a worthy creature, — rather sharp, to be sure, but, when her edge is turned the right way, none the worse for that, — and really I thought she had the right of it, to some extent.

People in general are so resigned to have other folks made burnt sacrifices, that it did not appear to me probable that there was a creature in Oldtown who would do anything more than rejoice that Deacon Badger felt able to take the children. After I had made some rather bitter reflections on the world, and its selfishness, in the style that we all practise, the thought suddenly occurred to me, What do you, more than others? and that idea, together with the beauty and charms of the poor little waif, decided me to take this bold step. I shut my eyes, and took it, — not without quaking in my shoes for fear of Polly; but I have carried my point in her very face, without so much as saying by your leave.

The little one has just been taken up stairs and tucked up warmly in my own bed, with one of our poor little Emily's old nightgowns on. They fit her exactly, and I exult over her as one that findeth great spoil.

Polly has not yet declared herself, except by slamming the door very hard when she first made the discovery of the child's presence in the house. I presume there is an equinoctial gale gathering, but I say nothing; for, after all, Polly is a good creature, and will blow herself round into the right quarter, in time, as our northeast rainstorms generally do. People always accommodate themselves to certainties.

I cannot but regard the coming of this child to me at this time as a messenger of mercy from God, to save me from sinking into utter despair. I have been so lonely, so miserable, so utterly, inexpressibly wretched of late, that it has seemed that, if something did not happen to help me, I must lose my reason. Our family disposition to melancholy is a hard enough thing to manage under the most prosperous circumstances. I remember my father's paroxysms of gloom: they used to frighten me when I was a little girl, and laid a heavy burden on the heart of our dear angel mother. Whatever that curse is, we all inherit it. In the heart of every one of us children there is that fearful *black drop*, like that which the Koran says the angel showed to Mahomet. It is an inexplicable something which always predisposes us to sadness, but in which any real, appreciable sorrow strikes a terribly deep and long root. Shakespeare describes this thing, as he does everything else: —

"In sooth, I know not why I am so sad:
It wearies me, — you say it wearies you;
But how I caught it, found it, or came by it,
What stuff 't is made of, whereof it is born,
I am to learn."

You have struggled with it by the most rational means, — an active out-of-door life, by sea voyages and severe manual labor. A *man* can fight this dragon as a woman cannot. We women are helpless, — tied to places, forms, and rules, — chained to our stake. We must meet him as we can.

Of late I have not been able to sleep, and, lying awake all night long in darkness and misery, have asked, if *this* be life, whether an immortal existence is not a curse to be feared, rather than a blessing to be hoped, and if the wretchedness we fear in the eternal world can be worse than what we sometimes suffer now, — such sinking of heart, such helplessness of fear, such a vain calling for help that never comes. Well, I will not live it over again, for I dare say you know it all too well. I think I finally wore myself out in trying to cheer poor brother Theodore's darksome way down to death. Can you wonder that he would take opium? God alone can judge people that suffer as he did, and, let people say what they please, I must, I will, think that God has some pity for the work of his hands.

Now, brother, I must, I will, write to you about Emily; though you have said you never wished to hear her name again. What right had you, her brother, to give her up so, and to let the whole burden of this dreadful mystery and sorrow come down on me alone? You are not certain that she has gone astray in the worst sense that a woman can. We only know that she has broken away from us and gone, — but where, how, and with whom, you cannot say, nor I. And certainly there was great excuse for her. Consider how the peculiar temperament and constitution of our family wrought upon her. Consider the temptations of her wonderful beauty, her highly nervous, wildly excitable organization. Her genius was extraordinary; her strength and vigor of character quite as much so. Altogether, she was a perilously constituted human being, — and what did we do with her? A good, common girl might have been put with Uncle and Aunt Farnsworth with great advantage. We put her there for the simple reason that they were her aunt and uncle, and had money enough to educate her. But in all other respects they were about the most unsuited that could be conceived. I must say that I think that glacial, gloomy, religious training in Uncle Farnsworth's family was, for her, peculiarly unfortunate. She sat from Sunday to Sunday under Dr. Stern's preaching. With a high-keyed, acute mind, she could not help listening and thinking; and such thinking is unfortunate, to say the least.

It always seemed to me that he was one of those who experiment on the immortal soul as daring doctors experiment on the body, — using the most violent and terrible remedies, — remedies that must kill or cure. His theory was, that a secret enemy to God was lying latent in every soul, which, like some virulent poisons in the body, could only be expelled by being brought to the surface; and he had sermon after sermon, whose only object appeared to be to bring into vivid consciousness what he calls the natural opposition of the human heart.

But, alas! in some cases the enmity thus aroused can never be subdued; and Emily's was a nature that would break before it would bow. Nothing could have subdued her but love, — and love she never heard. These appalling doctrines were presented with such logical clearness, and apparently so established from the Scriptures, that, unable to distinguish between the word of God and the cruel deductions of human logic, she trod both under foot in defiant despair. Then came in the French literature, which is so fascinating, and which just now is having so wide an influence on the thinking of our country. Rousseau and Voltaire charmed her, and took her into a new world. She has probably gone to France for liberty, with no protection but her own virgin nature. Are we at once to infer the worst, when we know so little? I, for one, shall love her and trust in her to the end; and if ever she should fall, and do things that I and all the world must condemn, I shall still say, that it will be less her fault than that of others; that she will be one of those who fall by their higher, rather than their lower nature.

I have a prophetic instinct in my heart that some day, poor, forlorn, and forsaken, she will look back with regret to the old house where she was born: and then she shall be welcome here.

This is why I keep this solitary old place, full of bitter and ghostly memories; because, as long as I keep it, there is one refuge that Emily may call her own, and one heart that will be true to her, and love her and believe in her to the end.

I think God has been merciful to me in sending me this child, to be to me as a daughter. Already her coming has been made a means of working in me that great moral change for which all my life I have been blindly seeking. I have sought that *conversion* which our father taught us to expect as alchemists seek the philosopher's stone.

What have I not read and suffered at the hands of the theologians? How many lonely hours, day after day, have I bent the knee in fruitless prayer that God would grant me this great, unknown grace! for without it how dreary is life!

We are in ourselves so utterly helpless, — life is so hard, so inexplicable, that we stand in perishing need of some helping hand, some sensible, appreciable connection with God. And yet for years every cry of misery, every breath of anguish, has been choked by the logical proofs of theology; — that God is my enemy, or that I am his; that every effort I make toward Him but aggravates my offence; and that this unknown gift, which no child of Adam ever did compass of himself, is so completely in my own power, that I am every minute of my life to blame for not possessing it.

How many hours have I gone round and round this dreary track, — chilled, weary, shivering, seeing no light, and hearing no voice! But within this last hour it seems as if a divine ray had shone upon me, and the great gift had been given me by the hand of a little child. It came in the simplest and most unexpected manner, while listening to a very homely hymn, repeated by this dear little one. The words themselves were not much in the way of poetry; it was merely the simplest statement of the truth that in Jesus Christ, ever living, ever present, every human soul has a personal friend, divine and almighty.

This thought came over me with such power, that it seemed as if all my doubts, all my intricate, contradictory theologies, all those personal and family sorrows which had made a burden on my soul greater than poor Christian ever staggered under, had gone where his did, when, at the sight of the Cross, it loosed from his back and rolled down into the sepulchre, to be seen no more. Can it be, I asked myself, that this mighty love, that I feel so powerfully and so sweetly, has been near me all these dark, melancholy years? Has the sun been shining behind all these heavy clouds, under whose shadows I have spent my life?

When I laid my little Tina down to sleep to-night, I came down here to think over this strange, new thought, — that I, even I, in my joyless old age, my poverty, my perplexities, my loneliness, am no longer alone! I am beloved. There is One who does love me, — the One Friend, whose love, like the sunshine, can be the portion of each individual of the human race, without exhaustion. This is the great mystery of faith, which I am determined from this hour to keep whole and undefiled.

My dear brother, I have never before addressed to you a word on this subject. It has been one in which I saw only perplexity. I have, it is true, been grieved and disappointed that you did not see your way clear to embrace the sacred ministry, which has for so many generations been the appointed work of our family. I confess for many years I did hope to see you succeed, not only to the library, but to the work of our honored, venerated father and grandfather. It was my hope that, in this position, I should find in you a spiritual guide to resolve my doubts and lead me aright. But I have gathered from you at times, by chance words dropped, that you could not exactly accept the faith of our fathers. Perhaps difficulties like my own have withheld you. I know you too well to believe that the French scepticism that has blown over here with the breath of our political revolution can have had the least influence over you. Whatever your views of doctrines may be, you are not a doubter. You are not — as poor Emily defiantly called herself — a deist, an alien from all that our fathers came to this wilderness to maintain. Yet when I see you burying your talents in a lonely mountain village, satisfied with the work of a poor schoolmaster, instead of standing forth to lead our New England in the pulpit, I ask myself, Why is this?

Speak to me, brother! tell me your innermost thoughts, as I have told you mine. Is not life short and sad and bitter enough, that those who could help each other should neglect the few things they can do to make it tolerable? Why do we travel side by side, lonely and silent, — each, perhaps, hiding in that silence the bread of life that the other needs? Write to me as I have written to you, and let me know that I have a brother in soul, as I have in flesh.

Your affectionate sister,

M. R.

MY DEAR SISTER: — I have read your letter. Answer it justly and truly how can I? How little we know of each other in outside intimacy! but when we put our key into the door of the secret chamber, who does not tremble and draw back? — *that* is the true haunted chamber!

First, about Emily, I will own I am wrong. It is from no want of love, though, but from too much. I was and am too sore and bitter on that subject to trust myself. I have a heart full of curses, but don't know exactly where to fling them; and, for aught I see, we are utterly helpless. Every clew fails; and what is the use of torturing ourselves? It is a man's nature to act, to do, and, where nothing can be done, to forget. It is a woman's nature to hold on to what can only torture, and live all her despairs over. Women's tears are their meat; men find the diet too salt, and won't take it.

Tell me anything I can *do*, and I'll do it; but talk I cannot, — every word burns me. I admit every word you say of Emily. We were mistaken in letting her go to the Farnsworths, and be baited and tortured with ultra-Calvinism; but we were blind, as we mortals always are, — fated never to see what we should have done, till seeing is too late.

I am glad you have taken that child, — first, because it's a good deed in itself, and, secondly, because it's good for you. That it should have shed light on your relations to God is strictly philosophical. You have been trying to find your way to Him by definitions and by logic; one might as well make love to a lady by the first book of Euclid. "He that loveth not his brother whom he hath seen, how can he love God whom he hath not seen?" That throb of protecting, all-embacing love which thrilled through your heart for this child taught you more of God than father's whole library. "He that loveth not knoweth not God." The old Bible is philosophical, and eminent for its common sense. Of course this child will make a fool of you. Never mind; the follies of love are remedial.

As to a system of education, it will be an amusement for you to get that up. Every human being likes to undertake to dictate for some other one. Go at it with good cheer. But, whatever you do, don't teach her *French*. Give her a good Saxon-English education; and, if she needs a pasture-land of foreign languages, let her learn Latin, and, more than that, Greek. Greek is the morning-land of languages, and has the freshness of early dew in it which will never exhale.

The French helped us in our late war: for that I thank them; but from French philosophy and French democracy, may the good Lord deliver us. They slew their Puritans in the massacre of St. Bartholomew, and the nation ever since has been without a moral sense. French literature is like an eagle with one broken wing. What the Puritans did for us English people, in bringing in civil liberty, they lacked. Our revolutions have been gradual. I predict theirs will come by and by with an explosion.

Meanwhile, our young men who follow after French literature become rakes and profligates. Their first step in liberty is to repeal the ten commandments, especially the seventh. Therefore I consider a young woman in our day misses nothing who does not read French. Decorous French literature is stupid, and bright French literature is too wicked for anything. So let French alone.

She threatens to be pretty, does she? So much the worse for you and her. If she makes you too much trouble by and by, send her up to my academy, and I will drill her, and make a Spartan of her.

As to what you say about religion, and the ministry, and the schoolmaster, what can I say on this sheet of paper? Briefly then. No, I am *not* in any sense an unbeliever in the old Bible; I would as soon disbelieve my own mother. And I am in my nature a thorough Puritan. I am a Puritan as thoroughly as a hound is a hound, and a pointer a pointer, whose pedigree of unmixed blood can be traced for generations back. I feel within me the preaching instinct, just as the hound snuffs, and the pointer points; but as to the pulpit in these days, — well, thereby hangs a tale.

What should I preach, supposing I were a minister, as my father, and grandfather, and great-grandfather were before me? What they preached was true to them, was fitted for their times, was loyally and sincerely said, and of course did a world of good. But when I look over their sermons, I put an interrogation point to almost everything they say; and what was true to them is not true to me; and if I should speak out as honestly as they did what *is* true to me, the world would not understand or receive it, and I think it would do more harm than good. I believe I am thinking ahead of the present generation, and if I should undertake to push my thoughts I should only bother people, — just as one of my bright boys in the latter part of the algebra sometimes worries a new beginner with his advanced explanations.

Then again, our late Revolution has wrought a change in the ministry that will soon become more and more apparent. The time when ministers were noblemen by divine right, and reigned over their parishes by the cocked hat and gold-headed cane, is passing away. Dr. Lothrop, and Dr. Stern, and a few others, keep up the prestige, but that sort of thing is going by; and in the next generation the minister will be nothing but a citizen; his words will come without prestige, and be examined and sifted just like the words of any other citizen.

There is a race of ministers rising up who are fully adequate to meet this exigency; and these men are going to throw Calvinism down into the arena, and discuss every inch of it, hand to hand and knee to knee, with the common people; and we shall see what will come of this.

I, for my part, am not prepared to be a minister on these terms. Still, as I said, I have the born instinct of preaching; I am dictatorial by nature, and one of those who need constantly to see themselves reflected in other people's eyes; and so I have got an academy here, up in the mountains, where I have a set of as clear, bright-eyed, bright-minded boys and girls as you would wish to see, and am in my way a pope. Well, I enjoy being a pope. It is one of my weaknesses.

As to society, we have the doctor, — a quiet little wrinkled old man, a profound disbeliever in medicines, who gives cream-of tartar for ordinary cases, and camomile tea when the symptoms become desperate, and reads Greek for his own private amusement. Of course he doesn't get very rich, but here in the mountains one can afford to be poor. One of our sunsets is worth half a Boston doctor's income.

Then there's the lawyer and squire, who draws the deeds, and makes the wills, and settles the quarrels; and the minister, who belongs to the new dispensation. He and I are sworn friends; he is

my Fidus Achates. His garden joins mine, and when I am hoeing
my corn he is hoeing his, and thence comes talk. As it gets more
eager I jump the fence and hoe in his garden, or he does the same
to mine. We have a strife on the matter of garden craft, who shall
with most skill outwit our Mother Nature, and get cantelopes and
melons under circumstances in which she never intended them to
grow. This year I beat the parson, but I can see that he is secretly
resolved to revenge himself on me when the sweet corn comes in.
One evening every week we devote to reading the newspaper and
settling the affairs of the country. We are both stanch Federalists,
and make the walls ring with our denunciations of Jacobinism and
Democracy. Once a month we have the Columbian Magazine and
the foreign news from Europe, and then we have a great deal on
our hands; we go over affairs, every country systematically, and
settle them for the month. In general we are pretty well agreed, but
now and then our lines of policy differ, and then we fight it out with
good courage, not sparing the adjectives. The parson has a sly humor of his own, and our noisiest discussions generally end in a
hearty laugh.

So much for the man and friend, — now for the clergyman. He
is neither the sentimental, good parson of Goldsmith, nor the plaintive, ascetic parish priest of Romanism, nor the cocked hat of the
theocracy, but a lively, acute, full-blooded *man,* who does his duty
on equal terms among men. He is as singlehearted as an unblem-
ished crystal, and in some matters sacredly simple; but yet not
without a thrifty practical shrewdness, both in things temporal and
things spiritual. He has an income of about two hundred and fifty
dollars, with his wood. The farmers about here consider him as
rolling in wealth, and I must say that, though the parsonage is
absolutely bare of luxuries, one is not there often unpleasantly reminded that the parson is a poor man. He has that golden faculty
of enjoying the work he does so utterly, and believing in it so entirely, that he can quite afford to be poor. He whose daily work is
in itself a pleasure ought not to ask for riches: so I tell myself about
my school-keeping, and him about his parish. He takes up the conversion of sinners as an immediate practical business, to be done
and done now; he preaches in all the little hills and dales and hollows and brown school-houses for miles around, and chases his
sinners up and down so zealously, that they have, on the whole, a

lively time of it. He attacks drinking and all our small forms of country immorality with a vigor sufficient to demolish sins of double their size, and gives nobody even a chance to sleep in meeting. The good farmers around here, some of whom would like to serve Mammon comfortably, are rather in a quandary what to do. They never would bear the constant hounding which he gives them, and the cannonades he fires at their pet sins, and the way he chases them from pillar to post, and the merciless manner in which he breaks in upon their comfortable old habit of sleeping in meeting, were it not that they feel that they are paying him an enormous salary, and ought to get their money's worth out of him, which they are certain they are doing most fully. Your Yankee has such a sense of values, that, if he pays a man to thrash him, he wants to be thrashed thoroughly.

My good friend preaches what they call New Divinity, by which I understand the Calvinism which our fathers left us, in the commencing process of disintegration. He is thoroughly and enthusiastically in earnest about it, and believes that the system, as far as Edwards and Hopkins have got it, is almost absolute truth; but, for all that, is cheerfully busy in making some little emendations and corrections, upon which he values himself, and which he thinks of the greatest consequence. What is to the credit of his heart is, that these emendations are generally in favor of some original-minded sheep who can't be got into the sheep-fold without some alteration in the paling. In these cases I have generally noticed that he will loosen a rail or tear off a picket, and let the sheep in, it being his impression, after all, that the sheep are worth more than the sheep-fold.

In his zeal to catch certain shy sinners, he has more than once preached sermons which his brethren about here find fault with, as wandering from old standards; and it costs abundance of bustle and ingenuity to arrange his system so as to provide for exceptional cases, and yet to leave it exactly what it was before the alterations were made.

It is, I believe, an admitted thing among theologians, that, while theology must go on improving from age to age, it must also remain exactly what it was a hundred years ago.

The parson is my intimate friend, and it is easy for me to see that he has designs for the good of my soul, for which I sincerely love him. I can see that he is lying in wait for me patiently, as sometimes we do for trout, when we go out fishing together. He reconnoitres me, approaches me carefully, makes nice little logical traps to catch me in, and baits them with very innocent-looking questions, which I, being an old theological rat, skilfully avoid answering.

My friend's forte is logic. Between you and me, if there is a golden calf worshipped in our sanctified New England, its name is Logic; and my good friend the parson burns incense before it with a most sacred innocence of intention. He believes that sinners can be converted by logic, and that, if he could once get me into one of these neat little traps aforesaid, the salvation of my soul would be assured. He has caught numbers of the shrewdest infidel foxes among the farmers around, and I must say that there is no trap for the Yankee like the logic-trap.

I must tell you a story about this that amused me greatly. You know everybody's religious opinions are a matter of discussion in our neighborhood, and Ezekiel Scranton, a rich farmer who lives up on the hill, enjoys the celebrity of being an atheist, and rather values himself on the distinction. It takes a man of courage, you know, to live without a God; and Ezekiel gives himself out as a plucky dog, and able to hold the parson at bay. The parson, however, had privately prepared a string of questions which he was quite sure would drive Ezekiel into strait quarters. So he meets him the other day in the store.

"How's this, Mr. Scranton? they tell me that you're an atheist!"

"Well I guess I be, Parson," says Ezekiel, comfortably.

"Well, Ezekiel, let's talk about this. You believe in your own existence, don't you?"

"No, I don't."

"What! not believe in your own existence?"

"No, I don't." Then, after a moment, "Tell you what, Parson, ain't a going to be twitched up by none o' your syllogisms."

Ezekiel was quite in the right of it; for I must do my friend the parson the justice to say, that, if you answer one of his simple-looking questions, you are gone. You must say B after saying A, and the whole alphabet after that.

For my part, I do not greatly disbelieve the main points of Calvinism. They strike me, as most hard and disagreeable things do, as quite likely to be true, and very much in accordance with a sensible man's observation of facts as they stand in life and nature. My doubts come up, like bats, from a dark and dreadful cavern that underlies all religion, natural or revealed. They are of a class abhorrent to myself, smothering to my peace, imbittering to my life.

What must he be who is tempted to deny the very right of his Creator to the allegiance of his creatures? — who is tempted to feel that his own conscious existence is an inflicted curse, and that the whole race of men have been a set of neglected, suffering children, bred like fish-spawn on a thousand shores, by a Being who has never interested himself to care for their welfare, to prevent their degradation, to interfere with their cruelties to each other, as they have writhed and wrangled into life, through life, and out of life again? Does this look like being a Father in any sense in which we poor mortals think of fatherhood? After seeing nature, can we reason against any of the harshest conclusions of Calvinism, from the character of its Author?

Do we not consider a man unworthy the name of a good father who, from mere blind reproductive instinct, gives birth to children for whose improvement, virtue, and happiness he makes no provision? and yet does not this seem to be the way more than half of the human race actually comes into existence?

Then the laws of nature are an inextricable labyrinth, — puzzling, crossing, contradictory; and ages of wearisome study have as yet hardly made a portion of them clear enough for human comfort; and doctors and ministers go on torturing the body and the soul, with the most devout good intentions. And so forth, for there is no end to this sort of talk.

Now my friend the parson is the outgrowth of the New England theocracy, about the simplest, purest, and least objectionable state of society that the world ever saw. He has a good digestion, a healthy mind in a healthy body; he lives in a village where there is no pauperism, and hardly any crime, — where all the embarrassing, dreadful social problems and mysteries of life scarcely exist. But I, who have been tumbled up and down upon all the shores of earth, lived in India, China, and Polynesia, and seen the human race as they breed like vermin, in their filth and their contented degradation, — how can I think of applying the measurements of any theological system to a reality like this?

Now the parts of their system on which my dear friend the parson, and those of his school, specially value themselves, are their explanations of the reasons why evil was permitted, and their vindications of the Divine character in view of it. They are specially earnest and alert in giving out their views here, and the parson has read to me more than one sermon, hoping to medicate what he supposes to be my secret wound. To me their various theories are, as my friend the doctor once said to me, "putting their bitter pill in a chestnut-burr; the pill is bad, — there is no help for that, — but the chestnut-burr is impossible."

It is incredible, the ease and cheerfulness with which a man in his study, who never had so much experience of suffering as even a toothache would give him, can arrange a system in which the everlasting torture of millions is casually admitted as an item. But I, to whom, seriously speaking, existence has been for much of my life nothing but suffering, and who always looked on my existence as a misfortune, must necessarily feel reasonings of this kind in a different way. This soul-ache, this throb of pain, that seems as if it were an actual anguish of the immaterial part itself, is a dreadful teacher, and gives a fearful sense of what the chances of an immortal existence might be, and what the responsibilities of originating such existence.

I am not one of the shallow sort, who think that everything for everybody must or ought to end with perfect bliss at death. On the contrary, I do not see how anything but misery in eternal ages is to come from the outpouring into their abyss, of wrangling, undisciplined souls, who were a torment to themselves and others here, and who would make this world unbearable, were they not all swept off in their turn by the cobweb brush of Death.

So you see it's all a hopeless muddle to me. Do I then believe nothing? Yes, I believe in Jesus Christ with all my heart, all my might. He stands before me the one hopeful phenomenon of history. I adore him as Divine, or all of the Divine that I can comprehend; and when he bids me say to God, "Our Father which art in heaven," I smother all my doubts and say it. Those words are the rope thrown out to me, choking in the waters, — the voice from the awful silence. "God *so* loved the world that he gave his own Son." I try to believe that he *loves* this world, but I have got only so far as "Help thou mine unbelief."

Now, as to talking out all this to the parson, what good would it do? He is preaching well and working bravely. His preaching suits the state of advancement to which New England has come; and the process which he and ministers of his sort institute, of having every point in theology fully discussed by the common people, is not only a capital drill for their minds, but it will have its effect in the end on their theologies, and out of them all the truth of the future will arise.

So you see my position, and why I am niched here for life, as a schoolmaster. Come up and see me some time. I have a house-keeper who is as ugly as Hecate, but who reads Greek. She makes the best bread and cake in town, keeps my stockings mended and my shirt-ruffles plaited and my house like wax, and hears a class in Virgil every day, after she has "done her dinner-dishes." I shall not fall in love with her, though. Come some time to see me, and bring your new acquisition.

Your brother,
JONATHAN ROSSITER.

I have given these two letters as the best means of showing to the reader the character of the family with whom my destiny and that of Tina became in future life curiously intertwisted.

Among the peculiarly English ideas which the Colonists brought to Massachusetts, which all the wear and tear of democracy have not been able to obliterate, was that of *family*. Family feeling, family pride, family hope and fear and desire, were, in my early day, strongly-marked traits. Genealogy was a thing at the tip of every person's tongue, and in every person's mind; and it is among my most vivid remembrances, with what a solemn air of intense interest my mother, grandmother, Aunt Lois, and Aunt Keziah would enter into minute and discriminating particulars with regard to the stock, intermarriages, and family settlements of the different persons whose history was under their consideration. "Of

a very respectable family," was a sentence so often repeated at
the old fireside that its influence went in part to make up my character. In our present days, when every man is emphatically the
son of his own deeds, and nobody cares who his mother or grandmother or great-aunt was, there can scarcely be an understanding
of this intense feeling of race and genealogy which pervaded simple colonial Massachusetts.

As I have often before intimated, the aristocracy of Massachusetts consisted of two classes, the magistracy and the ministry;
and these two, in this theocratic State, played into each other's
hands continually. Next to the magistrate and the minister, in the
esteem of that community, came the schoolmaster; for education
might be said to be the ruling passion of the State.

The history of old New England families is marked by strong
lights and deep shadows of personal peculiarity. We appeal to
almost every old settler in New England towns, if he cannot remember stately old houses, inhabited by old families, whose histories might be brought to mind by that of Miss Mehitable and
her brother. There was in them a sort of intellectual vigor, a ceaseless activity of thought, a passion for reading and study, and a
quiet brooding on the very deepest problems of mental and moral
philosophy. The characteristic of such families is the greatly dis-
proportioned force of the internal, intellectual, and spiritual life
to the external one. Hence come often morbid and diseased forms
of manifestation. The threads which connect such persons with
the real life of the outer world are so fine and so weak, that they
are constantly breaking and giving way here and there, so that, in
such races, oddities and eccentricities are come to be accepted only
as badges of family character. Yet from stock of this character have
come some of the most brilliant and effective minds in New England; and from them also have come hermits and recluses, —
peculiar and exceptional people, — people delightful to the student
of human nature, but excessively puzzling to the every-day judgment of mere conventional society.

The Rossiter family had been one of these. It traced its origin
to the colony which came out with Governor Winthrop. The eldest
Rossiter had been one of the ejected ministers, and came from a
good substantial family of the English gentry. For several succes-

sive generations there had never been wanting a son in the Rossiter family to succeed to the pulpit of his father. The Rossiters had been leaned on by the magistrates and consulted by the governors, and their word had been law down to the time of Miss Mehitable's father.

The tendency of the stately old families of New England to constitutional melancholy has been well set forth by Dr. Cotton Mather, that delightful old New England grandmother, whose nursery tales of its infancy and childhood may well be pondered by those who would fully understand its far-reaching maturity. As I have before remarked, I have high ideas of the wisdom of grandmothers, and therefore do our beloved gossip, Dr. Cotton Mather, the greatest possible compliment in granting him the title.

The ministers of the early colonial days of New England, though well-read, scholarly men, were more statesmen than theologians. Their minds ran upon the actual arrangements of society, which were in a great degree left in their hands, rather than on doctrinal and metaphysical subtilties. They took their confession of faith just as the great body of Protestant reformers left it, and acted upon it as a practical foundation, without much further discussion, until the time of President Edwards. He was the first man who began the disintegrating process of applying rationalistic methods to the accepted doctrines of religion, and he rationalized far more boldly and widely than any publishers of his biography have ever dared to let the world know. He sawed the great dam and let out the whole waters of discussion over all New England, and that free discussion led to all the shades of opinion of our modern days. Little as he thought it, yet Waldo Emerson and Theodore Parker were the last results of the current set in motion by Jonathan Edwards.

Miss Mehitable Rossiter's father, during the latter part of his life, had dipped into this belt of New Divinity, and been excessively and immoderately interested in certain speculations concerning them. All the last part of his life had been consumed in writing a treatise in opposition to Dr. Stern, another rigorous old cocked-hat of his neighborhood, who maintained that the Deity had created sin on purpose, because it was a necessary means of the greatest good. Dr. Rossiter thought that evil had only *been permitted,* because it could be overruled for the greatest good; and each of them fought their battle as if the fate of the universe was to be decided by its results.

Considered as a man, in his terrestrial and mundane relations, Dr. Rossiter had that wholesome and homely interest in the things of this mortal life which was characteristic of the New England religious development. While the Puritans were intensely interested in the matters of the soul, they appeared to have a realizing sense of the fact that a soul without a body, in a material world, is at a great disadvantage in getting on. So they exhibited a sensible and commendable sense of the worth of property. They were especially addicted to lawful matrimony, and given to having large families of children; and, if one wife died, they straightway made up the loss by another, — a compliment to the virtues of the female sex which womankind appear always gratefully to appreciate.

Parson Rossiter had been three times married; first, to a strong-grained, homely, highly intellectual woman of one of the first Boston families, of whom Miss Mehitable Rossiter was the only daughter. The Doctor was said to be one of the handsomest men of his times. Nature, with her usual perversity in these matters, made Miss Mehitable an exact reproduction of all the homely traits of her mother, with the addition of the one or two physical defects of her handsome father. No woman with a heart in her bosom ever feels marked personal uncomeliness otherwise than as a great misfortune. Miss Mehitable bore it with a quaint and silent pride. Her brother Jonathan, next to herself in age, the son of a second and more comely wife, was far more gifted in personal points, though not equal to his father. Finally, late in life, after a somewhat prolonged widowhood, Parson Rossiter committed the folly of many men on the downhill side of life, that of marrying a woman considerably younger than himself. She was a pretty, nervous, excitable, sensitive creature, whom her homely elder daughter, Miss Mehitable, no less than her husband, petted and caressed on account of her beauty, as if she had been a child. She gave birth to two more children, a son named Theodore, and a daughter named Emily, and then died.

All the children had inherited from their father the peculiar constitutional tendency to depression of spirits of which we have spoken. In these last two, great beauty and brilliant powers of mind were united with such a singular sensitiveness and way-wardness of nature as made the prospect for happiness in such a life as this, and under the strict requirements of New England society, very problematical.

Theodore ran through a brilliant course in college, notwith-standing constant difficulties with the college authorities, but either could not or would not apply himself to any of the accepted modes of getting bread and butter which a young man must adopt who means to live and get on with other men. He was full of dis-gusts, and repulsions, and dislikes; everything in life wounded and made him sore; he could or would do nothing reasonably or rationally with human beings, and, to deaden the sense of pain in existence, took to the use of opiates, which left him a miserable wreck on his sister's hands, the father being dead.

Thus far the reader has the history of this family, and intima-tions of the younger and more beautiful one whose after fate was yet to be connected with ours.

Miss Mehitable Rossiter has always been to me a curious study. Singularly plain as she was in person, old, withered, and poor, she yet commanded respect, and even reverence, through the whole of a wide circle of acquaintance; for she was well known to some of the most considerable families in Boston, with whom, by her mother's side, she was connected. The interest in her was some-what like that in old lace, old china, and old cashmere shawls; which, though often excessively uncomely, and looking in the eyes of uninterested people like mere rubbish, are held by connoisseurs to be beyond all price.

Miss Mehitable herself had great pride of character, in the sense in which pride is an innocent weakness, if not a species of virtue. She had an innate sense that she belonged to a good family, — a perfectly quiet conviction that she was a Bradford by her mother's side, and a Rossiter by her father's side, come what might in this world. She was too well versed in the duties of good blood not to be always polite and considerate to the last degree to all well-meaning common people, for she felt the *noblesse oblige* as much as if she had been a duchess. And, for that matter, in the circles of Oldtown everything that Miss Mehitable did and said had a certain weight, quite apart from that of her really fine mental powers. It was the weight of past generations, of the whole Colony of Massachusetts; all the sermons of five generations of ministers were in it, which to a God-fearing community is a great deal.

But in her quaint, uncomely body was lodged, not only a most active and even masculine mind, but a heart capable of those passionate extremes of devotion which belong to the purely feminine side of woman. She was capable of a romantic excess of affection, of an extravagance of hero-worship, which, had she been personally beautiful, might perhaps have made her the heroine of some poem of the heart. It was among the quietly accepted sorrows of her life, that for her no such romance was possible.

Men always admired her as they admired other men, and talked to her as they talked with each other. Many, during the course of her life, had formed friendships with her, which were mere relations of comradeship, but which never touched the inner sphere of the heart. That heart, so warm, so tender, and so true, she kept, with a sort of conscious shame, hidden far behind the intrenchments of her intellect. With an instinctive fear of ridicule, she scarcely ever spoke a tender word, and generally veiled a soft emotion under some quaint phrase of drollery. She seemed forever to feel the strange contrast between the burning, romantic heart and the dry and withered exterior.

Like many other women who have borne the curse of marked plainness, Miss Mehitable put an extravagant valuation on personal beauty. Her younger sister, whose loveliness was uncommon, was a sort of petted idol to her, during all her childish years. At the time of her father's death, she would gladly have retained her with her, but, like many other women who are strong on the intellectual side of their nature, Miss Mehitable had a sort of weakness and helplessness in relation to mere material matters, which rendered her, in the eyes of the family, unfit to be trusted with the bringing up of a bright and wilful child. In fact, as regarded all the details of daily life, Miss Mehitable was the servant of Polly, who had united the offices of servant-of-all-work, housekeeper, nurse, and general factotum in old Parson Rossiter's family, and between whom and the little wilful Emily grievous quarrels had often arisen. For all these reasons, and because Mrs. Farnsworth of the neighboring town of Adams was the only sister of the child's mother, was herself childless, and in prosperous worldly circumstances, it would have been deemed a flying in the face of Providence to refuse her, when she declared her intention of adopting her sister's child as her own.

Of what came of this adoption I shall have occasion to speak hereafter.

CHAPTER XX

---◄◎►---

MISS ASPHYXIA GOES IN PURSUIT, AND MY GRANDMOTHER GIVES HER VIEWS ON EDUCATION

When Miss Asphyxia Smith found that both children really had disappeared from Needmore so completely that no trace of them remained, to do her justice, she felt some solicitude to know what had become of them. There had not been wanting instances in those early days, when so large a part of Massachusetts was unbroken forest, of children who had wandered away into the woods and starved to death; and Miss Asphyxia was by no means an ill-wisher to any child, nor so utterly without bowels as to contemplate such a possibility without some anxiety.

Not that she in the least doubted the wisdom and perfect propriety of her own mode of administration, which she had full faith would in the end have made a "smart girl" of her little charge. "That 'ere little limb didn't know what was good for herself," she said to Sol, over their evening meal of cold potatoes and boiled beef.

Sol looked round-eyed and stupid, and squared his shoulders, as he always did when this topic was introduced. He suggested, "You don't s'pose they could 'a' wandered off to the maountains where Bijah Peters' boy got lost?"

There was a sly satisfaction in observing the anxious, brooding expression which settled down over Miss Asphyxia's dusky features at the suggestion.

"When they found that 'ere boy," continued Sol, "he was all worn to skin and bone; he'd kep' himself a week on berries and ches'nuts and sich, but a boy can't be kep' on what a squirrel can."

"Well," said Miss Asphyxia, "I know one thing; it ain't my fault if they do starve to death. Silly critters, they was; well provided for, good home, good clothes, plenty and plenty to eat. I'm sure you can bear witness ef I ever stinted that 'ere child in her victuals."

"I'll bear you out on that 'ere," said Sol.

"And well you may; I'd scorn not to give any one in my house a good bellyful," quoth Miss Asphyxia.

"That's true enough," said Sol; "everybody'll know that."

"Well, it's jest total depravity," said Miss Asphyxia. "How can any one help bein' convinced o' that, that has anything to do with young uns?"

But the subject preyed upon the severe virgin's mind; and she so often mentioned it, with that roughening of her scrubby eyebrows which betokened care, that Sol's unctuous good-nature was somewhat moved, and he dropped at last a hint of having fallen on a trace of the children. He might as well have put the tips of his fingers into a rolling-mill. Miss Asphyxia was so wide-awake and resolute about anything that she wanted to know, that Sol at last was obliged to finish with informing her that he had heard of the children as having been taken in at Deacon Badger's, over in Oldtown. Sol internally chuckled, as he gave the information, when he saw how immediately Miss Asphyxia bristled with wrath. Even the best of human beings have felt that transient flash when anxiety for the fate of a child supposed to be in fatal danger gives place to unrestrained vexation at the little culprit who has given such a fright.

"Well, I shall jest tackle up and go over and bring them children home agin, at least the girl. Brother, he says he don't want the boy; he wa'n't nothin' but a plague; but I'm one o' them persons that when I undertake a thing I mean to go through with it. Now I undertook to raise that 'ere girl, and I mean to. She needn't think she's goin' to come round me with any o' her shines, going over to Deacon Badger's with lying stories about me. Mis' Deacon Badger needn't think she's goin' to hold up her head over me, if she *is* a deacon's wife and I *ain't* a perfessor of religion. I guess I *could* be a perfessor if I chose to do as some folks do. That's what I told Mis' Deacon Badger once when she asked me why I didn't jine the church. 'Mis' Badger,' says I, 'perfessin ain't possessin, and I'd ruther stand outside the church than go on as some people do inside on 't.'"

Therefore it was that a day or two after, when Miss Mehitable was making a quiet call at my grandmother's, and the party, consisting of my grandmother, Aunt Lois, and Aunt Keziah, were peacefully rattling their knitting-needles, while Tina was playing by the river-side, the child's senses were suddenly paralyzed by the sight of Miss Asphyxia driving with a strong arm over the bridge near my grandmother's.

In a moment the little one's heart was in her throat. She had such an awful faith in Miss Asphyxia's power to carry through anything she undertook, that all her courage withered at once at sight of her. She ran in at the back door, perfectly pale with fright, and seized hold imploringly of Miss Mehitable's gown.

"O, she's coming! she's coming after me. Don't let her get me!" she exclaimed.

"What's the matter now?" said my grandmother. "What ails the child?"

Miss Mehitable lifted her in her lap, and began a soothing course of inquiry; but the child clung to her, only reiterating, "Don't let her have me! she is dreadful! don't!"

"As true as you live, mother," said Aunt Lois, who had tripped to the window, "there's Miss Asphyxia Smith hitching her horse at our picket fence."

"She is?" said my grandmother, squaring her shoulders, and setting herself in fine martial order. "Well, let her come in; she's welcome, I'm sure. I'd like to talk to that woman! It's a free country, and everybody's got to speak their minds," — and my grandmother rattled her needles with great energy.

In a moment more Miss Asphyxia entered. She was arrayed in her best Sunday clothes, and made the neighborly salutations with an air of grim composure. There was silence, and a sense of something brooding in the air, as there often is before the outburst of a storm.

Finally, Miss Asphyxia opened the trenches. "I come over, Mis' Badger, to see about a gal o' mine that has run away." Here her eye rested severely on Tina.

"Run away!" quoth my grandmother, briskly; "and good reason she should run away; all I wonder at is that you have the face to come to a Christian family after her, — that's all. Well, she is provided for, and you've no call to be inquiring anything about *her*. So I advise you to go home, and attend to your own affairs, and leave children to folks that know how to manage them better than you do."

"I expected this, Mis' Badger," said Miss Asphyxia, in a towering wrath, "but I'd have you to know that I ain't a person that's going to take sa'ace from no one. No deacon nor deacon's wife, nor perfesser of religion, 's a goin' to turn up their noses at me! I can hold up my head with any on 'em, and I think your religion might teach you better than takin' up stories agin your neighbors, as a little lyin', artful hussy'll tell." Here there was a severe glance at Miss Tina, who quailed before it, and clung to Miss Mehitable's gown. "Yes, indeed, you may hide your head," she continued, "but you can't git away from the truth; not when I'm round to bring you out. Yes, Mis' Badger, I defy her to say I hain't done well by her, if she says the truth; for I say it now, this blessed minute, and would say it on my dyin' bed, and you can ask Sol ef that 'ere child hain't had everything pervided for her that a child could want, — a good clean bed and plenty o' bedclothes, and good whole clothes to wear, and her belly full o' good victuals every day; an' me a teachin' and a trainin' on her, enough to wear the very life out o' me, — for I always hated young uns, and this ere's a perfect little limb as I ever did see. Why, what did she think I was a goin' to do for her? I didn't make a lady on her; to be sure I didn't: I was a fetchin' on her up to work for her livin' as I was fetched up. I hadn't nothin' more'n she; an' just look at me now; there ain't many folks that can turn off as much work in a day as I can, though I say it that shouldn't. And I've got as pretty a piece of property, and as well seen to, as most any round; and all I've got — house and lands — is my own arnin's, honest, so there! There's folks, I s'pose, that thinks they can afford to keep tavern for all sorts of stragglers and runaways, Injun and white. I never was one o' them sort of folks, an' I should jest like to know ef those folks is able, — that's all. I guess if 'counts was added up, my 'counts would square up better'n theirn."

Here Miss Asphyxia elevated her nose and sniffed over my grandmother's cap-border in a very contemptuous manner, and the cap-border bristled defiantly, but undismayed, back again.

"Come now, Mis' Badger, have it out; I ain't afraid of you! I'd just like to have you tell me what I could ha' done more nor better for this child."

"Done!" quoth my grandmother, with a pop like a roasted chestnut bursting out of the fire. "Why, you've done what you'd no business to. You'd no business to take a child at all; you haven't got a grain of motherliness in you. Why, look at natur', that might teach you that more than meat and drink and clothes is wanted for a child. Hens brood their chickens, and keep 'em warm under their wings; and cows lick their calves and cosset 'em, and it's a mean shame that folks will take 'em away from them. There's our old cat will lie an hour on the kitchen floor and let her kittens lug and pull at her, atween sleeping and waking, just to keep 'em warm and comfortable, you know. 'T ain't just feedin' and clothin' back and belly that's all; it's *broodin'* that young creeturs wants; and you hain't got a bit of broodin' in you; your heart's as hard as the nether mill-stone. Sovereign grace may soften it some day, but nothin' else can; you're a poor, old, hard, worldly woman, Miss Asphyxia Smith: that's what *you* are! If Divine grace could have broken in upon you, and given you a heart to love the child, you might have brought her up, 'cause you are a smart woman, and an honest one; that nobody denies."

Here Miss Mehitable took up the conversation, surveying Miss Asphyxia with that air of curious attention with which one studies a human being entirely out of the line of one's personal experience. Miss Mehitable was, as we have shown, in every thread of her being and education an aristocrat, and had for Miss Asphyxia that polite, easy tolerance which a sense of undoubted superiority gives, united with a shrewd pleasure in the study of a new and peculiar variety of the human species.

"My good Miss Smith," she observed, in conciliatory tones, "by your own account you must have had a great deal of trouble with this child. Now I propose for the future to relieve you of it altogether. I do not think you would ever succeed in making as efficient a person as yourself of her. It strikes me," she added, with a humorous twinkle of her eye, "that there are radical differences of nature, which would prevent her growing up like yourself. I don't doubt you conscientiously intended to do your duty by her, and I beg you to believe that you need have no further trouble with her."

"Goodness gracious knows," said Miss Asphyxia, "the child ain't much to fight over, — she was nothin' but a plague; and I'd rather have done all she did any day, than to 'a' had her round under my feet. I hate young uns, anyway."

"Then why, my good woman, do you object to parting with her?"

"Who said I did object? I don't care nothin' about parting with her; all is, when I begin a thing I like to go through with it."

"But if it isn't worth going through with," said Miss Mehitable, "it's as well to leave it, is it not?"

"And I'd got her clothes made, — not that they're worth so very much, but then they're worth just what they *are* worth, anyway," said Miss Asphyxia.

Here Tina made a sudden impulsive dart from Miss Mehitable's lap, and ran out of the back door, and over to her new home, and up into the closet of the chamber where was hanging the new suit of homespun in which Miss Asphyxia had arrayed her. She took it down and rolled the articles all together in a tight bundle, which she secured with a string, and, before the party in the kitchen had ceased wondering at her flight, suddenly reappeared, with flushed cheeks and dilated eyes, and tossed the bundle into Miss Asphyxia's lap. "There's every bit you ever gave me," she said; "I don't want to keep a single thing."

"My dear, is that a proper way to speak?" said Miss Mehitable, reprovingly; but Tina saw my grandmother's broad shoulders joggling with a secret laugh, and discerned twinkling lines in the reproving gravity which Miss Mehitable tried to assume. She felt pretty sure of her ground by this time.

"Well, it's no use talkin'," said Miss Asphyxia, rising. "If folks think they're able to bring up a beggar child like a lady, it's their lookout and not mine. I wasn't aware," she added, with severe irony, "that Parson Rossiter left so much of an estate that you could afford to bring up other folks' children in silks and satins."

"Our estate isn't much," said Miss Mehitable, good-naturedly, "but we shall make the best of it."

"Well, now, you just mark my words, Miss Rossiter," said Miss Asphyxia, "that 'ere child will never grow up a smart woman with *your* bringin' up; she'll jest run right over *you*, and you'll let her have her head in everything. I see jest how 't'll be; I don't want nobody to tell me."

"I dare say you are quite right, Miss Smith," said Miss Mehitable; "I haven't the slightest opinion of my own powers in that line; but she may be happy with me, for all that."

"Happy?" repeated Miss Asphyxia, with an odd intonation, as if she were repeating a sound of something imperfectly comprehended, and altogether out of her line. "O, well, if folks is goin' to begin to talk about *that,* I hain't got time; it don't seem to me that *that*'s what this 'ere world's for."

"What is it for, then?" said Miss Mehitable, who felt an odd sort of interest in the human specimen before her.

"Meant for? Why, for hard work, I s'pose; that's all I ever found it for. Talk about coddling! it's little we get o' that, the way the Lord fixes things in this world, dear knows. He's pretty up and down with us, by all they tell us. You must take things right off, when they're goin'. Ef you don't, so much the worse for you; they won't wait for you. Lose an hour in the morning, and you may chase it till ye drop down, you never'll catch it! That's the way things goes, and I should like to know who's a going to stop to quiddle with young uns? 'T ain't me, that's certain; so, as there's no more to be made by this 'ere talk, I may's well be goin'. You're welcome to the young un, ef you say so; I jest wanted you to know that what I begun I'd 'a' gone through with, ef you hadn't stepped in; and I didn't want no reflections on my good name, neither, for I had my ideas of what's right, and can have 'em yet, I s'pose, if Mis' Badger does think I've got a heart of stone. I should like to know how I'm to have any other when I ain't elected, and I don't see as I am, or likely to be, and I don't see neither why I ain't full as good as a good many that be."

"Well, well, Miss Smith," said Miss Mehitable, "we can't any of us enter into those mysteries, but I respect your motives, and would be happy to see you any time you will call, and I'm in hopes to teach this little girl to treat you properly," she said, taking the child's hand.

"Likely story," said Miss Asphyxia, with a short, hard laugh. "She'll get ahead o' you, you'll see that: but I don't hold malice, so good morning," — and Miss Asphyxia suddenly and promptly departed, and was soon seen driving away at a violent pace.

"Upon my word, that woman isn't so bad, now," said Miss Mehitable, looking after her, while she leisurely inhaled a pinch of snuff.

"O, I'm so glad you didn't let her have me!" said Tina.

"To think of a creature so dry and dreary, so devoid even of the conception of enjoyment in life," said Miss Mehitable, "hurrying through life without a moment's rest, — without even the capacity of resting if she could, — and all for what?"

"For my part, mother, I think you were down too hard on her," said Aunt Lois.

"Not a bit," said my grandmother, cheerily. "Such folks ought to be talked to; it may set her to thinking, and do her good. I've had it on my heart to give that woman a piece of my mind ever since the children came here. Come here, my poor little dear," said she to Tina, with one of her impulsive outgushes of motherliness. "I know you must be hungry by this time; come into the buttery, and see what I've got for you."

Now there was an indiscreet championship of Miss Tina, a backing of her in her treatment of Miss Asphyxia, in this overflow, which Aunt Lois severely disapproved, and which struck Miss Mehitable as not being the very best thing to enforce her own teachings of decorum and propriety.

The small young lady tilted into the buttery after my grandmother, with the flushed cheeks and triumphant air of a victor, and they heard her little tongue running with the full assurance of having a sympathetic listener.

"Now mother will spoil that child, if you let her," said Aunt Lois. "She's the greatest hand to spoil children; she always lets 'em have what they ask for. I expect Susy's boys'll be raising Cain round the house; they would if it wasn't for me. They have only to follow mother into that buttery, and out they come with great slices of bread and butter, any time of day, — yes, and even sugar on it, if you'll believe me."

"And does 'em good, too," said my grandmother, who reappeared from the buttery, with Miss Tina tilting and dancing before her, with a confirmatory slice of bread and butter and sugar in her hand. "Tastes good, don't it, dear?" said she, giving the child a jovial chuck under her little chin.

"Yes, indeed," said Miss Tina; "I'd like to have old nasty Sphyxy see me now."

"Tut, tut! my dear," said grandmother; "good little girls don't call names"; — but at the same time the venerable gentle-woman nodded and winked in the most open manner across the curly head at Miss Mehitable, and her portly shoulders shook with laughter, so that the young culprit was not in the least abashed at the reproof.

"Mother, I do wonder at you!" said Aunt Lois, indignantly.

"Never you mind, Lois; I guess I've brought up more children than ever you did," said my grandmother, cheerily. "There, my little dear," she added, "you may run down to your play now, and never fear that anybody's going to get *you*."

Miss Tina, upon this hint, gladly ran off to finish an architectural structure of pebbles by the river, which she was busy in building at the time when the awful vision of Miss Asphyxia appeared; and my grandmother returned to her buttery to attend to a few matters which had been left unfinished in the morning's work.

"It is a very serious responsibility," said Miss Mehitable, when she had knit awhile in silence, "at my time of life, to charge one's self with the education of a child. One treats one's self to a child as one buys a picture or a flower, but the child will not remain a picture or a flower, and then comes the awful question, what it may grow to be, and what share you may have in determining its future."

"Well, old Parson Moore used to preach the best sermons on family government that ever I heard," said Aunt Lois. "He said you must begin in the very beginning and break a child's will, — short off, — nothing to be done without that. I remember he whipped little Titus, his first son, off and on, nearly a whole day, to make him pick up a pocket-handkerchief."

Here the edifying conversation was interrupted by a loud explosive expletive from the buttery, which showed that my grandmother was listening with anything but approbation.

"Fiddlesticks!" quoth she.

"And did he succeed in entirely subduing the child's will in that one effort?" said Miss Mehitable, musingly.

"Well, no. Mrs. Moore told me he had to have twenty or thirty just such spells before he brought him under; but he persevered, and he broke his will at last, — at least so far that he always minded when his father was round."

"FIDDLESTICKS!" quoth my grandmother, in a yet louder and more explosive tone.

"Mrs. Badger does not appear to sympathize with your views," said Miss Mehitable.

"O, mother? Of course she don't; she has her own ways and doings, and she won't hear to reason," said Aunt Lois.

"Come, come, Lois; I never knew an old maid who didn't think she knew just how to bring up children," said my grandmother. "Wish you could have tried yourself with that sort of doxy when you was little. Guess if I'd broke your will, I should ha' had to break you for good an' all, for your will is about all there is of you! But I tell you, I had too much to do to spend a whole forenoon making you pick up a pocket-handkerchief. When you didn't mind, I hit you a good clip, and picked it up myself; and when you wouldn't go where I wanted you, I picked you up, neck and crop, and put you there. That was my government. I let your will take care of itself. I thought the Lord had given you a pretty strong one, and he knew what 't was for, and could take care of it in his own time, which hain't come yet, as I see."

Now this last was one of those personal thrusts with which dear family friends are apt to give arguments a practical application; and Aunt Lois's spare, thin cheeks flushed up as she said, in an aggrieved tone: "Well, I s'pose I'm dreadful, of course. Mother always contrives to turn round on me."

"Well, Lois, I hate to hear folks talk nonsense," said my grandmother, who by this time had got a pot of cream under her arm, which she was stirring with the pudding-stick; and this afforded her an opportunity for emphasizing her sentences with occasional dumps of the same.

"People don't need to talk to me," she said, "about Parson Moore's government. Tite Moore wasn't any great shakes, after all the row they made about him. He was well enough while his father was round, but about the worst boy that ever I saw when his eye was off from him. Good or bad, my children was about the same behind my back that they were before my face, anyway."

"Well, now, there was Aunt Sally Morse," said Aunt Lois, steadily ignoring the point of my grandmother's discourse. "There was
a woman that brought up children exactly to suit me. Everything
went like clock-work with her babies; they were nursed just so
often, and no more; they were put down to sleep at just such a
time, and nobody was allowed to rock 'em, or sing to 'em, or fuss
with 'em. If they cried, she just whipped them till they stopped;
and when they began to toddle about, she never put things out of
their reach, but just slapped their hands whenever they touched
them, till they learnt to let things alone."

"Slapped their hands!" quoth my grandmother, "and learnt them
to let things alone! I'd like to ha' seen that tried on my children.
Sally had a set of white, still children, that were all just like
dipped candles by natur', and she laid it all to her management;
and look at 'em now they're grown up. They're decent, respectable
folks, but noways better than other folks' children. Lucinda Morse
ain't a bit better than you are, Lois, if she was whipped and made
to lie still when she was a baby, and you were taken up and rocked
when you cried. All is, they had hard times when they were little,
and cried themselves to sleep nights, and were hectored and worried when they ought to have been taking some comfort. Ain't the
world hard enough, without fighting babies, I want to know? I
hate to see a woman that don't want to rock her own baby, and is
contriving ways all the time to shirk the care of it. Why, if all the
world was that way, there would be no sense in Scriptur'. 'As one
whom his mother comforteth, so will I comfort you,' the Bible says,
taking for granted that mothers were made to comfort children
and give them good times when they are little. Sally Morse was
always talking about her system. She thought she did wonders,
'cause she got so much time to piece bedquilts, and work counter-
panes, and make pickles, by turning off her children; but I took
my comfort in mine, and let them have their comfort as they went
along. It's about all the comfort there is in this world, anyway,
and they're none the worse for it now, as I see."

"Well, in all these cases there is a medium, if we could hit it,"
said Miss Mehitable. "There must be authority over these ignorant,
helpless little folks in early years, to keep them from ruining themselves."

"O yes. Of course there must be government," said my grandmother. "I always made my children mind me; but I wouldn't pick quarrels with 'em, nor keep up long fights to break their will; if they didn't mind, I came down on 'em and had it over with at once, and then was done with 'em. They turned out pretty fair, too," said my grandmother complacently, giving an emphatic thump with her pudding-stick.

"I was reading Mr. John Locke's treatise on education yesterday," said Miss Mehitable. "It strikes me there are many good ideas in it."

"Well, one live child puts all your treatises to rout," said my grandmother. "There ain't any two children alike; and what works with one won't with another. Folks have just got to open their eyes, and look and see what the Lord meant when he put the child together, if they can, and not stand in his way; and after all we must wait for sovereign grace to finish the work: if the Lord don't keep the house, the watchman waketh but in vain. Children are the heritage of the Lord, — that's all you can make of it."

My grandmother, like other warm-tempered, impulsive, dictatorial people, had formed her theories of life to suit her own style of practice. She was, to be sure, autocratic in her own realm, and we youngsters knew that, at certain times when her blood was up, it was but a word and a blow for us, and that the blow was quite likely to come first and the word afterward; but the temporary severities of kindly-natured, generous people never lessen the affection of children or servants, any more than the too hot rays of the benignant sun, or the too driving patter of the needful rain. When my grandmother detected us in a childish piece of mischief, and soundly cuffed our ears, or administered summary justice with immediate polts of her rheumatic crutch, we never felt the least rising of wrath or rebellion, but only made off as fast as possible, generally convinced that the good woman was in the right of it, and that we got no more than we deserved.

I remember one occasion when Bill had been engaged in making some dressed chickens dance, which she had left trussed up with the liver and lights duly washed and replaced within them. Bill set them up on their pins, and put them through active gymnastics, in course of which these interior treasures were rapidly scattered out upon the table. A howl of indignation from grandmother announced coming wrath, and Bill darted out of the back door, while I was summarily seized and chastised.

"Grandmother, grandmother! *I* didn't do it, — it was Bill."

"Well, but I can't catch Bill, you see," said my venerable monitor, continuing the infliction.

"But I didn't do it."

"Well, let it stand for something you did do, then," quoth my grandmother, by this time quite pacified: "you do bad things enough that you ain't whipped for, any day."

The whole resulted in a large triangle of pumpkin pie, administered with the cordial warmth of returning friendship, and thus the matter was happily adjusted. Even the prodigal son Bill, when, returning piteously, and standing penitent under the milk-room window, he put in a submissive plea, "Please, grandmother, I won't do so any more," was allowed a peaceable slice of the same comfortable portion, and bid to go in peace.

I remember another funny instance of my grandmother's discipline. It was when I was a little fellow, seated in the chimney-corner at my grandfather's side. I had discovered a rising at the end of my shoe-sole, which showed that it was beginning to come off. It struck me as a funny thing to do to tear up the whole sole, which piece of mischief my grandfather perceiving, he raised his hand to chastise.

"Come here, Horace, quick!" said my grandmother, imperatively, that she might save me from the impending blow.

I lingered, whereat she made a dart at me, and seized me. Just as my grandfather boxed my ear on one side, she hit me a similar cuff on the other.

"Why didn't you come when I called you," she said; "now you've got your ears boxed both sides."

Somewhat bewildered, I retreated under her gown in disgrace, but I was after a relenting moment lifted into her lap, and allowed to go to sleep upon her ample bosom.

"Mother, why don't you send that boy to bed nights?" said Aunt Lois. "You never have any regular rules about anything."

"Law, he likes to sit up and see the fire as well as any of us, Lois; and do let him have all the comfort he can as he goes along, poor boy! there ain't any too much in this world, anyway."

"Well for my part, I think there ought to be *system* in bringing up children," said Aunt Lois.

"Wait till you get 'em of your own, and then try it, Lois," said my grandmother, laughing with a rich, comfortable laugh which rocked my little sleepy head up and down, as I drowsily opened my eyes with a delicious sense of warmth and security.

From all these specimens it is to be inferred that the theorists on education will find no improvement in the contemplation of my grandmother's methods, and will pronounce her a pig-headed, passionate, impulsive, soft-hearted body, as entirely below the notice of a rational, inquiring mind as an old brooding hen, which model of maternity in many respects she resembled. It may be so, but the longer I live, the more faith I have in grandmothers and grandmotherly logic, of which, at some future time, I shall give my views at large.

CHAPTER XXI

———◆———

WHAT IS TO BE DONE
WITH THE BOY?

"Well," said my Aunt Lois, as she gave the last sweep to the hearth, after she had finished washing up the supper-dishes; "I've been up to Ebal Scran's store this afternoon, to see about soling Horace's Sunday shoes. Ebal will do 'em as reasonable as any one; and he spoke to me to know whether I knew of any boy that a good family would like to bind out to him for an apprentice, and I told him I'd speak to you about Horace. It'll be time pretty soon to think of putting him at something."

Among the many unexplained and inexplicable woes of childhood, are its bitter antagonisms, so perfectly powerless, yet often so very decided, against certain of the grown people who control it. Perhaps some of us may remember respectable, well-meaning people, with whom in our mature years we live in perfect amity, but who in our childhood appeared to us bitter enemies. Children are remarkably helpless in this respect, because they cannot choose their company and surroundings as grown people can; and are sometimes entirely in the power of those with whom their natures are so unsympathetic that they may be almost said to have a constitutional aversion to them. Aunt Lois was such a one to me, principally because of her forecasting, untiring, pertinacious, caretaking propensities. She had already looked over my lot in life, and set down in her own mind what was to be done with me, and went at it with a resolute energy that would not wait for the slow development of circumstances.

That I should want to study, as my father did, — that I should for this cause hang as an unpractical, unproductive, dead weight on the family, — was the evil which she saw in prospective, against which my grandfather's placid, easy temper, and my grandmother's impulsive bountifulness, gave her no security. A student in the family, and a son in college, she felt to be luxuries to which a poor widow in dependent circumstances had no right to look forward, and therefore she opened the subject betimes, with prompt energy, by the proposition above stated.

My mother, who sat on the other side of the fireplace, looked at me with a fluttering look of apprehension. I flushed up in a sort of rage that somehow Aunt Lois always succeeded in putting me into. "I don't want to be a shoemaker, and I won't neither," I said.

"Tut, tut," said my grandfather, placidly, from his corner; "we don't let little boys say 'won't' here."

I now burst out crying, and ran to my grandmother, sobbing as if my heart would break.

"Lois, *can't* you let this boy alone?" said my grandmother, vengefully; "I do wonder at you. Poor little fellow! his father ain't quite cold in his grave yet, and you want to pitch him out into the world," — and my grandmother seized me in her strong arms, and lulled me against her ample bosom. "There, poor boy, don't you cry; you sha'n't, no, you sha'n't; you shall stay and help grandma, so you shall."

"Great help he is," said Aunt Lois, contemptuously; "gets a book in his hand and goes round with his head in a bag; never gives a message right, and is always stumbling over things that are right in his way. There's Harry, now, is as handy as a girl, and if he says he'll do a thing, I know 't'll be done," — and Aunt Lois illustrated her doctrine by calling up Harry, and making him stretch forth his arms for a skein of blue-mixed yarn which she was going to wind. The fire-light shone full on his golden curls and clear blue eyes, as he stood obediently and carefully yielding to Aunt Lois's quick, positive movements. As she wound, and twitched, and pulled, with certainly twice the energy that the work in hand required, his eyes followed her motions with a sort of quiet drollery; there was a still, inward laugh in them, as if she amused him greatly.

Such open comparisons between two boys might have gone far to destroy incipient friendship; but Harry seemed to be in a wonderful degree gifted with the faculties that made him a universal favorite. All the elders of the family liked him, because he was quiet and obedient, always doing with cheerful promptness exactly what he was bidden, unless, as sometimes happened in our family circle, he was bidden to do two or three different things at one

and the same time, when he would stand looking innocently puzzled, till my grandmother and Aunt Lois and Aunt Keziah had
settled it among them whose was to be the ruling will. He was
deft and neat-handed as a girl about any little offices of a domestic
nature; he was thoughtful and exact in doing errands; he was
delicately clean and neat in his personal habits; he never tracked
Aunt Lois's newly scoured floor with the traces of unwiped shoes;
he never left shavings and litter on a cleanly swept hearth, or
tumbled and deranged anything, so that he might safely be trusted
on errands even to the most sacred precincts of a housekeeper's
dominions. What boy with all these virtues is not held a saint by
all women-folk? Yet, though he was frequently commended in all
those respects, to my marked discredit, Harry was to me a sort of
necessary of life. There was something in his nature that was wanting to mine, and I attached myself to him with a pertinacity
which had never before marked my intercourse with any boy.

A day or two after the arrival of the children, the minister and
Lady Lothrop had called on my grandmother in all the dignity of
their station, and taken an approving view of the boy. Lady
Lothrop had engaged to take him under her care, and provide a
yearly sum for his clothing and education. She had never had a
child of her own, and felt that diffidence about taking the entire
charge of a boy which would be natural to a person of fastidious
and quiet habits, and she therefore signified that it would be more
agreeable to her if my grandmother would allow him to make one
of her own family circle, — a proposal to which she cheerfully
assented, saying, that "one more chick makes little difference to
an old hen."

I immediately petitioned that I might have Harry for a bedfellow, and he and I were allowed a small bedroom to ourselves
at the head of the back stairs. It was a rude little crib, roughly
fenced off from the passage-way by unplaned boards of different
heights. A pine table, two stools, a small trundle-bed, and a rude
case of drawers, were all its furniture. Harry's love of order was
strikingly manifest in the care which he took of this little apartment. His few articles of clothing and personal belongings all had
their exact place, and always were bestowed there with scrupulous
regularity. He would adjust the furniture, straighten the bedclothing, and quietly place and replace the things that I in my

fitful, nervous eagerness was always disarranging; and when, as
often happened in one of my spasms of enthusiasm, I turned everything in the room topsy-turvy, searching for something I had lost,
or projecting some new arrangement, he would wait peaceably till
I had finished, and then noiselessly get everything back again into
its former order. He never quarrelled with me, or thwarted me in
my turbulent or impatient moods, but seemed to wait for me to
get through whatever I was doing, when he would come in and
silently rearrange. He was, on the whole, a singularly silent child,
but with the kind of silence which gives a sense of companionship.
It was evident that he was always intensely observant and interested in whatever was going on before him, and ready at any
moment to take a friendly part when he was wanted; but for the
most part his place in the world seemed that of an amused listener
and observer. Life seemed to present itself to him as a curious
spectacle, and he was never tired of looking and listening, watching the ways and words of all our family circle, and often smiling
to himself as if they afforded him great diversion. Aunt Lois, with
her quick, sharp movements, her determined, outspoken ways,
seemed to amuse him as much as she irritated me, and I would
sometimes see him turn away with a droll smile when he had been
watching one of her emphatic courses round the room. He had a
certain tact in avoiding all the sharp corners and angles of her
character, which, in connection with his handiness and his orderly
ways, caused him at last to become a prime favorite with her.
With his quiet serviceableness and manual dexterity, he seemed to
be always the one that was exactly wanting to do an odd turn, so
that at last he came to be depended on for many little inferior
offices, which he rendered with a good-will none the less cheerful
because of his silence.

"There's time enough to think about what Horace is to do another year," said my grandfather, having reflected some moments
after the passage of arms between my grandmother and Aunt Lois.
"He's got to have some schooling. The boys had both better go to
school for this winter, and then we'll see what next."

"Well, I just mentioned about Ebal Scran, because he's a good
man to take a boy, and he wants one now. If we don't take that
chance it may not come again."

"Wal, Miss Lois," said Sam Lawson, who had sat silent in a dark corner of the chimney, "ef I was to say about Horace, I'd say he'd do better for somethin' else 'n shoemakin'. He's the most amazin' little fellow to read I ever see. As much as a year ago Jake Marshall and me and the other fellers round to the store used to like to get him to read the Columbian Sentinel to us; he did it off slicker than any of us could, he did, — there wa'n't no kind o' word could stop him. I should say such a boy as that ought to have a liberal education."

"And who's going to pay for it?" said Aunt Lois, turning round on him sharply. "I suppose you know it costs something to get a man through college. *We* never can afford to send him to college. It's all we can do to bring his Uncle Bill through."

"Well, well," said my grandmother, "there's no use worrying the child, one way or the other."

"They can both go to district school this winter," said my grandfather.

"Well," said Aunt Lois, "the other day I found him down in a corner humping his back out over a Latin grammar that I'd put away with all the rest of his father's books on the back side of the upper shelf in our closet, and I took it away from him. If he was going to college, why, it's well enough to study for it; but if he isn't we don't want him idlin' round with scraps of Latin in his head like old Jock Twitchel, — got just Latin enough to make a fool of his English, and he's neither one thing nor another."

"I do wonder, Lois, what there is under the sun that you don't feel called to see to," said my grandmother. "What do you want to quarrel with the child for? He shall have his Latin grammar if he wants it, and any of the rest of his father's books, poor child. I s'pose he likes 'em because they were his poor father's."

I leaped for joy in my grandmother's lap, for my father's precious books had been in a state of blockade ever since we had been in the house, and it was only by putting a chair on a table one day, when Aunt Lois and my mother were out, that I had managed to help myself to the Latin grammar, out of which my father had begun to teach me before he died.

"Well, well," said Aunt Lois, "at any rate it's eight o'clock, and time these boys went to bed."

Upon this hint Harry and I went to our little bedroom without the ceremony of a candle. It was a frosty autumn night, but a good, clear square of moonlight lay on the floor.

Now Harry, in common with many other very quiet-natured people, was remarkable for a peculiar persistency in all his ways and manners. Ever since I had roomed with him, I had noticed with a kind of silent wonder the regularity of his nightly devotional exercises, to which he always addressed himself before he went to bed, with an appearance of simple and absorbed fervor, kneeling down by the bed, and speaking in a low, earnest tone of voice, never seeming to hurry or to abbreviate, as I was always inclined to do whenever I attempted similar performances. In fact, as usually I said no prayers at all, there was often an awkward pause and stillness on my part, while I watched and waited for Harry to be through with his devotions, so that I might resume the thread of worldly conversation.

Now to me the perseverance with which he performed these nightly exercises was unaccountable. The doctrines which in that day had been gaining ground in New England, with regard to the utter inutility and unacceptableness of any prayers or religious doings of the unregenerate, had borne their legitimate fruits in causing parents to become less and less particular in cultivating early habits of devotion in children; and so, when I had a room to myself, my mother had ceased to take any oversight of my religious exercises; and as I had overheard my Aunt Lois maintaining very stringently that there was no use in it so long as my heart was not changed, I very soon dropped the form. So, when night after night I noticed Harry going on with his devotions, it seemed to me, from my more worldly point of view, that he gave himself a great deal of unnecessary trouble, particularly if, after all, his prayers did no good. I thought I would speak with him about it, and accordingly this night I said to him, "Harry, do you think it does any good to say your prayers?"

"To be sure I do," he said.

"But if your heart hasn't been changed, your prayer is an abomination to the Lord. Aunt Lois says so," I said, repeating a Scriptural form I had often heard quoted.

Harry turned over, and in the fading daylight I saw his eyes, large, clear, and tranquil. There was not the shadow of a cloud in them. "I don't know anything about that," he said quietly. "You see I don't believe that sort of talk. God is our Father; he loves us. If we want things, and ask him for them, he will give them to us if it is best; mother always told me so, and I find it is so. I promised her always to say these prayers, and to believe that God loves us. I always shall."

"Do you *really* think so, Harry?" I said.

"Why, yes; to be sure I do."

"I mean, do you ever ask God for things you want? I don't mean saying prayers, but asking for anything."

"Of course I do. I always have, and he gives them to me. He always has taken care of me, and he always will."

"Now, Harry," said I, "I want to go to college, and Aunt Lois says there isn't any money to send me there. She wants mother to bind me out to a shoemaker; and I'd rather die than do that. I love to study, and I mean to learn. Now do you suppose if I ask God he will help me?"

"Certainly he will," said Harry, with an incredible firmness and quietness of manner. "Just you try it."

"Don't you want to study and go to college?" said I.

"Certainly I do. I ask God every night that I may *if it is best*," he said with simplicity.

"It will be a great deal harder for you than for me," I said, "because you haven't any relations."

"Yes, but God *can* do anything he pleases," said Harry, with a sort of energetic simplicity.

The confidence expressed in his manner produced a kind of effect upon me. I had urgent needs, too, — longings which I was utterly helpless ever to fulfil, — particularly that visionary desire to go to college and get an education. "Harry," I said, "you ask God that I may go to college."

"Yes, I will," he answered, — "I'll ask every night. But then," he added, turning over and looking at me, "why don't you ask yourself, Horace?"

It was difficult for me to answer that question. I think that the differences among human beings in the natural power of *faith* are as great as any other constitutional diversity, and that they begin in childhood. Some are born believers, and some are born sceptics. I was one of the latter. There was an eternal query, — an habitual interrogation-point to almost every proposition in my mind, even from childhood, — a habit of looking at everything from so many sides, that it was difficult to get a settled assent to anything.

Perhaps the curious kind of double life that I led confirmed this sceptical tendency. I was certain that I constantly saw and felt things, the assertion of whose existence as I saw them drew down on me stinging reproofs and radical doubts of my veracity. This led me to distrust my own perceptions on all subjects, for I was no less certain of what I saw and felt in the spiritual world than of what I saw and felt in the material; and, if I could be utterly mistaken in the one, I could also be in the other.

The repression and silence about this which became the habit of my life formed a covering for a constant wondering inquiry. The habit of reserve on these subjects had become so intense, that even to Harry I never spoke of it. I think I loved Harry more than I loved anything; in fact, before he came to us, I do not think I knew anything of love as a sentiment. My devotion to my father resembled the blind, instinctive worship of a dog for his master. My feeling toward my mother and grandmother was that impulse of want that induces a chicken to run to a hen in any of its little straits. It was an animal instinct, — a commerce of helplessness with help.

For Harry I felt a sort of rudimentary, poetical tenderness, like the love of man for woman. I admired his clear blue eyes, his curling golden hair, his fair, pure complexion, his refined and quiet habits, and a sort of unconsciousness of self that there was about him. His simplicity of nature was incorruptible; he seemed always to speak, without disguise, exactly what he thought, without the least apparent consideration of anything but its truth; and this gave him a strange air of innocency. A sort of quaint humor always bubbling up in little quiet looks and ways, and in harmless practical jokes, gave me a constant sense of amusement in his society.

As the reader may have observed, we were a sharp-cut and peculiar set in our house, and sometimes, when the varied scenes of family life below stairs had amused Harry more than common, he would, after we had got into our chamber by ourselves, break into a sudden flow of mimicry, — imitating now Aunt Lois's sharp, incisive movements and decided tones, or flying about like my venerated grandmother in her most confused and hurried moments, or presenting a perfect image of Uncle Fliakim's frisky gyrations, till he would set me into roars of laughter; when he would turn gravely round and ask what I was laughing at. He never mentioned a name, or made remarks about the persons indicated, — the sole reflection on them was the absurd truthfulness of his imitation; and when I would call out the name he would look at me with eyes brimful of mischief, but in utter silence.

Generally speaking, his language was characterized by a peculiar nicety in the selection of words, and an avoidance of clownish or vulgar phraseology, and was such as marks a child whose early years have all been passed in the intercourse of refined society; but sometimes he would absurdly introduce into his conversation scraps from Sam Lawson's vocabulary, with flashes of mimicry of his shambling gait, and the lanky droop of his hands; yet these shifting flashes of imitation were the only comment he ever made upon him.

After Harry began to share my apartment, my nightly visions became less frequent, because, perhaps, instead of lying wide-awake expecting them, I had him to talk to. Once or twice, indeed, I saw standing by him, after he had fallen asleep, that same woman whose blue eyes and golden hair I had remarked when we were lost in the forest. She looked down on him with an inexpressible tenderness, and seemed to bless him; and I used to notice that he spoke oftener of his mother the next day, and quoted her words to me with the simple, unquestioning veneration which he always showed for them.

One thing about Harry which was striking to me, and which he possessed in common with many still, retiring people, was great vigor in maintaining his individuality. It has been the experience of my life that it is your quiet people who, above all other children of men, are set in their ways and intense in their opinions. Their very reserve and silence are a fortification behind which all their peculiarities grow and thrive at their leisure, without encountering those blows and shocks which materially modify more outspoken natures. It is owing to the peculiar power of quietness that one sometimes sees characters fashioning themselves in a manner the least to be expected from the circumstances and associates which surround them. As a fair white lily grows up out of the bed of meadow muck, and, without note or comment, rejects all in the soil that is alien from her being, and goes on fashioning her own silver cup side by side with weeds that are drawing coarser nutriment from the soil, so we often see a refined and gentle nature by some singular internal force unfolding itself by its own laws, and confirming itself in its own beliefs, as wholly different from all that surround it as is the lily from the rag-weed. There are persons, in fact, who seem to grow almost wholly from within, and on whom the teachings, the doctrines, and the opinions of those around them produce little or no impression.

Harry was modest in his bearing; he never put forth an opinion opposed to those around him, unless a special question was asked him; but, even from early childhood, the opinion of no human being seemed to have much power to modify or alter certain convictions on which his life was based.

I remember, one Sunday, our good Parson Lothrop took it into his head to preach one of those cool, philosophical sermons in which certain scholarly and rational Christians in easy worldly circumstances seem to take delight, — a sort of preaching which removes the providence of God as far off from human sympathy as it is possible to be. The amount of the matter as he stated it seemed to be, that the Creator had devised a very complicated and thorough-working machine, which he had wound up and set going ages ago, which brought out results with the undeviating accuracy of clock-work. Of course there was the declaration that "not a sparrow falleth to the ground without our Father," and that "the very hairs of our head are numbered," standing square across his way. But we all know that a text of Scripture is no embarrassment at all in the way of a thorough-paced theologian, when he has a favorite idea to establish.

These declarations were explained as an Oriental, metaphorical way of stating that the All-wise had started a grand world-machine on general laws which included the greatest good to the least of his creation.

I noticed that Harry sat gazing at him with clear, wide-open eyes and that fixed attention which he always gave to anything of a religious nature. The inference that I drew from it was, that Harry must be mistaken in his confidence in prayer, and that the kind of Fatherly intervention he looked for and asked for in his affairs was out of the question. As we walked home I expected him to say something about it, but he did not. When we were in our room at night, and he had finished his prayers, I said, "Harry, did you notice Dr. Lothrop's sermon?"

"Yes, I noticed it," he said.

"Well, if that is true, what good does it do to pray?"

"It isn't true," he said, simply.

"How do you know it isn't?"

"O, I *know* better," he said.

"But, Harry, — Dr. Lothrop, you know, — why, he's the minister," — and what could a boy of that day say more?

"He's mistaken there, though," said Harry, quietly, as he would speak of a man who denied the existence of the sun or moon. He was too positive and too settled to be in any frame to argue about it, and the whole of the discourse, which had seemed to me so damaging to his opinions, melted over him like so much moonshine. He fell asleep saying to himself, "The Lord is my shepherd, I shall not want," and I lay awake, wondering in my own mind whether this was the way to live, and, if it were, why my grandmother and Aunt Lois, and my father and mother, and all the good people I had ever known, had so many troubles and worries.

Ages ago, in the green, flowery hollows of the hills of Bethlehem, a young shepherd boy took this view of life, and began his days singing, "The Lord is my shepherd, I shall not want," and ended them by saying, "Thou hast taught me from my youth up, and hitherto have I declared thy wondrous works"; and his tender communings with an unseen Father have come down to our days as witnesses of green pastures and still waters to be found in this weary work-a-day world, open ever to those who are simple-hearted enough to seek them. It would seem to be the most natural thing in the world that the child of an ever-present Father should live in this way, — that weakness and ignorance, standing within call and reach of infinite grace and strength, should lay hold of that divine helpfulness, and grow to it and by it, as the vine climbs upon the rock; but yet such lives are the exception rather than the rule, even among the good. But the absolute faith of Harry's mind produced about him an atmosphere of composure and restfulness which was, perhaps, the strongest attraction that drew me to him.

I was naturally nervous, sensitive, excitable, and needed the repose which he gave me. His quiet belief that all would be right had a sort of effect on me, and, although I did not fall into his way of praying, I came to have great confidence in it for him, and to indulge some vague hopes that something good might come of it for me.

CHAPTER XXII

DAILY LIVING IN OLDTOWN

Henceforth my story must be a cord with three strands, inexplicably intertwisted, and appearing and disappearing in their regular intervals, as each occupies for the moment the prominent place. And this threefold cord is composed of myself, Harry, and Tina. To show how the peculiar life of old Massachusetts worked upon us, and determined our growth and character and destinies, is a theme that brings in many personages, many subjects, many accessories. It is strange that no human being grows up who does not so intertwist in his growth the whole idea and spirit of his day, that rightly to dissect out his history would require one to cut to pieces and analyze society, law, religion, the metaphysics and the morals of his times; and, as all these things run back to those of past days, the problem is still further complicated. The humblest human being is the sum total of a column of figures which go back through centuries before he was born.

Old Crab Smith and Miss Asphyxia, if their biographies were rightly written, would be found to be the result and out-come of certain moral and social forces, justly to discriminate which might puzzle a philosopher. But be not alarmed, reader; I am not going to puzzle you, but to return in the briefest time possible to my story.

Harry was adopted into our family circle early in the autumn; and, after much discussion, it was resolved in the family synod that he and I should go to the common school in the neighborhood that winter, and out of school-hours share between us certain family tasks or "chores," as they were called at home.

Our daily life began at four o'clock in the morning, when the tapping of Aunt Lois's imperative heels on the back stairs, and her authoritative rap at our door, dispelled my slumbers. I was never much of a sleeper; my slumbers at best were light and cat-like; but Harry required all my help and my nervous wakefulness to

get him to open his drowsy blue eyes, which he always did with
the most perfectly amiable temper. He had that charming gift of
physical good-humor which is often praised as a virtue in children
and in grown people, but which is a mere condition of the animal
nature. We all know that there are good-natured animals and
irritable animals, — that the cow is tranquil and gentle, and the
hyena snarly and fretful; but we never think of praising and re-
warding the one, or punishing the other, for this obvious conformation. But in the case of the human animal it always happens
that he who has the good luck to have a quiet, imperturbable
nature has also the further good luck of being praised for it as for
a Christian virtue, while he who has the ill fortune to be born with
irritable nerves has the further ill fortune of being always considered a sinner on account of it.

Nobody that has not suffered from such causes can tell the
amount of torture that a child of a certain nervous formation undergoes in the mere process of getting accustomed to his body, to
the physical forces of life, and to the ways and doings of that world
of grown-up people who have taken possession of the earth before
him, and are using it, and determined to go on using it, for their
own behoof and convenience, in spite of his childish efforts to
push in his little individuality and seize his little portion of existence. He is at once laid hold upon by the older majority as an
instrument to work out their views of what is fit and proper for
himself and themselves; and if he proves a hard-working or creaking instrument, has the further capability of being rebuked and
chastened for it.

My first morning feeling was generally one of anger at the sound
of Aunt Lois's heels, worthy soul! I have lived to see the day when
the tap of those efficient little instruments has seemed to me a
most praiseworthy and desirable sound; but in those days they
seemed only to be the reveille by which I was awakened to that
daily battle of my will with hers which formed so great a feature
in my life. It imposed in the first place the necessity of my quitting
my warm bed in a room where the thermometer must have stood
below zero, and where the snow, drifting through the loosely
framed window, often lay in long wreaths on the floor.

As Aunt Lois always opened the door and set in a lighted candle,
one of my sinful amusements consisted in lying and admiring the

forest of glittering frost-work which had been made by our breath freezing upon the threads of the blanket. I sometimes saw rainbow colors in this frost-work, and went off into dreams and fancies about it, which ended in a doze, from which I was awakened, perhaps, by some of the snow from the floor rubbed smartly on my face, and the words, "How many times must you be called?" and opened my eyes to the vision of Aunt Lois standing over me indignant and admonitory.

Then I would wake Harry. We would spring from the bed and hurry on our clothes, buttoning them with fingers numb with cold, and run down to the back sink-room, where, in water that flew off in icy spatters, we performed our morning ablutions, refreshing our faces and hands by a brisk rub upon a coarse rolling-towel of brown homespun linen. Then with mittens, hats, and comforters, we were ready to turn out with old Cæsar to the barn to help him fodder the cattle. I must say that, when it came to this, on the whole it began to be grand fun for us. As Cæsar went ahead of us with his snow-shovel, we plunged laughing and rolling into the powdery element, with which we plentifully pelted him. Arrived at the barn we climbed, like cats, upon the mow, whence we joyously threw down enough for all his foddering purposes, and with such superabundant good-will in our efforts, that, had need so required, we would have stayed all day and flung off all the hay upon the mow; in fact, like the broomstick in the fable, which would persist in bringing water without rhyme or reason, so we overwhelmed our sable friend with avalanches of hay, which we cast down upon him in an inconsiderate fury of usefulness, and out of which we laughed to see him tear his way, struggling, gesticulating and remonstrating, till his black face shone with perspiration, and his woolly head bristled with hay-seeds and morsels of clover.

Then came the feeding of the hens and chickens and other poultry, a work in which we especially delighted, going altogether beyond Cæsar in our largesses of corn, and requiring a constant interposition of his authority to prevent our emptying the crib on every single occasion.

In very severe weather we sometimes found hens or turkeys so overcome with the cold as to require, in Cæsar's view, hospital treatment. This awoke our sympathies, and stimulated our sense of personal importance, and we were never so happy as when trudging back through the snow, following Cæsar with a great cock-turkey lying languidly over his shoulder like a sick baby, his long neck drooping, his wattles, erst so fiery red with pride and valor, now blue and despairing. Great on such occasions were our zeal and excitement, as the cavalcade burst into the kitchen with much noise, and upturning of everything, changing Aunt Lois's quiet arrangements into an impromptu sanitary commission. My grandmother bestirred herself promptly, compounding messes of Indian-meal enlivened with pepper-corns, which were forced incontinently down the long throat, and which in due time acted as a restorative.

A turkey treated in this way soon recovered his wonted pride of demeanor, and, with an ingratitude which is like the ways of this world, would be ready to bully my grandmother and fly at her back when she was picking up chips, and charge down upon us children with vociferous gobblings, the very first warm day afterwards. Such toils as these before breakfast gave a zest to the smoking hot brown bread, the beans and sausages, which formed our morning meal.

The great abundance of *food* in our New England life is one subject quite worthy of reflection, if we consider the hardness of the soil, the extreme severity of the climate, and the shortness of the growing season between the late frosts of spring and those of early autumn. But, as matter of fact, good, plain food was everywhere in New England so plentiful, that at the day I write of nobody could really suffer for the want of it. The theocracy of New England had been so thoroughly saturated with the humane and charitable spirit of the old laws of Moses, in which, dealing "bread to the hungry" is so often reiterated and enforced as foremost among human duties, that no one ever thought of refusing food to any that appeared to need it; and a traveller might have walked on foot from one end of New England to the other, as sure of a meal in its season as he was that he saw a farm-house. Even if there was now and then a Nabal like Crab Smith, who, from a native viciousness, hated to do kindness, there was always sure to be in his family an Abigail, ashamed of his baseness, who redeemed the credit of the house by a surreptitious practice of the Christian virtues.

I mention all this because it strikes me, in review of my childhood, that, although far from wealth, and living in many respects in a hard and rough way, I remember great enjoyment in that part of our physical life so important to a child, — the eating and drinking. Our bread, to be sure, was the black compound of rye and Indian which the economy of Massachusetts then made the common form, because it was the result of what could be most easily raised on her hard and stony soil; but I can inform all whom it may concern that rye and Indian bread smoking hot, on a cold winter morning, together with savory sausages, pork, and beans, formed a breakfast fit for a king, if the king had earned it by getting up in a cold room, washing in ice-water, tumbling through snow-drifts, and foddering cattle. We partook of it with a thorough cheeriness; and black Cæsar, seated on his block in the chimney-corner, divided his rations with Bose, the yellow dog of our establishment, with a contentment which it was pleasant to behold.

After breakfast grandfather conducted family prayers, commencing always by reading his chapter in the Bible. He read regularly through in course, as was the custom in those days, without note, comment, or explanation. Among the many insensible forces which formed the minds of New England children, was this constant, daily familiarity with the letter of the Bible. It was for the most part read twice a day in every family of any pretensions to respectability, and it was read as a reading-book in every common school, — in both cases without any attempt at explanation. Such parts as explained themselves were left to do so. Such as were beyond our knowledge were still read, and left to make what impression they would. For my part, I am impatient of the theory of those who think that nothing that is not understood makes any valuable impression on the mind of a child. I am certain that the constant contact of the Bible with my childish mind was a very great mental stimulant, as it certainly was a cause of a singular and vague pleasure. The wild, poetic parts of the prophecies, with their bold figures, vivid exclamations, and strange Oriental names and images, filled me with a quaint and solemn delight. Just as a child brought up under the shadow of the great cathedrals of the Old World, wandering into them daily, at morning, or eventide, beholding the many-colored windows flamboyant with strange legends of saints and angels, and neither understanding the legends, nor comprehending the architecture, is yet stilled and impressed, till the old minster grows into his growth and fashions his nature, so this wonderful old cathedral book insensibly wrought a sort of mystical poetry into the otherwise hard and sterile life of New England. Its passionate Oriental phrases, its quaint, pathetic stories, its wild, transcendent bursts of imagery, fixed an indelible mark in my imagination. Where Kedar and Tarshish and Pul and Lud, Chittim and the Isles, Dan and Beersheba, were, or what they were, I knew not, but they were fixed stations in my realm of cloud-land. I knew them as well as I knew my grandmother's rocking-chair, yet the habit of hearing of them only in solemn tones, and in the readings of religious hours, gave to them a mysterious charm. I think no New-Englander, brought up under the *régime* established by the Puritans, could really estimate how much of himself had actually been formed by this constant face-to-face intimacy with Hebrew literature. It is worthy of remark, too, that, although in details relating to human crime and vice, the Old Bible is the most plain-spoken book conceivable, it never violated the chastity of a child's mind, or stimulated an improper curiosity. I have been astonished in later years to learn the real meaning of passages to which, in family prayers, I listened with innocent gravity.

My grandfather's prayers had a regular daily form, to which, in time, I became quite accustomed. No man of not more than ordinary capacity ever ministered twice a day the year round, in the office of priest to his family, without soon learning to repeat the same ideas in the same phrases, forming to himself a sort of individual liturgy. My grandfather always prayed standing, and the image of his mild, silvery head, leaning over the top of the high-backed chair, always rises before me as I think of early days. There was no great warmth or fervor in these daily exercises, but rather a serious and decorous propriety. They were Hebraistic in their form; they spoke of Zion and Jerusalem, of the God of Israel, the God of Jacob, as much as if my grandfather had been a veritable Jew; and except for the closing phrase, "for the sake of thy Son, our Saviour," might all have been uttered in Palestine by a well-trained Jew in the time of David.

When prayers were over every morning, the first move of the day, announced in Aunt Lois's brief energetic phrases, was to "get the boys out of the way." Our dinner was packed in a small splint basket, and we were started on our way to the district school, about a mile distant. We had our sleds with us, — dear winter companions of boys, — not the gayly painted, genteel little sledges with which Boston boys in these days enliven the Common, but rude, coarse fabrics, got up by Cæsar in rainy days out of the odds and ends of old sleigh-runners and such rough boards as he could rudely fashion with saw and hatchet. Such as they were, they suited us well, — mine in particular, because upon it I could draw Tina to school; for already, children as we were, things had naturally settled themselves between us. She was supreme mistress, and I the too happy slave, only anxious to be permitted to do her bidding. With Harry and me she assumed the negligent airs of a little empress. She gave us her books to carry, called on us to tie her shoes, charged us to remember her errands, got us to learn her lessons for her, and to help her out with whatever she had no mind to labor at; and we were only too happy to do it. Harry was the most doting of brothers, and never could look on Tina in any other light than as one whom he must at any price save from every care and every exertion; and as for me, I never dreamed of disputing her supremacy.

One may, perhaps, wonder how a person so extremely aristocratic in all her ideas of female education as Miss Mehitable should commit her little charge to the chance comradeship and unselect society of the district school. But Miss Mehitable, like many another person who has undertaken the task of bringing up a human being, found herself reduced to the doing of a great many things which she had never expected to do. She prepared for her work in the most thorough manner; she read Locke and Milton, and Dr. Gregory's "Legacy to his Daughter," and Mrs. Chapone on the bringing up of girls, to say nothing of Miss Hannah More and all the other wise people; and, after forming some of the most carefully considered and select plans of operation for herself and her little charge, she was at length driven to the discovery that in education, as in all other things, people who cannot do as they would must do as they can. She discovered that a woman between fifty and sixty years of age, of a peculiar nature, and with very fixed, set habits, could not undertake to be the sole companion and educator of a lively, wilful, spirited little pilgrim of mortality, who was as active as a squirrel, and as inconsequent and uncertain in all her movements as a butterfly.

By some rare good fortune of nature or of grace, she found her little *protégée* already able to read with fluency, and a tolerable mistress of the use of the needle and thimble. Thus she possessed the key of useful knowledge and of useful feminine practice. But truth compels us to state that there appeared not the smallest prospect, during the first few weeks of Miss Mehitable's educational efforts, that she would ever make a good use of either. In vain Miss Mehitable had written a nice card, marking out regular hours for sewing, for reading, for geography and grammar, with suitable intervals of amusement; and in vain Miss Tina, with edifying enthusiasm, had promised, with large eyes and most abundant eloquence, and with many overflowing caresses, to be "so good." Alas! when it came to carrying out the programme, all alone in the house, Mondays, Tuesdays, Wednesdays, Thursdays, Fridays, and all days, Tina gaped and nestled, and lost her thimble and her needle, and was infinite in excuses, and infinite in wheedling caresses, and arguments, enforced with flattering kisses, in favor of putting off the duties now of this hour and then of that, and substituting something more to her fancy. She had a thousand plans of her own for each passing hour, and no end of argument and eloquence to persuade her old friend to follow her ways, — to hear her read an old ballad instead of applying herself to her arithmetic lesson, or listen to her recital of something that she had just picked out of English history, or let her finish a drawing that she was just inspired to commence, or spend a bright, sunny hour in flower-gatherings and rambles by the brown river-side; whence she would return laden with flowers, and fill every vase in the old, silent room till it would seem as if the wilderness had literally blossomed as the rose. Tina's knack for the arranging of vases and twining of vines and sorting of wild-flowers amounted to a species of genius; and, as it was something of which Miss Mehitable had not the slightest comprehension, the child took the lead in this matter with a confident assurance. And, after all, the effect was so cheerful and so delightful, that Miss Mehitable could not find it in her heart to call to the mind of the little wood-fairy how many hours these cheerful decorations had cost.

Thus poor Miss Mehitable found herself daily being drawn, by the leash that held this gay bird, into all sorts of unseemly gyrations and wanderings, instead of using it to tether the bird to her own well-considered purposes. She could not deny that the child was making her old days pass in a very amusing manner, and it was so much easier to follow the lively little sprite in all her airy ways and caprices, seeing her lively and spirited and happy, than to watch the *ennui* and the yawns and the restlessness that came over her with every effort to conform to the strict letter of the programme, that good Miss Mehitable was always yielding. Every night she went to bed with an unquiet conscience, sensible that, though she had had an entertaining day, she had been letting Tina govern her, instead of governing Tina.

Over that grave supposed necessity of governing Tina, this excellent woman groaned in spirit on many a night after the little wheedling tongue had become silent, and the bright, deluding eyes had gone down under their fringy lashes. "The fact is," said the sad old woman, "Miss Asphyxia spoke the truth. It is a fact, I am not fit to bring up a child. She does rule over me, just as she said she would, and I'm a poor old fool; but then, what am I to do? She is so bright and sweet and pretty, and I'm a queer-looking, dry, odd old woman, with nobody to love me if she doesn't. If I cross her and tie her to rules, and am severe with her, she won't love me, and I am too selfish to risk that. Besides, only think what came of using severe measures with poor Emily! people can be spoilt by severity just as much as by indulgence, and more hopelessly. But what shall I do?"

Miss Mehitable at first had some hope of supporting and backing up the weaknesses of her own heart by having recourse to Polly's well-known energy. Polly was a veritable dragon of education, and strong in the most efficient articles of faith. Children must have their wills *broken*, as she expressed it, "short off"; they must mind the very first time you speak; they must be kept under and made to go according to rule, and, if they swerved, Polly recommended measures of most sanguinary severity.

But somehow or other Tina had contrived to throw over this grimmest and most Calvinistic of virgins the glamour of her presence, so that she ruled, reigned, and predominated in the most awful sanctuaries of Polly's kitchen, with a fearfully unconcerned and negligent freedom. She dared to peep into her yeast-jug in the very moment of projection, and to pinch off from her downy puffs of newly raised bread sly morsels for her own cooking experiments; she picked from Polly's very hand the raisins which the good woman was stoning for the most awfully sacred election cake, and resolutely persisted in hanging on her chair and chattering in her ear during the evolution of high culinary mysteries with which the Eleusinian, or any other heathen trumperies of old, were not to be named. Hadn't the receipt for election cake been in the family for one hundred years? and was not Polly the sacred ark and tabernacle in which that divine secret resided? Even Miss Mehitable had always been politely requested to step out of the kitchen when Polly was composing her mind for this serious work, but yet Tina neglected her geography and sewing to be present, chattered all the time, as Polly remarked, like a grist-mill, tasted the sugar and spices, and helped herself at intervals to the savory composition as it was gradually being put together, announcing her opinions, and giving Polly her advice, with an effrontery to which Polly's submission was something appalling.

It really used to seem to Miss Mehitable, as she listened to Polly's dissonant shrieks of laughter from the kitchen, as if that venerable old girl must be slightly intoxicated. Polly's laughter was in truth something quite formidable. All the organs in her which would usually be employed in this exercise were so rusty for want of use, so choked up with theological dust and *débris*, that when brought into exercise they had a wild, grating, dissonant sound, rather calculated to alarm. Miss Mehitable really wondered if this could be the same Polly of whom she herself stood in a certain secret awe, whose premises she never invaded, and whose will over and about her had been always done instead of her own; but if she ventured to open the kitchen door and recall Tina, she was sure to be vigorously snubbed by Polly, who walked over all her own precepts and maxims in the most shameless and astonishing manner.

Polly, however, made up for her own compliances by heaping up censures on poor Miss Mehitable when Tina had gone to bed at night. When the bright eyes were fairly closed, and the little bewitching voice hushed in sleep, Polly's conscience awoke like an armed man, and she atoned for her own sins of compliance and indulgence by stringently admonishing Miss Mehitable that she must be more particular about that child, and not let her get her own head so much, — most unblushingly ignoring her own share in abetting her transgressions, and covering her own especial sins under the declaration that "*she* never had undertaken to bring the child up, — she had to get along with her the best way she could, — but the child never would make anything if she was let to go on so." Yet, in any particular case that arose, Polly was always sure to go over to Tina's side and back her usurpations.

For example, it is to be confessed that Tina never could or would be got to bed at those hours which are universally admitted to be canonical for well-brought up children. As night drew on, the little one's tongue ran with increasing fluency, and her powers of entertainment waxed more dizzy and dazzling; and so, oftentimes, as the drizzling, freezing night shut in, and the wind piped and howled lonesomely round the corners of the dusky old mansion, neither of the two forlorn women could find it in her heart to extinguish the little cheerful candle of their dwelling in bed; and so she was to them ballet and opera as she sung and danced, mimicked the dog, mimicked the cat and the hens and the tom-turkey, and at last talked and flew about the room like Aunt Lois, stirred up butter and pshawed like grandma, or invented imaginary scenes and conversations, or improvised unheard-of costumes out of strange old things she had rummaged out of Miss Mehitable's dark closets. Neither of the two worthy women had ever seen the smallest kind of dramatic representation, so that Tina's histrionic powers fascinated them by touching upon dormant faculties, and seemed more wonderful for their utter novelty; and more than once, to the poignant self-reproach of Miss Mehitable, and Polly's most moral indignation, nine o'clock struck, in the inevitable tones of the old family timepiece, before they were well aware what they were doing. Then Tina would be hustled off to bed, and Polly would preach Miss Mehitable a strenuous discourse on the necessity of keeping children to regular hours, interspersed with fragments of quotations from one of her venerable father's early sermons on the Christian bringing up of households. Polly would grow inexorable as conscience on these occasions, and when Miss Mehitable humbly pleaded in extenuation how charming a little creature it was, and what a pleasant evening she had given, Polly would shake her head, and declare that the ways of sin were always pleasant for a time, but at the last it would "bite like a serpent and sting like

an adder"; and when Miss Mehitable, in the most delicate manner, would insinuate that Polly had been sharing the forbidden
fruit, such as it was, Polly would flare up in sudden wrath, and declare that "everything that went wrong was always laid to her."

In consequence of this, though Miss Mehitable found the first
few weeks with her little charge altogether the gayest and brightest that had diversified her dreary life, yet there was a bitter sense
of self-condemnation and perplexity with it all. One day she opened
her mind to my grandmother.

"Laws a massy! don't try to teach her yourself," said that plain-
spoken old individual, — "send her to school with the boys. Children have to go in droves. What's the use of fussing with 'em all
day? let the schoolmaster take a part of the care. Children have
to be got rid of sometimes, and we come to them all the fresher
for having them out of our sight."

The consequence was, that Tina rode to school on our sleds in
triumph, and made more fun, and did more mischief, and learned
less, and was more adored and desired, than any other scholar of
us all.

CHAPTER XXIII

WE TAKE A STEP UP
IN THE WORLD

One of my most vivid childish remembrances is the length of our winters, the depth of the snows, the raging fury of the storms that used to whirl over the old farm-house, shrieking and piping and screaming round each angle and corner, and thundering down the chimney in a way that used to threaten to topple all down before it.

The one great central kitchen fire was the only means of warming known in the house, and duly at nine o'clock every night *that* was raked up, and all the family took their way to bed-chambers that never knew a fire, where the very sheets and blankets seemed so full of stinging cold air that they made one's fingers tingle; and where, after getting into bed, there was a prolonged shiver, until one's own internal heat-giving economy had warmed through the whole icy mass. Delicate people had these horrors ameliorated by the application of a brass warming-pan, — an article of high respect and repute in those days, which the modern conveniences for warmth in our houses have entirely banished.

Then came the sleet storms, when the trees bent and creaked under glittering mail of ice, and every sprig and spray of any kind of vegetation was reproduced in sparkling crystals. These were cold days *par excellence,* when everybody talked of the weather as something exciting and tremendous, — when the cider would freeze in the cellar, and the bread in the milk-room would be like blocks of ice, — when not a drop of water could be got out of the sealed well, and the very chimney-back over the raked-up fire would be seen in the morning sparkling with a rime of frost crystals. How the sledges used to squeak over the hard snow, and the breath freeze on the hair, and beard, and woolly comforters around the necks of the men, as one and another brought in news of the wonderful, unheard-of excesses of Jack Frost during the foregone night! There was always something exhilarating about those extremely cold days, when a very forest of logs, heaped up and burning in the great chimney, could not warm the other side of the kitchen; and when Aunt Lois, standing with her back so near the blaze as to be uncomfortably warm, yet found her dish-towel freezing in her hand, while she wiped the teacup drawn from the almost boiling water. When things got to this point, we little folks were jolly. It was an excitement, an intoxication; it filled life full of talk. People froze the tips of their noses, their ears, their toes; we froze our own. Whoever touched a door-latch incautiously, in the early morning, received a skinning bite from Jack. The axe, the saw, the hatchet, all the iron tools, in short, were possessed of a cold devil ready to snap out at any incautious hand that meddled with him. What ponderous stalactites of ice used to hang from the eaves, and hung unmelted days, weeks, and months, dripping a little, perhaps, towards noon, but hardening again as night came on! and how long all this lasted! To us children it seemed ages.

Then came April with here and there a sunny day. A bluebird would be vaguely spoken of as having appeared. Sam Lawson was usually the first to announce the fact, to the sharp and sceptical contempt of his helpmeet.

On a shimmering April morning, with a half-mind to be sunshiny, Sam saw Harry and myself trotting by his door, and called to us for a bit of gossip.

"Lordy massy, boys, ain't it pleasant? Why, bless your soul and body, I do believe spring's a comin', though Hepsy she won't believe it," he said, as he leaned over the fence contemplatively, with the axe in his hand. "I heard a bluebird last week, Jake Marshall and me, when we was goin' over to Hopkinton to see how Ike Saunders is. You know he is down with the measles. I went over to offer to sit up with him. Where be ye goin' this mornin'?"

"We're going to the minister's. Grandfather isn't well, and Lady Lothrop told us to come for some wine."

"Jes' so," said Sam. "Wal, now, he orter take something for his stomach's sake, Scriptur' goes in for that. A little good hot spiced wine, it's jest the thing; and Ma'am Lothrop, she has the very best. Why, some o' that 'ere wine o' hern come over from England years ago, when her fust husband was living; and he was a man that knew where to get his things. Wal, you mustn't stop to play; allers remember when you're sent on errands not to be a idlin' on the road."

"Sam Lawson, will you split me that oven-wood or won't you?" said a smart, cracking voice, as the door flew open and Hepsy's thin face and snapping black eyes appeared, as she stood with a weird, wiry, sharp-visaged baby exalted on one shoulder, while in the other hand she shook a dish-cloth.

"Lordy massy, Hepsy, I'm splittin' as fast as I can. There, run along, boys; don't stop to play."

We ran along, for, truth to say, the vision of Hepsy's sharp features always quickened our speed, and we heard the loud, high-pitched storm of matrimonial objurgation long after we had left them behind.

Timidly we struck the great knocker, and with due respect and modesty told our errand to the black doctor of divinity who opened the door.

"I'll speak to Missis," he said; "but this 'ere's Missis' great day; it's Good Friday, and she don't come out of her room the whole blessed day."

"But she sent word that we should come," we both answered in one voice.

"Well, you jest wait here while I go up and see," — and the important messenger creaked up stairs on tiptoe with infinite precaution, and knocked at a chamber door.

Now there was something in all this reception that was vaguely solemn and impressive to us. The minister's house of itself was a dignified and august place. The minister was in our minds great and greatly to be feared, and to be had in reverence of them that were about him. The minister's wife was a very great lady, who wore very stiff silks, and rode in a coach, and had no end of unknown wealth at her control, so ran the village gossip. And now what this mysterious Good Friday was, and why the house was so still, and why the black doctor of divinity tiptoed up stairs so stealthily, and knocked at her door so timidly, we could not exactly conjecture; — it was all of a piece with the general marvellous and supernatural character of the whole establishment.

We heard above the silvery well-bred tones that marked Lady Lothrop.

"Tell the children to come up."

We looked at each other, and each waited a moment for the other to lead the way; finally I took the lead, and Harry followed.

We entered a bedroom shaded in a sombre gloom which seemed to our childish eyes mysterious and impressive. There were three windows in the room, but the shutters were closed, and the only light that came in was from heart-shaped apertures in each one. There was in one corner a tall, solemn-looking, high-post bedstead with heavy crimson draperies. There were heavy carved bureaus and chairs of black, solid oak.

At a table covered with dark cloth sat Lady Lothrop, dressed entirely in black, with a great Book of Common Prayer spread out before her. The light from the heart-shaped hole streamed down upon this prayer-book in a sort of dusky shaft, and I was the more struck and impressed because it was not an ordinary volume, but a great folio bound in parchment, with heavy brass knobs and clasps, printed in black-letter, of that identical old edition first prepared in King Edward's time, and appointed to be read in churches. Its very unusual and antique appearance impressed me with a kind of awe.

There was at the other end of the room a tall, full-length mirror, which, as we advanced, duplicated the whole scene, giving back faithfully the image of the spare figure of Lady Lothrop, her grave and serious face, and the strange old book over which she seemed to be bending, with a dusky gleaming of crimson draperies in the background.

"Come here, my children," she said, as we hesitated; "how is your grandfather?"

"He is not so well to-day; and grandmamma said — "

"Yes, yes; I know," she said, with a gentle little wave of the hand; "I desired that you might be sent for some wine; Pompey shall have it ready for you. But tell me, little boys, do you know what day this is?"

"It's Friday, ma'am," said I, innocently.

"Yes, my child; but do you know *what* Friday it is?" she said.

"No, ma'am," said I, faintly.

"Well, my child, it is Good Friday; and do you know why it is called Good Friday?"

"No, ma'am."

"This is the day when our Lord and Saviour Jesus Christ died on the cross for our salvation; so we call it Good Friday."

I must confess that these words struck me with a strange and blank amazement. That there had been in this world a personage called "Our Lord and Saviour Jesus Christ," I had learned from the repetition of his name as the usual ending of prayers at church and in the family; but the real literal fact that he had lived on earth had never presented itself to me in any definite form before; but this solemn and secluded room, this sombre woman shut out from all the ordinary ways of the world, devoting the day to lonely musing, gave to her words a strange reality.

"When did he die?" I said.

"More than a thousand years ago," she answered.

Insensibly Harry had pressed forward till he stood in the shaft of light, which fell upon his golden curls, and his large blue eyes now had that wide-open, absorbed expression with which he always listened to anything of a religious nature, and, as if speaking involuntarily, he said eagerly, "But he is not dead. He is living; and we pray to him."

"Why, yes, my son," said Lady Lothrop, turning and looking with pleased surprise, which became more admiring as she gazed, — "yes, he rose from the dead."

"I know. Mother told me all about that. Day after to-morrow will be Easter day," said Harry; "I remember."

A bright flush of pleased expression passed over Lady Lothrop's face as she said, "I am glad, my boy, that *you* at least have been taught. Tell me, boys," she said at last, graciously, "should you like to go with me in my carriage to Easter Sunday, in Boston?"

Had a good fairy offered to take us on the rainbow to the palace of the sunset, the offer could not have seemed more unworldly and dream-like. What Easter Sunday was I had not the faintest idea, but I felt it to be something vague, strange, and remotely suggestive of the supernatural.

Harry, however, stood the thing in the simple, solemn, gentlemanlike way which was habitual with him.

"Thank you, ma'am, I shall be very happy, if grandmamma is willing."

It will be seen that Harry slid into the adoptive familiarity which made my grandmother his, with the easy good faith of childhood.

"Tell your grandmamma if she is willing I shall call for you in my coach to-morrow," — and we were graciously dismissed.

We ran home in all haste with our bottle of wine, and burst into the kitchen, communicating our message both at once to Aunt Lois and Aunt Keziah. The two women looked at each other mysteriously; there was a slight flush on Aunt Lois's keen, spare face.

"Well, if she's a mind to do it, Kezzy, I don't see how we can refuse."

"Mother never would consent in the world," said Aunt Keziah.

"Mother *must*," said Aunt Lois, with decision. "We can't afford to offend Lady Lothrop, with both these boys on our hands. Besides, now father is sick, what a mercy to have 'em both out of the house for a Sunday!"

Aunt Lois spoke this with an intensive earnestness that deepened my already strong convictions that we boys were a daily load upon her life, only endured by a high and protracted exercise of Christian fortitude.

She rose and tapped briskly into the bedroom where my grandmother was sitting reading by my grandfather's bed. I heard her making some rapid statements in a subdued, imperative tone. There were a few moments of a sort of suppressed, earnest hum of conversation, and soon we heard sundry vehement interjections from my grandmother, — "Good Friday! — Easter! — pish, Lois! — don't tell me! — old cast-off rags of the scarlet woman, — nothing else.

> 'Abhor the arrant whore of Rome,
> And all her blasphemies;
> Drink not of her accursed cup,
> Obey not her decrees.' "

"Now, mother, how absurd!" I heard Aunt Lois say. "Who's talking about Rome? I'm sure, if Dr. Lothrop can allow it, we can. It's all nonsense to talk so. We don't want to offend our minister's wife; we must do the things that make for peace"; and then the humming went on for a few moments more and more earnestly, till finally we heard grandmother break out: —

"Well, well, have it your own way, Lois, — you always did and always will, I suppose. Glad the boys'll have a holiday, anyhow. She means well, I dare say, — thinks she's doing right."

I must say that this was a favorite formula with which my grandmother generally let herself down from the high platform of her own sharply defined opinions to the level of Christian charity with her neighbors.

"Who is the whore of Rome?" said Harry to me, confidentially, when we had gone to our room to make ready for our jaunt the next day.

"Don't you know?" said I. "Why, it's the one that burnt John Rogers, in the Catechism. I can show it to you"; and, forthwith producing from my small stock of books my New England Primer, I called his attention to the picture of Mr. John Rogers in gown and bands, standing in the midst of a brisk and voluminous coil of fire and smoke, over which an executioner, with a supernatural broad-axe upon his shoulders, seemed to preside with grim satisfaction. There was a woman with a baby in her arms and nine children at her side, who stood in a row, each head being just a step lower than the preceding, so that they made a regular flight of stairs. The artist had represented the mother and all the children with a sort of round bundle on each of their heads, of about the same size as the head itself, — a thing which I always interpreted as a further device of the enemy in putting stones on their heads to crush them down; and I pointed it out to Harry as an aggravating feature of the martyrdom.

"Did the whore of Rome do that?" said Harry, after a few moments' reflection.

"Yes, she did, and it tells about it in the poetry which he wrote here to his children the night before his execution"; and forthwith I proceeded to read to Harry that whole poetical production, delighted to find a gap in his education which I was competent to fill. We were both wrought up into a highly Protestant state by reading this.

"Horace," said Harry, timidly, "*she* wouldn't like such things, would she? she is such a good woman."

"What, Lady Lothrop? of course she's a good woman; else she wouldn't be our minister's wife."

"What was grandma talking about?" said Harry.

"O, I don't know; grandmother talks about a great many things," said I. "At any rate, we shall see Boston, and I've always wanted to see Boston. Only think, Harry, we shall go in a coach!"

This projected tour to Boston was a glorification of us children in the eyes of the whole family. To go, on the humblest of terms, *to Boston,* — but to be taken thither in Lady Lothrop's coach, to be trotted in magnificently behind her fat pair of carriage-horses, — that was a good fortune second only to translation.

Boston lay at an easy three hours' ride from Oldtown, and Lady Lothrop had signified to my grandmother that we were to be called for soon after dinner. We were to spend the night and the Sunday following at the house of Lady Lothrop's mother, who still kept the old family mansion at the north end, and Lady Lothrop was graciously pleased to add that she would keep the children over Easter Monday, to show them Boston. Faithful old soul, she never omitted the opportunity of reminding the gainsaying community among whom her lot was cast of the solemn days of her church and for one *I* have remembered Easter Sunday and Monday to this day.

Our good fortune received its crowning stroke in our eyes when, running over to Miss Mehitable's with the news, we found that Lady Lothrop had considerately included Tina in the invitation.

"Well, she must like children better than I do," was Aunt Lois's comment upon the fact, when we announced it. "Now, boys, mind and behave yourselves like young gentlemen," she added, "for you are going to one of the oldest families of Boston, among real genteel people."

"They're Tories, Lois," put in Aunt Keziah, apprehensively.

"Well, what of that? that thing's over and gone now," said Aunt Lois, "and nobody lays it up against the Kitterys, and everybody knows they were in the very first circles in Boston before the war, and connected with the highest people in England, so it was quite natural they should be Tories."

"I shouldn't wonder if Lady Widgery should be there," said Aunt Keziah, musingly, as she twitched her yarn; "she always used to come to Boston about this time o' the year."

"Very likely she will," said my mother. "What relation is she to Lady Lothrop?"

"Why, bless me, don't you know?" said Aunt Lois. "Why, she was Polly Steadman, and sister to old Ma'am Kittery's husband's first wife. She was second wife to Sir Thomas; his first wife was one of the Keatons of Penshurst, in England; she died while Sir Thomas was in the custom-house; she was a poor, sickly thing. Polly was a great beauty in her day. People said he admired her rather too much before his wife died, but I don't know how that was."

"I wonder what folks want to say such things for," quoth my grandmother. "I hate backbiters, for my part."

"We aren't backbiting, mother. I only said how the story ran. It was years ago, and poor Sir Thomas is in his grave long ago."

"Then you might let him rest there," said my grandmother. "Lady Widgery was a pleasant-spoken woman, I remember."

"She's quite an invalid now, I heard," said Aunt Lois. "Our Bill was calling at the Kitterys' the other day, and Miss Deborah Kittery spoke of expecting Lady Widgery. The Kitterys have been very polite to Bill; they've invited him there to dinner once or twice this winter. That was one reason why I thought we ought to be careful how we treat Lady Lothrop's invitation. It's entirely through her influence that Bill gets these attentions."

"I don't know about their being the best thing for him," said my grandmother, doubtfully.

"Mother, how can you talk so? What can be better than for a young man to have the run of good families in Boston?" said Aunt Lois.

"I'd rather see him have intimacy with one godly minister of old times," said my grandmother.

"Well, that's what Bill isn't likely to do," quoth Aunt Lois, with a slight shade of impatience. "We must take boys as we find 'em."

"I haven't anything against Tories or Episcopalians," said my grandmother; "but they ain't our sort of folks. I dare say they mean as well as they know how."

"Miss Mehitable visits the Kitterys when she is in Boston," said Aunt Lois, "and thinks everything of them. She says that Deborah Kittery is a very smart, intelligent woman, — a woman of a very strong mind."

"I dare say they're well enough," said my grandmother. "I'm sure I wish 'em well with all my heart."

"Now, Horace," said Aunt Lois, "be careful you don't sniff, and be sure and wipe your shoes on the mat when you come in, and never on any account speak a word unless you are spoken to. Little boys should be seen and not heard; and be very careful you never touch anything you see. It is very good of Lady Lothrop to be willing to take all the trouble of having you with her, and you must make her just as little as possible."

I mentally resolved to reduce myself to a nonentity, to go out of existence, as it were, to be nobody and nowhere, if only I might escape making trouble.

"As to Harry, he is always a good, quiet boy, and never touches things, or forgets to wipe his shoes," said my aunt. "I'm sure he will behave himself."

My mother colored slightly at this undisguised partiality for Harry, but she was too much under Aunt Lois's discipline to venture a word.

"Lordy massy, Mis' Badger, how do ye all do?" said Sam Lawson, this moment appearing at the kitchen door. "I saw your winders so bright, I thought I'd jest look in and ask after the Deacon. I ben into Miss Mehitable's, and there's Polly, she told me about the chillen goin' to Boston to-morrow. Tiny, she's jest flying round and round like a lightning-bug, most out of her head, she's so tickled; and Polly, she was ai'nin' up her white aprons to get her up smart. Polly, she says it's all pagan flummery about Easter, but she's glad the chillen are goin' to have the holiday." And with this Sam Lawson seated himself on his usual evening roost in the corner, next to black Cæsar, and we both came and stood by his knee.

"Wal, boys, now you're goin' among real, old-fashioned gentility. Them Kitterys used to hold their heads 'mazin' high afore the war, and they've managed by hook and crook to hold on to most what they got, and now by-gones is by-gones. But I believe they don't go out much, or go into company. Old Ma'am Kittery, she's kind o' broke up about her son that was killed at the Delaware."

"Fighting on the wrong side, poor woman," said my grandmother. "Well, I s'pose he thought he was doing right."

"Yes, yes," said Sam, "there's all sorts o' folks go to make up a world, and, lordy massy, we mustn't be hard on nobody; can't 'spect everybody to be right all round; it's what I tell Polly when she sniffs at Lady Lothrop keepin' Christmas and Easter and sich. 'Lordy massy, Polly,' says I, 'if she reads her Bible, and's good to the poor, and don't speak evil o' nobody, why, let her have her Easter; what's the harm on 't?' But, lordy massy bless your soul an' body! there's no kind o' use talkin' to Polly. She fumed away there, over her i'nin' table; she didn't believe in folks that read their prayers out o' books; and then she hed it all over about them tew thousan' ministers that was all turned out o' the church in one day in old King Charles's time. Now, raily, Mis' Badger, I don't see why Lady Lothrop should be held 'sponsible for that are, if she is 'Piscopalian."

"Well, well," said my grandmother; "they did turn out the very best men in England, but the Lord took 'em for seed to plant America with. But no wonder we feel it: burnt children dread the fire. I've nothing against Lady Lothrop, and I don't wish evil to the Episcopalians nor to the Tories. There's good folks among 'em all, and 'the Lord knoweth them that are his.' But I do hope, Horace, that, when you get to Boston, you will go out on to Copps Hill and see the graves of the Saints. There are the men that I want my children to remember. You come here, and let me read you about them in my 'Magnaly' * here." And with this my grandmother produced her well-worn copy; and, to say the truth, we were never tired of hearing what there was in it. What legends, wonderful and stirring, of the solemn old forest life, — of fights with the Indians, and thrilling adventures, and captivities, and distresses, — of encounters with panthers and serpents, and other wild beasts, which made our very hair stand on end! Then there were the weird witch-stories, so wonderfully attested; and how Mr. Peter So-and-so did visibly see, when crossing a river, a cat's head swimming in front of the boat, and the tail of the same following behind; and how worthy people had been badgered and harassed by a sudden friskiness in all their household belongings, in a manner not unknown in our modern days. Of all these fascinating legends my grandmother was a willing communicator, and had, to match them, numbers of corresponding ones from her own personal observation and experience; and sometimes Sam Lawson would chime in with long-winded legends, which, being told by flickering firelight, with the wind rumbling and tumbling down the great chimney, or shrieking and yelling and piping around every corner of the house, like an army of fiends trying with tooth and claw to get in upon us, had power to send cold chills down our backs in the most charming manner.

For my part, I had not the slightest fear of the supernatural; it was to me only a delightful stimulant, just crisping the surface

* Dr. Cotton Mather's "Magnalia."

of my mind with a pleasing horror. I had not any doubt of the
stories of apparitions related by Dr. Cotton, because I had seen
so many of them myself; and I did not doubt that many of the
witnesses who testified in these cases really *did see* what they
said they saw, as plainly as I had seen similar appearances. The
consideration of the fact that there really are people in whose lives
such phenomena are of frequent occurrence seems to have been
entirely left out of the minds of those who have endeavored to
explain that dark passage in our history.

In my maturer years I looked upon this peculiarity as something resulting from a physical idiosyncrasy, and I have supposed
that such affections may become at times epidemics in communities, as well as any other affection of the brain and nervous system. Whether the things thus discerned have an objective reality
or not, has been one of those questions at which, all my life, the
interrogation point has stood unerased.

On this evening, however, my grandmother thought fit to edify
us by copious extracts from "The Second Part, entitled *Sepher-
Jearim,* i.e. *Liber Deum Timentium*; or, Dead Abels; — yet speaking and spoken of."

The lives of several of these "Dead Abels" were her favorite
reading, and to-night she designed especially to fortify our minds
with their biographies; so she gave us short dips and extracts here
and there from several of them, as, for example: "*Janus Nov.-
Anglicus*; or, The Life of Mr. Samuel Higginson"; — "*Cadmus
Americanus*; or, Life of Mr. Charles Chauncey"; — "*Cygnea Can-
tio*; or, The Death of Mr. John Avery"; — "*Fulgentius*; or, The
Life of Mr. Richard Mather"; and "*Elisha's Bones*; or, Life of Mr.
Henry Whitefield."

These Latin titles stimulated my imagination like the sound of
a trumpet, and I looked them out diligently in my father's great
dictionary, and sometimes astonished my grandmother by telling
her what they meant.

In fact, I was sent to bed that night thoroughly fortified against
all seductions of the gay and worldly society into which I was
about to be precipitated; and my reader will see that there was
need enough of this preparation.

All these various conversations in regard to differences of religion went on before us children with the freedom with which

older people generally allow themselves to go on in the presence of the little non-combatants of life. In those days, when utter silence and reserve in the presence of elders was so forcibly inculcated as one of the leading virtues of childhood, there was little calculation made for the effect of such words on the childish mind. With me it was a perfect hazy mist of wonder and bewilderment; and I went to sleep and dreamed that John Rogers was burning Lady Lothrop at the stake, and Polly, as executioner, presided with a great broadaxe over her shoulder, while grandmother, with nine small children, all with stone bundles on their heads, assisted at the ceremony.

Our ride to Boston was performed in a most proper and edifying manner. Lady Lothrop sat erect and gracious on the back seat, and placed Harry, for whom she seemed to have conceived a special affection, by her side. Tina was perched on the knee of my lady's maid, a starched, prim woman who had grown up and dried in all the most sacred and sanctified essences of genteel propriety. She was the very crispness of old-time decorum, brought up to order herself lowly and reverently to all her betters, and with a secret conviction that, aside from Lady Lothrop, the whole of the Oldtown population were rather low Dissenters, whom she was required by the rules of Christian propriety to be kind to. To her master, as having been honored with the august favor of her mistress's hand, she looked up with respect, but her highest mark of approbation was in the oft-repeated burst which came from her heart in moments of confidential enthusiasm, — "Ah, ma'am, depend upon it, master is a churchman in his heart. If 'e 'ad only 'ad the good fortune to be born in Hengland, 'e would 'ave been a bishop!"

Tina had been talked to and schooled rigorously by Miss Mehitable as to propriety of manner during this ride; and, as Miss Mehitable well knew what a chatterbox she was, she exacted from her a solemn promise that she would only speak when she was spoken to. Being perched in Mrs. Margery's lap, she felt still further the stringent and binding power of that atmosphere of frosty decorum which encircled this immaculate waiting-maid. A more well-bred, inoffensive, reverential little trio never surrounded a lady patroness; and as Lady Lothrop was not much of a talker, and, being a childless woman, had none of those little arts of drawing out children which the maternal instinct alone teaches, our ride, though undoubtedly a matter of great enjoyment, was an enjoyment of a serious and even awful character. Lady Lothrop addressed a few kind inquiries to each one of us in turn, to which we each of us replied, and then the conversation fell into the hands of Mrs. Margery, and consisted mainly in precise details as to where and how she had packed her mistress's Sunday cap and velvet dress; in doing which she evinced the great fluency and fertility of language with which women of her class are gifted on the one subject of their souls. Mrs. Margery felt as if the Sunday cap of the only supporter of the true Church in the dark and heathen parish of Oldtown was a subject not to be lightly or unadvisedly considered; and, therefore, she told at great length how she had intended to pack it first all together, — how she had altered her mind and taken off the bow, and packed that in a little box by itself, and laid the strings out flat in the box, — what difficulties had met her in folding the velvet dress, — and how she had at first laid it on top of the trunk, but had decided at last that the black lutestring might go on top of that, because it was so much lighter, &c., &c., &c.

Lady Lothrop was so much accustomed to this species of monologue, that it is quite doubtful if she heard a word of it; but poor Tina, who felt within herself whole worlds of things to say, from the various objects upon the road, of which she was dying to talk and ask questions, wriggled and twisted upon Mrs. Margery's knee, and finally gave utterance to her pent-up feelings in deep sighs.

"What's the matter, little dear?" said Lady Lothrop.

"O dear! I was just wishing I could go to church."

"Well, you are going to-morrow, dear."

"I just wish I could go now to say *one* prayer."

"And what is that, my dear?"

"I just want to say, 'O Lord, open thou my lips,'" said Tina, with effusion.

Lady Lothrop smiled with an air of innocent surprise, and Mrs. Margery winked over the little head.

"I'm *so* tired of not talking!" said Tina, pathetically; "but I promised Miss Mehitable I wouldn't speak unless I was spoken to," she added, with an air of virtuous resolution.

"Why, my little dear, you *may* talk," said Lady Lothrop. "It won't disturb me at all. Tell us now about anything that interests you."

"O, thank you ever so much," said Tina; and from this moment, as a little elfin butterfly bursts from a cold, gray chrysalis, Tina rattled and chattered and sparkled, and went on with *verve* and gusto that quite waked us all up. Lady Lothrop and Mrs. Margery soon found themselves laughing with a heartiness which surprised themselves; and, the icy chains of silence being once broken, we all talked, almost forgetting in whose presence we were. Lady Lothrop looked from one to another in a sort of pleased and innocent surprise. Her still, childless, decorous life covered and concealed many mute feminine instincts which now rose at the voice and touch of childhood; and sometimes in the course of our gambols she would sigh, perhaps thinking of her own childless hearth.

CHAPTER XXIV

WE BEHOLD GRANDEUR

It was just at dusk that our carriage stood before the door of a respectable mansion at the north end of Boston.

I remember our alighting and passing through a wide hall with a dark oaken staircase, into a low-studded parlor, lighted by the blaze of a fire of hickory logs, which threw out tongues of yellow flame, and winked at itself with a thousand fanciful flashes, in the crinkles and angles of a singularly high and mighty pair of brass andirons.

A lovely, peaceful old lady, whose silvery white hair and black dress were the most striking features of the picture, kissed Lady Lothrop, and then came to us with a perfect outgush of motherly kindness. "Why, the poor little dears! the little darlings!" she said, as she began with her trembling fingers to undo Tina's bonnet-strings. "Did they want to come to Boston and see the great city? Well, they should. They must be cold; there, put them close by the fire, and grandma will get them a nice cake pretty soon. Here, I'll hold the little lady," she said, as she put Tina on her knee.

The child nestled her head down on her bosom as lovingly and confidingly as if she had known her all her days. "Poor babe," said the old lady to Lady Lothrop, "who could have had a heart to desert such a child? and this is the boy," she said, drawing Harry to her and looking tenderly at him. "Well, a father of the fatherless is God in his holy habitation." There was something even grand about the fervor of this sentence as she uttered it, and Tina put up her hand with a caressing gesture around the withered old neck.

"Debby, get these poor children a cake," said the lady to a brisk, energetic, rather high-stepping individual, who now entered the apartment.

"Come now, mother, do let it rest till supper-time. If we let you alone, you would murder all the children in your neighborhood with cake and suger-plums; you'd be as bad as King Herod."

Miss Debby was a well-preserved, up-and-down, positive, cheery, sprightly maiden lady of an age lying somewhere in the indeterminate region between forty and sixty. There was a positive, brusque way about all her movements, and she advanced to the fire, rearranged the wood, picked up stray brands, and whisked up the coals with a brush, and then, seating herself bolt upright, took up the business of making our acquaintance in the most precise and systematic manner.

"So this is Master Horace Holyoke. How do you do, sir?"

As previously directed, I made my best bow with anxious politeness.

"And this is Master Harry Percival, is it?" Harry did the same.

"And this," she added, turning to Tina, "is Miss Tina Percival, I understand? Well, we are very happy to see *good* little children in this house always." There was a rather severe emphasis on the *good,* which, together with the somewhat martial and disciplinary air which invested all Miss Deborah's words and actions, was calculated to strike children with a wholesome awe.

Our resolution "to be very good indeed" received an immediate accession of strength. At this moment a serving-maid appeared at the door, and, with eyes cast down, and a stiff, respectful courtesy, conveyed the information, "If you please, ma'am, tea is ready."

This humble, self-abased figure — the utter air of self-abnegation with which the domestic seemed to intimate that, unless her mistress pleased, tea was not ready, and that everything in creation was to be either ready or not ready according to her sovereign will and good pleasure — was to us children a new lesson in decorum.

"Go tell Lady Widgery that tea is served," said Miss Deborah, in a loud, resounding voice. "Tell her that we will wait her ladyship's convenience."

The humble serving-maid courtesied, and closed the door softly with reverential awe. On the whole, the impression upon our minds was deeply solemn; we were about to see her ladyship.

Lady Widgery was the last rose of summer of the departed

aristocracy. Lady Lothrop's title was only by courtesy; but Sir Thomas Widgery was a live baronet; and as there were to be no more of these splendid dispensations in America, one may fancy the tenderness with which old Tory families cherished the last lingering remnants.

The door was soon opened again, and a bundle of black silk appeared, with a pale, thin face looking out of it. There was to be seen the glitter of a pair of sharp, black eyes, and the shimmer of a thin white hand with a diamond ring upon it. These were the items that made up Lady Widgery, as she dawned upon our childish vision.

Lest the reader should conceive any false hopes or impressions, I may as well say that it turned out, on further acquaintance, that these items were about all there was of Lady Widgery. It was one of the cases where Nature had picked up a very indifferent and commonplace soul, and shut it up in a very intelligent-looking body. From her youth up, Lady Widgery's principal attraction consisted in looking as if there was a great deal more in her than there really was. Her eyes were sparkling and bright, and had a habit of looking at things in this world with keen, shrewd glances, as if she were thinking about them to some purpose, which she never was. Sometimes they were tender and beseeching, and led her distracted admirers to feel as if she were melting with emotions that she never dreamed of. Thus Lady Widgery had always been rushed for and contended for by the other sex; and one husband had hardly time to be cold in his grave before the air was filled with the rivalry of candidates to her hand; and after all the beautiful little hoax had nothing for it but her attractive soul-case. In her old age she still looked elegant, shrewd, and keen, and undeniably high-bred, and carried about her the prestige of rank and beauty. Otherwise she was a little dry bundle of old prejudices, of faded recollections of past conquests and gayeties, and weakly concerned about her own health, which, in her view and that of everybody about her, appeared a most sacred subject. She had a somewhat entertaining manner of rehearsing the gossip and scandals of the last forty years, and was, so far as such a person could be, religious: that is to say, she kept all the feasts and fasts of the Church scrupulously. She had, in a weakly way, a sense of some responsibility in this matter, because she was Lady Widgery, and because infidelity was prevailing in the land, and it became Lady Widgery to cast her influence against it. Therefore it was that, even at the risk of her precious life, as she thought, she had felt it imperative to come to Boston to celebrate Easter Sunday.

When she entered the room there was an immediate bustle of welcome. Lady Lothrop ran up to her, saluting her with an appearance of great fondness, mingled, I thought, with a sort of extreme deference. Miss Deborah was pressing in her attentions. "Will you sit a moment before tea to get your feet warm, or will you go out at once? The dining-room is quite warm."

Lady Widgery's feet were quite warm, and everybody was *so* glad to hear it, that we were filled with wonder.

Then she turned and fixed her keen, dark eyes on us, as if she were reading our very destiny, and asked who we were. We were all presented circumstantially, and the brilliant eyes seemed to look through us shrewdly, as we made our bows and courtesies. One would have thought that she was studying us with a deep interest, which was not the case.

We were now marshalled out to the tea-table, where we children had our plates put in a row together, and were waited on with obsequious civility by Mrs. Margery and another equally starched and decorous female, who was the attendant of Lady Widgery. We stood at our places a moment, while the lovely old lady, raising her trembling hand, pronounced the words of the customary grace: "For what we are now about to receive, the Lord make us truly thankful." Her voice trembled as she spoke, and somehow the impression of fragility and sanctity that she made on me awoke in me a sort of tender awe. When the blessing was over, the maids seated us, and I had leisure to notice the entirely new scene about me.

It was all conducted with an inexpressible stateliness of propriety, and, in an undefined way, the impression was produced upon my mind that the frail, shivery, rather thin and withered little being, enveloped in a tangle of black silk wraps, was something inexpressibly sacred and sublime. Miss Deborah waited on her constantly, pressingly, energetically; and the dear, sweet old white-haired lady tended her with obsequiousness, which, like everything else that she did, was lost in lovingness; and Lady

Lothrop, to me the most awe-inspiring of the female race, paled her ineffectual fires, and bowed her sacred head to the rustling little black silk bundle, in a way that made me inwardly wonder. The whole scene was so different from the wide, rough, noisy, free-and-easy democracy of my grandmother's kitchen, that I felt crusted all over with an indefinite stiffness of embarrassment, as if I had been dipped in an alum-bath. At the head of the table there was an old silver tea-urn, looking heavy enough to have the weight of whole generations in it, into which, at the moment of sitting down, a serious-visaged waiting-maid dropped a red-hot weight, and forthwith the noise of a violent boiling arose. We little folks looked at each other inquiringly, but said nothing. All was to us like an enchanted palace. The great, mysterious tea-urn, the chased silver tea-caddy, the precise and well-considered movements of Miss Deborah as she rinsed the old embossed silver tea-pots in the boiling water, the India-china cups and plates, painted with the family initials and family crest, all were to us solemn signs and symbols of that upper table-land of gentility, into which we were forewarned by Aunt Lois we were to enter.

"There," said Miss Deborah, with emphasis, as she poured and handed to Lady Widgery a cup of tea, — "there's some of the tea that my brother saved at the time of that disgraceful Boston riot, when Boston Harbor was floating with tea-chests. His cargo was rifled in the most scandalous manner, but he went out in a boat and saved some at the risk of his life."

Now my most sacred and enthusiastic remembrance was of the glow of patriotic fervor with which, seated on my grandfather's knee, I had heard the particulars of that event at a time when names and dates and dress, and time, place, and circumstance, had all the life and vividness of a recent transaction. I cannot describe the clarion tones in which Miss Deborah rung out the word *disgraceful*, in connection with an event which had always set my blood boiling with pride and patriotism. Now, as if convicted of sheep-stealing, I felt myself getting red to the very tips of my ears.

"It was a shameful proceeding," sighed Lady Widgery, in her pretty, high-bred tones, as she pensively stirred the amber fluid in her teacup. "I never saw Sir Thomas so indignant at anything in all my life, and I'm sure it gave me a sick-headache for three days, so that I had to stay shut up in a dark room, and couldn't keep the least thing on my stomach. What a mysterious providence it is that such conduct should be suffered to lead to success!"

"Well," said Lady Lothrop, sipping her tea on the other side, "clouds and darkness are about the Divine dispensations; but let us hope it will be all finally overruled for the best."

"O, come," said Miss Debby, giving a cheerful, victorious crow of defiance from behind her teapots. "Dorothy will be down on us with the tip-end of one of her husband's sermons, of course. Having married a Continental Congress parson, she has to say the best she can; but I, Deborah Kittery, who was never yet in bondage to any man, shall be free to have *my* say to the end of my days, and I *do* say that the Continental Congress is an abomination in the land, and the leaders of it, if justice had been done, they would all have been hanged high as Haman; and that there is one house in old Boston, at the North End, and not far from the spot where we have the honor to be, where King George now reigns as much as ever he did, and where law and order prevail in spite of General Washington and Mrs. Martha, with her court and train. It puts me out of all manner of patience to read the papers, — receptions to 'em here, there, and everywhere; — I should like to give 'em a reception."

"Come, come, Deborah, my child, you must be patient," said the old lady. "The Lord's ways are not as our ways. He knows what is best."

"I dare say he does, mother, but we know he does let wickedness triumph to an awful extent. I think myself he's given this country up."

"Let us hope not," said the mother, fervently.

"Just look at it," said Miss Deborah. "Has not this miserable rebellion broken up the true Church in this country just as it was getting a foothold? has it not shaken hands with French infidelity? Thomas Jefferson is a scoffing infidel, and he drafted their old Declaration of Independence, which, I will say, is the most abominable and blasphemous document that ever sinners dared to sign."

"But General Washington was a Churchman," said Lady Widgery, "and they were always very careful about keeping the feasts and fasts. Why, I remember, in the old times, I have been there to Easter holidays, and we had a splendid ball."

"Well, then, if he was in the true Church, so much the worse for him," said Miss Deborah. "There is some excuse for men of Puritan families, because their ancestors were schismatics and disorganizers to begin with, and came over here because they didn't like to submit to lawful government. For my part, I have always been ashamed of having been born here. If I'd been consulted I should have given my voice against it."

"Debby, child, how you do talk!" said the old lady.

"Well, mother, what can I do but talk? and it's a pity if I shouldn't be allowed to do that. If I had been a man, I'd have fought; and, if I could have my way now, I'd go back to England and live, where there's some religion and some government."

"I don't see," said the old lady, "but people are doing pretty well under the new government."

"Indeed, mother, how can you know anything about it? There's a perfect reign of infidelity and immorality begun. Why, look here, in Boston and Cambridge things are going just as you might think they would. The college fellows call themselves D'Alembert, Rousseau, Voltaire, and other French heathen names; and there's Ellery Davenport! just look at him, — came straight down from generations of Puritan ministers, and hasn't half as much religion as my cat there; for Tom does know how to order himself lowly and reverently to all his betters."

Here there was such a burst of pleading feminine eloquence on all hands as showed that general interest which often pervades the female breast for some bright, naughty, wicked prodigal son. Lady Widgery and old Mrs. Kittery and Lady Lothrop all spoke at once. "Indeed, Miss Deborah," — "Come, come, Debby," — "You are too bad, — he goes to church with us sometimes."

"To church, does he?" said Miss Debby, with a toss; "and what does he go for? Simply to ogle the girls."

"We should be charitable in our judgments," said Lady Widgery.

"Especially of handsome young men," said Miss Debby, with strong irony. "You all know he doesn't believe as much as a heathen. They say he reads and speaks French like a native, and that's all I want to know of anybody. I've no opinion of such people; a good honest Christian has no occasion to go out of his own language, and when he does you may be pretty sure it's for no good."

"O, come now, Deborah, you are too sweeping altogether," said Lady Lothrop; "French is of course an elegant accomplishment."

"I never saw any good of the French language, for my part, I must confess," said Miss Debby, "nor, for that matter, of the French nation either; they eat frogs, and break the Sabbath, and are as immoral as the old Canaanites. It's just exactly like them to aid and abet this unrighteous rebellion. They always hated England, and they take delight in massacres and rebellions, and every kind of mischief, ever since the massacre of St. Bartholomew. Well, well, we shall see what'll come of these ungodly levelling principles in time. 'All men created free and equal,' forsooth. Just think of that! clearly against the church catechism."

"Of course that is all infidelity," said Lady Widgery, confidently. "Sir Thomas used to say it was the effect on the lower classes he dreaded. You see these lower classes are something dreadful; and what's to keep them down if it isn't religion? as Sir Thomas used to say when he always would go to church Sundays. He felt such a responsibility."

"Well," said Miss Deborah, "you'll see. I predict we shall see the time when your butcher and your baker, and your candlestick-maker will come into your parlor and take a chair as easy as if they were your equals, and every servant-maid will be thinking she must have a silk gown like her mistress. That's what we shall get by our revolution."

"But let us hope it will be all overruled for good," said Lady Lothrop.

"O, overruled, overruled!" said Miss Deborah. "Of course it will be overruled. Sodom and Gomorrah were overruled for good, but 't was a great deal better not to be living there about those times." Miss Debby's voice had got upon so high a key, and her denunciations began to be so terrifying, that the dear old lady interposed.

"Well, children, do let's love one another, whatever we do," she said; "and, Debby, you mustn't talk so hard about Ellery, — he's your cousin, you know."

"Besides, my dear," said Lady Widgery, "great allowances should be made for his domestic misfortunes."

"I don't see why a man need turn infidel and rebel because his wife has turned out a madwoman," said Miss Debby; "what did he marry her for?"

"O my dear, it was a family arrangement to unite the two properties," said Lady Widgery. "You see all the great Pierrepoint estates came in through her, but then she was quite shocking, — very peculiar always, but after her marriage her temper was dreadful, — it made poor Ellery miserable, and drove him from home; it really was a mercy when it broke out into real insanity, so that they could shut her up. I've always had great tenderness for Ellery on that account."

"Of course you have, because you're a lady. Did I ever know a lady yet that didn't like Ellery Davenport, and wasn't ready to go to the stake for him? For my part I hate him, because, after all, he humbugs me, and will make me like him in spite of myself. I have to watch and pray against him all the time."

And as if, by the odd law of attraction which has given birth to the proverb that somebody is always nearest when you are talking about him, at this moment the dining-room door was thrown open, and the old man-servant announced "Colonel Ellery Davenport."

"Colonel!" said Miss Debby, with a frown and an accent of contempt. "How often must I tell Hawkins not to use those titles of the old rebel mob army? Insubordination is beginning to creep in, I can see."

These words were lost in the bustle of the entrance of one on whom, after listening to all the past conversation, we children looked with very round eyes of attention. What we saw was a tall, graceful young man, whose air and movements gave a singular impression of both lightness and strength. He carried his head on his shoulders with a jaunty, slightly haughty air, like that of a thorough-bred young horse, and there was quality and breeding in every movement of his body. He was dressed in the imposing and picturesque fashion of those times, with a slight military suggestion in its arrangements. His hair was powdered to a dazzling whiteness, and brushed off his low Greek forehead, and the powder gave that peculiar effect to the eye and complexion which was one of the most dinstinctive traits of that style of costume. His eyes were of a deep violet blue, and of that lively, flashing brilliancy which a painter could only represent by double lights. They seemed to throw out light like diamonds. He entered the room bowing and smiling with the gay good-humor of one sure of pleasing. An inspiring sort of cheerfulness came in with him, that seemed to illuminate the room like a whole stream of sunshine. In short, he fully justified all Miss Deborah's fears.

In a moment he had taken a rapid survey of the party; he had kissed the hand of the dear old lady; he had complimented Lady Widgery; he had inquired with effusion after the health of Parson Lothrop, and ended all by an adroit attempt to kiss Miss Deborah's hand, which earned him a smart little cuff from that wary belligerent.

"No rebels allowed on these premises," said Miss Debby, sententiously.

"On my soul, cousin, you forget that peace has been declared," he said, throwing himself into a chair with a *nonchalant* freedom.

"Peace! not in our house. *I* haven't surrendered, if Lord Cornwallis has," said Miss Debby, "and I consider you as the enemy."

"Well, Debby, we must love our enemies," said the old lady, in a pleading tone.

"Certainly you must," he replied quickly; "and here I've come to Boston on purpose to go to church with you to-morrow."

"That's right, my boy," said the old lady. "I always knew you'd come into right ways at last."

"O, there are hopes of me, certainly," he said; "if the gentler sex will only remember their mission, and be guardian angels, I think I shall be saved in the end."

"You mean that you are going to wait on pretty Lizzie Cabot to church to-morrow," said Miss Debby; "that's about all the religion there is in it."

"Mine is the religion of beauty, fair cousin," said he. "If I had had the honor of being one of the apostles, I should have put at least one article to that effect into our highly respectable creed."

"Ellery Davenport, you are a scoffer."

"What, I? because I believe in the beautiful? What is goodness but beauty? and what is sin but bad taste? I could prove it to you out of my grandfather Edwards's works, *passim*, and I think nobody in New England would dispute him."

"I don't know anything about him," said Miss Debby, with a toss. "He wasn't in the Church."

"Mere matter of position, cousin. Couldn't very well be when the Church was a thousand miles across the water; but he lived and died a stanch loyalist, — an aristocrat in the very marrow of his bones, as anybody may see. The whole of his system rests on the undisputed right of big folks to eat up little folks in proportion to their bigness, and the Creator, being biggest of all, is dispensed from all obligation to seek anything but his own glory. Here you have the root-doctrine of the divine right of kings and nobles, who have only to follow their Maker's example in their several spheres, as his blessed Majesty King George has of late been doing with his American colonies. If he had got the treatise on true virtue by heart, he could not have carried out its principles better."

"Well, now, I never knew that there was so much good in President Edwards before," said Lady Widgery, with simplicity. "I must get my maid to read me that treatise some time."

"Do, madam," said Ellery. "I think you will find it exactly adapted to your habits of thought, and extremely soothing."

"It will be a nice thing for her to read me to sleep with," said Lady Widgery, innocently.

"By all means," said Ellery, with an indescribable mocking light in his great blue eyes.

For my own part, having that strange, vibrating susceptibility of constitution which I have described as making me peculiarly impressible by the moral sphere of others, I felt in the presence of this man a singular and painful contest of attraction and repulsion, such as one might imagine to be produced by the near approach of some beautiful but dangerous animal. His singular grace and brilliancy awoke in me an undefined antagonism akin to antipathy, and yet, as if under some enchantment, I could not keep my eyes off from him, and eagerly listened to everything that he had to say.

With that quick insight into human nature which enabled him, as by a sort of instinct, to catch the reflex of every impression which he made on any human being, he surveyed the row of wide-open, wondering, admiring eyes, which followed him at our end of the table.

"Aha, what have we here?" he said, as he advanced and laid his hand on my head. I shuddered and shook it off with a feeling of pain and dislike amounting to hatred.

"How now, my little man?" he said; "what's the matter here?" and then he turned to Tina. "Here's a little lady will be more gracious, I know," and he stooped and attempted to kiss her.

The little lady drew her head back and repulsed him with the dignity of a young princess.

"Upon my word," he said, "we learn the tricks of our trade early, don't we? Pardon me, petite mademoiselle," he said as he retreated, laughing. "So you don't like to be kissed?"

"Only by proper persons," said Tina, with that demure gravity which she could at times so whimsically assume, but sending with the words a long mischievous flash from under her downcast eyelashes.

"Upon my word, if there isn't one that's perfect in Mother Eve's catechism at an early age," said Ellery Davenport. "Young lady, I hope for a better acquaintance with you one of these days."

"Come Ellery, let the child alone," said Miss Debby; "why should you be teaching all the girls to be forward? If you notice her so much she will be vain."

"That's past praying for, anyhow," said he, looking with admiration at the dimpling, sparkling face of Tina, who evidently was dying to answer him back. "Don't you see the monkey has her quiver full of arrows?" he said. "Do let her try her infant hand on me."

But Miss Debby, eminently proper, rose immediately, and broke up the tea-table session by proposing adjournment to the parlor.

After this we had family prayers, the maid-servants and man-servant being called in and ranged in decorous order on a bench that stood prepared for exactly that occasion in a corner of the room. Miss Deborah placed a stand, with a great quarto edition of the Bible and prayer-book, before her mother, and the old lady read in a trembling voice the psalm, the epistle, and the gospel for Easter evening, and then, all kneeling, the evening prayers. The sound of her tremulous voice, and the beauty of the prayers themselves, which I vaguely felt, impressed me so much that I wept, without knowing why, as one sometimes does at plaintive music. One thing in particular filled me with a solemn surprise; and that was the prayers, which I had never heard before, for "The Royal Family of England." The trembling voice rose to fervent clearness on the words, "We beseech Thee, with Thy favor, to behold our most Sovereign Lord, King George, and so replenish him with the grace of Thy Holy Spirit, that he may alway incline to Thy will, and walk in Thy way. Endue him plenteously with heavenly gifts, grant him in health and wealth long to live, strengthen him that he may vanquish and overcome all his enemies, and finally after this life may attain everlasting joy and felicity, through Jesus Christ our Lord."

The loud "Amen" from Miss Debby which followed this, heartily chorussed as it was by the well-taught man-servant and maid-servants, might have done any king's heart good. For my part, I was lost in astonishment; and when the prayer followed "for the gracious Queen Charlotte, their Royal Highnesses, George, Prince of Wales, the Princess Dowager of Wales, and all the Royal Family," my confusion of mind was at its height. All these unknown personages were to be endued with the Holy Spirit, enriched with heavenly grace, and brought to an everlasting kingdom, through Jesus Christ, our Lord. I must confess that all I had heard of them previously, in my education, had not prepared me to see the propriety of any peculiar celestial arrangements in their favor; but the sweet and solemn awe inspired by the trembling voice which pleaded went a long way towards making me feel as if there must have been a great mistake in my bringing up hitherto.

When the circle rose from their knees, Ellery Davenport said to Miss Debby, "It's a pity the King of England couldn't know what stanch supporters he has in Boston."

"I don't see," said the old lady, "why they won't let us have that prayer read in churches now; it can't do any harm."

"I don't, either," said Ellery. "For my part, I don't know any one who needs praying for more than the King of England; but the prayers of the Church don't appear to have been answered in his case. If he had been in the slightest degree 'endowed with heavenly gifts,' he needn't have lost these American colonies."

"Come, Ellery, none of your profane talk," said Miss Debby; "*you* don't believe in anything good."

"On the contrary, I always insist on seeing the good before I believe; I should believe in prayer, if I saw any good come from it."

"For shame, Ellery, when children are listening to you!" said

Miss Debby. "But come, my little folks," she added, rising briskly, "it's time for these little eyes to be shut."

The dear old lady called us all to her, and kissed us "good night," laying her hand gently on our heads as she did so. I felt the peaceful influence of that hand go through me like music, and its benediction even in my dreams.

CHAPTER XXV

EASTER SUNDAY

For a marvel, even in the stormy clime of Boston, our Easter Sunday was one of those celestial days which seem, like the New Jerusalem of the Revelations, to come straight down from God out of heaven, to show us mortals what the upper world may be like. Our poor old Mother Boston has now and then such a day given to her, even in the uncertain spring-time; and when all her bells ring together, and the old North Church chimes her solemn psalm-tunes, and all the people in their holiday garments come streaming out towards the churches of every name which line her streets, it seems as if the venerable dead on Copps Hill must dream pleasantly, for "Blessed are the dead that die in the Lord," and even to this day, in dear old Boston, their works do follow them.

At an early hour we were roused, and dressed ourselves with the most anxious and exemplary care. For the first time in my life I looked anxiously in the looking-glass, and scanned with some solicitude, as if it had been a third person, the little being who called himself "I." I saw a pair of great brown eyes, a face rather thin and pale, a high forehead, and a great profusion of dark curls, — the combing out of which, by the by, was one of the morning trials of my life. In vain Aunt Lois had cut them off repeatedly, in the laudable hope that my hair would grow out straight. It seemed a more inextricable mat at each shearing; but as Harry's flaxen poll had the same peculiarity, we consoled each other, while we labored at our morning toilet.

Down in the sunny parlor, a little before breakfast was on the table, we walked about softly with our hands behind us, lest Satan, who we were assured had always some mischief still for idle hands to do, should entice us into touching some of the many curious articles which we gazed upon now for the first time. There was the picture of a very handsome young man over the mantel-piece, and beneath it hung a soldier's sword in a large loop of black crape, a significant symbol of the last great sorrow which had overshadowed the household. On one side of the door, framed and glazed, was a large coat of arms of the Kittery family, worked in chenille and embroidery, — the labor of Miss Deborah's hands during the course of her early education. In other places on the walls hung oil paintings of the deceased master of the mansion, and of the present venerable mistress, as she was in the glow of early youth. They were evidently painted by a not unskilful hand, and their eyes always following us as we moved about the room gave us the impression of being overlooked, even while as yet there was nobody else in the apartment. Conspicuously hung on one side of the room was a copy of one of the Vandyck portraits of Charles the First, with his lace ruff and peaked beard. Underneath this was a printed document, framed and glazed; and I, who was always drawn to read anything that could be read, stationed myself opposite to it and began reading aloud: —

"The Twelve Good Rules of the Most Blessed Martyr, King Charles First, of Blessed Memory."

I was reading these in a loud, clear voice, when Miss Debby entered the room. She stopped and listened to me, with a countenance beaming with approbation.

"Go on, sonny!" she said, coming up behind me, with an approving nod, when I blushed and stopped on seeing her. "Read them through; those are good rules for a man to form his life by."

I wish I could remember now what these so highly praised rules were. The few that I can recall are not especially in accordance with the genius of our modern times. They began: —

"1st. Profane no Divine Ordinances.

"2d. Touch no State Matter.

"3d. Pick no Quarrels.

"4th. Maintain no ill Opinions."

Here my memory fails me, but I remember that, stimulated by Miss Deborah's approbation, I did commit the whole of them to memory at the time, and repeated them with a readiness and fluency which drew upon me warm commendations from the dear old lady, and in fact from all in the house, though Ellery Davenport did shrug his shoulders contumaciously and give a sort of suppressed whistle of dissent.

"If we had minded those rules," he said, "we shouldn't be where we are now."

"No, indeed, you wouldn't; the more's the pity you didn't," said Miss Debby. "If I'd had the bringing of you up, you should be learning things like that, instead of trumpery French and democratic nonsense."

"Speaking of French," said Ellery, "I declare I forgot a package of gloves that I brought over especially for you and Aunty here, — the very best of Paris kid."

"You may spare yourself the trouble of bringing them, cousin," said Miss Deborah, coldly. "Whatever others may do, I trust *I* never shall be left to put a French glove on *my* hands. They may be all very fine, no doubt, but English gloves, made under her Majesty's sanction, will always be good enough for me."

"O, well, in that case I shall have the honor of presenting them to Lady Lothrop, unless her principles should be equally rigid."

"I dare say Dorothy will take them," said Miss Deborah. "When a woman has married a Continental parson, what can you expect of her? but, for *my* part, I should feel that I dishonored the house of the Lord to enter it with gloves on made by those atheistical French people. The fact is, we must put a stop to worldly conformities somewhere."

"And you draw the line at French gloves," said Ellery.

"No, indeed," said Miss Deborah; "by no means French gloves. French novels, French philosophy, and, above all, French morals, or rather want of morals, — *these* are what I go against, Cousin Ellery."

So saying, Miss Debby led the way to the breakfast-table, with an air of the most martial and determined moral principle.

I remember only one other incident of that morning before we went to church. The dear old lady had seemed sensibly affected by the levity with which Ellery Davenport generally spoke upon sacred subjects, and disturbed by her daughter's confident assertions of his infidel sentiments. So she administered to him an admonition in her own way. A little before church-time she was sitting on the sofa, reading in her great Bible spread out on the table before her.

"Ellery," she said, "come here and sit down by me. I want you to read me this text."

"Certainly, Aunty, by all means," he said, as he seated himself by her, bent his handsome head over the book, and, following the lead of her trembling finger, read: —

"And thou, Solomon, my son, know thou the God of thy fathers, and serve him with a perfect heart and a willing mind. If thou seek him, he will be found of thee, but if thou forsake him, he will cast thee off forever."

"Ellery," she said, with trembling earnestness, "think of that, my boy. O Ellery, remember!"

He turned and kissed her hand, and there certainly were tears in his eyes. "Aunty," he said, "you must pray for me; I may be a good boy one of these days, who knows?"

There was no more preaching, and no more said; she only held his hand, looked lovingly at him, and stroked his forehead. "There have been a great many good people among your fathers, Ellery."

"I know it," he said.

At this moment Miss Debby came in with the summons to church. The family carriage came round for the old lady, but we were better pleased to walk up the street under convoy of Ellery Davenport, who made himself quite delightful to us. Tina obstinately refused to take his hand, and insisted upon walking only with Harry, though from time to time she cast glances at him over her shoulder, and he called her "a little chip of mother Eve's block," — at which she professed to feel great indignation.

The reader may remember my description of our meeting-house at Oldtown, and therefore will not wonder that the architecture of the Old North and its solemn-sounding chimes, though by no means remarkable compared with European churches, appeared to us a vision of wonder. We gazed with delighted awe at the chancel and the altar, with their massive draperies of crimson looped back with heavy gold cord and tassels, and revealing a cloud of little winged cherubs, whereat Tina's eyes grew large with awe, as if she had seen a vision. Above this there was a mystical Hebrew word emblazoned in a golden halo, while around the galleries of the house were marvellous little colored statuettes of angels blowing long golden trumpets. These figures had been taken from a privateer and presented to the church by a British man-of-war, and no child that saw them would ever forget them. Then there was the organ, whose wonderful sounds were heard by me for the first time in my life. There was also an indefinable impression of stately people that worshipped there. They all seemed to me like Lady Lothrop, rustling in silks and brocades; with gentlemen like Captain Brown, in scarlet cloaks and powdered hair. Not a crowded house by any means, but a well-ordered and select few, who performed all the responses and evolutions of the service with immaculate propriety. I was struck with every one's kneeling and bowing the head on taking a seat in the church; even gay Ellery Davenport knelt down and hid his face in his hat, though what he did it for was a matter of some speculation with us afterward. Miss Debby took me under her special supervision. She gave me a prayer-book, found the places for me, and took me up and down with her through the whole service, giving her responses in such loud, clear, and energetic tones as entirely to acquit herself of her share of responsibility in the matter. The "true Church" received no detriment, so far as she was concerned. I was most especially edified and astonished by the deep courtesies which she and several distinguished-looking ladies made at the name of the Saviour in the Creed; so much so, that she was obliged to tap me on the head to indicate to me my own part in that portion of the Church service.

I was surprised to observe that Harry appeared perfectly familiar with the ceremony; and Lady Lothrop, who had him under her particular surveillance, looked on with wonder and approbation, as he quietly opened his prayer-book and went through the service with perfect regularity. Tina, who stood between Ellery Davenport and the old lady, seemed, to tell the truth, much too conscious of the amused attention with which he was regarding her little movements, notwithstanding the kindly efforts of her venerable guardian to guide her through the service. She resolutely refused to allow him to assist her, half-turning her back upon him, but slyly watching him from under her long eyelashes, in a way that afforded him great amusement.

The sermon which followed the prayers was of the most droning and sleepy kind. But as it was dispensed by a regularly ordained successor of the Apostles, Miss Deborah, though ordinarily the shrewdest and sharpest of womankind, and certainly capable of preaching a sermon far more to the point herself, sat bolt upright and listened to all those slumberous platitudes with the most reverential attention.

It yet remains a mystery to my mind, how a church which retains such a stimulating and inspiring liturgy *could* have such drowsy preaching, — how men could go through with the "Te Deum," and the "Gloria in Excelsis," without one thrill of inspiration, or one lift above the dust of earth, and, after uttering words which one would think might warm the frozen heart of the very dead, settle sleepily down into the quietest commonplace. Such, however, has been the sin of ritualism in all days, principally because human nature is, above all things, lazy, and needs to be thorned and goaded up those heights where it ought to fly.

Harry and I both had a very nice little nap during sermon-time, while Ellery Davenport made a rabbit of his pocket-handkerchief by way of paying his court to Tina, who sat shyly giggling and looking at him.

After the services came the Easter dinner, to which, as a great privilege, we were admitted from first to last; although children in those days were held to belong strictly to the dessert, and only came in with the nuts and raisins. I remember Ellery Davenport seemed to be the life of the table, and kept everybody laughing. He seemed particularly fond of rousing up Miss Debby to those rigorous and energetic statements concerning Church and King which she delivered with such freedom.

"I don't know how we are any of us to get to heaven now," he said to Miss Debby. "Supposing I wanted to be confirmed, there isn't a bishop in America."

"Well, don't you think they will send one over?" said Lady Widgery, with a face of great solicitude.

"Two, madam; it would take two in order to start the succession in America. The apostolic electricity cannot come down through one."

"I heard that Dr. Franklin was negotiating with the Archbishop of Canterbury," said Lady Lothrop.

"Yes, but they are not in the best humor toward us over there," said Ellery. "You know what Franklin wrote back, don't you?"

"No," said Lady Widgery; "what was it?"

"Well, you see, he found Canterbury & Co. rather huffy, and

somewhat on the high-and-mighty order with him, and, being a democratic American, he didn't like it. So he wrote over that he didn't see, for his part, why anybody that wanted to preach the Gospel couldn't preach it, without sending a thousand miles across the water to ask leave of a cross old gentleman at Canterbury."

A shocked expression went round the table, and Miss Debby drew herself up. "That's what I call a profane remark, Ellery Davenport," she said.

"I didn't make it, you understand."

"No, dear, you didn't," said the old lady. "Of course you wouldn't say such a thing."

"Of course I shouldn't, Aunty, — O no. I'm only concerned to know how I shall be confirmed, if ever I want to be. Do you think there really is no other way to heaven, Miss Debby? Now, if the Archbishop of Canterbury won't repent, and I do, — if he won't send a bishop, and I become a good Christian, — don't you think now the Church might open the door a little crack for me?"

"Why, of course, Ellery," said Lady Lothrop. "We believe that many good people will be saved out of the Church."

"My dear madam, that's because you married a Congregational parson; you are getting illogical."

"Ellery, you know better," said Miss Debby, vigorously. "You know we hold that many good persons out of the Church are saved, though they are saved by uncovenanted mercies. There are no direct promises to any but those in the Church; they had no authorized ministry or sacraments."

"What a dreadful condition these American colonies are in!" said Ellery; "it's a result of our Revolution which never struck me before."

"You can sneer as much as you please, it's a solemn fact, Ellery; it's the chief mischief of this dreadful rebellion."

"Come, come, children," said the old lady; "let's talk about something else. We've been to the communion, and heard about 'peace on earth and good-will to men.' I always think of our blessed King George every time I take the communion wine out of those cups that he gave to our church."

"Yes, indeed," said Miss Debby; "it will be a long time before you get the American Congress to giving communion services, like our good, pious King George."

"It's a pity pious folks are so apt to be pig-headed," said Ellery, in a tone just loud enough to stir up Miss Debby, but not to catch the ear of the old lady.

"I suppose there never was such a pious family as our royal family," said Lady Widgery. "I have been told that Queen Charlotte reads prayers with her maids regularly every night, and we all know how our blessed King read prayers beside a dying cottager."

"I do not know what the reason is," said Ellery Davenport, reflectively, "but political tyrants as a general thing are very pious men. The worse their political actions are, the more they pray. Perhaps it is on the principle of compensation, just as animals that are incapacitated from helping themselves in one way have some corresponding organ in another direction."

"I agree with you that kings are generally religious," said Lady Widgery, "and you must admit that, if monarchy makes men religious, it is an argument in its favor, because there is nothing so important as religion, you know."

"The argument, madam, is a profound one, and does credit to your discernment; but the question now is, since it has pleased Providence to prosper rebellion, and allow a community to be founded without any true church, or any means of getting at true ordinances and sacraments, what young fellows like us are to do about it."

"I'll tell you, Ellery," said the old lady, laying hold of his arm. "'Know the God of thy fathers, and serve him with a perfect heart and willing mind,' and everything will come right."

"But, even then, I couldn't belong to 'the true Church,'" said Ellery.

"You'd belong to the church of all good people," said the old lady, "and that's the main thing."

"Aunty, you are always right," he said.

Now I listened with the sharpest attention to all this conversation, which was as bewildering to me as all the rest of the scenery and surroundings of this extraordinary visit had been.

Miss Debby's martial and declaratory air, the vigorous faith in her statements which she appeared to have, were quite a match, it seemed to me, for similar statements of a contrary nature which I had heard from my respected grandmother; and I couldn't help wondering in my own mind what strange concussions of the elementary powers would result if ever these two should be brought together. To use a modern figure, it would be like the meeting of two full-charged railroad engines, from opposite directions, on the same track.

After dinner, in the evening, instead of the usual service of family prayers, Miss Debby catechised her family in a vigorous and determined manner. We children went and stood up with the row of men and maid servants, and Harry proved to have a very good knowledge of the catechism, but Tina and I encompassed our answers by repeating them after Miss Debby; and she applied herself to teaching us as if this were the only opportunity of getting the truth we were ever to have in our lives.

In fact, Miss Debby made a current of electricity that, for the time being, carried me completely away, and I exerted myself to the utmost to appear well before her, especially as I had gathered from Aunt Lois and Aunt Keziah's conversations, that whatever went on in this mansion belonged strictly to upper circles of society, dimly known and revered. American democracy had not in those days become a practical thing, so as to outgrow the result of generations of reverence for the upper classes. And the man-servant and the maid-servants seemed so humble, and Miss Debby so victorious and dominant, that I couldn't help feeling what a grand thing the true Church must be, and find growing in myself the desires of a submissive catechumen.

As to the catechism itself, I don't recollect that I thought one moment what a word of it meant, I was so absorbed and busy in the mere effort of repeating it after Miss Debby's rapid dictation.

The only comparison I remember to have made with that which I had been accustomed to recite in school every Saturday respected the superior case of answering the first question; which required me, instead of relating in metaphysical terms what "man's chief end" was in time and eternity, to give a plain statement of what my own name was on this mortal earth.

This first question, as being easiest, was put to Tina, who dimpled and colored and flashed out of her eyes, as she usually did when addressed, looked shyly across at Ellery Davenport, who sat with an air of negligent amusement contemplating the scene, and then answered with sufficient precision and distinctness, "Eglantine Percival."

He gave a little start, as if some sudden train of recollection had been awakened, and looked at her with intense attention; and when Ellery Davenport fixed his attention upon anybody, there was so much fire and electricity in his eyes that they seemed to be felt, even at a distance; and I saw that Tina constantly colored and giggled, and seemed so excited that she scarcely knew what she was saying, till at last Miss Debby, perceiving this, turned sharp round upon him, and said, "Ellery Davenport, if you haven't any religion yourself, I wish you wouldn't interrupt my instructions."

"Bless my soul, cousin! what was I doing? I have been sitting here still as a mouse; but I'll turn my back, and read a good book"; — and round he turned, accordingly, till the catechising was finished.

When it was all over, and the servants had gone out, we grouped ourselves around the fire, and Ellery Davenport began: "Cousin Debby, I'm going to come down handsomely to you. I admit that your catechism is much better for children than the one I was brought up on. I was well drilled in the formulas of the celebrated Assembly of *dry*vines of Westminster, and dry enough I found it. Now it's a true proverb, 'Call a man a thief, and he'll steal'; 'give a dog a bad name, and he'll bite you'; tell a child that he is 'a member of Christ, a child of God, and an inheritor of the kingdom of heaven,' and he feels, to say the least, civilly disposed towards religion; tell him 'he is under God's wrath and curse, and so made liable to all the miseries of this life, to death itself, and the pains of hell forever,' because somebody ate an apple five thousand years ago, and his religious associations are not so agreeable, — especially if he has the answers whipped into him, or has to go to bed without his supper for not learning them."

"You poor dear!" said the old lady; "did they send you to bed without your supper? They ought to have been whipped themselves, every one of them."

"Well, you see, I was a little fellow when my parents died, and brought up under brother Jonathan, who was the bluest kind of blue; and he was so afraid that I should mistake my naturally sweet temper for religion, that he instructed me daily that I was a child of wrath, and couldn't, and didn't, and never should do one right thing till I was regenerated, and when that would happen no mortal knew; so I thought, as my account was going to be scored off at that time, it was no matter if I did run up a pretty long one; so I lied and stole whenever it came handy."

"O Ellery, I hope not!" said the old lady; "certainly you never stole anything!"

"Have, though, my blessed aunt, — robbed orchards and watermelon patches; but then St. Augustine did that very thing himself, and he didn't turn about till he was thirty years old, and I'm a good deal short of that yet; so you see there is a great chance for me."

"Ellery, why don't you come into the true Church?" said Miss Debby. "That's what you need."

"Well," said Ellery, "I must confess that I like the idea of a nice old motherly Church, that sings to us, and talks to us, and prays with us, and takes us in her lap and coddles us when we are sick and says, —

'Hush, my dear, lie still and slumber.'

Nothing would suit me better, if I could get my reason to sleep; but the mischief of a Calvinistic education is, it wakes up your reason, and it never will go to sleep again, and you can't take a pleasant humbug if you would. Now, in this life, where nobody knows anything about anything, a capacity for humbugs would be a splendid thing to have. I wish to my heart I'd been brought up a Roman Catholic! but I have not, — I've been brought up a Calvinist, and so here I am."

"But if you'd try to come into the Church and believe," said Miss Debby, energetically, "grace would be given you. You've been baptized, and the Church admits your baptism. Now just assume your position."

Miss Debby spoke with such zeal and earnestness, that I, whom she was holding in her lap, looked straight across with the expectation of hearing Ellery Davenport declare his immediate conversion then and there. I shall never forget the expression of his face. There was first a flash of amusement, as he looked at Miss Debby's strong, sincere face, and then it faded into something between admiration and pity; and then he said to himself in a musing tone:

"I a 'member of Christ, a child of God, and an inheritor of the kingdom of heaven.'" And then a strange, sarcastic expression broke
over his face, as he added: "Couldn't do it, cousin; not exactly my
style. Besides, I shouldn't be much of a credit to any church, and
whichever catches me would be apt to find a shark in the net. You
see," he added, jumping up and walking about rapidly, "I have the
misfortune to have an extremely exacting nature, and, if I set out
to be religious at all, it would oblige me to carry the thing to as
great lengths as did my grandfather Jonathan Edwards. I should
have to take up the cross and all that, and I don't want to, and
don't mean to; and as to all these pleasant, comfortable churches,
where a fellow can get to heaven without it, I have the misfortune
of not being able to believe in them; so there you see precisely my
situation."

"These horrid old Calvinistic doctrines," said Miss Debby, "are
the ruin of children."

"My dear, they are all in the Thirty-nine Articles as strong as
in the Cambridge platform, and all the other platforms, for the
good reason that John Calvin himself had the overlooking of them.
And, what is worse, there is an abominable sight of truth in them.
Nature herself is a high Calvinist, old jade; and there never was a
man of energy enough to feel the force of the world he deals with
that wasn't a predestinarian, from the time of the Greek Tragedians
down to the time of Oliver Cromwell, and ever since. The hardest
doctrines are the things that a fellow sees with his own eyes going
on in the world around him. If you had been in England, as I have,
where the true Church prevails, you'd see that pretty much the
whole of the lower classes there are predestinated to be conceived
and born in sin, and shapen in iniquity; and come into the world
in such circumstances that to expect even decent morality of them
is expecting what is contrary to all reason. This is your Christian
country, after eighteen hundred years' experiment of Christianity.
The elect, by whom I mean the bishops and clergy and upper
classes, have attained to a position in which a decent and religious
life is practicable, and where there is leisure from the claims of the
body to attend to those of the soul. These, however, to a large extent are smothering in their own fat, or, as your service to-day had
it, 'Their heart is fat as brawn'; and so they don't, to any great
extent, make their calling and election sure. Then, as for heathen

countries, they are a peg below those of Christianity. Taking the mass of human beings in the world at this hour, they are in such circumstances, that, so far from its being reasonable to expect the morals of Christianity of them, they are not within sight of ordinary human decencies. Talk of purity of heart to a Malay of Hottentot! Why, the doctrine of a clean shirt is an uncomprehended mystery to more than half the human race at this moment. That's what I call visible election and reprobation, get rid of it as we may or can."

"Positively, Ellery, I am not going to have you talk so before these children," said Miss Debby, getting up and ringing the bell energetically. "This all comes of the vile democratic idea that people are to have opinions on all subjects, instead of believing what the Church tells them; and, as you say, it's Calvinism that starts people out to be always reasoning and discussing and having opinions. I hate folks who are always speculating and thinking, and having new doctrines; all I want to know is *my duty*, and to do it. I want to know what *my* part is, and it's none of my business whether the bishops and the kings and the nobility do theirs or not, if I only do mine. 'To do my duty in that state of life in which it has pleased God to call me,' is all I want, and I think it is all anybody need want."

"*Amen!*" said Ellery Davenport, "*and so be it.*"

Here Mrs. Margery appeared with the candles to take us to bed.

In bidding our adieus for the night, it was customary for good children to kiss all round; but Tina, in performing this ceremony both this night and the night before, resolutely ignored Ellery Davenport, notwithstanding his earnest petitions; and, while she would kiss with ostentatious affection those on each side of him, she hung her head and drew back whenever he attempted the familiarity, yet, by way of reparation, turned back at the door as she was going out, and made him a parting salutation with the air of a princess; and I heard him say, "Upon my word, how she does it!"

After we left the room (this being a particular which, like tellers of stories in general, I learned from other sources), he turned to Lady Lothrop and said: "Did I understand that she said her name was Eglantine Percival, and that she is a sort of foundling?"

"Certainly," said Lady Lothrop; "both these children are orphans, left on the parish by a poor woman who died in a neighboring town. They appear to be of good blood and breeding, but we have no means of knowing who they are."

"Well," said Ellery Davenport, "I knew a young English officer by the name of Percival, who was rather a graceless fellow. He once visited me at my country-seat, with several others. When he went away, being, as he often was, not very fit to take care of himself, he dropped and left a pocket-book, so some of the servants told me, which was thrown into one of the drawers, and for aught I know may be there now: it's just barely possible that it may be, and that there may be some papers in it which will shed light on these children's parentage. If I recollect rightly, he was said to be connected with a good English family, and it might be possible, if we were properly informed, to shame him, or frighten him into doing something for these children. I will look into the matter myself, when I am in England next winter, where I shall have some business; that is to say, if we can get any clew. The probability is that the children are illegitimate."

"O, I hope not," said Lady Lothrop; "they appear to have been so beautifully educated."

"Well," said Ellery Davenport, "he may have seduced his curate's daughter; that's a very simple supposition. At any rate, he never produced her in society, never spoke of her, kept her in cheap, poor lodgings in the country, and the general supposition was that she was his mistress, not his wife."

"No," said a little voice near his elbow, which startled every one in the room, — "no, Mr. Davenport, my mother was my father's wife."

The fire had burnt low, and the candles had not been brought in, and Harry, who had been sent back by Mrs. Margery to give a message as to the night arrangements, had entered the room softly, and stood waiting to get a chance to deliver it. He now came forward, and stood trembling with agitation, pale yet bold. Of course all were very much shocked as he went on: "They took my mother's wedding-ring, and sold it to pay for her coffin; but she always wore it and often told me when it was put on. But," he added, "she told me, the night she died, that I had no father but God."

"And he is Father enough!" said the old lady, who, entirely

broken down and overcome, clasped the little boy in her arms. "Never you mind it, dear, God certainly will take care of you."

"I know he will," said the boy, with solemn simplicity; "but I want you all to believe the truth about my mother."

It was characteristic of that intense inwardness and delicacy which were so peculiar in Harry's character, that, when he came back from this agitating scene, he did not tell me a word of what had occurred, nor did I learn it till years afterwards. I was very much in the habit of lying awake nights, long after he had sunk into untroubled slumbers, and this night I remember that he lay long but silently awake, so very still and quiet, that it was some time before I discovered that he was not sleeping.

The next day Ellery Davenport left us, but we remained to see the wonders of Boston. I remembered my grandmother's orders, and went on to Copps Hill, and to the old Granary burying-ground, to see the graves of the saints, and read the inscriptions. I had a curious passion for this sort of mortuary literature, even as a child, — a sort of nameless, weird, strange delight, — so that I accomplished this part of my grandmother's wishes *con amore*.

Boston in those days had not even arrived at being a city, but, as the reader may learn from contemporary magazines, was known as the Town of Boston. In some respects, however, it was even more attractive in those days for private residences than it is at present. As is the case now in some of our large rural towns, it had many stately old houses, which stood surrounded by gardens and grounds, where fruits and flowers were tended with scrupulous care. It was sometimes called "the garden town." The house of Madam Kittery stood on a high eminence overlooking the sea, and had connected with it a stately garden, which, just at the time of year I speak of, was gay with the first crocuses and snowdrops.

In the eyes of the New England people, it was always a sort of mother-town, — a sacred city, the shrine of that religious enthusiasm which founded the States of New England. There were the graves of her prophets and her martyrs, — those who had given their lives through the hardships of that enterprise in so ungenial a climate.

On Easter Monday Lady Lothrop proposed to take us all to see the shops and sights of Boston, with the bountiful intention of purchasing some few additions to the children's wardrobes. I was invited to accompany the expedition, and all parties appeared not a little surprised, and somewhat amused, that I preferred, instead of this lively tour among the living, to spend my time in a lonely ramble in the Copps Hill burying-ground.

I returned home after an hour or two spent in this way, and found the parlor deserted by all except dear old Madam Kittery. I remember, even now, the aspect of that sunny room, and the perfect picture of peace and love that she seemed to me, as she sat on the sofa with a table full of books drawn up to her, placidly reading.

She called me to her as soon as I came in, and would have me get on the sofa by her. She stroked my head, and looked lovingly at me, and called me "Sonny," till my whole heart opened toward her as a flower opens toward the sunshine.

Among all the loves that man has to woman, there is none so sacred and saint-like as that toward these dear, white-haired angels, who seem to form the connecting link between heaven and earth, who have lived to get the victory over every sin and every sorrow, and live perpetually on the banks of the dark river, in that bright, calm land of Beulah, where angels daily walk to and fro, and sounds of celestial music are heard across the water.

Such have no longer personal cares, or griefs, or sorrows. The tears of life have all been shed, and therefore they have hearts at leisure to attend to every one else. Even the sweet, guileless child-ishness that comes on in this period has a sacred dignity; it is a seal of fitness for that heavenly kingdom which whosoever shall not receive as a little child, shall not enter therein.

Madam Kittery, with all her apparent simplicity, had a sort of simple shrewdness. She delighted in reading, and some of the best classical literature was always lying on her table. She began questioning me about my reading, and asking me to read to her, and seemed quite surprised at the intelligence and expression with which I did it.

I remember, in the course of the reading, coming across a very simple Latin quotation, at which she stopped me. "There," said she, "is one of those Latin streaks that always trouble me in books, because I can't tell what they mean. When George was alive, he used to read them to me."

Now, as this was very simple, I felt myself quite adequate to its interpretation, and gave it with a readiness which pleased her.

"Why! how came you to know Latin?" she said.

Then my heart opened, and I told her all my story, and how my poor father had always longed to go to college, "and died without the sight," and how he had begun to teach me Latin; but how he was dead, and my mother was poor, and grandpapa could only afford to keep Uncle Bill in college, and there was no way for me to go, and Aunt Lois wanted to bind me out to a shoemaker. And then I began to cry, as I always did when I thought of this.

I shall never forget the overflowing, motherly sympathy which had made it easy for me to tell all this to one who, but a few hours before, had been a stranger; nor how she comforted me, and cheered me, and insisted upon it that I should immediately eat a piece of cake, and begged me not to trouble myself about it, and she would talk to Debby, and something should be done.

Now I had not the slightest idea of what Madam Kittery could do in the situation, but I was exceedingly strengthened and consoled, and felt sure that there had come a favorable turn in my fortunes; and the dear old lady and myself forthwith entered into a league of friendship.

I was thus emboldened, now that we were all alone, and Miss Debby far away, to propound to her indulgent ear certain political doubts, raised by the conflict of my past education with the things I had been hearing for the last day or two.

"If King George was such a good man, what made him oppress the Colonies so?" said I.

"Why, dear, he didn't," she said, earnestly. "That's all a great mistake. Our King is a dear, pious, good man, and wished us all well, and was doing just the best for us he knew how."

"Then was it because he didn't know how to govern us?" said I.

"My dear, you know the King can do no wrong; it was his ministers, if anybody. I don't know exactly how it was, but they got into a brangle, and everything went wrong; and then there was so much evil feeling and fighting and killing, and 'there was confusion, and every evil work.' There's my poor boy," she said, pointing to the picture with a trembling hand, and to the sword hanging in its crape loop, — "he died for his King, doing his duty in that state of life in which it pleased God to call him. I mustn't be sorry for that, but O, I wish there hadn't been any war, and we could have had it all peaceful, and George could have stayed with us. I don't see, either, the use of all these new-fangled notions, but then I try to love everybody, and hope for the best."

So spoke my dear old friend; and has there ever been a step in human progress that has not been taken against the prayers of some good soul, and been washed by tears, sincerely and despondently shed? But, for all this, is there not a true unity of the faith in all good hearts? and when they have risen a little above the mists of earth, may not both sides — the conqueror and the conquered — agree that God hath given them the victory in advancing the cause of truth and goodness?

Only one other conversation that I heard during this memorable visit fixed itself very strongly in my mind. On the evening of this same day, we three children were stationed at a table to look at a volume of engravings of beautiful birds, while Miss Debby, Lady Widgery and Madam Kittery sat by the fire. I heard them talking of Ellery Davenport, and, though I had been instructed that it was not proper for children to listen when their elders were talking among themselves, yet it really was not possible to avoid hearing what Miss Debby said, because all her words were delivered with such a sharp and determinate emphasis.

As it appeared, Lady Widgery had been relating to them some of the trials and sorrows of Ellery Davenport's domestic life. And then there followed a buzz of some kind of story which Lady Widgery seemed relating with great minuteness. At last I heard Miss Deborah exclaim earnestly: "If I had a daughter, catch me letting her be intimate with Ellery Davenport! I tell you that man hasn't read French for nothing."

"I do assure you, his conduct has been marked with perfect decorum," said Lady Widgery.

"So are your French novels," said Miss Deborah; "they are always talking about decorum; they are full of decorum and piety! why, the kingdom of heaven is nothing to them! but somehow they all end in adultery."

"Debby," said the old lady, "I can't bear to hear you talk so. I think your cousin's heart is in the right place, after all; and he's a good, kind boy as ever was."

"But, mother, he's a liar! that's just what he is."

"Debby, Debby! how can you talk so?"

"Well, mother, people have different names for different things. I hear a great deal about Ellery Davenport's tact and knowledge of the world, and all that; but he does a great deal of what *I* call lying, — so there! Now there are some folks who lie blunderingly, and unskilfully, but I'll say for Ellery Davenport that he can lie as innocently and sweetly and prettily as a French woman, and I can't say any more. And if a woman doesn't want to believe him, she just mustn't listen to him, that's all. I always believe him when he is around, but when he's away and I think him over, I know just what he is, and see just what an old fool he has made of me."

These words dropped into my childish mind as if you should accidentally drop a ring into a deep well. I did not think of them much at the time, but there came a day in my life when the ring was fished up out of the well, good as new.

CHAPTER XXVI

WHAT "OUR FOLKS" SAID AT OLDTOWN

We children returned to Oldtown, crowned with victory, as it were. Then, as now, even in the simple and severe Puritanical village, there was much incense burnt upon the altar of gentility, — a deity somewhat corresponding to the unknown god whose altar Paul found at Athens, and probably more universally worshipped in all the circles of this lower world than any other idol on record.

Now we had been taken notice of, put forward, and patronized, in undeniably genteel society. We had been to Boston and come back in a coach; and what well-regulated mind does not see that that was something to inspire respect?

Aunt Lois was evidently dying to ask us all manner of questions, but was restrained by a sort of decent pride. To exhibit any undue eagerness would be to concede that she was ignorant of good society, and that the ways and doings of upper classes were not perfectly familiar to her. That, my dear reader, is what no good democratic American woman can for a moment concede. Aunt Lois therefore, for once in her life, looked complacently on Sam Lawson, who continued to occupy his usual roost in the chimney-corner, and who, embarrassed with no similar delicate scruples, put us through our catechism with the usual Yankee thoroughness.

"Well, chillen, I suppose them Kitterys has everythin' in real grander, don't they? I've heerd tell that they hes Turkey carpets on th' floors. You know Josh Kittery, he was in the Injy trade. Turkey carpets is that kind, you know, that lies all up thick like a mat. They had that kind, didn't they?"

We eagerly assured him that they did.

"Want to know, now," said Sam, who always moralized as he went along. "Wal, wal, some folks does seem to receive their good thin's in this life, don't they? S'pose the tea-things all on 'em was solid silver, wa'n't they? Yeh didn't ask them, did yeh?"

"O no," said I; "you know we were told we mustn't ask questions."

"Jes so; very right, — little boys shouldn't ask questions. But I've heerd a good 'eal about the Kittery silver. Jake Marshall, he knew a fellah that had talked with one of their servants, that helped bury it in the cellar in war-times, and he said theh was porringers an' spoons an' tankards, say nothing of tablespoons, an' silver forks, an' sich. That 'ere would ha' been a haul for Congress, if they could ha' got hold on 't in war-time, wouldn't it? S'pose yeh was sot up all so grand, and hed servants to wait on yeh, behind yer chairs, didn't yeh?"

"Yes," we assured him, "we did."

"Wal, wal; yeh mustn't be carried away by these 'ere glories: they's transitory, arter all: ye must jest come right daown to plain livin'. How many servants d'yeh say they kep'?"

"Why, there were two men and two women, besides Lady Widgery's maid and Mrs. Margery."

"And all used to come in to prayers every night," said Harry.

"Hes prayers reg'lar, does they?" said Sam. "Well, now, that 'ere beats all! Didn't know as these gran' families wus so pious as that comes to. Who prayed?"

"Old Madam Kittery," said I. "She used to read prayers out of a large book."

"O yis; these 'ere gran' Tory families is 'Piscopal, pretty much all on 'em. But now readin' prayers out of a book, that 'ere don' strike me as just the right kind o' thing. For my part, I like prayers that come right out of the heart better. But then, lordy massy, folks hes theh different ways; an' I ain't so set as Polly is. Why, I b'lieve, if that 'ere woman had her way, theh wouldn't nobody be 'lowed to do nothin', except just to suit her. Yeh didn't notice, did yeh, what the Kittery coat of arms was?"

Yes, we had noticed it; and Harry gave a full description of an embroidered set of armorial bearings which had been one of the ornaments of the parlor.

"So you say," said Sam, " 't was a lion upon his hind legs, — that 'ere is what they call 'the lion rampant,' — and then there was a key and a scroll. Wal! coats of arms is curus, and I don't wonder folks kind o' hangs onter um; but then, the Kitterys bein' Tories, they nat'ally has more interest in sech thin's. Do you know where Mis' Kittery keeps her silver nights?"

"No, really," said I; "we were sent to bed early, and didn't see."

Now this inquiry, from anybody less innocent than Sam Lawson, might have been thought a dangerous exhibition of burglarious proclivities; but from him it was received only as an indication of that everlasting thirst for general information which was his leading characteristic.

When the rigor of his cross-examination had somewhat abated, he stooped over the fire to meditate further inquiries. I seized the opportunity to propound to my grandmother a query which had been the result of my singular experiences for a day or two past. So, after an interval in which all had sat silently looking into the great coals of the fire, I suddenly broke out with the inquiry, "Grandmother, what is *The True Church?*"

I remember the expression on my grandfather's calm, benign face as I uttered this query. It was an expression of shrewd amusement, such as befits the face of an elder when a younger has propounded a well-worn problem; but my grandmother had her answer at the tip of her tongue, and replied, "It is the whole number of the elect, my son."

I had in my head a confused remembrance of Ellery Davenport's tirade on election, and of the elect who did or did not have clean shirts; so I pursued my inquiry by asking, "Who are the elect?"

"All good people," replied my grandfather. "In every nation he that feareth God and worketh righteousness is accepted of Him."

"Well, how came you to ask that question?" said my grandmother, turning on me.

"Why," said I, "because Miss Deborah Kittery said that the war destroyed the true Church in this country."

"O, pshaw!" said my grandmother; "that's some of her Episcopal nonsense. I really should like to ask her, now, if she thinks there ain't any one going to heaven but Episcopalians."

"O no, she doesn't think so," said I, rather eagerly. "She said a great many good people would be saved out of the Church, but they would be saved by uncovenanted mercies."

"*Uncovenanted fiddlesticks!*" said my grandmother, her very cap-border bristling with contempt and defiance. "Now, Lois, you just see what comes of sending children into Tory Episcopal families, — coming home and talking nonsense like that!"

"Mercy, mother! what odds does it make?" said Aunt Lois. "The children have got to learn to hear all sorts of things said, — may as well hear them at one time as another. Besides, it all goes into one ear and out at the other."

My grandmother was better pleased with the account that I hastened to give her of my visit to the graves of the saints and martyrs, in my recent pilgrimage. Her broad face glowed with delight, as she told over again to our listening ears the stories of the faith and self-denial of those who had fled from an oppressive king and church, that they might plant a new region where life should be simpler, easier, and more natural. And she got out her "Cotton Mather," and, notwithstanding Aunt Lois's reminder that she had often read it before, read to us again, in a trembling yet audible voice, that wonderful document, in which the reasons for the first planting of New England are set forth. Some of these reasons I remember from often hearing them in my childhood. They speak thus quaintly of the old countries of Europe: —

"*Thirdly.* The land grows weary of her inhabitants, insomuch that *man*, which is the most precious of all creatures, is here more vile than the earth he treads upon, — children, neighbors, and friends, especially the *poor*, which, if things were right, would be the greatest earthly blessings.

"*Fourthly.* We are grown to that intemperance in all *excess of riot*, as no mean estate will suffice a man to keep sail with his *equals*, and he that fails in it must live in scorn and contempt: hence it comes to pass that all *arts* and *trades* are carried in that deceitful manner and uprighteous course, as it is almost impossible for a good, upright man to maintain his constant charge, and live comfortably in them.

"*Fifthly.* The schools of learning and religion are so corrupted as (besides the insupportable charge of education) most children of the best, wittiest, and of the fairest hopes are perverted, corrupted, and utterly overthrown by the multitude of evil examples and licentious behaviours in these *seminaries*.

"*Sixthly.* The *whole earth* is the Lord's *garden*, and he hath given it to the sons of Adam to be tilled and improved by them. Why then should we stand starving here for places of habitation, and

in the mean time suffer whole countries as profitable for the use of
man to lie waste without any improvement?"

Language like this, often repeated, was not lost upon us. The
idea of self-sacrifice which it constantly inculcated, — the reverence for self-denial, — the conception of a life which should look,
not mainly to selfish interests, but to the good of the whole human
race, prevented the hardness and roughness of those early New
England days from becoming mere stolid, material toil. It was toil
and manual labor ennobled by a new motive.

Even in those very early times there was some dawning sense of
what the great American nation was yet to be. And every man,
woman, and child was constantly taught, by every fireside, to feel
that he or she was part and parcel of a great new movement in
human progress. The old aristocratic ideas, though still lingering
in involuntary manners and customs, only served to give a sort of
quaintness and grace of Old-World culture to the roughness of
new-fledged democracy.

Our visit to Boston was productive of good to us such as we little
dreamed of. In the course of a day or two Lady Lothrop called,
and had a long private interview with the female portion of the
family; after which, to my great delight, it was announced to us
that Harry and I might begin to study Latin, if we pleased, and if
we proved bright, good boys, means would be provided for the
finishing of our education in college.

I was stunned and overwhelmed by the great intelligence, and
Harry and I ran over to tell it to Tina, who jumped about and
hugged and kissed us both with an impartiality which some years
later she quite forgot to practise.

"I'm glad, because you like it," she said; "but I should think it
would be horrid to study Latin."

I afterwards learned that I was indebted to my dear old friend
Madam Kittery for the good fortune which had befallen me. She
had been interested in my story, as it appears, to some purpose,
and, being wealthy and without a son, had resolved to console
herself by appropriating to the education of a poor boy a portion
of the wealth which should have gone to her own child.

The searching out of poor boys, and assisting them to a liberal
education, had ever been held to be one of the appropriate works
of the minister in a New England town. The schoolmaster who

taught the district school did not teach Latin; but Lady Lothrop was graciously pleased to say that, for the present, Dr. Lothrop would hear our lessons at a certain hour every afternoon; and the reader may be assured that we studied faithfully in view of an ordeal like this.

I remember one of our favorite places for study. The brown, sparkling stream on which my grandfather's mill was placed had just below the mill-dam a little island, which a boy could easily reach by wading through the shallow waters over a bed of many-colored pebbles. The island was overshadowed by thick bushes, which were all wreathed and matted together by a wild grape-vine; but within I had hollowed out for myself a green little arbor, and constructed a rude wigwam of poles and bark, after the manner of those I had seen among the Indians. It was one of the charms of this place, that nobody knew of it: it was utterly secluded; and being cut off from land by the broad belt of shallow water, and presenting nothing to tempt or attract anybody to its shores, it was mine, and mine alone. There I studied, and there I read; there I dreamed and saw visions.

Never did I find it in my heart to tell to any other boy the secret of this woodland shelter, this fairy-land, so near to the real outer world; but Harry, with his refinement, his quietude, his sympathetic silence, seemed to me as unobjectionable an associate as the mute spiritual companions whose presence had cheered my lonely, childish sleeping-room.

We moved my father's Latin books into a rough little closet that we constructed in our wigwam; and there, with the water dashing behind us, and the afternoon sun shining down through the green grape-leaves, with bluebirds and bobolinks singing to us, we studied our lessons. More than that, we spent many pleasant hours in reading; and I have now a *résumé*, in our boyish handwriting, of the greater part of Plutarch's Lives, which we wrote out during this summer.

As to Tina, of course she insisted upon it that we should occasionally carry her in a lady-chair over to this island, that she might inspect our operations and our housekeeping, and we read some of these sketches to her for her critical approbation; and if any of them pleased her fancy, she would immediately insist that we should come over to Miss Mehitable's, and have a dramatic representation of them up in the garret.

Saturday afternoon, in New England, was considered, from time immemorial, as the children's perquisite; and hard-hearted must be that parent or that teacher who would wish to take away from them its golden hours. Certainly it was not Miss Mehitable, nor my grandmother, that could be capable of any such cruelty.

Our Saturday afternoons were generally spent as Tina dictated; and, as she had a decided taste for the drama, one of our most common employments was the improvising of plays, with Miss Tina for stage manager. The pleasure we took in these exercises was inconceivable; they had for us a vividness and reality past all expression.

I remember our acting, at one time, the Book of Esther, with Tina, very much be-trinketed and dressed out in an old flowered brocade that she had rummaged from a trunk in the garret, as Queen Esther. Harry was Mordecai, and I was Ahasuerus.

The great trouble was to find a Haman; but, as the hanging of Haman was indispensable to any proper moral effect of the tragedy, Tina petted and cajoled and coaxed old Bose, the yellow dog of our establishment, to undertake the part, instructing him volubly that he must sulk and look cross when Mordecai went by, — a thing which Bose, who was one of the best-natured of dogs, found difficulty in learning. Bose would always insist upon sitting on his haunches, in his free-and-easy, jolly manner, and lolling out his red tongue in a style so decidedly jocular as utterly to spoil the effect, till Tina, reduced to desperation, ensconced herself under an old quilted petticoat behind him, and brought out the proper expression at the right moment by a vigorous pull at his tail. Bose was a dog of great constitutional equanimity, but there were some things that transcended even his powers of endurance, and the snarl that he gave to Mordecai was held to be a triumphant success; but the thing was, to get him to snarl when Tina was in front of him, where she could see it; and now will it be believed that the all-conquering little mischief-maker actually kissed and flattered and bejuggled old Polly into taking this part behind the scenes?

No words can more fitly describe the abject state to which that vehemently moral old soul was reduced.

When it came to the hanging of Haman, the difficulties thickened. Polly warned us that we must by no means attempt to hang Bose by the neck, as "the crittur was heavy, and 't was sartin to be the death of him." So we compromised by passing the rope under his fore paws, or, as Tina called it, "under his arms." But Bose was rheumatic, and it took all Tina's petting and caressing, and obliged Polly to go down and hunt out two or three slices of meat from her larder, to induce him fairly to submit to the operation; but hang him we did, and he ki-hied with a vigor that strikingly increased the moral effect. So we soon let him down again, and plentifully rewarded him with cold meat.

In a similar manner we performed a patriotic drama, entitled "The Battle of Bunker Hill," in which a couple of old guns that we found in the garret produced splendid effects, and salvoes of artillery were created by the rolling across the garret of two old cannon-balls; but this was suppressed by order of the authorities, on account of the vigor of the cannonade. Tina, by the by, figured in this as the "Genius of Liberty," with some stars on her head cut out of gilt paper, and wearing an old flag which we had pulled out of one of the trunks.

We also acted the history of "Romulus and Remus," with Bose for the she-wolf. The difference in age was remedied by a vigorous effort of the imagination. Of course, operations of this nature made us pretty familiar with the topography of the old garret. There was, however, one quarter, fenced off by some barrels filled with pamphlets, where Polly strictly forbade us to go.

What was the result of such a prohibition, O reader? Can you imagine it to be any other than that that part of the garret became at once the only one that we really cared about investigating? How we hung about it, and considered it, and peeped over and around and between the barrels at a pile of pictures, that stood with their faces to the wall! What were those pictures, we wondered. When we asked Polly this, she drew on a mysterious face and said, "*Them* was things we mustn't ask about."

We talked it over among ourselves, and Tina assured us that she dreamed about it nights; but Polly had strictly forbidden us even to mention that corner of the garret to Miss Mehitable, or to ask her leave to look at it, alleging, as a reason, that " 't would bring on her hypos."

We didn't know what "hypos" were, but we supposed of course they must be something dreadful; but the very fearfulness of the consequences that might ensue from our getting behind those fatal barrels only made them still more attractive. Finally, one rainy Saturday afternoon, when we were tired of acting plays, and the rain pattered on the roof, and the wind howled and shook the casings, and there was a generally wild and disorganized state of affairs out of doors, a sympathetic spirit of insubordination appeared to awaken in Tina's bosom. "I declare, I am going inside of those barrels!" she said. "I don't care if Polly does scold us; I know I can bring her all round again fast enough. I can do about what I like with Polly. Now you boys just move this barrel a little bit, and I'll go in and see!"

Just at this moment there was one of those chance lulls in the storm that sometimes occur, and as Tina went in behind the barrels, and boldly turned the first picture, a ray of sunshine streamed through the dusky window and lit it up with a watery light.

Harry and Tina both gave an exclamation of astonishment.

"O Tina! it's the lady in the closet!"

The discovery seemed really to frighten the child. She retreated quickly to the outside of the barrels again, and stood with us, looking at the picture.

It was a pastel of a young girl in a plain, low-necked white dress, with a haughty, beautiful head, and jet-black curls flowing down her neck, and deep, melancholy black eyes, that seemed to fix themselves reproachfully on us.

"O dear me, Harry, what shall we do?" said Tina. "How she looks at us! This certainly is the very same one that we saw in the old house."

"You ought not to have done it, Tina," said Harry, in a rather low and frightened voice; "but I'll go in and turn it back again."

Just at this moment we heard what was still more appalling, — the footsteps of Polly on the garret stairs.

"Well! now I should like to know if there's any mischief you wouldn't be up to, Tina Percival," she said, coming forward, reproachfully. "When I give you the run of the whole garret, and wear my life out a pickin' up and puttin' up after you, I sh'd think you might let this 'ere corner alone!"

"Oh! but, Polly, you've no idea how I wanted to see it, and *do* pray tell me who it is, and how came it here? Is it anybody that's dead?" said Tina, hanging upon Polly caressingly.

"Somebody that's dead to us, I'm afraid," said Polly, solemnly.

"Do tell us, Polly, *do!* who was she?"

"Well, child, you mustn't *never* tell nobody, nor let a word about it come out of your lips; but it's Parson Rossiter's daughter Emily, and where she's gone to, the Lord only knows. I took that 'ere pictur' down myself, and put it up here with Mr. Theodore's, so 't Miss Mehitable needn't see 'em, 'cause they always give her the hypos."

"And don't anybody know where she is," said Tina, "or if she's alive or dead?"

"Nobody," said Polly, shaking her head solemnly. "All I hope is, she may never come back here again. You see, children, what comes o' follerin' the nateral heart; it's deceitful above all things, and desperately wicked. She followed her nateral heart, and nobody knows where she's gone to."

Polly spoke with such sepulchral earnestness that, what with gloomy weather and the consciousness of having been accessory to an unlawful action, we all felt, to say the least, extremely sober.

"Do you think I have got such a heart as that?" said Tina, after a deep-drawn sigh.

"Sartain, you have," said the old woman. "We all on us has. Why, if the Lord should give any on us a sight o' our own heart just as it is, it would strike us down dead right on the spot."

"Mercy on us, Polly! I hope he won't, then," said Tina. "But, Polly," she added, getting her arms round her neck and playing with her gold beads, "*you* haven't got such a very bad heart now; I don't believe a word of it. I'm sure you are just as *good* as can be."

"Law, Miss Tina, you don't see into me," said Polly, who, after all, felt a sort of ameliorating gleam stealing over her. "You mustn't try to wheedle me into thinking better of myself than I be; that would just lead to carnal security."

"Well, Polly, don't tell Miss Mehitable, and I'll try and not get you into carnal security."

Polly went behind the barrels, gently wiped the dust from the picture, and turned the melancholy, beseeching face to the wall again; but we pondered and talked many days as to what it might be.

CHAPTER XXVII

HOW WE KEPT THANKSGIVING
AT OLDTOWN

On the whole, about this time in our life we were a reasonably happy set of children. The Thanksgiving festival of that year is particularly impressed on my mind as a white day.

Are there any of my readers who do not know what Thanksgiving day is to a child? Then let them go back with me, and recall the image of it as we kept it in Oldtown.

People have often supposed, because the Puritans founded a society where there were no professed public amusements, that therefore there was no fun going on in the ancient land of Israel, and that there were no cakes and ale, because they were virtuous. They were never more mistaken in their lives. There was an abundance of sober, well-considered merriment; and the hinges of life were well oiled with that sort of secret humor which to this day gives the raciness to real Yankee wit. Besides this, we must remember that life itself is the greatest possible amusement to people who really believe they can do much with it, — who have that intense sense of what can be brought to pass by human effort, that was characteristic of the New England colonies. To such it is not exactly proper to say that life is an amusement, but it certainly is an engrossing interest that takes the place of all amusements.

Looking over the world on a broad scale, do we not find that public entertainments have very generally been the sops thrown out by engrossing upper classes to keep lower classes from inquiring too particularly into their rights, and to make them satisfied with a stone, when it was not quite convenient to give them bread? Wherever there is a class that is to be made content to be plundered of its rights, there is an abundance of fiddling and dancing, and amusements, public and private, are in great requisition. It may also be set down, I think, as a general axiom, that people feel the need of amusements less and less, precisely in proportion as they have solid reasons for being happy.

Our good Puritan fathers intended to form a state of society of such equality of conditions, and to make the means of securing the goods of life so free to all, that everybody should find abundant employment for his faculties in a prosperous seeking of his fortunes. Hence, while they forbade theatres, operas, and dances, they made a state of unparalleled peace and prosperity, where one could go to sleep at all hours of day or night with the house door wide open, without bolt or bar, yet without apprehension of any to molest or make afraid.

There were, however, some few national fêtes: — Election day, when the Governor took his seat with pomp and rejoicing, and all the housewives outdid themselves in election cake, and one or two training days, when all the children were refreshed, and our military ardor quickened, by the roll of drums, and the flash of steel bayonets, and marchings and evolutions, — sometimes ending in that sublimest of military operations, a sham fight, in which nobody was killed. The Fourth of July took high rank, after the Declaration of Independence; but the king and high priest of all festivals was the autumn Thanksgiving.

When the apples were all gathered and the cider was all made, and the yellow pumpkins were rolled in from many a hill in billows of gold, and the corn was husked, and the labors of the season were done, and the warm, late days of Indian Summer came in, dreamy and calm and still, with just frost enough to crisp the ground of a morning, but with warm trances of benignant, sunny hours at noon, there came over the community a sort of genial repose of spirit, — a sense of something accomplished, and of a new golden mark made in advance on the calendar of life, — and the deacon began to say to the minister, of a Sunday, "I suppose it's about time for the Thanksgiving proclamation."

Rural dress-makers about this time were extremely busy in making up festival garments, for everybody's new dress, if she was to have one at all, must appear on Thanksgiving day.

Aunt Keziah and Aunt Lois and my mother talked over their bonnets, and turned them round and round on their hands, and discoursed sagely of ribbons and linings, and of all the kindred bonnets that there were in the parish, and how they would probably appear after Thanksgiving. My grandmother, whose mind had long ceased to wander on such worldly vanities, was at this time officiously reminded by her daughters that her bonnet wasn't respectable, or it was announced to her that she *must* have a new gown. Such were the distant horizon gleams of the Thanksgiving festival.

We also felt its approach in all departments of the household, — the conversation at this time beginning to turn on high and solemn culinary mysteries and receipts of wondrous power and virtue. New modes of elaborating squash pies and quince tarts were now ofttimes carefully discussed at the evening fireside by Aunt Lois and Aunt Keziah, and notes seriously compared with the experiences of certain other Aunties of high repute in such matters. I noticed that on these occasions their voices often fell into mysterious whispers, and that receipts of especial power and sanctity were communicated in tones so low as entirely to escape the vulgar ear. I still remember the solemn shake of the head with which my Aunt Lois conveyed to Miss Mehitable Rossiter the critical properties of *mace*, in relation to its powers of producing in corn fritters a suggestive resemblance to oysters. As ours was an oyster-getting district, and as that charming bivalve was perfectly easy to come at, the interest of such an imitation can be accounted for only by the fondness of the human mind for works of art.

For as much as a week beforehand, "we children" were employed in chopping mince for pies to a most wearisome fineness, and in pounding cinnamon, allspice, and cloves in a great lignum-vitæ mortar; and the sound of this pounding and chopping re-echoed through all the rafters of the old house with a hearty and vigorous cheer, most refreshing to our spirits.

In those days there were none of the thousand ameliorations of the labors of housekeeping which have since arisen, — no ground and prepared spices and sweet herbs; everything came into our hands in the rough, and in bulk, and the reducing of it into a state for use was deemed one of the appropriate labors of childhood. Even the very salt that we used in cooking was rock-salt, which we were required to wash and dry and pound and sift, before it became fit for use.

At other times of the year we sometimes murmured at these

labors, but those that were supposed to usher in the great Thanksgiving festival were always entered into with enthusiasm. There were signs of richness all around us, — stoning of raisins, cutting of citron, slicing of candied orange-peel. Yet all these were only dawnings and intimations of what was coming during the week of real preparation, after the Governor's proclamation had been read.

The glories of that proclamation! We knew beforehand the Sunday it was to be read, and walked to church with alacrity, filled with gorgeous and vague expectations.

The cheering anticipation sustained us through what seemed to us the long waste of the sermon and prayers; and when at last the auspicious moment approached, — when the last quaver of the last hymn had died out, — the whole house rippled with a general movement of complacency, and a satisfied smile of pleased expectation might be seen gleaming on the faces of all the young people, like a ray of sunshine through a garden of flowers.

Thanksgiving now was dawning! We children poked one another, and fairly giggled with unreproved delight as we listened to the crackle of the slowly unfolding document. That great sheet of paper impressed us as something supernatural, by reason of its mighty size, and by the broad seal of the State affixed thereto; and when the minister read therefrom, "By his Excellency, the Governor of the Commonwealth of Massachusetts, a Proclamation," our mirth was with difficulty repressed by admonitory glances from our sympathetic elders. Then, after a solemn enumeration of the benefits which the Commonwealth had that year received at the hands of Divine Providence, came at last the naming of the eventful day, and, at the end of all, the imposing heraldic words, "God save the Commonwealth of Massachusetts." And then, as the congregation broke up and dispersed, all went their several ways with schemes of mirth and feasting in their heads.

And now came on the week in earnest. In the very watches of the night preceding Monday morning, a preternatural stir below stairs, and the thunder of the pounding-barrel, announced that the washing was to be got out of the way before daylight, so as to give "ample scope and room enough" for the more pleasing duties of the season.

The making of *pies* at this period assumed vast proportions that verged upon the sublime. Pies were made by forties and fifties and hundreds, and made of everything on the earth and under the earth.

The pie is an English institution, which, planted on American soil, forthwith ran rampant and burst forth into an untold variety of genera and species. Not merely the old traditional mince pie, but a thousand strictly American seedlings from that main stock, evinced the power of American housewives to adapt old institutions to new uses. Pumpkin pies, cranberry pies, huckleberry pies, cherry pies, green-currant pies, peach, pear, and plum pies, custard pies, apple pies, Marlborough-pudding pies, — pies with top crusts, and pies without, — pies adorned with all sorts of fanciful flutings and architectural strips laid across and around, and otherwise varied, attested the boundless fertility of the feminine mind, when once let loose in a given direction.

Fancy the heat and vigor of the great pan-formation, when Aunt Lois and Aunt Keziah, and my mother and grandmother, all in ecstasies of creative inspiration, ran, bustled, and hurried, — mixing, rolling, tasting, consulting, — alternately setting us children to work when anything could be made of us, and then chasing us all out of the kitchen when our misinformed childhood ventured to take too many liberties with sacred mysteries. Then out we would all fly at the kitchen door, like sparks from a blacksmith's window.

On these occasions, as there was a great looseness in the police department over us children, we usually found a ready refuge at Miss Mehitable's with Tina, who, confident of the strength of her position with Polly, invited us into the kitchen, and with the air of a mistress led us around to view the proceedings there.

A genius for entertaining was one of Tina's principal characteristics; and she did not fail to make free with raisins, or citron, or whatever came to hand, in a spirit of hospitality at which Polly seriously demurred. That worthy woman occasionally felt the inconvenience of the state of subjugation to which the little elf had somehow or other reduced her, and sometimes rattled her chains fiercely, scolding with a vigor which rather alarmed us, but which Tina minded not a whit. Confident of her own powers, she would, in the very midst of her wrath, mimic her to her face with such irresistible drollery as to cause the torrent of reproof to end in a dissonant laugh, accompanied by a submissive cry for quarter.

"I declare, Tina Percival," she said to her one day, "you're saucy enough to physic a horn-bug! I never did see the beater of you! If Miss Mehitable don't keep you in better order, I don't see what's to become of any of us!"

"Why, what did become of you before I came?" was the undismayed reply. "You know, Polly, you and Aunty both were just as lonesome as you could be till I came here, and you never had such pleasant times in your life as you've had since I've been here. You're a couple of old beauties, both of you, and know just how to get along with me. But come, boys, let's take our raisins and go up in the garret and play Thanksgiving."

In the corner of the great kitchen, during all these days, the jolly old oven roared and crackled in great volcanic billows of flame, snapping and gurgling as if the old fellow entered with joyful sympathy into the frolic of the hour; and then, his great heart being once warmed up, he brooded over successive generations of pies and cakes, which went in raw and came out cooked, till butteries and dressers and shelves and pantries were literally crowded with a jostling abundance.

A great cold northern chamber, where the sun never shone, and where in winter the snow sifted in at the window-cracks, and ice and frost reigned with undisputed sway, was fitted up to be the storehouse of these surplus treasures. There, frozen solid, and thus well preserved in their icy fetters, they formed a great repository for all the winter months; and the pies baked at Thanksgiving often came out fresh and good with the violets of April.

During this eventful preparation week, all the female part of my grandmother's household, as I have before remarked, were at a height above any ordinary state of mind, — they moved about the house rapt in a species of prophetic frenzy. It seemed to be considered a necessary feature of such festivals, that everybody should be in a hurry, and everything in the house should be turned bottom upwards with enthusiasm, — so at least we children understood it, and we certainly did our part to keep the ball rolling.

At this period the constitutional activity of Uncle Fliakim increased to a degree that might fairly be called preternatural. Thanksgiving time was the time for errands of mercy and beneficence through the country; and Uncle Fliakim's immortal old rubber horse and rattling wagon were on the full jump, in tours of investigation into everybody's affairs in the region around. On returning, he would fly through our kitchen like the wind, leaving open the doors, upsetting whatever came in his way, — now a pan of milk, and now a basin of mince, — talking rapidly, and forgetting only the point in every case that gave it significance, or enabled any one to put it to any sort of use. When Aunt Lois checked his benevolent effusions by putting the test questions of practical efficiency, Uncle Fliakim always remembered that he'd "forgotten to inquire about that," and skipping through the kitchen, and springing into his old wagon, would rattle off again on a full tilt to correct and amend his investigations.

Moreover, my grandmother's kitchen at this time began to be haunted by those occasional hangers-on and retainers, of uncertain fortunes, whom a full experience of her bountiful habits led to expect something at her hand at this time of the year. All the poor, loafing tribes, Indian and half-Indian, who at other times wandered, selling baskets and other light wares, were sure to come back to Oldtown a little before Thanksgiving time, and report themselves in my grandmother's kitchen.

The great hogshead of cider in the cellar, which my grandfather called the Indian Hogshead, was on tap at all hours of the day; and many a mugful did I draw and dispense to the tribes that basked in the sunshine at our door.

Aunt Lois never had a hearty conviction of the propriety of these arrangements; but my grandmother, who had a prodigious verbal memory, bore down upon her with such strings of quotations from the Old Testament that she was utterly routed.

"Now," says my Aunt Lois, "I s'pose we've got to have Betty Poganut and Sally Wonsamug, and old Obscue and his wife, and the whole tribe down, roosting around our doors, till we give 'em something. That's just mother's way; she always keeps a whole generation at her heels."

"How many times must I tell you, Lois, to read your Bible?" was my grandmother's rejoinder; and loud over the sound of pounding and chopping in the kitchen could be heard the voice of her quotations: "If there be among you a poor man in any of the gates of the land which the Lord thy God giveth thee, thou shalt not harden thy heart, nor shut thy hand, from thy poor brother. Thou shalt surely give him; and thy heart shall not be grieved when thou givest to him, because that for this thing the Lord thy God shall bless thee in all thy works; for the poor shall never cease from out of the land."

These words seemed to resound like a sort of heraldic proclamation to call around us all that softly shiftless class, who, for some reason or other, are never to be found with anything in hand at the moment that it is wanted.

"There, to be sure," said Aunt Lois, one day when our preparations were in full blast, — "there comes Sam Lawson down the hill, limpsy as ever; now he'll have his doleful story to tell, and mother'll give him one of the turkeys."

And so, of course, it fell out.

Sam came in with his usual air of plaintive assurance, and seated himself a contemplative spectator in the chimney-corner, regardless of the looks and signs of unwelcome on the part of Aunt Lois.

"Lordy massy, how prosperous everything does seem here!" he said, in musing tones, over his inevitable mug of cider; "so different from what 'tis t' our house. There's Hepsy, she's all in a stew, an' I've just been an' got her thirty-seven cents' wuth o' nutmegs, yet she says she's sure she don't see how she's to keep Thanksgiving, an' she's down on me about it, just as ef 't was my fault. Yeh see, last winter our old gobbler got froze. You know, Mis' Badger, that 'ere cold night we hed last winter. Wal, I was off with Jake Marshall that night; ye see, Jake, he hed to take old General Dearborn's corpse into Boston, to the family vault, and Jake, he kind o' hated to go alone; 't was a drefful cold time, and he ses to me, 'Sam, you jes' go 'long with me'; so I was sort o' sorry for him, and I kind o' thought I'd go 'long. Wal, come 'long to Josh Bissel's tahvern, there at the Half-way House, you know, 't was so swinging cold we stopped to take a little suthin' warmin', an' we sort o' sot an' sot over the fire, till, fust we knew, we kind o' got asleep; an' when we woke up we found we'd left the old General hitched up t' th' post pretty much all night. Wal, didn't hurt him none, poor man; 't was allers a favorite spot o' his'n. But, takin' one thing with another, I didn't get home till about noon next day, an', I tell you, Hepsy she was right down on me. She said the baby was sick, and there hadn't been no wood split, nor the barn fastened up, nor nothin'. Lordy massy, I didn't mean no harm; I thought there was wood enough, and I thought likely Hepsy'd git out an' fasten up the barn. But Hepsy, she was in one o' her contrary streaks, an' she wouldn't do a thing; an', when I went out to look, why, sure 'nuff, there was our old tom-turkey froze as stiff as a stake, — his claws jist a stickin' right straight up like this." Here Sam struck an expressive attitude, and looked so much like a frozen turkey as to give a pathetic reality to the picture.

"Well now, Sam, why need you be off on things that's none of your business?" said my grandmother. "I've talked to you plainly about that a great many times, Sam," she continued, in tones of severe admonition. "Hepsy is a hard-working woman, but she can't be expected to see to everything, and you oughter 'ave been at home that night to fasten up your own barn and look after your own creeturs."

Sam took the rebuke all the more meekly as he perceived the stiff black legs of a turkey poking out from under my grandmother's apron while she was delivering it. To be exhorted and told of his shortcomings, and then furnished with a turkey at Thanksgiving, was a yearly part of his family programme. In time he departed, not only with the turkey, but with us boys in procession after him, bearing a mince and a pumpkin pie for Hepsy's children.

"Poor things!" my grandmother remarked; "they ought to have something good to eat Thanksgiving day; 't ain't their fault that they've got a shiftless father."

Sam, in his turn, moralized to us children, as we walked beside him: "A body'd think that Hepsy'd learn to trust in Providence," he said, "but she don't. She allers has a Thanksgiving dinner pervided; but that 'ere woman ain't grateful for it, by no manner o' means. Now she'll be jest as cross as she can be, 'cause this 'ere ain't *our* turkey, and these 'ere ain't our pies. Folks doos lose so much, that hes sech dispositions."

A multitude of similar dispensations during the course of the week materially reduced the great pile of chickens and turkeys which black Cæsar efforts in slaughtering, picking, and dressing kept daily supplied.

Besides these offerings to the poor, the handsomest turkey of the flock was sent, dressed in first-rate style, with Deacon Badger's dutiful compliments, to the minister; and we children, who were happy to accompany black Cæsar on this errand, generally received a seed-cake and a word of acknowledgment from the minister's lady.

Well, at last, when all the chopping and pounding and baking and brewing, preparatory to the festival, were gone through with, the eventful day dawned. All the tribes of the Badger family were to come back home to the old house, with all the relations of every degree, to eat the Thanksgiving dinner. And it was understood that in the evening the minister and his lady would look in upon us, together with some of the select aristocracy of Oldtown.

Great as the preparations were for the dinner, everything was so contrived that not a soul in the house should be kept from the morning service of Thanksgiving in the church, and from listening to the Thanksgiving sermon, in which the minister was expected to express his views freely concerning the politics of the country, and the state of things in society generally, in a somewhat more secular vein of thought than was deemed exactly appropriate to the Lord's day. But it is to be confessed, that, when the good man got carried away by the enthusiasm of his subject to extend these exercises beyond a certain length, anxious glances, exchanged between good wives, sometimes indicated a weakness of the flesh, having a tender reference to the turkeys and chickens and chicken pies, which might possibly be over-doing in the ovens at home. But your old brick oven was a true Puritan institution, and backed up the devotional habits of good housewives, by the capital care which he took of whatever was committed to his capacious bosom. A truly well-bred oven would have been ashamed of himself all his days, and blushed redder than his own fires, if a God-fearing house-matron, away at the temple of the Lord, should come home and find her piecrust either burned or underdone by his over or under zeal; so the old fellow generally managed to bring things out exactly right.

When sermons and prayers were all over, we children rushed home to see the great feast of the year spread.

What chitterings and chatterings there were all over the house, as all the aunties and uncles and cousins came pouring in, taking off their things, looking at one another's bonnets and dresses, and mingling their comments on the morning sermon with various opinions on the new millinery outfits, and with bits of home news, and kindly neighborhood gossip.

Uncle Bill, whom the Cambridge college authorities released, as they did all the other youngsters of the land, for Thanksgiving day, made a breezy stir among them all, especially with the young cousins of the feminine gender.

The best room on this occasion was thrown wide open, and its habitual coldness had been warmed by the burning down of a great stack of hickory logs, which had been heaped up unsparingly since morning. It takes some hours to get a room warm, where a family never sits, and which therefore has not in its walls one particle of the genial vitality which comes from the in-dwelling of human beings. But on Thanksgiving day, at least, every year, this marvel was effected in our best room.

Although all servile labor and vain recreation on this day were by law forbidden, according to the terms of the proclamation, it was not held to be a violation of the precept, that all the nice old aunties should bring their knitting-work and sit gently trotting their needles around the fire; nor that Uncle Bill should start a full-fledged romp among the girls and children, while the dinner was being set on the long table in the neighboring kitchen. Certain of the good elderly female relatives, of serious and discreet demeanor, assisted at this operation.

But who shall do justice to the dinner, and describe the turkey, and chickens, and chickens pies, with all that endless variety of vegetables which the American soil and climate have contributed to the table, and which, without regard to the French doctrine of courses, were all piled together in jovial abundance upon the smoking board? There was much carving and laughing and talking and eating, and all showed that cheerful ability to despatch the provisions which was the ruling spirit of the hour. After the meat came the plum-puddings, and then the endless array of pies, till human nature was actually bewildered and overpowered by the tempting variety; and even we children turned from the profusion offered to us, and wondered what was the matter that we could eat no more.

When all was over, my grandfather rose at the head of the table, and a fine venerable picture he made as he stood there, his silver hair flowing in curls down each side of his clear, calm face, while, in conformity to the old Puritan custom, he called their attention to a recital of the mercies of God in his dealings with their family.

It was a sort of family history, going over and touching upon the various events which had happened. He spoke of my father's death, and gave a tribute to his memory; and closed all with the application of a time-honored text, expressing the hope that as years passed by we might "so number our days as to apply our hearts unto wisdom"; and then he gave out that psalm which in those days might be called the national hymn of the Puritans.

"Let children hear the mighty deeds
    Which God performed of old,
Which in our younger years we saw,
    And which our fathers told.

"He bids us make his glories known,
    His works of power and grace.
And we'll convey his wonders down
    Through every rising race.

"Our lips shall tell them to our sons,
    And they again to theirs;
That generations yet unborn
    May teach them to their heirs.

"Thus shall they learn in God alone
    Their hope securely stands;
That they may ne'er forget his works,
    But practise his commands."

This we all united in singing to the venerable tune of St. Martin's, an air which, the reader will perceive, by its multiplicity of quavers and inflections gave the greatest possible scope to the cracked and trembling voices of the ancients, who united in it with even more zeal than the younger part of the community.

Uncle Fliakim Sheril, furbished up in a new crisp black suit, and with his spindle-shanks trimly incased in the smoothest of black silk stockings, looking for all the world just like an alert and spirited black cricket, outdid himself on this occasion in singing *counter*, in that high, weird voice that he must have learned from the wintry winds that usually piped around the corners of the old house. But any one who looked at him, as he sat with his eyes closed, beating time with head and hand, and, in short, with every limb of his body, must have perceived the exquisite satisfaction which he derived from this mode of expressing himself. I much regret to be obliged to state that my graceless Uncle Bill, taking advantage of the fact that the eyes of all his elders were devotionally closed, stationing himself a little in the rear of my Uncle Fliakim, performed an exact imitation of his *counter*, with such a killing facility that all the younger part of the audience were nearly dead with suppressed laughter. Aunt Lois, who never shut her eyes a moment on any occasion, discerned this from a distant part of the room, and in vain endeavored to stop it by vigorously shaking her head at the offender. She might as well have shaken it at a bobolink tilting on a clover-top. In fact, Uncle Bill was Aunt Lois's weak point, and the corners of her own mouth were observed to twitch in such a suspicious manner that the whole moral force of her admonition was destroyed.

And now, the dinner being cleared away, we youngsters, already excited to a tumult of laughter, tumbled into the best room, under the supervision of Uncle Bill, to relieve ourselves with a game of "blind-man's-buff," while the elderly women washed up the dishes and got the house in order, and the menfolks went out to the barn to look at the cattle, and walked over the farm and talked of the crops.

In the evening the house was all open and lighted with the best of tallow candles, which Aunt Lois herself had made with especial care for this illumination. It was understood that we were to have a dance, and black Cæsar, full of turkey and pumpkin pie, and giggling in the very jollity of his heart, had that afternoon rosined his bow, and tuned his fiddle, and practised jigs and Virginia reels, in a way that made us children think him a perfect Orpheus.

As soon as the candles were lighted came in Miss Mehitable with her brother Jonathan, and Tina, like a gay little tassel, hanging on her withered arm.

Mr. Jonathan Rossiter was a tall, well-made man, with a clear-cut, aquiline profile, and high round forehead, from which his powdered hair was brushed smoothly back and hung down behind in a long cue. His eyes were of a piercing dark gray, with that peculiar expression of depth and intensity which marks a melancholy temperament. He had a large mouth, which he kept

shut with an air of firmness that suggested something even hard
and dictatorial in his nature. He was quick and alert in all his
movements, and his eyes had a searching quickness of observation,
which seemed to lose nothing of what took place around him.
There was an air of breeding and self-command about him; and
in all his involuntary ways he bore the appearance of a man more
interested to make up a judgment of others than concerned as to
what their judgment might be about himself.

Miss Mehitable hung upon his arm with an evident admiration
and pride, which showed that when he came he made summer
at least for her.

After them soon arrived the minister and his lady, — she in a
grand brocade satin dress, open in front to display a petticoat
brocaded with silver flowers. With her well-formed hands shining out of a shimmer of costly lace, and her feet propped on high-
heeled shoes, Lady Lothrop justified the prestige of good society
which always hung about her. Her lord and master, in the spotless
whiteness of his ruffles on wrist and bosom, and in the immaculate
keeping and neatness of all his clerical black, and the perfect *pose*
of his grand full-bottomed clerical wig, did honor to her conjugal
cares. They moved through the room like a royal prince and
princess, with an appropriate, gracious, well-considered word for
each and every one. They even returned, with punctilious civility,
the awe-struck obeisance of black Cæsar, who giggled over
straightway with joy and exultation at the honor.

But conceive of my Aunt Lois's pride of heart, when, following in the train of these august persons, actually came Ellery
Davenport, bringing upon his arm Miss Deborah Kittery. Here
was a situation! Had the whole island of Great Britain waded
across the Atlantic Ocean to call on Bunker Hill, the circumstance could scarcely have seemed to her more critical.

"Mercy on us!" she thought to herself, "all these Episcopalians
coming! I do hope mother'll be careful; I hope she won't feel it
necessary to give them a piece of her mind, as she's always doing."

Miss Deborah Kittery, however, knew her soundings, and was
too genuine an Englishwoman not to know that "every man's
house is his castle," and that one must respect one's neighbor's
opinions on his own ground.

As to my grandmother, her broad and buxom heart on this

evening was so full of motherliness, that she could have patted the
very King of England on the head, if he had been there, and
comforted his soul with the assurance that she supposed he meant
well, though he didn't exactly know how to manage; so, although
she had a full consciousness that Miss Deborah Kittery had turned
all America over to uncovenanted mercies, she nevertheless shook
her warmly by the hand, and told her she hoped she'd make herself at home. And I think she would have done exactly the same
by the Pope of Rome himself, if that poor heathen sinner had
presented himself on Thanksgiving evening. So vast and billowy
was the ocean of her loving-kindness, and so firmly were her feet
planted on the rock of the Cambridge Platform, that on it she
could stand breathing prayers for all Jews, Turks, Infidels, Tories,
Episcopalians, and even Roman Catholics. The very man that burnt
Mr. John Rogers might have had a mug of cider in the kitchen on
this evening, with an exhortation to go and sin no more.

You may imagine the astounding wassail among the young
people, when two such spirits as Ellery Davenport and my Uncle
Bill were pushing each other on, in one house. My Uncle Bill
related the story of "the Wry-mouth Family," with such twists
and contortions and killing extremes of the ludicrous as perfectly
overcame even the minister; and he was to be seen, at one period
of the evening, with a face purple with laughter, and the tears
actually rolling down over his well-formed cheeks, while some of
the more excitable young people almost fell in trances, and rolled
on the floor in the extreme of their merriment. In fact, the assemblage was becoming so tumultuous, that the scrape of Cæsar's
violin, and the forming of sets for a dance, seemed necessary to
restore the peace.

Whenever or wherever it was that the idea of the sinfulness of
dancing arose in New England, I know not; it is a certain fact that
at Oldtown, at this time, the presence of the minister and his lady
was held not to be in the slightest degree incompatible with this
amusement. I appeal to many of my readers, if they or their parents
could not recall a time in New England when in all the large towns
dancing assemblies used to be statedly held, at which the minister
and his lady, though never uniting in the dance, always gave an
approving attendance, and where all the decorous, respectable old
church-members brought their children, and stayed to watch an

amusement in which they no longer actively partook. No one looked on with a more placid and patronizing smile than Dr. Lothrop and his lady, as one after another began joining the exercise, which, commencing first with the children and young people, crept gradually upwards among the elders.

Uncle Bill would insist on leading out Aunt Lois, and the bright color rising to her thin cheeks brought back a fluttering image of what might have been beauty in some fresh, early day. Ellery Davenport insisted upon leading forth Miss Deborah Kittery, notwithstanding her oft-repeated refusals and earnest protestations to the contrary. As to Uncle Fliakim, he jumped and frisked and gyrated among the single sisters and maiden aunts, whirling them into the dance as if he had been the little black gentleman himself. With that true spirit of Christian charity which marked all his actions, he invariably chose out the homeliest and most neglected, and thus worthy Aunt Keziah, dear old soul, was for a time made quite prominent by his attentions.

Of course the dances in those days were of a strictly moral nature. The very thought of one of the round dances of modern times would have sent Lady Lothrop behind her big fan in helpless confusion, and exploded my grandmother like a full-charged arsenal of indignation. As it was, she stood, her broad, pleased face radiant with satisfaction, as the wave of joyousness crept up higher and higher round her, till the elders, who stood keeping time with their heads and feet, began to tell one another how they had danced with their sweethearts in good old days gone by, and the elder women began to blush and bridle, and boast of steps that they could take in their youth, till the music finally subdued them, and into the dance they went.

"Well, well!" quoth my grandmother; "they're all at it so hearty, I don't see why I shouldn't try it myself." And into the Virginia reel she went, amid screams of laughter from all the younger members of the company.

But I assure you my grandmother was not a woman to be laughed at; for whatever she once set on foot, she "put through" with a sturdy energy befitting a daughter of the Puritans.

"Why shouldn't I dance?" she said, when she arrived red and resplendent at the bottom of the set. "Didn't Mr. Despondency and Miss Muchafraid and Mr. Readytohalt all dance together in the Pilgrim's Progress?" — and the minister in his ample flowing wig, and my lady in her stiff brocade, gave to my grandmother a solemn twinkle of approbation.

As nine o'clock struck, the whole scene dissolved and melted; for what well-regulated village would think of carrying festivities beyond that hour?

And so ended our Thanksgiving at Oldtown.

CHAPTER XXVIII

THE RAID ON OLDTOWN,
AND UNCLE FLIAKIM'S BRAVERY

The next morning after Thanksgiving, life resumed its usual hard, laborious course, with a sharp and imperative reaction, such as ensues when a strong spring, which has been for some time held back, is suddenly let fly again.

Certainly Aunt Lois appeared to be astir fully an hour earlier than usual, and dispelled all our golden visions of chicken pies and dancings and merry-makings, by the flat, hard summons of every-day life. We had no time to become demoralized and softened.

Breakfast this next morning was half an hour in advance of the usual time, because Aunt Lois was under some vague impression of infinite disturbances in the house, owing to the latitude of the last two weeks, and of great furbishings and repairs to be done in the best room, before it could be again shut up and condemned to silence.

While we were eating our breakfast, Sam Lawson came in, with an air of great trepidation.

"Lordy massy, Mis' Badger! what *do* you s'pose has happened?" he exclaimed, holding up his hands. "Wal! if I ever — no, I never did!" — and, before an explanation could be drawn out of him, in fluttered Uncle Fliakim, and began dancing an indignant rigadoon round the kitchen.

"Perfectly abominable! the selectmen ought to take it up!" he exclaimed, — "ought to make a State affair of it, and send to the Governor."

"Do for mercy's sake, Fliakim, sit down, and tell us what the matter is," said my grandmother.

"I can't! I can't!! I can't!!! I've just got to hitch right up and go on after 'em; and mebbe I'll catch 'em before they get over the State line. I just wanted to borrow your breech-band, 'cause ours is broke. Where is it? Is it out in the barn, or where?"

By this time we had all arisen from table, and stood looking at one another, while Uncle Fliakim had shot out of the back door toward the barn. Of course our information must now be got out of Sam Lawson.

"Wal, you see, Deacon, who ever would ha' thought of it? They've took every child on 'em, every one!"

"Who's taken? what children?" said my grandmother. "Do pray begin at the right end of your story, and not come in here scaring a body to death."

"Wal, it's Aunt Nancy Prime's children. Last night the kidnappers come to her house an' took her an' every single one of the child'en, an' goin' to carry 'em off to York State for slaves. Jake Marshall, he was round to our house this mornin', an' told me 'bout it. Jake, he'd ben over to keep Thanksgivin', over t' Aunt Sally Proddy's; an' way over by the ten-mile tahvern he met the waggin, an' Aunt Nancy, she called out to him, an' he heerd one of the fellers swear at her. The' was two fellers in the waggin, an' they was a drivin' like mad, an' I jest come runnin' down to Mr. Sheril's, 'cause I know his horse never gits out of a canter, an' 's pretty much used to bein' twitched up sudden. But, Lordy massy, s'posin' he could ketch up with 'em, what could he do? He couldn't much more'n fly at 'em like an old hen; so I don't see what's to be done."

"Well," said my grandfather, rising up, "if that's the case, it's time we should all be on the move; and I'll go right over to Israel Scran's, and he and his two sons and I'll go over, and I guess there'll be enough of us to teach them reason. These kidnappers always make for the New York State line. Boys, you go out and tackle the old mare, and have our wagon round to the house; and, if Fliakim's wagon will hold together, the two will just carry the party."

"Lordy massy! I should like to go 'long too," said Sam Lawson. "I hain't got no special business to-day but what could be put off as well as not."

"You never do have," said Aunt Lois. "That's the trouble with you."

"Wal, I was a thinkin'," said Sam, "that Jake and me hes been over them roads so often, and we kind o' know all the ups an' downs an' cross-roads. Then we's pretty intimate with some o' them Injun fellers, an' ye git them sot out on a trail arter a body, they's like a huntin' dog."

"Well, father," said Aunt Lois, "I think it's quite likely that Sam may be right here. He certainly knows more about such things than any decent, industrious man ought to, and it's a pity you shouldn't put him to some use when you can."

"Jes' so!" said Sam. "Now, there's reason in that 'ere; an' I'll jes' go over to Israel's store with the Deacon. Yeh see ye can't take both the boys, 'cause one on 'em'll have to stay and tend the store; but I tell you what 'tis, I ain't no bad of a hand a hittin' a lick at kidnappers. I could pound on 'em as willingly as ever I pounded a horseshoe; an' a woman's a woman, an' child'en's child'en, ef they be black; that's jes' my 'pinion."

"Sam, you're a good fellow," said my grandmother, approvingly. "But come, go right along."

Here, now, was something to prevent the wave of yesterday's excitement from flatting down into entire insipidity

Harry and I ran over instantly to tell Tina; and Tina with all her eloquence set it forth to Miss Mehitable and Polly, and we gave vent to our emotions by an immediate rush to the garret and a dramatic representation of the whole scene of the rescue, conducted with four or five of Tina's rag-dolls and a little old box wagon, with which we cantered and re-cantered across the garret floor in a way that would have been intolerable to any less patient and indulgent person than Miss Mehitable.

The fact is, however, that she shared in the universal excitement to such a degree, that she put on her bonnet immediately, and rushed over to the minister's to give vent to her feelings, while Polly, coming up garret, shouldered one of the guns lovingly, and declared she'd "like nothing better than to fire it off at one o' them fellers"; and then she told us how, in her young days, where she was brought up in Maine, the painters (panthers) used to come round their log cabin at night, and howl and growl; and how they always had to keep the guns loaded; and how once her mother, during her father's absence, had treed a painter, and kept him up in his perch for hours by threatening him whenever he offered to come down, until her husband came home and shot him.

Pretty stanch, reliant blood, about those times, flowed in the bosoms of the women of New England, and Polly relieved the excitement of her mind this morning by relating to us story after story of the wild forest life of her early days.

While Polly was thus giving vent to her emotions at home, Miss Mehitable had produced a corresponding excitement in the minister's family. Ellery Davenport declared his prompt intention of going up and joining the pursuing party, as he was young and strong, with all his wits about him; and, with the prestige of rank in the late Revolutionary war, such an accession to the party was of the greatest possible importance. As to Miss Deborah Kittery, she gave it as her opinion that such uprisings against law and order were just what was to be expected in a democracy. "The lower classes, my dear, you know, need to be kept down with a strong hand," she said with an instructive nod of the head; "and I think we shall find that there's no security in the way things are going on now."

Miss Mehitable and the minister listened with grave amusement while the worthy lady thus delivered herself; and, as they did not reply, she had the comfort of feeling that she had given them something to think of.

All the village, that day, was in a ferment of expectation; for Aunt Nancy was a general favorite in all the families round, and was sent for in case of elections or weddings or other high merry-makings, so that meddling with her was in fact taking away part of the vested property of Oldtown. The loafers who tilted, with their heels uppermost, on the railings of the tavern veranda, talked stringently of State rights, and some were of opinion that President Washington ought to be apprised of the fact without loss of time. My grandmother went about house in a state of indignation all day, declaring it was a pretty state of things, to be sure, and that, next they should know, they should wake up some morning and find that Cæsar had been gobbled up in the night and run off with. But Harry and I calmed the fears which this seemed to excite in his breast, by a vivid description of the two guns over in Miss Mehitable's garret, and of the use that we should certainly make of them in case of an attack on Cæsar.

The chase, however, was conducted with such fire and ardor that before moonrise on the same night the captives were brought back in triumph to Oldtown village, and lodged for safe-keeping in my grandmother's house, who spared nothing in their entertainment.

A happy man was Sam Lawson that evening, as he sat in the

chimney-corner and sipped his mug of cider, and recounted his adventures.

"Lordy massy! well, 't was providential we took Colonel Devenport 'long with us, I tell you; he talked to them fellers in a way that made 'em shake in their shoes. Why, Lordy massy, when we fust came in sight on 'em, Mr. Sheril an' me, we wus in the foremost waggin, an' we saw 'em before us just as we got to the top of a long, windin' hill, an' I tell you if they didn't whip up an' go lickity-split down that 'ere hill, — I tell you, they rattled them child'en as ef they'd ben so many punkins, an' I tell you one of 'em darned old young-uns flew right over the side of the waggin, an' jest picked itself up as lively as a cricket, an' never cried. We didn't stop to take it up, but jes' kep' right along arter; an' Mr. Sheril, he hollers out, 'Whoa! whoa! stop! stop thief!' as loud as he could yell; but they jes' laughed at him; but Colonel Devenport, he come ridin' by on horseback, like thunder, an' driv' right by 'em, an' then turned round an' charged down on their horses so it driv' 'em right out the road, an' the waggin was upsot, an' the fellers, they were pitched out, an' in a minute Colonel Devenport had one on 'em by the collar an' his pistol right out to the head o' t'other. 'Now,' ses he, 'if you stir you're a dead man!'

"Wal, Mr. Sheril, he made arter the other one, — he always means mighty well, Mr. Sheril does, — he gin a long jump, he did, an' he lit right in the middle of a tuft of blackberry-bushes, an' tore his breeches as ef the heavens an' 'arth was a goin' asunder. Yeh see, they never 'd a got 'em ef 't hadn't ben for Colonel Devenport. He kep' the other feller under range of his pistol, an' told him he'd shoot him ef he stirred; an' the feller, he was scart to death, an' he roared an' begged for mercy in a way 't would ha' done your heart good to hear.

"Wal, wal! the upshot on 't all was, when Israel Scran come down with his boy (they was in the back waggin), they got out the ropes an' tied 'em up snug, an' have ben a fetchin' on 'em along to jail, where I guess they'll have one spell o' considerin their ways. But, Lordy massy, yeh never see such a sight as your uncle's breeches wus. Mis' Sheril, she says she never see the beater of him for allus goin' off in his best clothes, 'cause, you see, he heard the news early, an' he jes' whips on his Thanksgivin' clothes an' went off in 'em just as he was. His intentions is allus so good. It's a pity, though, he don't take more time to consider. Now I think folks ought to take things more moderate. Yeh see, these folks that hurries allus, they gits into scrapes, is just what I'm allus a tellin' Hepsy."

"Who were the fellows, do you know?" said my grandmother.

"Wal, one on 'em was one, of them Hessians that come over in the war times, — he is a stupid crittur; but the other is Widdah Huldy Miller's son, down to Black Brook there."

"Do tell," said my grandmother, with the liveliest concern; "has Eph Miller come to that?"

"Yes, yes!" said Sam, "it's Eph, sure enough. He was exalted to heaven in p'int o' privilege, but he took to drink and onstiddy ways in the army, and now here he is in jail. I tell you, I tried to set it home to Eph, when I was a bringin' on him home in the waggin, but, Lordy massy, we don't none of us like to have our sins set in order afore us. There was David, now, he was crank as could be when he thought Nathan was a talkin' about other people's sins. Says David, 'The man that did that shall surely die'; but come to set it home, and say, 'Thou art the man,' David caved right in. 'Lordy massy bless your soul and body, Nathan,' says he, 'I don't want to die.'"

It will be seen by these edifying moralizings how eminently Scriptural was the course of Sam's mind. In fact, his turn for long-winded, pious reflection was not the least among his many miscellaneous accomplishments.

As to my grandmother, she busied herself in comforting the hearts of Aunt Nancy and the children with more than they could eat of the relics of the Thanksgiving feast, and bidding them not to be down-hearted nor afeard of anything, for the neighbors would all stand up for them, confirming her words with well-known quotations from the Old Testament, to the effect that "the triumphing of the wicked is short," and that "evil-doers shall soon be cut off from the earth."

This incident gave Ellery Davenport a wide-spread popularity in the circles of Oldtown. My grandmother was predisposed to look on him with complacency as a grandson of President Edwards, although he took, apparently, a freakish delight in shocking the respectable prejudices, and disappointing the reasonable expectations, of people in this regard, by assuming in every conversation precisely the sentiments that could have been least expected of him in view of such a paternity.

In fact, Ellery Davenport was one of those talkers who delight to maintain the contrary of every proposition started, and who enjoy the bustle and confusion which they thus make in every circle.

In good, earnest, intense New England, where every idea was taken up and sifted with serious solemnity, and investigated with a view to an immediate practical action upon it as true or false, this glittering, fanciful system of fencing which he kept up on all subjects, maintaining with equal brilliancy and ingenuity this to-day and that to-morrow, might possibly have drawn down upon a man a certain horror, as a professed scoffer and a bitter enemy of all that is good; but Ellery Davenport, with all his apparent carelessness, understood himself and the world he moved in perfectly. He never lost sight of the effect he was producing on any mind, and had an intuitive judgment, in every situation, of exactly how far he might go without going too far.

The position of such young men as Ellery Davenport, in the theocratic state of society in New England at this time, can be understood only by considering the theologic movements of their period.

The colonists who founded Massachusetts were men whose doctrine of a Christian church in regard to the position of its children was essentially the same as that of the Church of England. Thus we find in Doctor Cotton Mather this statement: —

"They did all agree with their brethren at Plymouth in this point: that the children of the faithful were church-members with their parents; and that their baptism was a seal of their being so; only, before their admission to fellowship in any particular church, it was judged necessary that, being free from scandal in life, they should be examined by the elders of the church, upon whose approbation of their fitness they should publicly and personally own the covenant, and so be received unto the table of the Lord. And accordingly the eldest son of Mr. Higginson, being about fifteen years of age, and laudably answering all the characters expected in a communicant, was then so received."

The colony under Governor Winthrop and Thomas Dudley was, in fact, composed of men in all but political opinion warmly attached to the Church of England; and they published, on their departure, a tract called "The Humble Request of His Majesty's Loyal Subjects, the Governor and Company lately gone for New England, for the Obtaining of their Prayers, and the Removal of Suspicions and Misconstruction of their Intentions"; and in this address they called the Church of England their dear mother, acknowledging that such hope and part as they had attained in the common salvation, they had sucked from her breasts; and entreating their many reverend fathers and brethren to recommend them unto the mercies of God, in their constant prayers, as a church now springing out of their own bowels. Originally, therefore, the first young people who grew up in New England were taught in their earliest childhood to regard themselves as already members of the church, as under obligations to comport themselves accordingly, and at a very early age it was expected of them that they would come forward by their own act and confirm the action of their parents in their baptism, in a manner much the same in general effect as confirmation in England. The immediate result of this was much sympathy on the part of the children and young people with the religious views of their parents, and a sort of growing up into them from generation to generation. But, as the world is always tending to become unspiritual and mechanical in its views and sentiments, the defect of the species of religion thus engendered was a want of that vitality and warmth of emotion which attend the convert whose mind has come out of darkness into marvellous light, — who has passed through interior conflicts which have agitated his soul to the very depths. So there was always a party in New England who maintained that only those who could relate a change so marked as to be characterized as supernatural should hope that they were the true elect of God, or be received in churches and acknowledged as true Christians.

Many pages of Cotton Mather record the earnest attention which not only the ministers, but the governors and magistrates, of New England, in her early days, gave to the question, "What is the true position of the baptized children of the Church?" and Cotton Mather, who was warmly in favor of the Church of England platform in this respect, say: "It was the study of those prudent men who might be called our seers, that the children of the faithful should be kept, as far as may be, under a church watch, in expectation that they might be in a fairer way to receive the grace of God;

so that the prosperous condition of religion in our churches might not be a matter of one age alone."

Old Cotton waxes warm in arguing this subject, as follows: —

"The Scriptures tell us that men's denying the children of the Church to have any part in the Lord hath a strong tendency in it to make them cease from fearing the Lord, and harden their hearts from his fear. But the awful obligations of covenant interest have a great tendency to soften the heart and break it, and draw it home to God. Hence, when the Lord would powerfully win men to obedience, he often begins with this: that he *is* their God. The way of the Anabaptists, to admit none unto membership and baptism but adult professors, is the straitest way. One would think it should be a way of great purity, but experience hath shown that it has been an inlet unto great corruption, and a troublesome, dangerous underminer of reformation."

And then old Cotton adds these words, certainly as explicit as even the modern Puseyite could desire: —

"If we do not keep in the way of a converting, grace-giving *covenant,* and keep persons *under those church dispensations wherein grace is given,* the Church will die of a lingering, though not a violent death. The Lord hath not set up churches, only that a few old Christians may keep one another warm while they live and then carry away the Church into the cold grave with them when they die. No; but that they might with all care and with all the obligations and advantages to that care that may be, nurse up another generation of subjects to our Lord, that may stand up in his kingdom when they are gone."

It was for some time doubtful whether the New England Church would organize itself and seek its own perpetuation on the educational basis which has been the foundation of the majority of the Christian Church elsewhere; and the question was decided, as such society questions often are, by the vigor and power of one man. Jonathan Edwards, a man who united in himself the natures of both a poet and a metaphysician, all whose experiences and feelings were as much more intense than those of common men as Dante's or Milton's, fell into the error of making his own constitutional religious experience the measure and standard of all others, and revolutionizing by it the institutions of the Pilgrim Fathers.

Regeneration, as he taught it in his "Treatise on the Affections," was the implantation by Divine power of a new spiritual sense in the soul, as diverse from all the other senses as seeing is from hearing, or tasting from smelling. No one that had not received this new, divine, supernatural sense, could properly belong to the Church of Christ, and all men, until they did receive it, were naturally and constitutionally enemies of God to such a degree, that, as he says in a sermon to that effect, "If they had God in their power, they would kill him."

It was his power and his influence which succeeded in completely upsetting New England from the basis on which the Reformers and the Puritan Fathers had placed her, and casting out of the Church the children of the very saints and martyrs who had come to this country for no other reason than to found a church.

It is remarkable that, in all the discussions of depravity inherited from Adam, it never seemed to occur to any theologian that there might also be a counter-working of the great law of descent, by which the feelings and habits of thought wrought in the human mind by Jesus Christ might descend through generations of Christians, so that, in course of time, many might be born predisposed to good, rather than to evil. Cotton Mather fearlessly says that *the seed of the Church are born holy*," — not, of course, meaning it in a strictly theological sense, but certainly indicating that, in his day, a mild and genial spirit of hope breathed over the cradle of infancy and childhood.

Those very persons whom President Edwards addresses in such merciless terms of denunciation in his sermons, telling them that it is a wonder the sun does not refuse to shine upon them, — that the earth daily groans ot open under them, — and that the wind and the sun and the waters are all weary of them and longing to break forth and execute the wrath of God upon them, — were the children for uncounted generations back of fathers and mothers nursed in the bosom of the Church, trained in habits of daily prayer, brought up to patience and self-sacrifice and self-denial as the very bread of their daily being, and lacking only this supernatural sixth sense, the want of which brought upon them a guilt so tremendous. The consequence was, that, immediately after the time of President Edwards, there grew up in the very bosom of the New England Church a set of young people who were not merely indifferent to religion, but who hated it with the whole energy of their being.

Ellery Davenport's feeling toward the Church and religion had all the bitterness of the disinherited son, who likes nothing better than to point out the faults in those favored children who enjoy the privileges of which he is deprived. All the consequences that good, motherly Cotton Mather had foreseen as likely to result from the proposed system of arranging the Church were strikingly verified in his case. He had not been able entirely to rid himself of a belief in what he hated. The danger of all such violent recoils from the religion of one's childhood consists in this fact, — that the person is always secretly uncertain that he may not be opposing truth and virtue itself; he struggles confusedly with the faith of his mother, the prayers of his father, with whatever there may be holy and noble in the profession of that faith from which he has broken away; and few escape a very serious shock to conscience and their moral nature in doing it.

Ellery Davenport was at war with himself, at war with the traditions of his ancestry, and had the feeling that he was regarded in the Puritan community as an apostate; but he took a perverse pleasure in making his position good by a brilliancy of wit and grace of manner which few could resist; and, truth to say, his success, even with the more rigid, justified his self-confidence. As during these days there were very few young persons who made any profession of religion at all, the latitude of expression which he allowed himself on these subjects was looked upon as a sort of spiritual sowing of wild oats. Heads would be gravely shaken over him. One and another would say, "Ah! that Edwards blood is smart; it runs pretty wild in youth, but the Lord's time may come by and by"; and I doubt not that my grandmother that very night, before she slept, wrestled with God in prayer for his soul with all the enthusiasm of a Monica for a St. Augustine.

Meantime, with that easy facility which enabled him to please everybody, he became, during the course of a somewhat extended visit which he made at the minister's, rather a hero in Oldtown. What Colonel Davenport said, and what Colonel Davenport did, were spoken of from mouth to mouth. Even his wicked wit was repeated by the gravest and most pious, — of course with some expressions of disclaimer, but, after all, with that genuine pleasure which a Yankee never fails to feel in anything smartly and neatly hit off in language.

He cultivated a great friendship with Miss Mehitable, — talking with her of books and literature and foreign countries, and advising her in regard to the education of Tina, with great unction and gravity. With that little princess there was always a sort of half whimsical flirtation, as she demurely insisted on being treated by him as a woman, rather than as a child, — a caprice which amused him greatly.

Miss Mehitable felt herself irresistibly drawn, in his society, as almost everybody else was, to make a confidant of him. He was so winning, so obliging, so gentle, and knew so well just where and how to turn the conversation to avoid anything that he didn't like to hear, and to hear anything that he did. So gently did his fingers run over the gamut of everybody's nature, that nobody dreamed of being played on.

Such men are not, of course, villains; but, if they ever should happen to wish to become so, their nature gives them every facility.

Before she knew what she was about, Miss Mehitable found herself talking with Ellery Davenport on the strange, mysterious sorrow which imbittered her life, and she found a most sympathetic and respectful listener.

Ellery Davenport was already versed in diplomatic life, and had held for a year or two a situation of importance at the court of France; was soon to return thither, and also to be employed on diplomatic service in England. Could he, would he, find any traces of the lost one there? On this subject there were long, and, on the part of Miss Mehitable, agitating interviews, which much excited Miss Tina's curiosity.

CHAPTER XXIX

MY GRANDMOTHER'S BLUE BOOK

Reader, this is to be a serious chapter, and I advise all those people who want to go through the world without giving five minutes' consecutive thought to any subject to skip it. They will not find it entertaining, and it may perhaps lead them to think on puzzling subjects, even for so long a time as half an hour; and who knows what may happen to their brains, from so unusual an exercise?

My grandmother, as I have shown, was a character in her way, full of contradictions and inconsistencies, brave, generous, energetic, large-hearted, and impulsive. Theoretically she was an ardent disciple of the sharpest and severest Calvinism, and used to repeat Michael Wigglesworth's "Day of Doom" to us in the chimney-corner, of an evening, with a reverent acquiescence in all its hard sayings, while practically she was the most pitiful, easy-to-be-entreated old mortal on earth, and was ever falling a prey to any lazy vagabond who chose to make an appeal to her abounding charity. She could not refuse a beggar that asked in a piteous tone; she could not send a child to bed that wanted to sit up; she could not eat a meal in peace when there were hungry eyes watching her; she could not, in cool, deliberate moments, even inflict transient and necessary pain for the greater good of a child, and resolutely shut her eyes to the necessity of such infliction. But there lay at the bottom of all this apparent inconsistency a deep cause that made it consistent, and that cause was the theologic stratum in which her mind, and the mind of all New England, was embedded.

Never, in the most intensely religious ages of the world, did the insoluble problem of the WHENCE, the WHY, and the WHITHER of mankind receive such earnest attention. New England was founded by a colony who turned their backs on the civilization of the Old World, on purpose that they might have nothing else to think of. Their object was to form a community that should think of nothing else.

Working on a hard soil, battling with a harsh, ungenial climate, everywhere being treated by Nature with the most rigorous severity, they asked no indulgence, they got none, and they gave none. They shut out from their religious worship every poetic drapery, every physical accessory that they feared would interfere with the abstract contemplation of hard, naked truth, and set themselves grimly and determinately to study the severest problems of the unknowable and the insoluble. Just as resolutely as they made their farms by blasting rocks and clearing land of ledges of stone, and founded thrifty cities and thriving money-getting communities in places which one would think might more properly have been left to the white bears, so resolutely they pursued their investigations amid the grim mysteries of human existence, determined to see and touch and handle everything for themselves, and to get at the absolute truth if absolute truth could be got at.

They never expected to find truth agreeable. Nothing in their experience of life had ever prepared them to think it would be so. Their investigations were made with the courage of the man who hopes little, but determines to know the worst of his affairs. They wanted no smoke of incense to blind them, and no soft opiates of pictures and music to lull them; for what they were after was *truth*, and not happiness, and they valued *duty* far higher than *enjoyment*.

The underlying foundation of life, therefore, in New England, was one of profound, unutterable, and therefore unuttered, melancholy, which regarded human existence itself as a ghastly risk, and, in the case of the vast majority of human beings, an inconceivable misfortune.

My grandmother believed in statements which made the fortunate number who escaped the great catastrophe of mortal life as few and far between as the shivering, half-drowned mariners, who crawl up on to the shores of some desert island, when all else on board have perished. In this view she regarded the birth of an infant with a suppressed groan, and the death of one almost with satisfaction. That more than half the human race die in infancy, — that infanticide is the general custom in so many heathen lands, —

was to her a comforting consideration, for so many were held to escape at once the awful ordeal, and to be gathered into the numbers of the elect.

As I have said, she was a great reader. On the round table that stood in her bedroom, next to the kitchen, there was an ample supply of books. Rollin's Ancient History, Hume's History of England, and President Edwards's Sermons, were among these.

She was not one of those systematic, skilful housewives who contrive with few steps and great method to do much in little time; she took everything the hardest end first, and attacked difficulties by sheer inconsiderate strength. For example, instead of putting on the great family pot, filling it with water, and afterwards putting therein the beef, pork, and vegetables of our daily meal, she would load up the receptacle at the sink in the back room, and then, with strong arm and cap-border erect, would fly across the kitchen with it and swing it over the fire by main strength. Thus inconsiderately she rushed at the daily battle of existence. But there was one point of system in which she never failed. There was, every day, a period, sacred and inviolable, which she gave to reading. The noon meal came exactly at twelve o'clock; and immediately after, when the dishes were washed and wiped, and the kitchen reduced to order, my grandmother changed her gown, and retired to the sanctuary of her bedroom to read. In this way she accomplished an amount which a modern house-keeper, with four servants, would pronounce to be wholly incredible.

The books on her table came in time to be my reading as well as hers; for, as I have said, reading was with me a passion, a hunger, and I read all that came in my way.

Her favorite books had different-colored covers, thriftily put on to preserve them from the wear of handling; and it was by these covers they were generally designated in the family. Hume's History of England was known as "the brown book"; Rollin's History was "the green book"; but there was one volume which she pondered oftener and with more intense earnestness than any other, which received the designation of "the blue book." This was a volume by the Rev. Dr. Bellamy of Connecticut, called "True Religion delineated, and distinguished from all Counter-feits." It was originally published by subscription, and sent out into New England with a letter of introduction and recommendation from the Rev. Jonathan Edwards, who earnestly set it forth as being a condensed summary, in popular language, of what it is vital and important for human beings to know for their spiritual progress. It was written in a strong, nervous, condensed, popular style, such as is fallen into by a practical man speaking to a practical people, by a man thoroughly in earnest to men as deeply in earnest, and lastly, by a man who believed without the shadow of a doubt, and without even the comprehension of the possibility of a doubt.

I cannot give a better idea of the unflinching manner in which the deepest mysteries of religion were propounded to the common people than by giving a specimen of some of the headings of this book.

Page 288 considers, "Were we by the Fall brought into a State of Being worse than Not to Be?"

The answer to this comprehensive question is sufficiently explicit.

"Mankind were by their fall brought into a state of being worse than not to be. The damned in hell, no doubt, are in such a state, else their punishment would not be infinite, as justice requires it should be. But mankind, by the fall, were brought into a state, *for substance,* as bad as that which the damned are in."

The next inquiry to this is, "How could God, consistent with his perfections, put us into a state of being worse than not to be? And how can we ever thank God for such a being?"

The answer to this, as it was read by thousands of reflecting minds like mine, certainly shows that these hardy and courageous investigators often raised spirits that they could not lay. As, for instance, this solution of the question, which never struck me as satisfactory.

"Inasmuch as God did virtually give being to all mankind, when he blessed our first parents and said, 'Be fruitful and multiply'; and inasmuch as *Being,* under the circumstances that man was *then* put in by God, was very desirable: we ought, therefore, to thank God for our being, considered in this light, and justify God for all the evil that has come upon us by apostasy."

On this subject the author goes on to moralize thus: —

"Mankind, by the fall, were brought into a state of being infinitely worse than not to be; and were they but so far awake as to be sensible of it, they would, no doubt, all over the earth, murmur and blaspheme the God of Heaven. But what then? there would be no just ground for such conduct. We have no reason to think hard of God, — to blame him or esteem him e'er the less. What he has done was fit and right. His conduct was beautiful, and he is worthy to be esteemed for it. For that constitution was holy, just, and good, as has been proved. And, therefore, a fallen world ought to ascribe to themselves all the evil, and to justify God and say: 'God gave us being under a constitution holy, just, and good, and it was a mercy. We should have accounted it a great mercy in case Adam had never fallen; but God is not to blame for this, nor, therefore, is he the less worthy of thanks.'"

After this comes another and quite practical inquiry, which is stated as follows: —

"But if mankind are thus by nature children of wrath, in a state of being worse than not to be, how can men have the heart to propagate their kind?"

The answer to this inquiry it is not necessary to give at length. I merely state it to show how unblinking was the gaze which men in those days fixed upon the problems of life.

The objector is still further represented as saying, —

"It cannot be thought a blessing to have children, if most of them are thought to be likely to perish."

The answer to this is as follows: —

"The most of Abraham's posterity for these three thousand years, no doubt, have been wicked and perished. And God knew beforehand how it would be, and yet he promised such a numerous posterity under the notion of a great blessing. For, considering children as to this life, they may be a great blessing and comfort to their parents; and we are certain that God will do them no wrong in the life to come. All men's murmuring thoughts about this matter arise from their not liking God's way of governing the world."

I will quote but one more passage, as showing the hardy vigor of assertion on the darkest of subjects, — the origin of evil. The author says: —

"When God first designed the world, and laid out his scheme of government, it was easy for him to have determined that neither angels nor men should ever sin, and that misery should never be heard of in all his dominions; for he could easily have prevented both sin and misery. Why did not he? Surely not for want of goodness in his nature, for that is infinite; not from anything like cruelty, for there is no such thing in him; not for want of a suitable regard to the happiness of his creatures, for that he always has: but because in his infinite wisdom he did not think it best on the whole.

"But why was it not best? What could he have in view, preferable to the happiness of his creatures? And, if their happiness was to him above all things most dear, how could he bear the thoughts of their ever any of them being miserable?

"It is certain that he had in view something else than merely the happiness of his creatures. It was something of greater importance. But what was that thing that was of greater worth and importance, and to which he had the greatest regard, making all other things give way to this? What was his great end in creating and governing the world? Why, look what end he is at last likely to obtain, when the whole scheme is finished, and the Day of Judgment passed, and heaven and hell filled with all their proper inhabitants. What will be the final result? What will he get by all? Why, this: that he will exert and display every one of his perfections to the life, and so by all will exhibit a most perfect and exact image of himself.

"Now it is evident that the fall of angels and of man, together with all those things which have and will come to pass in consequence thereof, from the beginning of the world to the Day of Judgment and throughout eternity, will serve to give a much more lively and perfect representation of God than could possibly have been given had there been no sin or misery."

This book also led the inquirer through all the mazes of mental philosophy, and discussed all the problems of mystical religion, such as, —

"Can a man, merely from self-love, love God more than himself?"

"Is our impotency only moral?"

"What is the most fundamental difference between Arminians and Calvinists?"

"How the love to our neighbor which is commanded by God is a thing different from natural compassion, from natural affection, from party-spirited love, from any love whatever that arises merely from self-love, and from the love which enthusiasts and heretics have for one another."

I give these specimens, that the reader may reflect what kind of population there was likely to be where such were the daily studies of a plain country farmer's wife, and such the common topics discussed at every kitchen fireside.

My grandmother's blue book was published and recommended to the attention of New England, August 4, 1750, just twenty-six years before the Declaration of Independence. How popular it was, and how widely read in New England, appears from the list of subscribers which stands at the end of the old copy which my grandmother actually used. Almost every good old Massachusetts or Connecticut family name is there represented. We have the Emersons, the Adamses, the Brattles of Brattle Street, the Bromfields of Bromfield Street, the Brinsmaids of Connecticut, the Butlers, the Campbells, the Chapmans, the Cottons, the Daggetts, the Hawleys, the Hookers, with many more names of families yet continuing to hold influence in New England. How they regarded this book may be inferred from the fact that some subscribed for six books, some for twelve, some for thirty-six, and some for fifty. Its dissemination was deemed an act of religious ministry, and there is not the slightest doubt that it was heedfully and earnestly read in every good family of New England; and its propositions were discussed everywhere and by everybody. This is one undoubted fact; the other is, that it was this generation who fought through the Revolutionary war. They were a set of men and women brought up to *think*, — to think not merely on agreeable subjects, but to wrestle and tug at the very severest problems. Utter self-renunciation, a sort of grand contempt for personal happiness when weighed with things greater and more valuable, was the fundamental principle of life in those days. They who could calmly look in the face, and settle themselves down to, the idea of being resigned and thankful for an existence which was not so good as non-existence, — who were willing to be loyal subjects of a splendid and powerful government which was conducted on quite other issues than a regard for their happiness, — were possessed of a courage and a fortitude which no mere earthly mischance could shake. They who had faced eternal ruin with an unflinching gaze were not likely to shrink before the comparatively trivial losses and gains of any mere earthly conflict. Being accustomed to combats with the Devil, it was rather a recreation to fight only British officers.

If any should ever be so curious as to read this old treatise, as well as most of the writings of Jonathan Edwards, they will perceive with singular plainness how inevitably monarchical and aristocratic institutions influence theology.

That "the king can do no wrong," — that the subject owes everything to the king, and the king nothing to the subject, — that it is the king's first duty to take care of himself, and keep up state, splendor, majesty, and royalty, and that it is the people's duty to give themselves up, body and soul, without a murmuring thought, to keep up this state, splendor, and royalty, — were ideas for ages so wrought into the human mind, and transmitted by ordinary generation, — they so reflected themselves in literature and poetry and art, and all the great customs of society, — that it was inevitable that systematic theology should be permeated by them.

The idea of God in which theologians delighted, and which the popular mind accepted, was not that of the Good Shepherd that giveth his life for the sheep, — of him that made himself of no reputation, and took unto himself the form of a servant, — of him who on his knees washed the feet of his disciples, and said that in the kingdom of heaven the greatest was he who served most humbly, — this aspect of a Divine Being had not yet been wrought into their systematic theology; because, while the Bible comes from God, theology is the outgrowth of the human mind, and therefore must spring from the movement of society.

When the Puritans arrived at a perception of the political rights of men in the state, and began to enunciate and act upon the doctrine that a king's right to reign was founded upon his power to promote the greatest happiness of his subjects, and when, in pursuance of this theory, they tried, condemned, and executed a king who had been false to the people, they took a long step forward in human progress. Why did not immediate anarchy follow, as when the French took such a step in regard to their king? It was because the Puritans transferred to God all those rights and immunities, all that unquestioning homage and worship and loyalty, which hitherto they had given to an earthly king.

The human mind cannot bear to relinquish more than a certain portion of its cherished past ideas in one century. Society falls into anarchy in too entire a change of base.

The Puritans had still a King. The French Revolutionists had nothing; therefore, the Puritan Revolution went on stronger and stronger. The French passed through anarchy back under despotism.

The doctrine of Divine sovereignty was the great rest to the human mind in those days, when the foundations of many generations were broken up. It is always painful to honest and loyal minds to break away from that which they have reverenced, — to put down that which they have respected. And the Puritans were by nature the most reverential and most loyal portion of the community. Their passionate attachment to the doctrine of Divine sovereignty, at this period, was the pleading and yearning within them of a faculty robbed of its appropriate object, and longing for support and expression.

There is something most affecting in the submissive devotion of these old Puritans to their God. Nothing shows more completely the indestructible nature of the filial tie which binds man to God, of the filial yearning which throbs in the heart of a great child of so great a Father, than the manner in which these men loved and worshipped and trusted God as the ALL LOVELY, even in the face of monstrous assertions of theology ascribing to him deeds which no father could imitate without being cast out of human society, and no governor without being handed down to all ages as a monster.

These theologies were not formed by the Puritans; they were their legacy from past monarchical and mediæval ages; and the principles of true Christian democracy upon which they founded their new state began, from the time of the American Revolution, to act upon them with a constantly ameliorating power; so that whosoever should read my grandmother's blue book now would be astonished to find how completely New England theology has changed its base.

The artist, in reproducing pictures of New England life during this period, is often obliged to hold his hand. He could not faithfully report the familiar conversations of the common people, because they often allude to and discuss the most awful and tremendous subjects. This, however, was the inevitable result of the honest, fearless manner in which the New England ministry of this second era discussed the Divine administration. They argued for it with the common people in very much the tone and with much the language in which they defended the Continental Congress and the ruling President; and every human being was addressed as a competent judge.

The result of such a mode of proceeding, in the long run, changed the theology of New England, from what it was when Jonathan Edwards recommended my grandmother's blue book, into what it is at this present writing. But, during the process of this investigation, every child born in New England found himself beaten backwards and forwards, like a shuttlecock, between the battledoors of discussion. Our kitchen used to be shaken constantly by what my grandfather significantly called "the battle of the Infinites," especially when my Uncle Bill came home from Cambridge on his vacations, fully charged with syllogisms, which he hurled like catapults back on the syllogisms which my grandmother had drawn from the armory of her blue book.

My grandmother would say, for example: "Whatever sin is committed against an infinite being is an infinite evil. Every infinite evil deserves infinite punishment; therefore every sin of man deserves an infinite punishment."

Then Uncle Bill, on the other side, would say: "No act of a finite being can be infinite. Man is a finite being; therefore no sin of man can be infinite. No finite evil deserve infinite punishment. Man's sins are finite evils; therefore man's sins do not deserve infinite punishment." When the combatants had got thus far, they generally looked at each other in silence.

As a result, my grandmother being earnest and prayerful, and my uncle careless and worldly, the thing generally ended in her believing that he was wrong, though she could not answer him; and in his believing that she, after all, might be right, though he *could* answer her; for it is noticeable, in every battle of opinion, that honest, sincere, moral earnestness has a certain advantage over mere intellectual cleverness.

It was inevitable that a people who had just carried through a national revolution and declared national independence on the principle that "governments owe their just power to the consent of the governed," and who recognized it as an axiom that the greatest good to the greatest number was the object to be held in view in all just governments, should very soon come into painful collision with forms of theological statement, in regard to God's government, which appeared to contravene all these principles, and which could be supported only by referring to the old notion of the divine right and prerogative of the King Eternal.

President Edwards had constructed a marvellous piece of logic to show that, while true virtue in man consisted in supreme devotion to the general good of all, true virtue in God consisted in supreme regard for himself. This "Treatise on True Virtue" was one of the strongest attempts to back up by reasoning the old monarchical and aristocratic ideas of the supreme right of the king and upper classes. The whole of it falls to dust before the one simple declaration of Jesus Christ, that, in the eyes of Heaven, one lost sheep is more prized than all the ninety and nine that went not astray, and before the parable in which the father runs, forgetful of parental prerogative and dignity, to cast himself on the neck of the far-off prodigal.

Theology being human and a reflection of human infirmities, nothing is more common than for it to come up point-blank in opposition to the simplest declarations of Christ.

I must beg my readers' pardon for all this, but it is a fact that the true tragedy of New England life, its deep, unutterable pathos, its endurances and its sufferings, all depended upon, and were woven into, this constant wrestling of thought with infinite problems which could not be avoided, and which saddened the days of almost every one who grew up under it.

Was this entire freedom of thought and discussion a bad thing, then? Do we not see that strength of mind and strength of will, and the courage and fortitude and endurance which founded this great American government, grew up out of characters formed thus to think and struggle and suffer? It seems to be the law of this present existence, that all the changes by which the world is made better are brought about by the struggle and suffering, and sometimes the utter shipwreck, of individual human beings.

In regard to our own family, the deepest tragedy in it, and the one which for a time brought the most suffering and sorrow on us all, cannot be explained unless we take into consideration this peculiar state of society.

In the neighboring town of Adams there lived one of the most remarkable clergymen that New England has ever produced. His career influenced the thinking of Massachusetts, both in regard to those who adopted his opinions, and in the violent reaction from those opinions which was the result of his extreme manner of pushing them.

Dr. Moses Stern's figure is well remembered by me as I saw it in my boyhood. Everybody knew him, and when he appeared in the pulpit everybody trembled before him. He moved among men, but seemed not of men. An austere, inflexible, grand indifference to all things earthly seemed to give him the prestige and dignity of a supernatural being. His Calvinism was of so severe and ultra a type, and his statements were so little qualified either by pity of human infirmity, or fear of human censure, or desire of human approbation, that he reminded one of some ancient prophet, freighted with a mission of woe and wrath, which he must always speak, whether people would hear or whether they would forbear.

The Revolutionary war had introduced into the country a great deal of scepticism, of a type of which Paine's "Age of Reason" was an exponent; and, to meet this, the ministry of New England was not slow or unskilful.

Dr. Stern's mode of meeting this attitude of the popular mind was by an unflinching, authoritative, vehement reiteration of all the most unpopular and unpleasant points of Calvinism. Now as Nature is, in many of her obvious aspects, notoriously uncompromising, harsh, and severe, the Calvinist who begins to talk to common-sense people has this advantage on his side, — that the things which he represents the Author of Nature as doing and being ready to do, are not very different from what the common-sense man sees that the Author of Nature is already in the habit of doing.

The farmer who struggles with the hard soil, and with drouth and frost and caterpillars and fifty other insect plagues, — who finds his most persistent and well-calculated efforts constantly thwarted by laws whose workings he never can fully anticipate, and which never manifest either care for his good intentions or sympathy for his losses, is very apt to believe that the God who created nature may be a generally benevolent, but a severe and unsympathetic being, governing the world for some great, unknown purpose of his own, of which man's private improvement and happiness may or may not form a part.

Dr. Stern, with characteristic independence and fearlessness, on his own simple authority cut loose from and repudiated the whole traditional idea of the fall in Adam as having anything to do with the existence of human depravity; and made up his own theory of the universe, and began preaching it to the farmers of Adams. It was simply this: that the Divine Being is the efficient cause of all things, not only in matter but in mind, — that every good and every evil volition of any being in the universe is immediately caused by Him and tends equally well in its way to carry on his great designs. But, in order that this might not interfere with the doctrines of human responsibility, he taught that all was accomplished by Omniscient skill and knowledge in such a way as not in the slightest degree to interfere with human free agency; so that the whole responsibility of every human being's actions must rest upon himself.

Thus was this system calculated, like a skilful engine of torture, to produce all the mental anguish of the most perfect sense of helplessness with the most torturing sense of responsibility. Alternately he worked these two great levers with an almost supernatural power, — on one Sunday demonstrating with the most logical clearness, and by appeals to human consciousness, the perfect freedom of man, and, on the next, demonstrating with no less precision and logic the perfect power which an Omniscient Being possessed and exercised of controlling all his thoughts and volitions and actions.

Individually, Dr. Stern, like many other teachers of severe, uncompromising theories, was an artless, simple-hearted, gentle-mannered man. He was a close student, and wore two holes in the floor opposite his table in the spot where year after year his feet were placed in study. He refused to have the smallest thing to do with any temporal affair of this life. Like the other clergymen, he lived on a small salary, and the support of his family depended largely on the proceeds of a farm. But it is recorded of

him, that once, when his whole summer's crop of hay was threatened with the bursting of a thunder-shower, and, farmhands being
short, he was importuned to lend a hand to save it, he resolutely
declined, saying, that, if he once began to allow himself to be
called on in any emergency for temporal affairs, he should become
forgetful of his great mission.

The same inflexible, unbending perseverance he showed in
preaching, on the basis of his own terrible theory, the most fearful doctrines of Calvinism. His sermons on Judas, on Jeroboam,
and on Pharaoh, as practical examples of the doctrine of reprobation, were pieces of literature so startling and astounding, that,
even in those days of interrupted travel, when there were neither
railroads nor good roads of any kind, and almost none of our
modern communicative system of magazines and newspapers, they
were heard of all over New England. So great was the revulsion
which his doctrines excited, that, when he exchanged with his
brother ministers, his appearance in the pulpit was the signal for
some of the most independent of the congregation to get up and
leave the meeting-house. But, as it was one of his maxims that the
minister who does not excite the opposition of the natural heart
fails to do his work, he regarded such demonstrations as evident
signs of a faithful ministry.

The science of Biblical criticism in his day was in its infancy;
the Bible was mostly read by ministers, and proof-texts quoted
from it as if it had been a treatise written in the English language
by New-Englanders, and in which every word must bear the exact
sense of a New England metaphysical treatise. And thus interpreting the whole wide labyrinth of poetry and history, and
Oriental allegory and hyperbole, by literal rules, Dr. Stern found
no difficulty in making it clear to those who heard him that there
was no choice between believing his hard doctrines and giving
up the Bible altogether. And it shows the deep and rooted attachment which the human heart has for that motherly book, that
even in this dreadful dilemma the majority of his hearers did not
revolt from the Bible.

As it was, in the town where he lived his preaching formed
the strongest, most controlling of all forces. No human being could
hear his sermons unmoved. He would not preach to an inattentive
audience, and on one occasion, observing a large number of his

congregation asleep, he abruptly descended from the pulpit and calmly walked off home, leaving the astonished congregation to their own reflections; nor would he resume public services until messages of contrition and assurances of better conduct had been sent him.

Dr. Stern was in his position irresistible, simply because he cared nothing at all for the things which men ordinarily care for, and which therefore could be used as motives to restrain the declarations and actions of a clergyman. He cared nothing about worldly prosperity; he was totally indifferent to money; he utterly despised fame and reputation; and therefore from none of these sources could he be in the slightest degree influenced. Such a man is generally the king of his neighborhood, — the one whom all look up to, and all fear, and whose word in time becomes law.

Dr. Stern never sought to put himself forward otherwise than by the steady preaching of his system to the farming population of Adams. And yet, so great were his influence and his fame, that in time it became customary for young theological students to come and settle themselves down there as his students. This was done at first without his desire, and contrary to his remonstrance.

"I can't engage to teach you," he said; but still, when scholars came and continued to come, he found himself, without seeking it, actually at the head of a school of theology.

Let justice be done to all; it is due to truth to state that the theological scholars of Dr. Stern, wherever they went in the United States, were always marked men, — marked for an un-flinching adherence to principle, and especially for a great power in supporting unpopular truths.

The Doctor himself lived to an extreme old age, always retaining and reiterating with unflinching constancy his opinions. He was the last of the New England ministers who preserved the old clerical dress of the theocracy. Long after the cocked hat and small-clothes, silk stockings and shoe-buckles, had ceased to appear in modern life, his venerable figure, thus apparelled, walked the ways of modern men, seeming like one of the primitive Puritans risen from the dead.

He was the last, also, of the New England ministers to claim for himself that peculiar position, as God's ambassador, which was such a reality in the minds of the whole early Puritan community.

To extreme old age, his word was law in his parish, and he calmly and positively felt that it should be so. In time, his gray hairs, his fine, antique figure and quaint costume came to be regarded with the sort of appreciative veneration that every one gives to the monuments of the past. When he was near his ninetieth year, he was invited to New York to give the prestige of his venerable presence to the religious anniversaries which then were in the flush of newly organized enthusiasm, and which gladly laid hold of this striking accessory to the religious picturesque.

Dr. Stern was invited and fêted in the most select upper circles of New York, and treated with attentions which would have been flattering had he not been too entirely simple-minded and careless of such matters even to perceive what they meant.

But at this same time the Abolitionists, who were regarded as most improper people to be recognized in the religious circles of good society, came to New York, resolving to have their anniversary also; and, knowing that Dr. Stern had always professed to be an antislavery man, they invited him to sit on the stage with them; and Dr. Stern went. Shocking to relate, and dreadful to behold, this very cocked hat and these picturesque gray hairs, that had been brought to New York on purpose to ornament religious anniversaries which were all agreed in excluding and ignoring the Abolitionists, had gone right over into the camp of the enemy! and he was so entirely ignorant and uninstructible on the subject, and came back, after having committed this abomination, with a face of such innocent and serene gravity, that nobody dared to say a word to him on the subject.

He was at this time the accepted guest in a family whose very religion consisted in a gracious carefulness and tenderness lest they should wake up the feelings of their Southern brethren on the delicate subject of slavery. But then Dr. Stern was a man that it did no good to talk to, since it was well known that, wherever there was an unpopular truth to be defended, his cocked hat was sure to be in the front ranks.

Let us do one more justice to Dr. Stern, and say that his utter inflexibility toward human infirmity and human feeling spared himself as little as it spared any other. In his early life he records, in a most affecting autobiography, the stroke which deprived him, within a very short space, of a beloved wife and two charming children. In the struggle of that hour he says, with affecting simplicity, "I felt that I should die if I did not submit; and I did submit then, once for all." Thence-forward the beginning and middle and end of his whole preaching was *submission,* — utter, absolute, and unconditional.

In extreme old age, trembling on the verge of the grave, and looking back over sixty years of intense labor, he said, "After all, it is quite possible that *I* may not be saved"; but he considered himself as but one drop in the ocean, and his personal salvation as of but secondary account. His devotion to the King Eternal had no reference to a matter so slight. In all this, if there is something terrible and painful, there is something also which is grand, and in which we can take pride, as the fruit of our human nature. Peace to his ashes! he has learned better things ere now.

If my readers would properly understand the real depth of sorrowful perplexity in which our friend Miss Mehitable Rossiter was struggling, they must go back with us some years before, to the time when little Emily Rossiter was given up to the guardianship and entire control of her Aunt Farnsworth.

Zedekiah Farnsworth was one of those men who embody qualities which the world could not afford to be without, and which yet are far from being the most agreeable. Uncompromising firmness, intense self-reliance, with great vigor in that part of the animal nature which fits man to resist and to subdue and to hold in subjection the forces of nature, were his prominent characteristics. His was a bold and granite formation, — most necessary for the stability of the earth, but without a flower.

His wife was a woman who had once been gay and beautiful, but who, coming under the dominion of a stronger nature, was perfectly magnetized by it, so as to assimilate and become a modified reproduction of the same traits. A calm, intense, severe conscientiousness, which judged alike herself and others with unflinching severity, was her leading characteristic.

Let us now imagine a child inheriting from the mother a sensitive, nervous organization, and from the father a predisposition to morbid action, with a mind as sensitive to external influence as a daguerreotype-plate, brought suddenly from the warmth of a too-indulgent household to the arctic regularity and frozen still-

ness of the Farnsworth mansion. It will be seen that the consequences must have been many conflicts, and many struggles of
nature with nature, and that a character growing up thus must of
course grow up into unnatural and unhealthy development.

The problem of education is seriously complicated by the peculiarities of womanhood. If we suppose two souls, exactly alike,
sent into bodies, the one of man, the other of woman, that mere
fact alone alters the whole mental and moral history of the two.

In addition to all the other sources of peril which beset the
little Emily, she early developed a beauty so remarkable as to
draw upon her constant attention, and, as she grew older, brought
to her all the trials and the dangers which extraordinary beauty
brings to woman. It was a part of her Aunt Farnsworth's system
to pretend to be ignorant of this great fact, with a view, as she
supposed, of checking any disposition to pride or vanity which
might naturally arise therefrom. The consequence was that the
child, hearing this agreeable news from every one else who surrounded her, soon learned the transparent nature of the hoax, and
with it acquired a certain doubt of her aunt's sincerity.

Emily had a warm, social nature, and had always on hand during her school days a list of enthusiastic friends whose admiration
of her supplied the light and warmth which were entirely wanting
from every other source.

Mrs. Farnsworth was not insensible to the charms of her niece.
She was, in fact, quite proud of them, but was pursuing conscientiously the course in regard to them which she felt that duty required of her. She loved the child, too, devotedly, but her own
nature had been so thoroughly frozen by maxims of self-restraint,
that this love seldom or never came into outward forms of expression.

It is sad to be compelled to trace the ill effects produced by the
overaction and misapplication of the very noblest faculties of the
human mind.

The Farnsworth family was one in which there was the fullest
sympathy with the severest preaching of Dr. Stern. As Emily
grew older, it was exacted of her, as one of her Sabbath duties,
to take notes of his discourses at church, which were afterwards
to be read over on Sunday evening by her aunt and uncle, and
preserved in an extract-book.

The effect of such kinds of religious teaching on most of the children and young people in the town of Adams was to make them consider religion, and everything connected with it, as the most disagreeable of all subjects, and to seek practically to have as little to do with it as possible; so that there was among the young people a great deal of youthful gayety and of young enjoyment in life, notwithstanding the preaching from Sunday to Sunday of assertions enough to freeze every heart with fear. Many formed the habit of thinking of something else during the sermon-time, and many heard without really attaching any very definite meaning to what they heard.

The severest utterances, if constantly reiterated, lose their power and come to be considered as nothing. But Emily Rossiter had been gifted with a mind of far more than ordinary vigor, and with even a Greek passion for ideas, and with capabilities for logical thought which rendered it impossible for her to listen to discourses so intellectual without taking in their drift and responding to their stimulus by a corresponding intellectual activity.

Dr. Stern set the example of a perfectly bold and independent manner of differing from the popular theology of his day in certain important respects; and, where he did differ, it was with a hardihood of self-assertion, and an utter disregard of popular opinion, and a perfect reliance on his own powers of discovering truth, which were very apt to magnetize these same qualities in other minds. People who thus set the example of free and independent thinking in one or two respects, and yet hope to constrain their disciples to think exactly as they do on all other subjects, generally reckon without their host; and there is no other region in Massachusetts where all sorts of hardy free-thinking are so rife at the present day as in the region formerly controlled by Dr. Stern.

Before Emily was fourteen years old she had passed through two or three of those seasons of convulsed and agonized feeling which are caused by the revolt of a strong sense of justice and humanity against teachings which seem to accuse the great Father of all of the most frightful cruelty and injustice. The teachings were backed up by literal quotations from the Bible, which in those days no common person possessed the means, or the habits of thought, for understanding, and thus were accepted by her at first as Divine declarations.

When these agonized conflicts occurred, they were treated by her aunt and uncle only as active developments of the natural opposition of the human heart to God. Some such period of active contest with the Divine nature was on record in the lives of some of the most eminent New England saints. President Edwards recorded the same; and therefore they looked upon them hopefully, just as the medical faculty of those same uninstructed times looked upon the writhings and agonies which their administration of poison produced in the human body.

The last and most fearful of these mental struggles came after the death of her favorite brother Theodore; who, being supposed to die in an unregenerate state, was forthwith judged and sentenced, and his final condition spoken of with a grim and solemn certainty, by her aunt and uncle.

How far the preaching of Dr. Stern did violence to the most cherished feelings of human nature on this subject will appear by an extract from a sermon preached about this time.

The text was from Rev. xix, 3. "And again they said Alleluia. And her smoke rose up for ever and ever."

The subject is thus announced: —

"The heavenly hosts will praise God for punishing the finally impenitent forever."

In the *improvement* or practical application of this text, is the following passage: —

"Will the heavenly hosts praise God for all the displays of his vindictive justice in the punishment of the damned? then we may learn that there is an essential difference between saints and sinners. Sinners often disbelieve and deny this distinction; and it is very difficult to make them see and believe it. . . . . They sometimes freely say that they do not think that heaven is such a place as has been described; or that the inhabitants of it say 'Amen, Alleluia,' while they see the smoke of the torments of the damned ascend up for ever and ever. They desire and hope to go to heaven, without ever being willing to speak such a language, or to express such feelings in the view of the damned. And is not this saying that their hearts are essentially different from those who feel such a spirit, and are willing to adopt the language of heaven? Good men do adopt the language of heaven before they arrive there. And all who are conscious that they cannot say 'Amen, Alleluia,' may know that they are yet sinners, and essentially different from saints, and altogether unprepared to go with them to heaven and join with them in praising God for the vindictive justice he displays in dooming all unholy creatures to a never-ending torment."

It was this sermon that finally broke those cords which years of pious descent had made so near and tender between the heart of Emily and her father's Bible.

No young person ever takes a deliberate and final leave of the faith of the fathers without a pang; and Emily suffered so much in the struggle, that her aunt became alarmed for her health. She was sent to Boston to spend a winter under the care of another sister of her mother's, who was simply a good-natured woman of the world, who was proud of her niece's beauty and talents, and resolved to make the most of them in a purely worldly way.

At this time she formed the acquaintance of a very interesting French family of high rank, who for certain family reasons were just then exiled to America. She became fascinated with their society, and plunged into the study of the French language and literature with all the enthusiasm of a voyager who finds himself among enchanted islands. And French literature at this time was full of the life of a new era, — the era which produced both the American and the French Revolution.

The writings of Voltaire were too cold and cynical for her enthusiastic nature; but Rousseau was to her like a sudden translation from the ice and snow of Massachusetts to the tropical flowers of a February in Florida. In "La Nouvelle Héloïse," she found, not merely a passionate love story, but the consideration, on the author's side, of just such problems as had been raised by her theological education.

When she returned from this visit she was apparently quiet and at peace. Her peace was the peace of a river which has found an underground passage, and therefore chafes and frets no more. Her philosophy was the philosophy of Émile, her faith the faith of the Savoyard vicar, and she imitated Dr. Stern only in utter self-reliance and fearlessness of consequences in pursuit of what she believed true.

Had her aunt and uncle been able to read the French language, they would have found her note-book of sermons sometimes interspersed by quotations from her favorite author, which certainly were quite in point; as, for instance, at the foot of a severe sermon on the doctrine of reprobation was written: —

"Quand cette dure et décourageante doctrine se déduit de l'Écriture elle-même, mon premier devoir n'est-il pas d'honorer Dieu? Quelque respect que je doive au texte sacré, j'en dois plus encore à son Auteur; et *j'aimerais mieux croire la Bible falsifée ou inintelligible, que Dieu injuste ou malfaisant.* St. Paul ne veut pas que le vase dise au potier, Pourquoi m'as-tu fait ainsi? Cela est fort bien si le potier n'exige du vase que des services qu'il l'a mis en état de lui rendre; mais s'il s'en prenait au vase de n' être pas propre à un usage pour lequel il ne l'aurait pas fait, le vase aurait-il tort de lui dire, Pourquoi m'as-tu fait ainsi?" *

After a period of deceitful quiet and calm, in which Emily read and wrote and studied alone in her room, and moved about in her daily circle like one whose heart is afar off, she suddenly disappeared from them all. She left ostensibly to go on a visit to Boston to her aunt, and all that was ever heard from her after that was a letter of final farewell to Miss Mehitable, in which she told her briefly, that, unable any longer to endure the life she had been leading, and to seem to believe what she could not believe, and being importuned to practise what she never intended to do, she had chosen her lot for herself, and requested her neither to seek her out nor to inquire after her, as all such inquiries would be absolutely vain.

All that could be ascertained on the subject was, that about this time the Marquis de Conté and his lady were found to have sailed for France.

This was the sad story which Miss Mehitable poured into the sympathetic ear of Ellery Davenport.

* "When this harsh, discouraging doctrine is deduced from the Scriptures themselves, is not my first duty to honor God? Whatever respect I owe to the sacred text, I owe still more to its Author, *and I should prefer to believe the Bible falsified or unintelligible to believing God unjust or cruel.* St. Paul would not that the vase should say to the potter, Why hast thou made me thus? That is all very well if the potter exacts of the vase only such services as he has fitted it to render; but if he should require of it a usage for which he has not fitted it, would the vase be in the wrong for saying, Why hast thou made me thus?"

CHAPTER XXX

WE BEGIN TO BE
GROWN-UP PEOPLE

We begin to be grown-up people. We cannot always remain in the pleasant valley of childhood. I myself, good reader, have dwelt on its scenes longer, because, looking back on it from the extreme end of life, it seems to my weary eyes so fresh and beautiful; the dew of the morning-land lies on it, — that dew which no coming day will restore.

Our childhood, as the reader has seen, must be confessed to have been reasonably enjoyable. Its influences were all homely, innocent, and pure. There was no seductive vice, no open or covert immorality. Our worst form of roaring dissipation consisted in being too fond of huckleberry parties, or in the immoderate pursuit of chestnuts and walnuts. Even the vagrant associates of uncertain social standing who abounded in Oldtown were characterized by a kind of woodland innocence, and were not much more harmful than woodchucks and squirrels.

Sam Lawson, for instance, though he dearly loved lazy lounging, and was devoted to idle tramps, was yet a most edifying vagrant. A profane word was an abomination in his sight; his speculations on doctrines were all orthodox, and his expositions of Scripture as original and abundant as those of some of the dreamy old fathers. As a general thing he was a devout Sunday keeper and a pillar of the sanctuary, playing his bass-viol to the most mournful tunes with evident relish.

I remember being once left at home alone on Sunday, with an incipient sore-throat, when Sam volunteered himself as my nurse. In the course of the forenoon stillness, a wandering Indian came in, who, by the joint influence of a large mug of cider and the weariness of his tramp, fell into a heavy sleep on our kitchen floor, and somehow Sam was beguiled to amuse himself by tickling his nose with a broom-straw, and laughing, until the tears rolled down his cheeks, at the sleepy snorts and struggles and odd contortions of visage which were the results. Yet so tender was Sam's conscience, that he had frequent searchings of heart, afterward, on account of this profanation of sacred hours, and indulged in floods of long-winded penitence.

Though Sam abhorred all profanity, yet for seasons of extreme provocation he was well provided with that gentler Yankee litany which affords to the irritated mind the comfort of swearing, without the commission of the sin. Under great pressure of provocation Sam Lawson freely said, "Darn it!" The word "darn," in fact, was to the conscientious New England mind a comfortable resting-place, a refreshment to the exacerbated spirit, that shrunk from that too similar word with an *m* in it.

In my boyhood I sometimes pondered that other hard word, and vaguely decided to speak it, with that awful curiosity which gives to an unknown sin a hold upon the imagination. What would happen if I should say "damn"? I dwelt on that subject with a restless curiosity which my grandmother certainly would have told me was a temptation of the Devil. The horrible desire so grew on me, that once, in the sanctity of my own private apartment, with all the doors shut and locked, I thought I would boldly try the experiment of saying "damn" out loud, and seeing what would happen. I did it, and looked up apprehensively to see if the walls were going to fall on me, but they didn't, and I covered up my head in the bedclothes and felt degraded. I had committed the sin, and got not even the excitement of a catastrophe. The Lord apparently did not think me worth his notice.

In regard to the awful questions of my grandmother's blue book, our triad grew up with varying influences. Harry, as I have said, was one of those quiet human beings, of great force in native individuality, who silently draw from all scenes and things just those elements which their own being craves, and resolutely and calmly think their own thoughts, and live their own life, amid the most discordant influences; just as the fluid, sparkling waters of a mountain brook dart this way and that amid stones and rubbish, and hum to themselves their own quiet, hidden tune.

A saintly woman, whose heart was burning itself away in the torturing fires of a slow martyrdom, had been for the first ten years of his life his only companion and teacher, and, dying, had sealed him with a seal given from a visibly opened heaven; and thenceforward no theologies, and no human authority, had the power and weight with him that had the remembrance of those dying eyes, and the sanctity of those last counsels.

By native descent Harry was a gentleman of the peculiarly English stock. He had the shy reserve, the silent, self-respecting pride and delicacy, which led him to keep his own soul as a castle, and that interested, because it left a sense of something veiled and unexpressed.

We were now eighteen years old, and yet, during all these years that he had lived side by side with me in closest intimacy, he had never spoken to me freely and frankly of that which I afterwards learned was always the intensest and bitterest mortification of his life, namely, his father's desertion of his mother and himself. Once only do I remember ever to have seen him carried away by anger, and that was when a coarse and cruel bully among the school-boys applied to him a name which reflected on his mother's honor. The anger of such quiet people is often a perfect convulsion, and it was so in this case. He seemed to blaze with it, — to flame up and redden with a delirious passion; and he knocked down and stamped upon the boy with a blind fury which it was really frightful to see, and which was in singular contrast with his usual unprovokable good-humor.

Ellery Davenport had made good his promise of looking for the pocket-book which Harry's father had left in his country-seat, and the marriage certificate of his mother had been found in it, and carefully lodged in the hands of Lady Lothrop; but nothing had been said to us children about it; it was merely held quietly, as a document that might be of use in time in bringing some property to the children. And even at the time of this fight with the school-boy, Harry said so little afterward, that the real depth of his feeling on this subject was not suspected.

I have reason to believe, also, that Ellery Davenport did succeed in making the father of Harry and Tina aware of the existence of two such promising children, and of the respectability of the families into which they had been adopted. Captain Percival, now Sir Harry Percival, had married again in England, so Ellery Davenport had informed Miss Mehitable in a letter, and had a son by this marriage, and so had no desire to bring to view his former connection. It was understood, I believe, that a sum of money was to be transmitted yearly to the hands of the guardians of the children, for their benefit, and that they were to be left undisturbed in the possession of those who had adopted them.

Miss Mehitable had suffered so extremely herself by the conflict of her own earnest, melancholy nature with the theologic ideas of her time, that she shrunk with dread from imposing them on the gay and joyous little being whose education she had undertaken. Yet she was impressed by that awful sense of responsibility which is one of the most imperative characteristics of the New England mind; and she applied to her brother earnestly to know what she should teach Tina with regard to her own spiritual position. The reply of her brother was characteristic, and we shall give it here: —

"My dear Sister: — I am a Puritan, — the son, the grandson, the great-grandson of Puritans, — and I say to you, Plant the footsteps of your child on the ground of the old Cambridge Platform, and teach her as Winthrop and Dudley and the Mathers taught their children, — that she 'is already a member in the Church of Christ, — that she is in covenant with God, and hath the seal thereof upon her, to wit, baptism; and so, if not regenerate, is yet in a more hopeful way of attaining regeneration and all spiritual blessings, both of the covenant and seal.' * By teaching the child this, you will place her mind in natural and healthful relations with God and religion. She will feel in her Father's house, and under her Father's care, and the long and weary years of a sense of disinheritance with which you struggled will be spared to her.

"I hold Jonathan Edwards to have been the greatest man, since St. Augustine, that Christianity has turned out. But when a great man, instead of making himself a great ladder for feeble folks to climb on, strikes away the ladder and bids them come to where he stands at a step, his greatness and his goodness both may prove unfortunate for those who come after him. I go for the good old Puritan platform.

"Your affectionate brother,
"Jonathan Rossiter."

The consequence of all this was, that Tina adopted in her glad and joyous nature the simple, helpful faith of her brother, — the

* Cambridge Platform. Mather's Magnalia, page 227, article 7.

faith in an ever good, ever present, ever kind Father, whose child she was and in whose household she had grown up. She had a most unbounded faith in prayer, and in the indulgence and tenderness of the Heavenly Power. All things to her eyes were seen through the halo of a cheerful, sanguine, confiding nature. Life had for her no cloud or darkness or mystery.

As to myself, I had been taught in the contrary doctrines, — that I was a disinherited child of wrath. It is true that this doctrine was contradicted by the whole influence of the minister, who, as I have said before, belonged to the Arminian wing of the Church, and bore very mildly on all these great topics. My grandmother sometimes endeavored to stir him up to more decisive orthodoxy, and especially to a more vigorous presentation of the doctrine of native human depravity. I remember once, in her zeal, her quoting to him as a proof-text the quatrain of Dr. Watts: —

> "Conceived in sin, O woful state!
>   Before we draw our breath,
>   The first young pulse begins to beat
>   Iniquity and death."

"That, madam," said Dr. Lothrop, who never forgot to be the grand gentleman under any circumstances, — "that, madam, is not the New Testament, but Dr. Isaac Watts, allow me to remind you."

"Well," said my grandmother, "Dr. Watts got it from the Bible."

"Yes, madam, a *very long way* from the Bible, allow me to say."

And yet, after all, though I did not like my grandmother's Calvinistic doctrines, I must confess that she, and all such as thought like her, always impressed me as being more earnestly religious than those that held the milder and more moderate belief.

Once in a while old Dr. Stern would preach in our neighborhood, and I used to go to hear him. Everybody went to hear him. A sermon on reprobation from Dr. Stern would stir up a whole community in those days, just as a presidential election stirs one up now. And I remember that he used to impress me as being more like a messenger from the other world than most ministers. Dr. Lothrop's sermons, by the side of his, were like Pope's Pastorals beside the Tragedies of Æschylus. Dr. Lothrop's discourses were smooth, they were sensible, they were well worded, and everybody went to sleep under them; but Dr. Stern shook and swayed his audience like a field of grain under a high wind. There was no possibility of not listening to him, or of hearing him with indifference, for he dealt in assertions that would have made the very dead turn in their graves. One of his sermons was talked of for months afterward, with a sort of suppressed breath of supernatural awe, such as men would use in discussing the reappearance of a soul from the other world.

But meanwhile I believed neither my grandmother, nor Dr. Stern, nor the minister. The eternal questions seethed and boiled and burned in my mind without answer. It was not my own personal destiny that lay with weight on my mind; it was the incessant, restless desire to know the real truth from some unanswerable authority. I longed for a visible, tangible communion with God; I longed to see the eternal beauty, to hear a friendly voice from the eternal silence. Among all the differences with regard to doctrinal opinion, I could see clearly that there were two classes of people in the world, — those who had found God and felt him as a living power upon their spirits, and those who had not; and that unknown experience was what I sought.

Such, then, were we three children when Harry and I were in our eighteenth year and Tina in her fifteenth. And just at this moment there was among the high consulting powers that regulated our destiny a movement as to what further was to be done with the three that had hitherto grown up together.

Now, if the reader has attentively read ancient and modern history, he will observe that there is a class of women to be found in this lower world, who, wherever they are, are sure to be in some way the first or the last cause of everything that is going on. Everybody knows, for instance, that Helen was the great instigator of the Trojan war, and if it had not been for her we should have had no Homer. In France, Madame Récamier was, for the time being, reason enough for almost anything that any man in France did; and yet one cannot find out that Madame Récamier had any uncommon genius of her own, except the sovereign one of charming every human being that came in her way, so that all became her humble and subservient subjects. The instance is a marked one, because it operated in a wide sphere, on very celebrated men, in an interesting historic period. But it individualizes a kind of faculty which, generally speaking, is peculiar to women, though it is in some instances exercised by men, — a faculty of charming and controlling every person with whom one has to do.

Tina was now verging toward maturity; she was in just that delicious period in which the girl has all the privileges and graces of childhood, its freedom of movement and action, brightened with a sort of mysterious aurora by the coming dawn of womanhood; and everything indicated that she was to be one of this powerful class of womankind. Can one analyze the charm which such women possess? I have a theory that, in all cases, there is a certain amount of genius with it, — genius which does not declare itself in literature, but in social life, and which devotes itself to pleasing, as other artists devote themselves to painting or to poetry.

Tina had no inconsiderable share of self-will; she was very pronounced in her tastes, and fond of her own way; but she had received from nature this passion for entertaining, and been endowed with varied talents in this line which made her always, from early childhood, the coveted and desired person in every circle. Not a visage in Oldtown was so set in grimness of care, that it did not relax its lines when it saw Tina coming down the street; for Tina could mimic and sing and dance, and fling back joke for joke in a perfect meteoric shower. So long as she entertained, she was perfectly indifferent who the party was. She would display her accomplishments to a set of strolling Indians, or for Sam Lawson and Jake Marshall, as readily as for any one else. She would run up and catch the minister by the elbow as he solemnly and decorously moved down street, and his face always broke into a laugh at the sight of her.

The minister's lady, and Aunt Lois, and Miss Deborah Kittery, while they used to mourn in secret places over her want of decorum in thus displaying her talents before the lower classes, would afterward laugh till the tears rolled down their cheeks and their ancient whalebone stays creaked, when she would do the same thing over in a select circle for them.

We have seen how completely she had conquered Polly, and what difficulty Miss Mehitable found in applying the precepts of Mrs. Chapone and Miss Hannah More to her case. The pattern young lady of the period, in the eyes of all respectable females, was expressed by Lucilla Stanley, in "Cœlebs in Search of a Wife." But when Miss Mehitable, after delighting herself with the Johnsonian balance of the rhythmical sentences which described this paragon as "not so much perfectly beautiful as perfectly elegant," — this model of consistency, who always blushed at the right moment, spoke at the right moment, and stopped at the right moment, and was, in short, a woman made to order, precisely to suit a bachelor who had traversed the whole earth, "not expecting perfection, but looking for consistency," — when, after all these charming visions, she looked at Tina, she was perfectly dismayed at contemplating her scholar. She felt the power by which Tina continually charmed and beguiled her, and the empire which she exercised over her; and, with wonderful good sense, she formally laid down the weapons of authority when she found she had no heart to use them.

"My child," she said to her one day, when that young lady was about eleven years of age, "you are a great deal stronger than I. I am weak because I love you, and because I have been broken by sorrow, and because, being a poor old woman, I don't trust myself. And you are young and strong and fearless; but remember, dear, the life you have to live is yours and not mine. I have not the heart to force you to take my way instead of your own, but I shall warn you that it will be better you should do so, and then leave you free. If you don't take my way, I shall do the very best for you that I can in your way, and you must take the responsibility in the end."

This was the only kind of system which Miss Mehitable was capable of carrying out. She was wise, shrewd, and loving, and she gradually controlled her little charge more and more by simple influence, but she had to meet in her education the opposition force of that universal petting and spoiling which everybody in society gives to an entertaining child.

Life is such a monotonous, dull affair, that anybody who has the gift of making it pass off gayly is in great demand. Tina was sent for to the parsonage, and the minister took her on his knee and encouraged her to chatter all sorts of egregious nonsense to him. And Miss Deborah Kittery insisted on having her sent for to visit them in Boston, and old Madam Kittery overwhelmed her with indulgence and caresses. Now Tina loved praises and caresses; incense was the very breath of her nostrils; and she enjoyed being fêted and petted as much as a cat enjoys being stroked.

It will not be surprising to one who considers the career of this kind of girl to hear that she was not much of a student. What she learned was by impulses and fits and starts, and all of it immediately used for some specific purpose of entertainment, so that among simple people she had the reputation of being a prodigy of information, on a very small capital of actual knowledge. Miss Mehitable sighed after thorough knowledge and discipline of mind for her charge, but she invariably found all Tina's teachers becoming accomplices in her superficial practices by praising and caressing her when she had been least faithful, always apologizing for her deficiencies, and speaking in the most flattering terms of her talents. During the last year the schoolmaster had been observed always to walk home with her and bring her books, with a humble, trembling subserviency and prostrate humility which she rewarded with great apparent contempt; and finally she announced to Miss Mehitable that she "didn't intend to go to school any more, because the master acted so silly."

Now Miss Mehitable, during all her experience of life, had always associated with the men of her acquaintance without ever being reminded in any particular manner of the difference of sex, and it was a subject which, therefore, was about the last to enter into her calculations with regard to her little charge. So she said, "My dear, you shouldn't speak in that way about your teacher; he knows a great deal more than you do."

"He may know more than I do about arithmetic, but he doesn't know how to behave. What right has he to put his old hand under my chin? and I won't have him putting his arm round me when he sets my copies! and I told him to-day he shouldn't carry my books home any more, — so there!"

Miss Mehitable was struck dumb. She went that afternoon and visited the minister's lady.

"Depend upon it, my dear," said Lady Lothrop, "it's time to try a course of home reading."

A bright idea now struck Miss Mehitable. Her cousin, Mr. Mordecai Rossiter, had recently been appointed a colleague with the venerable Dr. Lothrop. He was a young man, finely read, and of great solidity and piety, and Miss Mehitable resolved to invite him to take up his abode with them for the purpose of assisting her educational efforts. Mr. Mordecai Rossiter accordingly took up his abode in the family, used to conduct family worship, and was expected now and then to drop words of good advice and wholesome counsel to form the mind of Miss Tina. A daily hour was appointed during which he was to superintend her progress in arithmetic.

Mr. Mordecai Rossiter was one of the most simple-minded, honest, sincere human beings that ever wore a black coat. He accepted his charge in sacred simplicity, and took a prayerful view of his young catechumen, whom he was in hopes to make realize, by degrees, the native depravity of her own heart, and to lead through a gradual process to the best of all results.

Miss Tina also took a view of her instructor, and without any evil intentions, simply following her strongest instinct, which was to entertain and please, she very soon made herself an exceedingly delightful pupil. Since religion was evidently the engrossing subject in his mind, Tina also turned her attention to it, and instructed and edified him with flights of devout eloquence which were to him perfectly astonishing. Tina would discourse on the goodness of God, and ornament her remarks with so many flowers, and stars, and poetical fireworks, and be so rapt and carried away with her subject, that he would sit and listen to her as if she was an inspired being, and wholly forget the analysis which he meant to propose to her, as to whether her emotions of love to God proceeded from self-love or from disinterested benevolence.

As I have said, Tina had a genius for poetry, and had employed the dull hours which children of her age usually spend in church in reading the psalm-book and committing to memory all the most vividly emotional psalms and hymns. And these she was fond of repeating with great fervor and enthusiasm to her admiring listener.

Miss Mehitable considered that the schoolmaster had been an ill-taught, presumptuous man, who had ventured to take improper liberties with a mere child; but, when she established this connection between this same child and a solemn young minister, it never occurred to her to imagine that there would be any embarrassing consequences from the relation. She considered Tina as a mere infant, — as not yet having approached the age when the idea of anything like love or marriage could possibly be suggested to her.

In course of time, however, she could not help remarking that her cousin was in some respects quite an altered man. He reformed many little negligences in regard to his toilet which Miss Tina had pointed out to him with the nonchalant freedom of a young empress. And he would run and spring and fetch and carry in her service with a zeal and alertness quite wonderful to behold. He expressed privately to Miss Mehitable the utmost astonishment at her mental powers, and spoke of the wonderful work of divine grace which appeared to have made such progress in her heart. Never had he been so instructed and delighted before by the exercises of any young person. And he went so far as to assure Miss Mehitable that in many things he should be only too happy to sit at her feet and learn of her.

"Good gracious me!" said Miss Mehitable to herself, with a sort of half start of awakening, though not yet fully come to consciousness; "what does ail everybody that gets hold of Tina?"

What got hold of her cousin in this case she had an opportunity of learning, not long after, by overhearing him tell her young charge that she was an angel, and that he asked nothing more of Heaven than to be allowed to follow her lead through life. Now Miss Tina accepted this, as she did all other incense, with great satisfaction. Not that she had the slightest idea of taking this clumsy-footed theological follower round the world with her; but having the highest possible respect for him, knowing that Miss Mehitable and the minister and his wife thought him a person of consideration, she had felt it her duty to *please* him, — had taxed her powers of pleasing to the utmost, in his own line, and had met with this gratifying evidence of success.

Miss Mehitable was for once really angry. She sent for her cousin to a private interview, and thus addressed him: —

"Cousin Mordecai, I thought you were a man of sense when I put this child under your care! My great trouble in bringing her up is, that everybody flatters her and defers to her; but I thought that in you I had got a man that could be depended on!"

"I do *not* flatter her, cousin," replied the young minister, earnestly.

"You pretend you don't flatter her? didn't I hear you calling her an angel?"

"Well, I don't care if I did; she *is* an angel," said Mr. Mordecai Rossiter, with tears in his eyes; "she is the most perfectly heavenly being I ever saw!"

"Ah! bah!" said Miss Mehitable, with intense disgust; "what fools you men are!"

Miss Mehitable now, much as she disliked it, felt bound to have some cautionary conversation with Miss Tina.

"My dear," she said; "you must be very careful in your treatment of Cousin Mordecai. I overheard some things he said to you this morning which I do not approve of."

"O yes, Aunty, he does talk in a silly way sometimes. Men always begin to talk that way to me. Why, you've no idea the things they will say. Well, of course I don't believe them; it's only a foolish way they have, but they all talk just alike."

"But I thought my cousin would have had his mind on better things," said Miss Mehitable. "The idea of his making love to you!"

"I know it; only think of it, Aunty! how very funny it is! and there, I haven't done a single thing to make him. I've been just as religious as I could be, and said hymns to him, and everything, and given him good advice, — ever so much, — because, you see, he didn't know about a great many things till I told him."

"But, my dear, all this is going to make him too fond of you; you know you ought not to be thinking of such things now."

"What things, Aunty?" said the catechumen, innocently.

"Why, love and marriage; that's what such feelings will come to, if you encourage them."

"Marriage! O dear me, what nonsense!" and Tina laughed till the room rang again. "Why, dear Aunty, what absurd ideas have got into your head! Of course you can't think that he's thinking of any such thing; he's only getting very fond of me, and I'm trying to make him have a good time, — that's all."

But Miss Tina found that was not all, and was provoked beyond endurance at the question proposed to her in plain terms, whether she would not look upon her teacher as one destined in a year or two to become her husband. Thereupon at once the whole gay fabric dissolved like a dream. Tina was as vexed at the proposition as a young unbroken colt is at the sight of a halter. She cried, and said she didn't like him, she couldn't bear him, and she never wanted to see him again, — that he was silly and ridiculous to talk so to a little girl. And Miss Mehitable sat down to write a long letter to her brother, to inquire what she should do next.

CHAPTER XXXI

WHAT SHALL WE DO
WITH TINA?

"My dear Brother: — I am in a complete *embarras* what to do with Tina. She is the very light of my eyes, — the sweetest, gayest, brightest, and best-meaning little mortal that ever was made; but somehow or other I fear I am not the one that ought to have undertaken to bring her up.

"She has a good deal of self-will; so much that I have long felt it would be quite impossible for me to control her merely by authority. In fact I laid down my sceptre long ago, such as it was. I never did have much of a gift in that way. But Tina's self-will runs in the channel of a most charming persuasiveness. She has all sorts of pretty phrases, and would talk a bird off from a bush, or a trout out of a brook, by dint of sheer persistent eloquence; and she is always so delightfully certain that her way is the right one and the best for me and all concerned. Then she has no end of those peculiar gifts of entertainment which are rather dangerous things for a young woman. She is a born mimic, she is a natural actress, and she has always a repartee or a smart saying quite *apropos* at the tip of her tongue. All this makes her an immense favorite with people who have no responsibility about her, — who merely want to be amused with her drolleries, and then shake their heads wisely when she is gone, and say that Miss Mehitable Rossiter ought to keep a close hand on that girl.

"It seems to be the common understanding that everybody but me is to spoil her; for there isn't anybody, not even Dr. Lothrop and his wife, that won't connive at her mimicking and fripperies, and then talk gravely with me afterward about the danger of these things, as if I were the only person to say anything disagreeable to her. But then, I can see very plainly that the little chit is in danger on all sides of becoming trivial and superficial, — of mistaking wit for wisdom, and thinking she has answered an argument when she has said a smart thing and raised a laugh.

"Of late, trouble of another kind has been added. Tina is a little turned of fifteen; she is going to be very beautiful; she is very pretty now; and, in addition to all my other perplexities, the men are beginning to talk that atrocious kind of nonsense to her which they seem to think they must talk to young girls. I have had to take her away from the school on account of the schoolmaster, and when I put her under the care of Cousin Mordecai Rossiter, whom I thought old enough, and discreet enough, to make a useful teacher to her, he has acted like a natural fool. I have no kind of patience with him. I would not have believed a man could be so devoid of common sense. I shall have to send Tina somewhere, — though I can't bear to part with her, and it seems like taking the very sunshine out of the house; so I remember what you told me about sending her up to you.

"Lady Lothrop and Lois Badger and I have been talking together, and we think the boys might as well go up too to your academy, as our present schoolmaster is not very competent, and you will give them a thorough fitting for college."

To this came the following reply: —

"Sister Mehitable: — The thing has happened that I have foreseen. Send her up here; she shall board in the minister's family; and his daughter Esther, who is wisest, virtuousest, discreetest, best, shall help keep her in order.

"Send the boys along, too; they are bright fellows, as I remember, and I would like to have a hand at them. One of them might live with us and do the out-door chores and help hoe in the garden, and the other might do the same for the minister. So send them along.

"Your affectionate brother,
"Jonathan Rossiter."

This was an era in our lives. Harry and I from this time felt ourselves to be *men*, and thereafter adopted the habit of speaking of ourselves familiarly as "a man of my character," "a man of my

age," and "a man in my circumstances." The comfort and dignity
which this imparted to us were wonderful. We also discussed Tina
in a very paternal way, and gravely considered what was best for
her. We were, of course, properly shocked at the behavior of the
schoolmaster, and greatly applauded her spirit in defending herself
against his presumption.

Then Tina had told Harry and me all about her trouble with the
minister, and I remember at this time how extremely aged and
venerable I felt, and what quantities of good advice I gave to
Tina, which was all based on the supposition of her dangerously
powerful charms and attractions. This is the edifying kind of
counsel with which young gentlemen of my age instruct their lady
friends, and it will be seen at once that advice and admonition
which rest on the theory of superhuman excellence and attractions
in the advised party are far more agreeable than the rough, common admonitions, generally addressed to boys at this time of life,
which are unseasoned by any such pleasing hallucination.

There is now a general plea in society that women shall be educated more as men are, and we hear much talk as if the difference
between them and our sex is merely one of difference in education.
But how could it be helped that Tina should be educated and
formed wholly unlike Harry and myself, when every address made
to her from her childhood was of necessity wholly different from
what would be made to a boy in the same circumstances? and
particularly when she carried with her always that dizzying, blinding charm which turned the head of every boy and man that
undertook to talk reason to her?

In my own mind I had formed my plan of life. I was to go to
college, and therefrom soar to an unmeasured height of literary
distinction, and when I had won trophies and laurels and renown,
I was to come back and lay all at Tina's feet. This was what Harry
and I agreed on, in many a conversation, as the destined result of
our friendship.

Harry and I had sworn friendship by all the solemn oaths and
forms known in ancient or modern history. We changed names
with each other, and in our private notes and letters addressed
each by the name of the other, and felt as if this was some sacred
and wonderful peculiarity. Tina called us both brothers, and this
we agreed was the best means of preserving her artless mind un-

alarmed and undisturbed until the future hour of the great declaration. As for Tina, she absolutely could not keep anything to herself if she tried. Whatever agitated her mind or interested it had to be told to us. She did not seem able to rest satisfied with herself till she had proved to us that she was exactly right, or made us share her triumphs in her achievements, or her perplexity in her failures.

At this crisis Miss Mehitable talked very seriously and sensibly with her little charge. She pointed out to her the danger of living a trivial and superficial life, — of becoming vain, and living merely for admiration. She showed her how deficient she had been in those attainments which require perseverance and steadiness of mind, and earnestly recommended her now to devote herself to serious studies.

Nobody was a better subject to preach such a sermon to than Tina. She would even take up the discourse and enlarge upon it, and suggest new and fanciful illustrations; she entered into the project of Miss Mehitable with enthusiasm; she confessed all her faults, and resolved hereafter to become a pattern of the contrary virtues. And then she came and related the whole conversation to us, and entered into the project of devoting herself to study with such a glow of enthusiasm, that we formed at once the most brilliant expectations.

The town of Cloudland, whither we were going, was a two days' journey up into the mountains; and, as travelling facilities then were, it was viewed as such an undertaking to send us there, that the whole family conclave talked gravely of it and discussed it in every point of view, for a fortnight before we started. Our Uncle Jacob, the good, meek, quiet farmer of whom I have spoken, had a little business in regard to some property that had been left by a relative of his wife in that place, and suggested the possibility of going up with us himself. So weighty a move was at first thrown out as a mere proposal to be talked of in the family circle. Grandmother and Aunt Lois and Aunt Keziah and my mother picked over and discussed this proposition for days, as a lot of hens will pick over an ear of corn, turning it from side to side, and looking at it from every possible point of view. Uncle Fliakim had serious thoughts of offering his well-worn equipage, but it was universally admitted that his constant charities had kept it in such a condition of frailty that the mountain roads would finish it, and thus deprive multitudes of the female population of Oldtown of an establishment which was about as much their own as if they had the care and keeping of it.

I don't know anybody who could have been taken from Oldtown whose loss would have been more universally felt and deplored than little Miss Tina's. In the first place, Oldtown had come into the way of regarding her as a sort of Child of the Regiment, and then Tina was one of those sociable, acquaintance-making bodies that have visited everybody, penetrated everybody's affairs, and given a friendly lift now and then in almost everybody's troubles.

"Why, lordy massy!" said Sam Lawson, "I don't know nothin' what we're any on us goin' to do when Tiny's gone. Why, there ain't a dog goes into the meetin'-house but wags his tail when he sees her a comin'. I expect she knows about every yellow-bird's nest an' blue jay's an' bobolink's an' meadow-lark's that there's ben round here these five years, an' how they's goin' to set an' hatch without her's best known to 'emselves, I s'pose. Lordy massy! that child can sing so like a skunk blackbird that you can't tell which is which. Wal, I'll say one thing for her; she draws the fire out o' Hepsy, an' she's 'bout the only livin' critter that can; but some nights when she's ben inter our house a playin' checkers or fox an' geese with the child'en, she'd railly git Hepsy slicked down so that 't was kind o' comfortable bein' with her. I'm sorry she's goin', for my part, an' all the child'en'll be sorry."

As for Polly, she worked night and day on Tina's outfit, and scolded and hectored herself for certain tears that now and then dropped on the white aprons that she was ironing. On the night before Tina was to depart, Polly came into her room and insisted upon endowing her with her string of gold beads, the only relic of earthly vanity in which that severe female had ever been known to indulge. Tina was quite melted, and fell upon her neck.

"Why, Polly! No, no; you dear old creature, you, you've been a thousand times too good for me, and I've nearly plagued the life out of you, and you sha'n't give me your poor, dear, old gold beads, but keep them yourself, for you're as good as gold any day, and so it's a great deal better that you should wear them."

"O Tina, child, you don't know my heart," said Polly, shaking her head solemnly; "if you could see the depths of depravity that there are there!"

"I don't believe a word of it, Polly."

"Ah! but, you see, the Lord seeth not as man sees, Tina."

"I know he don't," said Tina; "he's a thousand times kinder, and makes a thousand more excuses for us than we ever do for ourselves or each other. You know the Bible says, 'He knoweth our frame, he remembereth that we are dust.'"

"O Tina, Tina, you always was a wonderful child to talk," said Polly, shaking her head doubtfully; "but then you know the heart is so deceitful, and then you see there's the danger that we should mistake natural emotions for grace."

"O, I dare say there are all sorts of dangers," said Tina; "of course there are. I know I'm nothing but just a poor little silly bird; but He knows it too, and he's taken care of ever so many such little silly people as I am, so that I'm not afraid. He won't let me deceive myself. You know, when that bird got shut in the house the other day, how much time you and I and Miss Mehitable all spent in trying to keep it from breaking its foolish head against the glass, and flying into the fire, and all that, and how glad we were when we got it safe out into the air. I'm sure we are not half as good as God is, and, if we take so much care about a poor little bird that we didn't make and had nothing to do with, he must care a good deal more about us when we are his children. And God is all the Father I have or ever knew."

This certainly looked to Polly like very specious reasoning, but, after all, the faithful creature groaned in spirit. Might not this all be mere natural religion and not the supernatural grace? So she said trembling: "O Tina, did you always feel so towards God? wa'n't there a time when your heart rose in opposition to him?"

"O, certainly," said Tina, "when Miss Asphyxia used to talk to me about it, I thought I never wanted to hear of him, and I never said my prayers; but as soon as I came to Aunty, she was so loving and kind that I began to see what God must be like, — because I know he is kinder than she can be, or you, or anybody can be. That's so, isn't it? You know the Bible says his loving-kindness is infinite."

The thing in this speech which gave Polly such peculiar satisfaction was the admission that there had been a definite point of time in which the feelings of her little friend had undergone a distinct change. Henceforth she was better satisfied, — never reflecting how much she was trusting to a mere state of mind in the child, instead of resting her faith on the Almighty Friend who so evidently had held her in charge during the whole of her short history.

As for me, the eve of my departure was to me one of triumph. When I had seen all my father's Latin books fairly stowed away in my trunk, with the very simple wardrobe which belonged to Harry and me, and the trunk had been shut and locked and corded, and we were to start at sunrise the next morning, I felt as if my father's unfulfilled life-desire was at last going to be accomplished in me.

It was a bright, clear, starlight night in June, and we were warned to go to bed early, that we might be ready in season the next morning. As usual, Harry fell fast asleep, and I was too nervous and excited to close my eyes. I began to think of the old phantasmagoria of my childish days, which now so seldom appeared to me. I felt stealing over me that peculiar thrill and vibration of the great central nerves which used to indicate the approach of those phenomena, and, looking up, I saw distinctly my father, exactly as I used to see him, standing between the door and the bed. It seemed to me that he entered by passing through the door, but there he was, every line and lineament of his face, every curl of his hair, exactly as I remembered it. His eyes were fixed on mine with a tender human radiance. There was something soft and compassionate about the look he gave me, and I felt it vibrating on my nerves with that peculiar electric thrill of which I have spoken. I learned by such interviews as these how spirits can communicate with one another without human language.

The appearance of my father was vivid and real even to the clothing that he used to wear, which was earthly and home-like, precisely as I remembered it. Yet I felt no disposition to address him, and no need of words. Gradually the image faded; it grew thinner and fainter, and I saw the door through it as if it had been a veil, and then it passed away entirely.

What are these apparitions? I know that this will be read by many who have seen them quite as plainly as I have, who, like me, have hushed back the memory of them into the most secret and silent chambers of their hearts.

I know, with regard to myself, that the sight of my father was accompanied by such a vivid conviction of the reality of his presence, such an assurance radiated from his serene eyes that he had at last found the secret of eternal peace, such an intense conviction of continued watchful affection and of sympathy in the course that I was now beginning, that I could not have doubted if I would. And when we remember that, from the beginning of the world, some such possible communication between departed love and the beloved on earth has been among the most cherished legends of humanity, why must we always meet such phenomena with a resolute determination to account for them by every or any supposition but that which the human heart most craves? Is not the great mystery of life and death made more cruel and inexorable by this rigid incredulity? One would fancy, to hear some moderns talk, that there was no possibility that the departed, even when most tender and most earnest, could, if they would, recall themselves to their earthly friends.

For my part, it was through some such experiences as these that I learned that there are truths of the spiritual life which are intuitive, and above logic, which a man must believe because he cannot help it, — just as he believes the facts of his daily experience in the world of matter, though most ingenious and unanswerable treatises have been written to show that there is no proof of its existence.

CHAPTER XXXII

THE JOURNEY TO CLOUDLAND

The next morning Aunt Lois rapped at our door, when there was the very faintest red streak in the east, and the birds were just in the midst of that vociferous singing which nobody knows anything about who isn't awake at this precise hour. We were forward enough to be up and dressed, and, before our breakfast was through, Uncle Jacob came to the door.

The agricultural population of Massachusetts, at this time, were a far more steady set as regards locomotion than they are in these days of railroads. At this time, a journey from Boston to New York took a fortnight, — a longer time than it now takes to go to Europe, — and my Uncle Jacob had never been even to Boston. In fact, the seven-mile tavern in the neighborhood had been the extent of his wanderings, and it was evident that he regarded the two days' journey as quite a solemn event in his life. He had given a fortnight's thought to it; he had arranged all his worldly affairs, and given charges and messages to his wife and children, in case, as he said, "anything should happen to him." And he informed Aunt Lois that he had been awake the biggest part of the night thinking it over. But when he had taken Tina and her little trunk on board, and we had finished all our hand-shakings, and Polly had told us over for the fourth or fifth time exactly where she had put the cold chicken and the biscuits and the cakes and pie, and Miss Mehitable had cautioned Tina again and again to put on her shawl in case a shower should come up, and my grandmother and Aunt Lois had put in their share of parting admonitions, we at last trolled off as cheery and merry a set of youngsters as the sun ever looked upon in a dewy June morning.

Our road lay first along the beautiful brown river, with its sweeping bends, and its prattling curves of water dashing and chattering over mossy rocks. Towards noon we began to find ourselves winding up and up amid hemlock forests, whose solemn shadows were all radiant and aglow with clouds of blossoming laurel. We had long hills to wind up, when we got out and walked, and gathered flowers, and scampered, and chased the brook up stream from one little dashing waterfall to another, and then, suddenly darting out upon the road again, we would meet the wagon at the top of the hill.

Can there be anything on earth so beautiful as these mountain rides in New England? At any rate we were full in the faith that there could not. When we were riding in the wagon, Tina's powers of entertainment were brought into full play. The great success of the morning was her exact imitation of a squirrel eating a nut, which she was requested to perform many times, and which she did, with variations, until at last Uncle Jacob remarked, with a grin, that "if he should meet her and a squirrel sitting on a stone fence together, he believed he shouldn't know which was which."

Besides this, we acted various impromptu plays, assuming characters and supporting them as we had been accustomed to do in our theatrical rehearsals in the garret, till Uncle Jacob declared that he never did see such a musical set as we were. About nightfall we came to Uncle Sim Geary's tavern, which had been fixed upon for our stopping-place. This was neither more nor less than a mountain farm-house, where the few travellers who ever passed that way could find accommodation.

Uncle Jacob, after seeing to his horses, and partaking of a plentiful supper, went immediately to bed, as was his innocent custom every evening, as speedily as possible. To bed, but not to sleep, for when, an hour or two afterward, I had occasion to go into his room, I found him lying on his bed with his clothes on, his shoes merely slipped off, and his hat held securely over the pit of his stomach.

"Why, Uncle Jacob," said I, "aren't you going to bed?"

"Well, I guess I'll just lie down as I be; no knowin' what may happen when you're travelling. It's a very nice house, and a very respectable family, but it's best always to be prepared for anything that may happen. So I think you children had better all go to bed and keep quiet."

What roars of laughter there were among us when I described this scene and communicated the message of Uncle Jacob! It seemed as if Tina could not be got to sleep that night, and we

could hear her giggling, through the board partition that separated our room from hers, every hour of the night.

Happy are the days when one can go to sleep and wake up
laughing. The next morning, however, Uncle Jacob reaped the
reward of his vigilance by finding himself ready dressed at six
o'clock, when I came in and found him sleeping profoundly.
The fact was, that, having kept awake till near morning, he was
sounder asleep at this point of time than any of us, and was
snoring away like a grist-mill. He remarked that he shouldn't
wonder if he had dropped asleep, and added, in a solemn tone,
"We've got through the night wonderfully, all things considered."

The next day's ride was the same thing over, only the hills
were longer; and by and by we came into great vistas of mountains, whose cloudy purple heads seemed to stretch and veer
around our path like the phantasmagoria of a dream. Sometimes
the road seemed to come straight up against an impenetrable
wall, and we would wonder what we were to do with it; but lo!
as we approached, the old mountain seemed gracefully to slide
aside, and open to us a passage round it. Tina found ever so many
moralities and poetical images in these mountains. It was like
life, she said. Your way would seem all shut up before you, but,
if you only had faith and went on, the mountains would move
aside for you and let you through.

Towards night we began to pull in earnest up a series of as-
cents toward the little village of Cloudland. Hill after hill, hill
after hill, how long they seemed! but how beautiful it was when
the sun went down over the distant valleys! and there was such
a pomp and glory of golden clouds and rosy vapors wreathing
around the old mountain-tops as one must go to Cloudland to
know anything about.

At last we came to a little terrace of land, where were a white
meeting-house, and a store, and two or three houses, and to the
door of one of these our wagon drove. There stood Mr. Jonathan
Rossiter and the minister and Esther. You do not know Esther,
do you? neither at this minute did we. We saw a tall, straight,
graceful girl, who looked at us out of a pair of keen, clear, hazel
eyes, with a sort of inquisitive yet not unkindly glance, but as if
she meant to make up her mind about us; and when she looked
at Tina I could see that her mind was made up in a moment.

"CLOUDLAND, June 6.

"Here we are, dear Aunty, up in the skies, in the most beautiful place that you can possibly conceive of. We had such a good time coming! you've no idea of the fun we had. You know I am going to be very sober, but I didn't think it was necessary to begin while we were travelling, and we kept Uncle Jacob laughing so that I really think he must have been tired.

"Do you know, Aunty, I have got so that I can look exactly like a squirrel? We saw ever so many on the way, and I got a great many new hints on the subject, and now I can do squirrel in four or five different attitudes, and the boys almost killed themselves laughing.

"Harry is an old sly-boots. Do you know, he is just as much of a mimic as I am, for all he looks so sober; but when we get him a going he is perfectly killing. He and I and Horace acted all sorts of plays on the way. We agreed with each other that we'd give a set of Oldtown representations, and see if Uncle Jacob would know who they were, and so Harry was Sam Lawson and I was Hepsy, and I made an unexceptionable baby out of our two shawls, and Horace was Uncle Fliakim come in to give us moral exhortations. I do wish you could hear how we did it. Uncle Jacob isn't the brightest of all mortals, and not very easily roused, but we made him laugh till he said his sides were sore; and to pay for it he made us laugh when we got to the tavern where we stopped all night. Do you believe, Aunty, Uncle Jacob really was frightened, or care-worn, or something, so that he hardly slept any all night? It was just the quietest place that ever you saw, and there was a good motherly woman, who got us the nicest kind of supper, and a peaceable, slow, dull old man, just like Uncle Jacob. There wasn't the least thing that looked as if we had fallen into a cave of banditti, or a castle in the Apennines, such as Mrs. Radcliffe tells about in the Mysteries of Udolpho; but, for all that, Uncle Jacob's mind was so oppressed with care that he went to bed with all his clothes on, and lay broad awake with his hat in his hand all night. I didn't think before that Uncle Jacob had such a brilliant imagination. Poor man! I should have thought he would have lain down and slept as peacefully as one of his own oxen.

"We got up into Cloudland about half past six o'clock in the afternoon, the second day; and such a sunset! I thought of a good subject for a little poem, and wrote two or three verses, which I'll send you some time; but I must tell you now about the people here.

"I don't doubt I shall become very good, for just think what a place I am in, — living at the minister's! and then I room with Esther! You ought to see Esther. She's a beautiful girl; she's tall, and straight, and graceful, with smooth black hair, and piercing dark eyes that look as if they could read your very soul. Her face has the features of a statue, at least such as I think some of the beautiful statues that I've read about might have; and what makes it more statuesque is, that she's so very pale; she is perfectly healthy, but there doesn't seem to be any red blood in her cheeks; and, dear Aunty, she is alarmingly good. She knows so much, and does so much, that it is really discouraging to me to think of it. Why, do you know, she has read through Virgil, and is reading a Greek tragedy now with Mr. Rossiter; and she teaches a class in mathematics in school, besides being her father's only house-keeper, and taking care of her younger brothers.

"I should be frightened to death at so much goodness, if it were not that she seems to have taken the greatest possible fancy to me. As I told you, we room together; and such a nice room as it is! everything is just like wax; and she gave me half of everything, — half the drawers and half the closet, and put all my things so nicely in their places, and then in the morning she gets up at unheard-of hours, and she was beginning to pet me and tell me that I needn't get up. Now you know, Aunty, that's just the way people are always doing with me, and the way poor dear old Polly would spoil me; but I told Esther all about my new resolutions and exactly how good I intended to be, and that I thought I couldn't do better than to do everything that she did, and so when she gets up I get up; and really, Aunty, you've no idea what a sight the sunrise is here in the mountains; it really is worth getting up for.

"We have breakfast at six o'clock, and then there are about three hours before school, and I help Esther wash up the break-fast things, and we make our bed and sweep our room, and put everything up nice, and then I have ever so long to study, while Esther is seeing to all her family cares and directing black Dinah about the dinner, and settling any little cases that may arise among her three younger brothers. They are great, strong, nice boys, with bright red cheeks, and a good capacity for making a noise, but she manages them nicely. Dear Aunty, I hope some of her virtues will rub off on to me by contact; don't you?

"I don't think your brother likes me much. He hardly noticed me at all when I was first presented to him, and seemed to have forgotten that he had ever seen me. I tried to talk to him, but he cut me quite short, and turned round and went to talking to Mr. Avery, the minister, you know. I think that these people that know so much might be civil to us little folks, but then I dare say it's all right enough; but sometimes it does seem as if he wanted to snub me. Well, perhaps it's good for me to be snubbed: I have such good times generally that I ought to have something that isn't quite so pleasant.

"Life is to me such a beautiful story! and every morning when I open my eyes and see things looking so charming as they do here, I thank God that I am alive.

"Mr. Rossiter has been examining the boys in their studies. He isn't a man that ever praises anybody, I suppose, but I can see that he is pretty well pleased with them. We have a lady principal, Miss Titcomb. She is about forty years old, I should think, and very pleasant and affable. I shall tell you more about these things by and by.

"Give my love to dear old Polly, and to grandma and Aunt Lois, and all the nice folks in Oldtown.

"Dear Aunty, sometimes I used to think that you were depressed, and had troubles that you did not tell me; and something you said once about your life being so wintry made me quite sad. Do let me be your little Spring, and think always how dearly I love you, and how good I am going to try to be for your sake.

"Your own affectionate little

"TINA."

CHAPTER XXXIII

SCHOOL-LIFE IN CLOUDLAND

The academy in Cloudland was one of those pure wells from which the hidden strength of New England is drawn, as her broad rivers are made from hidden mountain brooks. The first object of every colony in New England, after building the church, was to establish a school-house; and a class of the most superior men of New England, in those days of simple living, were perfectly satisfied to make it the business of their lives to teach in the small country academies with which the nooks and hollows of New England were filled.

Could materials be got as profuse as Boswell's Life of Johnson to illustrate the daily life and table-talk of some of the academy schoolmasters of this period, it would be an acquisition for the world.

For that simple, pastoral germ-state of society is a thing forever gone. Never again shall we see that union of perfect repose in regard to outward surroundings and outward life with that intense activity of the inward and intellectual world, that made New England, at this time, the vigorous, germinating seed-bed for all that has since been developed of politics, laws, letters, and theology, through New England to America, and through America to the world. The hurry of railroads, and the rush and roar of business that now fill it, would have prevented that germinating process. It was necessary that there should be a period like that we describe, when villages were each a separate little democracy, shut off by rough roads and forests from the rest of the world, organized round the church and school as a common centre, and formed by the minister and the schoolmaster.

The academy of Cloudland had become celebrated in the neighborhood for the skill and ability with which it was conducted, and pupils had been drawn, even from as far as Boston, to come and sojourn in our mountain town to partake of these advantages.

They were mostly young girls, who were boarded at very simple rates in the various families of the place. In all, the pupils of the academy numbered about a hundred, equally divided between the two sexes. There was a class of about fifteen young men who were preparing for college, and a greater number of boys who were studying with the same ultimate hope.

As a general rule, the country academies of Massachusetts have been equally open to both sexes. Andover and Exeter, so far as I know, formed the only exceptions to this rule, being by their charters confined rigorously to the use of the dominant sex. But, in the generality of country academies, the girls and boys studied side by side, without any other restriction as to the character of their studies than personal preference. As a general thing, the classics and the higher mathematics were more pursued by the boys than the girls. But if there were a daughter of Eve who wished, like her mother, to put forth her hand to the tree of knowledge, there was neither cherubim nor flaming sword to drive her away.

Mr. Rossiter was always stimulating the female part of his subjects to such undertakings, and the consequence was that in his school an unusual number devoted themselves to these pursuits, and the leading scholar in Greek and the higher mathematics was our new acquaintance, Esther Avery.

The female principal, Miss Titcomb, was a thorough-bred, old-fashioned lady, whose views of education were formed by Miss Hannah More, and whose style, like Miss Hannah More's, was profoundly Johnsonian. This lady had composed a set of rules for the conduct of the school, in the most ornate and resounding periods. The rules, briefly epitomized, required of us *only* absolute moral perfection, but they were run into details which caused the reading of them to take up about a quarter of an hour every Saturday morning. I would that I could remember some of the sentences. It was required of us all, for one thing, that we should be perfectly polite. "Persons truly polite," it was added, "invariably treat their superiors with reverence, their equals with exact consideration, and their inferiors with condescension." Again, under the head of manners, we were warned, "not to consider romping as indicative of sprightliness, or loud laughter a mark of wit."

The scene every Saturday morning, when these rules were read to a set of young people on whom the mountain air acted like champagne, and among whom both romping and loud laughter were fearfully prevalent, was sufficiently edifying.

There was also a system of marks, quite complicated, by which our departure from any of these virtuous proprieties was indicated. After a while, however, the reciting of these rules, like the reading of the Ten Commandments in churches, and a great deal of other good substantial reading, came to be looked upon only as a Saturday morning decorum, and the Johnsonian periods, which we all knew by heart, were principally useful in pointing a joke. Nevertheless, we were not a badly behaved set of young people.

Miss Titcomb exercised a general supervision over the manners, morals, and health of the young ladies connected with the institution, taught history and geography, and also gave especial attention to female accomplishments. These, so far as I could observe, consisted largely in embroidering mourning pieces, with a family monument in the centre, a green ground worked in chenille and floss silk, with an exuberant willow-tree, and a number of weeping mourners, whose faces were often concealed by flowing pocket-handkerchiefs.

Pastoral pieces were also in great favor, representing fair young shepherdesses sitting on green chenille banks, with crooks in their hands, and tending some animals of an uncertain description, which were to be received by faith as sheep. The sweet, confiding innocence which regarded the making of objects like these as more suited to the tender female character than the pursuit of Latin and mathematics, was characteristic of the ancient *régime*. Did not Penelope embroider, and all sorts of princesses, ancient and modern? and was not embroidery a true feminine grace? Even Esther Avery, though she found no time for works of this kind, looked upon it with respect, as an accomplishment for which nature unfortunately had not given her a taste.

Mr. Rossiter, although he of course would not infringe on the kingdom of his female associate, treated these accomplishments with a scarce concealed contempt. It was, perhaps, the frosty atmosphere of scepticism which he breathed about him touching those works of art, that prevented his favorite scholars from going far in the direction of such accomplishments. The fact is, that Mr. Rossiter, during the sailor period of his life, had been to the Mediterranean, had seen the churches of Spain and Italy, and knew what Murillos and Titians were like, which may account somewhat for the glances of civil amusement which he sometimes cast over into Miss Titcomb's department, when the adjuncts and accessories of a family tombstone were being eagerly discussed.

Mr. Jonathan Rossiter held us all by the sheer force of his personal character and will, just as the ancient mariner held the wedding guest with his glittering eye. He so utterly scorned and contemned a lazy scholar, that trifling and inefficiency in study were scorched and withered by the very breath of his nostrils. We were so awfully afraid of his opinion, we so hoped for his good word and so dreaded his contempt, and we so verily believed that no such man ever walked this earth, that he had only to shake his ambrosial locks and give the nod, to settle us all as to any matter whatever.

In an age when in England schools were managed by the grossest and most brutal exercise of corporal punishment, the schoolmasters of New England, to a great extent, had entirely dropped all resort to such barbarous measures, and carried on their schools as republics, by the sheer force of moral and intellectual influences. Mr. Jonathan Rossiter would have been ashamed of himself at even the suggestion of caning a boy, — as if he were incapable of any higher style of government. And yet never was a man more feared and his will had in more awful regard. Mr. Rossiter was sparing of praise, but his praise bore a value in proportion to its scarcity. It was like diamonds and rubies, — few could have it, but the whole of his little commonwealth were working for it.

He scorned all conventional rules in teaching, and he would not tolerate a mechanical lesson, and took delight in puzzling his pupils and breaking up all routine business by startling and unexpected questions and assertions. He compelled every one to think, and to think for himself. "Your heads may not be the best in the world," was one of his sharp, off-hand sayings, "but they are the best God has given you, and you must use them for yourselves."

To tell the truth, he used his teaching somewhat as a mental gratification for himself. If there was a subject he wanted to investigate, or an old Greek or Latin author that he wanted to dig out, he would put a class on it, without the least regard to whether it was in the course of college preparation or not, and if a word was said by any poor mechanical body, he would blast out upon him with a sort of despotic scorn.

"Learn to read Greek perfectly," he said, "and it's no matter what you read"; or, "Learn to use your own heads, and you can learn anything."

There was little idling and no shirking in his school, but a slow, dull, industrious fellow, if he showed a disposition to work steadily, got more notice from him than even a bright one.

Mr. Rossiter kept house by himself in a small cottage adjoining that of the minister. His housekeeper, Miss Minerva Randall, generally known to the village as "Miss Nervy Randall," was one of those preternaturally well-informed old mermaids who, so far as I know, are a peculiar product of the State of Maine. Study and work had been the two passions of her life, and in neither could she be excelled by man or woman. Single-handed, and without a servant, she performed all the labors of Mr. Jonathan Rossiter's little establishment. She washed for him, ironed for him, plaited his ruffled shirts in neatest folds, brushed his clothes, cooked his food, occasionally hoed in the garden, trained flowers around the house, and found, also, time to read Greek and Latin authors, and to work out problems in mathematics and surveying and navigation, and to take charge of boys in reading Virgil.

Miss Minerva Randall was one of those female persons who are of Sojourner Truth's opinion, — that if women want any rights they had better take them, and say nothing about it. Her *sex* had never occurred to her as a reason for doing or not doing anything which her hand found to do. In the earlier part of her life, for the mere love of roving and improving her mind by seeing foreign countries, she had gone on a Mediterranean voyage with her brother Zachariah Randall, who was wont to say of her that she was a better mate than any man he could find. And true enough, when he was confined to his berth with a fever, Miss Minerva not only nursed him, but navigated the ship home in the most matter-of-fact way in the world. She had no fol-de-rol about woman's rights, but she was always wide-awake to perceive when a thing was to be done, and to do it. Nor did she ever after in her life talk of this exploit as a thing to be boasted of, seeming to regard it as a matter too simple, and entirely in the natural course of things, to be mentioned. Miss Minerva, however, had not enough of the external illusive charms of her sex, to suggest to a casual spectator any doubt on that score of the propriety of her doing or not doing anything. Although she had not precisely the air of a man, she had very little of what usually suggests the associations of femininity. There was a sort of fishy quaintness about her that awakened grim ideas of some unknown ocean product, — a wild and withered appearance, like a wind-blown juniper on a sea promontory, — unsightly and stunted, yet not, after all, commonplace or vulgar. She was short, square, and broad, and the circumference of her waist was if anything greater where that of other females decreases. What the color of her hair might have been in days of youthful bloom was not apparent; but she had, when we knew her, thin tresses of a pepper-and-salt mixture of tint, combed tightly, and twisted in a very small nut on the back of her head, and fastened with a reddish-yellowish horn comb. Her small black eyes were overhung by a grizzled thicket of the same mixed color as her hair. For the graces of the toilet, Miss Nervy had no particular esteem. Her clothing and her person, as well as her housekeeping and belongings, were of a scrupulous and wholesome neatness; but the idea of any other beauty than that of utility had never suggested itself to her mind. She wore always a stuff petticoat of her own spinning, with a striped linen short gown, and probably in all her life never expended twenty dollars a year for clothing; and yet Miss Nervy was about the happiest female person whose acquaintance it has ever been my fortune to make. She had just as much as she wanted of exactly the two things she liked best in the world, — books and work, and when her work was done, there were the books, and life could give no more. Miss Nervy had no sentiment, — not a particle of romance, — she was the most perfectly contented mortal that could possibly be imagined. As to station and position, she was as well known and highly respected in Cloudland as the schoolmaster himself: she was one of the fixed facts of the town, as much as the meeting-house. Days came and went, and spring flowers and autumn leaves succeeded each other, and boys and girls, like the spring flowers and autumn leaves, came and went in Cloudland Academy, but there was always Miss Nervy Randall, not a bit older, not a bit changed, doing her spinning and her herb-drying, working over her butter and plaiting Mr. Jonathan's ruffled shirts and teaching her Virgil class. What gave a piquancy to Miss Nervy's discourse was, that she always clung persistently to the racy Yankee dialect of her childhood, and when she was discoursing of Latin and the classics the idioms made a droll mixture. She was the most invariably good-natured of mortals, and helpful to the last degree; and she would always stop her kitchen work, take her hands out of the bread, or turn away from her yeast in a critical moment, to show a puzzled boy the way through a hard Latin sentence.

"Why, don't you know what that 'ere is?" she would say. "That 'ere is part of the gerund in *dum;* you've got to decline it, and then you'll find it. Look here!" she'd say; "run that 'ere through the moods an' tenses, and ye'll git it in the subjunctive"; or, "Massy, child! that 'ere is one o' the deponent verbs. 'T ain't got any active form; them deponent verbs allus does trouble boys till they git used to 'em."

Now these provincialisms might have excited the risibles of so keen a set of grammarians as we were, only that Miss Randall was a dead shot in any case of difficulty presented by the learned languages. No matter how her English phrased it, she had taught so many boys that she knew evey hard rub and difficult stepping-stone and tight place in the Latin grammar by heart, and had relief at her tongue's end for any distressed beginner.

In the cottage over which Miss Randall presided, Harry and I had our room, and we were boarded at the master's table; and so far we were fortunate. Our apartment, which was a roof-room of a gambrel-roofed cottage, was, to be sure, unplastered and carpet-less; but it looked out through the boughs of a great apple-tree, up a most bewildering blue vista of mountains, whence the sight of a sunset was something forever to be remembered. All our physical appointments, though rustically plain, were kept by Miss Nervy in the utmost perfection of neatness. She had as great a passion for soap and sand as she had for Greek roots, and probably for the same reason. These wild sea-coast countries seemed to produce a sort of superfluity of energy which longed to wreak itself on something, and delighted in digging and delving mentally as well as physically.

Our table had a pastoral perfection in the articles of bread and butter, with honey furnished by Miss Minerva's bees, and game and fish brought in by the united woodcraft of the minister and Mr. Rossiter.

Mr. Rossiter pursued all the natural sciences with an industry and enthusiasm only possible to a man who lives in so lonely and retired a place as Cloudland, and who has, therefore, none of the thousand dissipations of time resulting from our modern system of intercommunication, which is fast producing a state of shallow and superficial knowledge. He had a ponderous herbarium, of some forty or fifty folios, of his own collection and arrangement, over which he gloated with affectionate pride. He had a fine mineralogical cabinet; and there was scarcely a ledge of rocks within a circuit of twelve miles that had not resounded to the tap of his stone hammer and furnished specimens for his collection; and he had an entomologic collection, where luckless bugs impaled on steel pins stuck in thin sheets of cork struggled away a melancholy existence, martyrs to the taste for science. The tenderhearted among us sometimes ventured a remonstrance in favor of these hapless beetles, but were silenced by the authoritative dictum of Mr. Rossiter. "Insects," he declared, "are unsusceptible of pain, the structure of their nervous organization forbidding the idea, and their spasmodic action being simply nervous contraction." As nobody has ever been inside of a beetle to certify to the contrary, and as the race have no mode of communication, we all found it comfortable to put implicit faith in Mr. Rossiter's statements till better advised.

It was among the awe-inspiring legends that were current of Mr. Rossiter in the school, that he corresponded with learned men in Norway and Sweden, Switzerland and France, to whom he sent specimens of American plants and minerals and insects, receiving in return those of other countries. Even in that remote day, little New England had her eyes and her thoughts and her hands everywhere where ship could sail.

Mr. Rossiter dearly loved to talk and to teach, and out of school-hours it was his delight to sit surrounded by his disciples, to answer their questions, and show them his herbarium and his cabinet, to organize woodland tramps, and to start us on researches similar to his own. It was fashionable in his school to have private herbariums and cabinets, and before a month was passed our garret-room began to look quite like a grotto. In short, Mr. Rossiter's system resembled that of those gardeners who, instead of bending all their energies toward making a handsome head to a young tree, encourage it to burst out in suckers clear down to the root, bringing every part of it into vigorous life and circulation.

I still remember the blessed old fellow, as he used to sit among us on the steps of his house, in some of those resplendent moonlight nights which used to light up Cloudland like a fairy dream. There he still sits, in memory, with his court around him, — Esther, with the thoughtful shadows in her eyes and the pensive Psyche profile, and Tina, ever restless, changing, enthusiastic, Harry with his sly, reticent humor and silent enjoyment, and he, our master, talking of everything under the sun, past, present, and to come, — of the cathedrals and pictures of Europe, describing those he had not seen apparently with as minute a knowledge as those he had, — of plants and animals, — of the ancients and the moderns, — of theology, metaphysics, grammar, rhetoric, or whatever came uppermost, — always full and suggestive, startling us with paradoxes, provoking us to arguments, setting us out to run eager tilts of discussion with him, yet in all holding us in a state of unmeasured admiration. Was he conscious, our great man and master, of that weakness of his nature which made an audience, and an admiring one, always a necessity to him? Of a soul naturally self-distrustful and melancholy, he needed to be constantly reinforced and built up in his own esteem by the suffrage of others. What seemed the most trenchant self-assertion in him was, after all, only the desperate struggles of a drowning man to keep his head above water; and, though he seemed at times to despise us all, our good opinion, our worship and reverence, were the raft that kept him from sinking in despair.

The first few weeks that Tina was in school, it was evident that Mr. Rossiter considered her as a spoiled child of fortune, whom the world had conspired to injure by over-much petting. He appeared resolved at once to change the atmosphere and the diet. For some time in school it seemed as if she could do nothing to please him. He seemed determined to put her through a sort of Spartan drill, with hard work and small praise.

Tina had received from nature and womanhood that inspiration in dress and toilet attraction which led her always and instinctively to some little form of personal adornment. Every wild spray or fluttering vine in our woodland rambles seemed to suggest to her some caprice of ornamentation. Each day she had some new thing in her hair, — now a feathery fern-leaf, and anon some wild red berry, whose presence just where she placed it was as picturesque as a French lithograph; and we boys were in the habit of looking each day to see what she would wear next. One morning she came into school, fair as Ariadne, with her viny golden curls rippling over and around a crown of laurel-blossoms. She seemed to us like a little woodland poem. We all looked at her, and complimented her, and she received our compliments, as she always did coin of that sort, with the most undisguised and radiant satisfaction. Mr. Rossiter was in one of his most savage humors this morning, and eyed the pretty toilet grimly. "If you had only an equal talent for ornamenting the *inside* of your head," he said to her, "there might be some hopes of you."

Tears of mortification came into Tina's eyes, as she dashed the offending laurel-blossoms out of the window, and bent resolutely over her book. At recess-time she strolled out with me into the pine woods back of the school-house, and we sat down on a mossy log together, and I comforted her and took her part.

"I don't care, Horace," she said, — "I don't care!" and she dashed the tears out of her eyes. "I'll *make* that man like me yet, — you see if I don't. He shall like me before I'm done with him, so there! I don't care how much he scolds. I'll give in to him, and do exactly as he tells me, but I'll conquer him, — you see if I don't."

And true enough Miss Tina from this time brushed her curly hair straight as such rebellious curls possibly could be brushed, and dressed herself as plainly as Esther, and went at study as if her life depended on it. She took all Mr. Rossiter's snubs and despiteful sayings with the most prostrate humility, and now we began to learn, to our astonishment, what a mind the little creature had. In all my experience of human beings, I never saw one who learned so easily as she. It was but a week or two after she began the Latin grammar before, jumping over all the intermediate books, she alighted in a class in Virgil among scholars who had been studying for a year, and kept up with them, and in some respects stood clearly as the first scholar. The *vim* with which the little puss went at it, the zeal with which she turned over the big dictionary and whirled the leaves of the grammar, the almost inspiration which she showed in seizing the poetical shading of words over which her more prosaic companions blundered, were matters of never-ending astonishment and admiration to Harry and myself. At the end of the first week she gravely announced to us that she intended to render Virgil into English verse; and we had not the smallest doubt that she would do it, and were so immensely wrought up about it that we talked of it after we went to bed that night. Tina, in fact, had produced quite a clever translation of the first ten lines of "Arma virumque," &c. and we wondered what Mr. Rossiter would say to it. One of us stepped in and laid it on his writing-desk.

"Which of you boys did this?" he said the next morning, in not a disapproving tone.

There was a pause, and he slowly read the lines aloud.

"Pretty fair!" he said, — "pretty fair! I shouldn't be surprised if that boy should be able to write English one of these days."

"If you please, sir," said I, "it's Miss Tina Percival that wrote that."

Tina's cheeks were red enough as he handed her back her poetry.

"Not bad," he said, — "not bad; keep on as you've begun, and you may come to something yet."

This scanty measure of approbation was interpreted as high praise, and we complimented Tina on her success. The project of making a poetical translation of Virgil, however, was not carried out, though every now and then she gave us little jets and spurts, which kept up our courage.

Bless me, how we did study everything in that school! English grammar, for instance. The whole school was divided into a certain number of classes, each under a leader, and at the close of every term came on a great examination, which was like a tournament or passage at arms in matters of the English language. To beat in this great contest of knowledge was what excited all our energies. Mr. Rossiter searched out the most difficult specimens of English literature for us to parse, and we were given to understand that he was laying up all the most abstruse problems of grammar to propound to us. All that might be raked out from the coarse print and the fine print of grammar was to be brought to bear on us; and the division that knew the most — the division that could not be puzzled by any subtlety, that had anticipated every possible question, and was prepared with an answer — would be the victorious division, and would be crowned with laurels as glorious in our eyes as those of the old Olympic games. For a week we talked, spoke, and dreamed of nothing but English grammar. Each division sat in solemn, mysterious conclave, afraid lest one of its mighty secrets of wisdom should possibly take wing and be plundered by some of the outlying scouts of another division.

We had for a subject Satan's address to the sun, in Milton, which in our private counsels we tore limb from limb with as little remorse as the anatomist dissects a once lovely human body. The town doctor was a noted linguist and grammarian, and his son was contended for by all the divisions, as supposed to have access to the fountain of his father's wisdom on these subjects; and we were so happy in the balloting as to secure him for our side. Esther was our leader, and we were all in the same division, and our excitement was indescribable. We had also to manage a quotation from Otway, which I remember contained the clause, "Were the world on fire." To parse "on fire" was a problem which kept the eyes of the whole school waking. Each division had its theory, of which it spoke mysteriously in the presence of outsiders; but we had George Norton, and George had been in solemn consultation with Dr. Norton. Never shall I forget the excitement as he came rushing up to our house at nine o'clock at night with the last results of his father's analysis. We shut the doors and shut the windows, — for who knew what of the enemy might be listening? — and gathered breathlessly around him, while in a low, mysterious voice he unfolded to us how to parse "on fire." At that moment George Norton enjoyed the full pleasure of being a distinguished individual, if he never did before or after.

Mr. Rossiter all this while was like the Egyptian Sphinx, perfectly unfathomable, and severely resolved to sift and test us to the utmost.

Ah, well! to think of the glories of the day when our division beat! — for we did beat. We ran along neck and neck with Ben Baldwin's division, for Ben was an accomplished grammarian, and had picked up one or two recondite pieces of information wherewith he threatened for a time to turn our flank, but the fortunes of the field were reversed when it came to the phrase "on fire," and our success was complete and glorious. It was well to have this conflict over, for I don't believe that Tina slept one night that week without dreams of particles and prepositions, — Tina, who was as full of the enthusiasm of everything that was going on as a flossy evening cloud is of light, and to whose health I really do believe a defeat might have caused a serious injury.

Never shall I forget Esther, radiant, grave, and resolved, as she sat in the midst of her division through all the fluctuations of the contest. A little bright spot had come in each of her usually pale cheeks, and her eyes glowed with a fervor which showed that she had it in her to have defended a fortress, or served a cannon, like the Maid of Saragossa. We could not have felt more if our division had been our country and she had led us in triumph through a battle.

Besides grammar, we gave great attention to rhetoric. We studied Dr. Blair with the same kind of thoroughness with which we studied the English grammar. Every week a division of the school was appointed to write compositions; but there was, besides, a call for volunteers, and Mr. Rossiter had a smile of approbation for those who volunteered to write every week; and so we were always among that number.

It was remarkable that the very best writers, as a general thing, were among the female part of the school. There were several young men, of nineteen and twenty years of age, whose education had been retarded by the necessity of earning for themselves the money which was to support them while preparing for college. They were not boys, they were men, and, generally speaking, men of fine minds and fine characters. Some of them have since risen to distinction, and acted leading parts at Washington. But, for all that, the best writers of the school, as I have before said, were the girls. Nor was the standard of writing low: Mr. Rossiter had the most withering scorn for ordinary sentimental nonsense and school-girl platitudes. If a bit of weakly poetry got running among the scholars, he was sure to come down upon it with such an absurd parody that nobody could ever recall it again without a laugh.

We wrote on such subjects as "The Difference between the Natural and Moral Sublime," "The Comparative Merits of Milton and Shakespeare," "The Comparative Merits of the Athenian and

Lacedæmonian Systems of Education." Sometimes, also, we wrote criticisms. If, perchance, the master picked up some verbose Fourth of July oration, or some sophomorical newspaper declamation, he delivered it over to our tender mercies with as little remorse as a huntsman feels in throwing a dead fox to the dogs. Hard was the fate of any such composition thrown out to us. With what infinite zeal we attacked it! how we riddled and shook it! how we scoffed, and sneered, and jeered at it! how we exposed its limping metaphors, and hung up in triumph its deficient grammar! Such a sharp set of critics we became that our compositions, read to each other, went through something of an ordeal.

Tina, Harry, Esther, and I were a private composition club. Many an hour have we sat in the old school-room long after all the other scholars had gone, talking to one another of our literary schemes. We planned poems and tragedies; we planned romances that would have taken many volumes to write out; we planned arguments and discussions; we gravely criticised each other's style, and read morsels of projected compositions to one another.

It was characteristic of the simple, earnest fearlessness of those times in regard to all matters of opinion, that the hardest theological problems were sometimes given out as composition subjects, and we four children not unfrequently sat perched on the old high benches of the school-room during the fading twilight hours, and, like Milton's fallen angels, —

> "Reasoned high
> Of providence, foreknowledge, will, and fate;
> Fixed fate, free will, foreknowledge absolute, ...
> Of happiness and final misery."

Esther, Harry, and I were reading the "Prometheus Bound" with Mr. Rossiter. It was one of his literary diversions, into which he carried us; and the Calvinism of the old Greek tragedian mingling with the Calvinism of the pulpit and of modern New England life, formed a curious admixture in our thoughts.

Tina insisted on reading this with us, just as of old she insisted on being carried in a lady chair over to our woodland study in the island. She had begun Greek with great zeal under Mr. Rossiter, but of course was in no situation to venture upon any such heights; but she insisted upon always being with us when we were digging out our lesson, and in fact, when we were talking over doubtfully the meaning of a passage, would irradiate it with such a flood of happy conjecture as ought to have softened the stern facts of moods and tenses, and *made* itself the meaning. She rendered some parts of it into verse much better than any of us could have done it, and her versifications, laid on Mr. Rossiter's desk, called out a commendation that was no small triumph to her.

"My forte lies in picking knowledge out of other folks and using it," said Tina, joyously. "Out of the least bit of ore that you dig up, I can make no end of gold-leaf!" O Tina, Tina, you never spoke a truer word, and while you were with us you made everything glitter with your "no end of gold-leaf."

It may seem to some impossible that, at so early an age as ours, our minds should have striven with subjects such as have been indicated here; but let it be remembered that these problems are to every human individual a part of an unknown tragedy in which he is to play the rôle either of the conqueror or the victim. A ritualistic church, which places all souls under the guardianship of a priesthood, of course shuts all these doors of discussion so far as the individual is concerned. "The Church" is a great ship, where you have only to buy your ticket and pay for it, and the rest is none of your concern. But the New England system, as taught at this time, put on every human being the necessity of crossing the shoreless ocean alone on his own raft; and many a New England child of ten or twelve years of age, or even younger, has trembled at the possibilities of final election or reprobation.

I remember well that at one time the composition subject given out at school was, "Can the Benevolence of the Deity be proved by the Light of Nature?" Mr. Rossiter generally gave out the subject, and discussed it with the school in an animated conversation, stirring up all the thinking matter that there was among us by vigorous questions, and by arguing before us first on one side and then on the other, until our minds were strongly excited about it; and, when he had wrought up the whole school to an intense interest, he called for volunteers to write on either side. Many of these compositions were full of vigor and thought; two of those on the above-mentioned subject were very striking. Harry took the affirmative ground, and gave a statement of the argument, so lucid, and in language so beautiful, that it has remained fixed in my mind like a gem ever since. It was the statement of a nature harmonious and confiding, naturally prone to faith in goodness, harmonizing and presenting all those evidences of tenderness, mercy, and thoughtful care which are furnished in the workings of natural laws. The other composition was by Esther; it was on the other and darker side of the subject, and as perfect a match for it as the "Penseroso" to the "Allegro." It was condensed and logical, fearfully vigorous in conception and expression, and altogether a very melancholy piece of literature to have been conceived and written by a girl of her age. It spoke of that fearful law of existence by which the sins of parents who often themselves escape punishment are visited on the heads of innocent children, as a law which seems made specifically to protect and continue the existence of vice and disorder from generation to generation. It spoke of the apparent injustice of an arrangement by which human beings, in the very outset of their career in life, often inherit almost uncontrollable propensities to evil. The sorrows, the perplexities, the unregarded wants and aspirations, over which the unsympathetic laws of nature cut their way regardless of quivering nerve or muscle, were all bitterly dwelt upon. The sufferings of dumb animals, and of helpless infant children, apparently so useless and so needless, and certainly so undeserved, were also energetically mentioned. There was a bitter intensity in the style that was most painful. In short, the two compositions were two perfect pictures of the world and life as they appear to two classes of minds. I remember looking at Esther while her composition was read, and being struck with the expression of her face, — so pale, so calm, so almost hopeless, — its expression was very like despair. I remember that Harry noticed it as well as I, and when school was over he took a long and lonely ramble with her, and from that time a nearer intimacy arose between them.

Esther was one of those intense, silent, repressed women that have been a frequent outgrowth of New England society. Moral traits, like physical ones, often intensify themselves in course of descent, so that the child of a long line of pious ancestry may sometimes suffer from too fine a moral fibre, and become a victim to a species of morbid *spiritual ideality*.

Esther looked to me, from the first, less like a warm, breathing, impulsive woman, less like ordinary flesh and blood, than some half-spiritual organization, every particle of which was a thought.

Old Dr. Donne says of such a woman, "One might almost say her body thought"; and it often came in my mind when I watched the movements of intense yet repressed intellect and emotion in Esther's face.

With many New England women at this particular period, when life was so retired and so cut off from outward sources of excitement, *thinking* grew to be a disease. The great subject of thought was, of course, theology; and woman's nature has never been consulted in theology. Theologic systems, as to the expression of their great body of ideas, have, as yet, been the work of man alone. They have had their origin, as in St. Augustine, with men who were utterly ignorant of moral and intellectual companionship with woman, looking on her only in her animal nature as a temptation and a snare. Consequently, when, as in this period of New England, the theology of Augustine began to be freely discussed by every individual in society, it was the women who found it hardest to tolerate or to assimilate it, and many a delicate and sensitive nature was utterly wrecked in the struggle.

Plato says somewhere that the only perfect human thinker and philosopher who will ever arise will be the MAN-WOMAN, or a human being who unites perfectly the nature of the two sexes. It was Esther's misfortune to have, to a certain degree, this very conformation. From a long line of reasoning, thinking, intellectual ancestry she had inherited all the strong logical faculties, and the tastes and inclinations for purely intellectual modes of viewing things, which are supposed to be more particularly the characteristic of man. From a line of saintly and tender women, half refined to angel in their nature, she had inherited exquisite moral perceptions, and all that flattering host of tremulous, half-spiritual, half-sensuous intuitions that lie in the borderland between the pure intellect and the animal nature. The consequence of all this was the internal strife of a divided nature. Her heart was always rebelling against the conclusions of her head. She was constantly being forced by one half of her nature to movements, inquiries, and reasonings which brought only torture to the other half.

Esther had no capacity for illusions; and in this respect her constitution was an unfortunate one.

Tina, for example, was one of those happily organized human beings in whom an intellectual proposition, fully assented to, might lie all her life dormant as the wheat-seed which remained thousands of years ungerminate in the wrappings of a mummy. She thought only of what she liked to think of; and a disagreeable or painful truth in her mind dropped at once out of sight, — it sank into the ground and roses grew over it.

Esther never could have made one of those clinging, submissive, parasitical wives who form the delight of song and story, and are supposed to be the peculiar gems of womanhood. It was her nature always to be obliged to see her friends clearly through the understanding, and to judge them by a refined and exquisite conscientiousness. A spot or stain on the honor of the most beloved could never have become invisible to her. She had none of that soft, blinding, social aura, — that blending, blue haze, such as softens the sharp outlines of an Italian landscape, and in life changes the hardness of reality into illusive and charming possibilities. Her clear, piercing hazel eyes seemed to pass over everything with a determination to know only and exactly the truth, hard and cold and unwelcome though it might be.

Yet there is no doubt that the warm, sunny, showery, rainbow nature of Tina acted as a constant and favorable alterative upon her. It was a daily living poem acting on the unused poetical and imaginative part of her own nature; for Esther had a suppressed vigor of imagination, and a passionate capability of emotion, stronger and more intense than that of Tina herself.

I remarked this to Harry, as we were talking about them one day. "Both have poetical natures," I said; "both are intense; but how different they are!"

"Yes," said Harry, "Tina's is electricity, and that snaps and sparkles and flashes; Esther's is galvanism, that comes in long, intense waves, and shakes and convulses; she both thinks and feels too much on all subjects."

"That was a very strange composition," I said.

"It is an unwholesome course of thought," said Harry, after thinking for a few moments with his head on his hands; "none but bitter berries grow on those bushes."

"But the reasoning was very striking," said I.

"Reasoning!" said Harry, impatiently; "we must trust the intuition of our hearts above reason. That is what I am trying to persuade Esther to do. To me it is an absolute demonstration, that

God never could make a creature who would be *better* than himself. We must look at the noblest, best human beings. We must see what generosity, what tenderness, what magnanimity can be in man and woman, and believe all that and more in God. All that there is in the best fathers and best mothers *must* be in him."

"But the world's history does not look like this, as Mr. Rossiter was saying."

"We have not seen the world's history yet," said Harry. "What does this green aphid, crawling over this leaf, know of the universe?"

CHAPTER XXXIV

OUR MINISTER IN CLOUDLAND

The picture of our life in Cloudland, and of the developing forces which were there brought to bear upon us, would be incomplete without the portrait of the minister.

Even during the course of my youth, the principles of democratic equality introduced and maintained in the American Revolution were greatly changing the social position and standing of the clergy. Ministers like Dr. Lothrop, noble men of the theocracy, men of the cocked hat, were beginning to pass away, or to appear among men only as venerable antiquities, and the present order of American citizen clergy was coming in.

Mr. Avery was a cheerful, busy, manly man, who posed himself among men as a companion and fellow-citizen, whose word on any subject was to go only so far as its own weight and momentum should carry it. His preaching was a striking contrast to the elegant Addisonian essays of Parson Lothrop. It was a vehement address to our intelligent and reasoning powers, — an address made telling by a back force of burning enthusiasm. Mr. Avery preached a vigorous system of mental philosophy in theology, which made our Sundays, on the whole, about as intense an intellectual drill as any of our week-days. If I could describe its character by any one word, I should call it *manly* preaching.

Every person has a key-note to his mind which determines all its various harmonies. The key-note of Mr. Avery's mind was "the free agency of man." Free agency was with him the universal solvent, the philosopher's stone in theology; every line of his sermons said to every human being, "You are free, and you are able." And the great object was to intensify to its highest point, in every human being, the sense of individual, personal responsibility.

Of course, as a Calvinist, he found food for abundant discourse in reconciling this absolute freedom of man with those declarations in the standards of the Church which assert the absolute government of God over all his creatures and all their actions. But the cheerfulness and vigor with which he drove and interpreted and hammered in the most contradictory statements, when they came in the way of his favorite ideas, was really quite inspiring.

During the year we had a whole course of systematic theology, beginning with the history of the introduction of moral evil, the fall of the angels, and the consequent fall of man and the work of redemption resulting therefrom. In the treatment of all these subjects, the theology and imagery of Milton figured so largely that one might receive the impression that Paradise Lost was part of the sacred canon.

Mr. Avery not only preached these things in the pulpit, but talked them out in his daily life. His system of theology was to him the vital breath of his being. His mind was always running upon it, and all nature was, in his sight, giving daily tributary illustrations to it. In his farming, gardening, hunting, or fishing, he was constantly finding new and graphic forms of presenting his favorite truths. The most abstract subject ceased to be abstract in his treatment of it, but became clothed upon with the homely, every-day similes of common life.

I have the image of the dear good man now, as I have seen him, seated on a hay-cart, mending a hoe-handle, and at the same moment vehemently explaining to an inquiring brother minister the exact way that Satan first came to fall, as illustrating how a perfectly holy mind can be tempted to sin. The familiarity that he showed with the celestial arcana, — the zeal with which he vindicated his Maker, — the perfect knowledge that he seemed to have of the strategic plans of the evil powers in the first great insurrection, — are traits strongly impressed on my memory. They seemed as vivid and as much a matter of course to his mind as if he had read them out of a weekly newspaper.

Mr. Avery indulged the fond supposition that he had solved the great problem of the origin of evil in a perfectly satisfactory manner. He was fond of the Socratic method, and would clench his reasoning in a series of questions, thus: —

"Has not God power to make any kind of thing he pleases?"
"Yes."

"Then he can make a kind of being incapable of being governed except by motive?"

"Yes."

"Then, when he has made that kind of being, he cannot govern them except by motive, can he?"

"No."

"Now if there is no motive in existence strong enough to govern them by, he cannot keep them from falling, can he?"

"No."

"You see then the necessity of moral evil: there must be experience of evil to work out motive."

The Calvinism of Mr. Avery, though sharp and well defined, was not dull, as abstractions often are, nor gloomy and fateful like that of Dr. Stern. It was permeated through and through by cheerfulness and hope.

Mr. Avery was one of the kind of men who have a passion for saving souls. If there is such a thing as apostolic succession, this passion is what it ought to consist in. It is what ought to come with the laying on of hands, if the laying on of hands is what it is sometimes claimed to be.

Mr. Avery was a firm believer in hell, but he believed also that nobody need go there, and he was determined, so far as he was concerned, that nobody should go there if he could help it. Such a tragedy as the loss of any one soul in his parish he could not and would not contemplate for a moment; and he had such a firm belief in the truths he preached, that he verily expected with them to save anybody that would listen to him.

Goethe says, "Blessed is the man who believes that he has an idea by which he may help his fellow-creatures." Mr. Avery was exactly that man. He had such faith in what he preached that he would have gone with it to Satan himself, could he have secured a dispassionate and unemployed hour, with a hope of bringing him round.

Generous and ardent in his social sympathies, Mr. Avery never would be brought to believe that any particular human being had finally perished. At every funeral he attended he contrived to see a ground for hope that the departed had found mercy. Even the slightest hints of repentance were magnified in his warm and hopeful mode of presentation. He has been known to suggest

to a distracted mother, whose thoughtless boy had been suddenly
killed by a fall from a horse, the possibilities of the merciful old
couplet, —

> "Between the saddle and the ground,
> Mercy was sought, and mercy found."

Like most of the New England ministers, Mr. Avery was a warm
believer in the millennium. This millennium was the favorite
recreation ground, solace, and pasture land, where the New England ministry fed their hopes and courage. Men of large hearts
and warm benevolence, their theology would have filled them with
gloom, were it not for this overplus of joy and peace to which
human society on earth was in their view tending. Thousands of
years, when the poor old earth should produce only a saintly race
of perfected human beings, were to them some compensation for
the darkness and losses of the great struggle.

Mr. Avery believed, not only that the millennium was coming,
but that it was coming fast, and, in fact, was at the door. Every
political and social change announced it. Our Revolution was a
long step towards it, and the French Revolution, now in progress,
was a part of that distress of nations which heralded it; and every
month, when the Columbia Magazine brought in the news from
Europe, Mr. Avery rushed over to Mr. Rossiter, and called him
to come and hear how the thing was going.

Mr. Rossiter took upon himself that right which every free-
born Yankee holds sacred, — the right of contravening his minister. Though, if he caught one of his boys swelling or ruffling with
any opposing doctrine, he would scath and scorch the youngster
with contemptuous irony, and teach him to comport himself
modestly in talking of his betters, yet it was the employment of
a great many of his leisure hours to run argumentative tilts against
Mr. Avery. Sometimes, when we were sitting in our little garret
window digging out the Greek lessons, such a war of voices and
clangor of assertion and contradiction would come up from among
the tassels of the corn, where the two were hoeing together in the
garden, as would have alarmed people less accustomed to the
vigorous manners of both the friends.

"Now, Rossiter, that will never do. Your system would upset

moral government entirely. Not an angel could be kept in his place upon your supposition."

"It is not my supposition. I haven't got any supposition, and I don't want any; but I was telling you that, if you must have a theory of the universe, Origen's was a better one than yours."

"And I say that Origen's system would upset everything, and you ought to let it alone."

"I sha'n't let it alone!"

"Why, Rossiter, you will destroy responsibility, and annihilate all the motives of God's government."

"That's just what you theologians always say. You think the universe will go to pieces if we upset your pine-shingle theology."

"Rossiter, you must be careful how you spread your ideas."

"I don't want to spread my ideas; I don't want to interfere with your system. It's the best thing you can make your people take, but you ought to know that no system is anything more than human theory."

"It's eternal truth."

"There's truth in it, but it isn't eternal truth."

"It's Bible."

"Part, and part Milton and Edwards, and part Mr. Avery."

Harry and I were like adopted sons in both families, and the two expressed their minds about each other freely before us. Mr. Avery would say: "The root of the matter is in Rossiter. I don't doubt that he's a really regenerate man, but he has a head that works strangely. We must wait for him, he'll come along by and by."

And Mr. Rossiter would say of Mr. Avery: "That's a growing man, boys; he hasn't made his terminal buds yet. Some men make them quick, like lilac-bushes. They only grow a little way and stop. And some grow all the season through, like locust-trees. Avery is one of that sort: he'll never be done thinking and growing, particularly if he has me to fight him on all hands. He'll grow into different opinions on a good many subjects, before he dies."

It was this implied liberty of growth — the liberty to think and to judge freely upon all subjects — that formed the great distinctive educational force of New England life, particularly in this period of my youth. Monarchy, aristocracy, and theocracy, with their peculiar trains of ideas, were passing away, and we were coming within the sweep of pure republican influences, in which the *individual* is *everything*. Mr. Avery's enthusiastic preaching of free agency and personal responsibility was more than an *individual impulse*. It was the voice of a man whose ideas were the reflection of a period in American history. While New England theology was made by loyal monarchists, it reflected monarchical ideas. The rights and immunities of divine sovereignty were its favorite topics. When, as now, the government was becoming settled in the hands of the common people, the freedom of the individual, his absolute power of choice, and the consequent reasonableness of the duties he owed to the Great Sovereign Authority, began to be the favorite subjects of the pulpit.

Mr. Avery's preaching was immensely popular. There were in Cloudland only about half a dozen families of any prestige as to ancestral standing or previous wealth and cultivation. The old aristocratic idea was represented only in the one street that went over Cloudland Hill, where was a series of wide, cool, roomy, elm-shadowed houses, set back in deep door-yards, and flanked with stately, well-tended gardens. The doctor, the lawyer, the sheriff of the county, the schoolmaster, and the minister, formed here a sort of nucleus; but outlying in all the hills and valleys round were the mountain and valley farmers. Their houses sat on high hills or sunk in deep valleys, and their flaming windows at morning and evening looked through the encircling belts of forest solitudes as if to say, "We are here, and we are a power." These hard-working farmers formed the body of Mr. Avery's congregation. Sunday morning, when the little bell pealed out its note of invitation loud and long over the forest-feathered hills, it seemed to evoke a caravan of thrifty, well-filled farm-wagons, which, punctual as the village-clock itself, came streaming from the east and west, the north and south. Past the parsonage they streamed, with the bright cheeks and fluttering ribbons of the girls, and the cheery, rubicund faces of children, and with the inevitable yellow dog of the family faithfully pattering in the rear. The audience that filled the rude old meeting-house every Sunday would have astonished the men who only rode through the village of a week-day. For this set of shrewd, toil-hardened, vigorous, full-blooded republicans I can think of no preaching more admirably adapted than Mr.

Avery's. It was preaching that was on the move, as their minds were, and which was slowly shaping out and elaborating those new forms of doctrinal statement that inevitably grow out of new forms of society. Living, as these men did, a lonely, thoughtful, secluded life, without any of the thousand stimulants which railroads and magazine and newspaper literature cast into our existence, their two Sunday sermons were the great intellectual stimulus which kept their minds bright, and they were listened to with an intense interest of which the scattered and diversified state of modern society gives few examples. They felt the compliment of being talked to as if they were capable of understanding the very highest of subjects, and they liked it. Each hard, heroic nature flashed like a flint at the grand thought of a free agency with which not even their Maker would interfere. Their God himself asked to reign over them, not by force, but by the free, voluntary choice of their own hearts. "*Choose* you this day whom ye will serve. If the Lord be God, serve him, and if Baal be God, serve him," was a grand appeal, fit for freemen.

The reasoning on moral government, on the history of man, — the theories of the universe past, present, and to come, — opened to these men a grand Miltonic poem, in which their own otherwise commonplace lives shone with a solemn splendor. Without churches or cathedrals or physical accessories to quicken their poetic nature, their lives were redeemed only by this poetry of ideas.

Calvinism is much berated in our days, but let us look at the political, social, and materialistic progress of Calvinistic countries, and ask if the world is yet far enough along to dispense with it altogether. Look at Spain at this hour, and look back at New England at the time of which I write, — both having just finished a revolution, both feeling their way along the path of national independence, — and compare the Spanish peasantry with the yeomen of New England, such as made up Mr. Avery's congregation; — the one set made by reasoning, active-minded Calvinism, the other by pictures, statues, incense, architecture, and all the sentimental paraphernalia of ritualism.

If Spain had had not a single cathedral, if her Murillos had been all sunk in the sea, and if she had had, for a hundred years past, a set of schoolmasters and ministers working together as I

have described Mr. Avery and Mr. Rossiter as working, would
not Spain be infinitely better off for this life at least, whether
there is any life to come or not? This is a point that I humbly
present to the consideration of society.

Harry and I were often taken by Mr. Avery on his preaching
tours to the distant farm parishes. There was a brown school-
house in this valley, and a red school-house in that, and another
on the hill, and so on for miles around, and Mr. Avery kept a
constant stream of preaching going in one or other of these every
evening. We liked these expeditions with him, because they were
often excursions amid the wildest and most romantic of the mountain scenery, and we liked them furthermore because Mr. Avery
was a man that made himself, for the time being, companionable
to every creature of human shape that was with him.

With boys he was a boy, — a boy in the vigor of his animal life,
his keen delight in riding, hunting, fishing. With farmers he was
a farmer. Brought up on a farm, familiar during all his early days
with its wholesome toils, he still had a farmer's eye and a farmer's
estimates, and the working-people felt him bone of their bone, and
flesh of their flesh. It used to be a saying among them, that, when
Mr. Avery hoed more than usual in his potato-field, the Sunday
sermon was sure to be better.

But the best sport of all was when some of Mr. Avery's preaching tours would lead up the course of a fine mountain trout-brook
in the vicinity. Then sometimes Mr. Rossiter, Mr. Avery, Harry,
and I would put our supper in our pockets, and start with the sun
an hour or two high, designing to bring up at the red school-house,
as the weekly notice phrased it, at "early candle-lighting."

A person who should accidentally meet Mr. Avery on one of
these tours, never having seen him before, might imagine him to
be a man who had never thought or dreamed of anything but
catching trout all his days, he went into it with such *abandon*.
Eye, voice, hand, thought, feeling, all were concentrated on trout.
He seemed to have the quick perception, the rapid hand, and the
noiseless foot of an Indian, and the fish came to his hook as if
drawn there by magic. So perfectly absorbed was he that we
would be obliged to jog his memory, and, in fact, often to drag
him away by main force, when the hour for the evening lecture
arrived. Then our spoils would be hid away among the bushes,

and with wet feet he would hurry in; but, once in, he was as completely absorbed in his work of saving sinners as he had before been in his temporal fishery. He argued, illustrated, stated, guarded, answered objections, looking the while from one hard, keen, shrewd face to another, to see if he was being understood. The phase of Calvinism shown in my grandmother's blue book had naturally enough sowed through the minds of a thoughtful community hosts of doubts and queries. A great part of Mr. Avery's work was to remove these doubts by substituting more rational statements. It was essential that he should feel that he had made a hit somewhere, said something that answered a purpose in the minds of his hearers, and helped them at least a step or two on their way.

After services were over, I think of him and Mr. Rossiter cheerily arguing with and contradicting each other a little beyond us in the road, while Harry and I compared our own notes behind. Arrived at the parsonage, there would be Tina and Esther coming along the street to meet us. Tina full of careless, open, gay enthusiasm, Esther with a shy and wistful welcome, that said far less, and perhaps meant more. Then our treasures were displayed and exulted over; the supper-table was laid, and Mr. Avery, Mr. Rossiter, and we boys applied ourselves to dressing our fish; and then Mr. Avery, disdaining Dinah, and, in fact, all female supervision, presided himself over the frying-pan, and brought our woodland captives on the table in a state worthy of a trout brook. It should have comforted the very soul of a trout taken in our snares to think how much was made of him, and how perfectly Mr. Avery respected his dignity, and did him justice in his cookery.

We two boys were in fact domesticated as sons in the family. Although our boarding-place was with the master, we were almost as much with the minister as if we had been of his household. We worked in his garden, we came over and sat with Esther and Tina. Our windows faced their windows, so that in study hours we could call to one another backward and forward, and tell where the lesson began, and what the root of the verb was, or any other message that came into our heads. Sometimes, of a still summer morning, while we were gravely digging at our lessons, we would hear Esther in tones of expostulation at some madcap impulse of Tina, and, looking across, would see her bursting out in some freak of droll pantomimic performance, and then an immediate whirlwind of gayety would seize us all. We would drop our dictionaries and grammars, rush together, and have a general outbreak of jollity.

In general, Tina was a most praiseworthy and zealous student, and these wild, sudden whisks of gayety seemed only the escape-valves by which her suppressed spirits vented themselves; but, when they came, they were perfectly irresistible. She devoted herself to Esther with that sympathetic adaptation which seemed to give her power over every nature. She was interested in her housekeeping, in all its departments, as if it had been her own glory and pride; and Tina was one that took glory and pride in everything of her friends, as if it had been her own. Esther had been left by the death of her mother only the year before the mistress of the parsonage. The great unspoken sorrow of this loss lay like a dark chasm between her and her father, each striving to hide from the other its depth and coldness by a brave cheerfulness.

Esther, strong as was her intellectual life, had that intense sense of the worth of a well-ordered household, and of the dignity of house-economies, which is characteristic of New England women. Her conscientiousness pervaded every nook and corner of her domestic duties with a beautiful perfection; nor did she ever feel tempted to think that her fine mental powers were a reason why these homely details should be considered a slavery. Household cares are a drudgery only when unpervaded by sentiment. When they are an offering of love, a ministry of care and devotion to the beloved, every detail has its interest.

There were certain grand festivals of a minister's family which fill a housekeeper's heart and hands, and in which all of us made common interest with her. The Association was a reunion when all the ministers of the county met together and spent a social day with the minister, dining together, and passing their time in brotherly converse, such as reading essays, comparing sermons, taking counsel with each other in all the varied ups and downs of their pastoral life. The Consociation was another meeting of the clergy, but embracing also with each minister a lay delegate, and thus uniting, not only the ministry, but the laymen of the county, in a general fraternal religious conference.

The first Association that Esther had to manage quite alone as sole mistress of the parsonage occurred while we were with her. Like most solemn festivals of New England, these seasons were announced under the domestic roof by great preparatory pound- ings and choppings, by manufacture, on a large scale, of cakes, pies, and provisions for the outer man; and at this time Harry, Tina, and I devoted all our energies, and made ourselves every- where serviceable. We ran to the store on errands, we chopped mince for pies with a most virtuous pertinacity, we cut citron and stoned raisins, we helped put up curtains and set up bedsteads. We were all of us as resolved as Esther that the housekeeping of the little parsonage should be found without speck or flaw, and should reflect glory upon her youthful sovereignty.

Some power or other gilded and glorified these happy days, — for happy enough they were. What was it that made everything that we four did together so harmonious and so charming? "Friend- ship, only friendship," sang Tina, with silver tongue. "Such a *per- fect* friendship," she remarked, "was *never* known except just in our particular case"; it exceeded all the classical records, all the annals, ancient and modern.

But what instinct or affinity in friendship made it a fact that when we four sat at table together, with our lessons before us, Harry somehow was always found on Esther's side? I used to notice it because his golden-brown mat of curls was such a con- trast to the smooth, shining black satin bands of her hair as they bent together over the dictionary, and looked up innocently into each other's eyes, talking of verbs and adjectives and terminations, innocently conjugating "amo, amare" to each other. Was it friend- ship that made Esther's dark, clear eyes, instinctively look towards Harry for his opinion, when we were reading our compositions to one another? Was it friendship, that starry brightness that began to come in Harry's eyes, and made them seem darker and bluer and deeper, with a sort of mysterious meaning, when he looked at Esther? Was it friendship that seemed to make him feel taller, stronger, more manly, when he thought of her, and that always placed him at her hand when there was some household task that required a manly height or handiness? It was Harry and Esther together who put up the white curtains all through the parsonage that spring, that made it look so trim and comely for the ministers' meeting. Last year, Esther said, innocently, she had no one to help her, and the work tired her so. How happy, how busy, how bright they were as they measured and altered, and Harry, in boundless complacency, went up and down at her orders, and changed and altered and arranged, till her fastidious eye was satisfied, and every fold hung aright! It was Harry who took down and cleansed the family portraits, and hung them again, and balanced them so nicely; it was Harry who papered over a room where the walls had been disfigured by an accident, and it was Esther by him who cut the paper and trimmed the bordering and executed all her little sovereignties of taste and disposal by his obedient hands. And Tina and I at this time gathered green boughs and ground-pine for the vases, and made floral decorations without end, till the bare little parsonage looked like a woodland bower.

I have pleasant recollections of those ministers' meetings. Calvinistic doctrines, in their dry, abstract form, are, I confess, rather hard; but Calvinistic ministers, so far as I have ever had an opportunity to observe, are invariably a jolly set of fellows. In those early days the ministry had not yet felt the need of that generous decision which led them afterwards to forego all dangerous stimulants, as an example to their flock. A long green wooden case, full of tobacco-pipes and a quantity of papers of tobacco, used to be part of the hospitable stock prepared for the reception of the brethren. No less was there a quantity of spirituous liquor laid in. In those days its dispensation was regarded as one of the inevitable duties of hospitality. The New England ministry of this period were men full of interest. Each one was the intellectual centre of his own district, and supplied around him the stimulus which is now brought to bear through a thousand other sources. It was the minister who overlooked the school, who put parents upon the idea of giving their sons liberal educations. In poor districts the minister often practised medicine, and drew wills and deeds, thus supplying the place of both lawyer and doctor. Apart from their doctrinal theology, which was a constant source of intellectual activity to them, their secluded life led them to many forms of literary labor.

As a specimen of these, it is recorded of the Rev. Mr. Taylor of Westfield, that he took such delight in the writings of Origen, that, being unable to purchase them, he copied them in four quarto volumes, that he might have them for his own study. These are still in the possession of his descendants. Other instances of literary perseverance and devotion, equally curious, might be cited.

The lives that these men led were simple and tranquil. Almost all of them were practical farmers, preserving about them the fresh sympathies and interests of the soil, and laboring enough with their hands to keep their muscles in good order, and prevent indigestion. Mingling very little with the world, each one a sort of autocrat in his way, in his own district, and with an idea of stability and perpetuity in his office, which, in these days, does not belong to the position of a minister anywhere, these men developed many originalities and peculiarities of character, to which the simple state of society then allowed full scope. They were humorists, — like the mossy old apple-trees which each of them had in his orchard, bending this way and turning that, and throwing out their limbs with quaint twists and jerks, yet none the less acceptable, so long as the fruit they bore was sound and wholesome.

We have read of "Handkerchief Moody," who for some years persisted in always appearing among men with his face covered with a handkerchief, — an incident which Hawthorne has worked up in his weird manner into the story of "The Minister with the Black Veil."

Father Mills, of Torringford, was a gigantic man who used to appear in the pulpit in a full-bottomed white horse-hair wig. On the loss of a beloved wife, he laid aside his wig for a year, and appeared in the pulpit with his head tied up in a black handkerchief, representing to the good housewives of his parish that, as he always dressed in black, he could in no other way testify to his respect for his dear wife's memory; and this tribute was accepted by his parish with the same innocent simplicity with which it was rendered.

On the whole, the days which brought all the brother ministers to the parsonage were days of enlivenment to all us young people. They seemed to have such a hearty joy in their meeting, and to deliver themselves up to mirth and good-fellowship with such a free and hearty *abandon,* and the jokes and stories which they brought with them were chorused by such roars of merriment, as made us think a ministers' meeting the most joyous thing on earth.

I know that some say this jocund mirthfulness indicated a want of faith in the doctrines they taught. But do not you and I, honest friends, often profess our belief in things which it would take away our appetite and wither our strength to realize, but notwithstanding which we eat and drink and sleep joyously? You read in your morning paper that the city of so-and-so has been half submerged by an earthquake, and that after the earthquake came a fire and burnt the crushed inhabitants alive in the ruins of their dwellings. Nay, if you are an American, you may believe some such catastrophe to have happened on the Erie Railroad a day or two before, and that men, women, and children have been cooped up and burnt, in lingering agonies, in your own vicinity. And yet, though you believe these things, you laugh and talk and are gay, and plan for a party in the evening and a ride on the same road the next week.

No; man was mercifully made with the power of ignoring what he believes. It is all that makes existence in a life like this tolerable. And our ministers, conscious of doing the very best they can to keep the world straight, must be allowed their laugh and joke, sin and Satan to the contrary notwithstanding.

There was only one brother, in the whole confraternity that used to meet at Mr. Avery's, who was not a married man; and he, in spite of all the snares and temptations which must beset a minister who guides a female flock of parishioners, had come to the afternoon of life in the state of bachelorhood. But O the jokes and witticisms which always set the room in a roar at his expense! It was a subject that never wearied or grew old. To clap Brother Boardman on the back and inquire for Mrs. Boardman, — to joke him about some suitable widow, or bright-eyed young lamb of his flock, at each ministers' meeting, — was a provocative of mirth ever fresh and ever young. But the undaunted old bachelor was always a match for these attacks, and had his rejoinder ready to fling back into the camp of the married men. He was a model of gallant devotion to womanhood in the abstract, and seemed loath to give up to one what was meant for womankind. So, the last that I ever heard of him, he was still unmarried, — a most unheard-of thing for a New England parson.

Mr. Avery was a leader among the clergy of his State. His zeal, enthusiasm, eloquence, and doctrinal vigor, added to a capacity for forming an indefinite number of personal friendships, made him a sort of chief among them.

What joyous hours they spent together in the ins and the outs, the highways and by-ways, of metaphysics and theology! Harry and Esther and Tina and I learned them all. We knew all about the Arminians and Pelagians and the Tasters and the Exercisers, and made a deal of fun with each other over it in our private hours. We knew precisely every shade of difference between tweedle-dum and tweedle-dee which the different metaphysicians had invented, and tossed our knowledge joyously back and forward at one another in our gayer hours, just as the old ministers did, when they smoked and argued in the great parsonage dining-room. Everything is joyful that is learned by two young men in company with two young women with whom they are secretly in love. Mathematics, metaphysics, or no matter what of dry and desolate, buds and blossoms as the rose under such circumstances.

Did you ever go out in the misty gray of morning dawn, when the stars had not yet shut their eyes, and still there were rosy bands lying across the east? And then have you watched a trellis of morning-glories, with all the buds asleep, but ready in one hour to waken? The first kiss of sunlight and they will be open! That was just where we were.

CHAPTER XXXV

THE REVIVAL OF RELIGION

No New England boy or girl comes to maturity without a full understanding of what is meant by the term at the head of this chapter.

Religion was, perhaps, never so much the governing idea in any Commonwealth before. Nowhere has there been a people, the mass of whom acted more uniformly on considerations drawn from the unseen and future life; yet nowhere a people who paid a more earnest attention to the life that is seen and temporal.

The New England colonies were, in the first instance, the outgrowth of a religious enthusiasm. Right alongside of them, at the same period of time, other colonies were founded from a religious enthusiasm quite as intense and sincere. The French missionary settlers in Canada had a grandeur of self-sacrifice, an intensity of religious devotion, which would almost throw in the shade that of the Pilgrim Fathers; and the sole reason why one set of colonists proved the seed of a great nation, and the other attained so very limited success, is the difference between the religions taught by the two.

The one was the religion of asceticism, in view of which contempt of the body and of material good was taught as a virtue, and its teachers were men and women to whom marriage and its earthly relations were forbidden. The other was the spirit of the Old Testament, in which material prosperity is always spoken of as the lawful reward of piety, in which marriage is an honor, and a numerous posterity a thing to be desired. Our forefathers were, in many essential respects, Jews in their thoughts and feelings with regard to this life, but they superadded to this broad physical basis the intense spiritualism of the New Testament. Hence came a peculiar race of men, uniting the utmost extremes of the material and the spiritual.

Dr. Franklin represents that outgrowth of the New England mind which moves in the material alone, and scarcely ever rises to the spiritual. President Edwards represents the mind so risen to the spiritual as scarcely to touch the material. Put these two together, and you have the average New England character, — that land in which every *ism* of social or religious life has had its origin, — that land whose hills and valleys are one blaze and buzz of material and manufacturing production.

A revival of religion in New England meant a time when that deep spiritual undercurrent of thought and emotion with regard to the future life, which was always flowing quietly under its intense material industries, exhaled and steamed up into an atmosphere which pervaded all things, and made itself for a few weeks the only thought of every person in some town or village or city. It was the always-existing spiritual becoming visible and tangible.

Such periods would come in the labors of ministers like Mr. Avery. When a man of powerful mind and shrewd tact and great natural eloquence lives among a people already thoughtfully predisposed, for no other purpose than to stir them up to the care of their souls, it is evident that there will come times when the results of all his care and seeking, his public ministrations, his private conversations with individuals, will come out in some marked social form; and such a period in New England is called a revival of religion.

There were three or four weeks in the autumn of the first year that we spent in Cloudland, in which there was pervading the town a sort of subdued hush of emotions, — a quiet sense of something like a spiritual presence brooding through the mild autumn air. This was accompanied by a general inclination to attend religious services, and to converse on religious subjects. It pervaded the school; it was to be heard at the store. Every kind of individual talked on and about religion in his own characteristic way, and in a small mountain town like Cloudland everybody's characteristic way is known to every one else.

Ezekiel Scranton, the atheist of the parish, haunted the store where the farmers tied up their wagons when they brought their produce, and held, after his way, excited theological arguments with Deacon Phineas Simons, who kept the store, — arguments to which the academy boys sometimes listened, and of which they brought astounding reports to the school-room.

Tina, who was so intensely sympathetic with all social influences that she scarcely seemed to have an individuality of her own, was now glowing like a luminous cloud with religious zeal.

"I could convert that man," she said; "I know I could! I wonder Mr. Avery hasn't converted him long ago!"

At this time, Mr. Avery, who had always kept a watchful eye upon us, had a special conversation with Harry and myself, the object of which was to place us right in our great foundation relations. Mr. Avery stood upon the basis that most good New England men, since Jonathan Edwards, have adopted, and regarded all young people, as a matter of course, out of the fold of the Church, and devoid of anything truly acceptable to God, until they had passed through a mental process designated, in well-known language, as conviction and conversion.

He began to address Harry, therefore, upon this supposition. I well remember the conversation.

"My son," he said, "is it not time for you to think seriously of giving your heart to God?"

"I have given my heart to God," replied Harry, calmly.

"Indeed!" said Mr. Avery, with surprise; "when did that take place?"

"I have always done it."

Mr. Avery looked at him with a gentle surprise.

"Do you mean to say, my son, that you have always loved God?"

"Yes, sir," said Harry, quietly.

Mr. Avery felt entirely incredulous, and supposed that this must be one of those specious forms of natural piety spoken of depreciatingly by Jonathan Edwards, who relates in his own memoirs similar exercises of early devotion as the mere fruits of the ungrafted natural heart. Mr. Avery, therefore, proceeded to put many theological questions to Harry on the nature of sin and holiness, on the difference between manly, natural affections and emotions, and those excited by the supernatural movement of a divine power on the soul, — the good man begging him to remember the danger of self-deception, saying that nothing was more common than for young people to mistake the transient movements of mere natural emotions for real religion.

I observed that Harry, after a few moments, became violently agitated. Two large blue veins upon his forehead swelled out, his eyes had that peculiar flash and fire that they had at rare intervals, when some thought penetrated through the usual gentle quietude of his surface life to its deepest internal recesses. He rose and walked up and down the room, and finally spoke in a thick, husky voice, as one who pants with emotion. He was one of the most reserved human beings I have ever known. There was a region of emotion deep within him, which it was almost like death to him to express. There is something piteous and even fearful in the convulsions by which such natures disclose what is nearest to their hearts.

"Mr. Avery," he said, "I have heard your preaching ever since I have been here, and thought of it all. It has done me good, because it has made me think deeply. It is right and proper that our minds should be forced to think on all these subjects; but I have not thought, and cannot think, exactly like you, nor exactly like any one that I know of. I must make up my opinions for myself. I suppose I am peculiar, but I have been brought up peculiarly. My lot in life has been very different from that of ordinary boys. The first ten years of my life, all that I can remember is the constant fear and pain and distress and mortification and want through which my mother and I passed together, — she a stranger in this strange land, — her husband and my father worse than nothing to us, oftentimes our greatest terror. We should both of us have died, if it had not been for one thing: she believed that her Saviour loved her, and loved us all. She told me that these sorrows were from him, — that he permitted them because he loved us, — that they would be for good in the end. She died at last alone and utterly forsaken by everybody but her Saviour, and yet her death was blessed. I saw it in her eyes, and she left it as her last message to me, whatever happened to me, *never to doubt God's love,* — in all my life to trust him, to seek his counsel in all things, and to believe that all that happened to me was ordered by him. This was and is my religion; and, after all that I have heard, I can have no other. I do love God because he is good, and because he has been good to me. I believe that Jesus Christ is God, and I worship God

always through him, and I leave everything for myself, for life
and death are in his hands. I know that I am not very good. I
know, as you say, I am liable to make mistakes, and to deceive
myself in a thousand ways; but *He* knows all things, and he can
and will teach me; he will not let me lose myself, I feel sure."

"My son," said Mr. Avery, "you are blessed. I thank God with
all my heart for you. Go on, and God be with you!"

It is to be seen that Mr. Avery was a man who always corrected
theory by common sense. When he perceived that a child could be
trained up a Christian, and grow into the love of a Heavenly
Father as he grows into the love of an earthly one, by a daily and
hourly experience of goodness, he yielded to the perceptions of his
mind in that particular case.

Of course our little circle of four had, at this time, deep communings. Tina was buoyant and joyous, full of poetic images,
delighted with the news of every conversion, and taking such an
interest in Mr. Avery's preaching that she several times suggested
to him capital subjects for sermons. She walked up to Ezekiel
Scranton's, one afternoon, for no other object than to convert him
from his atheism, and succeeded so far as to exact a promise from
him that he would attend all Mr. Avery's meetings for a fortnight.
Ezekiel was one of the converts of that revival, and Harry and I,
of course, ascribed it largely to Tina's influence.

A rough old New England farmer, living on the windy side of a
high hill, subsisting largely on codfish and hard cider, does not
often win the flattering attention of any little specimen of humanity
like Tina; and therefore it was not to be wondered at that the
results of her missionary zeal appeared to his mind something like
that recorded in the New Testament, where "an angel went down
at a certain season and troubled the waters."

But, while Tina was thus buoyant and joyous, Esther seemed to
sink into the very depths of despondency. Hers, as I have already
intimated, was one of those delicate and sensitive natures, on
which the moral excitements of New England acted all the while
with too much power. The work and care of a faithful pastor are
always complicated by the fact that those truths, and modes of
presenting truths, which are only just sufficient to arouse the attention of certain classes of hearers, and to prevent their sinking into

apathetic materialism, are altogether too stimulating and exciting for others of a more delicate structure.

Esther Avery was one of those persons for whom the peculiar theory of religious training which prevailed in New England at this period, however invigorating to the intellect of the masses, might be considered as a personal misfortune. Had she been educated in the tender and paternal manner recommended by the Cambridge platform, and practised among the earlier Puritans, recognized from infancy as a member of Christ's Church, and in tender covenant relations with him, her whole being would have responded to such an appeal; her strongest leading faculties would have engaged her to fulfil, in the most perfect manner, the sacred duties growing out of that relation, and her course into the full communion of the Church would have been gentle and insensible as a flowing river.

" 'T is a tyranny," says old Dr. Cotton Mather, "to impose upon every man a record of the precise time and way of their conversion to God. Few that have been restrained by a religious education can give such an one."

Esther, however, had been trained to expect a marked and decided period of conversion, — a change that could be described in the same language in which Paul described the conversion of the heathen at dissolute Corinth and Ephesus. She was told, as early as she was capable of understanding language, that she was by nature in a state of alienation from God, in which every thought of her heart and action of her life was evil, and evil only; and continually that she was entirely destitute of holiness, and exposed momently to the wrath of God; and that it was her immediate duty to escape from this state by an act of penitence for sin and supreme love to God.

The effort to bring about in her heart that state of emotion was during all her youth a failure. She was by constitution delicately, intensely self-analytic, and her analysis was guided by the most exacting moral ideality. Every hopeful emotion of her higher nature, as it rose, was dissolved in this keen analysis, as diamond and pearls disappeared in the smelting furnaces of the old alchemists. We all know that self-scrutiny is the death of emotion, and that the analytic, self-inspective habit is its sure preventive.

Had Esther applied to her feelings for her own beloved father the same tests by which she tried every rising emotion of love to the Divine Being, the result would have been precisely the same.

Esther was now nineteen years of age; she was the idol of her father's heart; she was the staff and stay of her family; she was, in all the duties of life, inspired by a most faultless conscientiousness. Her love of the absolute right was almost painful in its excess of minuteness, and yet, in her own view, in the view of the Church, in the view even of her admiring and loving father, she was no Christian. Perfectly faultless in every relation so far as human beings could observe, reverent to God, submissive to his will, careful in all outward religious observances, yet wanting in a certain emotional experience, she judged herself to be, and was judged to be by the theology which her father taught, utterly devoid of virtue or moral excellence of any kind in the sight of God. The theology of the times also taught her that the act of grace which should put an end to this state, and place her in the relation of a forgiven child with her Heavenly Father, was a voluntary one, momently in her power, and that nothing but her own persistent refusal prevented her performing it; yet taught at the same time that, so desperate was the obstinacy of the human heart, no child of Adam ever would, or ever could, perform it without a special interposition of God, — an interposition which might or might not come. Thus all the responsibility and the guilt rested upon her. Now, when a nature intensely conscientious is constantly oppressed by a sense of unperformed duty, that sense becomes a gnawing worm at the very root of life. Esther had in vain striven to bring herself into the required state of emotion. Often for weeks and months she offered daily, and many times a day, prayers which brought no brightness and no relief, and read conscientiously that Bible, all whose tender words and comforting promises were like the distant vision of Eden to the fallen exiles, guarded by a flaming sword which turned every way. Mute and mournful she looked into the paradise of peace possessed by the favored ones whom God had chosen to help through the mysterious passage, and asked herself, would that helping hand ever open the gate to her?

Esther had passed through two or three periods of revival of religion, and seen others far less consistent gathered into the fold of the Church, while she only sunk at each period into a state of hopeless gloom and despondency which threatened her health. Latterly, her mind, wounded and bruised, had begun to turn in bitter reactions. From such experiences as hers come floods of distracting intellectual questions. Scepticism and doubt are the direct children of unhappiness. If she had been, as her standards stated, born "utterly indisposed, disabled, and made opposite to all good, and wholly inclined to all evil," was not this an excuse for sin? Was it *her* fault that she was born so? and, if her Creator had brought her into being in this state, was it not an act of simple justice to restore her mind to a normal condition?

When she addressed these questions to her father, he was alarmed, and warned her against speculation. Mr. Avery did not consider that the Assembly's catechism and the Cambridge platform and a great part of his own preaching were, after all, but human speculation, — the uninspired *inferences* of men from the Bible, and not the Bible itself, — and that minds once set going in this direction often cannot help a third question after a second, any more than they can help breathing; and that third question may be one for which neither God nor nature has an answer. Such inquiries as Esther's never arose from reading the parables of Christ, the Sermon on the Mount: they are the legitimate children of mere human attempts at systematic theology.

How to deliver a soul that has come from excessive harassments, introspections, self-analysis, into that morbid state of half-sceptical despondency, was a problem over which Mr. Avery sighed in vain. His cheerful hopefulness, his sympathetic vitality, had drawn many others through darkness into light, and settled them in cheerful hope. But with his own daughter he felt no power, — his heart trembled, — his hand was weak as the surgeon's who cannot operate when it is the life of his best beloved that lies under his hands.

Esther's deliverance came through that greatest and holiest of all the natural sacraments and means of grace, — Love.

An ancient gem has upon it a figure of a Psyche sitting with bound wings and blindfolded and weeping, whose bonds are being sundered by Love. It is an emblem of what often occurs in woman's life.

It has sometimes been thrown out as a sneer on periods of religious excitement, that they kindle the enthusiasm of man and woman towards each other into earthly attachments; but the sneer should wither as something satanic before the purity of love as it comes to noble natures. The man who has learned to think meanly of *that*, to associate it with vulgar thoughts and low desires, — the man who has not been lifted by love to aspire after unworldly excellence, to sigh for unworldly purity, to reverence unworldly good, — has lost his one great chance of regeneration.

Harry and Esther had moved side by side for months, drawn daily to each other, — showing each other their compositions, studying out of the same book, arguing together in constant friendly differences, — and yet neither of them exactly conscious whither they were tending. A great social, religious excitement has often this result, that it throws open between friends the doors of the inner nature. How long, how long we may live in the same house, sit at the same table, hold daily converse with friends to whom and by whom these inner doors are closed! We cannot even tell whether we should love them more or less if they were open, — they are a mystery. But a great, pure, pervading, social excitement breaks like some early spring day around us; the sun shines, the birds sing; and forthwith open fly all the doors and windows, and let in the sunshine and the breeze and the bird-song!

In such an hour Esther saw that she was beloved! — beloved by a poet soul, — one of that rare order to whom the love of woman is a religion! — a baptism! — a consecration!

Her life, hitherto so chill and colorless, so imprisoned and bound in the chains of mere and cold intellect, awoke with a sudden thrill of consciousness to a new and passionate life. She was as changed as the poor and silent Jungfrau of the Swiss mountains, when the gray and ghostly cold of the night bursts into rosy light, as the morning sunbeams rise upon it. The most auspicious and beautiful of all phenomena that ever diversify this weary life is that wonderful moment in which two souls, who hitherto have not known each other, suddenly, by the lifting of a veil or the falling of a barrier, become in one moment and forever after one. Henceforth each soul has in itself the double riches of the other. Each weakness is made strong by some corresponding strength in the other; for the truest union is where each soul has precisely the faculty which the other needs.

Harry was by nature and habit exactly the reverse of Esther. His conclusions were all intuitions. His religion was an emanation from the heart, a child of personal experience, and not a formula of the head. In him was seen the beginning of that great *reaction* which took place largely in the young mind of New England against the tyranny of mere logical methods as applied to the ascertaining of moral truths.

The hour of full heart union that made them one placed her mind under the control of his. His simple faith in God's love was an antidote to her despondent fears. His mind bore hers along on its current. His imagination awakened hers. She was like one carried away by a winged spirit, lifted up and borne heavenward by his faith and love. She was a transfigured being. An atmosphere of joy brightened and breathed around her; her eyes had a mysterious depth, her cheeks a fluttering color. The winter was over and past for her, and the time of the singing of birds had come.

Mr. Avery was in raptures. The long agony was past. He had gained a daughter and a son, and he was too joyful, too willing to believe, to be analytic or critical. Long had he secretly hoped that such faultless consistency, such strict attention to duty, might perhaps indicate a secret work of divine grace, which would spring into joy if only recognized and believed in. But now, when the dove that had long wandered actually bent her white wings at the window of the ark, he stretched forth his hand and drew her in with a trembling eagerness.

CHAPTER XXXVI

AFTER THE REVIVAL

But the revival could not always last. The briefness of these periods, and the inevitable gravitation of everybody back to the things of earth, has sometimes been mentioned with a sneer.

"Where's your revival now?"

The deacon whose face was so radiant as he talked of the love of Christ now sits with the same face drawn into knots and puckers over his account-book; and he thinks the money for the mortgage is due, and the avails for the little country store are small; and somehow a great family of boys and girls eat up and wear out; and the love of Christ seems a great way off, and the trouble about the mortgage very close at hand; and so the deacon is cross, and the world has its ready sneer for the poor man. "He can talk about the love of Christ, but he's a terrible screw at a bargain," they say. Ah, brother, have mercy! the world screws us, and then we are tempted to screw the world. The soil is hard, the climate cold, labor incessant, little to come of it, and can you sneer that a poor soul has, for a brief season, forgotten all this and risen out of his body and above his cares, and been for a little while a glorified deacon instead of a poor, haggling, country store-keeper?

Plato says that we all once had wings, and that they still tend to grow out in us, and that our burnings and aspirations for higher things are like the teething pangs of children. We are trying to cut our wings. Let us not despise these teething seasons. Though the wings do not become apparent, they may be starting under many a rough coat, and on many a clumsy pair of shoulders.

But in our little town of Cloudland, after the heavenly breeze had blown over, there were to be found here and there immortal flowers and leaves from the tree of life, which had blown into many a dwelling.

Poor old drunken Culver, who lived under the hill, and was said to beat his wife, had become a changed man, and used to come out to weekly prayer-meetings. Some tough old family quarrels, such as follow the settlement of wills in a poor country, had at last been brought to an end, and brother had shaken hands with brother: the long root of bitterness had been pulled up and burned on the altar of love. It is true that nobody had become an angel. Poor sharp-tongued Miss Krissy Pike still went on reporting the wasteful excesses she had seen in the minister's swill-barrel. And some that were crabbed and cross-gained before were so still, and some, perhaps, were a little more snarly than usual, on account of the late over-excitement.

A revival of religion merely makes manifest for a time what religion there is in a community, but it does not exalt men above their nature or above their times. It is neither revelation nor inspiration; it is impulse. It gives no new faculties, and it goes at last into that general average of influences which go to make up the progress of a generation.

One terrestrial result of the revival in our academy was that about half a dozen of the boys fell desperately in love with Tina. I have always fancied Tina to be one of that species of womankind that used to be sought out for priestesses to the Delphic oracle. She had a flame-like, impulsive, ethereal temperament, a capacity for sudden inspirations, in which she was carried out of herself, and spoke winged words that made one wonder whence they came. Her religious zeal had impelled her to be the adviser of every one who came near her, and her sayings were quoted, and some of our shaggy, rough-coated mountain boys thought that they had never had an idea of the beauty of holiness before. Poor boys! they were so sacredly simple about it. And Tina came to me with wide brown eyes that sparkled like a cairngorm-stone, and told me that she believed she had found what her peculiar calling was: it was to influence young men in religion! She cited, with enthusiasm, the wonderful results she had been able to produce, the sceptical doubts she had removed, the conceptions of heavenly things that she had been able to pour into their souls.

The divine priestess and I had a grand quarrel one day, because I insisted upon it that these religious ministrations on the part of a beautiful young girl to those of the opposite sex would assuredly end in declarations of love and hopes of marriage.

Girls like Tina are often censured as flirts, — most unjustly so, too. Their unawakened nature gives them no power of perceiving what must be the full extent of their influence over the opposite sex. Tina was warmly social; she was enthusiastic and self-confident, and had precisely that spirit which should fit a woman to be priestess or prophetess, to inspire and to lead. She had a magnetic fervor of nature, an attractive force that warmed in her cheeks and sparkled in her eyes, and seemed to make summer around her. She excited the higher faculties, — poetry, ideality, blissful dreams seemed to be her atmosphere, — and she had a power of quick sympathy, of genuine, spontaneous outburst, that gave to her looks and words almost the value of a caress, so that she was an unconscious deceiver, and seemed always to say more for the individual than she really meant. All men are lovers of sunshine and spring gales, but they are no one's in particular; and he who seeks to hold them to one heart finds his mistake. Like all others who have a given faculty, Tina loved its exercise, — she loved to influence, loved to feel her power, alike, over man and woman. But who does not know that the power of the sibyl is doubled by the opposition of sex? That which is only acquiescence in a woman friend becomes devotion in a man. That which is admiration from a woman becomes adoration in a man. And of all kinds of power which can be possessed by man or woman, there is none which I think so absolutely intoxicating as this of personal fascination. You may as well blame a bird for wanting to soar and sing as blame such women for the instinctive pleasure they feel in their peculiar kind of empire. Yet, in simple good faith, Tina did not want her friends of the other sex to become lovers. She was willing enough that they should devote themselves, under all sorts of illusive names of brother and friend and what-not, but when they proceeded to ask her for herself there was an instant revulsion, as when some person has unguardedly touched a strong electric circle. The first breath of passion repelled her; the friend that had been so agreeable the hour before was unendurable. Over and over again have I seen her go to the same illusive round, always sure that in this instance it was understood that it was to be friendship, and only friendship, or brotherly or Christian love, till the hour came for the electric revulsion, and the friend was lost.

Tina had not learned the modern way of girls, who count their lovers and offers as an Indian does his scalps, and parade the number of their victims before their acquaintances. Every incident of this kind struck her as a catastrophe; and, as Esther, Harry, and I were always warning her, she would come to us like a guilty child, and seek to extenuate her offence. I think the girl was sincere in the wish she often uttered, that she could be a boy, and be loved as a comrade and friend only. "Why must, why would, they always persist in falling into this tiresome result?" "O Horace!" she would say to me, "if I were only Tom Percival, I should be perfectly happy! but it is so stupid to be a girl!"

In my own secret soul I had no kind of wish that she should be Tom Percival, but I did not tell her so. No, I was too wise for that. I knew that my only chance of keeping my position as father-confessor to this elastic young penitent consisted in a judicious suppression of all peculiar claims or hopes on my part, and I was often praised and encouraged for this exemplary conduct, and the question pathetically put to me, "Why couldn't the others do as I did?" O Tina, Tina! did your brown eyes see, and your quick senses divine, that there was something in me which you dreaded to awaken, and feared to meet?

There are some men who have a faculty of making themselves the confidants of women. Perhaps because they have a certain amount of the feminine element in their own composition. They seem to be able to sympathize with them on their feminine side, and are capable of running far in a friendship without running fatally into love.

I think I had this power, and on it I founded my hopes in this regard. I enjoyed, in my way, almost as much celebrity in our little circle for advising and guiding my friends of the other sex as Tina did, and I took care to have on hand such a list of intimates as would prevent my name from being coupled with hers in the school gossip.

In these modern times, when man's fair sister is asking admission at the doors of classic halls, where man has hitherto reigned in monastic solitude, the query is often raised by our modern sociologists, Can man and woman, with propriety, pursue their studies together? Does the great mystery of sex, with its wide laws of attraction, and its strange, blinding, dazzling influences, furnish a sufficient reason why the two halves of creation, made for each other, should be kept during the whole course of education rigorously apart? This question, like a great many others, was solved without discussion by the good sense of our Puritan ancestors, in throwing the country academies, where young men were fitted for college, open alike to both sexes, and in making the work of education of such dignity in the eyes of the community, that first-rate men were willing to adopt it for life. The consequences were, that, in some lonely mountain town, under some brilliant schoolmaster, young men and women actually were studying together the branches usually pursued in college.

"But," says the modern objector, "bring young men and young women together in these relations, and there will be flirtations and love affairs."

Even so, my friend, there will be. But flirtations and love affairs among a nice set of girls and boys, in a pure and simple state of community, where love is never thought of, except as leading to lawful marriage, are certainly not the worst things that can be thought of, — not half so bad as the grossness and coarseness and roughness and rudeness of those wholly male schools in which boys fight their way on alone, with no humanizing influences from the other sex.

There was, to be sure, a great crop of love affairs, always green and vigorous, in our academy, and vows of eternal constancy interchanged between boys and girls who afterwards forgot and outgrew them, without breaking their hearts on either side; but, for my own part, I think love-making over one's Latin and Greek much better than the fisting and cuffing and fagging of English schools, or than many another thing to which poor, blindly fermenting boyhood runs when separated from home, mother, and sister, and confined to an atmosphere and surroundings sharply and purely male. It is certain that the companionship of the girl improves the boy, but more doubt has been expressed whether the delicacy of womanhood is not impaired by an early experience of the flatteries and gallantries of the other sex. But, after all, it is no worse for a girl to coquette and flirt in her Latin and mathematical class than to do it in the German or the polka. The studies and drill of the school have a certain repressive influence, wholly wanting in the ball-room and under the gas-light of fashionable parties. In a good school, the standard of attraction is, to some extent, intellectual. The girl is valued for something besides her person; her disposition and character are thoroughly tested, the powers of her mind go for something, and, what is more, she is known in her every-day clothes. On the whole, I do not think a better way can be found to bring the two sexes together, without that false glamour which obscures their knowledge of each other, than to put them side by side in the daily drill of a good literary institution.

Certainly, of all the days that I look back upon, this academy life in Cloudland was the most perfectly happy. It was happier than college life, because of the constant intertwining and companionship with woman, which gave a domestic and family charm to it. It was happy because we were in the first flush of belief in ourselves, and in life.

O that first belief! those incredible first visions! when all things look possible, and one believes in the pot of gold at the end of the rainbow, and sees enchanted palaces in the sunset clouds!

What faith we had in one another, and how wonderful we were in one another's eyes! Our little clique of four was a sort of holy of holies in our view. We believed that we had secrets of happiness and progress known only to ourselves. We had full faith in one another's destiny; we were all remarkable people, and destined to do great things.

At the close of the revival, we four, with many others, joined Mr. Avery's church, — a step which in New England, at this time, meant a conviction of some spiritual experience gained, of some familiar communion with the Great Invisible. Had I found it then? Had I laid hold of that invisible hand, and felt its warmth and reality? Had I heard the beatings of a warm heart under the cold exterior of the regular laws of nature, and found a living God? I thought so. That hand and heart were the hand and heart of Jesus, — the brother, the friend, and the interpreting God for poor, blind, and helpless man.

As we stood together before the pulpit, with about fifty others, on that Sunday most joyful to Mr. Avery's heart, we made our religious profession with ardent sincerity. The dear man found in that day the reward of all his sorrows, and the fruit of all his labors. He rejoiced in us as first fruits of the millennium, which, having already dawned in his good honest heart, he thought could not be far off from the earth.

Ah! those days of young religion were vaguely and ignorantly beautiful, like all the rest of our outlook on life. We were sincere, and meant to be very good and true and pure, and we knew so little of the world we were living in! The village of Cloudland, without a pauper, with scarcely an ignorant person in it, with no temptation, no dissipation, no vice, — what could we know there of the appalling questions of real life? We were hid there together, as in the hollow of God's hand; and a very sweet and lovely hiding-place it was.

Harry had already chosen his profession; he was to be a clergyman, and study with Mr. Avery when his college course was finished. In those days the young aspirants for the pulpit were not gathered into seminaries, but distributed through the country, studying, writing, and learning the pastoral work by sharing the labors of older pastors. Life looked, therefore, very bright to Harry, for life was, at that age, to live with Esther. Worldly care there was none. Mr. Avery was rich on two hundred and fifty dollars, and there were other places in the mountains where birds sung and flowers grew, where Esther could manage another parsonage, as now her father's. She lived in the world of taste and intellect and thought. Her love of the beautiful was fed by the cheap delights of nature, and there was no onerous burden of care in looking forward to marriage, such as now besets a young man when he meditates taking to himself some costly piece of modern luxury, — some exotic bird, who must be fed on incense and odors, and for whom any number of gilded cages and costly surroundings may be necessary. Marriage, in the days of which I speak, was a very simple and natural affair, and Harry and Esther enjoyed the full pleasure of talking over and arranging what their future home should be; and Tina, quite as interested as they, drew wonderful pictures of it, and tinted them with every hue of the rainbow.

Mr. Avery talked with me many times to induce me to choose the same profession. He was an enthusiast for it; it was to him a calling that eclipsed all others, and he could wish the man he loved no greater blessedness than to make him a minister.

But I felt within myself a shrinking doubt of my own ability to be the moral guide of others, and my life-long habit of half-sceptical contemplation made it so impossible to believe the New England theology with the perfect, undoubting faith that Mr. Avery had, that I dared not undertake. I did not disbelieve. I would not for the world controvert; but I could not believe with his undoubting enthusiasm. His sword and spear, so effective in his hands, would tremble in mine. I knew that Harry would do something. He had a natural call, a divine impulse, that led him from childhood to sacred ministries; and though he did not more than I accept the system of new-school theology as complete truth, yet I could see that it would furnish to his own devotional nature a stock from which vigorous grafts would shoot forth.

Shall I say, also, that my future was swayed unconsciously by a sort of instinctive perception of what yet might be desired by Tina? Something a little more of this world I seemed to want to lay at her feet. I felt, somehow, that there was in her an aptitude for the perfume and brightness and gayeties of this lower world. And as there must be, not only clergymen, but lawyers, and as men will pay more for getting their own will than for saving their souls, I dreamed of myself, in the future, as a lawyer, — of course a rising one; of course I should win laurels at the bar, and win them by honorable means. I *would* do it; and Tina should be mistress of a fine, antique house in Boston, like the Kitterys', with fair, large gardens and pleasant prospects, and she should glitter and burn and twinkle like a gem, in the very front ranks of society. Yes, I was ambitious, but it was for her.

One thing troubled me: every once in a while, in the letters from Miss Mehitable, came one from Ellery Davenport, written in a free, gay, dashing, cavalier style, and addressing Tina with a kind of patronizing freedom that made me ineffably angry. I wanted to shoot him. Such are the risings of the ancient Adam in us, even after we have joined the Church. Tina always laughed at me because I scolded and frowned at these letters, and, I thought, seemed to take rather a perverse pleasure in them. I have often speculated on that trait wherein lovely woman slightly resembles a cat; she cannot, for the life of her, resist the temptation to play with her mouse a little, and rouse it with gentle pats of her velvet paw, just to see what it will do.

I was, of course, understood to be under solemn bond and promise to love Tina only as a brother; but was it not a brother's duty to watch over his sister? With what satisfaction did I remember all Miss Debby Kittery's philippics against Ellery Davenport! Did I not believe every word of them heartily? I hated the French language with all my soul, and Ellery Davenport's proficiency in it; and Tina could not make me more angry than by speaking with admiration of his graceful fluency in French, and expressing rather wilful determinations that, when she got away from Mr. Rossiter's dictation, she would study it. Mr. Davenport had said that, when he came back to America, he would give her French lessons. He was always kind and polite, and she didn't doubt that he'd give *me* lessons, too, if I'd take them. "French is the language of modern civilization," said Tina, with the decision of a professor. But she made me promise that I wouldn't say a word to her about it before Mr. Rossiter.

"Now, Horace dear, you know," she said, "that French to him is just like a red rag to a bull; he'd begin to roar and lash his sides the minute you said the words, and Mr. Rossiter and I are capital friends now. You've no idea, Horace, how good he is to me. He takes such an interest in the development of my mind. He writes me a letter or note almost every week about it, and I take his advice, you know, and I wouldn't want to hurt his feelings about French, or anything else. What do you suppose he hates the French so for? I should think he was a genuine Englishman, that had been kept awake nights during all the French wars."

"Well, Tina," I said, "you know there is a great deal of corrupt and dangerous literature in the French language."

"What nonsense, Horace! just as if there wasn't in the English language, too, and I none the worse for it. And I'm sure there are no ends of bad things in the classical dictionary, and in the mythology. He'd better talk about the French language! No, you may depend upon it, Horace, I shall learn French as soon as I leave school."

It will be inferred from this that my young lady had a considerable share of that quality which Milton represents to have been the ruin of our first mother; namely, a determination to go her own way and see for herself, and have little confidential interviews with the serpent, notwithstanding all that could be urged to the contrary by sober old Adam.

"Of course, Adam," said Eve, "I can take care of myself, and don't want you always lumbering after me with your advice. You think the serpent will injure me, do you? That just shows how little you know about me. The serpent, Adam, is a very agreeable fellow, and helps one to pass away one's time; but he don't take me in. O no! there's no danger of his ever getting around *me!* So, my dear Adam, go your own way in the garden, and let me manage for myself."

Whether in the celestial regions there will be saints and angels who develop this particular form of self-will, I know not; but in this world of what Mr. Avery called "imperfect sanctification," religion doesn't prevent the fair angels of the other sex from developing this quality in pretty energetic forms. In fact, I found that, if I was going to guide my Ariadne at all, I must let out my line fast, and let her feel free and unwatched.

CHAPTER XXXVII

THE MINISTER'S WOOD-SPELL

It was in the winter of this next year that the minister's "wood-spell" was announced.

"What is a wood-spell?" you say. Well, the pastor was settled on the understanding of receiving two hundred dollars a year and his wood; and there was a certain day set apart in the winter, generally in the time of the best sleighing, when every parishioner brought the minister a sled-load of wood; and thus, in the course of time, built him up a mighty wood-pile.

It was one of the great seasons of preparation in the minister's family, and Tina, Harry, and I had been busy for two or three days beforehand, in helping Esther create the wood-spell cake, which was to be made in quantities large enough to give ample slices to every parishioner. Two days beforehand, the fire was besieged with a row of earthen pots, in which the spicy compound was rising to the necessary lightness, and Harry and I split incredible amounts of oven-wood, and in the evening we sat together stoning raisins round the great kitchen fire, with Mr. Avery in the midst of us, telling us stories and arguing with us, and entering into the hilarity of the thing like a boy. He was so happy in Esther, and delighted to draw the shy color into her cheeks, by some sly joke or allusion, when Harry's head of golden curls came into close proximity with her smooth black satin tresses.

The cake came out victorious, and we all claimed the merit of it; and a mighty cheese was bought, and every shelf of the closet, and all the dressers of the kitchen, were crowded with the abundance.

We had a jewel of a morning, — one of those sharp, clear, sunny winter days, when the sleds squeak over the flinty snow, and the little icicles tingle along on the glittering crust as they fall from the trees, and the breath of the slow-pacing oxen steams up like a rosy cloud in the morning sun, and then falls back condensed in little icicles on every hair.

We were all astir early, full of life and vigor. There was a holiday in the academy. Mr. Rossiter had been invited over to the minister's to chat and tell stories with the farmers, and give them high entertainment. Miss Nervy Randall, more withered and wild in her attire than usual, but eminently serviceable, stood prepared to cut cake and cheese without end, and dispense it with wholesome nods and messages of comfort. The minister himself heated two little old andirons red-hot in the fire, and therewith from time to time stirred up a mighty bowl of flip, which was to flow in abundance to every comer. Not then had the temperance reformation dawned on America, though ten years later Mr. Avery would as soon have been caught in a gambling-saloon as stirring and dispensing a bowl of flip to his parishioners.

Mr. Avery had recently preached a highly popular sermon on agriculture, in which he set forth the dignity of the farmer's life, from the text, "For the king himself is served of the field"; and there had been a rustle of professional enthusiasm in all the mountain farms around, and it was resolved, by a sort of general consent, that the minister's wood-pile this year should be of the best: none of your old make-shifts, — loads made out with crooked sticks and snapping chestnut logs, most noisy, and destructive to good wives' aprons. Good straight shagbark-hickory was voted none too good for the minister. Also the axe was lifted up on many a proud oak and beech and maple. What destruction of glory and beauty there was in those mountain regions! How ruthlessly man destroys in a few hours that which centuries cannot bring again!

What an idea of riches in those glorious woodland regions! We read legends of millionnaires who fed their fires with cinnamon and rolled up thousand-dollar bills into lamp-lighters, in the very wantonness of profusion. But what was that compared to the prodigality which fed our great roaring winter fires on the thousand-leafed oaks, whose conception had been ages ago, — who were children of the light and of the day, — every fragment and fibre of them made of most celestial influences, of sunshine and raindrops, and night-dews and clouds, slowly working for centuries until they had wrought the wondrous shape into a gigantic miracle of beauty? And then snuffling old Heber Atwood, with his two hard-fisted boys, cut one down in a forenoon and made logs of it for the minister's wood-pile. If this isn't making light of serious things, we don't know what is. But think of your wealth, O ye farmers! — think what beauty and glory every year perish to serve your cooking-stoves and chimney-corners.

To tell the truth, very little of such sentiment was in Mr. Avery's mind or in any of ours. We lived in a woodland region, and we were *blasé* with the glory of trees. We did admire the splendid elms that hung their cathedral arches over the one central street of Cloudland Village, and on this particular morning they were all aflame like Aladdin's palace, hanging with emeralds and rubies and crystals, flashing and glittering and dancing in the sunlight. And when the first sled came squeaking up the village street, we did not look upon it as the funereal hearse bearing the honored corpse of a hundred summers, but we boys clapped our hands and shouted, "Hurrah for old Heber!" as his load of magnificent oak, well-bearded with gray moss, came scrunching into the yard. Mr. Avery hastened to draw the hot flip-iron from the fire and stir the foaming bowl. Esther began cutting the first loaf of cake, and Mr. Rossiter walked out and cracked a joke on Heber's shoulder, whereat all the cast-iron lineaments of his hard features relaxed. Heber had not the remotest idea at this moment that he was to be branded as a tree-murderer. On the contrary, if there was anything for which he valued himself, and with which his heart was at this moment swelling with victorious pride, it was his power of cutting down trees. Man he regarded in a physical point of view as principally made to cut down trees, and trees as the natural enemies of man. When he stood under a magnificent oak, and heard the airy rustle of its thousand leaves, to his ear it was always a rustle of defiance, as if the old oak had challenged him to single combat; and Heber would feel of his axe and say, "Next winter, old boy, we'll see, — we'll see!" And at this moment he and his two tall, slab-sided, big-handed boys came into the kitchen with an uplifted air, in which triumph was but just repressed by suitable modesty. They came prepared to be complimented, and they were complimented accordingly.

"Well, Mr. Atwood," said the minister, "you must have had pretty hard work on that load; that's no ordinary oak; it took strong hands to roll those logs, and yet I don't see but two of your boys. Where are they all now?"

"Scattered, scattered!" said Heber, as he sat with a great block of cake in one hand, and sipped his mug of flip, looking, with his grizzly beard and shaggy hair and his iron features, like a cross between a polar bear and a man, — a very shrewd, thoughtful, reflective polar bear, however, quite up to any sort of argument with a man.

"Yes, they're scattered," he said. "We're putty lonesome now 't our house. Nobody there but Pars, Dass, Dill, Noah, and 'Liakim. I ses to Noah and 'Liakim this mornin', 'Ef we had all our boys to hum, we sh'd haf to take up two loads to the minister, sartin, to make it fair on the wood-spell cake.'"

"Where are your boys now?" said Mr. Avery. "I haven't seen them at meeting now for a good while."

"Wal, Sol and Tim's gone up to Umbagog, lumberin'; and Tite, he's sailed to Archangel; and Jeduth, he's gone to th' West Injies for molasses; and Pete, he's gone to the West. Folks begins to talk now 'bout that 'ere Western kentry, and so Pete, he must go to Buffalo, and see the great West. He's writ back about Niagry Falls. His letters is most amazin'. The old woman, she can't feel easy 'bout him no way. She insists 'pon it them Injuns'll scalp him. The old woman is just as choice of her boys as ef she hadn't got just es many es she has."

"How many sons have you?" said Harry, with a countenance of innocent wonder.

"Wal," said Heber, "I've seen the time when I had fourteen good, straight boys, — all on 'em a turnin' over a log together."

"Dear me!" said Tina. "Hadn't you any daughters?"

"Gals?" said Heber, reflectively. "Bless you, yis. There's been a gal or two 'long, in between, here an' there, — don't jest remember where they come; but, any way, there's plenty of women-folks 't our house."

"Why!" said Tina, with a toss of her pretty head, "you don't seem to think much of women."

"Good in their way," said Heber, shaking his head; "but Adam was fust formed, and then Eve, you know." Looking more attentively at Tina as she stood bridling and dimpling before him, like a bird just ready to fly, Heber conceived an indistinct idea that he must say something gallant, so he added, "Give all honor to the women, as weaker vessels, ye know; that's sound doctrine, I s'pose."

Heber having now warmed and refreshed himself, and endowed his minister with what he conceived to be a tip-top, irreproachable load of wood, proceeded, also, to give him the benefit of a little good advice, prefaced by gracious words of encouragement. "I wus tellin' my old woman this mornin' that I didn't grudge a cent of my subscription, 'cause your preachin' lasts well and pays well. Ses I, 'Mr. Avery ain't the kind of man that strikes twelve the fust time. He's a man that'll wear.' That's what I said fust, and I've followed y' up putty close in yer preachin'; but then I've jest got one word to say to ye. Ain't free agency a gettin' a leetle too top-heavy in yer preachin'? Ain't it kind o' overgrowin' sovereignty? Now, ye see, divine sovereignty hes got to be took care of as well as free agency. That's all, that's all. I thought I'd jest drop the thought, ye know, and leave you to think on 't. This 'ere last revival you run along considerble on 'Whosoever will may come,' an' all that. Now, p'r'aps, ef you'd jest tighten up the ropes a leetle t'other side, and give 'em sovereignty, the hull load would sled easier."

"Well," said Mr. Avery, "I'm much obliged to you for your suggestions."

"Now there's my wife's brother, Josh Baldwin," said Heber; "he was delegate to the last Consociation, and he heerd your openin' sermon, and ses he to me, ses he, 'Your minister sartin doos slant a leetle towards th' Arminians; he don't quite walk the crack,' Josh says, ses he. Ses I, 'Josh, we ain't none on us perfect; but,' ses I, 'Mr. Avery ain't no Arminian, I can tell you. Yeh can't judge Mr. Avery by one sermon,' ses I. You hear him preach the year round, and ye'll find that all the doctrines gits their place.' Ye see I stood up for ye, Mr. Avery, but I thought 't wouldn't do no harm to kind o' let ye know what folks is sayin'."

Here the theological discussion was abruptly cut short by Deacon Zachary Chipman's load, which entered the yard amid the huzzahs of the boys. Heber and his boys were at the door in a minute. "Wal, railly, ef the deacon hain't come down with his shagbark! Wal, wal, the revival has operated on him some, I guess. Last year the deacon sent a load that I'd ha' been ashamed to had in my back yard, an' I took the liberty o' tellin' on him so. Good, straight-grained shagbark. Wal, wal! I'll go out an' help him onload it. Ef that 'ere holds out to the bottom, the deacon's done putty wal, an' I shall think grace *has* made some progress."

The deacon, a mournful, shivery-looking man, with a little round bald head, looking wistfully out of a great red comforter, all furry and white with the sharp frosts of the morning, and, with his small red eyes weeping tears through the sharpness of the air, looked as if he had come as chief mourner at the hearse of his beloved hickory-trees. He had cut down the very darlings of his soul, and come up with his precious load, impelled by a divine impulse like that which made the lowing kine, in the Old Testament story, come slowly bearing the ark of God, while their brute hearts were turning toward the calves that they had left at home. Certainly, if virtue is in proportion to sacrifice, Deacon Chipman's load of hickory had more of self-sacrifice in it than a dozen loads from old Heber; for Heber was a forest prince in his way of doing things, and, with all his shrewd calculations of money's worth, had an open-handed generosity of nature that made him take a pride in liberal giving.

The little man shrank mournfully into a corner, and sipped his tumbler of flip and ate his cake and cheese as if he had been at a funeral.

"How are you all at home, deacon?" said Mr. Avery, heartily.

"Just crawlin', thank you, — just crawlin'. My old woman don't git out much; her rheumatiz gits a dreadful strong hold on her; and, Mr. Avery, she hopes you'll be round to visit her 'fore long. Since the revival she's kind o' fell into darkness, and don't see no cheerin' views. She ses sometimes the universe ain't nothin' but blackness and darkness to her."

"Has she a good appetite?" said Mr. Avery.

"Wal, no. She don't enjoy her vittles much. Some say she's got the jaunders. I try to cosset her up, and git her to take relishin' things. I tell her ef she'd eat a good sassage for breakfast of a cold mornin', with a good hearty bit o' mince-pie, and a cup o' strong coffee, 't would kind o' set her up for the day; but, somehow, she don't git no nourishment from her food."

"There, Rossiter," we heard Mr. Avery whisper aside, "you see what a country minister has to do, — give cheering views to a dyspeptic that breakfasts on sausages and mince-pies."

And now the loads began coming thick and fast. Sometimes two and three, and sometimes four and five, came stringing along, one after another, in unbroken procession. For every one Mr. Avery had an appreciative word. Its especial points were noticed and commended, and the farmers themselves, shrewdest observers, looked at every load and gave it their verdict. By and by the kitchen was full of a merry, chatting circle, and Mr. Rossiter and Mr. Avery were telling their best stories, and roars of laughter came from the house.

Tina glanced in and out among the old farmers, like a bright tropical bird, carrying the cake and cheese to each one, laughing and telling stories, dispensing smiles to the younger ones, — treacherous smiles, which meant nothing, but made the hearts beat faster under the shaggy coats; and if she saw a red-fisted fellow in a corner, who seemed to be having a bad time, she would go and sit down by him, and be so gracious and warming and winning that his tongue would be loosened, and he would tell her all about his steers and his calves and his last crop of corn, and his load of wood, and then wonder all the way home whether he should ever have, in a house of his own, a pretty little woman like that.

By afternoon the minister's wood-pile was enormous. It stretched beyond anything before seen in Cloudland; it exceeded all the legends of neighboring wood-piles and wood-spells related by deacons and lay delegates in the late Consociation. And truly, among things picturesque and graceful, among childish remembrances, dear and cheerful, there is nothing that more speaks to my memory than the dear, good old mossy wood-pile. Harry, Tina, Esther, and I ran up and down and in and about the piles of wood that evening with a joyous satisfaction. How fresh and spicy and woodsy it smelt! I can smell now the fragrance of the hickory, whose clear, oily bark in burning cast forth perfume quite equal to cinnamon. Then there was the fragrant black birch, sought and prized by us all for the high-flavored bark on the smaller limbs, which was a favorite species of confectionery to us. There were also the logs of white birch, gleaming up in their purity, from which we made sheets of woodland parchment.

It is recorded of one man who stands in a high position at Washington, that all his earlier writing-lessons were performed upon leaves of the white birch bark, the only paper used in the family.

Then there were massive trunks of oak, veritable worlds of mossy vegetation in themselves, with tufts of green velvet nestled away in their bark, and sheets of greenness carpeting their sides, and little white, hoary trees of moss, with little white, hoary apples upon them, like miniature orchards.

One of our most interesting amusements was forming land-scapes in the snow, in which we had mountains and hills and valleys, and represented streams of water by means of glass, and clothed the sides of our hills with orchards of apple-trees made of this gray moss. It was an incipient practice at landscape-gardening, for which we found rich material in the wood-pile. Esther and Tina had been filling their aprons with these mossy treasures, for which we had all been searching together, and now we all sat chatting in the evening light. The sun was going down. The sleds had ceased to come, the riches of our woodland treasures were all in, the whole air was full of the trembling, rose-colored light that turned all the snow-covered landscape to brightness. All around us not a fence to be seen, — nothing but waving hollows of spotless snow, glowing with the rosy radiance, and fading away in purple and lilac shadows; and the evening stars began to twinkle, one after another, keen and clear through the frosty air, as we all sat together in triumph on the highest perch of the wood-pile. And Harry said to Esther, "One of these days they'll be bringing in our wood," and Esther's cheeks reflected the pink of the sky.

"Yes, indeed!" said Tina. "And then I am coming to live with you. I'm going to be an old maid, you know, and I shall help Esther as I do now. I never shall want to be married."

Just at this moment the ring of sleigh-bells was heard coming up the street. Who and what now? A little one-horse sleigh drove swiftly up to the door, the driver sprang out with a lively alacrity, hitched his horse, and came toward the house. In the same moment Tina and I recognized Ellery Davenport!

CHAPTER XXXVIII

ELLERY DAVENPORT

Tina immediately turned and ran into the house, laughing, and up stairs into her chamber, leaving Esther to go seriously forward, — Esther always tranquil and always ready. For myself, I felt such a vindictive hatred at the moment as really alarmed me. What had this good-natured man done, with his frank, merry face and his easy, high-bred air, that I should hate him so? What sort of Christian was I, to feel in this way? Certainly it was a temptation of the Devil, and I would put it down, and act like a reasonable being. So I went forward with Harry, and he shook hands with us.

"Hulloa, fellows!" he said, "you've made the great leap since I saw you, and changed from boys into men."

"Good evening, Miss Avery," he said, as we presented him to her. "May I trench on your hospitality a little? I am a traveller in these arctic regions, and Miss Mehitable charged me to call and see after the health and happiness of our young friends here. I see," he said, looking at us, "that there need be no inquiries after health; your looks speak for themselves."

"Why, Percival!" he said, turning to Harry, "what a pair of shoulders you are getting! Genuine Saxon blood runs in your veins plainly enough, and one of these days, when you get to be Sir Harry Percival, you'll do honor to the name."

The proud, reserved blood flushed into Harry's face, and his blue eyes, usually so bright and clear, sparkled with displeasure. I was pleased to see that Ellery Davenport had made him angry. Yes, I said to myself, "What want of tact for him to dare to touch on a subject that Harry's most intimate friends never speak of!"

Esther looked fixedly at him with those clear, piercing hazel eyes, as if she were mentally studying him. I hoped she would not like him; yet why should I hope so?

He saw in a moment that he had made a mistake, and glided off quickly to another subject.

"Where's my fair little enemy, Miss Tina?" he said.

His "fair little enemy" was at this moment attentively studying him through a crack in the window-curtain. Shall I say, too, that the first thing she did, on rushing up to her room, was to look at her hair, and study herself in the glass, wondering how she would look to him now. Well, she had not seen herself for some hours, and self-knowledge is a virtue, we all know. And then our scamper over the wood-pile, in the fresh, evening air, must have deranged something, for Tina had one of those rebellious heads of curls that every breeze takes liberties with, and that have to be looked after and watched and restrained. Esther's satin bands of hair could pass through a whirlwind, and not lose their gloss. It is curious how character runs even to the minutest thing, — the very hairs of our heads are numbered by it, — Esther, always in everything self-poised, thoughtful, reflective; Tina, the child of every wandering influence, tremulously alive to every new excitement, a wind-harp for every air of heaven to breathe upon.

It would be hard to say what mysterious impulse for good or ill made her turn and run when she saw Ellery Davenport. That turning and running in girls means something; it means that the electric chain has been struck in some way; but how?

Mr. Davenport came into the house, and was received with frank cordiality by Mr. Avery. He was a grandson of Jonathan Edwards, and the good man regarded him as, in some sort, a son of the Church, and had, no doubt, instantaneous promptings for his conversion. Mr. Avery, though he believed stringently in the doctrine of total depravity, was very innocent in his application of it to individuals. That Ellery Davenport was a sceptic was well known in New England, wherever the reputation of his brilliant talents and person had circulated, and Mr. Avery had often longed for an opportunity to convert him. The dear, good man had no possible idea that anybody could go wrong from anything but mistaken views, and he was sure, in the case of Ellery Davenport, that his mind must have been perplexed about free agency and decrees, and thus he hailed with delight the Providence which had sent him to his abode. He plunged into an immediate conversation with him about the state of France, whence he had just returned.

Esther, meanwhile, went upstairs to notify Tina of his arrival.

"Mr. Ellery Davenport is below, and has inquired for you."

Nobody could be more profoundly indifferent to any piece of news.

"Was that Mr. Ellery Davenport? How stupid of him to come here when we are all so tired! I don't think I can go down; I am too tired."

Esther, straightforward Esther, took the thing as stated. Tina, to be sure, had exhibited no symptoms of fatigue up to that moment; but Esther now saw that she had been allowing her to over-exert herself.

"My darling," she said, "I have been letting you do too much altogether. You are quite right; you should lie down here quietly, and I'll bring you up your tea. Perhaps by and by, in the evening, you might come down and see Mr. Davenport, when you are rested."

"O nonsense about Mr. Davenport! he doesn't come to see me. He wants to talk with your father, I suppose."

"But he has inquired for you two or three times," said Esther, "and he really seems to be a very entertaining, well-informed man; so by and by, if you feel rested, I should think you had better come down."

Now I, for my part, wondered then and wonder now, and always shall, what all this was for. Tina certainly was not a co-quette; she had not learned the art of trading in herself, and using her powers and fascinations as women do who have been in the world, and learnt the precise value of everything that they say and do. She was, at least now, a simple child of nature, yet she acted exactly as an artful coquette might have done.

Ellery Davenport constantly glanced at the door as he talked with Mr. Avery, and shifted uneasily on his chair; evidently he expected her to enter, and when Esther returned without her he was secretly vexed and annoyed. I was glad of it, too, like a fool as I was. It would have been a thousand times better for my hopes had she walked straight out to meet him, cool and friendly, like Esther. There was one comfort; he was a married man; but then that crazy wife of his might die, or might be dead now. Who knew? To be sure, Ellery Davenport never had the air of a married man, — that steady, collected, sensible, restrained air which be-longs to the male individual, conscious, wherever he moves, of a home tribunal, to which he is responsible. He had gone loose in society, pitied and petted and caressed by ladies, and everybody said, if his wife should die, Ellery Davenport might marry whom he pleased. Esther knew nothing about him, except a faint general outline of his history. She had no prepossessions for or against, and he laid himself out to please her in conversation, with that easy grace and quick perception of character which were habitual with him. Ellery Davenport had been a thriving young Jacobin, and Mr. Avery and Mr. Rossiter were fierce Federalists.

Mr. Rossiter came in to tea, and both of them bore down exultingly on Ellery Davenport in regard to the disturbances in France.

"Just what I always said!" said Mr. Rossiter. "French democracy is straight from the Devil. It's the child of misrule, and leads to anarchy. See what their revolution is coming to. Well, I may not be orthodox entirely on the question of total depravity, but I always admitted the total depravity of the whole French nation."

"O, the French are men of like passions with us!" said Ellery Davenport. "They have been ground down and debased and imbruted till human nature can bear no longer, and now there is a sudden outbreak of the lower classes, — the turning of the worm."

"Not a worm," said Mr. Rossiter, "a serpent, and a strong one."

"Davenport," said Mr. Avery, "don't you see that all this is because this revolution is in the hands of atheists?"

"Certainly I do, sir. These fellows have destroyed the faith of the common people, and given them nothing in its place."

"I am glad to see you recognize that," said Mr. Avery.

"Recognize, my dear sir! Nobody knows the worth of religion as a political force better than I do. Those French people are just like children, — full of sentiment, full of feeling, full of fire, but without the cold, judging, logical power that is frozen into men here by your New England theology. If I have got to manage a republic, give me Calvinists."

"You admit, then," said Mr. Avery, delightedly, "the worth of Calvinism."

"As a political agent, certainly I do," said Ellery Davenport. "Men must have strong, positive religious beliefs to give them vigorous self-government; and republics are founded on the self-governing power of the individual."

"Davenport," said Mr. Avery, affectionately laying his hand on his shoulder, "I should like to have said that thing myself, I couldn't have put it better."

"But do you suppose," said Esther, trembling with eagerness, "that they will behead the Queen?"

"Certainly I do," said Ellery Davenport, with that air of cheerful composure with which the retailer of the last horror delights to shock a listener. "O certainly! I wouldn't give a pin for her chance. You read the account of the trial, I suppose; you saw that it was a foregone conclusion?"

"I did, indeed," said Esther. "But, O Mr. Davenport! can nothing be done? There is Lafayette; can he do nothing?"

"Lafayette may think himself happy if he keeps his own head on his shoulders," said Davenport. "The fact is, that there is a wild beast in every human being. In our race it is the lion. In the French it is the tiger — hotter, more tropical, more blindly intense in rage and wrath. Religion, government, education, are principally useful in keeping the human dominant over the beast; but when the beast gets above the human in the community, woe be to it."

"Davenport, you talk like an apostle," said Mr. Avery.

"You know the devils believe and tremble," said Ellery.

"Well, I take it," said Mr. Rossiter, "you've come home from France disposed to be a good Federalist."

"Yes, I have," said Ellery Davenport. "We must all live and learn, you know."

And so in one evening Ellery witched himself into the good graces of every one in the simple parsonage; and when Tina at last appeared she found him reigning king of the circle. Mr. Rossiter, having drawn from him the avowal that he was a Federalist, now looked complacently upon him as a hopeful young neophyte. Mr. Avery saw evident marks of grace in his declarations in favor of Calvinism, while yet there was a spicy flavor of the prodigal son about him, — enough to engage him for his conversion. Your wild, wicked, witty prodigal son is to a spiritual huntsman an attractive mark, like some rare kind of eagle, whose ways must be studied, and whose nest must be marked, and in whose free, savage gambols in the blue air and on the mountain-tops he has a kind of hidden sympathy.

When Tina entered, it was with an air unusually shy and quiet. She took all his compliments on her growth and change of appearance with a negligent, matter-of-course air, seated herself in the most distant part of the room, and remained obstinately still and silent. Nevertheless, it was to be observed that she lost not a word that he said, or a motion that he made. Was she in that stage of attraction which begins with repulsion? or did she feel stirring within her that intense antagonism which woman sometimes feels toward man, when she instinctively divines that he may be the one who shall one day send a herald and call on her to surrender. Women are so intense, they have such prophetic, fore-reaching, nervous systems, that sometimes they appear to be endowed with a gift of prophecy. Tina certainly was an innocent child at this time, uncalculating, and acting by instinct alone, and she looked upon Ellery Davenport as a married man, who was and ought to be and would be nothing to her; and yet, for the life of her, she could not treat him as she treated other men.

If there was in him something which powerfully attracted, there was also something of the reverse pole of the magnet, that repelled, and inspired a feeling not amounting to fear, but having an undefined savor of dread, as if some invisible spirit about him gave mysterious warning. There was a sense of such hidden, subtile power under his suavities, the grasp of the iron hand was so plain through the velvet glove, that delicate and impressible natures felt it. Ellery Davenport was prompt and energetic and heroic; he had a great deal of impulsive good-nature, as his history in all our affairs shows. He was always willing to reach out the helping hand, and helped to some purpose when he did so; and yet I felt, rather than could prove, in his presence, that he could be very remorseless and persistently cruel.

Ellery Davenport inherited the whole Edwards nature, without its religious discipline, — a nature strong both in intellect and passion. He was an unbelieving Jonathan Edwards. It was this whole nature that I felt in him, and I looked upon the gradual interest which I saw growing in Tina toward him, in the turning of her thoughts on him, in her flights from him and attractions to him, as one looks on the struggles of a fascinated bird, who flees and returns, and flees and returns, each time drawn nearer and nearer to the diamond eyes.

These impressions which come to certain kinds of natures are so dim and cloudy, it is so much the habit of the counter-current of life to disregard them, and to feel that an impression of which you have no physical, external proof is of necessity an absurdity and a weakness, that they are seldom acted on, — seldom, at least, in New England, where the habit of logic is so formed from child-hood in the mind, and the believing of nothing which you cannot prove is so constant a portion of the life education. Yet with re-gard to myself, as I have stated before, there was always a sphere of impression surrounding individuals, for which often I could give no reasonable account. It was as if there had been an emana-tion from the mind, like that from the body. From some it was an emanation of moral health and purity and soundness; from others, the sickly effluvium of moral decay, sometimes penetrating through all sorts of outward graces and accomplishments, like the smell of death through the tube-roses and lilies on the coffin.

I could not prove that Ellery Davenport was a wicked man; but I had an instinctive abhorrence of him, for which I reproached myself constantly, deeming it only the madness of an unreasonable jealousy.

His stay with us at this time was only for a few hours. The next morning he took Harry alone and communicated to him some intelligence quite important to his future.

"I have been to visit your father," he said, "and have made him aware what treasures he possesses in his children."

"His children have no desire that he should be made aware of it," said Harry, coldly. "He has broken all ties between them and him."

"Well, well!" said Ellery Davenport, "the fact is Sir Harry has gone into the virtuous stage of an Englishman's life, where a man is busy taking care of his gouty feet, looking after his tenants, and repenting at his leisure of the sins of his youth. But you will find, when you come to enter college next year, that there will be a handsome allowance at your disposal; and between you and me, I'll just say to you that young Sir Harry is about as puny and feeble a little bit of mortality as I ever saw. To my thinking, they'll never raise him; and his life is all that stands between you and the estate. You know that I got your mother's marriage cer-tificate, and it is safe in Parson Lothrop's hands. So you see there may be a brilliant future before you and your sister. It is well enough for you to know it early, and keep yourself and her free from entanglements. School friendships and flirtations and all that sort of thing are pretty little spring flowers, — very charming in their way and time; but it isn't advisable to let them lead us into compromising ourselves for life. If your future home is to be England, of course you will want your marriage to strengthen your position there."

"My future home will never be England," said Harry, briefly. "America has nursed me and educated me, and I shall always be, heart and soul, an American. My life must be acted in this country."

The other suggestion contained in Ellery Davenport's advice was passed over without a word. Harry was not one that could discuss his private relations with a stranger. He could not but feel obliged to Ellery Davenport for the interest that he had manifested in him, and yet there was something about this easy, patronizing manner of giving advice that galled him. He was not yet old enough not to feel vexed at being reminded that he was young.

It seemed but a few hours, and Ellery Davenport was gone again; and yet how he had changed everything! The hour that he drove up, how perfectly innocently happy and united we all were! Our thoughts needed not to go beyond the present moment: the moss that we had gathered from the wood-pile, and the landscapes that we were going to make with it, were greater treasures than all those of that unknown world of brightness and cleverness and wealth and station, out of which Ellery Davenport had shot like a comet, to astonish us, and then go back and leave us in obscurity.

Harry communicated the intelligence given him by Ellery Davenport, first to me, then to Tina and Esther and Mr. Avery, but begged that it might not be spoken of beyond our little circle. It could and it should make no change, he said. But can expectations of such magnitude be awakened in young minds without a change?

On the whole, Ellery Davenport left a trail of brightness behind him, notwithstanding my sinister suspicions. "How openhanded and friendly it was of him," said Esther, "to come up here, when he has so much on his hands! He told father that he should have to be in Washington next week, to talk with them there about French affairs."

"And I hope he may do Tom Jefferson some good!" said Mr. Avery, indignantly, — "teach him what he is doing in encouraging this hideous, atheistical French revolution! Why, it will bring discredit on republics, and put back the cause of liberty in Europe a century! Davenport sees into that as plainly as I do."

"He's a shrewd fellow," said Mr. Rossiter. "I heard him talk three or four years ago, when he was over here, and he was about as glib-tongued a Jacobin as you'd wish to see; but now my young man has come round handsomely. I told him he ought to tell Jefferson just how the thing is working. I go for government by the respectable classes of society."

"Davenport evidently is not a regenerated man," said Mr. Avery, thoughtfully; "but as far as speculative knowledge goes, he is as good a theologian as his grandfather. I had a pretty thorough talk with him, before we went to bed last night, and he laid down the distinctions with a clearness and a precision that were astonishing. He sees right through that point of the difference between natural and moral inability, and he put it into a sentence that was as neat and compact and clear as a quartz crystal. I think there was a little rub in his mind on the consistency of the freedom of the will with the divine decrees, and I just touched him off with an illustration or two there, and I could see, by the flash of his eye, how quickly he took it. 'Davenport,' said I to him, 'you are made for the pulpit; you ought to be in it.'

" 'I know it,' he said, 'Mr. Avery; but the trouble is, I am not good enough. I think,' he said, 'sometimes I should like to have been as good a man as my grandfather; but then, you see, there's the world, the flesh, and the Devil, who all have something to say to that.'

" 'Well,' says I, 'Davenport, the world and the flesh last only a little while — '

" 'But the Devil and I last forever, I suppose you mean to say,' said he, getting up with a sort of careless swing; and then he said he must go to bed; but before he went he reached out his hand and smiled on me, and said, 'Good night, and thank you, Mr. Avery.' That man has a beautiful smile. It's like a spirit in his face."

Had Ellery Davenport been acting the hypocrite with Mr. Avery? Supposing a man is made like an organ, with two or three banks of keys, and ever so many stops, so that he can play all sorts of tunes on himself; is it being a hypocrite with each person to play precisely the tune, and draw out exactly the stop, which he knows will make himself agreeable and further his purposes? Ellery Davenport did understand the New England theology as thoroughly as Mr. Avery. He knew it from turret to foundation-stone. He knew all the evidences of natural and revealed religion, and, when he chose to do so, could make most conclusive arguments upon them. He had a perfect appreciation of devotional religion, and knew precisely what it would do for individuals. He saw into politics with unerring precision, and knew what was in men, and whither things were tending. His unbelief was purely and simply what has been called in New England the natural opposition of the heart to God. He loved his own will, and he hated control, and he determined, *per fas aut nefas*, to carry his own plans in this world, and attend to the other when he got into it. To have his own way, and to carry his own points, and to do as he pleased, were the ruling purposes of his life.

CHAPTER XXXIX

LAST DAYS IN CLOUDLAND

The day was coming now that the idyl of Cloudland must end, and our last term wound up with a grand dramatic entertainment.

It was a time-honored custom in New England academies to act a play once a year as the closing exercise, and we resolved that our performance should surpass all others in scenic effect.

The theme of the play was to be the story of Jephthah's daughter, from the Old Testament. It had been suggested at first to take Miss Hannah More's sacred drama upon this subject; but Tina insisted upon it that it would be a great deal better to write an original drama ourselves, each one taking a character, and composing one's own part.

Tina was to be Jephthah's daughter, and Esther her mother; and a long opening scene between them was gotten up by the two in a private session at their desks in the school-room one night, and, when perfected, was read to Harry and me for our critical judgment. The conversation was conducted in blank verse, with the usual appropriate trimmings and flourishes of that species of literature, and, on the whole, even at this time, I do not see but that it was quite as good as Miss Hannah More's.

There was some skirmishing between Harry and myself about our parts, Harry being, as I thought, rather too golden-haired and blue-eyed for the grim resolve and fierce agonies of Jephthah. Moreover, the other part was to be that of Tina's lover, and he was to act very desperate verses indeed, and I represented to Harry privately that here, for obvious reasons, I was calculated to succeed. But Tina overruled me with that easy fluency of good reasons which the young lady always had at command. "Harry would make altogether the best lover," she said; "he was just cut out for a lover. Then, besides, what does Horace know about it? Harry has been practising for six months, and Horace hasn't even begun to think of such things yet."

This was one of those stringent declarations that my young lady was always making with regard to me, giving me to understand that her whole confidence in me was built entirely on my discretion. Well, I was happy enough to let it go so, for Ellery Davenport had gone like an evening meteor, and we had ceased talking and thinking about him. He was out of our horizon entirely. So we spouted blank verse at each other, morning, noon, and night, with the most cheerful courage. Tina and Harry had, both of them, a considerable share of artistic talent, and made themselves very busy in drawing and painting scenery, — a work in which the lady principal, Miss Titcomb, gave every assistance; although, as Tina said, her views of scenery were mostly confined to what was proper for tombstones. "But then," she added, "let her have the whole planning of my grave, with a great weeping willow over it, — that'll be superb! I believe the weeping willows will be out by that time, and we can have real branches. Won't that be splendid!"

Then there was the necessity of making our drama popular, by getting in the greatest possible number of our intimate friends and acquaintances. So Jephthah had to marshal an army on the stage, and there was no end of paper helmets to be made. In fact, every girl in school who could turn her hand to anything was making a paper helmet.

There was to be a procession of Judæan maidens across the stage, bearing the body of Jephthah's daughter on a bier, after the sacrifice. This took in every leading girl in the school; and as they were all to be dressed in white, with blue ribbons, one may fancy the preparation going on in all the houses far and near. There was also to be a procession of youths, bearing the body of the faithful lover, who, of course, was to die, to keep the departed company in the shades.

We had rehearsals every night for a fortnight, and Harry, Tina, and I officiated as stage-managers. It is incredible the trouble we had. Esther acted the part of Judæan matron to perfection, — her long black hair being let down and dressed after a picture in the Biblical Dictionary, which Tina insisted upon must be authentic. Esther, however, rebelled at the nose-jewels. There was no making her understand the Oriental taste of the thing; she absolutely declined the embellishment, and finally it was agreed among us that the nose-jewels should be left to the imagination.

Harry looked magnificent, with the help of a dark mustache, which Tina very adroitly compounded of black ravelled yarn, arranging it with such delicacy that it had quite the effect of hair. The difficulty was that in impassioned moments the mustache was apt to get awry; and once or twice, while on his knees before Tina in tragical attitudes, this occurrence set her off into hysterical giggles, which spoiled the effect of the rehearsal. But at last we contrived a plaster which the most desperate plunges of agony could not possibly disarrange.

As my eyes and hair were black, when I had mounted a towering helmet overshadowed by a crest of bear-skin, fresh from an authentic bear that Heber Atwood had killed only two weeks before, I made a most fateful and portentous Jephthah, and flattered myself secretly on the tragical and gloomy emotions excited in the breasts of divers of my female friends.

I composed for myself a most towering and lofty entrance scene, when I came in glory at the head of my troops. I could not help plagiarizing Miss Hannah More's first line: —

"On Jordan's banks proud Ammon's banners wave."

Any writer of poems will pity me, when he remembers his own position, if he has ever tried to make a verse on some subject and been stuck and pierced through by some line of another poet, which so sticks in his head and his memory that there is no possibility of his saying the thing any other way. I tried beginning, —

"On Salem's plains the summer sun is bright";

but when I looked at my troop of helmets and the very startling banner which we were to display, and reflected that Josh Billings was to give an inspiring blast on a bugle behind the scenes, I perfectly longed to do the glorious and magnificent, and this resounding line stood right in my way.

"Well, dear me, Horace," said Tina, "take it, and branch off from it, — make a text of it."

And so I did. How martial and Miltonic I was! I really made myself feel quite serious and solemn with the pomp and glory of my own language; but I contrived to introduce into my resounding verses a most touching description of my daughter, in which I exhausted Oriental images and similes on her charms. Esther and I were to have rather a tender scene, on parting, as she was to be my wife; but then we minded it not a jot. The adroitness with which both these young girls avoided getting into relations that might savor of reality was an eminent instance of feminine tact. And while Harry was playing the impassioned lover at Tina's feet, Esther looked at him slyly, with just the slightest shade of consciousness, — something as slight as the quivering of an eyelash, or a tremulous flush on her fair cheek. There was fire under that rose-colored snow after all, and that was what gave the subtle charm to the whole thing.

We had an earnest discussion among us four as to what was proper to be done with the lover. Harry insisted upon it, that, after tearing his hair and executing all the other properties of despair, he should end by falling on his sword; and he gave us two or three extemporaneous representations of the manner in which he intended to bring out this last scene. How we screamed with laughter over these discussions, as Harry, whose mat of curls was somewhat prodigious, ran up and down the room, howling distractedly, running his fingers through his hair until each separate curl stood on end, and his head was about the size of a half-bushel! We nearly killed ourselves laughing over our tragedy, but still the language thereof was none the less broken-hearted and impassioned.

Tina was vindictive and bloodthirsty in her determination that the tragedy should be of the deepest dye. She exhibited the ferocity of a little pirate in her utter insensibility to the details of blood and murder, and would not hear of any concealment, or half-measures, to spare anybody's feelings. She insisted upon being stabbed on the stage, and she had rigged up a kitchen carving-knife with a handle of gilt paper, ornamented with various breast-pins of the girls, which was celebrated in florid terms in her part of the drama as a Tyrian dagger.

"Why Tyrian," objected Harry, "when it is the Jews that are fighting the Ammonites?"

"O nonsense, Harry! Tyrian sounds a great deal better, and the Ammonites, I don't doubt, had Tyrian daggers," said Tina, who displayed a feminine facility in the manufacture of facts.

"Tyre, you know," she added, "was the country where all sorts of things were made: Tyrian purple and Tyrian mantles, — why, of course they must have made daggers, and the Jews must have got them, — of course they must! I'm going to have it, not only a Tyrian dagger, but a sacred dagger, taken away from a heathen temple and consecrated to the service of the Lord. And only see what a sheath I have made for it! Why, at this distance it couldn't be told from gold! And how do you suppose that embossed work is made? Why, it's different-colored grains of rice and gilt paper rolled up!"

It must be confessed that nobody enjoyed Tina's successes more heartily than she did herself. I never knew anybody who had a more perfect delight in the work of her own hands.

It was finally concluded, in full concert, that the sacrifice was to be performed at an altar, and here came an opportunity for Miss Titcomb's proficiency in tombstones to exercise itself. Our altar was to be like the lower part of a monument, so we decided, and Miss Titcomb had numerous patterns of this kind, subject to our approval. It was to be made life-size, of large sheets of pasteboard, and wreathed with sacrificial garlands.

Tina was to come in at the head of a chorus of wailing maidens, who were to sing a most pathetic lamentation over her. I was to stand grim and resolved, with my eyes rolled up into my helmet, and the sacrificial Tyrian dagger in my hands, when she was to kneel down before the altar, which was to have real flame upon it. The top of the altar was made to conceal a large bowl of alcohol, and before the entering of the procession the lights were all to be extinguished, and the last scene was to be witnessed by the lurid glare of the burning light on the altar. Any one who has ever tried the ghostly, spectral, supernatural appearance which his very dearest friend may be made to have by this simple contrivance, can appreciate how very sanguine our hopes must have been of the tragical powers of this *dénouement*.

All came about quite as we could have hoped. The academy hall was packed and crammed to the ceiling, and our acting was immensely helped by the loudly expressed sympathy of the audience, who entered into the play with the most undisguised conviction of its reality. When the lights were extinguished, and the lurid flame flickered up on the altar, and Tina entered dressed in white with her long hair streaming around her, and with an inspired look of pathetic resignation in her large, earnest eyes, a sort of mournful shudder of reality came over me, and the words I had said so many times concerning the sacrifice of the victim became suddenly intensely real; it was a sort of stage illusion, an overpowering belief in the present.

The effect of the ghastly light on Tina's face, on Esther's and Harry's, as they grouped themselves around in the preconcerted attitudes, was really overwhelming.

It had been arranged that, at the very moment when my hand was raised, Harry, as the lover, should rush forward with a shriek, and receive the dagger in his own bosom. This was the last modification of our play, after many successive rehearsals, and the success was prodigious. I stabbed Harry to the heart, Tina gave a piercing shriek and fell dead at his side, and then I plunged the dagger into my own heart, and the curtain fell, amid real weeping and wailing from many unsophisticated, soft-hearted old women.

Then came the last scene, — the procession of youths and maidens across the stage, bearing the bodies of the two lovers, — the whole ending in an admirably constructed monument, over which a large willow was seen waving. This last gave to Miss Titcomb, as she said, more complete gratification than any scene that had been exhibited. The whole was a most triumphant success.

Heber Atwood's "old woman" declared that she caught her breath, and thought she "should ha' fainted clean away when she see that gal come in." And as there was scarely a house in which there was not a youth or a maiden who had borne part in the chorus, all Cloudland shared in the triumph.

By way of dissipating the melancholy feelings consequent upon the tragedy, we had a farce called "Our Folks," which was acted extemporaneously by Harry, Tina, and myself, consisting principally in scenes between Harry as Sam Lawson, Tina as Hepsie, and myself as Uncle Fliakim, come in to make a pastoral visit, and exhort them how to get along and manage their affairs more prosperously. There had been just enough strain upon our nerves, enough reality of tragic exultation, to excite that hysterical quickness of humor which comes when the nervous system is well up. I let off my extra steam in Uncle Fliakim with a good will, as I danced in in my black silk tights, knocking down the spinning-wheel, upsetting the cradle, setting the babies to crying, and starting Hepsie's tongue, which lost nothing of force or fluency in Tina's reproduction. How the little elf could have transformed herself in a few moments into such a peaked, sharp, wiry-featured, virulent-tongued virago, was matter of astonishment to us all; while Harry, with a suit of fluttering old clothes, with every joint dissolving in looseness, and with his bushy hair in a sort of dismayed tangle, with his cheeks sucked in and her eyes protruding, gave an inimitable Sam Lawson.

The house was convulsed; the screams and shrieks of laughter quite equalled the moans of distress in our tragedy.

And so the curtain fell on our last exhibition in Cloudland. The next day was all packing of trunks and taking of leave, and last words from Mr. Rossiter and Mr. Avery to the school, and settling of board-bills and school-bills, and sending back all the breastpins from the Tyrian dagger, and a confused kicking about of helmets, together with interchanges between various Johns and Joans of vows of eternal constancy, assurances from some fair ones that, "though they could not *love*, they should always regard as a brother," and from some of our sex to the same purport toward gentle-hearted Aramintas, — very pleasant to look upon and charming to dwell upon, — who were not, after all, our chosen Aramintas; and there was no end of three and four-paged notes written, in which Susan Ann told Susan Jane that "never, never shall we forget the happy hours we've spent together on Cloudland hill, — never shall the hand of friendship grow cold, or the heart of friendship cease to beat with emotion."

Poor dear souls all of us! We meant every word that we said.

It was only the other day that I called in a house on Beacon Street to see a fair sister, to whom on this occasion I addressed a most pathetic note, and who sent me a very pretty curl of golden-brown hair. Now she is Mrs. Boggs, and the sylph that was is concealed under a most enormous matron; the room trembles when she sets her foot down. But I found her heart in the centre of the ponderous mass, and, as I am somewhat inclining to be a stout old gentleman, we shook the room with our merriment. Such is life!

The next day Tina was terribly out of spirits, and had two or three hours of long and bitter crying, the cause of which none of our trio could get out of her.

The morning that we were to leave she went around bidding good by to everybody and everything, for there was not a creature in Cloudland that did not claim some part in her, and for whom she had not a parting word. And, finally, I proposed that we should go in to the schoolmaster together and have a last good time with him, and then, with one of her sudden impulsive starts, she turned her back on me.

"No, no, Horace! I don't want to see him any more!"

I was in blank amazement for a moment, and then I remembered the correspondence on the improvement of her mind.

"Tina, you don't tell me," said I, "that Mr. Rossiter has — "

She turned quickly round and faced on the defensive.

"Now, Horace, you need not talk to me, for it is *not my fault! Could* I dream of such a thing, now? *Could* I? Mr. Rossiter, of all the men on earth! Why, Horace, I do love him dearly. I never had any father — that cared for me, at least," she said, with a quiver in her voice; "and he was beginning to seem so like a father to me. I loved him, I respected him, I reverenced him, — and now was I wrong to express it?"

"Why, but, Tina," said I, in amazement, "Mr. Rossiter cannot — he could not mean to marry you!"

"No, no. He says that he would not. He asked nothing. It all seemed to come out before he thought what he was saying, — that he has been thinking altogether too much of me, and that when I go it will seem as if *all* was gone that he cares for. I can't tell you how he spoke, Horace; there was something fearful in it, and he trembled. O Horace, he loves me nobly, disinterestedly, truly; but I felt guilty for it. I felt that such a power of feeling never ought to rest on such a bit of thistle-down as I am. Oh! why wouldn't he stay on the height where I had put him, and let me reverence and admire him, and have him to love as my father?"

"But Tina, you cannot, you must not now — "

"I know it, Horace. I have lost him for a friend and father and guide because he will love me too well."

And so ends Mr. Jonathan Rossiter's Spartan training.

My good friends of the American Republic, if ever we come

to have mingled among the senators of the United States specimens of womankind like Tina Percival, we men remaining such as we by nature are and must be, will not the general hue of politics take a decidedly new and interesting turn?

Mr. Avery parted from us with some last words of counsel.

"You are going into college life, boys, and you must take care of your bodies. Many a boy breaks down because he keeps his country appetite and loses his country exercise. You must balance study and brain-work by exercise and muscle-work, or you'll be down with dyspepsia, and won't know what ails you. People have wondered where the seat of original sin is; I think it's in the stomach. A man eats too much and neglects exercise, and the Devil has him all his own way, and the little imps, with their long black fingers, play on his nerves like a piano. Never overwork either body or mind, boys. All the work that a man can do that can be *rested by one night's sleep is good for him,* but fatigue that goes into the next day is always bad. Never get discouraged at difficulties. I give you both this piece of advice. When you get into a tight place, and everything goes against you till it seems as if you couldn't hold on a minute longer, *never give up then,* for that's just the place and time that the tide'll turn. Never trust to prayer without using every means in your power, and never use the means without trusting in prayer. Get your evidences of grace by pressing forward to the mark, and not by groping with a lantern after the boundary-lines, — and so, boys, go, and God bless you!"

CHAPTER XL

WE ENTER COLLEGE

Harry and I entered Cambridge with honor. It was a matter of pride with Mr. Rossiter that his boys should go more than ready, — that an open and abundant entrance should be administered unto them in the classic halls; and so it was with us. We were fully prepared on the conditions of the sophomore year, and thus, by Mr. Rossiter's drill, had saved the extra expenses of one year of college life.

We had our room in common, and Harry's improved means enabled him to fit it up and embellish it in an attractive manner. Tina came over and presided at the inauguration, and helped us hang our engravings, and fitted up various little trifles of shell and moss work, — memorials of Cloudland.

Tina was now visiting at the Kitterys', in Boston, dispensing smiles and sunbeams, inquired after and run after by every son of Adam who happened to come in her way, all to no purpose, so far as her heart was concerned.

> "Favors to none, to all she smiles extends;
> Oft she rejects, but never once offends."

Tina's education was now, in the common understanding of society, looked upon as finished. Harry's and mine were commencing; we were sophomores in college. She was a young lady in society; yet she was younger than either of us, and had, I must say, quite as good a mind, and was fully as capable of going through our college course with us as of having walked thus far.

However, with her the next question was, Whom will she marry? — a question that my young lady seemed not in the slightest hurry to answer. I flattered myself on her want of susceptibility that pointed in the direction of marriage. She could feel so much friendship, — such true affection, — and yet was apparently so perfectly devoid of passion.

She was so brilliant, and so fitted to adorn society, that one would have thought she would have been *ennuyée* in the old Rossiter house, with only the society of Miss Mehitable and Polly; but Tina was one of those whose own mind and nature are sufficient excitement to keep them always burning. She loved her old friend with all her little heart, and gave to her all her charms and graces, and wound round her in a wild-rose garland, like the eglantine that she was named after.

She had cultivated her literary tastes and powers. She wrote and sketched and painted for Miss Mehitable, and Miss Mehitable was most appreciative. Her strong, shrewd, well-cultivated mind felt and appreciated the worth and force of everything there was in Tina, and Tina seemed perfectly happy and satisfied with one devoted admirer. However, she had two, for Polly still survived, being of the dry immortal species, and seemed, as Tina told her, quite as good as new. And Tina once more had uproarious evenings with Miss Mehitable and Polly, delighting herself with the tumults of laughter which she awakened.

She visited and patronized Sam Lawson's children, gave them candy and told them stories, and now and then brought home Hepsie's baby for a half-day, and would busy herself dressing it up in something new of her own invention and construction. Poor Hepsie was one of those women fated always to have a baby in which she seemed to have no more maternal pleasure than an old fowling-piece. But Tina looked at her on the good-natured and pitiful side, although, to be sure, she did study her with a view to dramatic representation, and made no end of capital of her in this way in the bosom of her own family.

Tina's mimicry and mockery had not the slightest tinge of contempt or ill-feeling in it; it was pure merriment, and seemed to be just as natural to her as the freakish instincts of the mockingbird, who sits in the blossoming boughs above your head, and sends back every sound that you hear with a wild and airy gladness.

Tina's letters to us were full of this mirthful, effervescent sparkle, to which everything in Oldtown afforded matter of amusement; and the margins of them were scrawled with droll and lifelike caricatures, in which we recognized Sam Lawson, and Hepsie, and Uncle Fliakim, and, in fact, all the Oldtown worthies, — not even excepting Miss Mehitable and Polly, the minister and his lady, my grandmother, Aunt Lois, and Aunt Keziah. What harm was there in all this, when Tina assured us that aunty read the letters before they went, and laughed until she cried over them?

"But, after all," I said to Harry one day, "it's rather a steep thing for girls that have kept step with us in study up to this point, and had their minds braced just as ours have been, with all the drill of regular hours and regular lessons, to be suddenly let down, with nothing in particular to do."

"Except to wait the coming man," said Harry, "who is to teach her what to do."

"Well," said I, "in the interval, while this man is coming, what has Tina to do but to make a frolic of life? — to live like a bobolink on a clover-head, to sparkle like a dewdrop in a thornbush, to whirl like a bubble on a stream? Why couldn't she as well find the coming man while she is doing something as while she is doing nothing? Esther and you found each other while you were *working* side by side, your minds lively and braced, toiling at the same great ideas, knowing each other in the very noblest part of your natures; and you are true companions; it is a mating of *souls* and not merely of bodies."

"I know that," said Harry, "I know, too, that in these very things that I set my heart on in the college course Esther is by far my superior. You know, Horace, that she was ahead of us in both Greek and mathematics; and why should she not go through the whole course with us as well as the first part? The fact is, a man never sees a subject thoroughly until he sees what a woman will think of it, for there is a woman's view of every subject, which has a different shade from a man's view, and that is what you and I have insensibly been absorbing in all our course hitherto. How splendidly Esther lighted up some of those passages of the Greek tragedy! and what a sparkle and glitter there were in some of Tina's suggestions! All I know, Horace, is that it is confoundedly dull being without them; these fellows are well enough, but they are cloddish and lumpish."

"Well," said I, "that isn't the worst of it. When such a gay creature of the elements as Tina is has nothing earthly to do to steady her mind and task her faculties, and her life becomes a mere glitter, and her only business to amuse the passing hour, it throws her open to all sorts of temptations from that coming man, whoever he may be. Can we wonder that girls love to flirt, and try their power on lovers? And then they are fair game for men who want to try their powers on them, and some man who has a vacation in his life purpose, and wants something to amuse him, makes an episode by getting up some little romance, which is an amusement to him, but all in all to her. Is that fair?"

"True," said Harry, "and there's everything about Tina to tempt one; she is so dazzling and bewildering and exciting that a man might intoxicate himself with her for the mere pleasure of the thing, as one takes opium or champagne; and that sort of bewilderment and intoxication girls often mistake for love! I would to Heaven, Horace, that I were as sure that Tina loves you as I am that Esther loves me."

"She does love me with her *heart*," said I, "but not with her imagination. The trouble with Tina, Harry, is this: she is a woman that can really and truly love a man as a sister, or as a friend, or as a daughter, and she is a woman that no man can love in that way long. She feels nothing but affection, and she always creates passion. I have not the slightest doubt that she loves me dearly, but I have a sort of vision that between her and me will come some one who will kindle her imagination; and all the more so that she has nothing serious to do, nothing to keep her mind braced, and her intellectual and judging faculties in the ascendant, but is fairly set adrift, just like a little flowery boat, without steersman or oars, on a bright, swift-rushing river. Did you ever notice, Harry, what a singular effect Ellery Davenport seems to have on her?"

"No," said Harry, starting and looking surprised. "Why, Horace, Ellery Davenport is a good deal older than she is, and a married man too."

"Well, Harry, didn't you ever hear of married men that liked to try experiments with girls? and in our American society they can do it all the more safely, because here, thank Heaven! nobody ever dreams but what marriage is a perfect regulator and safe-guard."

"But," said Harry, rubbing his eyes like a person just waking up, "Horace, it must be the mere madness of jealousy that would put such a thing into your head. Why, there hasn't been the slightest foundation for it."

"That is to say, Harry, you've been in love with Esther, and your eyes and ears and senses have all run one way. But I have lived in Tina, and I believe I have a sort of divining power, so that I can almost see into her heart. I *feel in myself* how things affect her, and I *know*, by feeling and sensation, that from her childhood Ellery Davenport has had a peculiar magnetic effect upon her."

"But, Horace, he is a married man," persisted Harry.

"A fascinating married man, victimized by a crazy wife, and ready to throw himself on the sympathies of womanhood in this affliction. The fair sex are such Good Samaritans that some fellows make capital of their wounds and bruises."

"Well, but," said Harry, "there's not the slightest thing that leads me to think that he ever cared particularly about Tina."

"That's because you are Tina's brother, and not her lover," said I. "I remember as long ago as when we were children, spending Easter at Madam Kittery's, how Ellery Davenport's eyes used to follow her, — how she used constantly to seem to excite and interest him; and all this zeal about your affairs, and his coming up to Oldtown, and cultivating Miss Mehitable's acquaintance so zealously, and making himself so necessary to her; and then he has always been writing letters or sending messages to Tina, and then, when he was up in Cloudland, didn't you see how constantly his eyes followed her? He came there for nothing but to see her, — I'm perfectly sure of it."

"Well, Horace, you are about as absurd as a lover need be!" said Harry. "Mr. Davenport is rather a conceited man of the world; I think he patronized me somewhat extensively; but all this about Tina is a romance of your own spinning, you may be sure of it."

This conversation occurred one Saturday morning, while we were dressing and arraying ourselves to go into Boston, where we had engaged to dine at Madam Kittery's.

From the first of our coming to Cambridge, we had remembered our old-time friendship for the Kitterys, and it was an arranged thing that we were to dine with them every Saturday. The old Kittery mansion we had found the same still, charming, quaint, inviting place that it seemed to us in our childhood. The years that had passed over the silvery head of dear old Madam Kittery had passed lightly and reverently, each one leaving only a benediction.

She was still to be found, when we called, seated, as in days long ago, on her little old sofa in the sunny window, and with her table of books before her, reading her Bible and Dr. Johnson, and speaking on "Peace and good-will to men."

As to Miss Debby, she was as up and down, as high-stepping and outspoken and pleasantly sub-acid as ever. The French Revolution had put her in a state of good-humor hardly to be conceived of. It was so delightful to have all her theories of the bad effects of republics on lower classes illustrated and confirmed in such a striking manner, that even her indignation at the destruction of such vast numbers of the aristocracy was but a slight feature in comparison with it.

She kept the newspapers and magazines at hand which contained all the accounts of the massacres, mobbings, and outrages, and read them, in a high tone of voice, to her serving-women, butler, and footman after family prayers. She catechized more energetically than ever, and bore more stringently on ordering one's self lowly and reverently to one's betters, enforcing her remarks by the blood-and-thunder stories of the guillotine in France.

We were hardly seated in the house, and had gone over the usual track of inquiries which fill up the intervals, when she burst forth on us, triumphant.

"Well, my English papers have come in. Have you seen the last news from France? They're at it yet, hotter than ever. One would think that murdering the king and queen might have satisfied them, but it don't a bit. Everybody is at it now, cutting everybody's else throat, and there really does seem to be a prospect that the whole French nation will become extinct."

"Indeed," said Harry, with an air of amusement. "Well, Miss Debby, I suppose you think that would be the best way of settling things."

"Don't know but it would," said Miss Debby, putting on her spectacles in a manner which pushed her cap-border up into a bristling, helmet-like outline, and whirling over her file of papers, seemingly with a view to edifying us with the most startling morsels of French history for the six months past.

"Here's the account of how they worshipped 'the Goddess of Reason'!" she cried, eying us fiercely, as if we had been part and party in the transaction. "Here's all about how their philosophers and poets, and what not, put up a drab, and worshipped her as their 'Goddess of Reason'! And then they annulled the Sabbath, and proclaimed that 'Death is an Eternal Sleep'! Now, that is just what Tom Jefferson likes; it's what suits him. I read it to Ellery Davenport yesterday, to show him what his principles come to."

Harry immediately hastened to assure Miss Debby that we were stanch Federalists, and not in the least responsible for any of the acts or policy of Thomas Jefferson.

"Don't know anything about that; you see it's the Democrats that have got the country, and are running as hard as they can after France. Ah, here it is," Miss Debby added, still turning over her files of papers. "Here are the particulars of the execution of the queen. You can see, — they had her on a common cart, hands tied behind her, rattling and jolting, with all the vile fishwomen and dirty drabs of Paris leering and jeering at her, and they even had the cruelty," she added, coming indignantly at us as if we were responsible for it, "to stop the cart in front of her palace, so that she might be agonized at seeing her former home, and they might taunt her in her agonies! Anybody that can read that, and not say the French are devils, I'd like to know what they are made of!"

"Well," said Harry, undismayed by the denunciations; "the French are an exceedingly sensitive and excitable people, who had been miseducated and mismanaged, and taught brutality and cruelty by the examples of the clergy and nobility."

"Excitable fiddlesticks!" said Miss Debby, who, like my grandmother, had this peculiar way of summing up an argument. "I don't believe in softening sin and iniquity by such sayings as that."

"But you must think," said Harry, "that the French are human beings, and only act as any human beings would under their circumstances."

"Don't believe a word of it!" said she, shortly. "I agree with the man who said, 'God made two kinds of nature, — human nature and French nature.' Voltaire, wasn't it, himself, that said the French were a compound of the tiger and the monkey? I wonder what Tom Jefferson thinks of his beautiful, darling French Republic now! I presume he likes it. I don't doubt it is just such a state of things as he is trying to bring to pass here in America."

"O," said I, "the Federalists will head him at the next election."

"I don't know anything about your Democrats and your Federalists," said she. "I thank Heaven I wash my hands of this government."

"And does King George still reign here?" said Harry.

"Certainly he does, young gentleman! Whatever happens to *this* government, *I* have no part in it."

Miss Debby, upon this, ushered us to the dinner-table, and said grace in a resounding and belligerent voice, and, sitting down, began to administer the soup to us with great determination.

Old Madam Kittery, who had listened with a patient smile to all the preceding conversation, now began in a gentle aside to me.

"I really don't think it is good for Debby to read those bloody-bone stories morning, noon, and night, as she does," she said. "She really almost takes away my appetite some days, and it does seem as if she wouldn't talk about anything else. Now, Horace," she said to me, appealingly, "the Bible says 'Charity rejoiceth not in iniquity,' and I can't help feeling that Debby talks as if she were really glad to see those poor French making such a mess of things. I can't feel so. If they are French, they're our brothers, you know, and Debby really seems to go against the Bible, — not that she means to, dear," she added, earnestly, laying her hand on mine; "Debby is an excellent woman; but, between you and me, I think she is a little excitable."

"What's that mother's saying?" said Miss Debby, who kept a strict survey over all the sentiments expressed in her household. "What was mother saying?"

"I was saying, Debby, that I didn't think it did any good for you to keep reading over and over those dreadful things."

"And who does keep reading them over?" said Miss Debby, "I should like to know. I'm sure I don't; except when it is absolutely necessary to instruct the servants and put them on their guard. I'm sure I am as averse to such details as anybody can be."

Miss Debby said this with that innocent air with which good sort of people very generally maintain that they never do things which most of their acquaintances consider them particular nuisances for doing.

"By the by, Horace," said Miss Debby, by way of changing the subject, "have you seen Ellery Davenport since he came home?"

"No," said I, with a sudden feeling as if my heart was sinking down into my boots. "Has he come home to stay?"

"O yes," said Miss Debby; "his dear, sweet, model, Republican France grew too hot to hold him. He had to flee to England, and now he has concluded to come home and make what mischief he can here, with his democratic principles and his Rousseau and all the rest of them."

"Debby isn't as set against Ellery as she seems to be," said the old lady, in an explanatory aside to me. "You know, dear, he's her cousin."

"And you really think he intends to live in this country for the future?" said I.

"Well, I suppose so," said Miss Debby. "You know that poor, miserable, crazy wife of his is dead, and my lord is turned loose on society as a widower at large, and all the talk here in good circles is, Who is the blessed woman that shall be Mrs. Ellery Davenport the second? The girls are all pulling caps for him, of course."

It was perfectly ridiculous and absurd, but I suddenly lost all appetite for my dinner, and sat back in my chair playing with my knife and fork, until the old lady said to me compassionately: —

"Why, dear, you don't seem to be eating anything! Debby, put an oyster-*paté* on Horace's plate; he don't seem to relish his chicken."

I had to submit to the oyster-*paté*, and sit up and eat it like a man, to avoid the affectionate importunity of my dear old friend. In despair, I plunged into the subject least agreeable to me, and remarked: —

"Mr. Davenport is a very brilliant man, and I suppose in very good circumstances; is he not?"

"Yes, enormously rich," said Miss Debby. "He still passes for young, with that face of his that never will grow old, I believe. And then he has a tongue that could wheedle a bird out of a tree; so I don't know what is to hinder him from having as many wives as Solomon, if he feels so disposed. I don't imagine there is anybody would say 'No' to him."

"Well, I hope he will marry a good girl," said the old lady, "poor dear boy. I always loved Ellery; and he would make any woman happy, I am sure."

"That depends," said Miss Debby, "on what the woman wants. If she wants laces and cashmere shawls, and horses and carriages, and a fine establishment, Ellery Davenport will give her those. But if she wants a man to love her all her life, that's what Ellery Davenport can't do for any woman. He is a man that never cares for anything he has got. It's always the thing that he hasn't got that he's after. It's the 'pot of money at the end of the rainbow,' or the 'philosopher's stone,' or any other thing that keeps a man all his life on a canter, and never getting anywhere. And no woman will ever be anything to him but a temporary diversion. He can amuse himself in too many ways to want *her*."

"Yes," said the old lady, "but when a man marries he promises to cherish her."

"My dear mother, that is in the Church Service, and I assure you Ellery Davenport has got beyond that. He's altogether too fine and wise and enlightened to think that a man should spend his days in cherishing a woman merely because he went through the form of marriage with her in church. Much cherishing his crazy wife got of him! but he used his affliction to get half a dozen girls in love with him, so that he might be cherished himself. I tell you what, — Ellery Davenport lays out to marry a real angel. He's to swear and she's to pray! He is to wander where he likes, and she is always to meet him with a smile and ask no questions. That is the part for Mrs. Ellery Davenport to act."

"I don't believe a word of it, Debby," said the old lady. "You'll see now, — you'll see."

CHAPTER XLI

---◆---

NIGHT TALKS

We walked home that night by starlight, over the long bridge between Boston and Cambridge, and watched the image of the great
round yellow moon just above the horizon, breaking and shimmering in the water into a thousand crystal fragments, like an orb
of golden glass. We stopped midway in the calm obscurity, with
ours arms around each other, and had one of those long talks that
friends, even the most confidential, can have only in the darkness.
Cheek to cheek under the soft dim mantle of the starlight, the
night flowers of the innermost soul open.

We talked of our loves, our hopes, of the past, the present, and
the great hereafter, in which we hoped forever to mingle. And
then Harry spoke to me of his mother, and told in burning words
of that life of bitterness and humiliation and sorrow through which
he had passed with her.

"O Harry," said I, "did it not try your faith, that God should
have left her to suffer all that?"

"No, Horace, no, because in all that suffering she conquered, —
she was more than conqueror. O, I have seen such divine peace
in her eyes, at the very time when everything earthly was failing
her! Can I ever doubt? I who saw into heaven when she entered?
No, I have seen her crowned, glorified, in my soul as plainly as if
it had been a vision."

At that moment I felt in myself that magnetic vibration of the
great central nerves which always prefaced my spiritual visions,
and looking up I saw that the beautiful woman I had seen once
before was standing by Harry, but now more glowing and phos-
phorescent than I saw her last; there was a divine, sweet, awful
radiance in her eyes, as she raised her hands above his head, he,
meanwhile, stooping down and looking intently into the water.

"Harry," said I, after a few moments of silence, "do you believe your mother sees and knows what you do in this world, and watches over you?"

"That has always been one of those things that I have believed without reasoning," said Harry, musingly. "I never could help believing it; and there have been times in my life when I felt so certain that she must be near me, that it seemed as though, if I spoke, she must answer, — if I reached out my hand, it would touch hers. It is one of my instinctive certainties. It is curious," he added, "that the difference between Esther and myself is just the reverse kind of that which generally subsists between man and woman. She has been all her life so drilled in what logicians call reasoning, that, although she has a glorious semi-spiritual nature, and splendid moral instincts, she never trusts them. She is like an eagle that should insist upon climbing a mountain by beak and claw instead of using wings. She must always see the syllogism before she will believe."

"For my part," said I, "I have always felt the tyranny of the hard New England logic, and it has kept me from really knowing what to believe about many phenomena of my own mind that are vividly real to me." Here I faltered and hesitated, and the image that seemed to stand by us slowly faded. I could not and did not say to Harry how often I had seen it.

"After all I have heard and thought on this subject," said Harry, "my religious faith is what it always was, — a deep, instinctive certainty, an embrace by the soul of *something* which it could not exist without. My early recollections are stronger than anything else of perfect and utter helplessness, of troubles entirely beyond all human aid. My father — " He stopped and shuddered. "Horace, he was one of those whom intemperance makes mad. For a great part of his time he was a madman, with all the cunning, all the ingenuity, the devilishness of insanity, and I have had to stand between him and my mother, and to hide Tina out of his way." He seemed to shudder as one convulsed. "One does not get over such a childhood," he said. "It has made all my religious views, my religious faith, rest on two ideas, — man's helplessness, and God's helpfulness. We are sent into this world in the midst of a blind, confused jangle of natural laws, which we cannot by any possibility understand, and which cut their way through and over and around us. They tell us nothing; they have no sympathy; they hear no prayer; they spare neither vice nor virtue. And if we have no friend above to guide us through the labyrinth, if there is no Father's heart, no helping hand, of what use is life? I would throw myself into this river, and have it over with at once."

"I always noticed your faith in prayer," said I. "But how can it consist with this known inflexibility of natural laws?"

"And what if natural laws were meant as servants of man's moral life? What if Jesus Christ and his redeeming, consoling work were the *first* thing, and all things made by him for this end? Inflexible physical laws are necessary; their very inflexibility is divine order; but 'what law cannot do, in that it is weak through the flesh, God did by sending his Son in the likeness of sinful flesh.' Christ delivers us from slavery to natural law; he comes to embody and make visible the paternal idea; and if you and I, with our small knowledge of physical laws, can so turn and arrange them that their inflexible course shall help, and not hinder, much more can their Maker."

"You always speak of Christ as God."

"I have never thought of God in any other way," he answered. "Christ is the God of sufferers; and those who learn religion by sorrow always turn to him. No other than a suffering God could have helped my mother in her anguish."

"And do you think," said I, "that prayer is a clew strong enough to hold amid the rugged realities of life?"

"I do," said Harry. "At any rate, there is my great venture; that is my life-experiment. My mother left me that as her only legacy."

"It certainly seems to have worked well for you so far, Harry," said I, "and for me too, for God has guided us to what we scarcely could have hoped for, two poor boys as we were, and so utterly helpless. But then, Harry, there must be a great many prayers that are never answered."

"Of course," said Harry, "I do not suppose that God has put the key of all the universe into the hand of every child; but it is a comfort to have a Father to ask of, even though he refuse five times out of six, and it makes all the difference between having a father and being an orphan. Yes," he added, after a few moments of thought, "my poor mother's prayers seemed often to be denied, for she prayed that my father might reform. She often prayed from day to day that we might be spared miseries that he still brought upon us. But I feel sure that she has seen by this time that her Father heard the prayers that he seemed to deny, and her faith in him never failed. What is that music?" he said.

At this moment there came softly over the gleaming water, from the direction of the sea, the faintest possible vibration of a sound, like the dying of an organ tone. It might be from some ship, hidden away far off in the mist, but the effect was soft and dreamy as if it came from some spirit-land.

"I often think," said Harry, listening for a moment, "that no one can pronounce on what this life has been to him until he has passed entirely through it, and turns around and surveys it from the other world. I think then we shall see everything in its true proportions; but till then we must walk by faith and not by sight, — faith that God loves us, faith that our Saviour is always near us, and that all things are working together for good."

"Harry," said I, "do you ever think of your father now?"

"Horace, there is where I wish I could be a more perfect Christian than I am. I have a bitter feeling toward him, that I fear is not healthful, and that I pray God to take away. To-night, since we have been standing here, I have had a strange, remorseful feeling about him, as if some good spirit were interceding for him with me, and trying to draw me to love and forgive him. I shall never see him, probably, until I meet him in the great Hereafter, and then, perhaps, I shall find that her prayers have prevailed for him."

It was past twelve o'clock when we got to our room that night, and Harry found lying on his table a great sealed package from England. He opened it and found in it, first, a letter from his father, Sir Harry Percival. The letter was as follows: —

"HOLME HOUSE.

"MY SON HARRY: —

"I have had a dozen minds to write to you before now, having had good accounts of you from Mr. Davenport; but, to say truth, have been ashamed to write. I did not do right by your mother, nor by you and your sister, as I am now free to acknowledge. She was not of a family equal to ours, but she was too good for me.

I left her in America, like a brute as I was, and God has judged me for it.

"I married the woman my father picked out for me, when I came home, and resolved to pull up and live soberly like a decent man. But nothing went well with me. My children died one after another; my boy lived to be seven years old, but he was feeble, and now he is dead too, and you are the heir. I am thinking that I am an old sinner, and in a bad way. Have had two turns of gout in the stomach that went hard with me, and the doctor don't think I shall stand many such. I have made my will with a provision for the girl, and you will have the estate in course. I do wish you would come over and see a poor old sinner before he dies. It isn't in the least jolly being here, and I am dev'lish cross, they say. I suppose I am, but if you were minded to come I'd try and behave myself, and so make amends for what's past beyond recall.

"Your father,

"HARRY PERCIVAL."

Accompanying this letter was a letter from the family lawyer, stating that on the 18th day of the month past Sir Harry Percival had died of an attack of gout. The letter went on to give various particulars about the state of the property, and the steps which had been taken in relation to it, and expressing the hope that the arrangements made would meet with his approbation.

It may well be imagined that it was almost morning before we closed our eyes, after so very startling a turn in our affairs. We lay long discussing it in every possible light, and now first I found courage to tell Harry of my own peculiar experiences, and of what I had seen that very evening. "It seems to me," said Harry, when I had told him all, "as if I *felt* what you saw. I had a consciousness of a sympathetic presence, something breathing over me like wind upon harp-strings, something particularly predisposing me to think kindly of my father. My feeling towards him has been the weak spot of my inner life always, and I had a morbid horror of him. Now I feel at peace with him. Perhaps her prayers have prevailed to save him from utter ruin."

CHAPTER XLII

———————◆❖◆———————

SPRING VACATION AT OLDTOWN

It was the spring vacation, and Harry and I were coming again to Oldtown; and ten miles back, where we changed horses, we had left the crawling old Boston stage and took a foot-path through a patch of land known as the Spring Pasture. Our road lay pleasantly along the brown, sparkling river, which was now just waked up, after its winter nap, as fussy and busy and chattering as a housekeeper that has overslept herself. There were downy catkins on the willows, and the water-maples were throwing out their crimson tassels. The sweet-flag was just showing its green blades above the water, and here and there, in nooks, there were yellow cowslips reflecting their bright gold faces in the dark water.

Harry and I had walked this way that we might search under the banks and among the dried leaves for the white waxen buds and flowers of the trailing arbutus. We were down on our knees, scraping the leaves away, when a well-known voice came from behind the bushes.

"Wal, lordy massy, boys! Here ye be! Why, I ben up to Siah's tahvern, an' looked inter the stage, an' didn't see yer. I jest thought I'd like to come an' kind o' meet yer. Lordy massy, they's all a lookin' out for yer 't all the winders; 'n' Aunt Lois, she's ben bilin' up no end o' doughnuts, an' tearin' round 'nough to drive the house out o' the winders, to git everything ready for ye. Why, it beats the Prodigal Son all holler, the way they're killin' the fatted calves for yer; an' everybody in Oldtown's a wantin' to see Sir Harry."

"O nonsense, Sam!" said Harry, coloring. "Hush about that! We don't have titles over here in America."

"Lordy massy, that's just what I wus a tellin' on 'em up to store. It's a pity, ses I, this yere happened arter peace was signed, 'cause we might ha' had a real live Sir Harry round among us. An' I think Lady Lothrop, she kind o' thinks so too."

"O nonsense!" said Harry. "Sam, are the folks all well?"

"O lordy massy, yes! Chirk and chipper as can be. An' there's Tiny, they say she's a goin' to be an heiress nowadays, an' there's no end of her beaux. There's Ellery Devenport ben down here these two weeks, a puttin' up at the tahvern, with a landau an' a span o' crack horses, a takin' on her out to ride every day, and Miss Mehitable, she's so sot up, she's reely got a bran new bonnet, an' left off that 'ere old un o' hern that she's had trimmed over spring an' fall goin' on these 'ere ten years. I thought that 'ere bonnet's going to last out my time, but I see it hain't. An' she's got a new Injy shawl, that Mr. Devenport gin her. Yeh see, he understan's courtin', all round."

This intelligence, of course, was not the most agreeable to me. I hope, my good friends, that you have never known one of those quiet hours of life, when, while you are sitting talking and smiling, and to all appearance quite unmoved, you hear a remark or learn a fact that seems to operate on you as if somebody had quietly turned a faucet that was letting out your very life. Down, down, down, everything seems sinking, the strength passing away from you as the blood passes when an artery is cut. It was with somewhat this sensation that I listened to Sam's chatter, while I still mechanically poked away the leaves and drew out the long waxy garlands that I had been gathering for *her!*

Sam seated himself on the bank, and, drawing his knees up to his chin and clasping his hands upon them, began moralizing in his usual strain.

"Lordy massy, lordy massy, what a changin' world this 'ere is! It's jest see-saw, teeter-tawter, up an' down. To-day it's I'm up an' you're down, an' to-morrow it's you're up and I'm down! An' then, by an' by, death comes an' takes us all. I've ben kind o' dwellin' on some varses to-day, —

> 'Death, like a devourin' delūge,
> Sweeps all away.
> The young, the old, the middle-aged,
> To him become a prey.'

That 'ere is what Betty Poganut repeated to me the night we sot up by Statiry's corpse. Yeh 'member Statiry Poganut? Well, she's dead at last. Yeh see, we all gits called in our turn. We hain't here no continuin' city."

"But, Sam," said I, "how does business get along? Haven't you anything to do but tramp the pastures and moralize?"

"Wal," said Sam, "I've hed some pretty consid'able spells of blacksmithin' lately. There's Mr. Devenport, he's sech a pleasant-spoken man, he told me he brought his team all the way up from Bostin a purpose so that I might 'tend to their huffs. I've ben a shoein' on 'em fresh all round, an' the off horse, he'd kind o' got a crack in his huff, an' I've been a doctorin' on 't; an' Mr. Devenport, he said he hadn't found nobody that knew how to doctor a horse's huffs ekal to me. Very pleasant-spoken man Mr. Devenport is; he's got a good word for everybody. They say there ain't no end to his fortin, an' he goes a flingin' on 't round, right an' left, like a prince. Why, when I'd done shoein' his hosses, he jest put his hand inter his pocket an' handed me out ten dollars! ripped it out, he did, jest as easy as water runs! But there was Tiny a standin' by; I think she kind o' sot him on. O lordy massy, it's plain to be seen that *she* rules him. It's all cap in hand to her, an' 'What you will, madam,' an' 'Will ye have the end o' the rainbow, or a slice out o' the moon, or what is it?' It's all ekal to him, so as Miss Tiny wants it. Lordy massy," he said, lowering his voice confidentially to Harry, "course these 'ere things is all temporal, an' our hearts oughtn't to be too much sot on 'em; still he's got about the most amazin' fortin there is round Bostin. Why, if you b'lieve me, 'tween you an' me, it's him as owns the Dench Place, where you and Tiny put up when you wus children! Don't ye 'member when I found ye? Ye little guessed whose house ye wus a puttin' up at then; did yer? Lordy massy, lordy massy, who'd ha' thought it? The wonderful ways of Providence! 'He setteth the poor on high, an' letteth the runagates continoo in scarceness.' Wal, wal, it's a kind o' instructive world."

"Do you suppose," said Harry to me, in a low voice, "that this creature knows anything of what he is saying?"

"I'm afraid he does," said I. "Sam seems to have but one talent, and that is picking up news; and generally his guesses turn out to be about true."

"Sam," said I, by way of getting him to talk of something else, rather than on what I dreaded to hear, "you haven't said a word about Hepsy and the children. How are they all?"

"Wal, the young uns hes all got the whoopin' cough," said Sam, "an' I'm e'en a'most beat out with 'em. For fust it's one barks, an' then another, an' then all together. An' then Hepsy, she gets riled, an' she scolds; an', take it all together, a feller's head gits kind o' turned. When ye hes a lot o' young uns, there's allus suthin' a goin' on among 'em; ef 't ain't whoopin' cough, it's measles; an' ef 't ain't measles, it's chicken-pox, or else it's mumps, or scarlet-fever, or suthin'. They's all got to be gone through, fust an' last. It's enough to wean a body from this world. Lordy massy, yest'day arternoon I see yer Aunt Keziah an' yer Aunt Lois out a cuttin' cowslip greens t'other side o' th' river, an' the sun it shone so bright, an' the turtles an' frogs they kind o' peeped so pleasant, an' yer aunts they sot on the bank so kind o' easy an' free, an' I stood there a lookin' on 'em, an' I couldn't help a thinkin', 'Lordy massy, I wisht' I wus an old maid.' Folks 'scapes a great deal that don't hev no young uns a hangin' onter 'em."

"Well, Sam," said Harry, "isn't there any news stirring round in the neighborhood?"

"S'pose ye hain't heerd about the great church-quarrel over to Needmore?" he said.

"Quarrel? Why, no," said Harry. "What is it about?"

"Wal, ye see, there's a kind o' quarrel ris 'tween Parson Perry and Deacon Bangs. I can't jest git the right on 't, but it's got the hull town afire. I b'lieve it cum up in a kind o' dispute how to spell Saviour. The Deacon he's on the school-committee, an' Parson Perry he's on 't; an' the Deacon he spells it *iour*, an' Parson Perry he spells it *ior*, an' they wouldn't neither on 'em give up. Wal, ye know Deacon Bangs, — I *s'pose* he's a Christian, — but, lordy massy, he's one o' yer dreadful ugly kind o' Christians, that, when they gits their backs up, will do worse things than sinners will. I reelly think they kind o' take advantage o' their position, an' think, es they're goin' to be saved by grace, grace shell hev enough on 't. Now, to my mind, ef either on 'em wus to give way, the Deacon oughter give up to the Parson; but the Deacon he don't think so. Between you and me," said Sam, "it's my opinion that ef Ma'am Perry hedn't died jest when she did, this 'ere thing would never ha' growed to where 'tis. But ye see Ma'am Perry she died, an' that left Parson Perry a widower, an' folks did talk about him an' Mahaley Bangs, an' fact was, 'long about last spring, Deacon Bangs an' Mis' Bangs an' Mahaley wus jest as thick with the Par-

son as they could be. Why, Granny Watkins told me about their
havin' on him to tea two an' three times a week, an' Mahaley'd
make two kinds o' cake, an' they'd have preserved watermelon
rinds an' peaches an' cranberry saace, an' then 't was all sugar an'
all sweet, an' the Deacon he talked 'bout raisin' Parson Perry's
salary. Wal, then, ye see, Parson Perry he went over to Oldtown
an' married Jerushy Peabody. Now, Jerushy's a nice, pious gal, an'
it's a free country, an' parsons hes a right to suit 'emselves as well's
other men. But Jake Marshall, he ses to me, when he heerd o' that,
ses he, 'They'll be findin' fault with Parson Perry's doctrines now
afore two months is up; ye see if they don't.' Wal, sure enuff, this
'ere quarrel 'bout spellin' Saviour come on fust, an' Deacon Bangs
he fit the Parson like a bulldog. An' next town-meetin' day he told
Parson Perry right out before everybody thet he was wuss then 'n
Armenian, — thet he was a rank Pelagian; 'n' he said there was
folks thet hed taken notes o' his sermons for two years back, 'n'
they could show thet he hedn't preached the real doctrine of total
depravity, nor 'riginal sin, an' thet he'd got the plan o' salvation out
o' j'int intirely; he was all kind o' flattin' out onter morality. An'
Parson Perry he sed he'd preached jest's he allers hed. 'Tween you
'n' me, we know he *must* ha' done that, 'cause these 'ere ministers
thet hev to go preachin' round 'n' round like a hoss in a cider-mill,
— wal, *course* they *must* preach the same sermons over. *I* s'pose
they kind o' trim 'em up with new collars 'n' wris'bands. But we
used to say thet Parson Lothrop hed a bar'l o' sermons, 'n' when
he got through the year he turned his bar'l t'other side up, and
begun at t'other end. Lordy massy, who's to know it, when half on
em's asleep? And I guess the preachin's full as good as the pay
anyhow! Wal, the upshot on 't all is, they got a gret counsel there,
an' they're a tryin' Mr. Perry for heresy an' what not. Wal, I don't
b'lieve there's a yaller dog goes inter the Needmore meetin'-house
now that ain't got his mind made up one way or t'other about it.
Yer don't hear nothin' over there now 'xcept about Armenians an'
Pelagians an' Unitarians an' total depravity. Lordy massy! wal,
they lives up to that doctrine any way. What do ye think of old
Sphyxy Smith's bein' called in as one o' the witnesses in council?
She don' know no more 'bout religion than an' old hetchel, but
she's ferce as can be on Deacon Bangs's side, an' Old Crab Smith
he hes to hev' his say 'bout it."

"Do tell," said Harry, wonderingly, "if that old creature is alive yet!"

" 'Live? Why, yis, ye may say so," said Sam. "Much alive as ever he was. Ye see he kind o' pickles himself in hard cider, an' I dunno but he may live to hector his wife till he's ninety. But he's gret on the trial now, an' very much interested 'bout the doctrines. He ses thet he hain't heard a sermon on sovereignty, or 'lection, or reprobation, sence he can remember. Wal, t'other side, they say they don't see what business Old Crab an' Miss Sphyxy hev to be meddlin' so much, when they ain't church-members. Why, I was over to Needmore town-meetin' day jest to hear 'em fight over it; they talked a darned sight more 'bout that than 'bout the turn-pikes or town business. Why, I heard Deacon Brown (he's on the parson's side) tellin' Old Crab he didn't see what business *he* had to *boss* the doctrines, when he warn't a church-member, and Old Crab said it *was* his bisness about the doctrines, 'cause he *paid* to hev 'em. 'Ef I *pay* for good strong doctrine, why, I want to *hev* good strong doctrine,' says Old Crab, says he. 'Ef I pays for hell-fire, I want to hev hell-fire, and hev it hot too. I don't want none o' your prophesyin' smooth things. Why,' says he, 'look at Dr. Stern. His folks hes the very hair took off their heads 'most every Sunday, and he don't get no more'n we pay Parson Perry. I tell yew,' says Old Crab, 'he's a lettin' on us all go to sleep, and it's no wonder I ain't in the church.' Ye see, Old Crab and Sphyxy, they seem to be kind o' settin' it down to poor old Parson Perry's door that he hain't converted 'em, an' made saints on 'em long ago, when they've paid up their part o' the salary reg'lar, every year. Jes' so onreasonable folks will be; they give a man two hunderd dollars a year an' his wood, an' spect him to git all on 'em inter the kingdom o' heaven, whether they will or no, jest as the angels got Lot's wife and daughters out o' Sodom."

"That poor little old woman!" said Harry. "Do tell if she is living yet!"

"O yis, she's all right," said Sam; "she's one o' these 'ere little thin, dry old women that keep a good while. But ain't ye heerd? their son Obid's come home an' bought a farm, an' married a nice gal, and he insists on it his mother shall live with him. An' so Old Crab and Miss Sphyxy, they fight it out together. So the old woman is delivered from him most o' the time. Sometimes he walks over there an' stays a week, an' takes a spell o' aggravatin' on 'er, that kind o' sets him up, but he's so busy now 'bout the quarrel 't I b'lieve he lets her alone."

By this time we had reached the last rail-fence which separated us from the grassy street of Oldtown, and here Sam took his leave of us.

"I promised Hepsy when I went out," he said, "thet I'd go to the store and git her some corn meal, but I'll be round agin in th' evening. Look 'ere," he added, "I wus out this mornin', an' I dug some sweet-flag root for yer. I know ye used ter like sweet-flag root. 'T ain't time for young wintergreen yit, but here's a bunch I picked yer, with the berries an' old leaves. Do take 'em, boys, jest for sake o' old times!"

We thanked him, of course; there was a sort of aroma of boyhood about these things, that spoke of spring days and melting snows, and long Saturday afternoon rambles that we had had with Sam years before. And we saw his lean form go striding off with something of an affectionate complacency.

"Horace," said Harry, the minute we were alone, "you mustn't mind too much about Sam's gossip."

"It is just what I have been expecting," said I; "but in a few moments we shall know the truth."

We went on until the square white front of the old Rossiter house rose upon our view. We stopped before it, and down the walk from the front door to the gate, amid the sweet budding lilacs, came gleaming and glancing the airy form of Tina. So airy she looked, so bright, so full of life and joy, and threw herself into Harry's arms, laughing and crying.

"O Harry, Harry! God has been good to us! And you, dear brother Horace," she said, turning to me and giving me both her hands, with one of those frank, loving looks that said as much as another might say by throwing herself into your arms. "We are all so happy!" she said.

I determined to have it over at once, and I said, "Am I then to congratulate you, Tina, on your engagement?"

She laughed and blushed, and held up her hand, on which glittered a great diamond, and hid her face for a moment on Harry's shoulder.

"I couldn't write to you about it, boys, — I couldn't! But I meant to tell you myself, and tell you the first thing too. I wanted to tell you about him, because I think you none of you know him, or half how noble and good he is! Come, come in," she said, taking us each by the hand and drawing us along with her. "Come in and see Aunty; she'll be so glad to see you!"

If there was any one thing for which I was glad at this moment, it was that I had never really made love to Tina. It was a comfort to me to think that she did not and could not possibly know the pain she was giving me. All I know is that, at the moment, I was seized with a wild, extravagant gayety, and rattled and talked and laughed with a reckless *abandon* that quite astonished Harry. It seemed to me as if every ludicrous story and every droll remark that I had ever heard came thronging into my head together. And I believe that Tina really thought that I was sincere in rejoicing with her. Miss Mehitable talked with us gravely about it while Tina was out of the room. It was most sudden and unexpected, she said, to her; she always had supposed that Ellery Davenport had admired Tina, but never that he had thought of her in this way. In a worldly point of view, the match was a more brilliant one than could ever have been expected. He was of the best old families in the country, — of the Edwards and the Davenport stock, — his talents were splendid, and his wealth would furnish everything that wealth could furnish. "There is only one thing," she continued gravely; "I am not satisfied about his religious principles. But Tina is an enthusiast, and has perfect faith that he will come all right in this respect. He seems to be completely dazzled and under her influence now," said Miss Mehitable, taking a leisurely pinch of snuff, "but then, you see, that's a common phenomenon, about this time in a man's life. But," she added, "where there is such a strong attachment on both sides, all we can do is to wish both sides well, and speed them on their way. Mr. Davenport has interested himself in the very kindest manner in regard to both Tina and Harry, and I suppose it is greatly owing to this that affairs have turned out as prosperously as they have. As you know, Sir Harry made a handsome provision for Tina in his will. I confess I am glad of that," she said, with a sort of pride. "I wouldn't want my little Tina to have passed into his arms altogether penniless. When first love is over, men sometimes remember those things."

"If my father had not done justice to Tina in his will," said Harry, "I should have done it. My sister should not have gone to any man a beggar."

"I know that, my dear," said Miss Mehitable, "but still it is a pleasure to think that your father did it. It was a justice to your mother's memory that I am glad he rendered."

"And when is this marriage to take place?" said I.

"Mr. Davenport wants to carry her away in June," said Miss Mehitable. "That leaves but little time; but he says he must go to join the English Embassy, certainly by midsummer, and as there seems to be a good reason for his haste, I suppose I must not put my feelings in the way. It seems now as if I had had her only a few days, and she has been so very sweet and lovely to me. Well," said she, after a moment, "I suppose the old sweetbrier-bushes feel lonesome when we cut their blossoms and carry them off, but the old thorny things mustn't have blossoms if they don't expect to have them taken. That's all we scraggly old people are good for."

CHAPTER XLIII

WHAT OUR FOLKS THOUGHT ABOUT IT

At home, that evening, before the great open fire, still the same subject was discussed. Tina's engagement to Ellery Davenport was spoken of as the next most brilliant stroke of luck to Harry's accession to the English property. Aunt Lois was all smiles and suavity, poor dear old soul! How all the wrinkles and crinkles of her face smoothed out under the influence of prosperity! and how providential everything appeared to her!

"Providence gets some pay-days," said an old divine. Generally speaking, his account is suffered to run on with very lax attention. But when a young couple make a fortunate engagement, or our worldly prospects take a sudden turn to go as we would, the account of Providence is gladly balanced; praise and thanksgiving come in over-measure.

For my part, I couldn't see the Providence at all in it, and found this looking into happiness through other people's eyes a very fatiguing operation.

My grandfather and grandmother, as they sat pictured out by the light of a magnificent hickory fire, seemed scarcely a year older; but their faces this evening were beaming complacently; and my mother, in her very quiet way, could scarcely help triumphing over Aunt Lois. I was a sophomore in Cambridge, and Harry a landed proprietor, and Tina an heiress to property in her own right, instead of our being three poor orphan children without any money, and with the up-hill of life to climb.

In the course of the evening, Miss Mehitable came in with Ellery Davenport and Tina. Now, much as a man will dislike the person who steps between him and the lady of his love, I could not help, this evening, myself feeling the power of that fascination by which Ellery Davenport won the suffrages of all hearts.

Aunt Lois, as usual, was nervous and fidgety with the thought that the call of the splendid Mr. Davenport had surprised them all at the great kitchen-fire, when there was the best room cold as Nova Zembla. She looked almost reproachfully at Tina, and said apologetically to Mr. Davenport, "We are rough working folks, and you catch us just as we are. If we'd known you were coming, we'd have had a fire in the parlor."

"Then, Miss Badger, you would have been very cruel, and deprived us of a rare enjoyment," said he. "What other land but our own America can give this great, joyous, abundant home-fire? The great kitchen-fire of New England," he added, seating himself admiringly in front of it, "gives you all the freshness and simplicity of forest life, with a sense of shelter and protection. It's like a camp-fire in the woods, only that you have a house over you, and a good bed to sleep in at hand; and there is nothing that draws out the heart like it. People never can talk to each other as they do by these great open fires. For my part," he said, "I am almost a Fire-worshipper. I believe in the divine properties of flame. It purifies the heart and warms the affections, and when people sit and look into the coals together, they feel a sort of glow of charity coming over them that they never feel anywhere else."

"Now, I should think," said Aunt Lois, "Mr. Davenport, that you must have seen so much pomp and splendor and luxury abroad, that our rough life here would seem really disagreeable to you."

"Quite the contrary," said Ellery Davenport. "We go abroad to appreciate our home. Nature is our mother, and the life that is lived nearest to nature is, after all, the one that is the pleasantest. I met Brant at court last winter. You know he was a wild Indian to begin with, and he has seen both extremes, for now he is Colonel Brant, and has been moving in fashionable society in London. So I thought he must be a competent person to decide on the great question between savage and civilized life, and he gave his vote for the savage."

"I wonder at him," said my grandmother.

"Well, I remember," said Tina, "we had one day and night of savage life — don't you remember, Harry? — that was very pleasant. It was when we stayed with the old Indian woman, — do you remember? It was all very well, so long as the sun shone; but then when the rain fell, and the wind blew, and the drunken Indian came home, it was not so pleasant."

"That was the time, young lady," said Ellery Davenport, looking at her with a flash in his blue eyes, "that you established yourself as housekeeper on my premises! If I had only known it, I might have picked you up then, as a waif on my grounds."

"It's well you did not," said Tina, laughing; "you would have found me troublesome to keep. I don't believe you would have been as patient as dear old Aunty, here," she added, laying her head on Miss Mehitable's shoulder. "I was a perfect brier-rose, — small leaves and a great many prickles."

"By the by," said Harry, "Sam Lawson has been telling us, this morning, about our old friends Miss Asphyxia Smith and Old Crab."

"Is it possible," said Tina, laughing, "that those creatures are living yet? Why, I look back on them as some awful pre-Adamite monsters."

"Who was Miss Asphyxia?" said Ellery Davenport. "I haven't heard of her."

"O, 't was a great threshing-machine of a woman that caught me between its teeth some years ago," said Tina. "What do you suppose would ever have become of me, Aunty, if she had kept me? Do you think she ever could have made me a great stramming, threshing, scrubbing, floor-cleaning machine, like herself? She warned Miss Mehitable," continued Tina, looking at Ellery and laughing shyly, "that I never should grow up to be good for anything; and she spoke a fatal truth, for, since she gave me up, every mortal creature has tried to pet and spoil me. Dear old Aunty and Mr. Rossiter have made some feeble attempts to make me good for something, but they haven't done much at it."

"Thank Heaven!" said Ellery Davenport. "Who would think of training a wild rose? I sometimes look at the way a sweetbrier grows over one of our rough stone walls, and think what a beautiful defiance it is to gardeners."

"That is all very pretty to say," said Tina, "when you happen to be where there are none but wild roses; but when you were among marchionesses and duchesses, how was it then?"

For answer, Ellery Davenport bent over her, and said something which I could not hear. He had the art, without seeming to whisper, of throwing a sentence from him so that it should reach but one ear; and Tina laughed and blushed and dimpled, and looked as if a thousand little graces were shaking their wings around her.

It was one of Tina's great charms that she was never for a moment at rest. In this she was like a bird, or a brook, or a young tree, in which there is always a little glancing shimmer of movement. And when anything pleased her, her face sparkled as a river does when something falls into it. I noticed Ellery Davenport's eyes followed all these little motions as if he had been enchanted. O, there was no doubt that the great illusion, the delicious magic, was in full development between them. And Tina looked so gladly satisfied, and glanced about the circle and at him with such a quiet triumph of possession, and such satisfaction in her power over him, that it really half reconciled me to see that she was so happy. And, after all, I thought to myself as I looked at the airy and *spirituel* style of her beauty, — a beauty that conveyed the impression of fragility and brilliancy united to the highest point, — such a creature as that is made for luxury, made for perfume and flowers and jewelry and pomp of living and obsequious tending, for old aristocratic lands and court circles, where she would glitter as a star. And what had I to offer, — I, a poor sophomore in Harvard, owing that position to the loving charity of my dear old friend? My love to her seemed a madness and a selfishness, — as if I had wished to take the evening star out of the heavens and burn it for a household lamp. "How fortunate, how fortunate," I thought to myself, "that I have never told her! For now I shall keep the love of her heart. We are friends, and she shall be the lady of my heart forever, — the lady of my dreams."

I knew, too, that I had a certain hold upon her; and even at this moment I saw her eye often, as from old habit, looking across to me, a little timidly and anxiously, to see what I thought of her prize. She was Tina still, — the same old Tina, that always needed to be approved and loved and sympathized with, and have all her friends go with her, heart and hand, in all her ways. So I determined to like him.

At this moment Sam Lawson came in. I was a little curious to know how he had managed it with his conscience to leave his domestic circle under their trying circumstances, but I was very soon satisfied as to this point.

Sam, who had watched the light flaring out from the windows, and flattened his nose against the window-pane while he announced to Hepsy that "Mr. Devenport and Miss Mehitable and Tiny were all a goin' into the Deacon's to spend th' evenin'," could not resist the inexpressible yearning to have a peep himself at what was going on there.

He came in with a most prostrate air of dejection. Aunt Lois frowned with stern annoyance, and looked at my grandmother, as much as to say, "To think *he* should come in when Mr. Davenport is making a call here!"

Ellery Davenport, however, received him with a patronizing cheerfulness, — "Why, hulloa, Sam, how are you?" It was Ellery Davenport's delight to start Sam's loquacity and develop his conversational powers, and he made a welcoming movement toward the block of wood in the chimney-corner. "Sit down," he said, — "sit down, and tell us how Hepsy and the children are."

Tina and he looked at each other with eyes dancing with merriment.

"Wal, wal," said Sam, sinking into the seat and raising his lank hands to the fire, while his elbows rested on his knees, "the children's middlin', — Doctor Merrill ses he thinks they've got past the wust on 't, — but Hepsy, she's clean tuckered out, and kind o' discouraged. An' I thought I'd come over an' jest ask Mis' Badger ef she wouldn't kind o' jest mix 'er up a little milk punch to kind o' set 'er up agin."

"What a considerate husband!" said Ellery Davenport, glancing around the circle with infinite amusement.

My grandmother, always prompt at any call on her charity, was already half across the floor toward her buttery, whence she soon returned with a saucepan of milk.

"I'll watch that 'ere, Mis' Badger," said Sam. "Jest rake out the coals this way, an' when it begins ter simmer I'll put in the sperits, ef ye'll gin 'em to me. 'Give strong drink ter him as is ready to perish,' the Scriptur' says. Hepsy's got an amazin' sight o' grit in 'er, but I 'clare for 't, she's ben up an' down nights so much lately with them young uns thet she's a'most clean wore out. An' I should be too, ef I didn't take a tramp now 'n' then to kind o' keep me up. Wal, ye see, the head o' the family, he *hes* to take car' o' himself, 'cause ye see, ef *he* goes down, all goes down. 'The man is the head o' the woman,' ye know," said Sam, as he shook his skillet of milk.

I could see Tina's eyes dancing with mirthfulness as Ellery Davenport answered, "I'm glad to see, Sam, that you have a proper care of your health. You are such an important member of the community, that I don't know what Oldtown would be without you!"

"Wal, now, Mr. Devenport, ye flatter me; but then everybody don't seem to think so. I don't think folks like me, as does for this one an' does for that one, an' kind o' spreads out permiskus, is appreciated allers. There's Hepsy, she's allers at me, a sayin' I don't do nothin' for her, an' yet there las' night I wus up in my shirt, a shiverin' an' a goin' round, fust ter one and then ter 'nuther, a hevin' on 'em up an' a thumpin' on their backs, an' clarin' the phlegm out o' their thruts, till I wus e'en a'most fruz; and Hepsy, she lay there abed scoldin' 'cause I hedn't sawed no wood thet arternoon to keep up the fire. Lordy massy, I jest went out ter dig a leetle sweet-flag root ter gin ter the boys, 'cause I wus so kind o' wore out. I don't think these 'ere women ever 'flects on *men's* trials. They railly don't keep count o' what we do for 'em."

"What a picture of conjugal life!" said Ellery Davenport, glancing at Tina. "Yes, Sam, it is to be confessed that the female sex are pretty exorbitant creditors. They make us pay dear for serving them."

"Jes' so! jes' so!" said Sam. "They don't know nothin' what we undergo. I don't think Hepsy keeps no sort o' count o' the nights an' nights I've walked the floor with the baby, whishin' an' shooin' on 't, and singin' to 't till my thrut wus sore, an' then hed to git up afore daylight to split oven-wood, an' then right to my black-smithin', jest to git a little money to git the meat an' meal an' suthin' comfort'ble fur dinner! An' then, ye see, there don't nothin' *last,* when there's so many mouths to eat it up; an' there 'tis, it's jest roun' an' roun'. Ye git a good piece o' beef Tuesday an' pay for 't, an' by Thursday it's all gone, an' ye hev to go to work agin! Lordy massy, this 'ere life don't seem hardly wuth hevin'. I s'pose, Mr. Devenport, you've been among the gret folks o' th' earth, over there in King George's court? Why, they say here that you've ben an' tuk tea with the king, with his crown on 's head! I s'pose they all goes roun' with their crowns on over there; don't they?"

"Well, no, not precisely," said Ellery Davenport. "I think they rather mitigate their splendors when they have to do with us poor republicans, so as not to bear us down altogether."

"Jes' so," said Sam, "like Moses, that put a veil over 's face 'cause th' Israelites couldn't bear the glory."

"Well," said Ellery Davenport, "I've not been struck with any particular resemblance between King George and Moses."

"The folks here 'n Oldtown, Mr. Devenport, 's amazin' curus to hear the partic'lars 'bout them grand things 't you must ha' seen; I's tellin' on 'em up to store how you'd ben with lords 'n' ladies 'n' dukes 'n' duchesses, 'n' seen all the kingdoms o' the world, an' the glory on 'em. I told 'em I didn't doubt you'd et off 'm plates o' solid gold, an' ben in houses where the walls was all a crust o' gold 'n' diamonds 'n' precious stones, 'n' yit ye didn't seem ter be one bit lifted up nor proud, so 't yer couldn't talk ter common folks. I s'pose them gret fam'lies they hes as much 's fifty ur a hunderd servants, don't they?"

"Well, sometimes," said Ellery Davenport.

"Wal, now," said Sam, "I sh'd think a man'd feel kind o' curus, — sort o' 's ef he was keepin' a hotel, an' boardin' all the lower classes."

"It is something that way, Sam," said Ellery Davenport. "That's one way of providing for the lower classes."

"Jest what th' Lord told th' Israelites when they would hev a king," said Sam. "Ses he, 'He'll take yer daughters to be confectioners 'n' cooks 'n' bakers, an' he'll take the best o' yer fields 'n' yer vineyards 'n' olive-yards, an' give 'em to his sarvints an' he'll take a tenth o' yer seed 'n' give 'em ter his officers, an' he'll take yer men-sarvints 'n' yer maid-sarvints, 'n' yer goodliest young asses, an' put 'em ter his works."

"Striking picture of monarchical institutions, Sam," said Ellery Davenport.

"Wal, now, I tell ye what," said Sam, slowly shaking his shimmering skillet of milk, "I shouldn't want ter git inter that 'ere pie, unless I could be some o' the top crust. It's jest like a pile o' sheepskins, — 's only the top un lies light. I guess th' undermost one's squeezed putty flat."

"I'll bet it is, Sam," said Ellery Davenport, laughing.

"Wal," said Sam, "I go for republics, but yit it's human natur' ter kind o' like ter hold onter titles. Now over here a man likes ter be a deacon 'n' a cap'n 'n' a colonel in the milishy 'n' a sheriff 'n' a judge, 'n' all thet. Lordy massy, I don't wonder them grand English folks sticks to their grand titles, an' the people all kind o' bows down to 'em, as they did to Nebuchadnezzar's golden image."

"Why, Sam," said Ellery Davenport, "your speculations on politics are really profound."

"Wal," said Sam, "Mr. Devenport, there's one pint I want ter consult ye 'bout, an' thet is, what the king o' England's name is. There's Jake Marshall 'n' me, we's argood that pint these many times. Jake ses his name is George Rix, — R-i-x, — an' thet ef he'd come over here, he'd be called Mr. Rix. I ses to him, 'Why, Jake, 't ain't *Rix*, it's Rex, an' 't ain't his name, it's his title,' ses I, — 'cause the boys told me that Rex was Latin 'n' meant king; but Jake's one o' them fellers thet allers thinks he knows. Now, Mr. Devenport, I'd like to put it down from you ter him, 'cause you've just come from the court o' England, an' you'd know."

"Well, you may tell your friend Jake that you are quite in the right," said Ellery Davenport. "Give him my regards, and tell him he's been mistaken."

"But you don't call the king Rex when ye speak to 'im, do yer?" said Sam.

"Not precisely," said Ellery Davenport.

"Mis' Badger," said Sam, gravely, "this 'ere milk 's come to the bile, 'n' ef you'll be so kind 's to hand me the sperits 'n' the sugar, I'll fix this 'ere. Hepsy likes her milk punch putty hot."

"Well, Sam," said my grandmother, as she handed him the bottle, "take an old woman's advice, and don't go stramming off another afternoon. If you'd been steady at your blacksmithin', you might have earned enough money to buy all these things yourself, and Hepsy'd like it a great deal better."

"I suppose it's about the two hundred and forty-ninth time mother has told him that," said Aunt Lois, with an air of weary endurance.

"Wal, Mis' Badger," said Sam, " 'all work an' no play makes Jack a dull boy,' ye know. I *hes* to recreate, else I gits quite wore out. Why, lordy massy, even a saw-mill hes ter stop sometimes ter be greased. 'T ain't everybody thet's like Sphyxy Smith, but she grits and screeches all the time, jest 'cause she keeps to work without bein' 'iled. Why, she could work on, day 'n' night, these twenty years, 'n' never feel it. But, lordy massy, I gits so 'xhausted, an' hes sech a sinking 't my stomach, 'n' then I goes out 'n' kind o' *Injunin'* round, an' git flag-root 'n' wintergreen 'n' spruce boughs 'n' gensing root 'n' sarsafrass 'n' sich fur Hepsy to brew up a beer. I ain't a wastin' my time ef I be enjoyin' myself. I say it's a part o' what we's made for."

"You are a true philosopher, Sam," said Ellery Davenport.

"Wal," said Sam, "I look at it this 'ere way, — ef I keep on a grindin' and a grindin' day 'n' night, I never shell hev nothin', but ef I takes now 'n' then an arternoon to lie roun' in the sun, *I gits suthin' 's I go 'long.* Lordy massy, it's jest all the comfort I hes, kind o' watchin' the clouds 'n' the birds, 'n' kind o' forgettin' all 'bout Hepsy 'n' the children 'n' the blacksmithin'.'"

"Well," said Aunt Lois, smartly, "I think you are forgetting all about Hepsy and the children now, and I advise you to get that milk punch home as quick as you can, if it's going to do her any good. Come, here's a tin pail to put it into. Cover it up, and do let the poor woman have some comfort as well as you!"

Sam received his portion in silence, and, with reluctant glances at the warm circle, went out into the night.

"I don't see how you all can bear to listen to that man's maundering!" said Aunt Lois. "He puts me out of all sort of patience. 'Head of the woman' to be sure! when Hepsy earns the most of what that family uses, except what we give 'em. And I know exactly how she feels; the poor woman is mad with shame and humiliation half the time at the charities he will accept from us."

"O come, Miss Lois," said Ellery Davenport, "you must take an æsthetic view of him. Sam's a genuine poet in his nature, and poets are always practically useless. And now Sam's about the only person in Oldtown, that I have seen, that has the least idea that life is meant, in any way, for enjoyment. Everybody else seems to be sword in hand, fighting against the possibility of future suffering, toiling and depriving themselves of all present pleasure, so that they may not come to want by and by. Now I've been in countries where the whole peasantry are like Sam Lawson."

"Good gracious!" said Aunt Lois, "what a time they must have of it!"

"Well, to say the truth, there's not much progress in such communities, but there is a great deal of clear, sheer animal enjoyment. And when trouble comes, it comes on them as it does on animals, unfeared and unforeseen, and therefore unprovided for."

"Well," said my grandmother, "you don't think that is the way for rational and immortal creatures to live?"

"Well," said Ellery Davenport, "taking into account the rational and immortal, perhaps not; but I think if we could mix the two races together it would be better. The Yankee lives almost entirely for the future, the Italian enjoys the present."

"Well, but do you think it is *right* to live merely to enjoy the present?" persisted Aunt Lois.

"The eternal question!" said Ellery. "After all, who knows anything about it? What *is* right, and what *is* wrong? Mere geographical accidents! What is right for the Greenlander is wrong for me; what is right for me is wrong for the Hindoo. Take the greatest saint on earth to Greenland, and feed him on train oil and candles, and you make one thing of him; put him under the equator, with the thermometer at one hundred in the shade, and you make another."

"But right is right and wrong is wrong," said Aunt Lois, persistently, "after all."

"I sometimes think," said Ellery Davenport, "that right and wrong are just like color, mere accidental properties. There is no color where there's no light, and a thing is all sorts of colors according to the position you stand in and the hour of the day. There's your rocking-chair in the setting sun becomes a fine crimson, and in the morning comes out dingy gray. So it is with human actions. There's nothing so bad that you cannot see a good side to it, nothing so good that you cannot see a bad side to it. Now we think it's shocking for our Indian tribes, some of them, to slay their old people; but I'm not sure, if the Indian could set forth his side of the case, with all the advantages of our rhetoric, but that he would have the best of it. He does it as an act of filial devotion, you see. He loves and honors his father too much to let him go through all that horrid process of draining out life drop by drop that we think the thing to protract in our high civilization. For my part, if I were an Indian chief, I should prefer, when I came to be seventy, to be respectfully knocked on the head by my oldest son, rather than to shiver and drivel and muddle and cough my life out a dozen years more."

"But God has given his commandments to teach us what is right," said Aunt Lois. " 'Honor thy father and mother.' "

"Precisely," said Ellery; "and my friends the Sioux would tell you that they *do* honor their fathers and mothers by respectfully putting them out of the way when there is no more pleasure in living. They send them to enjoy eternal youth in the hunting-grounds of the fathers, you know."

"Positively, Ellery," said Tina, "I sha'n't have this sort of heathen stuff talked any longer. Why, you put one's head all in a whirl! and you know you don't believe a word of it yourself. What's the use of making everybody think you're worse than you are?"

"My dear," said Ellery, "there's nothing like hearing all that can be said on both sides of subjects. Now there's my good grandfather made an argument on the will, that is, and forever will remain, unanswerable, because he proves both sides of a flat contradiction perfectly; that method makes a logic-trap out of which no mortal can get his foot."

"Well," said my grandmother, "Mr. Davenport, if you'll take an old woman's advice, you'll take up with your grandfather's *good resolutions*, and not be wasting your strength in such talk."

"I believe there were about seventy-five — or eighty, was it? — of those resolutions," said Ellery.

"And you wouldn't be the worse for this world or the next if you'd make them yourself," said my grandmother.

"Thank you, madam," said Ellery, bowing, "I'll think of it."

"Well, come," said Tina, rising, "it's time for us to go; and," she said, shaking her finger warningly at Ellery Davenport, "I have a private lecture for you."

"I don't doubt it," he said, with a shrug of mock apprehension; "the preaching capacities of the fair sex are something terrific. I see all that is before me."

They bade adieu, the fire was raked up in the great fireplace, all the members of the family went their several ways to bed, but Harry and I sat up in the glimmer and gloom of the old kitchen, lighted, now and then, by a sputtering jet of flame, which burst from the sticks. All round the large dark hearth the crickets were chirping as if life were the very merriest thing possible.

"Well, Harry," I said, "you see the fates have ordered it just as I feared."

"It is almost as much of a disappointment to me as it can be to you," said Harry. "And it is the more so because I cannot quite trust this man."

"I never trusted him," said I. "I always had an instinctive doubt of him."

"My doubts are not instinct," said Harry, "they are founded on things I have heard him say myself. It seems to me that he has formed the habit of trifling with all truth, and that nothing is sacred in his eyes."

"And yet Tina loves him," said I. "I can see that she has gone to him heart and soul, and she believes in him with all her heart, and so we can only pray that he may be true to her. As for me, I can never love another. It only remains to live worthily of my love."

CHAPTER XLIV

MARRIAGE PREPARATIONS

And now for a time there was nothing thought of or talked of but marriage preparations and arrangements. Letters of congratulation came pouring in to Miss Mehitable from her Boston friends and acquaintances.

When Harry and I returned to college, we spent one day with our friends the Kitterys, and found it the one engrossing subject there, as everywhere.

Dear old Madam Kittery was dissolved in tenderness, and whenever the subject was mentioned reiterated all her good opinions of Ellery, and her delight in the engagement, and her sanguine hopes of its good influence on his spiritual prospects.

Miss Debby took the subject up energetically. Ellery Davenport was a near family connection, and it became the Kitterys to make all suitable and proper advances. She insisted upon addressing Harry by his title, notwithstanding his blushes and disclaimers.

"My dear sir," she said to him, "it appears that you are an Englishman and a subject of his Majesty; and I should not be surprised, at some future day, to hear of you in the House of Commons; and it becomes you to reflect upon your position, and what is proper in relation to yourself; and, at least under this roof, you must allow me to observe these proprieties, however much they may be disregarded elsewhere. I have already informed the servants that they are always to address you as Sir Harry, and I hope that you will not interfere with my instructions."

"O certainly not," said Harry. "It will make very little difference with me."

"Now, in regard to this marriage," said Miss Debby, "as there is no *church* in Oldtown, and no clergyman, I have felt that it would be proper in me, as a near kinswoman to Mr. Davenport, to place the Kittery mansion at Miss Mehitable Rossiter's disposal, for the wedding."

"Well, I confess," said Harry, blushing, "I never thought but that the ceremony would be performed at home, by Parson Lothrop."

"My dear Sir Harry!" said Miss Debby, laying her hand on his arm with solemnity, "consider that your excellent parents, Sir Harry and Lady Percival, were both members of the Established Church of England, the only true Apostolic Protestant Church, — and can you imagine that their spirits, looking down from heaven, would be pleased and satisfied that their daughter should consummate the most solemn union of her life out of the Church? and in fact at the hands of a man who has never received ordination?"

It was with great difficulty that Harry kept his countenance during this solemn address. His blue eyes actually laughed, though he exercised a rigid control over the muscles of his face.

"I really had not thought about it at all, Miss Debby," he said. "I think you are exceedingly kind."

"And I'm sure," said she, "that you must see the propriety of it now that it is suggested to you. Of course, a marriage performed by Mr. Lothrop would be a legal one, so far as the civil law is concerned; but I confess I always have regarded marriage as a religious ordinance, and it would be a disagreeable thing to me to have any connections of mine united merely by a *civil* tie. These Congregational marriages," said Miss Debby, in a contemptuous voice, "I should think would lead to immorality. How can people feel as if they were married that don't utter any vows themselves, and don't have any wedding-ring put on their finger? In my view, it's not respectable; and, as Mrs. Ellery Davenport will probably be presented in the first circles of England, I desire that she should appear there with her wedding-ring on, like an honest woman. I have therefore despatched an invitation to Miss Mehitable to bring your sister and spend the month preceding the wedding with us in Boston. It will be desirable for other reasons, as all the shopping and dressmaking and millinery work must be done in Boston. Oldtown is a highly respectable little village, but, of course, affords no advantages for the outfit of a person of quality, such as your sister is and is to be. I have had a letter from Lady Widgery this morning. She is much delighted, and sends congratulations. She always, she said, believed that you had distinguished blood in your veins when she first saw you at our house."

There was something in Miss Debby's satisfied, confiding faith in everything English and aristocratic that was vastly amusing to us. The perfect confidence she seemed to have that Sir Harry Percival, after all the sins of his youth, had entered heaven *ex officio* as a repentant and glorified baronet, a member of the only True Church, was really *naïve* and affecting. What would a church be good for that allowed people of quality to go to hell, like the commonalty? Sir Harry, of course, repented, and made his will in a proper manner, doubtless received the sacrament and absolution, and left all human infirmities, with his gouty toes, under the family monument, where his body reposed in sure and certain hope of a blessed and glorious resurrection. The finding of his children under such fortunate circumstances was another evidence of the good Providence who watches over the fortunes of the better classes, and does not suffer the steps of good Churchmen to slide beyond recovery.

There were so many reasons of convenience for accepting Madam Kittery's hospitable invitation, it was urged with such warmth and affectionate zeal by Madam Kittery and Miss Debby, and seconded so energetically by Ellery Davenport, to whom this arrangement would secure easy access to Tina's society during the intervening time, that it was accepted.

Harry and I were glad of it, as we should thus have more frequent opportunities of seeing her. Ellery Davenport was refurbishing and refurnishing the old country house, where Harry and Tina had spent those days of their childhood which it was now an amusement to recall, and Tina was as gladly, joyously beautiful as young womanhood can be in which, as in a transparent vase, the light of pure love and young hope has been lighted.

"You like him, Horace, don't you?" she had said to me, coaxingly, the first opportunity after the evening we had spent together. What was I to do? I did not like him, that was certain; but have you never, dear reader, been over-persuaded to think and say you liked where you did not? Have you not scolded and hushed down your own instinctive distrusts and heart-risings, blamed and schooled yourself for them, and taken yourself sharply to task, and made yourself acquiesce in somebody that was dear and necessary to some friend? So did I. I called myself selfish, unreasonable, foolish. I determined to be generous to my successful rival, and to like him. I took his frankly offered friendship, and I forced myself to be even enthusiastic in his praise. It was a sure way of making Tina's cheeks glow and her eyes look kindly on me, and she told me so often that there was no person in the world whose good opinion she had such a value for, and she was *so* glad I liked him. Would it not be perfectly abominable after this to let sneaking suspicions harbor in my breast?

Besides, if a man cannot have love, shall he therefore throw away friendship? and may I not love with the love of chivalry, — the love that knights dedicated to queens and princesses, the love that Tasso gave to Leonard D'Este, the love that Dante gave to Beatrice, love that hopes little and asks nothing?

I was frequently in at the Kittery house in leisure hours, and when, as often happened, Tina was closeted with Ellery Davenport, I took sweet counsel with Miss Mehitable.

"We all stand outside now, Horace," she said. "I remember when *I* had the hearing of all these thousand pretty little important secrets of the hour that now must all be told in another direction. Such is life. What we want always comes to us with some pain. I wanted Tina to be well married. I would not for the world she should marry without just this sort of love; but of course it leaves me out in the cold. I wouldn't say this to her for the world, — poor little thing, it would break her heart."

One morning, however, I went down and found Miss Mehitable in a very excited state. She complained of a bad headache, but she had all the appearance of a person who is constantly struggling with something which she is doubtful of the expediency of uttering.

At last, just as I was going, she called me into the library. "Come here, Horace," she said; "I want to speak to you."

I went in, and she made a turn or two across the room in an agitated way, then sat down at a table, and motioned me to sit down. "Horace, my dear boy," she said, "I have never spoken to you of the deepest sorrow of my life, and yet it often seems to me as if you knew it."

"My dear Aunty," said I, for we had from childhood called her thus, "I think I do know it, — somewhat vaguely. I know about your sister."

"You know how strangely, how unaccountably she left us, and that nothing satisfactory has ever been heard from her. I told Mr. Davenport all about her, and he promiised to try to learn something of her in Europe. He was so successful in relation to Tina and Harry, I hoped he might learn something as to her; but he never seemed to. Two or three times within the last four or five years I have received letters from her, but without date, or any mark by which her position could be identified. They told me, in the vaguest and most general way, that she was well, and still loved me, but begged me to make no inquiries. They were always postmarked at Havre; but the utmost research gives no clew to her residence there."

"Well?" said I.

"Well," said Miss Mehitable, trembling in every limb, "yesterday, when Mr. Davenport and Tina had been sitting together in this room for a long time, they went out to ride. They had been playing at verse-making, or something of the kind, and there were some scattered papers on the floor, and I thought I would remove them, as they were rather untidy, and among them I found — " she stopped, and panted for breath — "I found THIS!"

She handed me an envelope that had evidently been around a package of papers. It was postmarked Geneva, Switzerland, and directed to Ellery Davenport.

"Horace," said Miss Mehitable, *that is Emily Rossiter's handwriting;* and look, the date is only two months back! What shall we do?"

There are moments when whole trains of thought go through the brain like lightning. My first emotion was, I confess, a perfectly fierce feeling of joy. Here was a clew! My suspicions had not then been unjust; the man was what Miss Debby had said, — deep, artful, and to be unmasked. In a moment I sternly rebuked myself, and thought what a wretch I was for my suspicions. The very selfish stake that I held in any such discovery imposed upon me, in my view, a double obligation to defend the character of my rival. I so dreaded that I should be carried away that I pleaded strongly and resolutely with myself for him. Besides, what would Tina think of me if I impugned Ellery Davenport's honor for what might be, after all, an accidental resemblance in handwriting.

All these things came in one blinding flash of thought as I held the paper in my hands. Miss Mehitable sat, white and trembling, looking at me piteously.

"My dear Aunty," I said, "in a case like this we cannot take one single step without being perfectly sure. This handwriting may accidentally resemble your sister's. Are you perfectly sure that it is hers? It is a very small scrap of paper to determine by."

"Well, I can't really say," said Miss Mehitable, hesitating. "It may be that I have dwelt on this subject until I have grown nervous and my very senses deceive me. I really cannot say, Horace; that was the reason I came to you to ask what I should do."

"Let us look the matter over calmly, Aunty."

"Now," she said, nervously drawing from her pocket two or three letters and opening them before me, "here are those letters, and your head is cool and steady. I wish you would compare the writing, and tell me what to think of it."

Now the letters and the directions were in that sharp, decided English hand which so many well-educated women write, and in which personal peculiarities are lost, to a great degree, in a general style. I could not help seeing that there was a resemblance which might strike a person, — especially a person so deeply interested, and dwelling with such intentness upon a subject, as Miss Mehitable evidently was.

"My dear Aunty," said I, "I see a resemblance; but have you not known a great many ladies who wrote hands like this?"

"Yes, I must say I have," said Miss Mehitable, still hesitating, — "only, somehow, this impressed me very strongly."

"Well," said I, "supposing that your sister has written to Ellery Davenport, may she not have intrusted him with communications under his promise of secrecy, which he was bound in honor not to reveal?"

"That may be possible," said Miss Mehitable, sighing deeply; "but O, why should she not make a confidante of me?"

"It may be, Aunty," said I, hesitatingly, "that she is living in relations that she feels could not be justified to you."

"O Horace!" said Miss Mehitable.

"You know," I went on, "that there has been a very great shaking of old established opinions in Europe. A great many things are looked upon there as open questions, in regard to morality, which we here in New England never think of discussing. Ellery Davenport is a man of the European world, and I can easily see that there may be circumstances in which your sister would more readily resort to the friendship of such a man than to yours."

"May God help me!" said Miss Mehitable.

"My dear Aunty, suppose you find that your sister has adopted a false theory of life, sincerely and conscientiously, and under the influence of it gone astray from what we in New England think to be right. Should we not make a discrimination between errors that come from a wrong belief and the mere weakness that blindly yields to passion? Your sister's letters show great decision and strength of mind. It appears to me that she is exactly the woman to be misled by those dazzling, unsettling theories with regard to social life which now bear such sway, and are especially propagated by French literature. She may really and courageously deem herself doing right in a course that she knows she cannot defend to you and Mr. Rossiter."

"Horace, you speak out and make plain what has been the secret and dreadful fear of my life. I never have believed that Emily could have gone from us all, and stayed away so long, without the support of some attachment. And while you have been talking I have become perfectly certain that it is so; but the thought is like death to me."

"My dear Aunty," I said, "our Father above, who sees all the history of our minds, and how they work, must have a toleration and a patience that we have not with each other. He says that he will bring the blind by a way they knew not, and 'make darkness light before them, and crooked things straight'; and he adds, 'These things will I do unto them, and will not forsake them.' That has always seemed to me the most godlike passage in the Bible."

Miss Mehitable sat for a long time, leaning her head upon her hand.

"Then, Horace, you wouldn't advise me," she said, after a pause, "to say anything to Ellery Davenport about it?"

"Supposing," said I, "that there are communications that he is bound in honor not to reveal, of what use could be your inquiries? It can only create unpleasantness; it may make Tina feel unhappy, who is so very happy now, and probably, at best, you cannot learn anything that would satisfy you."

"Probably not," said she, sighing.

"I can hand this envelope to him," I said after a moment's thought, "this evening, if you think best, and you can see how he looks on receiving it."

"I don't know as it will be of any use," said Miss Mehitable, "but you may do it."

Accordingly, that evening, as we were all gathered in a circle around the open fire, and Tina and Ellery, seated side by side, were carrying on that sort of bantering warfare of wit in which they delighted, I drew this envelope from my pocket and said, carelessly, "Mr. Davenport, here is a letter of yours that you dropped in the library this morning."

He was at that moment playing with a silk tassel which fluttered from Tina's wrist. He let it go, and took the envelope and looked at it carelessly.

"A letter!" said Tina, snatching it out of his hand with saucy freedom, — "dated at Geneva, and a lady's handwriting! I think I have a right to open it!"

"Do so by all means," said Ellery.

"O pshaw! there's nothing in it," said Tina.

"Not an uncommon circumstance in a lady's letter," said Ellery.

"You saucy fellow!" said Tina.

"Why," said Ellery, "is it not the very province and privilege of the fair sex to make nothing more valuable and more agreeable than something? that's the true secret of witchcraft."

"But I sha'n't like it," said Tina, half pouting, "if you call my letters nothing."

"Your letters, I doubt not, will be an exception to those of all the sex," said Ellery. "I really tremble, when I think how profound they will be!"

"You are making fun of me!" said she, coloring.

"I making fun of you? And what have you been doing with all your hapless lovers up to this time? Behold Nemesis arrayed in my form."

"But seriously, Ellery, I want to know whom this letter was from?"

"Why don't you look at the signature?" said he.

"Well, of course you know there is no signature, but I mean what came in this paper?"

"What came in the paper," said Ellery, carelessly, "was a neat little collection of Alpine flowers, that, if you are interested in botany, I shall have the honor of showing you one of these days."

"But you haven't told me who sent them," said Tina.

"Ah, ha! we are jealous!" said he, shaking the letter at her. "What would you give to know, now? Will you be *very* good if I will tell you? Will you promise me for the future not to order me to do more than forty things at one time, for example?"

"I sha'n't make any promises," said Tina; "you ought to tell me!"

"What an oppressive mistress you are!" said Ellery Davenport. "I begin to sympathize with Sam Lawson, — lordy massy, you dunno nothin' what I undergo!"

"You don't get off that way," said Tina.

"Well," said Ellery Davenport, "if you must know, it's Mrs. Breck."

"And who is she?" said Tina.

"Well, my dear, she was my boarding-house keeper at Geneva, and a very pretty, nice Englishwoman, — one that I should recommend as an example to her sex."

"Oh!" said Tina, "I don't care anything about it now."

"Of course," said Ellery. "Modest, unpretending virtue never excites any interest. I have labored under that disadvantage all my days."

The by-play between the two had brought the whole circle around the fire into a careless, laughing state. I looked across to Miss Mehitable; she was laughing with the rest. As we started to go out, Miss Mehitable followed me into the passage-way. "My dear Horace," she said, "I was very absurd; it comes of being nervous and thinking of one thing too much."

CHAPTER XLV

WEDDING BELLS

The fourteenth of June was as bright a morning as if it had been made on purpose for a wedding-day, and of all the five thousand inauspicious possibilities which usually encumber weddings, not one fell to our share.

Tina's dress, for example, was all done two days beforehand, and fitted to a hair; and all the invited guests had come, and were lodged in the spacious Kittery mansion.

Esther Avery was to stand as bridesmaid, with me as groomsman, and Harry, as nearest relative, was to give the bride away. The day before, I had been in and seen both ladies dressed up in the marriage finery, and we had rehearsed the situation before Harry, as clergyman, Miss Debby being present, in one of her most commanding frames of mind, to see that everything was done according to the Rubric. She surveyed Esther, while she took an approving pinch of snuff, and remarked to me, aside, "That young person, for a Congregational parson's daughter, has a surprisingly distinguished air."

Lady Widgery and Lady Lothrop, who were also in at the inspection, honored Esther with their decided approbation.

"She will be quite presentable at court," Lady Widgery remarked. "Of course Sir Harry will wish her presented."

All this *empressement* in regard to Harry's rank and title, among these venerable sisters, afforded great amusement to our quartette, and we held it a capital joke among ourselves to make Esther blush by calling her Lady Percival, and to inquire of Harry about his future parliamentary prospects, his rent-rolls and tenants. In fact, when together, we were four children, and played with life much as we used to in the dear old days.

Esther, under the influence of hope and love, had bloomed out into a beautiful woman. Instead of looking like a pale image of abstract thought, she seemed like warm flesh and blood, and

Ellery Davenport remarked, "What a splendid contrast her black hair and eyes will make to the golden beauty of Tina!"

All Oldtown respectability had exerted itself to be at the wedding. All, however humble, who had befriended Tina and Harry during the days of their poverty, were bidden. Polly had been long sojourning in the house, in the capacity of Miss Mehitable's maid, and assisting assiduously in the endless sewing and fine laundry work which precedes a wedding.

On this auspicious morning she came gloriously forth, rustling in a stiff changeable lutestring, her very Sunday best, and with her mind made up to enter an Episcopal church for the first time in her life. There had, in fact, occurred some slight theological skirmishes between Polly and the High Church domestics of Miss Debby's establishment, and Miss Mehitable was obliged to make stringent representations to Polly concerning the duty of sometimes repressing her testimony for truth under particular circumstances.

Polly had attended one catechising, but the shock produced upon her mind by hearing doctrines which seemed to her to have such papistical tendencies was so great that Miss Mehitable begged Miss Debby to allow her to be excused in future. Miss Debby felt that the obligations of politeness owed by a woman of quality to an invited guest in her own house might take precedence even of theological considerations. In this point of view, she regarded Congregationalists with a well-bred, compassionate tolerance, and very willingly acceded to whatever Miss Mehitable suggested.

Harry and I had passed the night before the wedding-day at the Kittery mansion, that we might be there at the very earliest hour in the morning, to attend to all those thousand and one things that always turn up for attention at such a time.

Madam Kittery's garden commanded a distant view of the sea, and I walked among the stately alleys looking at that splendid distant view of Boston harbor, which seemed so bright and sunny, and which swooned away into the horizon with such an ineffable softness, as an image of eternal peace.

As I stood there looking, I heard a light footstep behind me, and Tina came up suddenly and spattered my cheek with a dewy rose that she had just been gathering.

"You look as mournful as if it were you that is going to be married!" she said.

"Tina!" I said, "you out so early too?"

"Yes, for a wonder. The fact was, I had a bad dream, and would not sleep. I got up and looked out of my window, and saw you here, Horace, so I dressed me quickly and ran down. I feel a little bit uncanny, — and eerie, as the Scotch say, — and a little bit sad, too, about the dear old days, Horace. We have had such good times together, — first we three, and then we took Esther in, and that made four; and now, Horace, you must open the ranks a little wider and take in Ellery."

"But five is an uneven number," said I; "it leaves one out in the cold."

"O Horace! I hope you will find one worthy of you," she said. "I shall have a place in my heart all ready for her. She shall be my sister. You will write to me, won't you? Do write. I shall so want to hear of the dear old things. Every stick and stone, every sweetbrier-bush and huckleberry patch in Oldtown, will always be dear to me. And dear old precious Aunty, what ever set it into her good heart to think of taking poor little me to be her child? and it's too bad that I should leave her so. You know, Horace, I have a small income all my own, and that I mean to give to Aunty."

Now there were many points in this little valedictory of Tina to which I had no mind to respond, and she looked, as she was speaking, with tears coming in her great soft eyes, altogether too loving and lovely to be a safe companion to one forbidden to hold her in his arms and kiss her, and I felt such a desperate temptation in that direction that I turned suddenly from her. "Does Mr. Davenport approve such a disposition of your income?" said I, in a constrained voice.

"Mr. Davenport! Mr. High and Mighty," she said, mimicking my constrained tone, "what makes you so sulky to me this morning?"

"I am not sulky, Tina, only sad," I said.

"Come, come, Horace, don't be sad," she said, coaxingly, and putting her hand through my arm. "Now just be a good boy, and walk up and down with me here a few moments, and let me tell you about things."

I submitted and let her lead me off passively. "You see, Horace," she said, "I feel for poor old Aunty. Hers seems to me such a dry, desolate life; and I can't help feeling a sort of self-reproach when I think of it. Why should I have health and youth and strength and Ellery, and be going to see all the beauty and glory of Europe, while she sits alone at home, old and poor, and hears the rain drip off from those old lilac-bushes? Oldtown is a nice place, to be sure, but it does rain a great deal there, and she and Polly will be so lonesome without me to make fun for them. Now, Horace, you must promise me to go there as much as you can. You must cultivate Aunty for my sake; and her friendship is worth cultivating for its own sake."

"I know it," said I; "I am fully aware of the value of her mind and character."

"You and Harry ought both to visit her," said Tina, "and write to her, and take her advice. Nothing improves a young man faster than such female friendship; it's worth that of dozens of us girls."

Tina always had a slight proclivity for sermonizing, but a chapter in Ecclesiastes, coming from little preachers with lips and eyes like hers, is generally acceptable.

"You know," said Tina, "that Aunty has some sort of a trouble on her mind."

"I know all about it," said I.

"Did she tell you?"

"Yes," said I, "after I had divined it."

"I made her tell me," said Tina. "When I came home from school, I determined I would not be treated like a child by her any longer, — that she should tell me her troubles, and let me bear them with her. I am young and full of hope, and ought to have troubles to bear. And she is worn out and weary with thinking over and over the same sad story. What a strange thing it is that that sister treats her so! I have been thinking so much about her lately, Horace; and, do you know? I had the strangest dream about her last night. I dreamed that Ellery and I were standing at the altar being married, and, all of a sudden, that lady that we saw in the closet and in the garret rose up like a ghost between us."

"Come, come," said I, "Tina, you are getting nervous. One shouldn't tell of one's bad dreams, and then one forgets them easier."

"Well," said Tina, "it made me sad to think that she was a young girl like me, full of hope and joy. They didn't treat her rightly over in that Farnsworth family, — Miss Mehitable told me all about it. O, it was a dreadful story! they perfectly froze her heart with their dreary talk about religion. Horace, I think the most irreligious thing in the world is that way of talking, which takes away our Heavenly Father, and gives only a dreadful Judge. I should not be so happy and so safe as I am now, if I did not believe in a loving God."

"Tina," said I, "are you satisfied with the religious principles of Mr. Davenport?"

"I'm glad you asked me that, Horace, because Mr. Davenport is a man that is very apt to be misunderstood. Nobody really does understand him but me. He has seen so much of cant, and hypocrisy, and pretence of religion, and is so afraid of pretensions that do not mean anything, that I think he goes to the other extreme. Indeed, I have told him so. But he says he is always delighted to hear me talk on religion, and he likes to have me repeat hymns to him; and he told me the other day that he thought the Bible contained finer strains of poetry and eloquence than could be got from all other books put together. Then he has such a wonderful mind, you know. Mr. Avery said that he never saw a person that appreciated all the distinctions of the doctrines more completely than he did. He doesn't quite agree with Mr. Avery, nor with anybody; but I think he is very far from being an irreligious man. I believe he thinks very seriously on all these subjects, indeed."

"I am glad of it," said I, half convinced by her fervor, more than half by the magic of her presence, and the touch of the golden curls that the wind blew against my cheek, — true Venetian curls, brown in the shade and gold in the sun. Certainly, such things as these, if not argument, incline man to be convinced of whatever a fair preacher says; and I thought it not unlikely that Ellery Davenport liked to hear her talk about religion. The conversation was interrupted by the breakfast-bell, which rung us in to an early meal, where we found Miss Debby, brisk and crisp with business and authority, apologizing to Lady Widgery for the unusually early hour, "but, really, so much always to be done in cases like these."

Breakfast was hurried over, for I was to dress myself, and go to Mr. Davenport's house, and accompany him, as groomsman, to meet Tina and Harry at the church door.

I remember admiring Ellery Davenport, as I met him this morning, with his easy, high-bred, cordial air, and with that overflow of general benevolence which seems to fill the hearts of happy bridegrooms on the way to the altar. Jealous as I was of the love that ought to be given to the idol of my knight-errantry, I could not but own to myself that Ellery Davenport was most loyally in love.

Then I have a vision of the old North Church, with its chimes playing, and the pews around the broad aisle filled with expectant guests. The wedding had excited a great deal of attention in the upper circles of Boston. Ellery Davenport was widely known, having been a sort of fashionable meteor, appearing at intervals in the select circles of the city, with all the prestige of foreign travel and diplomatic reputation. Then the little romance of the children had got about, and had proved as sweet a morsel under the tongues of good Bostonians as such spices in the dulness of real life usually do. There was talk everywhere of the little story, and, as usual, nothing was lost in the telling; the beauty and cleverness of the children had been reported from mouth to mouth, until everybody was on tiptoe to see them.

The Oldtown people, who were used to rising at daybreak, found no difficulty in getting to Boston in season. Uncle Fliakim's almost exhausted wagon had been diligently revamped, and his harness assiduously mended, for days beforehand, during which process the good man might have been seen flying like a meteor in an unceasing round, between the store, the blacksmith's shop, my grandfather's, and his own dwelling; and in consequence of these arduous labors, not only his wife, but Aunt Keziah and Hepsy Lawson were secured a free passage to the entertainment.

Lady Lothrop considerately offered a seat to my grandmother and Aunt Lois in her coach; but my grandmother declined the honor in favor of my mother.

"It's all very well," said my grandmother, "and I send my blessing on 'em with all my heart; but my old husband and I are too far along to be rattling our old bones to weddings in Boston.

I shouldn't know how to behave in their grand Episcopal church."

Aunt Lois, who, like many other good women, had an innocent love of the pomps and vanities, and my mother, to whom the scene was an unheard-of recreation, were, on the whole, not displeased that her mind had taken this turn. As to Sam Lawson, he arose before Aurora had unbarred the gates of dawn, and strode off vigorously on foot, in his best Sunday clothes, and arrived there in time to welcome Uncle Fliakim's wagon, and to tell him that "he'd ben a lookin' out for 'em these two hours."

So then for as much as half an hour before the wedding coaches arrived at the church door there was a goodly assemblage in the church, and, while the chimes were solemnly pealing the tune of old Wells, there were bibbing and bobbing of fashionable bonnets, and fluttering of fans, and rustling of silks, and subdued creakings of whalebone stays, and a gentle undertone of gossiping conversation in the expectant audience. Sam Lawson had mounted the organ loft, directly opposite the altar, which commanded a most distinct view of every possible transaction below, and also gave a prominent image of himself, with his lanky jaws, protruding eyes, and shackling figure, posed over all as the inspecting genius of the scene. And every once in a while he conveyed to Jake Marshall pieces of intelligence with regard to the amount of property or private history — the horses, carriages, servants, and most secret internal belongings — of the innocent Bostonians, who were disporting themselves below, in utter ignorance of how much was known about them. But when a man gives himself seriously, for years, to the task of collecting information, thinking nothing of long tramps of twenty miles in the acquisition, never hesitating to put a question and never forgetting an answer, it is astonishing what an amount of information he may pick up. In Sam, a valuable reporter of the press has been lost forever. He was born a generation too soon, and the civilization of his time had not yet made a place for him. But not the less did he at this moment feel in himself all the responsibilities of a special reporter for Oldtown.

"Lordy massy," he said to Jake, when the chimes began to play, "how solemn that 'ere does sound!

> 'Life *is* the time to sarve the Lord,
> The time *to* insure the gret reward.'

I ben up in the belfry askin' the ringer what Mr. Devenport's goin' to give him for ringin' them 'ere chimes; and how much de ye think 't was? Wal, 't was jest fifty dollars, for jest this 'ere one time! an' the weddin' fee's a goin' t' be a hunderd guineas in a gold puss. I tell yer, Colonel Devenport's a man as chops his mince putty fine. There's Parson Lothrop down there; he's got a spick span new coat an' a new wig! That's Mis' Lothrop's scarlet Injy shawl; that 'ere cost a hunderd guineas in Injy, — her first husband gin 'er that. Lordy massy, ain't it a providence that Parson Lothrop's married her? 'cause sence the war that 'ere s'ciety fur sendin' the Gospil to furrin parts don't send nothin' to 'em, an' the Oldtown people they don't pay nothin'. All they can raise they gin to Mr. Mordecai Rossiter, 'cause they say ef they hev to s'port a colleague it's all they can do, 'specially sence he's married. Yeh see, Mordecai, he wanted to git Tiny, but he couldn't come it, and so he's tuk up with Delily Barker. The folks, some on 'em, kind o' hinted to old Parson Lothrop thet his sermons wasn't so interestin' 's they might be, 'n' the parson, ses he, 'Wal, I b'lieve the sermons 's about 's good 's the pay; ain't they?' He hed 'em there. I like Parson Lothrop, — he's a fine old figger-head, and keeps up stiff for th' honor o' the ministry. Why, folks 's gittin' so nowadays thet ministers won't be no more 'n common folks, 'n' everybody'll hev their say to 'em jest as they do to anybody else. Lordy massy, there's the orgin, — goin' to hev all the glories, orgins 'n' bells 'n' everythin'; guess the procession must ha' started. Mr. Devenport's got another spick an' new landau, 't he ordered over from England, special, for this 'casion, an' two prancin' white hosses! Yeh see I got inter Bostin 'bout daybreak, an' I's around ter his stables a lookin' at 'em a polishin' up their huffs a little, 'n' givin' 'n' 'em a wipe down, 'n' I asked Jenkins what he thought he gin for 'em, an' he sed he reely shouldn't durst to tell me. I tell ye, he's like Solomon, — he's a goin' to make gold as the stones o' the street."

And while Sam's monologue was going on, in came the bridal procession, — first, Harry, with his golden head and blue eyes, and, leaning on his arm, a cloud of ethereal gauzes and laces, but of which looked a face, pale now as a lily, with wandering curls of golden hair like little gleams of sunlight on white clouds;

then the tall, splendid figure of Ellery Davenport, his haughty blue eyes glancing all around with a triumphant assurance. Miss Mehitable hung upon his arm, pale with excitement and emotion. Then came Esther and I. As we passed up the aisle, I heard a confused murmur of whisperings and a subdued drawing in of breath, and the rest all seemed to me to be done in a dream. I heard the words, "Who giveth this woman to be married to this man?" and saw Harry step forth, bold, and bright, and handsome, amid the whisperings that pointed him out as the hero of a little romance. And he gave her away forever, — our darling, our heart of hearts. And then those holy, tender words, those vows so awful, those supporting prayers, all mingled as in a dream, until it was all over, and ladies, laughing and crying, were crowding around Tina, and there were kissing and congratulating and shaking of hands, and then we swept out of the church, and into the carriages, and were whirled back to the Kittery mansion, which was thrown wide open, from garret to cellar, in the very profuseness of old English hospitality.

There was a splendid lunch laid out in the parlor, with all the old silver in muster, and with all the delicacies that Boston confectioners and caterers could furnish.

Ellery Davenport had indeed tendered the services of his French cook, but Miss Debby had respectfully declined the offer.

"He may be a very good cook, Ellery; I say nothing against him. I am extremely obliged to you for your polite offer, but good English cooking is good enough for me, and I trust that whatever guests I invite will always think it good enough for them."

On that day, Aunt Lois and Aunt Keziah and my mother and Uncle Fliakim sat down in proximity to some of the very selectest families of Boston, comporting themselves, like good republican Yankees, as if they had been accustomed to that sort of thing all their lives, though secretly embarrassed by many little points of etiquette.

Tina and Ellery sat at the head of the table, and dispensed hospitalities around them with a gay and gracious freedom; and Harry, in whom the bridal dress of Esther had evidently excited distracting visions of future probabilities, was making his seat by her at dinner an opportunity, in the general clatter of conversation, to enjoy a nice little *tête-à-tête*.

Besides the brilliant company in the parlor, a long table was laid out upon the greensward at the back of the house, in the garden, where beer and ale flowed freely, and ham and bread and cheese and cake and eatables of a solid and sustaining description were dispensed to whomsoever would. The humble friends of lower degree — the particular friends of the servants, and all the numerous tribe of dependents and hangers-on, who wished to have some small share in the prosperity of the prosperous — here found ample entertainment. Here Sam Lawson might be seen, seated beside Hepsy, on a garden-seat near the festive board, gallantly pressing upon her the good things of the hour.

"Eat all ye want ter, Hepsy, — it comes free 's water; ye can hev 'wine an' milk without money 'n' without price,' as 't were. Lordy massy, 's jest what I wanted. I hed sech a stram this mornin', 'n' hain't hed nothin' but a two-cent roll, 't I bought 't to baker's. Thought I should ha caved in 'fore they got through with the weddin'. These 'ere 'Piscopal weddin's is putty long. What d'ye think on 'em, Polly?"

"I think I like our own way the best," said Polly, stanchly, "none o' your folderol, 'n' kneelin', 'n' puttin' on o' rings."

"Well," said Hepsy, with the spice of a pepper-box in her eyes, "I liked the part that said, 'With all my worldly goods, I thee endow.'"

"Thet's putty well, when a man hes any worldly goods," said Sam; "but how about when he hesn't?"

"Then he's no business to git married!" said Hepsy, definitely.

"So *I* think," said Polly; "but, for my part, I don't want no man's worldly goods, ef I've got to take him with 'em. I'd rather work hard as I have done, and hev 'em all to myself, to do just what I please with."

"Wal, Polly," said Sam, "I dare say the men 's jest o' your mind, — none on 'em won't try very hard to git ye' out on 't."

"There's bin those thet hes, though!" said Polly; "but 't ain't wuth talkin' about, any way."

And so conversation below stairs and above proceeded gayly and briskly, until at last the parting hour came.

"Now jest all on ye step round ter the front door, an' see 'em go off in their glory. Them two white hosses is imported fresh from England, 'n' they couldn't ha' cost less 'n' a thousan' dollars apiece, ef they cost a cent."

"A thousand!" said Jenkins, the groom, who stood in his best clothes amid the festive throng. "Who told you that?"

"Wal!" said Sam, "I thought I'd put the figger low enough, sence ye wouldn't tell me perticklers. I like to be accurate 'bout these 'ere things. There they be! they're comin' out the door now. She's tuk off her white dress now, an' got on her travellin' dress, don't ye see? Lordy massy, what a kissin' an' a cryin'! How women allers does go on 'bout these 'ere things! There, he's got 'er at last. See 'em goin' down the steps! ain't they a han'some couple! There, he's handin' on 'er in. The kerrige's lined with blue satin, 'n' never was sot in afore this mornin'. Good luck go with 'em! There they go."

And we all of us stood on the steps of the Kittery mansion, kissing hands and waving handkerchiefs, until the beloved one, the darling of our hearts, was out of sight.

CHAPTER XLVI

Wedding joys are commonly supposed to pertain especially to the two principal personages, and to be of a kind with which the world doth not intermeddle; but a wedding in such a quiet and monotonous state of existence as that of Oldtown is like a glorious sunset, which leaves a long after-glow, in which trees and rocks, farmhouses, and all the dull, common place landscape of real life have, for a while, a roseate hue of brightness. And then the long after-talks, the deliberate turnings and revampings, and the re-enjoying, bit by bit, of every incident!

Sam Lawson was a man who knew how to make the most of this, and for a week or two he reigned triumphant in Oldtown on the strength of it. Others could relate the bare, simple facts, but Sam Lawson could give the wedding, with variations, with marginal references, and explanatory notes, and enlightening comments, that ran deep into the history of everybody present. So that even those who had been at the wedding did not know half what they had seen until Sam told them.

It was now the second evening after that auspicious event. Aunt Lois and my mother had been pressed to prolong their stay over one night after the wedding, to share the hospitalities of the Kittery mansion, and had been taken around in the Kittery carriage to see the wonders of Boston town. But prompt, on their return, Sam came in to assist them in dishing up information by the evening fireside.

"Wal, Mis' Badger," said he, " 't was gin'ally agreed, on all hands, there hadn't ben no weddin' like it seen in Boston sence the time them court folks and nobility used to be there. Old Luke there, that rings the chimes, he told me he hedn't seen no sech couple go up the broad aisle o' that church. Luke, says he to me, 'I tell yew, the grander o' Boston is here to-day,' and ye'd better b'lieve every

one on 'em had on their Sunday best. There was the Boylstons, an'
the Bowdoins, an' the Brattles, an' the Winthrops, an' the Brad-
fords, an' the Penhallows up from Portsmouth, an' the Quinceys,
an' the Sewells. Wal, I tell yer, there was real grit there! — folks
that come in their grand kerridges I tell you! — there was such a
pawin' and a stampin' o' horses and kerridges round the church as
if all the army of the Assyrians was there!"

"Well, now, I'm glad I didn't go," said my grandmother. "I'm too
old to go into any such grandeur.'"

"Wal, I don't see why folks hes so much 'bjections to these here
'Piscopal weddin's, neither," said Sam. "I tell yer, it's a kind o'
putty sight now; ye see I was up in the organ loft, where I could
look down on the heads of all the people. Massy to us! the bunnets,
an' the feathers, an' the Injy shawls, an' the purple an' fine linen,
was all out on the 'casion. An' when our Harry come in with Tiny
on his arm, tha' was a gineral kind o' buzz, an' folks a risin' up all
over the house to look at 'em. Her dress was yer real Injy satin,
thick an' yaller, kind o' like cream. An' she had on the Pierpont
pearls an' diamonds — "

"How did you know what she had on?" said Aunt Lois.

"O, I hes ways o' findin' out!" said Sam. "Yeh know old Gineral
Pierpont, his gret-gret-grandfather, was a gineral in the British
army in Injy, an' he racketed round 'mong them nabobs out there,
an' got no end o' gold an' precious stones, an' these 'ere pearls an'
diamonds that she wore on her neck and in her ears hes come down
in the Devenport family. Mis' Delily, Miss Deborah Kittery's maid,
she told me all the partic'lars 'bout it, an' she ses there ain't no
family so rich in silver and jewels, and sich, as Ellery Devenport's
is, an' hes ben for generations back. His house is jest chock-full of
all sorts o' graven images and queer things from Chiny an' Japan,
'cause, ye see, his ancestors they traded to Injy, an' they seem to
hev got the abundance o' the Gentiles flowin' to 'em."

"I noticed those pearls on her neck," said Aunt Lois; "I never saw
such pearls."

"Wal," said Sam, "Mis' Delily, she ses she's tried 'em 'longside
of a good-sized pea, an' they're full as big. An' the earrings's them
pear-shaped pearls, ye know, with diamond nubs atop on 'em. Then
there was a great pearl cross, an' the biggest kind of a diamond
right in the middle on 't. Wal, Mis' Delily she told me a story 'bout

them 'ere pearls," said Sam. "For my part, ef it hed ben a daughter o' mine, I'd ruther she'd 'a' worn suthin' on her neck that was spic an' span new. I tell yew, these 'ere old family jewels, I think sometimes they gits kind o' struck through an' through with moth an' rust, so to speak."

"I'm sure I don't know what you mean, Sam," said Aunt Lois, literally, "since we know gold can't rust, and pearls and diamonds don't hurt with any amount of keeping."

"Wal, ye see, they do say that 'ere old Gineral Pierpont was a putty hard customer; he got them 'ere pearls an' diamonds away from an Injun princess; I s'pose she thought she'd as much right to 'em 's he hed; an' they say 't was about all she hed was her jewels, an' so nat'rally enough she cussed him for taking on 'em. Wal, dunno's the Lord minds the cusses o' these poor old heathen critturs; but 's ben a fact, Mis' Delily says, thet them jewels hain't never brought good luck. Gineral Pierpont, he gin 'em to his fust wife, an' she didn't live but two months arter she was married. He gin 'em to his second wife, 'n' she tuck to drink and le'd him sech a life 't he wouldn't ha' cared ef she had died too; 'n' then they come down to Ellery Devenport's first wife, 'n' she went ravin' crazy the fust year arter she was married. Now all that 'ere does look a little like a cuss; don't it?"

"O nonsense, Sam!" said Aunt Lois, "I don't believe there's a word of truth in any of it! You can hatch more stories in one day than a hen can eggs in a month."

"Wal, any way," said Sam, "I like the 'Piscopal sarvice, all 'ceppin' the minister's wearin' his shirt outside; that I don't like."

" 'T isn't a shirt!" said Aunt Lois, indignantly.

"O lordy massy!" said Sam, "I know what they calls it. I know it's a surplice, but it looks for all the world like a man in his shirt-sleeves; but the words is real solemn. I wondered when he asked 'em all whether they hed any objections to 't, an' told 'em to speak up ef they hed, what would happen ef anybody should speak up jest there."

"Why, of course 't would stop the wedding," said Aunt Lois, "until the thing was inquired into."

"Wal, Jake Marshall, he said thet he'd heerd a story when he was a boy, about a weddin' in a church at Portsmouth, that was stopped jest there, 'cause, ye see, the man he hed another wife livin'. He said 'twas old Colonel Penhallow. 'Mazin' rich the old Colonel was, and these 'ere rich old cocks sometimes does seem to strut round and cut up pretty much as if they hedn't heard o' no God in their parts. The Colonel he got his wife shet up in a lunatic asylum, an' then spread the word that she was dead, an' courted a gal, and come jest as near as that to marryin' of her."

"As near as what?" said Aunt Lois.

"Why, when they got to that 'ere part of the service, there was his wife, good as new. She'd got out o' the 'sylum, and stood up there 'fore 'em all. So you see that 'ere does some good."

"I'd rather stay in an asylum all my life than go back to that man," said Aunt Lois.

"Wal, you see she didn't," said Sam; "her friends they made him make a settlement on her, poor woman, and he cleared out t' England."

"Good riddance to bad rubbish," said my grandmother.

"Wal, how handsome that 'ere gal is that Harry's going to marry!" continued Sam. "She didn't have on nothin' but white muslin', an' not a snip of a jewel; but she looked like a queen. Ses I to Jake, ses I, there goes the woman 't'll be Lady Percival one o' these days, over in England, an' I bet ye, he'll find lots o' family jewels for her, over there. Mis' Delily she said she didn't doubt there would be."

"I hope," said my grandmother, "that she will have more enduring riches than that; it's small matter about earthly jewels."

"Lordy massy, yes, Mis' Badger," said Sam, "jes' so, jes' so; now that 'ere was bein' impressed on my mind all the time. Folks oughtenter lay up their treasures on airth; I couldn't help thinkin' on 't, when I see Tiny a wearin' them jewels, jest how vain an' transitory everythin' is, an' how the women 't has worn 'em afore is all turned to dust, an' lyin' in their graves. Lordy massy, these 'ere things make us realize what a transitory world we's a livin' in. I was tellin' Hepsy 'bout it, — she's so kind o' worldly, Hepsy is, — seemed to make her feel so kind o' gritty to see so much wealth 'n' splendor, when we hedn't none. Ses I, 'Hepsy, there ain't no use o' wantin' worldly riches, 'cause our lives all passes away like a dream, an' a hundred years hence 't won't make no sort o' diffurnce what we've hed, an' what we heven't hed.' But wal, Miss Lois, *did* ye see the kerridge?" said Sam, returning to temporal things with renewed animation.

"I just got a glimpse of it," said Aunt Lois, "as it drove to the door."

"Lordy massy," said Sam, "I was all over that 'ere kerridge that mornin' by daylight. 'T ain't the one he had up here, — that was jest common doin's, — this 'ere is imported spic an' span new from England for the 'casion, an' all made jest 's they make 'em for the nobility. Why, 't was all quilted an' lined with blue satin, ever so grand, an' Turkey carpet under their feet, an' the springs was easy 's a rockin'-chair. That's what they've gone off in. Wal, lordy massy! I don't grudge Tina nothin'! She's the chipperest, light-heartedest, darlin'est little creetur that ever did live, an' I hope she'll hev good luck in all things."

A rap was heard at the kitchen door, and Polly entered. It was evident from her appearance that she was in a state of considerable agitation. She looked pale and excited, and her hands shook.

"Mis' Badger," she said to my grandmother, "Miss Rossiter wants to know 'f you won't come an' set up with her to-night."

"Why, is she sick?" said grandmother. "What's the matter with her?"

"She ain't very well," said Polly, evasively; "she wanted Mis' Badger to spend the night with her."

"Perhaps, mother, I'd better go over," said Aunt Lois.

"No, Miss Lois," said Polly, eagerly, "Miss Rossiter don't wanter see anybody but yer mother."

"Wal, now I wanter know!" said Sam Lawson.

"Well, you can't know everything," said Aunt Lois, "so you *may* want!"

"Tell Miss Rossiter, ef I can do anythin' for 'er, I hope she'll call on me," said Sam.

My grandmother and Polly went out together. Aunt Lois bustled about the hearth, swept it up, and then looked out into the darkness after them. What could it be?

The old clock ticked drowsily in the kitchen corner, and her knitting-needles rattled.

"What do you think it is?" said my mother, timidly, to Aunt Lois.

"How should I know?" said Aunt Lois, sharply.

In a few moments Polly returned again.

"Miss Mehitable says she would like to see Sam Lawson."

"O, wal, wal, would she? Wal, I'll come!" said Sam, rising with joyful alertness. "I'm allers ready at a minute's warnin'!"

And they went out into the darkness together.

CHAPTER XLVII

———◆◆◆———

BEHIND THE CURTAIN

In the creed of most story-tellers marriage is equal to translation. The mortal pair whose fortunes are traced to the foot of the altar forthwith ascend, and a cloud receives them out of our sight as the curtain falls. Faith supposes them rapt away to some unseen paradise, and every-day toil girds up its loins and with a sigh prepares to return to its delving and grubbing.

But our story must follow the fortunes of our heroine beyond the prescribed limits.

It had been arranged that the wedding pair, after a sunny afternoon's drive through some of the most picturesque scenery in the neighborhood of Boston, should return at eventide to their country home, where they were to spend a short time preparatory to sailing for Europe. Even in those early days the rocky glories of Nahant and its dashing waves were known and resorted to by Bostonians, and the first part of the drive was thitherward, and Tina climbed round among the rocks, exulting like a sea-bird with Ellery Davenport ever at her side, laughing, admiring, but holding back her bold, excited footsteps, lest she should plunge over by some unguarded movement, and become a vanished dream.

So near lies the ever possible tragedy at the hour of our greatest exultation; it is but a false step, an inadvertent movement, and all that was joy can become a cruel mockery! We all know this to be so. We sometimes start and shriek when we see it to be so in the case of others, but who is the less triumphant in his hour of possession for this gloomy shadow of possibility that forever dogs his steps?

Ellery Davenport was now in the high tide of victory. The pursuit of the hour was a success; he had captured the butterfly. In his eagerness he had trodden down and disregarded many teachings and impulses of his better nature that should have made him hesitate; but now he felt that he *had* her; she was his, — his alone and forever.

But already dark thoughts from the past were beginning to flutter out like ill-omened bats, and dip down on gloomy wing between him and the innocent, bright, confiding face. Tina he could see had idealized him entirely. She had invested him with all her conceptions of knighthood, honor, purity, religion, and made a creation of her own of him; and sometimes he smiled to himself, half amused and half annoyed at the very young and innocent simplicity of the matter. Nobody knew better than himself that what she dreamed he was he neither was nor meant to be, — that in fact there could not be a bitterer satire on his real self than her conceptions; but just now, with her brilliant beauty, her piquant earnestness, her perfect freshness, there was an indescribable charm about her that bewitched him.

Would it all pass away and get down to the jog-trot dustiness of ordinary married life, he wondered, and then, ought he not to have been a little more fair with her in exchange for the perfect transparence with which she threw open the whole of her past life to him? Had he not played with her as some villain might with a little child, and got away a priceless diamond for a bit of painted glass? He did not allow himself to think in that direction.

"Come, my little sea-gull," he said to her, after they had wandered and rambled over the rocks for a while, "you must come down from that perch, and we must drive on, if we mean to be at home before midnight."

"O Ellery, how glorious it is!"

"Yes, but we cannot build here three tabernacles, and so we must say, *Au revoir*. I will bring you here again"; — and Ellery half led, half carried her in his arms back to the carriage.

"How beautiful it is!" said Tina, as they were glancing along a turfy road through the woods. The white pines were just putting out their long fingers, the new leaves of the silvery birches were twinkling in the light, the road was fringed on both sides with great patches of the blue violet, and sweet-fern, and bayberry, and growing green tips of young spruce and fir were exhaling a spicy perfume. "It seems as if we two alone were flying through fairy-land." His arm was around her, tightening its grasp of possession as he looked down on her.

"Yes," he said, "we two are alone in our world now; none can enter it; none can see into it; none can come between us."

Suddenly the words recalled to Tina her bad dream of the night before. She was on the point of speaking of it, but hesitated to introduce it; she felt a strange shyness in mentioning that subject.

Ellery Davenport turned the conversation upon things in foreign lands, which he would soon show her. He pictured to her the bay of Naples, the rocks of Sorrento, where the blue Mediterranean is overhung with groves of oranges, where they should have a villa some day, and live in a dream of beauty. All things fair and bright and beautiful in foreign lands were evoked, and made to come as a sort of airy pageant around them while they wound through the still, spicy pine-woods.

It was past sunset, and the moon was looking white and sober through the flush of the evening sky, when they entered the grounds of their own future home.

"How different everything looks here from what it did when I was here years ago!" said Tina, — "the paths are all cleared, and then it was one wild, dripping tangle. I remember how long we knocked at the door, and couldn't make anyone hear, and the old black knocker frightened me, — it was a black serpent with his tail in his mouth. I wonder if it is there yet."

"O, to be sure it is," said Ellery; "that is quite a fine bit of old bronze, after something in Herculaneum, I think; you know serpents were quite in vogue among the ancients."

"I should think that symbol meant eternal evil," said Tina, — "a circle is eternity, and a serpent is evil."

"You are evidently prejudiced against serpents, my love," said Ellery. "The ancients thought better of them; they were emblems of wisdom, and the ladies very appropriately wore them for bracelets and necklaces."

"I wouldn't have one for the world," said Tina. "I always hated them, they are so bright, and still, and sly."

"Mere prejudice," said Ellery, laughing. "I must cure it by giving you, one of these days, an emerald-green serpent for a bracelet, with ruby crest and diamond eyes; you've no idea what pretty fellows they are. But here, you see, we are coming to the house; you can smell the roses."

"How lovely and how changed!" said Tina. "O, what a world of white roses over that portico, — roses everywhere, and white lilacs. It is a perfect paradise!"

"May you find it so, my little Eve," said Ellery Davenport, as the carriage stopped at the door. Ellery sprang out lightly, and, turning, took Tina in his arms and set her down in the porch.

They stood there a moment in the moonlight, and listened to the fainter patter of the horses' feet as they went down the drive.

"Come in, my little wife," said Ellery, opening the door, "and may the black serpent bring you good luck."

The house was brilliantly lighted by wax candles in massive silver candlesticks.

"O, how strangely altered!" said Tina, running about, and looking into the rooms with the delight of a child. "How beautiful everything is!"

The housekeeper, a respectable female, now appeared and offered her services to conduct her young mistress to her rooms. Ellery went with her, almost carrying her up the staircase on his arm. Above, as below, all was light and bright. "This room is ours," said Ellery, drawing her into that chamber which Tina remembered years before as so weirdly desolate. Now it was all radiant with hangings and furniture of blue and silver; the open windows let in branches of climbing white roses, the vases were full of lilies. The housekeeper paused a moment at the door.

"There is a lady in the little parlor below that has been waiting more than an hour to see you and madam," she said.

"A lady!" said both Tina and Ellery, in tones of surprise. "Did she give her name?" said Ellery.

"She gave no name; but she said that you, sir, would know her."

"I can't imagine who it should be," said Ellery. "Perhaps, Tina, I had better go down and see while you are dressing," said Ellery.

"Indeed, that would be a pretty way to do! No, sir, I allow no private interviews," said Tina, with authority, — "no, I am all ready and quite dressed enough to go down."

"Well, then, little positive," said Ellery, "be it as you will; let's go together."

"Well, I must confess," said Tina, "I didn't look for wedding callers out here to-night; but never mind, it's a nice little mystery to see what she wants."

They went down the staircase together, passed across the hall, and entered the little boudoir, where Tina and Harry had spent their first night together. The door of the writing cabinet stood open, and a lady all in black, in a bonnet and cloak, stood in the doorway.

As she came forward, Tina exclaimed, "O Ellery, it is she, — the lady in the closet!" and sank down pale and half fainting.

Ellery Davenport turned pale too; his cheeks, his very lips were blanched like marble; he looked utterly thunderstruck and appalled.

"Emily!" he said. "Great God!"

"Yes, Emily!" she said, coming forward slowly and with dignity. "You did not expect to meet ME here and now, Ellery Davenport!"

There was for a moment a silence that was perfectly awful. Tina looked on without power to speak, as in a dreadful dream. The ticking of the little French mantel clock seemed like a voice of doom to her.

The lady walked close up to Ellery Davenport, drew forth a letter, and spoke in that fearfully calm way that comes from the very white-heat of passion.

"Ellery," she said, "here is your letter. You did not *know* me — you could not know me — if you thought, after *that letter*, I would accept anything from you! *I* live on your bounty! I would sooner work as a servant!"

"Ellery, Ellery!" said Tina, springing up and clasping his arm, "O, tell me who she is! What is she to you? Is she — is she — "

"Be quiet, my poor child," said the woman, turning to her with an air of authority. "I have no claims; I come to make none. Such as this man is, *he is your husband*, not mine. You believe in him; so did I, — love him; so did I. I gave up all for him, — country, home, friends, name, reputation, — for I thought him such a man that a woman might well sacrifice her whole life to him! He is the father of my child! But fear not. The world, of course, will approve *him* and condemn *me*. They will say he did well to give up his mistress and take a wife; it's the world's morality. What woman will think the less of him, or smile the less on him, when she hears it? What woman will not feel herself too good even to touch my hand?"

"Emily," said Ellery Davenport, bitterly, "if you thought I deserved this, you might, at least, have spared this poor child."

"*The truth* is the best foundation in married life, Ellery," she said, "and the truth you have small faculty for speaking. I do her a favor in telling it. Let her start fair from the commencement, and then there will be no more to be told. Besides," she added, "I shall not trouble you long. *There*," she said, putting down a jewel-case, — "there are your gifts to me, — there are your letters." Then she threw on the table a miniature set in diamonds, "There is your picture. And now God help me! Farewell."

She turned and glided swiftly from the room.

      *   *   *   *   *

Readers who remember the former part of this narrative will see at once that it was, after all, Ellery Davenport with whom, years before, Emily Rossiter had fled to France. They had resided there, and subsequently in Switzerland, and she had devoted herself to him, and to his interests, with all the single hearted fervor of a true wife.

On her part, there was a full and conscientious belief that the choice of the individuals alone constituted a true marriage, and that the laws of human society upon this subject were an oppression which needed to be protested against.

On his part, however, the affair was a simple gratification of passion, and the principles, such as they were, were used by him as he used all principles, — simply as convenient machinery for carrying out his own purposes. Ellery Davenport spoke his own convictions when he said that there was no subject which had not its right and its wrong side, each of them capable of being unanswerably sustained. He had played with his own mind in this manner until he had entirely obliterated conscience. He could at any time dazzle and confound his own moral sense with his own reasonings; and it was sometimes amusing, but, in the long run, tedious and vexatious to him, to find that what he maintained merely for convenience and for theory should be regarded by Emily so seriously, and with such an earnest eye to logical consequences. In short, the two came, in the course of their intimacy, precisely to the spot to which many people come who are united by an indissoluble legal tie. Slowly, and through an experience of many incidents, they had come to perceive an entire and irrepressible conflict of natures between them.

Notwithstanding that Emily had taken a course diametrically opposed to the principles of her country and her fathers, she remained largely the Puritan nature. Instances have often been seen in New England of men and women who had renounced every particle of the Puritan theology, and yet retained in their fibre and composition all the moral traits of the Puritans — their uncompromising conscientiousness, their inflexible truthfulness, and their severe logic in following the convictions of their understandings. And the fact was, that while Emily had sacrificed for Ellery Davenport her position in society, — while she had exposed herself to the very coarsest misconstructions of the commonest minds, and made herself liable to be ranked by her friends in New England among abandoned outcasts, — she was really a woman standing on too high a moral plane for Ellery Davenport to consort with her in comfort. He was ambitious, intriguing, unscrupulous, and it was an annoyance to him to be obliged to give an account of himself to her. He was tired of playing the moral hero, the part that he assumed and acted with great success during the time of their early attachment. It annoyed him to be held to any consistency in principles. The very devotion to him which she felt, regarding him, as she always did, in his higher and nobler nature, vexed and annoyed him.

Of late years he had taken long vacations from her society, in excursions to England and America. When the prospect of being ambassador to England dawned upon him, he began seriously to consider the inconvenience of being connected with a woman unpresentable in society. He dared not risk introducing her into those high circles as his wife. Moreover, he knew that it was a falsehood to which he never should gain her consent; and running along in the line of his thoughts came his recollections of Tina. When he returned to America, with the fact in his mind that she would be the acknowledged daughter of a respectable old English family, all her charms and fascinations had a double power over him. He delivered himself up to them without scruple.

He wrote immediately to a confidential friend in Switzerland, enclosing money, with authority to settle upon Emily a villa near Geneva, and a suitable income. He trusted to her pride for the rest.

Never had the thought come into his head that she would return to her native country, and brave all the reproach and humiliation of such a step, rather than accept this settlement at his hands.

CHAPTER XLVIII

TINA'S SOLUTION

Harry and I had gone back to our college room after the wedding. There we received an earnest letter from Miss Mehitable, begging us to come to her at once. It was brought by Sam Lawson, who told us that he had got up at three o'clock in the morning to start away with it.

"There's trouble of some sort or other in that 'ere house," said Sam. "Last night I was in ter the Deacon's, and we was a talkin' over the weddin', when Polly came in all sort o' flustered, and said Miss Rossiter wanted to see Mis' Badger; and your granny she went over, and didn't come home all night. She sot up with somebody, and I'm certain 't wa'n't Miss Rossiter, 'cause I see her up tol'able spry in the mornin'; but, lordy massy, somethin' or other's ben a usin' on her up, for she was all wore out, and looked sort o' limpsy, as if there wa'n't no starch left in her. She sent for me last night. 'Sam,' says she, 'I want to send a note to the boys just as quick as I can, and I don't want to wait for the mail; can't you carry it?' 'Lordy massy, yes,' says I. 'I hope there ain't nothin' happened,' says I; and we see she didn't answer me; and puttin' that with Mis' Badger's settin' there all night, it 'peared to me there was suthin', I can't make out quite what."

Harry and I lost no time in going to the stage-house, and found ourselves by noon at Miss Mehitable's door.

When we went in, we found Miss Mehitable seated in close counsel with Mr. Jonathan Rossiter. His face looked sharp, and grave, and hard; his large gray eyes had in them a fiery, excited gleam. Spread out on the table before them were files of letters, in the handwriting of which I had before had a glimpse. The brother and sister had evidently been engaged in reading them, as some of them lay open under their hands.

When we came into the room, both looked up. Miss Mehitable rose, and offered her hands to us in an eager, excited way, as if she were asking something of us. The color flashed into Mr. Rossiter's cheeks, and he suddenly leaned forward over the papers and covered his face with his hands. It was a gesture of shame and humiliation infinitely touching to me.

"Horace," said Miss Mehitable, "the thing we feared has come upon us. O Horace, Horace! why could we not have known it in time?"

I divined at once. My memory, like an electric chain, flashed back over sayings and incidents of years.

"The villain!" I said.

Mr. Rossiter ground his foot on the floor with a hard, impatient movement, as if he were crushing some poisonous reptile.

"It's well for him that *I'm* not God," he said through his closed teeth.

Harry looked from one to the other of us in dazed and inquiring surprise. He had known in a vague way of Emily's disappearance, and of Miss Mehitable's anxieties, but it never had occurred to his mind to connect the two. In fact, our whole education had been in such a wholesome and innocent state of society, that neither of us had the foundation, in our experience or habits of thought, for the conception of anything like villany. We were far enough from any comprehension of the melodramatic possibilities suggested in our days by that heaving and tumbling modern literature, whose waters cast up mire and dirt.

Never shall I forget the shocked, incredulous expression on Harry's face as he listened to my explanations, nor the indignation to which it gave place.

"I would sooner have seen Tina in her grave than married to such a man," he said huskily.

"O Harry!" said Miss Mehitable.

"I would!" he said, rising excitedly. "There are things that men can do that still leave hope of them; but a thing like this is *final*, — it is decisive."

"That is my opinion, Harry," said Mr. Rossiter. "It is a sin that leaves no place for repentance."

"We have been reading these letters," said Miss Mehitable; "they were sent to us by Tina, and they do but confirm what I always said, — that Emily fell by her higher nature. She learned, under Dr. Stern, to think and to reason boldly, even when differing from received opinion; and this hardihood of mind and opinion she soon turned upon the doctrines he taught. Then we abandoned the Bible, and felt herself free to construct her own system of morals. Then came an intimate friendship with a fascinating married man, whose domestic misfortunes made a constant demand on her sympathy; and these charming French friends of hers — who were, as far as I see, disciples of the new style of philosophy, and had come to America to live in a union with each other which was not recognized by the laws of France — all united to make her feel that she was acting heroically and virtuously in sacrificing her whole life to her lover, and disregarding what they called the tyranny of human law. In Emily's eyes, her connection had all the sacredness of marriage."

"Yes," said Mr. Rossiter, "but see now how all these infernal, fine-spun, and high-flown notions always turn out to the disadvantage of the weaker party! It is *man* who always takes advantage of woman in relations like these; it is she that *gives* all, and he that *takes* all; it is she risks everything, and he risks nothing. Hard as marriage bonds bear in individual cases, it is for woman's interest that they should be as stringently maintained as the Lord himself has left them. When once they begin to be lessened, it is always the weaker party that goes to the wall!"

"But," said I, "suppose a case of confirmed and hopeless insanity on either side."

He made an impatient gesture. "Did you ever think," he said, "if men had the laws of nature in their hands, what a mess they would make of them? What treatises we should have against the cruelty of fire in *always* burning, and of water in *always* drowning! What saints and innocents has the fire tortured, and what just men made perfect has water drowned, making *no* exceptions! But who doubts that this inflexibility in natural law is, after all, the best thing? The laws of morals are in our hands, and so reversible, and, therefore, we are always clamoring for exceptions. I think they should cut their way like those of nature, *inflexibly* and *eternally!*"

Here the sound of wheels startled us. I went to the window, and, looking through the purple spikes of the tall old lilacs, which came up in a bower around the open window, I saw Tina alighting from a carriage.

"O Aunty," I said involuntarily, "it is she. *She* is coming, poor child."

We heard a light fluttering motion and a footfall on the stairs, and the door opened, and in a moment Tina stood among us.

She was very pale, and there was an expression such as I never saw in her face before. There had been a shock which had driven her soul inward, from the earthly upon the spiritual and the immortal. Something deep and pathetic spoke in her eyes, as she looked around on each of us for a moment without speaking. As she met Miss Mehitable's haggard, careworn face, her lip quivered. She ran to her, threw her arms round her, and hid her face on her shoulder, and sobbed out, 'O Aunty, Aunty! I didn't think I should live to make you this trouble."

"You, darling!" said Miss Mehitable. "It is not *you* who have made it."

"I am the cause," she said. "I know that he has done dreadfully wrong. I cannot defend him, but oh! I love him still. I cannot help loving him; it is my duty to," she added. "I promised, you know, before God, 'for better, for worse'; and what I promised I must keep. I am his wife; there is no going back from that."

"I know it, darling," said Miss Mehitable, stroking her head. "You are right, and my love for *you* will never change."

"I am come," she said, "to see what can be done."

"Nothing *can be done!*" spoke out the deep voice of Jonathan Rossiter. "She is lost and we disgraced beyond remedy!"

"You must not say that," Tina said, raising her head, her eyes sparkling through her tears with some of her old vivacity. "Your sister is a noble, injured woman. We must shield her and save her; there is every excuse for her."

"There is NEVER any excuse for such conduct," said Mr. Rossiter, harshly.

Tina started up in her headlong, energetic fashion. "What right have you to talk so, if you call yourself a Christian?" she said. "Think a minute. WHO was it said, 'Neither do I condemn thee'? and *whom* did he say it to? Christ was not afraid or ashamed to say *that* to a poor friendless woman, though he knew his words would never pass away."

"God bless you, darling, — God bless you!" said Miss Mehitable, clasping her in her arms.

"I have read those letters," continued Tina, impetuously. "He did not like me to do it, but I claimed it as my right, and I *would* do it, and I can see in all a noble woman, gone astray from noble motives. I can see that she was grand and unselfish in her love, that she was perfectly self-sacrificing, and I believe it was because Jesus understood these things in the hearts of women that he uttered those blessed words. The law was against that poor woman, the doctors, the Scribes and Pharisees, all respectable people, were against her, and Christ stepped between all and her; he sent them away abashed and humbled, and spoke those lovely words to her. O, I shall forever adore him for it! He is my Lord and my God!"

There was a pause for a few moments, and then Tina spoke again.

"Now, Aunty, hear my plan. You, perhaps, do not believe any good of *him,* and so I will not try to make you; only I will say that he is anxious to do all he can. He has left everything in my hands. This must go no farther than us few who now know it. Your sister refused the property he tried to settle on her. It was noble to do it. I should have felt just as she did. But, dear Aunty, *my* fortune I always meant to settle on you, and it will be enough for you both. It will make you easy as to money, and you can live together."

"Yes, my dear," said Miss Mehitable; "but how can this be kept secret when there is the child?"

"I have thought of that, Aunty. I will take the poor little one abroad with me, — children always love me. I can make her so happy; and O, it will be such a motive to make amends to her for all this wrong. Let me see your sister, Aunty, and tell her about it."

"Dear child," said Miss Mehitable, "you can do nothing with her. All last night I thought she was dying. Since then she seems to have recovered her strength; but she neither speaks nor moves. She lies with her eyes open, but notices nothing you say to her."

"Poor darling!" said Tina. "But, Aunty, let me go to her. I am so sure that God will help me, — that God sends me to her. I *must* see her!"

Tina's strong impulses seemed to carry us all with her. Miss Mehitable arose, and, taking her by the hand, opened the door of a chamber on the opposite side of the hall. I looked in, and saw that it was darkened. Tina went boldly in, and closed the door. We all sat silent together. We heard her voice, at times soft and pleading; then it seemed to grow more urgent and impetuous as she spoke continuously and in tones of piercing earnestness.

After a while, there were pauses of silence, and then a voice in reply.

"There," said Miss Mehitable, "Emily has begun to answer her, thank God! Anything is better than this oppressive silence. It is frightful!"

And now the sound of an earnest conversation was heard, waxing on both sides more and more ardent and passionate. Tina's voice sometimes could be distinguished in tones of the most pleading entreaty; sometimes it seemed almost like sobbing. After a while, there came a great silence, broken by now and then an indistinct word; and then Tina came out, softly closing the door. Her cheeks were flushed, her hair partially dishevelled, but she smiled brightly, — one of her old triumphant smiles when she had carried a point.

"I've conquered at last! I've won!" she said, almost breathless. "O, I prayed so that I might, and I did. She gives all up to me; she loves me. We love each other dearly. And now I'm going to take the little one with me, and by and by I will bring her back to her, and I will make her so happy. You must give me the darling at once, and I will take her away with us; for we are going to sail next week. We sail sooner than I thought," she said; "but this makes it best to go at once."

Miss Mehitable rose and went out, but soon reappeared, leading in a lovely little girl with great round, violet blue eyes, and curls of golden hair. The likeness of Ellery Davenport was plainly impressed on her infant features.

Tina ran towards her, and stretched out her arms. "Darling," she said, "come to me."

The little one, after a moment's survey, followed that law of attraction which always drew children to Tina. She came up confidingly, and nestled her head on her shoulder.

Tina gave her her watch to play with, and the child shook it about, well pleased.

"Emily want to go ride?" said Tina, carrying her to the window and showing her the horses.

The child laughed, and stretched out her hand.

"Bring me her things, Aunty," she said. "Let there not be a moment for change of mind. I take her with me this moment."

A few moments after, Tina went lightly tripping down the stairs, and Harry and I with her, carrying the child and its little basket of clothing.

"There, put them in," she said. "And now, boys," she said, turning and offering both her hands, "good by. I love you both dearly, and always shall."

She kissed us both, and was gone from our eyes before I awoke from the dream into which she had thrown me.

*   *   *   *   *

"Well," said Miss Mehitable, when the sound of wheels died away, "could I have believed that anything could have made my heart so much lighter as this visit?"

"She was inspired," said Mr. Rossiter.

"Tina's great characteristic," said I. "What makes her differ from others is this capacity of inspiration. She seems sometimes to rise, in a moment, to a level above her ordinary self, and to carry all up with her!"

"And to think that such a woman has thrown herself away on such a man!" said Harry.

"I foresee a dangerous future for her," said Mr. Rossiter. "With her brilliancy, her power of attraction, with the temptations of a new and fascinating social life before her, and with only that worthless fellow for a guide, I am afraid she will not continue *our* Tina."

"Suppose we trust in *Him* who has guided her hitherto," said Harry.

"People usually consider that sort of trust a desperate resort," said Mr. Rossiter. "'May the Lord help her,' means, 'It's all up with her.'"

"We see," said I, "that the greatest possible mortification and sorrow that could meet a young wife has only raised her into a higher plane. So let us hope for her future."

CHAPTER XLIX

———◄◆►———

WHAT CAME OF IT

The next week Mr. and Mrs. Ellery Davenport sailed for England.

I am warned by the increased quantity of manuscript which lies before me that, if I go on recounting scenes and incidents with equal minuteness, my story will transcend the limits of modern patience. Richardson might be allowed to trail off into seven volumes, and to trace all the histories of all his characters, even unto the third and fourth generations; but Richardson did not live in the days of railroad and steam, and mankind then had more leisure than now.

I am warned, too, that the departure of the principal character from the scene is a signal for general weariness through the audience, — for looking up of gloves, and putting on of shawls, and getting ready to call one's carriage.

In fact, when Harry and I had been down to see Tina off, and had stood on the shore, watching and waving our handkerchiefs, until the ship became a speck in the blue airy distance, I turned back to the world with very much the feeling that there was nothing left in it. What I had always dreamed of, hoped for, planned for, and made the object of all my endeavors, so far as this world was concerned, was gone, — gone, so far as I could see, hopelessly and irredeemably; and there came over me that utter languor and want of interest in every mortal thing, which is one of the worst diseases of the mind.

But I knew that it would never do to give way to this lethargy. I needed an alterative; and so I set myself, with all my might and soul, to learning a new language. There was an old German emigrant in Cambridge, with whom I became a pupil, and I plunged into German as into a new existence. I recommend everybody who wishes to try the waters of Lethe to study a new language, and learn to think in new forms; it is like going out of one sphere of existence into another.

Some may wonder that I do not recommend devotion for this grand alterative; but it is a fact, that, when one has to combat with the terrible lassitude produced by the sudden withdrawal of an absorbing object of affection, devotional exercises sometimes hinder more than they help. There is much in devotional religion of the same strain of softness and fervor which is akin to earthly attachments, and the one is almost sure to recall the other. What the soul wants is to be distracted for a while, — to be taken out of its old grooves of thought, and run upon entirely new ones. Religion must be sought in these moods, in its active and preceptive form, — what we may call its business character, — rather than in its sentimental and devotional one.

It had been concluded among us all that it would be expedient for Miss Mehitable to remove from Oldtown and take a residence in Boston.

It was desirable, for restoring the health of Emily, that she should have more change and variety, and less minute personal attention fixed upon her, than could be the case in the little village of Oldtown. Harry and I did a great deal of house-hunting for them, and at last succeeded in securing a neat little cottage on an eminence overlooking the harbor in the outskirts of Boston.

Preparing this house for them, and helping to establish them in it, furnished employment for a good many of our leisure hours. In fact, we found that this home so near would be quite an accession to our pleasures. Miss Mehitable had always been one of that most pleasant and desirable kind of acquaintances that a young man can have; to wit, a cultivated, intelligent, literary female friend, competent to advise and guide one in one's scholarly career. We became greatly interested in the society of her sister. The strength and dignity of character shown by this unfortunate lady in recovering her position commanded our respect. She was never aware, and was never made aware by anything in our manner, that we were acquainted with her past history.

The advice of Tina on this subject had been faithfully followed. No one in our circle, or in Boston, except my grandmother, had any knowledge of how the case really stood. In fact, Miss Mehitable had always said that her sister had gone abroad to study in France, and her reappearance again was only noticed among the few that inquired into it at all, at her return. Harry and I used to study French with her, both on our own account, and as a means of giving her some kind of employment. On the whole, the fireside circle at the little cottage became a cheerful and pleasant retreat. Miss Mehitable had gained what she had for years been sighing for, — the opportunity to devote herself wholly to this sister. She was a person with an enthusiastic power of affection, and the friendship that arose between the two was very beautiful.

The experiences of the French Revolution, many of whose terrors she had witnessed, had had a powerful influence on the mind of Emily, in making her feel how mistaken had been those views of human progress which come from the mere unassisted reason, when it rejects the guidance of revealed religion. She was in a mood to return to the faith of her fathers, receiving it again under milder and more liberal forms. I think the friendship of Harry was of great use to her in enabling her to attain to a settled religious faith. They were peculiarly congenial to each other, and his simplicity of religious trust was a constant corrective to the habits of thought formed by the sharp and pitiless logic of her early training.

A residence in Boston was also favorable to Emily's recovery, in giving to her what no person who has passed through such experiences can afford to be without, — an opportunity to help those poorer and more afflicted. Emily very naturally shrank from society; except the Kitterys, I think there was no family which she visited. I think she always had the feeling that she would not accept the acquaintance of any who would repudiate her were all the circumstances of her life known to them. But with the poor, the sick, and the afflicted, she felt herself at home. In their houses she was a Sister of Mercy, and the success of these sacred ministrations caused her, after a while, to be looked upon with a sort of reverence by all who knew her.

Tina proved a lively and most indefatigable correspondent. Harry and I heard from her constantly, in minute descriptions of the great gay world of London society, into which she was thrown as wife of the American minister. Her letters were like her old self, full of genius, of wit, and of humor, sparkling with descriptions and anecdotes of character, and sometimes scrawled on the edges with vivid sketches of places, or scenes, or buildings that hit her fancy. She was improving, she told us, taking lessons in drawing and music, and Ellery was making a capital French scholar of her. We could see through all her letters an evident effort to set forth everything relating to him to the best advantage; every good-natured or kindly action, and all the favorable things that were said of him, were put in the foreground, with even an anxious care.

To Miss Mehitable and Emily came other letters, filled with the sayings and doings of the little Emily, recording minutely all the particulars of her growth, and the incidents of the nursery, and showing that Tina, with all her going out, found time strictly to fulfil her promises in relation to her.

"I have got the very best kind of a maid for her," she wrote, — "just as good and true as Polly is, only she is formed by the Church Catechism instead of the Cambridge Platform. But she is faithfulness itself, and Emily loves her dearly."

In this record, also, minute notice was taken of all the presents made to the child by her father, — of all his smiles and caressing words. Without ever saying a word formally in her husband's defence, Tina thus contrived, through all her letters, to produce the most favorable impression of him. He was evidently, according to her showing, proud of her beauty and her talents, and proud of the admiration which she excited in society.

For a year or two there seemed to be a real vein of happiness running through all these letters of Tina's. I spoke to Harry about it one day.

"Tina," said I, "has just that fortunate kind of constitution, buoyant as cork, that will rise to the top of the stormiest waters."

"Yes," said Harry. "With some women it would have been an entire impossibility to live happily with a man after such a disclosure, — with Esther, for example. I have never told Esther a word about it; but I know that it would give her a horror of the man that she never could recover from."

"It is not," said I, "that Tina has not strong moral perceptions; but she has this buoyant hopefulness; she believes in herself, and she believes in others. She always feels adequate to manage the most difficult circumstances. I could not help smiling that dreadful day, when she came over and found us all so distressed and discouraged, to see what a perfect confidence she had in herself and in her own power to arrange the affair, — to make Emily consent, to make the child love her; in short, to carry out everything according to her own sweet will, just as she has always done with us all ever since we knew her."

"I always wondered," said Harry, "that, with all her pride, and all her anger, Emily did consent to let the child go."

"Why," said I, "she was languid and weak, and she was overborne by simple force of will. Tina was so positive and determined, so perfectly assured, and so warming and melting, that she carried all before her. There wasn't even the physical power to resist her."

"And do you think," said Harry, "that she will hold her power over a man like Ellery Davenport?"

"Longer, perhaps, than any other kind of woman," said I, "because she has such an infinite variety about her. But, after all, you remember what Miss Debby said about him, — that he never cared long for anything that he was sure of. Restlessness and pursuit are his nature, and therefore the time may come when she will share the fate of other idols."

"I regard it," said Harry, "as the most dreadful trial to a woman's character that can possibly be, to love, as Tina loves, a man whose moral standard is so far below hers. It is bad enough to be obliged to *talk* down always to those who are below us in intellect and comprehension; but to be obliged to *live down*, all the while, to a man without conscience or moral sense, is worse. I think often, 'What communion hath light with darkness?' and the only hope I can have is that she will fully find him out at last."

"And that," said I, "is a hope full of pain to her; but it seems to me likely to be realized. A man who has acted as he has done to one woman certainly never will be true to another."

Harry and I were now thrown more and more exclusively upon each other for society.

He had received his accession of fortune with as little exterior change as possible. Many in his situation would have rushed immediately over to England, and taken delight in coming openly into possession of the estate. Harry's fastidious reticence, however, hung about him even in this. It annoyed him to be an object of attention and gossip, and he felt no inclination to go alone into what seemed to him a strange country, into the midst of social manners and customs entirely different from those among which he had been brought up. He preferred to remain and pursue his course quietly, as he had begun, in the college with me; and he had taken no steps in relation to the property except to consult a lawyer in Boston.

Immediately on leaving college, it was his design to be married, and go with Esther to see what could be done in England. But I think his heart was set upon a home in America. The freedom and simplicity of life in this country were peculiarly suited to his character, and he felt a real vocation for the sacred ministry, not in the slightest degree lessened by the good fortune which had rendered him independent of it.

Two years of our college life passed away pleasantly enough in hard study, interspersed with social relaxations among the few friends nearest to us. Immediately after our graduation came Harry's marriage, — a peaceful little idyllic performance, which took us back to the mountains, and to all the traditions of our old innocent woodland life there.

After the wholesome fashion of New England clergymen, Mr. Avery had found a new mistress for the parsonage, so that Esther felt the more resigned to leaving him. When I had seen them off, however, I felt really quite alone in the world. The silent, receptive, sympathetic friend and brother of my youth was gone. But immediately came the effort to establish myself in Boston. And, through the friendly offices of the Kitterys, I was placed in connection with some very influential lawyers, who gave me that helping hand which takes a young man up the first steps of the profession. Harry had been most generous and liberal in regard to all our family, and insisted upon it that I should share his approved fortunes. There are friends so near to us that we can take from them as from ourselves. And Harry always insisted that he could in no way so repay the kindness and care that had hatched over his early years as by this assistance to me.

I received constant letters from him, and from their drift it became increasingly evident that the claims of duty upon him would lead him to make England his future home. In one of these he said: "I have always, as you know, looked forward to the ministry, and to such a kind of ministry as you have in America, where a man, for the most part, speaks to cultivated, instructed people, living in a healthy state of society, where a competence is the rule, and where there is a practical equality.

"I had no conception of life, such as I see it to be here, where there are whole races who appear born to poverty and subjection; where there are woes, and dangers, and miseries pressing on whole classes of men, which no one individual can do much to avert or alleviate. But it is to this very state of society that I feel a call to minister. I shall take orders in the Church of England, and endeavor to carry out among the poor and the suffering that simple Gospel which my mother taught me, and which, after all these years of experience, after all these theological discussions to which I have listened, remains in its perfect simplicity in my mind; namely, that every human soul on this earth has One Friend, and that Friend is Jesus Christ its Lord and Saviour.

"There is a redeeming power in being beloved, but there are many human beings who have never known what it is to be beloved. And my theology is, once penetrate any human soul with the full belief that *God loves him,* and you save him. Such is to be my life's object and end; and, in this ministry, Esther will go with me hand in hand. Her noble beauty and gracious manners make her the darling of all our people, and she is above measure happy in the power of doing good which is thus put into her hands.

"As to England, mortal heart cannot conceive more beauty than there is here. It is lovely beyond all poets' dreams. Near to our place are some charming old ruins, and I cannot tell you the delightful hours that Esther and I have spent there. Truly, the lines have fallen to us in pleasant places.

"I have not yet seen Tina, — she is abroad travelling on the Continent. She writes to us often; but, Horace, her letters begin to have the undertone of pain in them, — her skies are certainly beginning to fade. From some sources upon which I place reliance, I hear Ellery Davenport spoken of as a daring, plausible, but unscrupulous man. He is an *intrigant* in politics, and has no domestic life in him; while Tina, however much she loves and appreciates admiration, has a perfect woman's heart. Admiration without love would never satisfy her. I can see, through all the excuses of her letters, that he is going very much one way and she another, that he has his engagements, and she hers, and that they see, really, very little of each other, and that all this makes her sad and unhappy. The fact is, I suppose, he has played with his butterfly until there is no more down on its wings, and he is on the chase after new ones. Such is my reading of poor Tina's lot."

When I took this letter to Miss Mehitable, she told me that a similar impression had long since been produced on her mind by passages which she had read in hers. Tina often spoke of the little girl as very lovely, and as her greatest earthly comfort. A little one of her own, born in England, had died early, and her affections seemed thus to concentrate more entirely upon the child of her adoption. She described her with enthusiasm, as a child of rare beauty and talent, with capabilities of enthusiastic affection.

"Let us hope," said I, "that she does take her heart from her mother. Ellery Davenport is just one of those men that women are always wrecking themselves on, — men that have strong capabilities of passion, and very little capability of affection, — men that have no end of sentiment, and scarcely the beginning of real feeling. They make bewitching lovers, but terrible husbands."

One of the greatest solaces of my life during this period was my friendship with dear old Madam Kittery. Ever since the time when I had first opened to her my boyish heart, she had seemed to regard me with an especial tenderness, and to connect me in some manner with the image of her lost son. The assistance that she gave me in my educational career was viewed by her as a species of adoption. Her eye always brightened, and a lovely smile broke out upon her face, when I came to pass an hour with her. Time had treated her kindly; she still retained the gentle shrewdness, the love of literature, and the warm kindness which had been always charms in her. Some of my happiest hours were passed in reading to her. Chapter after chapter in her well-worn Bible needed no better commentary than the sweet brightness of her dear old face, and her occasional fervent responses. Many Sabbaths, when her increasing infirmities detained her from church, I spent in a tender, holy rest by her side. Then I would read from her prayer-book the morning service, not omitting the prayer that she loved, for the King and the royal family, and then, sitting hand in hand, we talked together of sacred things, and I often wondered to see what *strength* and discrimination there were in the wisdom of love, and how unerring were the decisions that she often made in practical questions. In fact, I felt myself drawn to Madam

Kittery by a closer, tenderer tie than even to my own grand
mother. I had my secret remorse for this, and tried to quiet myself
by saying that it was because, living in Boston, I saw Madam
Kittery oftener. But, after all, is it not true that, as we grow older
the relationship of souls will make itself felt? I revered and loved
my grandmother, but I never idealized her; but my attachment to
Madam Kittery was a species of poetic devotion. There was
slight flavor of romance in it, such as comes with the attachment
of our maturer life oftener than with those of our childhood.

Miss Debby looked on me with eyes of favor. In her own way
she really was quite as much my friend as her mother. She fell
into the habit of consulting me upon her business affairs, and
asking my advice in a general way about the arrangements of life

"I don't see," I said to Madam Kittery, one day, "why Miss
Deborah always asks my advice; she never takes it."

"My dear," said she, with the quiet smile with which she often
looked on her daughter's proceedings, "Debby wants somebody
to *ask* advice of. When she gets it, she is settled at once as to what
she *don't* want to do; and that's something."

Miss Debby once came to me with a face of great perplexity

"I don't know what to do, Horace. Our Thomas is a very valuable
man, and he has always been in the family. I don't know anything
how we should get along without him, but he is getting into bad
ways."

"Ah," said I, "what?"

"Well, you see it all comes of this modern talk about the right
of the people. I've instructed Thomas as faithfully as ever a woman
could; but — do you believe me? — he goes to the primary meet
ings. I have positive, reliable information that he does."

"My dear Miss Kittery, I suppose it's his right as a citizen."

"O, fiddlestick and humbug!" said Miss Debby; "and it may be
my right to turn him out of my service."

"And would not that, after all, be more harm to you than to
him?" suggested I.

Miss Debby swept up the hearth briskly, tapped on her snuff
box, and finally said she had forgotten her handkerchief, and left
the room.

Old Madam Kittery laughed a quiet laugh. "Poor Debby," she
said, "she'll have to come to it; the world will go on."

Thomas kept his situation for some years longer, till, having bought a snug place, and made some favorable investments, he at last announced to Miss Debby that, having been appointed constable, with a commission from the governor, his official duties would not allow of his continuance in her service.

CHAPTER L

———◆———

THE LAST CHAPTER

It was eight years after Tina left us on the wharf in Boston when I met her again. Ellery Davenport had returned to the country, and taken a house in Boston. I was then a lawyer established there in successful business.

Ellery Davenport met me with open-handed cordiality, and Tina with warm sisterly affection; and their house became one of my most frequent visiting-places. Knowing Tina by a species of divination, as I always had, it was easy for me to see through to those sacred little hypocrisies by which good women instinctively plead and intercede for husbands whom they themselves have found out. Michelet says, somewhere, that "in marriage the maternal feeling becomes always the strongest in woman, and in time it is the motherly feeling with which she regards her husband." She cares for him, watches over him, with the indefatigable tenderness which a mother gives to a son.

It was easy to see that Tina's affection for her husband was no longer a blind, triumphant adoration for an idealized hero, nor the confiding dependence of a happy wife, but the careworn anxiety of one who constantly seeks to guide and to restrain. And I was not long in seeing the cause of this anxiety.

Ellery Davenport was smitten with that direst curse, which, like the madness inflicted on the heroes of some of the Greek tragedies, might seem to be the vengeance of some incensed divinity. He was going down that dark and slippery road, up which so few return. We were all fully aware that at many times our Tina had all the ghastly horrors of dealing with a mad man. Even when he was himself again, and sought, by vows, promises, and illusive good resolutions, to efface the memory of the past, and give security for the future, there was no rest for Tina. In her dear eyes I could read always that sense of overhanging dread, that helpless watchfulness, which one may see in the eyes of so many poor women in our modern life, whose days are haunted by a fear they dare not express, and who must smile, and look gay, and seem confiding, when their very souls are failing them for fear. Still these seasons of madness did not seem for a while to impair the vigor of Ellery Davenport's mind, nor the feverish intensity of his ambition. He was absorbed in political life, in a wild, daring, unprincipled way, and made frequent occasions to leave Tina alone in Boston, while he travelled around the country, pursuing his intrigues. In one of these absences, it was his fate at last to fall in a political duel.

❋　　❋　　❋　　❋　　❋

Ten years after the gay and brilliant scene in Christ Church, some of those who were present as wedding guests were again convened to tender the last offices to the brilliant and popular Ellery Davenport. Among the mourners at the grave, two women who had loved him truly stood arm in arm.

After his death, it seemed, by the general consent of all, the kindest thing that could be done for him, to suffer the veil of silence to fall over his memory.

❋　　❋　　❋　　❋　　❋

Two years after that, one calm, lovely October morning, a quiet circle of friends stood around the altar of the old church, when Tina and I were married. Our wedding journey was a visit to Harry and Esther in England. Since then, the years have come and gone softly.

Ellery Davenport now seems to us as a distant dream of another life, recalled chiefly by the beauty of his daughter, whose growing loveliness is the principal ornament of our home.

Miss Mehitable and Emily form one circle with us. Nor does the youthful Emily know why she is so very dear to the saintly woman whose prayers and teachings are such a benediction in our family.

❋　　❋　　❋　　❋　　❋

Not long since we spent a summer vacation at Oldtown, to explore once more the old scenes, and to show to young Master Harry and Miss Tina the places that their parents had told them of.

Many changes have taken place in the old homestead. The lone old head of my grandfather has been laid beneath the cold sod of the burying-ground; and my mother, shortly after, was laid by him.

Old Parson Lothrop continued for some years, with his antique dress and his antique manners, respected in Oldtown as the shadowy minister of the past; while his colleague, Mr. Mordecai Rossiter, edified his congregation with the sharpest and most stringent new school Calvinism. To the last, Dr. Lothrop remained faithful to his Arminian views, and regarded the spread of the contrary doctrines, as a decaying old minister is apt to, as a personal reflection upon himself. In his last illness, which was very distressing, he was visited by a zealous Calvinistic brother from a neighboring town, who, on the strength of being a family connection, thought it his duty to go over and make one last effort to revive the orthodoxy of his venerable friend. Dr. Lothrop received him politely, and with his usual gentlemanly decorum remained for a long time in silence listening to his somewhat protracted arguments and statements. As he gave no reply, his friend at last said to him, "Dr. Lothrop, perhaps you are weak, and this conversation disturbs you?"

"I should be weak indeed, if I allowed such things as you have been saying to disturb me," replied the stanch old doctor.

"He died like a philosopher, my dear," said Lady Lothrop to me, "just as he always lived."

My grandmother, during the last part of her life, was totally blind. One would have thought that a person of her extreme activity would have been restless and wretched under this deprivation; but in her case blindness appeared to be indeed what Milton expressed it as being, "an overshadowing of the wings of the Almighty." Every earthly care was hushed, and her mind turned inward, in constant meditation upon those great religious truths which had fed her life for so many years.

Aunt Lois we found really quite lovely. There is a class of women who are like winter apples, — all their youth they are crabbed and hard, but at the further end of life they are full of softness and refreshment. The wrinkles had really almost smoothed themselves out in Aunt Lois's face, and our children found in her the most indulgent and painstaking of aunties, ready to run, and wait, and tend, and fetch, and carry, and willing to put everything in the house at their disposal. In fact, the young gentleman and lady found the old homestead such very free and easy ground that they announced to us that they preferred altogether staying there to being in Boston, especially as they had the barn to romp in.

One Saturday afternoon, Tina and I drove over to Needmore with a view to having one more gossip with Sam Lawson. Hepsy, it appears, had departed this life, and Sam had gone over to live with a son of his in Needmore. We found him roosting placidly in the porch on the sunny side of the house.

"Why, lordy massy, bless your soul an' body, ef that ain't Horace Holyoke!" he said, when he recognized who I was.

"An' this 'ere's your wife, is it? Wal, wal, how this 'ere world does turn round! Wal, now, who would ha' thought it? Here you be, and Tiny with you. Wal, wal!"

"Yes," said I, "here we are."

"Wal, now, jest sit down," said Sam, motioning us to a seat in the porch. "I was jest kind o' 'flectin' out here in the sun; ben a readin' in the Missionary Herald; they've ben a sendin' missionaries to Otawhity, an' they say that there ain't no winter there, an' the bread jest grows on the trees, so 't they don't hev to make none, an' there ain't no wood-piles nor splittin' wood, nor nothin' o' that sort goin' on, an' folks don't need no clothes to speak on. Now, I's jest thinkin' that 'ere's jest the country to suit me. I wonder, now, ef they couldn't find suthin' for me to do out there. I could shoe the hosses, ef they hed any, and I could teach the natives their catechize, and kind o' help round gin'ally. These 'ere winters gits so cold here I'm e'en a'most crooked up with the rheumatiz —"

"Why, Sam," said Tina, "where is Hepsy?"

"Law, now, hain't ye heerd? Why, Hepsy, she's been dead, wal, let me see, 't was three year the fourteenth o' last May when Hepsy died, but she was clear wore out afore she died. Wal, jest half on her was clear paralyzed, poor crittur; she couldn't speak a word; that 'ere was a gret trial to her. I don't think she was resigned under it. Hepsy hed an awful sight o' grit. I used to talk to Hepsy, an' talk, an' try to set things afore her in the best way I could, so's to git 'er into a better state o' mind. D'you believe, one

day when I'd ben a talkin' to her, she kind o' made a motion to m
with her eye, an' when I went up to 'er, what do you think? why
she jest tuk and BIT me! she did so!"

"Sam," said Tina, "I sympathize with Hepsy. I believe'd I ha
to be talked to an hour, and couldn't answer, I should bite."

"Jes' so, jes' so," said Sam. "I 'spex 't is so. You see, women jus
talk, there's where 'tis. Wal, now, don't ye remember that Mis
Bell, — Miss Miry Bell? She was of a good family in Boston. The
used to board her out to Oldtown, 'cause she was 's crazy's a loor
They jest let 'er go 'bout, 'cause she didn't hurt nobody, but massy
her tongue used ter run 's ef 't was hung in the middle and run bot
ends. Ye really couldn't hear yourself think when she was round
Wal, she was a visitin' Parson Lothrop, an' ses he, 'Miss Bell, d
pray see ef you can't be still a minute.' 'Lord bless ye, Dr. Lothrop
I can't stop talking!' ses she. 'Wal,' ses he, 'you jest take a mouthfu
o' water an' hold in your mouth, an' then mebbe ye ken stop.' Wal
she took the water, an' she sot still a minute or two, an' it kind c
worked on 'er so 't she jumped up an' twitched off Dr. Lothrop'
wig an' spun it right acrost the room inter the fireplace. 'Bless me
Miss Bell,' ses he, 'spit out yer water an' talk, ef ye must!' I've offur
thought on 't," said Sam. "I s'pose Hepsy's felt a good 'eal so. Wal
poor soul, she's gone to 'er rest. We're all on us goin', one arter an
other. Yer grandther's gone, an' yer mother, an' Parson Lothrop
he's gone, an' Lady Lothrop, she's kind o' solitary. I went over t
see 'er last week, an' ses she to me, 'Sam, I dunno nothin' what
shell do with my hosses. I feed 'em well, an' they ain't workec
hardly any, an' yet they act so 't I'm 'most afeard to drive out witl
'em.' I'm thinkin' 't would be a good thing ef she'd give up tha
'ere place o' hern, an' go an' live in Boston with her sister."

"Well, Sam," said Tina, "what has become of Old Crab Smith'
Is he alive yet?"

"Law, yis, he's creepin' round here yit; but the old woman, she'
dead," said Sam. "I tell you she's a hevin' her turn o' hectorin' hin
now, 'cause she keeps appearin' to him, an' scares the old critte
'most to death."

"Appears to him?" said I. "Why, what do you mean, Sam?"

"Wal, jest as true's you live an' breathe, she does 'pear to him,
said Sam. "Why, 't was only last week my son Luke an' I, we wa
a settin' by the fire here, an' I was a holdin' a skein o' yarn fo

Malviny to wind (Malviny, she's Luke's wife), when who should come in but Old Crab, head first, lookin' so scart an' white about the gills thet Luke, ses he, 'Why, Mistur Smith! what ails ye?' ses he. Wal, the critter was so scared 't he couldn't speak, he jest set down in the chair, an' he shuk so 't he shuk the chair, an' his teeth, they chattered, an' 't was a long time 'fore they could git it out on him. But come to, he told us, 't was a bright moonlight night, an' he was comin' 'long down by the Stone pastur, when all of a suddin he looks up an' there was his wife walkin' right 'long-side on him, — he ses he never see nothin' plainer in his life than he see the old woman, jest in her short gown an' petticut 't she allers wore, with her gold beads round her neck, an' a cap on with a black ribbon round it, an' there she kep' a walkin' right 'long-side of 'im, her elbow a touchin' hisn, all 'long the road, an' when he walked faster, she walked faster, an' when he walked slower, she walked slower, an' her eyes was sot, an' fixed on him, but she didn't speak no word, an' he didn't darse to speak to her. Finally, he ses he gin a dreadful yell an' run with all his might, an' our house was the very fust place he tumbled inter. Lordy massy, wal, I couldn't help thinkin' 't served him right. I told Sol 'bout it, last town-meetin' day, an' Sol, I thought he'd ha' split his sides. Sol said he didn't know 's the old woman had so much sperit. 'Lordy massy,' ses he, 'ef she don't do nothin' more'n take a walk 'long-side on him now an' then, why, I say, let 'er rip, — sarves him right.' "

"Well," said Tina, "I'm glad to hear about Old Sol; how is he?"

"O, Sol? Wal, he's doin' fustrate. He married Deacon Bijah Smith's darter, an' he's got a good farm of his own, an' boys bigger'n you be, considerable."

"Well," said Tina, "how is Miss Asphyxia?"

"Wal, Sol told me 't she'd got a cancer or suthin' or other the matter with 'er; but the old gal, she jest sets her teeth hard, an' goes on a workin'. She won't have no doctor, nor nothin' done for 'er, an' I expect bimeby she'll die, a standin' up in the harness."

"Poor old creature! I wonder, Horace, if it would do any good for me to go and see her. Has she a soul, I wonder, or is she nothing but a 'working machine'?"

"Wal, I dunno," said Sam. "This 'ere world is cur'us. When we git to thinkin' about it, we think ef we'd ha' had the makin' on 't, things would ha' ben made someways diffurnt from what they be.

But then things *is* just *as* they is, an' we can't help it. Sometimes I think," said Sam, embracing his knee profoundly, "an' then agin I dunno. — There's all sorts o' folks hes to be in this 'ere world, an' I s'pose the Lord knows what he wants 'em fur; but I'm sure I don't. I kind o' hope the Lord'll fetch everybody out 'bout right some o' these 'ere times. He ain't got nothin' else to do, an' it's his lookout, an' not ourn, what comes of 'em all. — But I *should* like to go to Otawhity, an' ef you see any o' these missionary folks, Horace, I wish you'd speak to 'em about it."

THE JOHN HARVARD LIBRARY

The intent of
Waldron Phoenix Belknap, Jr.,
as expressed in an early will, was for
Harvard College to use the income from a
permanent trust fund he set up, for "editing and
publishing rare, inaccessible, or hitherto unpublished
source material of interest in connection with the
history, literature, art (including minor and useful
art), commerce, customs, and manners or way of
life of the Colonial and Federal Periods of the United
States . . . In all cases the emphasis shall be on the
presentation of the basic material." A later testament
broadened this statement, but Mr. Belknap's inter-
ests remained constant until his death.

In linking the name of the first benefactor of
Harvard College with the purpose of this later,
generous-minded believer in American culture the
John Harvard Library seeks to emphasize the impor-
tance of Mr. Belknap's purpose. The John Harvard
Library of the Belknap Press of Harvard University
Press exists to make books and documents
about the American past more readily
available to scholars and the
general reader.

Date Due